Three Str...

Rancher Tom McBride
Ranger Zeke Lonetree
Rancher Mac MacDougal

Three Unforgettable Stories...

Manhunting in Montana
Bachelor Father
Pure Temptation

One Irresistible Collection!

THE SILENT *Type*

by Request®

Three complete novels
by one of your favorite authors.

Dear Reader,

In my extremely unscientific opinion, I believe the American West tends to produce a man of few words, a man who'd rather take action than talk about it, a man who feels deeply yet shields his emotions from public view. In other words, The Silent Type. Maybe it's the wide-open spaces. Maybe it's the heritage of the cowboy. Maybe it's the call of the wild. Whatever breeds this type of man, I'm grateful for the process. It inspired me to create Tom McBride (*Manhunting in Montana*), Zeke Lonetree (*Bachelor Father*) and Mac MacDougal (*Pure Temptation*). Yum. After spending time with guys like these, I've concluded that talking is highly overrated. And when it comes to doing, these three can definitely get it done. In all areas. I think you'll agree.

Warmly,

Vicki Lewis Thompson

P.S. If you have a chance, swing on over to my Web site at www.vickilewisthompson.com and say hi!

VICKI LEWIS THOMPSON

THE SILENT *Type*

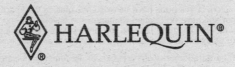

HARLEQUIN®

TORONTO • NEW YORK • LONDON
AMSTERDAM • PARIS • SYDNEY • HAMBURG
STOCKHOLM • ATHENS • TOKYO • MILAN • MADRID
PRAGUE • WARSAW • BUDAPEST • AUCKLAND

HARLEQUIN BOOKS

by Request—THE SILENT TYPE

Copyright © 2002 by Harlequin Books S.A.

ISBN 0-373-18508-1

The publisher acknowledges the copyright holder of the individual works as follows:

MANHUNTING IN MONTANA
Copyright © 1998 by Vicki Lewis Thompson
BACHELOR FATHER
Copyright © 1999 by Harlequin Books S.A.
PURE TEMPTATION
Copyright © 1999 by Vicki Lewis Thompson

This edition published by arrangement with Harlequin Books S.A.

Visit us at www.eHarlequin.com

Printed in U.S.A.

CONTENTS

MANHUNTING IN MONTANA

SHOOTING GORGEOUS GUYS really turned her on.

Cleo Griffin returned to her New York studio in the condition that usually followed a photo session—she wanted to grab the nearest man and get naked. Unfortunately there was no man in her studio, only her assistant and best friend, Bernadette Fairchild.

Bernie, a Rosie O'Donnell look-alike, glanced up from the computer screen. "You're flushed."

"Of course I'm flushed." Cleo took a bite of the soft pretzel she'd bought from a street vendor. Then, laying the pretzel on Bernie's desk, she eased the heavy camera bag off her shoulder onto an office chair.

"I take it Mr. December was well put-together?"

Cleo headed for the watercooler. "Bernie, the pecs on that guy would make you weep." She filled a paper cup with water and gulped it down. "If I don't get some action soon, I'm gonna self-combust."

Bernie stopped typing and swiveled her chair toward Cleo. "There's this new thing I just heard of. Dating."

"Don't have time." Cleo crumpled the paper cup and threw it in the trash before glancing at Bernie. "You're lucky. You have George to go home to."

"I invested *two years* in Project George. That's not luck, that's top-level strategy."

"I should have done the same thing when I was in school."

"Didn't I tell you that? Didn't I tell you those were the mating years? But would you listen?"

"It's not too late." Cleo pulled a chair over in front of Bernie's desk and sat down. "I can still find somebody. All I need is a nice guy who won't interfere with my work."

"But someone talented enough to take the edge off after a steamy session behind the lens, right?"

Cleo crossed her ankle over her knee and grinned. "That goes without saying." She picked up her pretzel again and took a generous bite.

"I'm afraid they don't offer those in the *Sharper Image* catalog," Bernie said. "By the way, your tickets arrived for the Montana trip. You're staying at a small, intimate yet authentic guest ranch, just like you specified. Six cabins, so it won't be crawling with tourists, and Tom McBride, the owner, runs a few head of cattle, so you'll have plenty of cowboys on the property and more at neighboring ranches." She pushed an envelope across the desk.

"Cowboys." Cleo picked up the envelope to look inside and check flight times. "How am I ever going to survive shooting twelve hunky cowhands, considering the shape I'm in after finishing this firefighter calendar?"

Bernie resumed typing. "Give in and take one to bed."

"No." She'd been tempted so many times, but it was totally unprofessional. She had a reputation to protect.

"You'll be at the ends of the earth in Montana." Bernie clicked the mouse on the print command and sat back in her chair. "I think they still communicate by Pony Express out there. Word would never get back to New York that you'd been naughty."

Cleo finished off the pretzel. "You know me better than that. I couldn't live with myself. Besides, it's almost as if I have to keep doing everything the same, with no deviation, to keep this calendar bonanza going."

"Chick, you're there. You've made it." Bernie picked up the letter that rolled out of the laser printer. "Are your hands clean?"

Cleo licked pretzel salt from her thumb. "Not exactly."

"Then don't touch this." She laid it in front of Cleo. "I just want you to read it and gloat."

Cleo read the letter explaining to the Van Cleefs that Ms. Griffin's schedule wouldn't allow her to photograph their daughter's very expensive, very prestigious wedding. Five years ago when the oldest daughter had gotten married, Bernie had practically crawled over broken glass trying to get Cleo the job, but another photographer had been chosen. Cleo knew she should be as impressed as Bernie that they didn't need the Van Cleefs anymore. She wanted to feel secure and confident with her success, but most of the time she felt more like a tightrope walker balancing a tray of Fabergé eggs.

She glanced up. "Okay, so I'm not begging to take society-wedding shots these days, but—"

"Your *Hard-Hat Heroes* calendar almost outsold *Calvin and Hobbes* last Christmas."

"Almost isn't good enough."

Bernie let out an exasperated sigh. "And would that be another maxim from the great Calvin Griffin?"

"Well, he's right." Cleo wadded up the paper the pretzel had come in and got out of the chair to throw it away. Talking about her father always made her edgy. "He didn't *almost* become the CEO of Sphinx Cosmetics. He's never *almost* done anything." Except once, she thought. He'd *almost* fathered a son, until Cleo's mother had miscarried, leaving him with only a daughter.

"Aren't you the CEO of Griffin Studios?" Bernie said quietly.

"It's not the same. It's not—"

"Enough?" Bernie prompted. "Listen, kid, you shouldn't have to prove anything to—"

"I need to get this film labeled and ready for the lab." Cleo picked up the camera bag by the strap. "The contact sheets won't be finished before I leave for Montana tomorrow, so you'll have to overnight them to me at the guest ranch. What's the name of it?"

"The Whispering Winds."

"Sounds way too romantic to be authentic. A ranch is supposed to be named something like the Triple Bar or the Rocking Z."

"I suggest you tell Tom McBride that. I'm sure he'd appreciate the tip from a New Yorker." Bernie returned to her keyboard.

"Well, I just might. The right name could improve his business." Cleo started toward her workroom. The studio was small—nine hundred square feet that included a reception area, Cleo's workroom and a seldom-used cubicle set up with umbrella lights for studio shots. Ever since Cleo had hit upon the idea of creating hunk calendars, she'd pretty much abandoned studio photography. She preferred shooting her men in their natural environment.

"Why not choose thirteen this time?" Bernie called after her.

Cleo turned back. "Thirteen what?"

"Cowboys. Pick out an extra one. Then if there's one of the thirteen you like personally, and he likes you, eliminate him from the calendar and make a little whoopee. You'll have some fun and you won't compromise your professional ethics."

Cleo rested the camera bag on the floor as she gazed at Bernie. The idea that was slowly forming terrified her, but it could be the answer to her prayers. "You just might have something there."

"That's my job. Facilitating your career and your happiness. You can have a wonderful romp in Montana and come home with a calendar and some great memories."

"I could also come home with a husband." God, that sounded bizarre. But what if her raging hormones caused her to forget herself during a shoot one of these days? She could ruin her reputation, her self-respect and her career in one fell swoop.

Bernie stared at her. "Hey, wait a minute, Cleo. That's not what I—"

"Why not?" Cleo met the fear churning inside with her usual weapon—an outward show of supreme confidence. "My interview for the bio note on the calendar can do double duty as a potential husband questionnaire. I can kill two birds with one stone. It's perfect."

"Love doesn't work on that kind of efficiency model, toots."

Cleo lifted her chin. "I say it can." Even Bernie didn't know how desperate she'd become for safe, steady sexual release with an understanding man, or how lonely her downtime had become when she was between projects. Marriage was the only solution. But she had to find some way to work the selection process into her schedule. Crazy as it seemed, this could be the answer.

Bernie didn't seem to appreciate the beauty of her plan. "Even if you managed such a thing, then what?" she argued. "You'll drag some poor cowboy back to New York? According to the movies, those ol' boys like the wide-open spaces, the howl of Wily Coyote, the smell of horse poop. You can't expect him to survive on the aroma of cab fumes."

"No, I wouldn't drag him back to New York. That's why it would be so perfect. He could stay in Montana, and I'd stay in New York, and we'd get together on weekends whenever it was convenient. I could go there, he could come here or we could each fly to a central spot like, say, Chicago."

Bernie stared at her with her mouth hanging open. "You're really serious."

"Of course." She was quivering inside, but she was deadly serious.

"What happens when the little bambinos show up? Will they be centrally located in Kansas?"

"No bambinos," she said quickly, thinking of how children could wreck her career. "That will be understood from the beginning. Not every guy wants to have kids, you know. Don't worry. I'll find one who thinks a commuter marriage is an exciting way to live."

"Cleo, are you nuts? This is too outrageous, my little bohemian friend, even for you."

"It is exactly what I need, and it is exactly what I'm going to get. Thanks for the idea, Bernie."

"That was *not* my idea. Don't you dare go pinning the rap on me. All I suggested was some R and R, not a husband-hunting expedition."

"But don't you see? I don't have time for R and R, but I have to solve this problem, and soon."

"What's wrong with you? Marriage is about sharing your life with someone! All you'd share would be sex and an accumulation of frequent-flier miles!"

"I'm going to do it, Bernie. I'm not saying it'll be easy finding a husband in two weeks, but you know how much I love challenges." Cleo swallowed the nervous lump in her throat. This had to work. "Somewhere in Montana, right this minute, my future husband is roping a steer, or sipping coffee beside a campfire, or riding a bucking bronco—one of those manly things cowboys do—unaware that his life is about to change forever."

"Or at least on alternate weekends," Bernie said.

"Tom, the toilet don't work in cabin six, and that photographer from New York is due in there tomorrow."

Tom McBride looked away from the computer terminal on his desk, more than happy to be interrupted. No matter how he juggled the figures, the Whispering Winds was sinking deeper in debt every year. He glanced up at the slim cowboy, Jeeter Neff, who stood just inside the open door of his office. Tom treated the men and women working for him on the ranch as equals, and the only people on the place who called him Mr. McBride were his cook Juanita's two kids, at Juanita's insistence.

"Is Hank around somewhere?" Tom asked. Hank Jacobs was the ranch's official handyman, a weathered old guy who'd been a school janitor before finally getting his wish to work and live as a cowboy.

"You gave him a week off to get his mother settled in that old folks' home."

"Oh yeah."

"I'd see to it, but I'm s'posed to take the Daniels bunch out on a trail ride in about ten minutes, and from what Luann said when she was in there gettin' the place ready, something needs to be done pronto."

Tom pushed back his chair, glad for an excuse to leave the office and the sea of red on the computer screen. He stood and grabbed his hat from the peg on the wall. "I'll do it."

"I'd recommend taking a plunger," Jeeter said with a grin. "Maybe a snake, too."

"On second thought, maybe I should wrangle the Daniels bunch and you can deal with the toilet."

Jeeter backed up, poised to hightail it out the front door of the ranch house. "You know, I never was much good at that job. Usually ended up making a worse mess than when I got started."

"Handy excuse, Jeeter." Another thought occurred to Tom. He hadn't considered the ramifications of giving Hank the time off. "I guess that means Hank can't pick up that photographer at the airport tomorrow, either."

"I guess not."

Tom sighed. "I might as well do it, then. Somebody needs to take a manure sample to the lab for a worm check, anyhow. Might as well get 'em both done at once."

"You gonna take that sample in before or after you go to the airport?"

"I don't know. Depends on traffic. Why?"

Jeeter's grin broke through again. "I just don't know if it'll do much for business, hauling around some fancy-dancy woman from New York with a plastic bag full of road apples on the seat between you."

"Hey, I talked to her secretary. This lady wants an *authentic* ranching experience." Tom didn't believe that for a minute. They all said that, until you handed them a shovel or asked them to stretch some barbed wire. "You just made up my mind, Jeeter. I'm taking in the sample after I pick her up. Let's see what she's made of."

Jeeter laughed and took off.

Moments later, armed with a plunger, Tom stepped out onto the wide front porch of the ranch house. He'd been born in this house, had learned to walk on this porch while clutching the railing. An errand had to be pretty damned important to keep him from pausing to appreciate the view from the top of the steps, and the toilet wasn't that important.

Although his dad had never been much for "standin' and gawkin'," his mother had taught him to treasure what lay before him—a meadow greening up after a rain, a corral of sleek horses, outbuildings nestled into the trees, and beyond, the proud sweep of the Gallatins still tipped with snow on this June morning. He knew the imprint of those mountains against the sky as well as he knew his mother's face. *Not many folks have paradise right out their front door, Tommy,* she'd said more times than he could count.

He took a deep breath of the pine-scented air. Friends had advised him to build more guest cabins to bring in the money he needed to stay solvent, but that would change the character of the ranch he loved more than anyone knew. Tugging at the brim of his Stetson, he left the porch and started toward cabin six. He wasn't good at compromise. And it might eventually get him kicked right out of paradise.

TOM HADN'T BEEN on airport duty for some time, and he arrived at the terminal with nothing more than the flight's arrival to go by. He'd forgotten to find the photographer's name in the computer before he left the Whispering Winds, but there couldn't be that many women on the plane with a big-city air and a camera bag over one shoulder.

Come to think of it, he hadn't been to the airport since the last time he'd met Deidre there two years ago. No wonder he was in a rotten mood, with memories of his ex-wife floating around the place. Deidre had looked fantastic coming down the jetway, he remembered, but professional models were supposed to look fantastic. Apparently they weren't supposed to look pregnant.

He'd waited for her, the medical report in his hand, hoping there had been some mistake. No mistake. She'd had the abortion in New York and never meant for him to know. The clinic had screwed up by accidentally sending the bill to her Montana address. Once Tom understood completely what had happened, it hadn't been Deidre's address any longer.

And here he was waiting for another woman who worked in New York. Unfair as it might be, he'd already branded the two as coming from the same herd. Although Deidre made her living in front of the camera and this woman made hers behind it, both of them had chosen a world in which image was everything.

Truth be told, he didn't much relish the idea of transporting this citified woman who wanted to photograph "authentic" cowboys. Jeeter would tell him he had a sizable chip on his shoulder about it, and Jeeter would be right. Tom had driven the truck through several mud puddles before he hit the main highway leading to the Bozeman airport, and the plastic bag of manure rested right on the dash, where the morning sun could bring out its special aroma. He'd worn his most faded blue work shirt, his most battered hat and the jeans that he'd torn up on the barbed wire the last time he'd been fixing fence.

As the plane carrying his New York guest landed, Tom remembered there was a little trick for notifying offloading folks that you were their ride home. He ought to be holding a sign, and because he didn't remember the woman's name he'd have to write Whispering Winds on it. He glanced around for something to write on, but there was precious little presenting itself.

Finally he noticed a newspaper in the trash. It turned

out to be a scandal sheet, and the biggest expanse of light-colored space to write on was that occupied by Loni Anderson's cleavage in a white sequined dress. Tom borrowed a pen from a businessman working a crossword puzzle and lettered a bold Whispering Winds across Loni's chest. Then in parentheses he added Run by Authentic Cowboys. Returning the pen, he folded the newspaper so the writing was facing toward the people getting off the plane.

There she was. He'd bet money that was her—a sleek brunette covered with gold jewelry and carrying nothing but one of those dumb little purses that looked as if it would barely hold a credit card and some loose change. Maybe she'd checked her camera equipment along with her luggage. Her outfit, tight jeans and a leather vest with lots of fringe, was exactly what New Yorkers might think they should wear in Montana.

He held up his tabloid sign and gazed at the brunette. She walked right past him, trailing clouds of heavy perfume. He was so surprised, so certain he'd been right, that he called after her, "Whispering Winds, ma'am!"

"I believe you're looking for me," said a low voice right beside him.

He turned and looked into her eyes. *Montana-sky blue.* The ranch hands would laugh themselves silly if they knew he'd thought such a thing, but it was true. He didn't have to look down very far to see into her eyes, either. She stood at least five-nine or ten, with curly golden hair falling in a jumble past her shoulders. It looked in need of a combing, and Tom had the crazy urge to straighten it out a little by running his fingers through it.

Over a blue work shirt almost as faded as his, she wore a canvas vest with all sorts of pockets, and her slacks were on the baggy side, not designed to show off what he suspected was a decent figure. She carried a heavy-looking camera bag over one shoulder, a backpack over the other, and held a wheeled carry-on by the handle. She was rumpled, appealing, and smelled as if she'd been rolling in wildflowers. She was nothing like what he'd expected.

He remembered the manure on the dash and winced.

"Cleo Griffin." Her clipped accent gave her away as a New Yorker and brought back memories of Deidre. She hoisted the camera bag more firmly on her shoulder and held out her hand.

He snapped out of his fog and realized that he'd been letting a ranch guest stand there laden down like a pack animal. "Let me take that, ma'am," he said, reaching for the camera-bag strap instead of accepting her handshake.

"I'll keep it, thanks." She made a quick grab for the strap and grabbed his hand instead.

Her grip was warm and firm, her skin smooth against his. As his gaze locked with hers for just an instant, he felt an unexpected rush of pleasure. All his memories of Deidre weren't bad, and this woman triggered the good ones, too.

She released his hand and took hold of the strap. "I need to be in charge of my equipment." Her tone was all business, but there was something going on in those blue eyes of hers that looked like more than business. She unhooked the backpack from her other shoulder. "I'd appreciate it if you'd take this, though. It's full of books, and it's getting very heavy."

He swung the backpack to his shoulder. "Is there more?"

She looked startled. "More what?"

"Luggage."

"Than this?" She gestured toward her rolling suitcase

and the backpack. "I should hope not. I'm not planning on attending any fancy-dress balls or—" She paused. "Oh, I get it. I'm a woman, so of course I've arrived with fourteen suitcases."

"Now, ma'am, I didn't mean—"

"Yes, you did, but never mind." She tapped the newspaper he still held in one hand. "Tell me, is this part of the dude treatment?"

He'd forgotten all about the sign he'd printed across Loni Anderson's cleavage. "I wanted to get your attention."

"Well, Loni's chest as an attention-getter is a little off the mark. Next time you're meeting a woman at the airport, try Matt McConaughey's chest and see if that doesn't work better."

He held back a grin. "Yes, ma'am."

She looked him up and down, her gaze amused. "From all these ma'ams you're tossing around, I gather you're one of the authentic cowboys who runs the Whispering Winds."

She had a smart mouth on her, but he was kind of enjoying the exchange. She might be more fun to have around than he'd thought. "Montana born and bred."

"Good. That's exactly what I'm looking for. Shall we leave?"

Tom touched the brim of his hat. "At your service, ma'am." This time when he thought about the manure on the dash, he smiled.

2

GOD, he was magnificent, Cleo thought, lengthening her stride to keep up with the lean cowboy beside her. She had to have him, chauvinism and all. Montana born and bred, indeed, unflappable as the rugged Rockies. His self-confidence would come across when she photographed him, making him a perfect cover model for the calendar.

Choosing him for the cover would eliminate him from the husband hunt, but he wouldn't have made the cut, anyway. He wasn't tame enough, which made him perfect cover material. The idea of capturing this man on film commanded her complete attention.

She'd begin with a full-length shot, maybe pose him leaning against a weathered fence with a coiled rope in one hand. She wanted to reach beneath the veneer of nonchalance he presented to the world and hint at the intensity simmering below the surface. The lens would love those broad shoulders and slim hips. Then she'd move in for some close-ups to bring out the flinty cast of his eyes and capture that mocking look he'd given her when she'd asked if he was an authentic cowboy.

As they crossed the parking lot in bright sunshine, she glanced over to see how the light affected the contours of his face. His battered hat shadowed most of it, but the sun found its way to the squared-off angle of his chin. Just below his lower lip a scar formed a white crescent against his tan. Beneath his hat, the hair at his temples and his nape was warm brown streaked with sun. The creases in his cheeks and the crinkle lines at the corners of his eyes revealed that he found life amusing a good deal of the time.

"Checking to see if I washed behind my ears this morning?" he asked without turning his head.

"No, I'm thinking of exactly how I'd like to photograph you."

He stopped abruptly and swung to face her. "No way, Ms. Griffin."

She backed up a step, amazed at the sudden hostility in his expression. "Let me put it this way. I pay really well, and it could easily be the best thing that ever happened to you. Men who've been in my calendars have been swamped with all sorts of offers, from movie contracts to marriage."

That mocking look reappeared in his gray eyes. "I have no desire to be in the movies, or to get married again. As for the money, you couldn't pay me enough to gallivant around in front of a camera and hang on the wall like some centerfold."

"My subject's don't *gallivant*, and they're not centerfolds, either. I shoot in black and white, and although the calendars are extremely commercial, I consider them art, a celebration of the beauty of the male body at work." Startled by her own outburst, she realized she'd never said those words out loud, and she was embarrassed to have spilled her creative guts in front of this cowboy. God knows why she had.

His tone gentled, and so did the look in his eyes. "Look, there are lots of men around here who will be overjoyed to pose for you. I'm just not in the market."

With every nuance of expression on his face, she became more sure that he could be one of the best subjects she'd ever photographed. Toughness and compassion didn't often go together, and her instincts told her that if she could portray that, she'd have done something worth the admiration of anyone...including her father.

She cleared her throat and tried again. "I don't think you understand. My calendars sell astronomically. The one I'm shooting now, *Montana Men,* promises to be the biggest seller of them all. I want to put you on the cover. It would literally change your life."

"Thank you, but I like my life just fine the way it is. Now I think we need to get going." He turned and started down a line of parked cars. "I have an errand to run before we head back to the ranch, and a pile of paperwork to do this afternoon."

The statement didn't sound like the kind usually made by a ranch hand. Cleo caught up with him, her suitcase wheels rattling over the asphalt. "You never did tell me your name."

"McBride. Tom McBride."

The owner of the Whispering Winds. That would explain the character she'd seen etched in his face and his uncommon poise. Putting him on the cover of the calendar would be more of a coup than she'd thought. The bio would practically compose itself and be the linchpin of her work. Tom McBride didn't know it yet, but she *would* have him for the cover.

What she needed was more information so she could plan her campaign. "I'm surprised that the owner of Whispering Winds is providing airport shuttle service," she said.

"The guy who usually does it is away on personal business, and I had an errand in Bozeman, anyway. We'll be taking a little detour back toward town before we start down to the ranch.''

"That's fine.'' She was a little reluctant to leave civilization, anyway. On the plane ride out here, she'd realized how much she depended on the amenities of the city to sustain her erratic eating and sleeping habits. She'd probably be expected to get up at cockcrow if she wanted breakfast at the Whispering Winds, and she doubted there was a corner deli within walking distance if she happened to oversleep.

Considering that Tom wasn't used to picking up guests at the airport, his story about finding the tabloid at the last minute so that he could make a sign to signal to her might be absolutely true. Maybe scrawling the message across Loni Anderson's chest hadn't been a chauvinistic gesture, after all. But she shouldn't forget that he'd added the words *Run by Authentic Cowboys,* which was a deliberate dig. And one he'd expected to get away with. He was one cool customer.

She watched as he approached the passenger side of a pickup truck so spattered with mud she wasn't sure what color it was. A person would have to deliberately hit puddles to get a truck that dirty, she thought.

After surveying the truck, his raggedy jeans and well-used cowboy hat, she came to a conclusion. "You know what I think, Tom?''

He paused in the act of opening the door of the unlocked truck and glanced at her. "I haven't the foggiest.''

"I think you've got a wee bit of attitude.''

His mouth twitched, and eventually a grin appeared. "Is that a fact?''

She approached the truck and turned over the handle of her suitcase to him so he could put it in the back. In the process, she looked directly into his eyes and smiled.

"The thing is, I'm a New York chick. I was weaned on attitude, and I refuse to take B.S. from anybody. I..." She paused and wrinkled her nose at an unpleasant smell coming from the cab. "What *is* that?"

Tom seemed to be working hard not to laugh. "That would be B.S., ma'am."

She looked inside and noticed a plastic bag on the dashboard that held a substance she vaguely recognized as appearing on the pavement after parades. The smell filled the cab, but it might all be coming from that bag, which was sitting in the sun.

She faced him again. "Is this your idea of cowboy humor?"

"No, ma'am." His voice was thick with repressed laughter. "It's my idea of a lab test to see if my cows have worms. That's my errand."

She stared at him dispassionately. "I don't believe you for a minute. You planted that there to see how I'd react."

"I'll prove my story by driving straight to the lab and taking the bag of manure inside."

"That won't prove a damn thing. Why is it in the cab instead of in the back?"

"Doesn't bother me to have it in the cab."

"I see." So it was a test, she thought. "If I ride all the way to the lab with this thing smelling up the atmosphere, will you let me take your picture for my calendar?"

"Nope."

"Then I see no need to make the sacrifice." She stepped around him, reached into the cab and took the bag by two fingers. Then she marched to the back and dropped the bag into the truck bed. Finally she climbed into the passenger seat. "I'll take my backpack and suitcase up here with me."

"You'll be mighty crowded."

"I'd rather be crowded than have my belongings shift around on that slippery truck bed and possibly smash into your bag of B.S."

"I'd hate that, too."

"Oh, sure you would."

"I would. I need that sample for the lab." He lifted her suitcase into the cab.

As she wedged it between her knees, she breathed in the woodsy scent of his aftershave, which was a welcome relief from *eau de manure*. "I'm surprised you didn't slap a little of the contents of that bag on yourself, for added effect."

He handed her the backpack. "That might have been taking things a little far."

"So you have limits to how much you tease the greenhorns?" She balanced the backpack on her suitcase and held her camera bag on her lap.

"To be honest, we don't usually tease them unless they specifically ask to meet some authentic cowboys." He closed the door and walked around to the driver's side.

"But my assistant had to ask!" she said once he got in. "Otherwise I might have ended up at some touristy place with a lot of rhinestone cowboys hanging around. I wanted the real thing."

Tom started the truck. "Well, I reckon that's what you'll get at the Whispering Winds, ma'am," he said, his voice an exaggerated drawl.

Not if I don't get you, she thought. And Cleo always got her man.

THEY WERE PACKED so tight into the cab that Tom kept brushing Cleo's knee when he shifted gears. She seemed totally unconcerned about it, but he found the constant contact unnerving because, fight it though he tried, he was attracted to her.

In fact, the evidence was mounting that he had a thing for city gals, possibly because they were different and brought variety to his country life. He remembered taking Deidre camping once, and making love to her under the stars. Just knowing the level of her sophistication, and that he'd stripped it all away along with her clothes, was a turn-on.

At Cleo's request he stopped for some fast-food hamburgers after he dropped the manure sample at the lab. From the way she tucked into hers as they started out of town, he figured she hadn't had much to eat on the plane ride.

He was a regular fool for beauty in a woman, and he couldn't help the enjoyment he felt watching Cleo do such a simple thing as unwrap her hamburger and take a bite of it with those even white teeth of hers. Her mouth was full and wide, a generous mouth, the kind that tempted a man to nibble and taste.

She took a napkin from the sack and wiped a dab of catsup from the corner of her mouth. "I need to ask about kitchen privileges," she said.

"Kitchen privileges? You fixing to cook while you're there?"

"Not cook, exactly, but I like to eat at odd times. I guess you could say I'm a snacker. I was wondering if I'd be allowed in the kitchen to fix myself something to eat."

Tom thought about Juanita's reign in the ranch kitchen. "I doubt it, but if you're real good to our cook, she might feed you between meals."

"I'd rather take care of myself, thanks. If you'll pull into that convenience store, I'll pick up some candy bars."

Tom swung the truck into the parking lot of the store and she began to untangle herself from her luggage.

"Hey, I'll get what you need," he said as he unbuckled his seat belt. "Don't go disturbing the balance there. Just tell me what you like."

"Okay." For the first time, she presented him with a genuine smile. "Anything with chocolate and nuts."

The result of that open smile was pretty impressive.

He totally forgot what she'd just told him about her candy-bar preferences. "Sorry, you'll have to repeat that."

"Chocolate and nuts." She gazed at him. "How did you get that scar on your chin?"

He touched the scar out of habit. "A little filly kicked me years back. She didn't mean to. Just scared."

"Tom, what would it take to convince you to be photographed?"

The effect of her smile wore off. "More than you can possibly imagine." He opened the door and got out of the truck. "How many candy bars?"

"At least thirty."

He ducked his head down to stare at her. "Thirty?"

"Yes." She dug in a pocket of her vest. "Let me get you some mon—"

"I'll cover it. I just never figured you wanted thirty candy bars."

"I told you. I like to snack."

"Slight understatement." Tom went inside and cleaned out the candy counter. He had to admit it was a refreshing change from most women he knew, who'd scarcely admit they ate candy, let alone send a man they barely knew into a store to buy them thirty bars of it.

When he returned with the plastic bag and gave it to

her, she thanked him and immediately delved into the assortment.

"You don't have some sort of condition, do you?" he asked.

She laughed. "Yes. It's called a high metabolism. I don't sleep much, but I sure do need to eat a lot to keep my energy level up. My dad's like that, too. I guess I inherited it."

As she unwrapped the candy, he pulled back into traffic. He was already tired of driving in it and longed for the lonely roads in the mountains. "I'd say it comes from living in New York City."

"You would, would you? Have you ever been there?"

"Yep."

"What for?"

"My ex-wife had an apartment there. Come to think of it, she probably still does."

"Now that's a fascinating bit of information." She took a bite of the candy bar.

He could tell she didn't want to drop the subject entirely, and sure enough, she brought it up again.

"I realize this is personal, and you don't have to answer, but would you consider telling me what your wife does in New York? It's a smaller town than you might think. I might even know her."

"Oh, I reckon you do. She's Deidre Anton."

Cleo sat up straighter. "The model?"

"Yep." He could almost hear the conclusions forming in her mind.

"And that's why you won't pose for me, isn't it?" she asked.

"That's the bulk of it. I've got nothing against you personally, but that whole world of glamour makes me sick to my stomach. Reality has been airbrushed right out of those pictures, but people think they're real, and then they try to be like those airbrushed folks, which they can't be, of course, so they're frustrated and unhappy with themselves."

"But I don't airbrush the men in my calendars. I like the character lines in their faces. If I photographed you, I'd want that little scar to stay in, because it's part of who you are. I'd want—"

"Cleo, I'm not doing it, so you can talk all day if you want, but it won't make any difference. I said Deidre was the main reason, but the other part is that I'm a very private man. I wouldn't want my picture all over the place."

She sighed and readjusted her knees around the suitcase. "That's a real shame."

"I can't see what the big problem is. I might be the first cowboy you've seen out here, but I won't be the last. Jeeter's going to love the idea of posing for you, I'll bet. And Stan's a pretty good-looking guy, and you might want to consider Jose, if he'll do it, which he probably will, especially if you give him that pitch about the movies. Is that part for real?"

"It's for real. I know of three guys I've used in calendars who've had small parts in movies. One just got his first speaking role."

Tom shuddered. "I'd rather be staked naked to an anthill."

"What a cool idea for a shot!"

"Not to a Montana man, it isn't. We're not that many generations removed from the pioneers who sometimes ended up that way. Anyway, you shouldn't have any trouble coming up with cowboys. There are lots of ranches around here. If this is a calendar, you only need twelve, right?"

"Well, I'd like to shoot an extra this time, in case someone doesn't work out. I don't want to have to come back."

"Yeah, that would be terrible." Tom cast her a sideways glance and was gratified that she had the sensitivity to blush, at least.

"I didn't mean it the way it sounded," she said.

"You have some beautiful country here." As if to prove that she meant it, she glanced out the window. "Really beautiful," she said with more conviction this time.

He remained silent and let the view of the mountains work on her some. Each section of Montana had something special about it, but Tom had a fierce love for Gallatin Canyon. A two-lane highway, partnered by the Gallatin River, wound between the Madison and Gallatin ranges and eventually entered Yellowstone Park. Between Bozeman and Yellowstone a person could see some damn fine scenery, in Tom's opinion.

This part of the state had been treated to some good rain the first couple of weeks of June, decorating the meadows with red Indian paintbrush, purple lupine, yellow bells and bluebells. Tom had always thought that the wildflowers, being temporary and delicate, gave a nice balance to the solid permanence of the mountains. The river flashed in the sun, reminding him of the hours he'd spent fly-fishing in its icy waters.

Cleo mumbled something as she continued to gaze out the window.

"I didn't catch that," Tom said.

"Should have brought a large-format," she said.

"Absolutely. I'm never without one, myself. What the hell is a large-format?"

She continued to be mesmerized by the view outside the truck. "It uses larger film and requires a tripod, so you can't be as spontaneous with it. I stick with the thirty-five millimeter for my calendar work, but for landscapes like this, a large format would be outstanding."

"I take it you like the view."

"I do. I've never seen anything like it, except in photos, of course. Too bad it's so far away from everything."

Tom smiled to himself. She obviously thought of New York City as the center of the universe. "It's not so far away," he said dryly. "Matter of fact, it's right outside my front door."

"Well, yeah, but I—oh my God. Stop the truck."

Tom pulled over to the shoulder as she scrambled to unfasten her seat belt and opened the door.

"Are you feeling sick? I'll bet it's all those candy—"

"I'm fine." She nearly fell out of the truck before she finally managed to climb around her gear and jump to the shoulder of the road. Shading her eyes with her hand, she gazed upward. "Come and look!"

Curious, he obliged, checking to make sure nobody was headed down the road behind them before he opened the door and got out.

"There." She pointed toward the blue sky.

He looked up, squinting a little. The large bird gliding above them was unmistakable, its seven-foot wingspan supported by the upward draft from the mountains, its white head and tail gleaming in the sun. His heart lifted every time he saw one.

"It's a bald eagle, isn't it?" she said in a hushed voice.

"Yep." Then he spotted the second one, the female of the pair, most likely. He touched her shoulder and pointed.

"There's his mate."

She clutched his arm. "Oh, Tom. They're... magnificent."

The catch in her voice caused him to look down at her, and sure enough, there were tears in her eyes. The sight of the bald eagles had stirred her in a way he understood all too well. For her, this was probably a first-time experience. He liked being around for that, just as he liked the way she'd grabbed his arm when she got excited.

"Well." She turned loose of his arm as the eagles soared out of sight and glanced at him. "Thanks. I've never seen an eagle before, except in the zoo."

"It's not quite the same."

Her smile was gentle "No, it's not quite the same."

In that moment Tom had his first premonition that this woman would become more than just another greenhorn visiting the Whispering Winds. He might not be interested in marriage anymore, but that didn't mean he'd given up on women altogether. An elemental connection tightened his gut. He made a practice of not getting involved with ranch guests, but this might be the time to make an exception.

3

CLEO HAD THOUGHT her decision to create a calendar featuring Montana cowboys had been pure marketing strategy, yet as the spectacular scenery unfolded with each bend in the road, she remembered an old childhood fantasy. She'd totally forgotten that one of her favorite pretend games had involved being a cowgirl living on a ranch surrounded by mountains. As Tom continued the drive to the Whispering Winds Ranch, he presented her with views of mountain meadows, streams and rose-colored bluffs right out of her youthful imagination.

Very few others shared the road with them, which surprised her. "Why is the traffic so light?" she asked finally.

"It's about normal for around here."

"But the road's practically deserted."

"You take eight hundred thousand people and spread them over a state the size of Montana, and you don't get much traffic."

"That's the state's population? But the city of New York has —"

"About ten times more people than the whole state of Montana. I'm well aware of that. I felt like a bull trapped in a rodeo chute whenever I went back there. Now, thank God, I don't have to go anymore."

"Are you kidding? New York is fantastic! Everywhere you look, there's something exciting to see."

"Not if you want to see this."

She had to concede his point. You couldn't find anything like Montana in Manhattan, but then she hadn't built her career on pretty pictures of mountain vistas and sparkling rivers, either. She gazed at the profile of the man beside her, and her trigger finger began to itch. She'd love to capture that decisive jawline, the curve of his ear, the aggressive line of his nose.

Her trusty thirty-five millimeter was loaded and ready inside her camera bag. She unzipped the bag slowly and eased the cap off the lens. Glancing down to check her settings, she lifted the camera out of the bag as noiselessly as possible.

"Don't." He hadn't moved his head even a fraction of an inch, yet he apparently knew what she was up to.

She put the lens cap back on. "What if I didn't use any of the photos for the calendar? What if I just took them for fun?"

"Don't forget, I was married to a model for five years, and I have some acquaintance with professional photographers. You don't usually shoot for fun."

She had to admit he was right. Although she enjoyed her work, she never took photos anymore just for the heck of it. No point in wasting time and film on something that wouldn't sell. "Okay, I wouldn't be doing it for the fun of it. I just think that if you saw what I could accomplish, you might change your mind about posing."

"Sorry. You'll have to find somebody with a bigger ego than mine if you want to succeed with that argument. I only look in the mirror so I won't nick myself when I shave."

Immediately she had a new idea for a shot—Tom, shirtless but wearing his Stetson, wielding a straight razor as he stood in front of a crockery washbasin. She'd love to know what he'd look like without a shirt. His open collar revealed a glimpse of chest hair that looked promising. Dammit, she wanted to get this man on film. She was so used to cooperative men that she was having a hard time with this one's refusal.

"Here we are," Tom said, swinging off the asphalt onto a dirt road. "Welcome to the Whispering Winds." He braked the truck to a stop in front of a metal gate and got out to open it. Barbed-wire fencing stretched into the distance on both sides of the gate, and wooden posts rose on either side of it. Suspended from a lodgepole that bridged the posts was a sign with Whispering Winds Ranch carved deep into the wood.

Tom climbed in, pulled the truck through and went back to close the gate, giving Cleo ample time to get the lay of the land. The road angled down to a wide meadow rimmed with evergreens and aspen. Beyond the meadow the terrain sloped upward as hills gave way to jagged, snowcapped mountain peaks.

It would have made a terrific postcard. Centered in the shot, if she were photographing the scene, was a log ranch house nestled against the trees. It reminded her of the Lincoln Log house she'd built as a kid during her cowgirl phase, and it had a weathered look that suggested it had been there for a long time. An aging barn and split-rail corrals occupied the right side of the meadow, and several rustic cabins clustered on the left. A string of riders appeared from among the trees and headed for the corrals, almost as if they'd been cued on stage when she arrived. To make the picture complete, a black-and-white dog ran out to greet the riders.

"This is *exactly* what I was looking for," Cleo said as Tom got back into the truck. "You don't mind if pieces of your ranch show up in my calendar, do you?"

"Pieces of my ranch are fine. Just no pieces of me." His

gaze held no compromise. "And don't think I haven't heard of zoom lenses. Take a picture of me and use it without my permission and I'll haul your fanny into court."

She was highly insulted. "I wouldn't dream of it. That's unethical."

His answering laugh was short and humorless. "When I was married to Deidre, we had paparazzi on our tail a few times. Don't preach to me about the ethics of photographers."

That got to her. She prided herself on her ethics. "Just because you didn't like being married to a successful model doesn't give you the right to be so prejudiced against photographers in general."

He negotiated around a puddle in the road. "It does give me the right. I earned it the hard way."

"For your information, I always get permission from my subjects before using the photographs. So do all the photographers I know."

"Good. You can be sure I won't give it."

"I've never met someone so phobic in my life."

He didn't respond.

Cleo sighed. If she had any sense, she'd give up on him, but that cover-shot possibility was seared into her brain. Now she wouldn't be satisfied with the calendar until she'd nailed down her concept. Maybe she'd find another cowboy who would project the image she wanted, but probably not. Tom was a rare find, and she'd photographed enough men to realize it.

Tom stopped the truck as the string of five riders crossed the road in front of them.

The lead rider, a lanky cowboy Cleo estimated to be in his mid-twenties, changed direction and headed for the truck. "Just take them on into the corral, folks," he called out to the riders—a man, woman and two kids. "I'll be right there."

Tom rolled down the window as the cowboy drew alongside. "How's it going, Jeeter?"

"Saw some cat tracks up along Settlers Creek. Looks like a big one, maybe looking to pick off a calf or two."

Cleo gasped. "A cougar?"

The cowboy named Jeeter leaned down to peer into the cab. He touched the brim of his hat in salute. "A cougar for sure, ma'am."

"Jeeter Neff, meet Cleo Griffin, our photographer from New York City," Tom said.

"Pleased to meet you," Jeeter said. "Listen, Tom, maybe somebody oughta go after that cat before something happens."

Tom rested his forearms on the steering wheel and frowned.

"That's what your dad would have done," Jeeter said.

Tom sighed. "I know. But in his day we had more of those cats. We planned to rotate the herd to a different pasture next month, anyway. Let's do it earlier, and see if we can get them out of range."

"You're the boss."

"We can take some of the dudes, give them a cattle-drive experience." Tom turned to Cleo. "Maybe you'd like to go along and take this cat's picture if it shows up."

She had no desire to come face-to-face with predatory wildlife, but going on a cattle drive might give her valuable background for the calendar. "Sounds like an interesting idea," she said, assessing Jeeter with a practiced eye. He didn't have Tom's seasoned ruggedness, but his blond good looks and mustache would definitely satisfy some woman's fantasy. "I'm doing a calendar called

Montana Men, and I'm here to photograph cowboys. Are you interested, Jeeter?"

"No joke?" Jeeter asked, pushing his hat back on his head. "You mean, I'd be like Mr. November or something?"

Cleo laughed. "I can't guarantee what month, but yes, something like that."

"Would I have to take off my clothes? I'm not saying I wouldn't do it, but I'd like to know beforehand."

"At the most, you'd only have to take off your shirt. I visualize the jeans as being part of the sex appeal."

'Yes, *ma'am!*" Jeeter grinned. "Just tell me where and when." He glanced at Tom. "That's if it's okay with you, Tom, and it fits into the schedule and everything."

"I'm sure we can work something out," Tom said, his tone dry.

"Are you gonna pose, Tom? I think you'd be—"

"No."

Jeeter gazed at his boss, then leaned down to look at Cleo again. "There's no catch to this, is there? Like I have to pay you, or something?"

"As a matter of fact, I'll pay you," Cleo said.

"If that don't beat all," Jeeter said. "I get to hang on somebody's wall and be paid for the privilege. Well, I'd better go check on the dudes." He touched his hat brim again. "Just let me know when you want me, ma'am." He cantered away.

"You sure put a swash in his buckle," Tom said as he lifted his foot from the brake.

"I hate to tell you, but that's the reaction I usually get. You're the only man who's ever refused to pose for me."

"And I intend to hold on to that distinction."

"You don't think you're being just a little stubborn? A little prejudiced? A little pigheaded?"

"You aren't going to flatter me into it, either. I suggest you drop the subject, Cleo, or we won't have much to do with each other while you're here."

"You're being ridiculous."

"Pardon me, ma'am, but on my ranch, I'll be whatever I want to be."

"Which is, difficult," Cleo muttered.

"I prefer to think of myself as an independent thinker. Well, here we are." Tom parked the truck next to a lovely little cabin tucked into the trees and more secluded than the other five. Red tulips and yellow daffodils bloomed by the doorstep and eyelet curtains hung at the windows.

"Well, the accommodations certainly are charming," Cleo said pointedly.

Tom paused before opening his door. "I can be charming, too, if someone's not threatening to point a camera in my face."

She met his determined gaze and decided to retreat for the time being. "Understood," she said. She had two weeks to wear him down. One thing she'd learned early in this game was patience. She opened her door and started to climb out around her gear.

"If you'll hold on, I'll be more than happy to help you out, ma'am," he said, all brusqueness gone from his manner. "I wouldn't want you to fall and break that pretty neck of yours."

She turned to him and lifted her eyebrows.

"See?" He grinned. "Charming."

Well, he was, she had to admit. Her insides did a funny little dance in the warmth of that smile. "Thanks," she said. "I could use some help, at that."

"Coming right up." He hopped out and walked around to her side.

She handed him the backpack and he set it on the

ground with no fuss, but the suitcase wedged between her knees was a more delicate matter. She had to spread her legs to make room to lift it out, and he kept brushing her inner thighs as he maneuvered it out of the cab. He acted as if he didn't notice, and she pretended not to, either, but her body noticed, all right. She grew very warm in certain strategic places, and her pulse rate skyrocketed.

This would never do. First of all, she wanted him as a subject for her calendar, which ruled out hanky-panky. Secondly, she had to save herself for the cowboy she'd ask to marry her while she was out here in the wilds of Montana. And that cowboy definitely wasn't Tom. He wasn't nearly docile enough for the role she had in mind.

"Are you about ready to come out of there, ma'am, or did you need a few more minutes to cogitate on the situation?"

She glanced over and found him watching her, his mouth curved in a smile and his thumbs hooked casually through his belt loops. It would make an excellent shot. She hoped to hell he hadn't been able to guess that she'd been staring into space because his accidental touch had turned her on. Grabbing her camera bag, she scrambled to the ground.

Tom led the way into the cabin, which wasn't locked. Cleo was fast learning that nobody bothered locking either house or car doors out here. That would take some getting used to, after the triple-lock system and the security alarm she had for her Greenwich Village apartment.

The interior of the cabin matched the charm of the exterior. The varnished log walls gave a honey-colored glow to the furnishings, which included a king-size bed, bureau and dressing table, all in whitewashed pine. A turquoise coverlet on the bed, western art on the walls and Indian-print rugs on the floor completed the frontier look.

Cleo nodded in satisfaction. "This is great."

"It's my favorite cabin," Tom said, "on account of its being back in the trees a little more. And then there's the hot tub just out the back door."

"Hot tub?" Cleo frowned at the vision of some plastic monster mucking up the rustic ambience of the place.

"The Whispering Winds is built on the site of natural hot springs," Tom said. "Didn't you read the brochure?"

"No, I left that to Bernie. She must have forgotten about the hot springs."

"Come on. I'll show you." Tom left her suitcase and backpack on the floor and walked back outside.

After some inner debate, Cleo left her camera bag there, too, before following him out the door. Surely no one would sneak in and steal her camera while she was out inspecting the hot tub, yet leaving it in an open cabin bothered her anyway. Big-city living had built caution into her. She wondered what it must be like to worry about a cougar killing your calves instead of a drug-crazed psycho killing you. That was one aspect of city life she could do without.

She hurried to catch up with Tom, who was striding down a narrow path that disappeared into the trees. Her shoes crunched pine needles underfoot, and the dusky scent of sun-warmed underbrush tickled her nose. A couple of perky little birds chirped and fluttered in the branches of a tree near the path, and overhead a breeze passed through the evergreens with a sound like gentle surf—the whispering winds the ranch was named after, she concluded.

Tom seemed to walk with even more assurance now that his boots touched down on his own land. *On my ranch, I'll be whatever I want to be.* It was a great line, and she'd love to use it in the bio printed next to his calendar photo. The calendar photo that would also appear on the cover of *Montana Men,* she vowed silently.

He glanced over his shoulder. "This is our most private hot tub. Some folks are spooked to be off here by themselves, but the dogs will always alert you if anything's around."

"Like what?" A little thrill of fear shot through her.

"Well, skunks, of course, and raccoons and deer. We've had a cougar down this far once in my lifetime, a few moose, wolves once in a while. Oh, and there was that one time a grizz showed up."

"A grizzly bear?" Cleo glanced around and her heart pounded faster. What had seemed like peaceful forest sounds took on a sinister cast. In her imagination, the crack of a twig became the warning of an approaching monster. "I thought they were all up in Alaska somewhere."

"We get a few down here now and then," Tom announced as if reporting on the migration of meadowlarks.

"When was the last time?"

"About five years ago." He stepped into a clearing where a redwood tub just right for two people bubbled away. "Here it is, a little bit of paradise."

"Unless a grizzly shows up." Cleo stepped forward to dip her hand into the warm water. After traveling all day, she'd like nothing better than to sink naked into it.

"The dogs would tell you if a bear was around." Tom trailed his hand through the water. "Unless the wind was wrong and they couldn't smell him, that is."

She glanced over at him. "Are you deliberately trying to scare me? Because you're doing a hell of a job."

His grin gave her the answer. "Okay, I'm laying it on a little thick. It's a bad habit I have with city people. You have a better chance of being mugged in New York than meeting a grizzly on this ranch."

"I don't find that a comforting comparison. I feel as if I should be armed with my canister of Mace."

Tom gave her a considering glance. "You know, all kidding aside, I can't remember the last time we've had a single woman as a guest. I didn't give much thought to the fact you might be scared staying out here alone. Maybe we should switch you over to the main house."

"I'd rather stay here." She'd already had fallen in love with her private little cabin. In addition to that, she really longed for a good long soak in this secluded hot tub, bears or no bears. "I'm sure pioneer women lived alone in the wilderness all the time."

"Modern-day women, too. My mother managed by herself lots of times when my dad and the hands went out on a roundup and took the cook along."

"This ranch used to belong to your parents?"

"And three generations before that. Mom and Dad would still be here running the place if Dad hadn't come down with Alzheimer's. They finally gave in and moved to Billings, where his specialist is located."

Five generations of McBrides on this spot. No wonder he looked so at home here. "Do you have brothers and sisters?"

"A sister. She fell in love with a Texan and moved to Austin."

The disbelief in his voice made Cleo smile. "Imagine that."

"Once she started a family, she lost interest in the ranch, so I bought her out."

"You really love the Whispering Winds, don't you?"

"It's home," he said quietly.

The warm water ran through Cleo's fingers as she remembered an essay she'd read in college about the importance of place in a person's life. She'd never understood the essay until now. Although she loved the city, she didn't feel the intense connection that Tom obviously felt to the ranch. He was different from the other men she'd known, including her father, who dedicated themselves to careers and business success. Curiosity had driven her to take up photography, and it drove her now—that and the hope that she would still get Tom to be part of her project.

"My time here is limited," she began, feeling her way toward the thought that was only half-formed in her mind. "I have a job to do, obviously, but while I'm here...I'd count it as a special favor if you'd show me what makes this place so special to you."

He contemplated her for a long moment. "I'd like that," he said at last. "Can you ride?"

"Some." She remembered English-riding lessons when she was ten, the struggle to win blue ribbons in competition and the sense of failure when all she could achieve was second place. She hadn't been on a horse since.

"Think you could handle a couple of days helping us move the cattle?" he said. "Tomorrow I have some chores to tend to, but the morning after that I'm planning to take a couple of hands and any guests who want to go. We'll see if we can get those calves out of harm's way."

"Sure." She'd never slept outside in her life, but cowboys did it all the time, and she was here to capture the spirit of being a cowboy. "I'll probably get some ideas for calendar shots."

"What you'll probably get is saddle-sore, if you

haven't ridden much lately. But we'll take a wagon along with sleeping bags and grub, so if you get tired, you can ride in—"

"I'll keep up."

He rubbed his chin and gazed at her. "This isn't a test, Cleo. I'm sorry if I gave you the idea that dudes have to prove themselves out here. You're supposed to relax and have a good time."

"But I'm not on vacation."

He studied her. "And I'll bet you don't take vacations."

"Nope. And I'll bet you don't, either."

"Nope." He smiled. "But it's mighty pretty country up there among the pines, so maybe we could both pretend a little."

By God, he was flirting with her. She wondered if she could entice him to participate in her calendar project with some innocent flirtation without compromising her principles. It would be tricky. "Okay, we'll pretend we're on vacation. But tomorrow I have to work. Can I borrow Jeeter for a couple of hours?"

"You can. I wouldn't want to stand in the way of his fame and fortune."

"You're free to watch me work if you're curious. You might change your mind about posing."

"I've seen photo shoots before, and I won't change my mind."

The challenge in his voice quickened her pulse and hardened her resolve. "We'll see."

TOM WAS SAILING on uncharted waters. As he stood by the hot tub and looked at Cleo, the sunlight filtering through the pine branches lighting up the gold in her hair, desire stirred in him with sweet persistence. He really shouldn't be having such thoughts about one of his guests, but he'd never had a guest quite like this one, either.

As he'd told Cleo, single women were a rarity at the ranch, with couples and families making up the biggest part of the guest roster. Years ago, two widows got in the habit of booking several weeks at the ranch each summer, but those sixty-something ladies were a far cry from a woman like Cleo. As he stood alone with her in this peaceful clearing, he fought the urge to step closer and snug up the line of tension between them. With a few well-chosen words and any encouragement from her, he might even risk taking her in his arms.

He wondered what she'd do. Push him away, most likely. Or maybe not. The interest she'd shown so far hinted that she might lift that full mouth to his. He probably should think the notion through a little more before he acted on it, though. A similar notion about a New York City woman had turned into major heartache. This one wanted to take his picture, and she might even be thinking that flirtation was a way to accomplish her ends.

"I'd better get to that paperwork I mentioned," he said. "Unless you need any help getting settled in."

Awareness flashed in her eyes.

He held his breath, wondering if she'd take him up on his offer. Now that he'd thrown out the comment, he wondered if it would be wise to follow through so quick. Reason told him it wouldn't be.

"No, I'll be fine," she said at last.

He let out his breath and discovered he was more disappointed than he'd expected under the circumstances. "I'll be going, then."

"Okay. By the way, when's dinner?"

He smiled. This constant appetite of hers amused him.

"At six, up at the house. We eat family style in the dining room."

"Speaking of all the families around here, is there a rule about wearing a bathing suit in the hot tub? I wouldn't want to embarrass anyone."

The rope of tension linking them snapped tight again.

Unless he missed his guess, she wanted him to know she planned to skinny-dip in the tub. He got the picture, and it scrambled his brains all the more. "The families don't use this one," he said. "Cabin six is set up for couples, and the private hot tub is part of the deal. You might want to wait until after dark, though, just to be on the safe side."

Cleo cupped water in her hand and let it run through her fingers. "Thanks. I'll keep that in mind."

"See you at dinner." He started out of the clearing.

"That's not the path we came in on," she called after him.

He paused and turned to her. "No. It's a shortcut to the house."

"So there are two paths leading to this clearing, one from the cabin and one from the main house?"

"That's right."

"Is that because you use this hot tub when nobody's staying in the cabin?"

"I've been known to."

"Maybe we can work out a system so we can share it."

Hellfire. This woman promised to be a handful, that is if he decided to take the considerable gamble of finding out. "Maybe so. Well, see you at dinner." He touched the brim of his hat and got himself out of there before he said or did something he wouldn't be able to take back. He'd like to share that hot tub with her, all right. Besides, if they decided to play games in the bubbling mineral water, he could be pretty sure she wouldn't have her damn camera hanging around her neck.

4

WIND GUSTS scented with rain pulled at Cleo's hair as she walked up to the main house for dinner. Clouds sat on the jagged crust of the mountains like scoops of blueberry ice cream, and the temperature had dropped by at least fifteen degrees. Even a greenhorn could tell a storm was on the way, Cleo thought, which probably doused her plans for a hot-tub experience tonight.

She was angry with herself for her part in the hot-tub discussion with Tom. His refusal to be part of her project stung, but she hoped a devilish sense of revenge was all that had motivated her to blurt out her intention of hot tubbing naked. She'd hate to think that she was unscrupulous enough to suggest sexual favors in exchange for his photo in her calendar, favors she'd never deliver. She wanted him on the cover, but she wouldn't sacrifice her character to get him there.

The sound of hammering drew her gaze to the roof of the two-story house, and there was Tom, kneeling to work on what must be a loose shingle. He wore no hat, and the wind whipped at his sun-streaked hair. Behind him rose the mountains and the darkening clouds. In his concentration on the task, she glimpsed the spirit of his pioneer ancestors, tough folks who had stood up to a tough country and won the right to live here.

She cupped her hands over her mouth. "Soup's on!"

He stopped hammering and looked down at her. "I'll

eat later. This flapping's been driving Juanita, our cook, crazy, and I promised her I'd fix it before the next storm hit. That should be shortly."

She hadn't realized how much she'd counted on seeing him during the meal until the prospect was taken away. "What do people do around here for fun in the evenings?" she asked.

He leaned his hammer arm on his bent knee. "Go to bed."

Had a New Yorker said that to her, she would have immediately got the double meaning, as intended, but Tom probably meant exactly what he'd said and nothing more. Being a city girl, and a sexually frustrated one, at that, she heard those simple words and immediately placed herself in a rumple of sheets and blankets with a certain rancher while the rain poured down outside. She really had to find a docile cowboy and get hitched, as they said in the Wild West.

"I just thought maybe there would be line-dancing lessons or something," she said.

"There's a ranch down the road that has all that. I could get Jeeter or someone to take you. Folks that book here prefer it quiet in the evenings."

"So they can hear the bears coming."

He grinned at her. "That's right. Now you'd better get in there. Juanita doesn't like people coming late to her table, and I know you want to get on her good side."

She'd been stalling, just to have an excuse to be around him, as if she were a teenager with a crush on the star football player. That was sickening behavior for a woman, and she vowed to stop it immediately. "Happy hammering," she called, and walked into the house without another glance at the roof. There were other cowboys on the range, and soon she'd have a baker's dozen from which to choose a man to ease her ache.

The main living area of the house was deserted, with all the noise coming from a doorway off to the right which led into the dining room. Although the aroma of food drew her, Cleo's artistic eye would never let her race through a room as interesting as this one.

The decor was more sensuous than she would have expected, a stimulating blend of masculine and feminine aspects. A native-rock fireplace with a rough-hewn mantel dominated one end of the room, and the scent of wood smoke and pipe tobacco hung in the air. The rugged ambience was balanced by overstuffed leather couches so plump they begged to be enjoyed. She ran a hand over the arm of the one nearest her and felt a jolt of pleasure at the butter-soft texture.

What fun it would be to roll around on one of these couches with— Cleo stopped herself with a grimace. She needed to get her plan up and running, and she needed to do it in a hurry, before she embarrassed herself.

A short, sturdy Hispanic woman wearing a food-stained apron came to the dining-room door. "Are you going to eat?" she asked.

"Yes, please." Cleo started toward the dining room. "You must be Juanita."

"And you're the photographer."

"That's right."

Juanita assessed her with dark eyes. "Tom said you brought a bunch of candy bars with you." It sounded like an indictment.

Thanks, Tom. "I like to eat at irregular times, and I didn't want to bother you."

Juanita looked her up and down. "If you keep eating

candy bars, instead of good food, you won't keep that figure for long."

Cleo tried to keep from smiling. If Juanita's figure was an indication of what good food could do to a person's figure, Cleo was better off with her candy bars. "I suppose you're right, but I honestly don't like bothering anyone when I want something to eat, and Tom said you didn't like to have people messing around in your kitchen when you're not there."

"Well, Tom's right. If I started letting the dudes, I mean the guests, go in there whenever they wanted, I'd have nothing but trouble."

"I don't want to louse up your program, and the candy bars will do just—"

"I could make you a deal."

Cleo looked at her in surprise. "What kind of deal?"

"I have two little ones, Rosa and Peter, and they're growing up so fast. My mother and father in Mexico are begging me for pictures, but I'm no good with a camera. If you'd take some special ones that I could send as Christmas presents, you can come into my kitchen and fix yourself whatever snacks you want."

"I don't usually take pictures of kids." Cleo didn't even know where she'd start.

Juanita waved her hand in a dismissive gesture. "I know. You take pictures of hunks. I have one of your calendars on my wall right now, the one with the construction guys on it." She winked. "*Muy bueno.*"

It was a moment Cleo had never experienced before— meeting a stranger who had bought one of her calendars. The sales figures had been numbers to her, not people. She felt gratified, but a little self-conscious. "Thanks."

"You can do a fine job with Rosa and Peter. Now come on in and eat dinner before everything gets cold." Juanita turned and started back into the dining room, as if the matter was settled.

Cleo shrugged and followed her. She'd have to remember to tell Bernie about this when she called her tomorrow. Her friend would get a kick out of it, the sophisticated Cleo Griffin snapping shots of rug rats.

TOM HAD TROUBLE getting to sleep that night. As he lay in bed, most of his thoughts involved excuses for checking on Cleo. The storm battered the ranch with enough force to scare a New York woman, he reasoned, and he wasn't absolutely sure her cabin didn't leak.

Finally he got up and went to the bedroom window. From his vantage point on the second floor, he could see one end of Cleo's cabin, and her light was still on. He hadn't left her with any buckets, so she might be frantically trying to find containers for drips. He'd never installed phones in the cabins, so of course she wouldn't have a way to call the main house if she had problems.

Then logic prevailed. Luann, his extremely efficient head housekeeper, would have reported any evidence of a leak when she mentioned the stopped-up toilet. In fact, he would have noticed stains on the floor when he was in the cabin fixing the toilet. The roof was secure.

He went back to bed and closed his eyes, but he was still too revved up to sleep. He listened to the storm blow itself out, and got up again to see if Cleo's light still shone from the window. It did, beckoning him with her presence, creating a restlessness he hadn't felt in some time.

Standing naked in the darkness staring out the window, he imagined how the yipping of coyotes and the rattle of raccoons trying to pry off garbage-can lids might frighten somebody who'd never heard them before. He should probably go down there and make sure she was okay.

Before he finished dressing, he reversed the process and took off his clothes again. He was too damn eager, and that meant trouble. That meant she might turn out to be more than a casual fling, and casual flings were all he was in the market for these days. Once upon a time he might have figured that a New York woman was a perfectly safe bet for a brief affair. Now he knew himself better.

If he started something with Cleo tonight, she'd have two weeks to burrow under his skin. It would be more than enough time to screw up his life but good. If he intended to get involved with her at all, he'd better pace himself so that before he started to fall for her, she'd be long gone.

He disciplined himself to take slow, deep breaths, and finally found sleep, but sleep also meant dreams. Dawn greeted him with an erection that required a cold shower before he could pull on his jeans. Impatient with himself, he headed down to help Jeeter and Stan with the morning feeding, and wished that his first thought hadn't been whether Cleo would make it to breakfast.

Sometime later, as he was on his second cup of coffee, he concluded that she wasn't going to show up. The other guests had come and gone, leaving Juanita and Luann to the cleanup chores in the big sunny dining room. Tom had checked with all of the dudes to find out who wanted to go on the cattle drive tomorrow, and he'd had five takers—one young childless couple and another couple with a fourteen-year-old daughter.

Now he sat alone at one end of the room's twin trestle tables and lingered over his coffee. He had no business taking it easy on this fine June morning, not with the amount of work to be done today, but he wanted to see Cleo again, if only for a moment.

Just as he was about to give up and tackle his list of chores, Cleo came through the double doors to the dining room looking like a zombie. A beautiful blond zombie, but a zombie nonetheless.

Juanita stopped wiping the table she'd just cleared and glanced up.

Tom braced himself for the tirade. Juanita considered tardiness at mealtime a personal insult, and it didn't matter if the offender was a paying guest or not. Fortunately, the Whispering Winds had a lot of return customers, and most everyone took Juanita's dictatorial ways in stride because she cooked like a goddess.

Juanita put down her dishcloth and walked over to Cleo. "You look like you could use a cup of coffee, *querida.*" She cupped Cleo's elbow and guided her to the bench at Tom's table. "Sit here and I'll bring you some. How about some toast? A soft-boiled egg?"

Tom's mouth hung open in amazement.

"Toast and black coffee is all I need, Juanita. Thanks so much." Cleo slid onto a bench and glanced down the table toward Tom. "Do mornings always come this early around here?"

Tom closed his mouth. "Generally speaking." That sleepy-eyed look of hers registered on his libido. He imagined waking up next to her and gradually, patiently kissing that sleepiness away.

Juanita bustled in with a steaming mug. "Here you go. Toast is on the way."

Tom was staring at Juanita in amazement, but she ignored him and hurried back out of the room.

"Thanks, Juanita," Cleo called after her. Then she took a long sip of coffee and closed her eyes.

"Are you all right?"

"I'm getting there." Her eyes drifted open again and she took another swallow of coffee. "My brain will start functioning any second now. I swear to God I heard a rooster crowing outside my window."

"That would be Rooster Cogburn. He pretty much has the run of the place and he does tend to crow when it gets light out. That's a rooster's job."

"I don't suppose you could give him a few days off? Send him to visit his brother in L.A. or something?"

"You're not a morning person."

"Doesn't look like it, does it?" She drank more coffee.

"How was your night?"

"Noisy."

He snorted. "Compared to New York with all the sirens and constant traffic? Are you kidding?"

"But I'm used to those noises. Here there's quiet, and then howling, and quiet, and then rustling, then more quiet, and yipping. Howling, rustling, yipping. Rustling, yipping, howling. All night long. I felt like I was sleeping on a bench at the Bronx Zoo."

"I wondered if I should check on you."

She looked more alert. "You did?"

"But then I decided a New York chick like you wouldn't be scared."

"I didn't say I was scared. Just awake."

Juanita swept back into the room. "Here's your toast, and some homemade apple jelly." She set a plate and a crock of jelly in front of Cleo and poured her some more coffee.

"This looks just fine. I appreciate it. And the coffee's great."

"If you want anything else, just call me." Juanita patted Cleo on the shoulder before starting back toward the kitchen.

"Hold it," Tom said. "If I may be so bold as to ask, what exactly is going on here?"

Juanita turned to him, the coffee carafe in one hand.

"I'm serving our guest a little breakfast. Isn't that what you hired me for?"

"Yeah, but you've never let anybody else get away with coming in late for a meal, unless it's some sort of emergency. And you're treating Cleo like...like Cleopatra on her barge, for God's sake."

"This woman is an artist," Juanita said disparagingly. "She can't be expected to live by the same schedule as the rest of us."

Tom looked down the table at Cleo, who was trying to hide a smile behind her coffee mug. He gazed at her for several seconds. "I see."

"I'll be back with a coffee refill in a little while, Cleo." Juanita started out of the room.

"I could use a coffee refill about now, myself," Tom called over his shoulder.

Juanita paused.

"If you can spare the time."

Juanita walked over and poured coffee into his mug. "Are you going to pose for her?"

"No, I'm not." He took a sip from his mug.

Juanita studied him for a moment. "I guess you're a little old for it."

He choked on his coffee. Thirty-eight wasn't old. Men hit their prime at his age, and he'd never felt better, more alive, more ready for...well, that wasn't the point. He cleared his throat. "As a matter of fact, she asked me."

"He turned you down?" she asked Cleo.

"Flat." Cleo had perked up considerably in the past few minutes and looked delighted with the conversation.

"Why on earth would he do that?" Juanita turned to him, her expression disbelieving. "You might not be the most handsome man in the world, but you're not bad for a cowhand. I'll bet she could make you look even better."

"As flattered as I am by that speech, Juanita, I'd rather clean the chicken coop with a toothbrush."

Juanita shrugged. "Some people wouldn't know a golden opportunity if it bit them in the backside."

"I guess not," Cleo said. "Thanks for breakfast."

"Anytime." Juanita left the room shaking her head.

"You've cast a spell on my cook," Tom said when Juanita was out of earshot.

Cleo laughed. "Apparently. Want to know my secret?"

"I imagine everyone in the county would like to know your secret. Juanita's the best cook in these parts, and she knows it. Why she hangs around the Whispering Winds is a mystery, except that I let her do whatever she wants. She doesn't dance to anyone's tune, but you seem to have her wrapped around your little finger."

"My trigger finger, to be more exact. She wants me to take pictures of her kids." Cleo bit into the toast and murmured her approval.

"Oh." Tom watched with pleasure as she sank her teeth into the crunchy bread and swiped her tongue over a spot of jelly that landed on her lower lip. "That makes sense. She dotes on those kids."

Cleo swallowed the bite of toast. "Where's the dad?"

"The marriage didn't work out, but they're both staunch Catholics, so divorce wasn't an option. He's on the rodeo circuit and stops by every month or so to see the kids, but she's pretty much on her own. She's hired a teenage girl to watch them when she's busy in the kitchen."

"Sounds like a difficult situation," Cleo said.

"It is."

"But she strikes me as pretty tough. And damn, she makes good coffee." Cleo took another long drink.

Tom wondered how long he could put off work without somebody coming to look for him. He was having a great time sharing this slice of morning with Cleo. "Juanita's tough, all right. I thought she was going to punch out Deidre once."

"Really? Did Deidre insult her cooking?"

"No. They...let's just say that Juanita didn't approve of Deidre's behavior." Deidre had imagined Juanita would back her on the abortion question, that they'd unite as two women who both faced the problems created by men. Deidre had miscalculated on that one.

Cleo gazed at him over her coffee mug. He figured she wanted to ask what behavior had caused Juanita to consider violence toward his ex-wife, but she held back. He probably shouldn't have brought up the subject, but the warm sun through the windows, the taste of Juanita's coffee and the quiet that had settled over the dining room all combined to give him the relaxed impression that he could tell her anything at all and she would understand. Still, Deidre's abortion wasn't the sort of topic you threw out to someone you'd known less than twenty-four hours.

With a sigh of regret, he pushed himself away from the table and stood. "I'd better get going."

"What's on the schedule for you today?"

He liked the feeling of having someone—someone soft and feminine—ask the question. He'd had an image of marriage that never came quite true with Deidre. They didn't spend enough time together to fall into a routine, and he'd discovered routine was comforting to him.

He adjusted his hat, a newer Stetson than the one he'd worn for her benefit yesterday. "Some repair work on the barn this morning, and we're breeding one of our mares this afternoon."

Her cheeks grew a shade pinker. "Really? Will it be one of those artificial insemination jobs?"

"No, we don't get that fancy around here. For the few times we get involved in the process, the old-fashioned way is good enough." He wondered if the conversation was affecting her the way it was affecting him. "You're going to take pictures of Jeeter today, aren't you?"

"We're scheduled for right after lunch, probably in the barn. I'm going to scout out some locations this morning. I'll make sure we don't get in the way of your... breeding."

"That's not until two-thirty. A neighbor's bringing his stallion over then."

"Love in the afternoon," Cleo said.

"It's not what I'd call love."

"Lust, then."

"That's closer, I guess. I sometimes feel sorry for animals. We can manipulate them so easily because of their biology." While *he* was so much more sophisticated, he thought. Sure he was. That's why he was picturing Cleo on her back in a pile of hay, wearing nothing but a smile. "Stop by the corral if you want, after your photography session," he said.

"Stop by the barn if you want, before your breeding session," she countered, putting down her mug and standing.

"We'll see." He glanced at her plate. "You'd better get

some more toast or something before you go. I doubt that will hold you until lunch."

She grinned at him. "You forget. It doesn't have to."

"Oh yeah." He rubbed the back of his neck. "I still can't believe all it took was a camera to make Juanita your devoted servant."

"A camera's a powerful tool."

"I guess you're right. You probably know that Native Americans used to believe it stole your spirit."

"I'd heard that." Her gaze was searching. "You half-way believe it yourself, don't you?"

He paused to think about the concept. At last he nodded. "Yeah, Cleo, I do. See you around."

5

CLEO MUNCHED her way through the morning, dropping by the kitchen several times to pilfer snacks. In the process she met Rosa, aged four, and Peter, aged two, when the baby-sitter brought them in for lunch. Cleo had no idea how she'd go about photographing the dark-eyed cherubs when the time came, but Juanita was so entranced with the idea that Cleo pretended more confidence than she felt.

Her morning snacking made her own lunch unnecessary, so while the hands and guests were inside the ranch house eating, Cleo took advantage of the deserted barn to set up for the photo session with Jeeter. During the morning, she'd figured out that light filtering through the big double doors would give her enough to shoot without a flash, which she preferred. Using ambient light instead of flashes or strobes was one of her trademarks, and she was vain about it.

Just inside the door the light fell just the way she wanted, and she positioned a bale of hay up against the weathered side of a vacant stall. All the stalls were empty on this warm summer day, now that the horses had been turned out to graze. Cleo wondered where the mare of the hour had been taken and if she was having her hooves painted and her mane curled for her big date. Cleo was dying with curiosity about the event, but she'd heard that watching such goings-on had an effect on the humans, and she didn't need any more of that certain effect, thank you very much.

With the horses gone from the barn, only a tortoiseshell cat and her newborn kittens remained to keep Cleo company as she arranged the hay bale and checked the light from different angles. She discovered the little family nestled inside a wooden box behind a hand cart. The saddle blanket tucked in the box looked deliberately placed there. Somebody had provided this kitten nursery, Cleo decided, and wondered if Tom was that much of a softie.

The scent of hay, oats and horses brought back bittersweet memories of her English-riding days. She'd loved the horses and had wanted one of her own. Her father had told her he'd buy her the horse of her dreams after she won her first blue ribbon. A man of his word, her father. She never got her horse.

Jeeter arrived right on time, interrupting her thoughts. Polished spurs jingling, he clomped into the barn wearing what she suspected was his Saturday-night going-to-town outfit—new jeans, ostrich-skin boots, a wildly patterned western shirt, a leather vest and a black Stetson that looked fresh out of the box.

He touched the brim in greeting. "Ma'am."

"Don't you look fine, Jeeter."

"I'm as nervous as a bull at cuttin' time," he admitted. She figured out that he was referring to the practice of castrating cattle. "Don't worry," she said. "This photo session will have the opposite effect. You'll be strutting around like Rooster Cogburn when it's over. The guys tell me it's very good for the ego." She pulled a small notebook out of her camera bag. "Before we start, I need a little background on you."

"Nothin' much to tell."

"Oh, I doubt that." She ran through her routine questions about age, birthplace, work experience and hobbies. Then she casually tossed in one tailored for this project alone. "Do you have a girlfriend?"

"How come you need to know that?"

Cleo had her answer ready. "I'd like to give her a complimentary copy of the calendar."

Jeeter grinned. "I don't know about that. A picture of me is okay, but I don't think I want Julie gawking at all those other guys for the rest of the year."

So he had a girlfriend. Cleo hadn't really expected him to make the cut as husband material, but this detail settled it. She wouldn't horn in on another woman's territory. "Then maybe she'd like a framed copy of the picture I use in the calendar."

"That would be great. I could sign it, and everything."

"You bet. Well, let's get started."

Jeeter smoothed his blond mustache and fiddled with a button on his vest. "Is this what I should be wearing? I wasn't sure."

"You look terrific." She gazed straight into his blue eyes as she spoke. "Did anyone ever tell you you're the spitting image of Alan Jackson?"

"A time or two." He stood a little taller, and the gleam in his eyes became a little brighter.

"Let's start with you sitting on that bale of hay over there," she said.

"Yes, ma'am." Perched self-consciously on the edge of the bale in his brand-new, totally buttoned-up clothes, he looked anything but sexy and relaxed.

In Cleo's experience, most guys started a session this way. After all, they weren't professional models, and they usually posed stiffly and stared straight at the camera as if they were having their picture taken at the driver's-license bureau. Her job was to get them to loosen up. She might waste an entire roll of film doing that, but if she succeeded, the second roll would be pure gold.

"That's nice," she said, looking through the viewfinder. "Lean back against the stall a little. Good." She clicked the shutter, knowing she wouldn't use the shot. "Now unbutton your vest."

Jeeter complied.

"You have a great build. Do you work out?" She snapped off a few more frames.

"Nope. Just regular cowboying." He pulled in his stomach and rolled his shoulders back.

Cleo had discovered that praising a man's body did wonders for the resulting photography. Fortunately, she didn't have to fake that praise. She loved looking at a well-built man, both as an artist and as a woman. "It's a shame to hide that physique. Let's try a few shots with the vest off."

"Yes, ma'am." His voice vibrated with sexual confidence now.

"And undo about four snaps on your shirt." She waited until he'd finished and was looking at her. Then she slowly licked her lips. "*Very* nice," she said, keeping her voice low and intimate. "Julie's a lucky woman."

"I'll tell her you said so."

"By all means." Cleo edged a little closer. "Lean down on your elbow and prop your boot on the hay. Mmm. I like that. I like that very much." Her implication, and men never failed to get it, was that she was enjoying the way the pose emphasized the bulge in their pants.

Jeeter's bulge stirred, and his breath was coming faster. "How about the shirt?" he said, his voice husky. "Do you want that off?"

"Unsnap it all the way and pull it out of the waistband," she murmured, clicking away. "We'll see what that looks like. Oh, I like that. As if you've just started to undress, just started the seduction. Cock your hips a little. What lovely muscles, Jeeter," she crooned, moving and clicking as she found different angles. "Look at me. Ah, that's perfect."

She might get what she wanted in the first roll, after all, she thought. His pupils were already dilated with sexual excitement, and there was a fine sheen of moisture on his bare chest.

"You must drive your girlfriend wild," she whispered. "You make her crazy with desire, don't you, Jeeter? You don't have to tell me. I know. Any woman who looks into your eyes would know."

His lips parted as he stared at her, thoroughly aroused and mesmerized by the sound of her voice. The problem was, she'd aroused herself in the process. It couldn't be helped, but it had to be controlled.

Yet she needed to feed this emotion building in him, because that was what women were looking for when they bought her calendars. "You're a fantastic lover, aren't you, Jeeter? You know how to please a woman so she can't get enough of you and your magnificent body."

He groaned softly.

"That's it," she said. "That's what I want. Give me what I want." She clicked the shutter rapidly, capturing the intensity before she ran out of film. Such a moment would never be sustained through reloading. She came to the end of the roll satisfied that she had her calendar shot. Sometimes, on a good day, it happened that way.

Slowly she straightened and brought the camera down. "That was fantastic, Jeeter."

"That's all?" His voice was rough with unexpressed passion.

"That should do it. You were wonderful." She turned to get the contract she'd tucked into her camera bag and saw Tom leaning in the doorway. In her current state, six feet of magnificent cowboy backlit by the sun was a powerful aphrodisiac. "Well, hello there."

"Hello, yourself." He didn't change position, just kept looking at her.

She thought it was encouraging that he'd been curious enough to come to the barn while she was shooting. She had to walk toward him to reach her camera bag. "How much of the session did you see?"

"Enough."

"Hey, boss," Jeeter said. "This is a real painless way to earn some cash."

"I imagine it is, Jeeter."

Cleo couldn't read his mood from his expression or the tone of voice, both of which seemed guarded. "Has the…uh…breeding started?"

"Not yet."

"Good." She swallowed. "I'd like to see how that's done."

"All right."

She leaned down and tucked her camera in the bag before pulling the contract out of a side pocket. "We're just about finished here."

"Take your time. They won't start anything until I get there."

"Okay." She turned and walked over to Jeeter, who was putting on his vest. "Here's the contract. I encourage you to take it home for the night and read everything. If you want a lawyer to see it, that's fine."

Jeeter straightened his vest and took the contract. "Or I could just sign it now and get it over with."

Tom spoke up. "Don't sign a contract until you've read it, Jeeter. You need to know what you've agreed to."

"I could read it back to front and not know what I'd agreed to, boss. That legal mumbo jumbo confuses the heck out of me."

Tom walked over to him. "Want me to take a look at it for you?"

"I'd be much obliged." He handed him the contract. "Say, boss, do you need me around here for anything in particular for the next couple of hours?"

"Any trail rides going out this afternoon?"

"Nope."

"Then I guess I don't have anything in particular for you to do. But I can always find—"

"I'd appreciate a couple of hours off." Jeeter tried to look nonchalant and failed. "Thought I'd ride over and see Julie."

Tom glanced at Cleo and back at Jeeter. "Yeah, go ahead, Ace."

"Thanks, boss." Jeeter turned to Cleo. "I'll get to see those pictures, right?"

"Of course. But I get the choice of which one to use."

"Don't forget about the one for Julie. And my mom might want one, too."

"We can talk about that." Cleo was careful about letting too many prints circulate. She wanted the pictures of her calendar boys to be unique. But sometimes she made exceptions for girlfriends and mothers.

"Yes, ma'am." Jeeter touched the brim of his hat. "It's been a pleasure." Then he left the barn with a decided swagger in his walk.

Cleo chuckled once he was out of earshot. "I think Julie just got lucky."

"And what if there had been no Julie?" Tom asked quietly.

Cleo glanced up into gray eyes that smoldered in a way that made her already keyed-up system kick into high gear. "That would be Jeeter's problem," she said. "I'm sure he would have found a way to take care of it."

"With you?"

She almost slapped him before she realized he didn't know about her code of ethics. After what he'd just seen, he couldn't be blamed for thinking she'd follow through on the seduction she'd begun if a man was single and available. "I have a rule. I don't sleep with my subjects."

He stepped closer. "Never?"

"Never." God, how she wanted him. Here. Now. On the floor of this barn, against that bale of hay. Anywhere. But that would ruin her cover plans, not to mention her husband hunt.

His voice rumbled low. "You get them all worked up and then leave them that way?"

She shrugged, trying to act as if her pulse wasn't beating a mile a minute just having him stand so close, teasing her with the scent of leather and sun and potent male. "It's no different for actors. They get all hot and bothered when they play love scenes, but they don't necessarily follow through with that behavior."

"Some do."

"Well, I don't. It's a reputation I'm proud of, and I intend to keep things that way."

"And what about you?"

She trembled at his caressing tone. "What about me?"

"How do you take care of all that tension boiling in that ripe body of yours?"

She swallowed. "What makes you think I'm affected at all?"

"Oh, I don't know." His glance flicked over her. "Maybe it's the scent of sex in the air. Maybe it's that look in your eyes that says you want a man's hands on you."

"Your enormous ego is working overtime."

"Is it?" He reached up and stroked a finger across her lower lip.

She gasped and stepped back.

"I didn't think so," he said.

"You surprised me."

"Then let's see how you react when you're not surprised." Tossing his hat and Jeeter's contract on the bale of hay, he closed the short distance between them and cupped her face in both hands.

She tried to draw away, but his touch was like rain falling on a parched field. She drank it in and wanted more, even though she knew it was a mistake. "No," she whispered as his head lowered.

"It's okay. I'm not one of your subjects."

"But I want you...to be."

"No way, baby." The touch of his lips was gentle, exploratory, tender.

Without warning, Cleo's restraint cracked wide open and she became the aggressor, clutching his head and deepening the kiss. He caught fire instantly, shifting the angle of his head for greater access and thrusting his tongue into her mouth.

The taste of him drove her wild. She matched him breath for ragged breath, sucking, licking, devouring what she needed, what they both needed. He pulled her close and she moaned at the full body contact. The man knew how to use his hands, and moisture rushed between her thighs as the ache to have him became almost unbearable.

Before she realized it, he'd backed her up against a rough wood wall and wrenched down the zipper of her jeans. His mouth was at her throat, his fingers unfastening her belt. Dimly, she realized he meant to take her, here in the barn.

"No!" The hoarse protest barely made it past her lips. "I don't want this." Her words were choked.

He paused and lifted his head to gaze into her eyes. He was panting. "The hell you don't."

"I don't." Summoning every reserve she had, she pushed him away.

He stared at her, chest heaving, the fly of his jeans stretched to the max. "You're a lousy liar, Cleo."

"I'm not lying. Once something like this happens between us, I can't use you for the cover of my calendar."

"Sweetheart, you can't use me anyway. Get over it and let us both have some relief."

She lifted her chin. "I'm not giving up. You'll pose for me before I leave."

"So you can treat me the way you just treated poor Jeeter?"

"It's business, Tom! Everyone benefits. It's the way I work."

"Well, you're not working that way with me." He turned away and propped his hands on his hips while he took several deep breaths. "Fasten your clothes. I have something you need to see."

She zipped her jeans and noticed he'd undone a couple of buttons on her blouse, too. She'd been so carried away she hadn't even known what he was doing. Her whole body ached and dripped with need, but she couldn't allow base instinct to rule her. Not if, by denying herself, she had a chance at a photo that would be the crown jewel in her career.

While she was straightening her clothes, he walked over and picked up his hat. He dusted it off and replaced it firmly on his head before picking up Jeeter's contract. He started flipping through it, paused and gave a low whistle.

"What?" she asked.

"I guess you do pay well."

"Of course." She wondered if money would make a difference to him. She had no idea of his financial situation, but unless he was independently wealthy, the money might come in handy. "And the amount is negotiable in your case, considering we're talking about a cover shot."

He glanced up from the contract. "I'm not doing it, Cleo." His smile beckoned to her. "And the sooner you accept that, the sooner we can get down to some good old-fashioned sex."

"I'm not interested."

"I think we just demonstrated how very interested you are."

"I mean mentally."

He laughed. "Making love isn't brain work. It's body work. Park your brain and have some fun with me, lady."

"No can do." She swung her camera bag to her shoulder. "A relationship with you would louse up...several things." She wasn't about to tell him that she was looking for a husband on this trip and didn't plan to settle for a brief affair. "Shall we go?"

"Absolutely. It's time for a little sex education." He folded the contract and tucked it in his hip pocket.

His comment, combined with the way the folded contract drew her gaze to his tight buns, had a predictable effect. Her nipples tightened and a warming trend began once again in her pelvic region. "Maybe this isn't such a great idea," she said as they started out of the barn. "I need to check and see if I have an overnight delivery from Bernie, anyway, and—"

"You don't. I would have found that out at lunch, because an overnight delivery out here in the country is a big deal. Nobody mentioned it."

"Oh. Well, speaking of lunch, I missed it because of the photo shoot, and I'm hungry."

He slanted a sideways glance at her as they walked side by side. "I'd say so. In fact, I'd say you were plum starved."

A flush warmed her cheeks. "Right after a photo shoot is a very vulnerable time for me. When you showed up, I just...reacted."

"Yes, ma'am, you sure did."

"It doesn't mean anything."

"If you say so."

"Now, if you'll excuse me, I'm going to the kitchen and find myself something to eat."

"Nope." Tom took her firmly by the arm and guided her toward the corral.

"What are you doing?" She tried to pull away from him, but his fingers remained clamped over her biceps like a manacle. "Tom, I said I've changed my mind about watching this little show. Let me go. I don't want to cause a scene."

"Neither do I. But after watching you with Jeeter, I think it's important for you to see what's about to happen in the corral. It should give you a better idea of why I won't pose for your calendar."

"My calendar? What on God's green earth would a couple of horses making whoopee have to do with my calendar?"

His smile was grim. "More than you think."

"Obviously," she muttered, but decided to go along, after all. If watching this spectacle would give her more insight into what made Tom tick, so much the better. "All right, I'll go with you."

"Good." He seemed to have forgotten that he still had a firm hold on her arm as they headed for the corral.

"You can turn me loose, Tom. I promise I won't bolt."

"Too bad." He grinned at her as he released her arm. "Might be kind of fun rounding you up again."

"Is that what you do with uncooperative women? Rope them and hog-tie them?"

"No, sweetheart." His glance was dangerously sexy. "I save that for the cooperative ones."

6

As soon as Tom arrived at the corral where a chestnut mare named Suzette pranced around, he asked Jose and Stan to bring Blaze, the scrub stallion, into the adjoining corral. A few of the hands and several of the guests had gathered on the far side of the corral, ready for the show. Tom had warned all the parents about the afternoon's event, in case they didn't want their kids to observe the breeding process, and he noticed none of the kids were around, either because they'd been kept away or because they didn't think mating horses were interesting enough to give up a swim for.

Cleo rested her arms on the top rail and propped her chin on her hands. Tom thought she looked really natural out here by the corral. Deidre never had, no matter how many weeks she'd spent on the ranch. Maybe it was Cleo's lack of heavy makeup, her unpolished nails and casual clothes. Or maybe it was the way she seemed to look at ranch life with an intensity of purpose, as if she wanted to understand how things worked around here. Deidre had never seemed to care.

Of course, Cleo had a purpose, and once that was satisfied, she might lose interest completely. He was impressed by Cleo's stubbornness when she got an idea. He didn't meet too many people he shared that trait with. Her stubbornness might cheat them both out of some really great sex, though, unless he used her special rule about mixing business with pleasure against her.

If he seduced her, he'd take himself out of the calendar project and end that debate once and for all. All he needed was the right set of circumstances, and she'd go up like a pile of dry kindling. A strand of golden hair blew across her cheek, and he resisted the impulse to comb it back for her. Now was not the time.

Blaze, an old palomino with too many conformation faults to be considered a good stud, came prancing into the corral next to Suzette's. Handling Blaze was a two-man job, so Stan and Jose each had a rope on the stallion.

"What's up with this?" Cleo asked. "He can't get to her."

"He's not supposed to. Blaze is the teaser."

Cleo turned to look at him. "Excuse me?"

He met her gaze. "We have to make sure Suzette's in heat before we bring in Chico, the stud. Otherwise she could bite him, or kick the devil out of him if she's not interested. I can't take a chance on that happening with Chico, who's worth a hell of a lot more than old Blaze."

"Oh." Cleo returned her attention to Suzette. "There've been a few times I could have used a set of hooves, myself."

Tom lowered his voice, although there was little danger of anyone overhearing. "Are you referring to recent history?"

She didn't look at him, but her throat moved in a swallow. "No. My attraction to you is real, and extremely inconvenient."

Or convenient, looking at the situation another way, he thought. "Just checking. I'd hate like hell to get kicked." He watched Suzette sidle over to the fence where Blaze strained at his ropes. Suzette lifted her tail and allowed Blaze a sniff. Good sign.

"I don't imagine you get kicked very often," Cleo murmured.

"Not if I can help it."

"He looks very eager," she said.

"Oh, he's eager, all right. Pretty soon it'll be very obvious how eager he is."

Blaze struggled against the ropes as he tried to lean over the fence, and his arousal became evident to anyone who cared to look between his hind legs.

"I...uh...see what you mean," Cleo muttered. "My goodness."

He gave her a sideways glance. "Males aren't built to keep secrets."

"What about her? How can you tell if she's in heat?"

"By the look in her eyes."

She turned her head and met his gaze.

He drew in a quick breath at the tumult in those blue depths. Oh, yes, she was ready. More than ready.

"Are we talking about horses?" she asked.

"You are." A high-pitched squeal from Suzette brought his attention back to the corral. Suzette humped her back in an awkward little bucking motion, laid her ears back and squealed again. "All right," Tom said. "We're in business." He raised his voice. "Jose, Stan— take him away and get Chico."

"Right, boss!" Jose said. He and Stan fought to pull the stallion away from the fence. Blaze fought back, whinnying and planting his haunches to brace himself against the tug of the ropes.

"That's terrible!" Cleo said. "Poor Blaze."

"That's business." Tom glanced at her. "Isn't that what you told me?"

She pushed away from the fence and faced him. "If you're implying that my photo sessions in any way resemble this...this..."

He kept his voice down. "I'm not implying. I'm saying it straight out. The whole time I watched you work with Jeeter, all I could think about was Blaze. I don't know if you have a boyfriend who gets the benefit of all those hormones flying around, but I refuse to be treated like some scrub stallion while another guy gets to take part in the main event."

Her lips were parted, her breath coming fast. Tom figured that if they weren't standing out in the wide-open spaces with eight or ten people as witnesses, now would be a fine time to touch a match to that dry kindling. From the corner of his eye he saw Chico, a magnificent dark bay, being brought into the corral with Suzette.

"I don't have a boyfriend," Cleo said, her gaze never leaving his face.

Damn, but that was good news. "Then you must get a little frustrated at times, darlin'." While he continued to keep his attention firmly on Cleo, he was also aware of the mare and stallion maneuvering through their courtship ritual—the sniffing, the little nips, the snorts and squeals. He remained alert to any signs of trouble, but all seemed to be going well.

"My frustrations aren't your concern," Cleo said.

"I could make them my concern."

"No." She licked her lips.

His groin tightened as he remembered how her tongue had felt inside his mouth and how hungry she'd been for his kiss. Instinct told him the horses would mate any moment now. "Hey, I don't want you to miss anything." He cupped her elbow and turned her to face the corral again just as Chico lunged over Suzette's hindquarters and buried himself in her. Tom felt the shudder go through Cleo.

He wondered if she might run from the blatant sexual message being spelled out in the corral, and this time he planned to let her go. He'd made his point. But she stayed through it all, trembling but focused.

Tom hated to leave her now. If he could walk her back to her cabin, they might settle things this afternoon. But he had duties connected with this breeding event. "I have to go," he murmured, squeezing her arm gently.

She nodded, not looking at him.

"If you need anything, you know where to find me."

She nodded again.

He walked away, wishing that just this once someone else could shoulder his responsibilities. He had no doubt that if he could take Cleo's hand and lead her to the nearest secluded place, she would make love with him until they were both exhausted. But an hour from now, the spell might be broken.

CLEO WASN'T SURE how she made it back to her cabin. Images of stallions and sexy cowboys swirled through her head as she stumbled away from the corral to find a measure of privacy so that she could think. She couldn't give in to this lust for Tom McBride, could she? Then she wouldn't be able to use him for the calendar, and she'd jeopardize her husband hunt in the bargain. But as she opened the door of her cabin and walked into the refreshing coolness, neither of those reasons seemed strong enough to deny herself the pleasure to be found in Tom's arms.

A courier packet lay on her bed—the contact sheets of her firefighters Bernie had shipped out yesterday. Relief flooded Cleo at the prospect of a familiar job. She knew from experience that choosing the photographs for a calendar didn't stir up the same cravings as the photo shoots themselves. The selection of prints required a dispassionate, critical eye, and one of the reasons she'd made it so far in her profession was her ability to coolly judge her own work.

Still standing beside the bed, she opened the packet and skimmed the note from Bernie, which contained nothing but routine information...until she came to the last paragraph.

> Your father called. He's interested in using your *Montana Men* calendar as a premium for Sphinx customers this Christmas. I told him I'd check with you. Frankly, although the extra exposure would be nice—I think the company's planning TV and print ads—I'd love you to tell him to go jump in the lake. This calendar will sell big without his help. By the way, found a husband yet?
>
> B.

Cleo sat on the bed and reread the paragraph. When her first calendar was scheduled, she'd asked her father if he'd consider using it as a giveaway for his cosmetics customers, which would have provided national and international exposure when she needed it most. Asking had been difficult for her. But listening to his refusal had been sheer hell.

Now that she had created her own fame, he was willing to link his company's name with hers. She wasn't sure what she would do yet, but one thing was certain—this calendar would be the best damn thing she'd ever done. And that meant getting Tom McBride on the cover.

Getting Tom to pose wouldn't be easy, but then nothing worth doing ever was. Her father had taught her that.

Cleo avoided Tom for the rest of the day and didn't go to the main house for dinner. Snacking from Juanita's refrigerator was more Cleo's style, anyway. She longed for a soak in the hot tub, but she couldn't take a chance that Tom might wander down to see if she was there. She didn't trust herself around him with all her clothes on at the moment, let alone when she was lounging naked in bubbling mineral water.

Instead, she used her evening to choose twelve firefighters from the contact sheets Bernie had sent. The task absorbed all her attention, and when she'd finished, she discovered she was tired enough to go to bed. After she packaged up her choices and sealed them into a return envelope, she crawled under the covers. She'd better enjoy the innerspring mattress tonight, she told herself, because the following night she'd be camped under the stars. Tom would be there, but so would a lot of other people, not to mention dogs, horses and cattle. Cleo judged the situation safe enough to keep her from falling into temptation.

She slipped easily toward sleep, despite the same yipping, rustling and howling she'd experienced the night before. Maybe the mountain air and sunshine had worked some sort of magic during the day, because she felt incredibly relaxed and peaceful. Or maybe, she thought briefly before she drifted off, she was getting used to Montana.

WHEN MORNING ARRIVED, bringing with it the prospect of seeing Tom constantly for the next two days, her stomach jumped around as if she'd just finished riding the Coney Island roller coaster. She missed breakfast because she spent a ridiculous amount of time deciding what to wear and what to pack. Finally, she settled on jeans, a chambray shirt and her vest. She packed a change of underwear, a few personal toiletries and several candy bars, all of which fit into the pockets of her camera bag. She put on her sunglasses and grabbed a jacket on her way out the door.

The sun had baked the dew from the grass, leaving behind a scent so fresh it triggered memories of a summer when she was fourteen. Normally she'd spent her school vacations in a round of music and dance lessons. Her father had never taken time off, and so neither had she or her mother, but that year she'd been invited by a girlfriend to spend two glorious weeks at the family's summer home in Connecticut. To Cleo, both then and now, the sun-warmed grass smelled of freedom.

She could see riders gathering beside the corral where mounts in the process of being saddled were lined up along the hitching post. The black-and-white dog she'd noticed the first day, whose name was Trixie, was trotting around the group in obvious anticipation of a trip. Nearby, a team of horses had been hitched to a wagon loaded with supplies.

Even from this distance, Cleo picked Tom out of the crowd. She recognized his walk, the set of his shoulders and the way he wore his hat. Forty-eight hours ago they'd been strangers, and already he'd become alarmingly familiar to her. Well, that was good, she decided, adjusting the strap of her camera bag on her shoulder as she started toward the corral. The more familiar he was, the better she'd photograph him when the time came.

As she approached, she recognized Jeeter and Jose, as well. That was lucky, she thought. Jose was a definite calendar possibility, and this would give her a chance to see if he was interested. She might even be able to set up a shoot while they were on the trail. *He's also a husband prospect*, she reminded herself. With that in mind, she tried to focus exclusively on Jose as he led another horse out of the corral, but her attention kept wandering in Tom's direction.

The scents and sounds of the corral brought back thoughts of yesterday, standing beside Tom while a stallion had his way with a willing mare. That man had known exactly what he was doing, piling that event on top of their encounter in the barn. If she succumbed to his considerable charms, she wouldn't get her cover photo. No matter how arousing the circumstances, she needed to remember that.

Luckily, for the next two days at least, she'd have chaperons. She glanced over the five guests who'd volunteered to help move the cattle. She remembered them vaguely from her first meal at the ranch and chance encounters during the day and a half she'd been at the Whispering Winds, but she'd zoned out on their names.

The young couple that looked fresh out of college had been married about a year and lived in Massachusetts. The second couple had a fourteen-year-old daughter, and Tom helped the girl adjust her stirrups while both her parents stood by and offered advice in a clipped Boston accent.

At one point, Tom turned his back to the parents, glanced up at the girl and winked.

She gave him a smile back, and Cleo figured Tom had just made a friend for life. No teenager appreciated that kind of parental hovering.

"That should do it, Laura." Tom positioned the girl's booted foot in the stirrup. "Stand up on the balls of your feet and let me check."

"I still think they should be shorter," her mother said.

Laura stood in the stirrups and got an approving nod from Tom. "Western riding is different from English, Mom," Laura said.

"Well, I want mine shorter than that."

Tom turned around to speak to her and noticed Cleo for the first time. An expression of welcome lit his face before he swung his attention to Laura's mother. "We'll adjust them any way you like, Mrs. Preston." He glanced down the row of horses. "Jose? Can you get the Prestons mounted up? And bring out Dynamite for Ms. Griffin?"

Dynamite? Cleo gulped.

"Sure thing, boss."

Cleo couldn't suppress feeling a flicker of desire as Tom walked over to her. He was one fine-looking cowboy.

He nudged his hat back with his thumb and smiled. "So you're going."

"I said I would. But about this horse you're putting me on. I—"

"I admire a woman of her word." His gaze traveled over her. "You need a hat."

"I don't have one. I'll be fine. Listen, is Dynamite a very—"

"Everybody in my outfit wears a hat." He took her arm. "Come on. Let's see what we can find."

"I don't like hats." She went along with him because it was less embarrassing than digging in her heels and creating a scene. "I never wear them."

"You will on this ride. I won't have you keeling over from sunstroke or burning that pretty little nose of yours."

"I have sunscreen. And lots of hair to protect me from sunstroke. And my nose isn't little."

He laughed as he towed her up the steps of the ranch house. "You're right. You've got one of those highborn sort of noses, but you won't look quite so regal if it's red as a bandanna."

"Oh, for heaven's sake. I feel like a little kid being told to wear her rubbers. I'm a big girl. I can take care of myself."

"In New York, maybe." Tom nodded to Luann, who was cleaning the ashes from the fireplace. "'Mornin', Luann."

"'Morning, Tom." She sat back on her heels and grinned at Cleo. "I'll bet he's getting you a hat."

"So he says."

Tom pulled her into his office and flipped the door closed. "You do need something to cover your head, but first I need this." He took off his hat and his mouth came down on hers.

They picked right up where they'd left off, and the barriers she'd worked so hard to construct, the reasons that she shouldn't allow this, crumpled before the onslaught of his lips. She should be pushing him away instead of reveling in the morning-coffee taste of him, breathing in the scent of his aftershave and the ever-present combination of leather and aroused male. God, he could kiss.

He held her tight against him and lifted his head to gaze down at her. "'Mornin', Cleo."

She tried to catch her breath. "You're trying to cause me trouble, aren't you, cowboy?"

"I'm trying to ease your troubles, lady. You've been dodging me since yesterday, haven't you?"

"I had work to do."

His hands slid down her back and cupped her bottom. "So did I, but I could have slipped you into my schedule."

She was turning into a molten mass of need, but she tried not to let him know how much he affected her. She took a deep breath. "I'm holding out for my cover photo, Tom."

His mouth curved in a slow, sensuous smile. "Damn, but you're a stubborn female."

And you're about the sexiest man I've ever met. Cleo looked into his mesmerizing gray eyes and gave thanks that Luann was just outside the door and seven people were waiting for them at the corral. Without those considerations, he might have been able to talk her into almost anything right now, including a session on top of his massive oak desk.

"We need to get going," she said.

"That's what I've been trying to tell you, woman. Life's too short."

"Back to the corral."

"Oh. Them."

"And after all this fuss I'd better show up with a hat."

"I was dead serious about the hat." He released her and walked over to a row of pegs where hats of various sizes and colors hung. "I was dead serious about the rest of it, too, but I intend to get your head covered first." He picked out a cream-colored Stetson and walked back to her. "Let's see how this suits you."

She held out her hand. "I'll put it on after we mount up."

"Nope. We'll make sure it fits right now, so I don't hear any excuses out on the trail as to why you're not wearing it. Hold still."

"Honestly." But with him that close, she had to hold still or risk throwing herself into his arms again.

He settled the hat on her head and tugged the brim down in front. Then he stood back, thumbs hooked in his belt loops, to survey the result. Slowly a grin creased his face.

"What?" She looked around for a mirror, but found none. "I look ridiculous, right?"

"Nope. You look like you were made to wear that hat. Keep it."

"Now that's *really* ridiculous. Once I leave here, I'll have no use for it." Once she left here, she wouldn't see Tom McBride again, either. The thought created such an empty feeling that she pushed it aside. "Because you're making such a big deal about this hat thing, I'll wear it for the cattle drive, but after that I'm returning it."

"I wouldn't be too hasty about that. The right hat is a rare discovery. Some people try on a hundred before they find the one that fits their head and personality. That one's perfect for you." He picked up his own from the desk and put it on. "Let's go." He strode over to the door and opened it.

Fascinated by his assessment, she hurried after him. "Why is it so perfect?"

He kept walking. "Frames your face real nice without dominating it. A face like yours doesn't need a lot of gee-gaws to distract people. The color's good against your blond hair. The crown's about right. Wouldn't want one too short, with those long legs of yours." He glanced at her as they crossed the ranch yard and headed toward the corrals. "It's classy, but that little feather in the hatband gives it spirit. Like I said, it's a great fit."

A warm glow settled over her as she absorbed his evaluation. His matter-of-fact delivery gave the elaborate compliment even more impact. If this was a line he was feeding her just to get what he wanted, he was very skilled at it—she was swallowing every single word without a single twinge of big-city cynicism.

By the time they arrived at the corrals, she'd decided that she positively loved the hat.

7

"PICK UP THE PACE, Dynamite. We're lagging behind again, horse." Finishing off her candy bar, Cleo nudged the buckskin mare in the ribs and clucked encouragingly. The truth was, their pokiness was as much her fault as Dynamite's. Riding up through a wildflower-strewn ravine—what Tom informed everyone was called a coulee out in these parts—Cleo lifted her gaze to snow-draped mountains that commanded a huge chunk of cobalt sky. Turning in her saddle, she watched the ranch transform into a child's diorama complete with a meandering stream that flashed silver in the sun.

The trail wound through a stand of aspens, their heart-shaped leaves quivering in the breeze. Beyond the aspen grove lay a meadow where a young buck lifted his antlered head, sniffed the air and bolted, his white tail lifting like a flag as he disappeared into the feathery protection of pine and spruce. Birds chattered and swooped through the trees, daubing color against the deep green of the forest, and the tangy scent of evergreens spiced the air.

Camera at the ready, Cleo was in no hurry to cover ground. She'd let everyone else go ahead of her while she used up one roll and started on another.

As for Dynamite, the mare was definitely in no hurry. Someone with a sense of humor had named this horse, Cleo decided as she dug her heels in again and clucked.

She was following Jeeter, who drove the wagon, and Tom, who rode alongside. Much as she enjoyed the leisurely pace and the chance to take some shots of the unbelievable scenery, she didn't want to lose sight of the group. Not when there could be cougars around.

"Move it, baby," Cleo said, getting more aggressive with her heels. "Bringing up the rear is one thing, but we're not even doing a credible job of that."

Dynamite's ears flicked back and her plodding stride accelerated slightly, but not much.

Ahead of them, Tom stopped talking with Jeeter and glanced over his shoulder. Then he wheeled his big chestnut and loped back toward Cleo. He looked mighty fine mounted on that flame-colored animal, Cleo thought, admiring how his body moved in rhythm with the gelding's stride. She'd never noticed before how much the rocking motion of a rider's hips mimicked the sexual act.

As he reached her and turned his mount to keep pace with Dynamite, all sorts of suggestive behavior leaped to Cleo's mind. The wagon had disappeared over a rise, leaving them in a tantalizingly private setting. But she must not allow herself to be tantalized.

"I can't seem to find the fuse on this horse of yours, McBride," she said.

He grinned. "I didn't know you wanted a Derby contender." He reined in his prancing horse. "Easy, Red."

"I didn't want a horse like yours, that's for sure. But with this mare, sweet as she is, I feel as if I may have to get out and push."

"I had the idea you hadn't ridden much recently, so I was thinking of your backside." He paused, glanced at her and laughed. "Let me rephrase that."

"Oh, I'll bet that's exactly what you were thinking of, cowboy."

His gray eyes twinkled. "Okay, it probably was. It's a damn good-looking backside, and I'd hate to see it damaged."

Not a good topic, Cleo thought as her body responded to the intimate discussion. "I think I could manage a little more speed without a problem. And what about when we find the cattle? Can she keep up?"

"She'll be fine. In her prime she was a good little cow pony, but she's semiretired now. I wanted you on a steady horse, and she's the steadiest one we have on the ranch. She won't spook and she'll stick by you if you happen to fall off."

Cleo was touched that he seemed to care so much about her welfare. "And what joker named this mare Dynamite?"

"I did."

"With tongue in cheek, right?"

"Nope." Tom kept his restless horse under a tight rein. "A kid doesn't joke around when he's naming his horse."

"She was your horse when you were a kid?" Cleo leaned down to examine Dynamite's muzzle for gray hairs and noticed quite a few. "Just how old is she?"

"Twenty-six."

"Yikes! Now I feel guilty for making her go faster. Shouldn't she be turned out to pasture or something?"

"Not when she's sound, and likes to get out and see a bit of the world, right, Dynamite?"

The mare's ears swiveled back at the mention of her name.

"I watched her being born," Tom continued. "When my dad gave her to me, he might as well have given me the world on a silver platter, I was so excited. She was a fast little pony and had the habit of exploding into a run, so I named her Dynamite. She has great-great-grandchildren on the ranch."

"Wow." Cleo had new respect for the mare, and a feeling of tenderness for the cowboy who was letting her ride his first horse. "All I ever had when I was a kid was a hamster."

"Never could figure that, keeping rodents as pets. Around here we have cats to get rid of the damn things."

"Ah, but you never knew Squeaky. He was an exceptional rodent. I taught him tricks." He'd been the only livestock on her Lincoln Log ranch, so she'd made do.

Tom chuckled. "I'll bet you did." He glanced at her. "I can just picture this little towhead training her hamster."

"He was good company." Cleo smiled at the memory of the furry little creature she hadn't thought about in years. She'd been devastated when he died.

"You don't have brothers or sisters?" Tom asked.

"Nope. It's up to me to carry the family banner."

"Sounds like a heavy one."

Cleo shrugged. "You're carrying your family banner, too, now that your sister isn't involved in the ranch."

"Yeah." He shook his head. "And I didn't know the true financial picture until a couple of years ago, when Dad finally had to turn everything over to me."

"Not good?"

"Not great. I—" He paused and looked at her in surprise. "How in hell did we get off on that?"

"It's weighing on your mind, isn't it?"

He stared off into the shadowy depths of the trees on either side of the trail. "Nah," he said, and gave her a cocky grin. "Not really."

She didn't believe him, but he was apparently too proud to reveal the true extent of his worry. "Pose for

me," she said. "As Jeeter mentioned, it's a painless way
to pick up some extra cash, and it might lead to other
monetary gain. It might even increase your business."

"Which would mean enlarging the ranch, and I like the
size it is now."

She did, too. She couldn't picture the Whispering
Winds as a giant operation. "Okay, then forget that. Just
think about your fee. I told you I'd negotiate a higher one
for you, because I really want you on the calendar."

He gazed at her. "I'd settle for having you really want
me, period."

Oh, she did. She certainly did. And they'd been alone
way too long. She cleared the huskiness from her voice.
"I think we'd better catch up to the others."

"Scared of me, Cleo?"

"Let's just say that your goal runs counter to mine."

"And you're afraid I might be able to talk you out of
that cover picture and into my bed, aren't you?"

Her nerves tightened and hummed, ready for action.
"The talking isn't what worries me."

His tone was low and easy on her ears. "I'll never take
you where you don't want to go."

"Then I think you'd better take me back to the others.
Now."

He sighed. "Probably so." As they passed a small pine,
he reached up, broke off a branch and held it out toward
her. "Whack Dynamite a few times on the rump with this
and she'll go for you."

Cleo shrank back from the offered stick. "Hit a great-
great-grandmother? I couldn't!"

"Somebody's got to. I have a powerful urge to pull you
off that horse and make love to you on a bed of pine needles this very minute."

She looked into his eyes, heavy with need, and her pulse raced at the picture he'd created in her mind.

"Hang on, Cleo."

She grasped the saddle horn just in time. The switch came down on Dynamite's rump at the same moment Tom whooped a command, and the little mare sprang straight out of her walk into a gallop. Cleo lost her stirrups but managed to regain them as the trees flashed by on either side of her. Pounding hooves behind her told her that Tom was following, making sure she was okay.

The speed felt good, once she was used to it. The forward momentum and whipping wind helped take her mind off her sexual frustration. But she couldn't ride like this for the entire time she was in Montana, and when she stopped, she'd want Tom all over again. She needed to create more distractions for herself, somehow, perhaps, by focusing on Jose and planning how she would pose him for the calendar, at least during this cattle drive.

WATCHING HER was sweet torture, Tom thought. She'd proved to be surprisingly good with the hazing of the cattle once they located the herd. When Dynamite demonstrated her cow-pony moves, Cleo managed to stay aboard and even work in a candy-bar break. Tom was so busy keeping a protective eye on Cleo, he ended up having to chase down a cow that slipped by him, much to Jose's amusement.

Jose happened to end up beside Tom while they were crossing a shallow stream. Next to them the cows flowed in a rust-brown river, the sound of their hooves splashing in a steady rhythm punctuated with irritated-sounding moos. "You like her, don't you, boss?" Jose asked.

Tom didn't bother to deny it. "I suppose I'm making a damn fool of myself, too."

"Not really," Jose said, loyal to the last. "It'd be easy to do, though, with a woman who looks like her." He guided his horse onto dry ground.

Tom followed and came alongside Jose again. He had a few questions for the cowboy. "Has she asked you to pose for the calendar yet?"

"Yep." Jose slapped his rope against his thigh as a cow tried to veer out of formation. "Hiya!" he shouted, heading the cow back into line.

"Gonna do it?" Tom felt a moment of unease, remembering the outrageous way Cleo had flirted with Jeeter.

"Guess so."

"Better talk to Jeeter and get a handle on how she works."

"I already did." Jose flicked a glance at his boss. "Jeeter says she comes on to the guy so she can get the right kind of picture. It's show business."

Tom's laugh was short. "That's one way of putting it."

"In your place, I wouldn't like the way she does things, either. But a dollar's a dollar, and Jeeter said you gave us the green light."

Tom pulled his hat lower over his eyes. "Hell, I can't stand in the way of your budding film career. I could be riding with the next Antonio Banderas, for all I know."

Jose laughed and shook his head. "I'm not counting on being a movie star, but I wouldn't mind the fee she's paying for the calendar. I could use a new saddle, and I've got my eye on a real beauty, silver-trimmed. I reckon I can flex my muscles for that." He grinned at Tom. "Not that you don't pay good, but I can't buy the rig I want on my wages from the Whispering Winds, boss."

"The way Cleo tells it, you make a pinup boy of yourself and your financial worries will be over. You'll head for Hollywood and that'll be the last I ever see of you."

"I couldn't leave this place," Jose said. "I've been working here ever since I turned sixteen."

"Which means you're in a rut, cowboy." In a way, Tom was relieved that a couple of his hands were getting this photo opportunity. Every time he looked at the ranch's debts, they cast a shadow bigger than the Madison Range they were riding into today. He was operating on such a small margin that if beef prices took a dive at market time, he'd go under, and so would the jobs of the people who were like family to him. Cleo might be unknowingly providing a cushion for Jose and Jeeter, at least.

"Jeeter says she asked you to pose, but you said no," Jose ventured.

"Jeeter's sure been flapping his jaws a lot. Guess I have to double up on that boy's duties, seeing as how he's got time to stand around and gossip." Tom headed off a calf who started to stray from the herd.

"Aw, Jeeter didn't mean any harm. He's just a kid, with stars in his eyes because he thinks he's going to be famous, and he thinks everyone else wants to be famous, too."

"But you don't."

"Nope. I know exactly what I want out of this."

Tom looked at him and wished the guy could be a little uglier. The idea of Cleo getting cozy with him was damn unsettling.

Jose returned the look. "Don't worry, boss. All I'm after is a saddle."

MOVING THE HERD took the rest of the afternoon. Cleo enjoyed every minute of the constant activity, which reminded her a lot of Manhattan at rush hour. But eventually the cattle were transferred to their new pasture and the riders recrossed the stream and started back down the mountain. About an hour later, as the sun dipped behind the Madisons, Tom announced it was time to set up camp.

Cleo didn't realize how saddle-sore she was until she dismounted, but nobody else was complaining, so she kept her mouth shut. Laura and her parents obviously rode all the time in Massachusetts, and the young couple had been at the ranch a week, so they were already toughened up. Cleo shuddered to think what shape she'd have been in if Tom hadn't given her the horseback equivalent of a BarcaLounger.

They were camped in an open meadow bisected by a bubbling brook, a truly picturesque spot, if Cleo could just forget that bears and cougars roamed free in this country, and that she'd be sleeping in a bedroll with not so much as a canvas tent between her and the great outdoors. Dynamite seemed unconcerned as Cleo turned her out to graze on the lush grass, so Cleo decided to try for the same nonchalance.

While Tom unhitched the team of horses from the wagon and led them out to join the others in the meadow, everyone else gathered around the fire Jose had built. He had a kerosene cookstove going with what smelled like beef stew in a large kettle. Cleo hoped that cougars didn't have a special fondness for stew, because the aroma seemed to fill the meadow, and night was coming on fast. She'd been counting on Trixie as an early-warning system, but the dog was flopped by the fire, apparently asleep.

She'd pulled on her jacket against the chill, but the darkness that began to surround them made her shiver more than the cool night air. She'd never seen anything so black as the edge of the forest. Fingers of mist curled over the meadow, further obscuring Cleo's view.

"Did anybody bring a flashlight?" she asked the group in general.

Jeeter looked up from where he was unloading camp stools from the back of the wagon. "We have a few. Want one?"

"Uh, not just at the moment. I just wondered if we...had some."

"I think the firelight is much more romantic," said Amy, cuddling next to her young husband, Nick.

Cleo would have been happy with a bank of flood-lights, say about the wattage of those used to illuminate Yankee Stadium.

"Yeah, this place is cool," Laura said. "It's exactly the sort of deserted spot aliens would pick to land."

"You've been watching too many movies," her father said. "Anything to drink in that wagon, Jeeter?"

"Sure. Everybody have a seat, and I'll take orders."

Cleo eyed the camp stools arranged around the fire cir-cle, then pictured herself inching down to sit on one and the grimace of pain that would give away her delicate condition. She elected to stand. Jeeter got around to her drink order just as Tom came back from seeing to the horses. When Tom materialized out of the darkness look-ing so solid and safe, she had the urge to run into the pro-tection of his arms. She'd actually moved a few steps in his direction before she caught herself and stopped.

"What'll you have, Cleo?" Jeeter asked.

Still watching Tom as he came toward her, she spoke without thinking, giving the response she would have in New York. "Perrier with a twist."

Tom grinned as he joined them. "Make sure you serve that in the Baccarat crystal while you're at it, Jeeter. You know where we keep it, don't you?"

"No, boss, I sure don't." Jeeter sounded totally mystified. "Isn't that some kind of board game?"

Cleo winced. Then she turned to Jeeter. "What do you
have to drink, Jeeter?"

"Beer and soda pop, ma'am."

"Then I'll take a beer, Jeeter. Thanks."

"Boss? Want something?"

"Sure." Tom shoved back his hat. "I'll take a beer."

Cleo turned to him after Jeeter left. "A cowboy who
knows his crystal. You're a fascinating combination,
Tom."

"Not fascinating enough, apparently."

"I'm the only daughter of a business tycoon. I have
personal discipline like you wouldn't believe."

"A tycoon, huh? And all you got was a hamster?"

"We lived in an elegant apartment in the city."

Tom nodded. "I know the kind." He paused as Jeeter
brought them each a beer. He tipped his can against hers.
"Here's looking at you, kid."

"*Casablanca*. Don't tell me you're a fan of old movies,
too."

"Okay, I won't tell you that."

As she took a sip from her beer can, she conjured an
image of curling up with him on the deep cushions of his
couch to watch Humphrey Bogart and Ingrid Bergman,
while a fire blazed on the hearth and snow whirled outside the windows. They'd have popcorn and beer, and
after the movie they'd... No, they wouldn't, because by
the time the winter snow arrived, she'd be long gone.

"How come you're not sitting over with the others on
the camp stools?" he asked.

"Standing's nice."

"Uh-huh. You got a little sore, after all, didn't you?"

"Maybe."

"We always bring along some sports cream for that problem. I'll get you a tube and you can go off a ways from the group and rub some on." He set his beer on a nearby rock and turned toward the wagon.

"Wait. What do you mean, go off a ways from the group?"

He glanced back at her. "I figured you wouldn't want to be pulling down your jeans in front of everybody."

"But it's dark out there." As if to make her point, something howled off in the distance.

"Then take somebody with you. One of the other women."

"Oh, sure. The blind leading the blind. Amy's in a romantic haze and Laura's looking for aliens. And I don't want to give Laura's mother the satisfaction of knowing I'm sore. When she wasn't correcting Laura's riding form, she was correcting mine."

He smiled. "Want me to go with you?"

"That's even more dangerous. I'll just put up with it."

"No, you won't. Hell, I'll send Jeeter out there with you, and have him take a rifle if it'll make you feel safer. He'll turn his back."

"Tom, please. I'd be embarrassed for Jeeter to know. Let's just keep this our little secret, okay?"

He shook his head. "You have to ride back to the ranch tomorrow, and you'll be so stiff you won't get your calendar work done. I've seen how much you move around when you're shooting. Here's the deal. I'll go with you. I'll take a rifle. Believe me, I'm not going to try anything funny with guests no more than thirty yards away."

"Oh, all right." Cleo decided she was becoming paranoid about the temptations he afforded. Of course they wouldn't get involved in hanky-panky when other people were so near. And she didn't want to be in worse shape tomorrow because she'd refused the treatment offered. She set her beer next to his on the rock.

Tom left and returned a few minutes later with a tube of ointment, a flashlight and a rifle. He handed her the ointment. "Let's go."

"After you."

He cradled the rifle under one arm, flicked on the flashlight and swung the beam back and forth across the grass as they walked into the darkness.

Cleo followed right on his heels. "Shouldn't you be shining that thing higher up, so it reflects off the eyes of the bear, or whatever comes along to eat us?"

He chuckled. "I'll hear something that big. I'm checking for snakes."

"That's it. I'm leaving." She whirled and started back.

He caught her by a finger through her belt loop and pulled her back. "Come on. Don't be a such a greenhorn."

She turned to face him. "I *am* a greenhorn. And proud of it."

He turned off the flashlight and tucked it in his pocket.

"Turn that thing on."

"In a minute." He nudged her hat back on her head and cupped her face in his free hand. "Kiss me, Cleo. It's gonna be a long night."

She wanted his kiss, no matter how much she tried to deny it. "I knew following you out here was a bad—"

His mouth came down on hers, ending her protest and playing hell with her self-control. There was nothing leisurely about his kiss. He ravaged her mouth, took possession with his tongue and left her pounding with desire. Then he pulled away, tugged her hat in place and reached in his pocket for the flashlight.

She could barely breathe.

"I thought you could use something else to think about besides critters," he said, switching on the flashlight and sweeping it around the area where they stood.

If that had been his strategy, it had worked really well, she thought. Two powerful emotions couldn't coexist within her, apparently, and lust had just obliterated fear.

He gestured with the beam of the flashlight. "Over there's as good a spot as any. I'll keep the light below your knees. Just walk about ten paces away and pull down your pants."

She took a shaky breath and followed his instructions. "I'll bet you say that to all the girls."

"Only the girls who look good in that hat."

"And how many has that been?"

"One."

8

TOM PULLED the last shift of guard duty, taking the few hours just before dawn. Jose, Jeeter and Tom had divided the night into thirds, as they always did when they had either people or animals to watch over. They didn't make a big deal of it, not wanting to alarm the dudes, but they couldn't afford to have a grizzly sneak up on the campsite. Tom had noticed that Cleo had looked immensely relieved when she'd discovered that someone would be patrolling the area all through the night.

He'd teased her about being a greenhorn, but he'd rather have the guests show her sort of caution than think they were in Disneyland and the animals could all talk and sing songs. Being out in the wilderness of Montana meant accepting some level of risk, but not everyone was willing to face that. Therefore, he took the responsibility for them and made sure someone stayed on guard, someone who could handle a rifle and keep a cool head.

It had been a quiet night. With the fire reduced to embers and the stars bright as the New York skyline after dark, visibility was pretty good. Jose had reported seeing a black bear venture partway out of the trees before heading back in. Tom had watched for the bear to reappear, but it hadn't. Bears weren't usually a problem unless they'd learned to raid campsites and had a taste for human junk food. Then they could be deadly in their search for the goodies they craved.

Tom was seeing more of that happening in his beloved wilderness, and he hated it, just as he hated the disappearance of the elegant cougars. He needed to keep his herd intact, but if at all possible, he'd do it without killing one of the giant cats.

As the stars lost some of their brilliance and the edge of the horizon began to lighten, he meandered over to the side of camp where Cleo slept. He took satisfaction in knowing that she slept, even though she'd stirred restlessly when the wolves had started in about an hour ago. Tom had always thought they sounded mournful instead of frightening. Wolves were another sore point with Montana ranchers now that the environmental faction had reintroduced them, but Tom figured they were part of the mix, just like cougars. Montana wouldn't be the same without predators.

The wolves had quieted, and Cleo looked peaceful now, her hand curled under her chin, her golden hair spilling over the rolled-up jacket she'd made into a pillow. She couldn't know that he'd sacrifice himself before letting anything happen to her. He wasn't sure exactly when it had clicked in, but he'd developed a protective feeling about her that probably spelled trouble. The minute he felt this urge to take care of a woman, it usually meant that he'd let down his guard and eventually she'd play him for a fool. Deidre sure as hell had.

He watched Cleo sleep and tried to pinpoint when he'd felt that telltale tug at his heart. Maybe when he'd seen how much like a cowgirl she looked in that hat, or when he'd noticed she was lagging behind and trying valiantly to coax Dynamite into a trot. Maybe it was the picture she'd painted of teaching her hamster tricks, or the plucky way she'd helped drive the cattle and then kept quiet about how sore she was.

In any case, more than lust drew him now, which could be dangerous. He could forget the lure of a woman's body, but once she'd started working on his mind, he'd remember her for the rest of his life.

From the corner of his eye, across the meadow, he caught a movement. Turning slowly, he glimpsed a huge bull moose coming out of the trees, headed for the brook. The moose was only an indistinct shadow now, his rack of antlers rising like an unattainable, perfect trophy in a hunter's dream. Tom never had developed a taste for hunting. He killed only when there was no choice—if an animal was a threat or very sick. He wouldn't lead guests on hunting trips, either, although many of his neighbors brought in extra money that way.

Moving carefully so as not to startle the moose, Tom crouched and gently shook Cleo's shoulder.

She opened her eyes at once, making him wonder if she'd been as fast asleep as he'd thought.

He leaned close to her ear and pushed the silky hair aside so he could whisper to her. Breathing in the flowery scent of her skin, he wanted to linger, to nibble and enjoy, but he knew she'd want this wildlife shot to take home to New York. "There's a bull moose approaching the stream," he murmured. "Move slowly and get your camera. It should be light enough soon for you to get a great picture of him."

She nodded and began crawling carefully out of her bedroll. He stood and kept an eye on the moose, and in no time Cleo stood beside him, shivering slightly, her camera hanging around her neck. He leaned down to her bedroll, shook out her bundled jacket and eased it over her arms.

She smiled her gratitude, and his heart turned over. She was a beauty in the morning. He took note of the breeze that lifted a lock of her hair. The wind was blowing toward them, which meant they might be able to sneak closer without being scented.

He mouthed *follow me,* and she nodded again. Watching each step to make sure he didn't step on a twig and shatter the morning silence, he crept forward. Looking like a ghost stepping slowly through the ground fog, the moose reached the rushing water and gazed around. Tom froze. As the moose lowered his head to drink, Tom started soundlessly forward again.

The moose lifted his head, water dripping from his muzzle, and Tom paused, knowing they dared go no closer or the animal would vanish back into the forest. Cleo put her hand on Tom's shoulder and squeezed, as if to signal to him that this was the spot. As they stood rigidly waiting, the first light of morning tipped the bull's mighty antlers with bronze.

Click. The sound of the camera's shutter was no louder than a cricket's chirp, but the moose swiveled his massive head and stared straight at them, as if he'd known of their presence all along. *Click.* The shutter opened and closed a second time. The moose turned and walked regally away, with no apparent haste, until he was lost in the shadows of the trees.

"Do you think you got it?" Tom asked, speaking softly as he watched the trees where the moose had disappeared.

"I got it." Her voice was rich with joy. "Oh, Tom, wasn't he magnificent?"

"Yeah." He turned toward her. "You asked me to show you what makes this place so special to me. I think I just did."

"Do you see stuff like that all the time?"

"Not all the time, but often enough to make all the hassles worthwhile."

"Thank you for waking me up."

"You're welcome." He couldn't help himself from touching her cheek. "How do you feel?"

"On the outside? A little stiff. On the inside? Like a kid at Christmas."

He smiled. "Welcome to the life of a cowpuncher. Most of the time you're stiff and sore from the work, but you have the most beautiful office in the world."

"No kidding." She gazed up at the mountains as sunlight gilded the snowy peaks. "I had no idea, Tom."

Easy, he cautioned himself. She might be falling in love with Montana. Lots of folks did that. It didn't mean much, in the long run. They went home, got back in their comfortable routine and forgot the wonder of a mountain morning like this one. Still, he'd never heard that awestruck tone in Deidre's voice. She'd liked the idea of being married to a Montana rancher because it sounded exotic to her New York friends. She hadn't liked the reality all that much.

"I have a very personal question to ask," Cleo said.

"Okay."

"You can tell me to mind my own business."

"Okay."

"Why...why did you get divorced?" She looked up at him and quickly glanced away. "Sorry. I shouldn't have asked."

That she had her mind on a question so close to his own thoughts shook him. "Why did you ask?"

"I don't know. It's just that you don't seem like the divorcing kind, and I can't believe a woman would give up...all this."

"I don't think it was so tough to give up. Deidre had her priorities. Being married to me wasn't one of them."

Something unreadable was going on behind those blue eyes of hers. "I guess you take the whole idea of marriage pretty seriously," she said.

"If you don't take it seriously, what's the point in getting married?"

She looked uncomfortable. "Well, of course, a person should take it seriously, to a point. But as for having a marriage control your whole life, I think that—"

"It damn well should control your whole life. It controlled mine, so why shouldn't it have controlled hers? I was standing here thinking that you weren't anything like her, but maybe I was wrong. Maybe you would have sided with her. Career comes first, and a husband is just a handy convenience."

She flushed. "Career has always come first for men, though, hasn't it? What did you do, expect her to give up modeling?"

"Just for a while." He tried to stem the tide of anger rising in him. "She could have gone back to it."

"Not likely!" Her eyes flashed blue fire. "That's not the kind of job where you take a leave of absence to play house. You miss a step and you're history. I don't suppose you ever considered giving up ranching, now, did you? The little woman has to make the adjustments, while the man—"

"The *man* finds out too late that the little *woman* aborted their baby! Since when did you get the idea that men have all the control? A woman has the ultimate control!"

She looked stricken. "Oh, Tom. Tom, I'm sorry. I didn't realize."

He stared down at the ground, where dew sparkled

like tears on the grass. "Nothing to be done about it now. Shouldn't have said anything." He was shaking, dammit. Worse yet, he could hear people stirring at the campsite. He'd probably woken them up with his shouting. Wonderful.

Cleo touched his arm. "Tom..."

"I need to check on the horses."

"I'll go with you."

"No." He gazed at her with regret. "It's probably just as well we got this argument out of the way. You'd think after going a few rounds with one New York woman I'd have sense enough to stay away from the next one who came along. Guess I'm a slow learner."

"Tom, I'm not..." She looked confused and didn't finish the sentence.

"I'm not saying you'd be sneaky, like Deidre. But you think like her. You've got a foothold on that success ladder, and you're not about to let some guy loosen that hold. You have a right to think like that. And I have a right to stay the hell away from you before I get myself in trouble again." He turned and headed out into the meadow where the horses grazed on the dew-soaked grass.

Thank God for this land, he thought as he took a deep, calming breath. The women might come and go, but the land never disappointed him.

THE CATTLE DRIVE seemed to have acted like a fountain of youth for Dynamite. Either that or the little mare was eager to get back to her corral, Cleo thought. Head up and steps light, Dynamite pranced near the head of the group heading down the mountain. That was fine with Cleo. She'd lost her taste for picture-taking.

Tom was absolutely right about her, she thought as she

rode along in the crisp air of a high-country morning. Career was her top priority, as it always had been for her father. Her mother had been a handy convenience. Growing up with that role model, Cleo had seen the advantages for the dominant person in the marriage, and she'd made up her mind to be that dominant person.

There was nothing wrong with her plan, she thought belligerently. Men had been working the system that way for years, so why shouldn't she turn the tables, find a docile man to play the supportive role, and get on with becoming famous? For the next few days all she needed to do was concentrate on her calendar and her husband-hunting. Not every cowboy in this valley thought like Tom. And if they didn't appeal to her quite as much as he did, well, that was the sacrifice she'd have to make. He wasn't the man for her.

Unfortunately, she wasn't making any progress getting Tom to pose for her calendar cover, either. In fact, after their blowup in the meadow, she doubted he'd want anything more to do with her, whether she had a camera in her hand or not. Well, good. She needed to forget him and get on with her work. Maybe Jose would make a good cover.

The sound of a trotting horse alerted her to someone coming from behind. Wondering if it could be Tom wanting to smooth things over, she turned expectantly and discovered Laura drawing alongside.

Pleasure glowed on Laura's fourteen-year-old face. "I ditched the mom and dad units. I found a wide place on the trail and rode around the wagon, but then the trail narrowed again and they're stuck behind it."

Cleo couldn't help laughing. It was so like the sort of thing she would have done at that age. "Parents can be a trial sometimes."

"Really. They treat me like a kid."

Cleo màde sure she didn't smile at that. Fourteen was a very tough age, as she well remembered.

"I'm buying one of your calendars when I get home," Laura said. "I think what you do is so cool."

"Thanks."

"I can hardly wait until I can get a job. And my own apartment." Her young jaw firmed. "And I'm going to college where I want to, and not where they want me to."

Cleo understood that tone of rebellion well. She'd used it herself enough times. "It's tough when they try to control your every move."

"Did your parents do that?"

"Oh, you bet. I'm an only daughter, too, and I know the pressures you're under. Your parents remind me of mine, always after me to be perfect."

"I know! I hate that!"

"Well, you're their only shot, Laura. They get to concentrate all their hopes on you. Part of the time I loved being the center of attention, but most of the time I wanted a brother or sister, just to take the heat off me."

Laura giggled. "I used to beg them to adopt a kid. I went into this whole routine about the poor children in the ghetto. But they never went for the idea. I think they count how many times I breathe each day."

"I uscd to think that, too. I used to think I couldn't sneeze without them knowing about it, and telling me how I could sneeze better next time."

"Yeah." Laura grinncd. "Anyway, I'll bet your parents don't control you anymore. You've got your life, your career, everything."

Laura thought of her father's latest offer, to use *Montana Men* as a premium for his customers. The hell of it was, she was tempted to go along with the idea. "They still try, Laura," she said. "Believe me, they still try."

WHEN SHE RETURNED to the ranch, Cleo called Bozeman and arranged for a rental convertible to be delivered. She should have reserved a car in the first place, she thought. Bernie had thought she'd get lost out here in the wilds, but she'd begun using the mountains to guide her in the same way she used the Chrysler Building and the Empire State Building in New York.

Of course, if she'd driven herself from Bozeman to the Whispering Winds, she would have missed seeing the pair of bald eagles. But she also would have missed that first intoxicating dose of Tom, and maybe she wouldn't have become so enamored of him so quickly.

She threw herself into her work, photographing Jose shirtless, his arm looped over the neck of a dark bay gelding. It was obvious from the expression she saw through her camera lens that Jose was no gelding, however. He was currently unattached, so Cleo put a star next to the interview notes, indicating Jose was a potential husband candidate.

Except for Tom, there was no one else on the Whispering Winds she wanted to photograph, so for the next several days she toured the neighboring ranches. She soon became known as the "camera lady," and cowboys began to seek her out and offer themselves as candidates. She had to gently reject a few, but she ended up with a good list of prospects, both for the calendar and for her matrimonial scheme. Stu, a red-haired wrangler with great buns, got a star, as did Bo, who was part Native American and had a mysterious sexuality that Cleo knew would drive women crazy. He could probably drive her crazy, too, she thought, if she could get Tom off her mind.

In trying to accomplish that, she stayed away from the Whispering Winds as much as possible. Several evenings she stopped for dinner at a steak house a few miles south of the ranch and didn't park her convertible beside her little cabin until bedtime. On one such occasion, when she'd put in a particularly long day and only wanted to get home and relax, she returned to her car after dinner and discovered it wouldn't start.

"Hey, camera lady!"

She glanced up to see Robert Henderson coming out of the restaurant. He was one of the cowboys she'd had to reject for the calendar because his round baby face wouldn't have photographed well.

"Looks like you got car problems," Robert said.

She smiled at him. "I'm afraid so."

"It's a rental, isn't it?"

"Yep."

"I could try to fix it, but you might get in trouble with the rental agency. Why don't I give you a lift to the Whispering Winds, and you can call the company from there? Let them deal with it."

"Great idea. And thanks."

Robert questioned her endlessly about life in New York for the entire drive home. By the time he finally dropped her off, and she'd thanked him profusely, she was completely drained. Nothing sounded better than a good night's sleep, unless...she glimpsed the row of decorative path lights that led behind her cottage to the area that contained a hot tub she had yet to use.

Moments later she slipped off her bathrobe in the privacy of the darkened forest, took her candy bar out of the robe pocket and mounted the steps to the steaming hot tub. She deserved this, she thought, climbing into the bubbling water with a sigh of contentment. She'd been working damn hard, and as always when she was in the midst of a project, the sexual frustration was building with each photo shoot.

As she settled onto a smooth bench and water swirled over her breasts, she sighed again. Somewhere in the darkness an owl hooted and a small creature scrabbled through the underbrush. Cleo leaned back and rested her head against the wood as she munched her chocolate. She was too tired to care what lurked in the forest. Unless Trixie started going crazy, she refused to worry about bears or cougars.

She just wanted the warm, bubbling water to ease her fatigue and mellow out the sharp edge of her desire. Damn that Tom McBride, anyway. Always before, her sexual hunger had been unfocused, but now, instead of longing for some anonymous lover, she wanted Tom. She compared every cowboy she photographed to him, and she found every one wanting.

Sliding in deeper, she murmured with delight. She'd been in Jacuzzis before, but never in natural hot springs. The soothing mineral water and the dim glow from the path lights coaxed her gently into an almost hypnotic state. "Don't fall asleep and drown, Griffin," she muttered to herself as her eyes threatened to close.

Yet there was an erotic nature to the experience that kept her on the edge of awareness. Maybe it was being outside, with the scent of pines and the soft whisper of the wind that made her feel a primitive oneness with nature. Finally she gave in to the mood, closed her eyes and allowed herself to drift closer and closer to sleep.

On the outer edge of consciousness, she sensed the presence of another, but felt no alarm, no thrill of danger. Floating in a fantasy world, she imagined that a warm breeze touched her eyelids, then her cheeks, and finally her mouth. The breeze became a brush of lips, and she didn't question, didn't open her eyes. For she knew. He was here.

9

TOM HAD SPENT the last few days stringing fence with
Stan. He'd given himself the relentless task to keep
thoughts of Cleo at bay, and his muscles were complaining. He'd noticed that Cleo didn't hang around the ranch
much, either, and he figured she was trying to avoid him
as much as he was trying to avoid her. When he didn't
see her convertible parked beside her cabin that evening,
he assumed she was out again, as usual.

He didn't like thinking about that, but he couldn't exactly stop her activities, whatever they might be. The
night had turned out to be fairly warm for Montana, so at
least he could pamper his aching muscles by taking a
nice long soak in the hot tub going to waste behind her
cabin. He'd walked down the path from the ranch house
wearing only his jeans and boots, with a towel slung over
his bare shoulder.

When he reached the clearing, he'd stopped in amazement, wondering if he'd started seeing visions in his des-
peration for a woman he couldn't have. But no, she was
real enough. Maybe something had happened to her convertible and she'd gotten a lift back to the ranch.

He could tell she had no idea he was standing there.
Her eyes were closed, and the sound of bubbling water
had muffled his footsteps on the path. If he could have
conjured up the most tempting image of Cleo he could
imagine, this would be it. He'd always been intrigued

with the way a woman piled her hair haphazardly on top of her head when she planned to soak in a tub. He found it endearing the way little tendrils fell out of that sort of arrangement, and how kissable a woman's neck seemed, when all her hair was pulled away to expose her soft skin.

Her shoulders were bare, and he suspected the rest of her was, too. After all, she'd announced that was the way she liked hot tubbing, and so did he, for that matter. He should turn around and walk back up that path and leave her to her solitary soak. He should...but even before he started across the little clearing, he knew he'd lost the willpower.

She didn't stir as he undressed and climbed slowly into the swirling water. He remembered how she'd seemed to play possum when he thought she was asleep that morning a few days ago at the campsite. She could be doing that now. A woman as headstrong as Cleo might have to pretend she was in a helpless trance before she could drop her defenses. Yet on some level, she knew what was happening, and she trusted him. He wouldn't betray that.

The steam surrounding them carried the citrus scent of her cologne, and he breathed deep as he eased down beside her on the wooden bench. Her face was flushed from the warmth of the water and her mouth curved slightly, on the brink of a smile. He leaned over and allowed his breath to caress her face. The barest of sighs parted her lips.

His heartbeat thundering in his ears, he touched his mouth to hers with the lightness of snow falling. Her lips were pliant and warm...receptive. Her mouth tasted of chocolate, and he smiled. She'd been snacking again. He sought firmer contact, and she responded, opening to him, inviting him deeper. He followed where she led, desire throbbing within him at the blatant suggestion of her kiss.

Yet his feathery touch betrayed no urgency as he trailed a finger down her throat and felt her pulse hammering in concert with his. For many long moments he stroked her throat, her shoulders, the nape of her neck, as if he were gentling a skittish filly. At last, when he felt she was ready for it, he slipped his hand beneath the water and cradled her breast. He captured her soft moan against his mouth as he continued his slow assault.

Ah, but the weight of her breast felt good in his palm. Her nipple was already taut with passion, as he'd thought it might be. As he stroked his thumb back and forth across the pebbled tip, he loved hearing the subtle hitch in her breathing.

Drawing out the newest stage of his seduction, he fondled her breasts, kneading and stroking as he lazily explored the moist recesses of her mouth with his tongue. Laying his hand over her heart, he could read the tumult he'd created as her chest pounded against his palm. Slowly, so as not to break the connection, he slid his lips away from hers. Her eyes remained closed, but her lashes fluttered. Her lips were parted, swollen from his kisses, and her breath came in agitated little puffs. Ah, Cleo.

Resisting the urge to return to the wonders of her mouth, he followed a path along her jaw and down her throat. He reached the surface of the water and lifted her breast until the water foamed just over the surface of her skin. With flicks of his tongue, he teased her nipple in tandem with the bubbling water, gratified with the way she trembled in his steady grip. At last he drew her, moist and quivering, into his mouth.

She gasped and arched upward, bringing both breasts

out of the water. He needed no more invitation than that. Cupping her with both hands, he tasted and savored, raking her gently with his teeth, laving her with his tongue. Touching him for the first time, she combed her damp fingers through his hair and held his head, silently urging him on.

When she began to whimper, he returned to kiss her whimpers away. Then he slid his hand slowly downward, parting her thighs. He marveled that she gave him no resistance. Taking her would be so easy. And such a mistake. She was swollen and ready as he slipped his fingers deep inside. He shook with the need to bury himself there, protection or no protection. But the consequences could bring him to his knees.

So he would settle for this—stroking her until she quivered and arched, touching her until she cried out and exploded in his arms. Perhaps this was all they'd ever share. He wouldn't think beyond this moment, which had appeared like a precious gift.

He lifted his head and spoke for the first time. "Open your eyes, Cleo."

She shook her head. Her breath came fast and shallow.

He pushed in deep and stilled the movement of his hand. "Feel how close I am, Cleo?"

She nodded.

"You let me touch the fire deep inside you," he murmured, kissing her jaw, her cheeks. "Let me see the fire in your eyes when I take you over the edge."

Slowly her eyes opened, pale yet glowing in the dim light of the clearing.

His breath caught in his throat. He'd maintained control of his grinding need to take her fully...until now. Now he wanted it all—the joining, the pleasure, the sweet release, the mating. From a nearby ridge a wolf howled, and the primitive cry echoed in his heart.

But he was a man, not a wolf. He would finish this and leave without taking what his body screamed to have. He increased the pressure, quickened the rhythm and watched with a fierce sense of possession as the flame leaped in her eyes.

"Yes," he whispered as he felt the contractions begin. Whether she knew it or not, he was staking a claim tonight.

Her eyes darkened. With a soft cry of surrender she lifted her hips, allowing him even deeper penetration as she shook with the force of her climax. He kissed her, plunging his tongue into her mouth as he absorbed her convulsions.

Gradually, she relaxed in his arms. He could bring her to the brink again, he knew. She was ready for more, and the slightest movement of his fingers would be enough to start all over again. She might be able to take it, but he couldn't.

He withdrew his hand, gave her one last lingering kiss and climbed out of the hot tub.

"Tom?" Her voice was dusky with spent passion.

Between being wet and aroused, he had a hell of a time getting his pants on, but he managed that and his boots, too. If he didn't get dressed, he wouldn't be able to look at her without wanting to jump back in and finish the job good and proper, the way it was meant to be done.

"You're...leaving?" she murmured. "But..."

He slung his towel over his shoulder and glanced at her. For a brief second he considered pulling her out of that tub and sitting her on the edge while he unfastened his jeans and...no. He wasn't taking those kinds of chances.

"I'm leaving," he said.

"But you didn't..."

He gazed at her. "A smart cowboy lets a filly get used to him before he tries to ride her for the first time." Then he turned and walked as best he could up the path. As an exit line, it was one of his more clever ones, he thought. Apparently, Cleo didn't appreciate it, though. A heaved stone landed somewhere behind him on the path. Maybe she wasn't as grateful as he thought she'd be.

CLEO HAD NO IDEA how she'd face Tom again. She slept like a zombie that night, though, and she'd always been an insomniac. She overslept, in fact, and as birds twittered outside and sun streamed through the window, she lay in bed and considered the ramifications of what she'd allowed to happen.

It was a murky ethical question. She'd hadn't actually *slept* with Tom, so technically she should be able to continue her husband hunt without feeling guilty. Oh, sure. What kind of woman would allow one man to caress her so intimately that she'd probably never forget the experience, and then within days ask another man if he'd be interested in marriage?

Maybe on this trip she could narrow down the prospects. Then in a few weeks she'd come back to Montana, staying somewhere else, of course, and look up the cowboy she'd set her sights on. In order to approach him with a clear conscience, she needed to put some distance between herself and the hot-tub incident.

As for photographing Tom for the calendar, she hadn't quite broken her rule there, either, but she couldn't imagine being able to maintain her professional demeanor after what they'd shared. Maybe *shared* was the wrong word. He'd played her like a concert pianist seated at a grand piano. It had been...awesome.

She threw back the covers and leaped out of bed. If she stayed there thinking about Tom's hands on her, she'd be in the same state in no time, and that would never do. Then she stood in the middle of the floor, astounded at her behavior. She never leaped out of bed. Crawling out, complaining every inch of the way, was more her style.

She stretched her arms over her head and smiled.

What she'd let happen in the hot tub was ill-advised, but she'd never felt better in her whole life. And she'd never felt less like shooting sexy cowboys. Maybe today would be the best time to take a roll of Juanita's kids, while the rental-car company sorted out what they wanted to do about her disabled convertible.

Dressing quickly, she kept an eye out for Tom as she went up to the back door of the ranch's kitchen and rapped gently. "Juanita?"

Juanita came to the screen door and opened it immediately. "Where have you been keeping yourself? You haven't been sneaking food from the kitchen in days!"

"I'd like to sneak some now," Cleo said. "I'm starving."

"Coming right up." Juanita motioned her inside and went over to open the pantry. "You look good." Her back to Cleo, she pulled out the makings for French toast. "Did you get some good news or something?"

Cleo made a mental note to tone down her pleased expression. She especially didn't want that look on her face if Tom showed up. "Oh, I guess I'm just enjoying the morning. Do you know if—uh—Tom or anybody is around?"

"Tom rode out of here before breakfast." Juanita

whipped eggs and milk together. "Did you need him for anything?"

"No! I mean, no. My car broke down last night at the Diamond Bar Steak House, and I—"

"He'd be glad to help you with that, I'm sure, but he didn't say when he'd be back."

"That's okay. I can handle it." She was afraid she sounded as distracted as she felt. "In fact, why don't I go call the rental company while the French toast is cooking?"

"Sure." Juanita gave her a strange look. "How'd you get home last night, then?"

"A cowboy gave me a lift. It worked out fine." Although Cleo knew that Juanita couldn't possibly figure out what happened after that, she still wanted to change the subject. "Listen, after breakfast, I thought I might try a few shots of the kids."

"Oh." Juanita looked bereft. "They're with their father. He took them down to the Gallatin River to fish today. If I'd known that you—"

"Never mind," Cleo said quickly. "I'll catch them another time."

"But you're so busy. And now that you haven't needed snacks during the day because you've been gone so much, I was afraid that you'd decide not to do it."

"I absolutely am going to do it." Cleo had been lukewarm about the idea before, but now that she understood how significant it was to Juanita, she'd make certain the job was accomplished. "Don't worry. I'll be around for a few more days. We'll find time."

Juanita kept pummeling the eggs and milk with the wire whisk, even though the mixture was frothy already. "Jeeter told me how much you paid him to take his picture. I...might have asked too big a favor, just in trade for a few meals. I'll bet you charge a lot for portraits, don't you?"

Cleo walked over and put her hands on Juanita's plump shoulders. "You let me into your kitchen," she said with a smile. "I figure that's beyond price."

Juanita stared at her for a minute, and finally her expression cleared and she grinned. "That's true. Go make your phone call while I fix you the best French toast west of the Mississippi."

Fifteen minutes later, her mouth full of the lightest, sweetest French toast she'd ever eaten, Cleo had to agree with her. She sat where Juanita had set her a place, on a stool drawn up to the butcher-block island in the center of the large kitchen. Juanita poured herself a cup of coffee and pulled up a stool to join her.

Cleo savored the bite a moment longer before swallowing it. "Tom is a lucky man," she said.

"Oh, I wouldn't say that."

"Why not? He's got this beautiful ranch, a fantastic cook and loyal hands to help him run the place."

"Assuming he can hang on."

Cleo took a sip of coffee so wonderful that it would set the standard for her from now on. "Are things really that bad? He mentioned something during the cattle drive about finances, but then he shrugged it off."

"He'd hate for me to talk to you about it."

"But you're dying to talk to somebody," Cleo guessed.

"I'm worried sick, to tell you the truth." Juanita waved at Cleo's plate. "Keep eating. I'll talk. You eat."

"You don't have to coax me. This is outstanding." Cleo pushed the edge of her fork through a golden slice of French toast dripping with maple syrup. "And I promise that whatever you say goes no further."

"I know that." Juanita cradled her mug of coffee. "I

have good instincts. Take that Deidre. I knew from the minute he brought her here she would be bad news."

"I heard what she did to Tom."

Juanita's brown eyes turned almost black with anger. "It was bad enough that she did it, but not even to tell him beforehand, to give him a chance to stop her...that was evil. Especially after all the money he wasted flying to New York once a month because he figured it was only fair that he do part of the traveling. Then when they split up, he had to pay her a cash settlement because he's the one who asked for the divorce, and Tom's not the type to sign a prenuptial agreement. He was already stretched pretty thin after buying his sister out, and then his dad's doctor bills started coming in."

"Wow. That does sound bad."

"I've pieced all this together on my own, but I see him in his office, hunched over the books. Unless he's got some gold buried somewhere on the ranch, he's in big trouble."

"You mean, he might lose the ranch?"

Juanita gazed at her. "It happens all the time around here. Ranching's tough, and taking in guests helps keep you even. But let an ex-wife take you to the cleaners, or let medical bills cut into your profits, and it's *adiós, muchachos.*"

"But this has been McBride land for five generations!"

Juanita nodded. "Can you imagine how that weighs on him? And he worries about all of us. I could get another job, but I don't want another one. I love this place as much as if it was my family that had been here for five generations. The first time I laid eyes on it, I recognized it as a real place, one that gets in your blood."

Cleo finished her meal and picked up her coffee mug. She knew what Juanita meant. She also knew that it didn't apply to any apartment she'd ever lived in in Manhattan. She felt a connection with the city in general, but it was far less personal than the one Tom had with the Whispering Winds.

She sent Juanita a rueful glance. "I thought if he'd just agree to pose for me, I could help him out. Sounds like that would be a drop in the bucket."

"Yes." Juanita smiled. "Although I'd give anything to see what you could do with him in a calendar pose. He has no idea what a sexy guy he is."

Cleo felt the heat rise to her cheeks.

"Aha!" Juanita set down her mug with a bang. "So I was right!"

Cleo stood and picked up her plate. "I really have to get going. I'm sure you have plenty to do before lunch. I—"

"I see you two ending up together, you know."

Cleo dumped her plate in the sink and ran water over it. She kept her back to Juanita. "That's ridiculous, and you know it. My life is in New York, just like Deidre's was. Even if Tom and I are somewhat attracted to each other, which you've obviously noticed, we'd both be crazy to act on it."

"You're no more like Deidre than I'm like Cruella De Ville."

"Tom thinks I'm like Deidre," Cleo said softly.

"Then Tom needs to look a little closer."

Cleo turned, bracing both hands behind her on the counter. "I am like her. I put my career ahead of everything else. Marriage, kids, a home—they're all secondary, just like with Deidre. I've worked hard to get where I am, and I don't intend to give it up."

Juanita gazed at her, her expression serene. "If you say so."

"I do. In fact, I need to use the telephone again, so I can call my assistant. Business is on my mind all the time."

"Uh-huh."

"It is, Juanita." She started out of the kitchen. "Thanks for a wonderful breakfast."

"Anytime."

Cleo had nothing specific to discuss with Bernie, but she needed to connect with that part of her life. She felt her grip on it slipping.

"How's the manhunt going?" Bernie asked cheerfully.

"I, uh, may have to make two trips to get the job accomplished," Cleo admitted. "It *is* pretty tough to get something like that settled in two weeks."

"Can't you find anybody who dreams of connubial bliss in a hotel room?"

"Stop it, Bernie. Honestly, you're sounding so old-fashioned. Did you get the rolls of film I shipped?"

"Of course. The contact sheets are on their way. You've got some cuties there. If I didn't have George, I might consider a guest-ranch vacation, myself."

"Yeah, there's something about cowboys." Especially one in particular, she thought.

"I have to ask. Are any of the ones on the rolls I saw husband candidates?"

"No." The answer came out too quickly, and there was no logic behind it, only emotion generated by a passionate man in a hot tub. She just couldn't think about marriage so soon after that. "I mean, probably not."

"I counted eight guys. If you've eliminated eight of your thirteen, you're not giving yourself much leeway."

"That's why I need another trip out here."

"That reservation wasn't easy to get," Bernie said. "You have some free time in September, so why don't I just schedule you at the same—"

"No!"

"What's the problem? You seemed to like it well enough in the beginning."

"It's okay. I just want to...branch out. Listen, don't schedule anything until I get back."

"All right. You sound funny. Is something wrong?"

Cleo cleared her throat. "Not a thing."

"You father called again. He wants an answer on whether he can count on the calendar as a premium."

"Tell him he can."

"Cleo, are you sure? You sound a little stressed, and bringing your father in on the project probably isn't—"

"I can handle it. In fact, I want to handle it. I've waited a long time for him to take me seriously. Now that he has, it would be childish to refuse."

Bernie sighed. "Okay. See you soon."

"Right. We'll take an afternoon off and go shopping on Fifth Avenue."

"We'll do *what*?"

"Go shopping," Cleo said. "Do lunch at the Four Seasons."

"You've never suggested a shopping trip in all the years we've known each other. What's up?"

"I just realized I'm not as appreciative of New York as I should be. Just because we don't have high mountains and moose and eagles and stuff doesn't mean we don't have lots of cool things in New York."

"Uh, okay, Cleo. Whatever you say. Shopping. Right. I gotta go now, toots. The other line's ringing. And the next time one of those cowboys rolls you a cigarette, ask what's in it. Sounds to me the mountains aren't the only thing that's high in Montana."

10

CLEO DID FEEL a little high after last night's episode. Compounding her sense of disorientation was having nothing to do. She'd always been in a rush, always on a schedule, but the rental-car situation wouldn't be straightened out for at least a couple of hours, so she had no wheels. She couldn't photograph Juanita's kids, and the phone call to Bernie had only used up a few minutes.

After a quick trip back to the kitchen for carrot chunks, she wandered down to the corral. Dynamite stood in the same sleepy-eyed position she'd been in when Cleo first saw her the morning of the cattle drive.

"Sandbagger," Cleo said. She clucked to the horse and reached in her pocket for a piece of carrot. "You just want everybody to think you're old and tired so they won't make you work too hard."

Dynamite walked over, and Cleo slipped her the carrot. She tried not to make a big deal about it and attract the attention of the other horses in the corral, although there weren't many. Jeeter had taken a big group out on a trail ride this morning, along with Trixie. She'd seen them head out as she walked up to the house for breakfast.

"Want to take her out for a spin?" Jose asked, ambling up to her with a posthole digger over his shoulder.

"Are you offering to go along?"

"Wish I could, but the boss needs some posts set this

morning. That doesn't mean you can't take a ride by yourself. It's a great day for it."

The idea appealed to her. "Aren't you afraid I'll get lost?"

"Find a fence and follow along. It'll lead you back home. Go out for about an hour, turn around and come back. I've seen you ride. You'll be fine."

"Okay, I'll go. Let me get my camera."

"I'll saddle Dynamite for you."

"I'll do that, too," Cleo said. "If I'm going out by myself, the least I can do is saddle my own horse."

Jose smiled at her. "Good for you."

She studied him and wondered if maybe he could be the one, after all. He was very handsome, and a nice guy. "Do you plan on having kids some day?" she asked. She hadn't figured out how to work that into the photo-shoot interview.

He blinked. "Excuse me?"

"Kids." Cleo managed a laugh. "Don't ask me why I thought of that, but I did."

Jose cleared his throat. "First I reckon I'd better find the right lady. Some of that decision would be up to her."

"What if she didn't want any?"

"Look, if you're trying to set me up with somebody in particular, then tell me who it is, and we can—"

"Nope. Just idle curiosity."

He swung the posthole digger from his shoulder and leaned on it, gazing at her in speculation. "Well, I've never considered that question, but it would depend on why she didn't want them, I guess. I'd understand a medical problem, or maybe she's worried about over-population, or the cost of college, things like that. But I always figured on being a father some day. Giving that up would be a sacrifice, and I wouldn't make it without a powerful reason."

"I see." That took care of Jose as a candidate.

He grinned. "And I still say you have somebody in mind you want to marry me off to. Send her on out. I'll change her mind about the kid thing."

Cleo waved her hands in front of her. "Nobody, really. I'll be right back with my camera."

"Don't forget your hat," he called out after her.

SOMETIME LATER, her hat firmly in place, Cleo guided Dynamite along a barbed-wire fence as it angled away from the ranch. She took a deep breath and smelled freedom, just as she had on the morning of the cattle drive. Out here there was no phone, no fax, no expectations.

She wondered where Tom was right now. Not that she'd ridden out here hoping to find him. In fact, he was the last person on earth she wanted to run into. But after last night, she'd rather their next encounter be in private, instead of when other people were around. Now that she knew Juanita had picked up on the attraction between the two of them, she was afraid others might do the same.

The longer she rode, the less any of that seemed to matter. She glanced at her watch and knew she'd better turn back, but she hated to do it just yet. Dynamite would accelerate on the way home, anyway, and the ride was so therapeutic. The majesty of her surroundings dwarfed human concerns. She remembered what Tom had called it—*the most beautiful office in the world.* Yet he might lose it. She didn't want to think about that. Tom belonged here, and the idea that he might lose the right to ride through this country really bothered her.

She leaned forward to pat Dynamite's soft neck. "It

won't happen, will it, Dynamite? The Whispering Winds will be McBride land for a long time yet, right?"

The mare's ears twitched back in acknowledgment of the conversation.

"You're a good pony, Dynamite. I'm going to miss you. In fact, I'm going to take your picture so I'll have something to remember you by." Pulling the mare to a halt beside the fence, she dismounted and dropped the reins to the ground, as Tom had instructed everyone to do during the cattle drive.

She walked a slight distance away, trying different camera angles. The horse stood in her typical half-asleep pose, looking like one disreputable nag. Cleo tried snapping her fingers, but nothing happened. "Open your eyes, Dynamite," she ordered. Then she remembered those had been Tom's exact words to her last night. She'd wanted to stay one step removed from what was happening in that hot tub. If she didn't open her eyes, she wasn't truly acknowledging that it was Tom there with her, touching her in all those forbidden ways. But he'd appealed to her sense of justice, and she'd opened her eyes, only to find herself drowning in the experience he was giving her.

Gazing into his eyes during those final moments of pleasure, she'd had the unmistakable feeling that he was binding her to him. That was ridiculous, of course. She wasn't bound to anyone. She was going back home soon, and putting together a calendar that would be her biggest hit yet. Sphinx Cosmetics would help make it so.

She crouched in the grass. "Okay, you sorry piece of horseflesh. If you don't perk up, all of New York will see what a lazy bag of bones you are, and they'll never believe you're the queen of the cow ponies. Is this the image you want carried to the Big Apple?"

Amazingly, Dynamite's ears flicked forward and she looked suddenly alert.

"Hey, that's more like it!" Cleo clicked the shutter.

Dynamite tossed her head and rolled her eyes.

"Go, baby! They're gonna love you on Broadway, sweetheart!"

Cleo kept shooting as Dynamite grew increasingly more animated, snorting and shaking her head. But when the mare let out a piercing scream and reared, Cleo decided something was wrong.

"Hey, leave that stuff to Trigger, okay, girl?" Taking the camera from around her neck and laying it on the ground, Cleo edged toward Dynamite, who reared again, coming down stiff-legged. The mare's eyes rolled as she reared once more, and Cleo's throat tightened with fear. She wondered if the camera had spooked Dynamite. Yet that didn't make much sense. Whatever had happened, Cleo had to get the horse calmed down.

She spoke in a low, soothing voice. "Look, if that little black box upsets you, we don't have to take any more pictures. I didn't mean to get you so worked up. Talk about camera-shy. You and your owner are two of a kind."

Dynamite seemed to pay no attention as she continued to rear, trampling the grass in front of her.

"Easy, girl." Cleo decided if she could get close enough to grab the reins, she could keep the horse from rearing, at least, and maybe work her out of the fit she'd thrown herself into. She reached cautiously toward the dangling reins.

And saw the snake.

Or what was left of it. The mangled carcass had once been a snake, but the torn-up mess that Dynamite had made of it caused Cleo to turn away and clutch her stomach.

Finally she took a deep breath and gathered the courage to survey the situation. Dynamite had stopped pounding the earth and backed up several steps. She stood quivering, her flanks heaving from the effort. Cleo made herself look closer at the carnage on the ground. She'd never seen a rattler before, but the tail of this snake was still intact, and it resembled the pictures she'd seen on television and in books.

Cleo began to shiver as she gazed at Dynamite. "I think you might have just saved my life, sweetheart. I probably walked right past that thing, greenhorn that I am." She glanced back to where she'd left her camera. "I hope they don't travel in pairs. Maybe we'll just ride over and get my camera. You've got a lot more sense about what's around here than I do."

Skirting the mangled snake, she gathered the reins and started to mount. That's when she noticed the barbed wire tangled around Dynamite's left hind leg. A strand had worked loose from the fence. In her frenzy to kill the snake, Dynamite had put her foot right through a loop that had been lying on the ground. Backing up to get away from the snake carcass had only made things worse.

Cleo felt horrible as she crouched to view the damage. Dynamite's leg was bleeding from several places where the barbs had been driven into the skin.

"I didn't see this loose wire, either, girl," she murmured. "I should have been watching the ground, but all I could do was stare at the mountains. You'll probably never want to ride out here with me again, and I wouldn't blame you." She sighed and laid her hat on the ground. "Guess we'd better see about getting you untangled. Let's hope to hell another snake doesn't show up while we're doing that."

With gloves, it would have been a tricky job, she thought. Without gloves, it would take a small miracle to accomplish, but she was out here by herself, with no one else to get her out of this fix. She'd just have to manage.

She got to her knees behind the horse. "Now don't kick me, sweetie," she cautioned, as she checked Dynamite to see if the horse had been bitten. "Ouch!" She pulled her bleeding finger back and stuck it in her mouth. "Damn, but that stuff hurts. I can just imagine what it feels like to have it wrapped around your leg. Easy, baby." Cleo was relieved to find no evidence of snakebite on Dynamite's leg. Now all she had to do was untangle the wire.

Gritting her teeth against the pain as the barbed wire continued to bite her, trying to pretend there were no more snakes within miles and hoping that Dynamite didn't kick her clear into next week, Cleo worked with the tangle. Sweat ran into her eyes and she wiped it away, belatedly realizing that she'd smeared blood from her cut fingers over her face.

She talked to Dynamite the whole time she worked with the wire to let the horse know exactly where she was, what she was doing and why she'd appreciate it if the mare would stand perfectly still. Once she felt a pair of eyes on her and glanced sideways to find a cottontail sitting beside the fence post staring at her.

"What'dya say, Thumper?"

The little rabbit twitched its nose and hopped away.

"Guess where there are bunnies, there aren't any snakes," she said to Dynamite. "Or at least we can hope, huh? Damn, but this wire hurts. We're getting somewhere, but it's slow going, girl," she said. "I think we're liable to be really late getting home."

ON HIS WAY BACK to the ranch for lunch, Tom stopped by to check Jose's progress with the postholes. "Looks good, Jose," he said, leaning on his saddle horn. "It's about time to knock off for lunch."

Jose took off his hat and wiped his forehead with a bandanna. "Yeah, I know. I thought I'd work until Cleo gets back and see if she wants any help putting away the tack."

The mention of Cleo's name started Tom's heart racing. He was in worse shape than he thought. "Where'd she go?" he asked, trying to sound casual. He wondered if he'd ridden near her this morning and not even known it. Except that he thought he would have known it, somehow. There was an electricity between them that would have alerted him to her presence.

"She took Dynamite out. Headed up along the northwest fence line," Jose said. "After the way she proved herself on the cattle drive, and knowing what a good horse Dynamite is, I figured it would be okay. I told her to follow the fence so she wouldn't get lost."

Tom nodded. "Sounds fine to me. When's she due in?"

Jose tilted his hat back and gazed up at the sun. "I'm expecting her any minute. She probably started taking pictures and forgot the time. She'll be along."

"So she's later than you thought she'd be?" He tried not to think in terms of disaster but couldn't seem to help himself. She was a greenhorn. *His* greenhorn.

"I guess she's a little late," Jose admitted. "Not enough to be worried about, though." He glanced at Tom. "We had a real strange conversation before she left. She asked if I wanted kids, and what I'd do if the woman I planned to marry didn't want any."

"Did she?"

"Yeah. I think she wants to fix me up with somebody."

"Could be." *And her name better not be Cleo,* he thought grimly. He'd be damned if another man would end up with her. "I think I'll ride up that way and see her home," he said, acting as if he'd just thought of it. He'd known from the minute Jose said where she'd gone that he'd go up and meet her. He'd done a lot of thinking this morning, and he and Cleo needed to talk.

"Okay," Jose said. "But I'm sure she's fine. She's a smart lady."

"That's for sure. Tell Juanita not to expect me for lunch." He wheeled Red and started off toward the fence line. Once he was out of Jose's sight, he kicked the horse into a gallop.

"THAT DOES IT, sweetheart." Cleo eased the last curl of wire from around the horse's leg and tossed the strand back toward the fence post. Her fingers ached and were covered with blood, both hers and Dynamite's. Her shoulders and legs were cramped from hunching in one position for so long. When she tried to stand, the blood roared in her ears and she was afraid she might pass out.

"Just give me a minute, Dynamite," she said, flopping back onto the grass and closing her eyes as the adrenaline surge that had carried her through the ordeal subsided. "Snakes, stay the hell away. I need a few seconds to rest here."

"Dear God."

At the soft, anguished cry, she opened her eyes and looked up to find Tom leaning over her, his face blanched white.

She'd expected to be embarrassed the first time she saw him again after the hot-tub encounter, but she was too grateful for his presence to waste time on embarrassment. "Hi, Tom," she said. "How's tricks?"

He dropped to his knees beside her, his expression grim. "Don't try to talk. Don't move. Something could be wrong with your back."

She sat up.

"I said don't move, woman!" he bellowed, grabbing her by the shoulders.

"Would you pipe down? You're scaring the horses, and Dynamite's been through enough for one day."

"To hell with Dynamite! She kicked you in the head!"

"No, she didn't. I—"

"Then why are you lying here covered with blood? Or at least, you were lying here." He gripped her more firmly. "Lie down, Cleo."

"Why?" She loved the way he'd ridden to her rescue, and having him hold her made all the trauma worthwhile. "So you can have your way with me?"

"Dammit, how can you think about sex at a time like this?"

"Because I'm fine."

"You look like the devil."

She supposed so. "I cut my fingers on the barbed wire when I was untangling it from Dynamite's leg. Then I wiped the sweat off my face and got blood on it."

He released her shoulders and picked up both her hands to examine them. "Aw, hell, Cleo. You're all torn up."

"I had to get the barbed wire off. Take a look at her leg, will you, Tom? I think it's mostly surface wounds, but I'm not an expert on these things."

"Don't move." He released her wrists and went to check on Dynamite. Then he came back and crouched in front of Cleo again. He looked into her eyes, his own dark with guilt. "She's not hurt too bad, but we'll ride double on Red, so we don't put any extra strain on her. I should have checked this section of fence today instead of riding off like some idiot this morning."

"Tom, this is not your fault." She suspected his solitary ride this morning had a lot to do with her. "Besides, I'm fine, and Dynamite will heal. The rattlesnake, now, that's a different story."

"The rattlesnake?" His gaze sharpened. "Are you bit?"

"No, thanks to Dynamite. She trampled it while I was engrossed in taking her picture. Big old snake, too. I wondered why she became so alert. Then when she reared—"

"You're sure it's dead?"

"Go look. About a yard in front of Dynamite you'll find what's left of it."

"Stay right there and don't move while I check it out."

"Okay." She was through trying to convince him she wasn't hurt. As soon as he stood up and walked away, she got to her feet and dusted herself off. After picking up her hat and tapping it against her thigh, she put it on and moved around to Dynamite's head. Wrapping an arm around the mare's neck, she scratched between the animal's ears. "You did great, sweetheart. Thanks for killing the snake, and not kicking me, and being the best horse on the planet." She gave the mare a kiss on the nose.

"Is that your idea of staying put?"

She turned and saw him standing with her camera in his hand.

"I found this lying in the grass," he said. "Knowing how much it means to you, I'm impressed that you left it to take care of your horse."

Cleo stroked the mare's neck. "The truth is, I love this little mare. I know she's technically yours, but we bonded today, so I feel as if she's a little bit my horse now."

"I understand." A faint smile touched his mouth and he shook his head. "But damned if you don't look like a massacre victim, Cleo." He handed her the camera and took her by the arm. "Come on, let me clean up your hands and face a little before we ride back, or you'll give everybody a heart attack."

"Was it a rattlesnake?"

He led her over to his horse. "It was. Timber rattler. Good-sized. Most of the time they go about their business and don't bother anyone. You had the bad luck to stop in the wrong place."

"And I didn't look around, Tom. If I had, I might have seen the snake, and I certainly would have seen the barbed wire. I should have picked a different place to take Dynamite's picture."

"Don't be too hard on yourself." He opened his saddlebag. "I can stow the camera in here if you want."

"Sure. Thanks. I really do feel like an idiot, though, Tom. Jose sent me out with such confidence, and I made a mess of things."

"Hey, you're new to this country." Pulling a red bandanna from his hip pocket, he wet it with water from his canteen. "You're not expected to think of everything the first few times. Now let me see those hands."

She held them out and pressed her lips together against the pain while he washed away the blood.

He shook his head. "You're tough, lady. Most people wouldn't have ripped up their hands like this to get that barbed wire off."

"I didn't see any alternative."

He frowned as he worked carefully on her wounds. "You could have waited until someone came to get you."

"I wasn't sure when that would be."

"I know," he said gently, glancing up at her. "And I admire your take-charge attitude. You reacted like a real cowgirl."

"Why, thank you." She smiled.

"God, but you look gruesome. Hold still, and let me get some of that dried blood off your face."

She lifted her face and closed her eyes.

He nudged her hat back on her head, cradled her chin in one hand and started wiping the cool cloth over her cheeks. "I'm sorry this had to happen to you. You're probably dying to get back to civilization about now."

"Not...exactly." Getting back to civilization was the last thing on her mind. All she could think of was the tenderness of his hand cupping her chin. And how much she wanted him to kiss her. After the trauma with the snake and the barbed wire, she needed to be held, and this was the man she wanted for the job.

Funny how battling for physical survival had rearranged her priorities in no time. Having Tom on the cover of her calendar didn't hold a candle to having him in her arms. New York seemed a million miles away from this sun-drenched meadow and this intriguing man.

"Speaking of things we shouldn't have done," he said. "That business last night..."

"Mmm." Her heart hammered as she replayed every detail. The memory moved through her body, arousing each portion it touched.

"That probably wasn't too bright of me." He'd stopped wiping her face, but he still cupped her face in his hand.

She opened her eyes and gazed up at him. "I don't think intelligence had much to do with it."

He brought his other hand to her face. "You got that right. And it looks like I'm going to keep on being stupid." His lips captured hers with an urgency that took her breath away.

She wrapped her arms around him and hung on to every taut inch of that glorious body. She'd been denied close contact with him the night before, denied the press of his erection and the rapid beat of his heart as he plunged his tongue into her mouth.

Beside them, Red snorted.

Tom lifted his mouth from hers. "We can't stay here. Jose will be coming along any minute to see what happened to us."

She groaned with frustration. "You're right. And we have to get Dynamite home and doctor her cuts."

He smiled. "You really are starting to think like a cowgirl." He kissed her more gently. "We'll settle this matter after we get back to the ranch."

She rubbed against him. "We're riding double all the way home, huh?"

"If I can survive it, we are. Damn, but you get me hot, woman."

Cleo felt her husband-hunting project slipping away, as well. Spending the next few nights with Tom outweighed every other consideration. "Want to do something about that when we get home, cowboy?"

11

DID HE EVER WANT to do something about it, Tom thought as they rode double on Red, with Cleo in the saddle holding the reins and Tom behind her, one arm wrapped around her rib cage just under her breasts, the other grasping Dynamite's lead rope. Her scent filled his nostrils and riding wasn't easy while a guy was aroused, he discovered. He looked longingly at shady glens they passed on the way to the ranch. Pine needles and a horse blanket would do just fine for what he was considering.

But they had to see to Dynamite. Besides, he wanted to discuss a few things with Cleo before he jumped into her bed. He'd managed to avoid giving her a straight answer to her proposition by kissing her hard and hoisting her up on Red. She probably thought that was a yes, when in fact it was a definite maybe.

He liked the way she'd reacted today, assuming responsibility for the accident with Dynamite and doing her best to rectify things. He winced every time he thought about her tender hands on that barbed wire, but he guessed a greenhorn had to earn her spurs somehow. He wondered if she realized how well she was adapting to this country. Then again, maybe she realized it all too well, which had prompted her questions to Jose. Maybe she was planning on roping herself a cowboy before she returned to New York, just like Deidre had done when she'd come to the ranch as a guest.

"Jose said you asked his opinion on a matrimonial issue this morning," he said. He felt the slight tenseness in her body.

"It's good to know my portrait subjects in depth," she said. "The more I know about them, the better job I'll do in choosing the shot that emphasizes their character."

His grip tightened and he leaned forward to murmur into her ear. "The day I picked you up at the airport, you said you don't take any B.S. from folks. Neither do I, and that last explanation was chock-full of it."

She shivered. "Don't breathe on my ear like that."

He blew softly. "Why not?"

"It gets me...worked up."

He rotated his forearm so he could cup her breast. "We might as well both be in that condition."

"Tom." It was more of a sigh than a command for him to stop.

So he didn't. He just kept his hand there, lazily stroking her breast. "Are you going to tell me why you asked Jose whether he wants to have kids after he gets married?"

She sighed again, deeper this time. "I might as well. The plan is in shambles, anyway, thanks to you."

"Oh?" He kept his tone level, his caress light, but his body went on alert at the word *plan*. "And what was your plan, sweetheart?"

"To find a husband."

He went totally still. "Is that right?"

"Don't worry. I wasn't after you."

He wanted to hit something and curse a blue streak. "You were after Jose," he said, his throat tight. He wondered how far things had gone between the two of them. He'd hate to have to fire the wrangler, but he'd do it.

"Not specifically Jose. And especially not after I found out how much he wants children."

Tom's head began to spin. "I don't get it."

"You're not going to like it, either, but please try to understand. You saw firsthand how shooting a calendar picture affects me. I...need somebody I can depend on, somebody to...work that out of my system so I don't end up seducing one of my subjects someday."

"Seems like you could hire that done," he said with more than a trace of bitterness.

"I was afraid you'd have that reaction. But it's more than sex, really. I need a friend, somebody in my corner, a person to be with during the lonely downtimes of the business. I'm looking for someone who doesn't think in rigid terms about what marriage is, someone who would consider a commuter marriage. We wouldn't even have to live together, just meet every couple of weeks."

"And get it on." Her concept of marriage horrified him, but damned if her idea wasn't also the most provocative one he'd ever come across.

"Well, I hope we'll also enjoy each other's company, but basically, I guess that's the bottom line."

"That isn't marriage. That's sex."

"I disagree. There would be love, and mutual respect, and commitment. I realize it's a little unusual, but that's what I need, and that's what I wanted to work toward on this trip. And then I met you."

"I still don't get it." He was beginning to understand, though. He just wanted her to lay it out for him so there could be no misunderstandings later.

"You told me right away you weren't interested in marriage," she said. "And even if you were, I can't imagine you agreeing to that arrangement."

"That's for damn sure. A guy would have to be a wimp to go for that deal. Like a puppy on a string."

She pushed his hand away from her breast. "Or a more flexible one than you are."

He snorted. "Like a pretzel, more likely."

"You can make fun of my idea all you want. Your opinion doesn't really matter. In fact, you have nothing to do with my plan, except..."

"Except what?"

"Except that I don't feel right looking for a husband when you and I have shared...certain moments."

"I see." Her standards were offbeat, but at least she had some, he thought. "Maybe I wasn't so dumb to climb in that hot tub, after all, if I've kept you from making a damn parlor pet out of one of our fine Montana boys."

"I don't know why I'm attracted to you, to be honest. You're way too macho for my tastes. If I was smart, I'd stay completely away from you."

"You said intelligence has nothing to do with it."

"I guess not. The minute you touch me, I don't have a brain cell working."

He pulled her close again. "The rest of you sure hums right along, though."

"Yes, it certainly does." She sighed and snuggled back against him.

Oh, God, he was in trouble. He was already imagining himself in her cabin this afternoon, making love in her king-size bed. Yet if he did that, he'd be dancing to her tune, providing a temporary physical release. He was worth more than that, and so was she. He just had to figure out a way to make her see how insulting her plan was to both of them.

She'd never be happy with a lapdog for a husband. She wasn't a halfway kind of person, no matter what she attempted. He'd seen that on the cattle drive and again when she did what she had to do for Dynamite just now. She needed somebody as strong as she was, someone who expected her to give herself completely to the relationship. Someone like...him. Not that he was interested in a career woman from New York who didn't want kids.

The hell he wasn't. She might be from New York, but Montana fit her personality like a glove. He would fit her like a glove. And as for kids, she'd love those, too. She just didn't know it yet.

"So I was wondering," she said, her voice low and sultry, "if you have some free time this afternoon?"

"I might." Even knowing he planned to throw a monkey wrench into her plans, he still felt his blood heat at the temptation she held out. "Don't you have some pictures to take or something?"

"I had an appointment, but my car gave out last night, and I don't know if it's fixed yet."

"What if it is?"

"I could pretend it wasn't."

She'd alter her schedule for him, he realized. That was telling, in itself. "How many more cowboys do you have to round up for this project?"

"I have eight so far."

"Then you need four more." An idea was forming, and he let it simmer for a while.

"I guess that's all I need now. I'd planned to find thirteen, so if one of them worked out as a husband, I could eliminate him from the calendar and still have twelve."

He blew out a breath. She'd apparently thought it would be that simple. She'd spent so much time behind a camera that she had no idea how the world worked. "And you really expected to get away with that?"

"Apparently I won't. Not on this trip, at any rate."

"I think having thirteen possibilities for your calendar is a good idea, anyway, in case somebody doesn't work out."

"Oh, they'll all work out. I screen my subjects pretty carefully, and the contract's binding."

"What if a subject didn't want to sign a contract?" he asked carefully.

"Then we wouldn't have a deal."

"Care to make an exception with me?"

She stiffened in his arms. "Are you saying you'll pose for me, after all?"

"I will, if I don't have to sign a contract until after I've seen the pictures and I can make my decision then."

All snuggling ended as she sat forward. "If there's a chance I can use you as a cover shot, that cancels out...anything between us."

"I guess that's your choice." He had no idea which way she'd go, but either way, he planned to show her that making love wasn't the simple bodily function she imagined. It wasn't a game, and it wasn't a career aid. It was the essence of life itself.

OFFERING TO POSE for the cover was the very last thing Cleo had expected of him. She recovered slowly from the shock as they neared the ranch. The choice was a no-brainer, really. A few times in bed with him, a casual affair that would end once she left Montana, versus a cover photo for her calendar that could guarantee her reputation, an image that would guarantee that the calendar she presented to Sphinx Cosmetics would be the best in her career.

He might deny her the use of the photos, of course, but she doubted it. No subject had ever been unhappy with the way he looked in one of her calendars. She had an eye for the shot that maximized a man's sexual charisma, and they loved seeing that quality reflected back to them. Even Tom, who only used a mirror to shave, would love it.

Looking at the question from Tom's angle, there was no doubt which way to go, either. The calendar could only help his financial situation. He might turn down the modeling contracts and the film deals, but business at the Whispering Winds would increase, especially with Jeeter and Jose in the calendar. Single women would flock to the ranch, and Tom would be able to raise his prices.

The fact that Tom himself would be mobbed with eligible women bothered her a little, but she couldn't allow herself to care about that. She and Tom had no future, and to begrudge him happiness in the arms of another woman was selfish and unfair. Her jaw might clench and plans for murder might run through her mind at the thought of him making love to someone else, but eventually she'd get over it. She'd have to.

She took a deep breath. "Okay, it's a deal. I'll take the shots and have them developed without a contract. When do you want to schedule a session?"

"Name your time."

"Let me think about it. I have to decide what setting and what kind of light I want to use."

"Just let me know."

She should be jubilant after gaining the prize she'd sought from the moment she'd walked out of the jetway and spied him waiting for her in the terminal. Instead, she wanted to cry. He'd be in front of her camera soon, but she wouldn't be able to feel his warm lips on hers, or his strong arms holding her tight, or his gentle touch ever again. It was more of a sacrifice than she'd counted on.

TIME WAS RUNNING OUT, and Cleo still hadn't figured out where to shoot Tom. Hoping inspiration would strike while she worked, she scheduled sessions with three of the four remaining cowboys. She took Eddie down to the Gallatin River and posed him standing in the water, jeans soaked and molding his lean hips. She got wet herself for that one, and welcomed the cold water on her heated body. Images of making love to Tom kept superimposing themselves over Eddie, but that only seemed to increase the electricity and bring out the best in the dark-haired cowboy, who had no idea she was imagining he was someone else.

She posed Ty in a cowboy bar and had him drink a little of the beer she used for a prop so he'd loosen up. He loosened up beautifully, giving her some great shots and another bad case of sexual frustration. If only Tom hadn't agreed to the cover shot, he could be easing that ache for her, but the cover would make the anguish all worthwhile, she told herself.

With Andy, she insisted he take off his shirt and lie in a field of wildflowers. He'd hated the idea at first, but as usual, Cleo played with his mind until he gazed up at her with exactly the degree of sensuality she wanted from him. When she returned from that shoot, she flung off her clothes and took the coldest shower in history.

That evening she took stock of the eleven poses she'd used so far and realized she still wasn't sure how to pose Tom. When she'd arrived, she'd visualized him leaning against a fence, but that seemed too common now, too much like some of her other portraits for the calendar. The pressure of taking the best photo of her career had cramped her mind, no doubt, but she had to uncramp it, and fast. She had exactly two days left. Two more days of Montana. She tried not to think about that. She could come back to Montana, of course, but not to this ranch. Never again to this ranch.

After a restless night that caused her to oversleep the next morning, she bummed some more carrots from Juanita and headed to the corral to see Dynamite. She'd agreed to shoot Juanita's kids on her last afternoon at the ranch, a relaxing windup to the schedule. She'd have a session with her final cowboy, Jake, in the morning and Juanita's kids in the afternoon. The next morning she'd leave for New York.

That left today and tonight for Tom's cover shot. Leaning against the corral fence, she scratched behind Dynamite's ears and wished for inspiration.

"Seems to me we're running out of time to get that picture taken."

She glanced up as Tom walked toward her. She hadn't seen him, except from a distance or in her dreams, since the day of the barbed-wire incident. The longing to hold him was so intense that she couldn't speak. Her body hungered for his in a way that made her wonder if she was coming down with something. She felt flushed and dizzy just looking at him.

"I've been waiting for you to let me know," he said softly, leaning an arm against the corral and standing very close to her. "Did you find a better prospect for that cover and decide to pass up my offer?"

"No." She sounded hoarse and nervous. "I just haven't been able to figure out the setting I want to use."

"You should have asked me for suggestions."

She hadn't thought of that. Usually she was reluctant to take ideas from her subjects because they seldom understood the requirements for the shots and then she was in the position of having to reject their suggestion. But she was so totally dry in this case that she decided to risk it with Tom.

"Okay," she said, looking at him from under the brim of her hat—his hat day after tomorrow. "What do you have in mind?"

"My bedroom."

She backed up a step, her pulse racing. "For the photo session, or for...something else?"

"For the photo session. You've made it clear what your rules are. Juanita has quite a collection of your calendars, and I've been studying them. If your aim is the sexual side of the men, why not show one of them in bed?"

"I've always concentrated on the work environment." And in Montana, that meant using the great outdoors, for the most part. "Besides, the light might not be any good in...there." She couldn't bring herself to say *your bedroom*, certain the words would come out sounding the way she felt—jumpy.

"Why not take a look yourself? The windows face south, so the light doesn't come directly in this time of year, but there's plenty of it."

"Do you have any other ideas?"

He shook his head. "That was it. The bed frame's made of lodgepole pine, and I have a Pendleton blanket, and I just thought maybe —"

"A Pendleton blanket?" She was already getting some ideas. The richly patterned blanket would be wonderful to design the shot with, even in black and white. And a massive bed like the one he was describing would add just the right masculine touch. Obvious as his suggestion was, it might be exactly what she needed. Tom McBride posed on a bed. The calendars would jump off the shelves.

He watched her, his gray eyes amused. "Want to go take a look?"

She considered the temptations involved. But it was the middle of the morning, for heaven's sake, and it wasn't as if they'd be alone in the house. Luann and Juanita would be around somewhere. "Okay, I'll take a look."

"How've the other sessions been coming along?" he asked as they walked side by side across the ranch yard.

"Just fine. I have one more scheduled tomorrow morning and Juanita's kids in the afternoon."

"Then I guess we need to get this accomplished today."

"I knew that, but without a solid idea about where to do the shoot, I hated to set something up with you. I didn't want to waste your time."

"Don't worry about that." He smiled. "Out here we don't have the same fixation on time that you do back East."

"My father taught me early that time is money."

"Hmm."

"I take it you don't agree with that."

"Let's just say I grew up with a different concept. My folks used to tell us that no matter where we were going, the most important thing to take was our time."

Cleo thought about that as they walked up on the porch and Tom opened the wide front door for her. Some of her best memories of Montana were the ones in which time hadn't been a factor. The cattle drive, for example, and taking the picture of the moose. Even her own solitary ride, though it had ended so dramatically, had been free of time restraints.

And, to be totally honest with herself, the moments with Tom in the warm mineral water had completely transcended time. She wouldn't have been able to say whether they'd spent an hour together or five minutes. She only knew that the experience would be part of her memories forever.

No one was in the large living room as they walked through and headed for the polished wooden staircase leading to the second floor. A little more activity would have made Cleo feel better about this encounter, but she'd look like a scared rabbit if she backed out of going up those stairs with Tom.

"Did you slide down this banister when you were a kid?" she asked, running her hand along the smooth wood.

"Yep. Taught my sister how to do it, too. We thought nobody knew what we were up to, until Dad caught us one day and admitted he and my uncle used to slide down it all the time, and so had my grandfather. That's why it's like satin—all those little fannies sailing down from the second floor."

Cleo laughed. "What a great tradition."

"Yeah, it was."

His use of the past tense told her that he thought the tradition was over, either because he wouldn't have children or because he wasn't sure he'd keep the ranch. He should do both, she thought. Yet in order to have children, he'd have to marry someone and father them. That idea didn't sit so well with her.

After passing a sign that said Guests Prohibited Beyond This Point, she walked with him down a long hallway that seemed to carry them farther and farther from the center of the house. "Kind of secluded up here, aren't you?"

"The guests have access to just about every other square foot of the Whispering Winds. This wing I keep for myself."

So they were in a private wing of an already large house, she thought uneasily. "You know, maybe this isn't such a good—"

"Here we are." He opened the door at the end of the hall and stepped back.

Moving through the doorway, she caught her breath at the magnificence of the large room that spanned the entire south side of the house. She always noticed light first, and the sunshine coming through the bank of windows was an artist's dream. The view itself was spectacular, but the light—she lusted after this sort of luminescent glow, knowing how it could infuse her shots with magic. As the light flowed into the room unfettered by window coverings, it gently picked out the details of furnishings that suited Tom perfectly.

The bed's massive headboard and footboard dominated the room. The spread, a nubby white, was only a backdrop for a huge Pendleton blanket that might have been custom-made. Its brown and orange print was faded from years of sunlight streaming into the room. Cleo walked closer and smoothed a hand over the wool, worn soft as velvet. Decorative pillows covered in a different Pendleton fabric were tossed against the headboard, along with fluffy bed pillows encased in snowy linen.

She turned to survey the rest of the room, finding it neat without being fussy. A plush towel hung from the knob of a door that led into the master bathroom. A flannel shirt was tossed over the back of a straight-backed oak chair, and a pair of worn boots sat in a corner near an oak dresser. The dresser top served as a gallery for several framed photos, many of them sepia-toned. As she walked over to look at the pictures, she took a deep breath and realized that the room held Tom's scent. That scent was making her more than a little crazy.

"Your family?" she asked, striving for nonchalance.

"About three generations' worth."

She studied the pictures and recognized the ranch house in the background of most of them. "Tom, is there a chance you could lose this place?" She turned to find him leaning in the doorway, watching her.

He adjusted the tilt of his Stetson. "I reckon you've been talking to Juanita."

"No, I—"

"Don't bother covering up for her. It's okay. When you two became chummy, I figured she might confide a few things in you. She's been wanting a woman around to talk to. Luann isn't quite her speed."

"Okay, Juanita told me she was worried. Does she have reason to be?"

He walked into the room, his boots echoing on the hardwood floor. "Why the concern? You'll be gone soon."

She looked into his eyes and knew she'd have to be very careful in this room. It would be too easy to forget herself and her code of ethics. "You're right. It's none of my business."

"It's nice of you to be concerned," he said, his expression softening. "I guess the place found its way into your heart a little bit."

"Of course it did." *And so did you.* She tried to pretend her pulse wasn't hammering. "You have a wonderful spot here. I don't know how precarious your finances are, but if you'll let this calendar work for you, it will increase your business among single women. With you on the cover, and Jose and Jeeter inside, the ranch will look very appealing to women who have a romantic image of cowboys."

He frowned. "I'm running a guest ranch, not an escort service."

"And I'm not saying these women will expect anything different. If they do, I'm sure all of you can handle it just fine."

"Meaning?" He stood close enough to kiss her.

She trembled. "Come on, Tom. I'm sure you don't live like a monk out here."

"I don't generally get involved with guests, either."

She tried to be flip. "Then the hot tub doesn't usually come with a cowboy included?"

"Only in your case." His gaze reached into hers for a long, tense moment. "Are you sure you want that calendar picture, Cleo?"

She swallowed and stepped back. "Yes. And you're right. This is the perfect place, just as you predicted. If you're free this afternoon, I'll—"

"I'm free."

"Then I'll meet you up here at three." She edged around him, heading toward the door.

"You don't want to get your camera and start now?"

"No, I...need to clean the lens." Lame, lame, lame. But it was all she could come up with to postpone the session. She needed time to shore up her defenses before she walked back into this pressure cooker of a bedroom. "I'll see you at three."

He touched the brim of his hat. "Yes, ma'am."

12

CLEO NEEDED one more bracing, career-oriented talk with Bernie before she walked back into Tom's bedroom. She needed to remind herself of her goals, and what was best for both her and Tom. She used the ranch-house phone while everyone else was eating lunch, because for the first time in recent memory she had no appetite.

"I'm glad you called," Bernie said. "I hated to wait until I picked you up at the airport, but it seemed silly to bother you on your last two days."

"What's up?"

"You know I wasn't overjoyed at the idea of bringing your father's company in for cross-promotion, but I have to tell you, it was a smart move."

"Really?"

"Instead of just offering the calendars as a premium for buying Sphinx cosmetics, he wants to go the other way, too, and offer Sphinx cosmetics as part of the calendar package. They're coming up with a whole line of products with a Western theme to coordinate with the calendar. Now that I see old Calvin Griffin in action, I understand why he's where he is. The man's a marketing genius. Everybody involved with this project is going to make money, lots of money."

Cleo thought immediately of how that might help Tom keep the ranch. "That's good, Bernie. And the best part is,

I've just about nailed my cover picture, and it's going to be hot."

"Just about? I figured you'd know who you were using by now. That Jose character wouldn't be bad, or—"

"You haven't seen the shot I want to use because I'm taking it this afternoon. I want Tom McBride for the cover, and he's agreed to let me use him if he sees the proofs first."

"Hold it. Proof approval? Who are you and what have you done with Cleo?"

"I know it's unusual for me to allow a subject to approve the proofs of a session, but—"

"Unusual? Try never in the history of your career. This makes me nervous, babe. We don't have a lot of time to jack around with this. You'll have to mail him proofs, and he'll probably be out rounding up cattle or something and not get to it for weeks, and production needs to start by—"

"Don't worry, I'm shooting thirteen cowboys, like I originally planned, so if Tom doesn't work out, we'll still have our calendar."

"Which reminds me. Should I start looking for a matron-of-honor dress?"

"I've, uh, sort of abandoned that plan for now."

"Good thing, because a wedding could really louse up the schedule for this calendar, and I'll tell you, we want to have our ducks in a row when Calvin comes to call with his Sphinx Cosmetics team."

"We'll be ready," Cleo said. "See you in two days."

TOM STOOD in front of his bedroom windows at five minutes before three. He'd cranked a couple of the windows open a few inches to let in the breeze and cool his heated body.

Right on time, Cleo stepped out of her cabin. She was hatless, and the sunlight danced like a spotlight on her jumble of blond curls. He admired the purposeful way she walked, as if she dared anyone to get in her way. He also admired her single-minded attitude and her courage in the face of adversity. They were good traits for a Montana woman to have. They were also the traits that might keep them apart.

He thought she needed more than a love of photography to keep her satisfied, but he could be wrong. What would happen between them, or not happen, was up to Cleo now. If she could maintain her professional distance throughout this photo shoot, that would be a pretty clear demonstration of her ability to put her career ahead of her emotional needs. She had a right to do that, and he'd respect her choice, but he had to know what that choice would be before he risked his heart.

He'd left strict instructions with Juanita and Jose that he was not to be disturbed, short of an emergency, until morning. They probably knew exactly what was going on, but neither of them had said a word or even lifted an eyebrow. Juanita's glance had communicated quite clearly that she thought it was about time.

Cleo had said she doubted that he lived like a monk. She might be surprised to discover he had been doing exactly that. She might be even more surprised to learn that she wasn't the only one dealing with the problem of sexual frustration.

To his amazement, he discovered he wasn't any good at casual sex anymore. Once upon a time, before Deidre, he'd cut a pretty wide swath through this valley, but marriage had shown him the joys of making love to the same woman, and he'd learned to treasure continuity. Although he mistrusted wedded bliss after the way Deidre had treated him, he wasn't ready to go back to his former sexual pursuits, either.

He was in a bind very similar to Cleo's, come to think of it.

"I'm here."

The sound of her voice skittered up his spine. He turned. "So I see."

She cleared her throat. "Well, I've been thinking about various poses, and I think we should start with—"

"I think we should start with closing the door."

She glanced around at the open doorway. "Oh, I don't think that's necessary, do you?"

"It's absolutely necessary. It isn't logical, considering that I may end up on a calendar the world is going to see, but I'll be damned if the photo session is going to be a public one."

"All right." She closed the door.

Instantly the atmosphere in the room intensified. His heart began chugging along like a freight train as he looked at her across the broad expanse of mattress separating them.

"I'd like you to sit on the bed," she said. "The side closest to the windows, so I can get that light falling on your face."

"Okay." He sat down and propped his hands behind him. "Now what?"

She licked her lips and took the lens cap off her camera. "Let me get a reading, here."

He looked straight into the lens as she crouched and pointed it at him.

"Nice," she said. "The light's perfect. Nudge your hat back a little."

He used his thumb to do what she asked, but he kept his gaze trained on that lens, because he knew she was looking into it and that was the only way to maintain eye contact with her.

"For someone who didn't want his picture taken, you seem pretty relaxed."

"Maybe because I finally got a few things straight, and I know what I want out of this."

She swallowed and clicked the shutter a couple of times. "Good. I talked to my assistant at noon, and we have some exciting cross-promotion lined up for the calendar." She moved a few steps and clicked the shutter again. She was going through the motions, but there was no style, no flair. "Bernie predicted that anyone connected with this project will make good money. That should be welcome news for you."

"That's assuming you'll be able to take a decent picture this afternoon."

"What?" She brought the camera down and stared at him.

"All this talk about cross-promotions and money isn't very sexy, and it isn't your usual approach, judging from what I've seen. You're holding back, Cleo."

"I just need to get warmed up!"

He spoke low and easy. "Can I help?"

"No! I mean..." She looked confused. Then she hung the camera from her neck and ran her fingers through her hair. "You're right. I'm tense. I've never shot a guy I...have feelings for. This is more awkward than I thought it would be."

"Maybe I can help, after all." He began unbuttoning his shirt.

"Wait!"

He almost smiled at the panic in her voice. He paused and lifted an eyebrow.

"Take...take off your boots. That's it. The rancher at

the end of the day sitting on the edge of his bed, taking off his boots. I like that."

"All right." He had the first boot off and was about to drop it to floor.

"Look at me," she commanded, crouching in front of him.

He did, although he deliberately didn't put a whole lot of expression into it. With her scent tantalizing him and her body almost within reach, keeping cool wasn't easy, but he'd do it. She was going to have to work to get what she wanted out of him.

She took the picture, but he could tell from her frown that she wasn't satisfied. "Okay, the other boot. Easy. Take it off slow. There. Look at me again. That's better."

Damn, but her voice was having an effect on him. He felt some heat transfer with that shot.

She stood and paced in front of him. "Let me think for a minute."

"You didn't have to think when you were shooting Jeeter."

"Don't you suppose I know that?" Her blue eyes flashed. "Jeeter was just another calendar page, but this...this has to be special."

"Then you'll have to go for it, Cleo," he said softly.

She stood in front of him, her gaze troubled, her body trembling slightly.

He lowered his voice another notch. "Unless you want to forget the calendar shot and just have a good time."

Her jaw clenched. "No, by God, we're going to do this. Take off your shirt."

He took his time unsnapping the cuffs and pulling the tail from the waistband of his jeans while he stared into the camera lens. He could hear the pattern of her breathing change when he finally took off the shirt and tossed it on the floor.

"Lean back on your elbows." Her tone was uneven, but there was a thread of determination running through it.

He gazed into the camera. "Aren't you going to tell me how good I look without a shirt?"

She swore softly, and he smiled. Click, click, click went the shutter as she moved closer, leaning over him slightly. "Undo the belt."

He was getting hard. Unhooking the belt buckle made him painfully aware of just how aroused he was.

"The top button." She clicked the shutter furiously now.

"I want you, Cleo."

"Don't tell me that." Her chest was heaving as she changed her camera angle. "Next button."

He complied, very slowly. "You can see how much I want you. Let me strip you naked and make love to you on this blanket."

"Stop it!" She took two more frames.

"Let me show you all the ways I can touch you, all the ways I can give you pleasure."

"No." She was breathing hard and kept shooting.

"I want to see the look on your face when I'm deep inside you."

"What are you doing?" she cried, the camera clutched in her shaking hands as she battled for control.

He sat up slowly, tossed his hat aside and took the camera from her unresisting fingers. "Trying to make you see," he murmured, lifting the strap over her head and laying the camera on the bedside table. "Did you get what you wanted?"

Her eyes were moist, her words choked. "I don't know."

"I believe you really don't." He drew her gently down and guided her back onto the blanket. "Let's see if maybe this could be it." He started on the buttons of her shirt.

"I can't." Her hair in disarray against the bold patterned wool, she gazed at him. "I can't, Tom." Yet she made no move to stop him.

"Yes, you can." He leaned down and kissed the soft skin of her throat as he continued to undress her.

"I've never...let one of my subjects..."

"This time you will." He worked her out of her clothes, caressing her firm breasts, her narrow waist, her silken thighs. She trembled and moaned beneath his touch, thrashing her head from side to side as if to deny what was happening, but she still didn't stop him.

Finally he lifted her more fully onto the bed and admired the contrast of her white skin against the bold colors of the blanket. "Perfect."

"No, Tom." She struggled for breath. "Really. We can't do this. We—"

He silenced her with a deep kiss that left her vibrating in his arms.

"But I don't want to," she wailed when her mouth was free again.

"Is that right?" he murmured against her breast.

With a downward stroke of his hand he sought the fevered dampness between her thighs. "I think you have a credibility problem, sweetheart."

"I'm so afraid that I'll..." She gasped as he probed deep.

"That you'll find out you're human? That a man can make you lose control of that famous discipline?"

"Yes!"

"That's why I'm here." He lifted his head to gaze into her eyes. "I need to see that happen."

"You planned this all along," she whispered.

"I wanted this all along. But I won't force you." He teased her lightly with his fingers. "Tell me to stop and I'll stop."

"St..."

He paused, his heartbeat thudding in his ears as he waited.

"Stay," she murmured at last, the word ending on a sigh. "Please stay. Love me until I can't think anymore."

Joy surged through him as he smiled tenderly down at her. "Yes, ma'am. I'd be happy to."

THE TOUCH OF HIS HANDS and mouth on her body swept away most of her control. The rest of it disappeared when he shucked his jeans and rolled a condom over his sizable erection.

"Now," she said, panting, needing him to fill the aching void within her. "Now, Tom."

"Yes, now."

She gazed upon the rugged beauty of him as he moved over her, and her throat tightened with the sudden urge to cry. She reached up to cup his face in both hands, to memorize the way he was looking at her with a perfect mix of tenderness and passion. And she knew she'd never capture that look with a camera.

He turned his head to kiss her palm that rested against his cheek. Then he looked down at her again. "The night in the hot tub was just fooling around," he murmured, stroking her with the tip of his shaft against her sensitive folds. "I'm through fooling around, Cleo."

"I'm not sure...what you mean." Her voice quivered.

"When we're finished here, you will be." He slid his

hands beneath her bottom, lifting her to meet him as he pushed in deep.

"*Oh.*" The cry rushed from her, propelled by a feeling of completeness she'd never known. He filled her, blotting out everything but the sensation of joining with her destiny.

"Ah, Cleo." He smiled gently as he drew back and completed the miracle once again.

"Tom," she said, gasping. "Tom, I—" Words failed her.

"Just enjoy, sweetheart." He moved slowly within her, setting off ripples of pleasure with every thrust. "Life doesn't give us times like this too often."

She'd always considered sex a frantic, sometimes confusing business. Tom was not the least bit confused. He knew exactly what he was doing, and what he was doing was incredible. Tension drained from all parts of her body to settle in one spot, and there he lavished all his attention. Marveling at the perfection of each movement, Cleo surrendered the last of her discipline, the last of her control, for the first time in her life.

"Now you're starting to give in to it," he murmured. "Just relax. We're going to take this slow and make it last."

For the first time she didn't question who was in command. He was solidly in charge, guiding her through a foreign and exciting land, one she'd never allowed herself to travel before, never trusted a man to navigate for her. Oh, she'd taken her pleasure, but always on her own terms, always with restraint.

Restraint slipped away. She arched against him, letting him know how she craved what he was giving her, shameless in her vulnerability.

"Yes, my darling. Yes," he whispered. Easing her bottom down to the blanket again, he braced his hands on either side of her head without breaking his steady rhythm. But his angle changed. The light sprinkle of hair that curled over his chest tickled her breasts as he created a new kind of friction with each thrust.

She gazed into his eyes, soft as rain clouds, yet she sensed the storm he kept in check while he led her through a garden of delights, building the tension within her. When he quickened the rhythm, she was helpless in his arms, swirling rapidly in an exotic river filled with frothy rapids and bright flowers. The waterfall rushed to meet her, wringing a cry from her lips as she tumbled over it.

He slowed the tempo, absorbed her convulsions against his body, and kept moving. Speechless, sated with the force of her climax, she looked at him in wonder.

His smile made her heart tremble. "I think that's what you wanted," he said gently as he eased back and forth, maintaining the thread of tension.

She thought so, too, but couldn't manage a single word.

"But there's even more." He wrapped his arms around her, snugged in tight and rolled to his back, bringing her with him.

Limp and languid though she was, she still found herself drawing her knees up on either side of his hips and bracing her hands beside his shoulders so that she could keep that delicious momentum going.

Gradually she found her capacity for speech return. Hair falling around her face, she met his gaze as she moved sensuously and deliberately toward another climax. "I feel wanton," she murmured. She felt far more than that, but lacked the courage to say it.

"That's the idea." He cupped her swaying breasts in both hands.

She loved the way he was touching her breasts, and the glow in his eyes as he looked at her naked body in the afternoon light. "But I've never…felt this way." *In love*.

"Then it's time you did. You… Mmm." He closed his eyes and clenched his jaw. "Wow. You nearly made me…oh, Cleo, take it easy."

"You put me on top, cowboy. Take the consequences."

He grasped her hips. "I can put you back on the bottom again, too. You're dealing with a steer wrestler."

"Don't." She leaned down and brushed her lips against his. "Let me take you with me this time."

He kept her close with a hand behind her head. "Your lips are so sweet," he said, urging her down to him. "Kiss me again. And make it count."

She did, telling him with the language of her lips and tongue what she dared not say out loud. His grip tightened on her bottom and his upward thrusts became more powerful. She took his moan of completion into her mouth as an answering explosion rocked her body. It was perfect. All of it. She'd broken her cardinal rule, and nothing had ever felt so right before.

ALL THE JANGLE of nerves that had kept Cleo from sleeping for years had quieted, and she dozed beside Tom as they lay sprawled on the patterned blanket. At last, the cool breeze from the window woke her. The wonderful light that had seduced her into coming into this bedroom was nearly gone.

She slipped out of bed without waking Tom and walked over to gaze at the ranch in the glow of late afternoon. The sound of a dog barking drew her gaze to the woods, where a group of riders came out of the trees headed for the corral. She stepped away from the window, although she was certain no one could see her from this distance.

Instead, she turned back to the bed and saw how the last light of day spilled across it, caressing the magnificent body of the cowboy sprawled there on his stomach, one arm flung out as if reaching for her.

She crept to the bedside table and picked up her camera. Five frames left on the roll. She sighted through the lens, moved a fraction and sighted again. In the orange light his sculpted body looked like bronze. The patterned blanket provided the perfect backdrop, and for once she wished she had a color roll. She'd love to be able to capture the rosy flush of his skin and the rich brown of his hair tipped with sunlight.

She took one shot, and another. Excitement rose within her. The composition, the light, the subject were all perfect. She moved to another vantage point and took a third shot. And a fourth. If what she saw through the viewfinder was what came out on film, these could be the best photos of her career.

On the fifth snap of the shutter, Tom's eyes opened.

"What are you doing?"

"Taking your picture."

The haze of sleep cleared from his eyes as he propped himself on one elbow. "Do you develop your own film?"

"No. I have a special lab that—"

"I guess that settles the question of whether I'll be in your calendar."

Uneasiness gripped her heart. "It does?"

"Sexy pictures are one thing. Nude pictures are a whole other subject."

"I wouldn't use these for the calendar!" No, she'd pictured putting them in an art show in the middle of Manhattan, and blowing them up to poster size.

"I don't care. My bare ass isn't going through some photo lab. You'll have to destroy the film."

13

"No! I won't destroy this film." Cleo held the camera to her chest, as if he might wrench it away from her.

Tom sighed and moved over to sit on the edge of the bed. This wasn't the mood he'd hoped to set when they awoke from the best lovemaking he'd ever experienced, and he hoped the best she'd ever known, too. She looked so damn good standing there, the light outlining her body like those auras he'd read about. "What did you plan to do with the pictures?"

She flushed, which made her look even more appealing. "Nothing without your permission, of course."

"And what did you plan to ask my permission for?"

"Nobody would recognize you. Your face was in shadow."

He saw red. "You wanted to *show* them to someone?"

"Tom, if I got what I think I did, they're wonderful. They're not just pictures, they're art. In a gallery, they could—"

"A *gallery?*" He came off the bed and started toward her.

"Don't yell," she said, backing away from him. "Somebody will hear you."

"I can yell if I damn well want to in my own house! And I want to!" He advanced on her. "Because that may be the only way you understand that my naked butt is never, and I mean never, going to be hanging in some gallery in New York City, or any other place on this planet! Got that?"

"Don't be so provincial." She backed up until she reached the oak chair, which halted her escape.

"I will be, because I am. I'm from rural Montana, lady, not the big city, and out here we don't go in for nude art, especially yours truly."

"Your name wouldn't be on it or anything. That's only for the calendar pictures, so they know the men are real. This is more like a fantasy, with the way the light fell, and I blurred the focus just slightly. It could very well be the best thing I've ever done. It could win awards."

He stared at her. "Let me get this straight. You objected to sleeping with me if you planned to put my picture in your calendar, but you don't mind sleeping with me and then parading my slightly blurred body all over New York?"

"That's right! Because the calendars are deliberately provocative, and the men are completely identified, so I have to make sure everyone knows I don't sleep with my subjects. That would be extremely unprofessional, and unfair to them, as well. In photography circles I would be called an artistic slut, with a great deal of justification."

"But sleeping with someone, taking his picture afterward and making it into an art print wouldn't be unprofessional?"

"No, it wouldn't, because the shots I took of you aren't provocative."

"Oh, no?" He glowered at her. "I have no clothes on, and I'm sprawled on a bed. That's pretty damn provocative, if you ask me."

"They're subtly sensuous, not overtly arousing, because I took them with tenderness and an eye for beauty."

He nearly choked. "Beauty?"

"Yes, beauty. Seeing you there, lying in that special shaft of light, with your hair all tousled, and shadows made by the muscles of your back, and your gentle hands spread out on the blanket..." She shrugged, making her breasts quiver. "The artist in me had to take those pictures. They weren't taken for gain, they were taken for love, and..." She glanced away. "What's the use? You don't understand me, anyway."

His heart squeezed. "I think I just understood some of it," he murmured, tilting her chin back around. "Come here a minute." He took her by the shoulders and turned her so he could slide onto the chair and ease her onto his lap. The pictures had been taken with love, she'd said. He'd gained more ground than he'd even hoped for.

She nestled against his shoulder, but she kept a firm hand on her camera. "Please don't ask me to destroy that film. You have every right to, of course. I said I wouldn't do it, but that was just bravado. I'd have to if you insisted, because I couldn't even develop the film without your consent."

"I told you from the beginning that I'm a private man. What we just shared is private." He breathed in the womanly scent of her and stroked her hair, working through the little tangles he'd helped create.

"I know. But you really won't be recognized. Besides, the lab doesn't pay attention to what it processes. It has a lot of clients who specialize in nude art, and I'm sure the people there have seen more naked bodies than a hospital staff. They're immune by now."

He was far from immune to one particular naked body. In fact, she was getting further with her argument by sitting on his lap than she had with all her logical reasoning. "Let me think about it," he said, knowing he probably wouldn't get much thinking done in this position, skin to skin with the sexiest woman he'd ever met. "Since you don't sleep with your calendar subjects, are you going to forget about using me for the cover?"

"Well, I violated my rule."

And how, he thought, trailing a finger down the slope of her breast and circling her nipple. It tightened in response. "Since it's your rule, I guess you have to decide what to do about it."

"Even if I want to use you in the calendar, you might decide against it when I send you the proofs."

"The proofs with my bare-butt shots included, I suppose." He teased the other nipple to erectness. A similar stiffening behavior was going on in his lap.

"Yes."

"But if I said the word, you'd take the film out and give it to me now?"

She stirred in his arms and sat up a little straighter. Her thighs rubbed sweetly against his erection.

"I'll give it to you now."

He wished she wasn't talking about film.

Apparently, she was. She opened the camera and took out the finished roll. "I'll leave it on your bedside table until tomorrow, so you have complete control over what happens to it." She stood, went to the bed and put the film on the table.

"Cleo, don't go yet. We—"

She set down the camera, opened the drawer and pulled out a condom. "Oh, I'm not leaving yet," she said, walking back to him with a decided sway to her hips. "The way I look at it, I might as well be hanged for a sheep as a lamb." Her gaze drifted to his lap. "And from the looks of things, you're ready to continue aiding my fall from grace."

He eyed the condom as she took it out of the package. "Do you have more film?"

"I always have more film. Want some kinky shots to remember me by?"

"God, no. I want you to promise me you won't reload that damn camera again."

"I promise." She dropped to her knees in front of him and rolled the condom over his hardened shaft. Standing again, she grasped the back of the chair and straddled both it and him. "I'll just concentrate on reloading you." With a smooth downward movement, she welcomed him back to paradise.

CLEO DECIDED she must be making up for lost time. Apparently Tom was, too. They couldn't seem to get enough of each other. Somewhere near midnight they pulled on enough clothes to cover the essentials and raided the refrigerator in Juanita's spotless kitchen. Afterward they tried to clean up the evidence.

"She'll still know we were here," Tom said after they gave the counter one last swipe and headed back upstairs.

"It's okay. I have kitchen privileges."

He slung an arm around her shoulders. "Do you realize that no one else has ever wangled that kind of treatment from Juanita?"

"She likes my calendars."

He pulled her over for a kiss as they walked down the hall toward his bedroom. "She likes you."

She savored the taste of him, flavored now with the roast beef and cheese sandwiches they'd just finished. "I like her, too. I like her coffee almost as much as I do her, and that's saying a lot. I'm going to miss both of them."

She could talk about missing Juanita. What she couldn't talk about, couldn't even think about, was missing Tom.

He guided her through the door and closed it tight before turning to her. "Cleo..."

She saw in his eyes what was coming next. She shook her head. "I can't do that to you."

"Do what?"

"Involve you with a New York woman again. Make you suffer going to the city because I couldn't always come out here. And there's something else. You're going to have children someday. You'll find the right woman and have those kids, because otherwise there won't be a McBride to take over the ranch." She waved a hand toward the photos on his dresser. "This place is full of continuity. You deserve to find someone who can help you create the next generation."

His gaze searched hers.

She felt her womb tighten and told herself it was mere sexual desire, not some primitive mating instinct. "Don't look at me like that. I'm not the maternal type."

"Aren't you?" Slipping the buttons free on her blouse, he cradled her breast and looked into her eyes as he stroked his thumb across her nipple.

In spite of herself, she pictured a tiny mouth there, seeking nourishment. A baby with Tom's eyes and her hair. Her voice grew husky. "You're the sort of man who would make any woman think of children, whether she wants to or not."

"That's not true." He cupped her bottom and pulled her against his erection. "But you're thinking of it."

Yes, she was. His arousal carried a different message this time, created a different sort of ache deep within her. "That's only because we've spent the past few hours in the activity that can result in babies, and now I brought

up the subject. It's only natural that I'm...aware of...of..."
She became lost in the depths of his gaze.

His tone was low and intense. "After what happened,
I never thought I'd want to make a woman pregnant
again."

She swallowed. The ache within her threatened to
overpower everything.

He stroked her belly as he looked deep into her eyes.
"It seems I was wrong."

Heat rushed through her, and she was suddenly desperate for his solid fullness deep inside her—all of him
loving her, with no barriers. She reached for the snap on
his jeans. "Make love to me."

They managed to get as far as the edge of the bed. He
leaned her back across the mattress, her feet still on the
floor as he shoved her slacks down. Insanity claimed her
as she released him from his jeans and opened her thighs.

"Wait. We need—"

"No." She kicked the slacks free and wrapped her legs
around his hips.

"Just for...a minute," he gasped. "Just until..."

She moaned aloud as he plunged inside her. In a few
quick strokes she exploded.

"Cleo, I can't...stop." He buried himself inside her
trembling body with a guttural cry of surrender.

"I SHOULDN'T HAVE done that." He'd refastened his jeans
and now stood in front of the windows looking into the
night.

"It takes two to be stupid." Cleo pulled on her clothes.
"You tried to stop me from behaving like a mare in season. I wouldn't let you." Her feelings were so jumbled,
she couldn't make sense of anything. She'd loved what

had just happened, yet it could ruin both their lives. She should be horrified, when instead she was filled with joy.

"I helped bring you into season," he said, "if you want to use that comparison. I saw that look in your eyes and I encouraged you."

"Don't worry," she said, coming over to put a hand on his arm. "One wild moment doesn't usually result in...an accident."

He turned and clasped his hands around her upper arms. "You're whistling in the dark, Cleo." His eyes were stormy. "You opened to me the way a flower opens for a bee, and you know it."

She did know it. Until now, all they'd done was make love. But this...this was mating. Still, the law of averages was on their side. She'd known couples who'd had unprotected sex for years and had never conceived the child they wanted. "You're a romantic," she said, smiling at him. "And you're also paranoid, which is understandable. We'll be fine."

His grip tightened. "And what if you're carrying our child?"

That would be a disaster, she thought, although she couldn't help continuing to smile at him. She was turning into a brainless twit who could only smile despite impending ruin. "I promise you that I won't do what Deidre did."

"Why not?"

Because I love you. But she didn't say those words. If she did, he might follow her to New York, and neglect the ranch again, as he probably had when Deidre was a part of his life. "Because you have rights, too," she said. "Rights that Deidre ignored. I would have the baby and turn the child immediately over to you. I can't think of a better place to grow up than the Whispering Winds, and

Juanita would take...really good care of..." She cleared the lump from her throat. "This is silly. I'm sure I'm not pregnant."

He drew her close and caressed her cheek. "I wouldn't just want the baby. I'd want you."

"I know." She gazed up at him. "But I'm the wrong woman."

"I don't think so." His kiss was desperate.

She couldn't help responding, because she was feeling pretty desperate, herself. But she had to get out of that room before she started agreeing to things that would be a mistake for both of them. With an effort she pulled away.

"I'm going back to my cabin."

"I'll walk you there."

"No. If you do, I'll want you to come in, and we'll just start all over again."

"So what? I promise we'll use protection." He reached for her.

She stepped back, away from the temptation of his strong arms. "That's the problem. I liked it too much without."

With a groan he moved quickly and hauled her back against him. "You belong with me, Cleo. Stop fighting it and—"

"And give up everything I've worked so hard for?" She looked into his beloved face, knowing this decision was as important for him as for her. "No. Let me go, Tom. Let me go so I can find the strength to walk away from you. You and this ranch have cast a spell over me. It's a glorious spell, but it's not what I want for the rest of my life. Let me go."

She looked away from the anguish in his eyes as he loosened his hold on her and stepped back. Then she walked over and picked up her camera bag. Not trusting herself to say anything more, she started from the room.

"Take the film."

She glanced back at him.

"You can have it. Develop the damn pictures and use them any way you want. At least that's one way I can stay in your life."

Swallowing back the tears, she went to the bedside table and picked up the roll of film. Now she had everything she wanted. Sure she did. "Thanks," she whispered, and walked out the door.

HE WATCHED HER walk across the yard back to her cabin, watched until she was safely inside the door. Well, at least he hadn't groveled. At least she had no idea how much he needed her at this very moment. Several times tonight he'd thought about telling her the latest news. Now he was glad he hadn't.

His mother's voice on the phone this morning had been teary. She'd found some papers his father had hidden, and in his mental deterioration, probably forgotten. If Tom had been paying more attention to such things instead of being so wrapped up in Deidre, and later in her secret abortion and the divorce, he might have been more aware of his father's activities.

But he'd left that angle to his dad, not wanting to admit that his father was losing his grip on reality and couldn't be trusted to handle the ranch finances. Now here was another banknote, another lien on the Whispering Winds. A balloon payment was due in two weeks, and if it wasn't paid, the ranch would be lost.

He'd had some crazy idea that with Cleo by his side he'd be able to stave off the inevitable. And even if he lost the ranch, having Cleo would make life seem worth living. But she didn't want to be a Montana rancher's wife. She'd made that perfectly clear.

If she turned out to be pregnant, and he had a gut feeling she was, she'd send the baby to him to raise, because she was a woman of her word. He'd go along with that, no matter what sacrifices he had to make in the process. But chances were, that kid wouldn't be raised, as she'd so lovingly described, on the Whispering Winds.

CLEO KEPT her appointment with the thirteenth cowboy the next morning as a safety measure. Considering her mental state when she'd been snapping those pictures of Tom, she didn't know if she'd have anything usable. The pictures she'd taken after they'd made love were a different story. But the calendar shots might be trash.

After her sleepless night she was running on pure adrenaline as she drove the replacement convertible the rental agency had delivered. She'd discovered a wooded area near a picnic grounds and had suggested meeting Jake there. The pose she had in mind involved him leaning against a ponderosa pine she'd discovered that already had a heart and initials carved into it. Perfect for February. Even if the shots of Tom worked, she might suggest to Bernie that they publish a thirteen-month calendar that began in December, so she could use everyone, including Jake.

She pulled into the parking area and cut the engine. Her hand went to her stomach, as it had been doing many times in the past few hours. Of course she wasn't pregnant. She just needed to get away from Tom, out of Montana, and these crazy notions would disappear. She didn't even want to think of how she'd tell her father such a thing. But that wouldn't be necessary because she wasn't carrying Tom's child.

Jake hadn't arrived, so she got out and walked the short distance to the tree she'd found. The scent of warm pine needles reminded her of the night in the hot tub. She put a hand on the tree's rough bark and looked up into branches that climbed fifty feet into the air. Then she traced the heart carved into the side of the tree, and the crude initials. B.R. + D.S. Tears filled her eyes as she pictured the earnest young lovers eager to tell the world of their bond.

It was a simple and elegant process. You found someone, fell in love and promised to cherish them forever. You didn't audition candidates in front of your camera. And you didn't, she realized now, meet on alternate weekends for sex. She'd never be able to stand so much time away from a man like Tom. More and more, she was realizing that she wouldn't get married at all. As he'd said, she wasn't capable of doing something halfway.

Jake arrived in his gleaming black pickup. He had a lot of swagger to him as he climbed down and walked toward her. She often looked for swagger, because it meant the subjects already knew how to project their sexuality.

He touched the brim of his white straw cowboy hat. "You're looking fine, ma'am."

"Thank you. You, too." And he did, she thought. Tight jeans, polished boots, a muscle shirt and the muscles to go with it. Intense black eyes and raven hair worn just a little long. Women would go wild looking at him next February. But she didn't feel a thing.

She'd work into it, she told herself. That little twinge of sexual excitement she always felt at the beginning of a shoot was just slightly late this time. "As I told you, I want to use this tree over here." She walked back toward the ponderosa and he followed her.

Jake chuckled. "I know the ol' boy who carved those initials."

"You do?"

"Yeah. Went to high school with him. Last I heard, he and Donna had about five kids."

Cleo touched her stomach again. "Really? How about you? Do you have any children?"

"No, ma'am! Don't know if I ever want any. Kids are a lot of trouble."

"And what does your girlfriend think of that?"

He glanced at her. "To be honest, Suzanne and I broke up over it. She's married now, and already has a baby on the way."

"Oh." She felt rotten for probing into his personal life. "I'm sorry. I shouldn't have asked."

He gave her a lazy grin. "Why not? That's what most women do when they're trying to find out if a guy's available, and that's exactly what I am. How about you? Somebody special in your life?"

Here he was, she thought. The perfect candidate to fall in with her husband-hunting plan. He was about her age, maybe a couple of years younger. Wanted a carefree existence. Looked great in jeans, and probably knew his way around a bedroom. He'd probably love the idea of a once-in-a-while wife. Too bad the concept didn't appeal to her at all anymore.

"Looks like I asked too personal a question, myself," he said. "Sorry."

"No, it's not too personal." She tried to push Tom out of her mind. She couldn't do it. "Yes, there is someone."

"I wondered. There's that certain glow women get when they're either in love or feverish. I'm glad you're not sick."

"Not sick," she said. "Just crazy. Come on, let's get the shots taken."

"I'm ready."

She instructed him to lean a shoulder and hip against the tree. Then she got below him, shooting upward to emphasize his crotch and the strong jut of the tree. It was an extremely sexual angle. Normally, she'd be reacting to the suggestive nature of the pose, but she might as well have been taking a photo of a haystack.

"You have a great physique," she said, but instead of the husky tone she normally used to work her men into a lather, the comment came out sounding like a clinical evaluation.

"Thanks."

She cursed to herself. She had to get into the mood somehow, and she didn't have all day to do it. "Tell me what you like best about a woman's body," she said.

He laughed. "Is this supposed to be X-rated or the family channel?"

"Make it sexy. That's what we're here for, to capture a little lust."

"Okay. Then I'd have to say a woman's breasts are my favorite. I love touching them, holding them, kissing them, especially if she really likes that, too." His eyes grew smoky with desire. "And her nipples, the way they get hard when I run my tongue around them. I love doing that when I'm inside her, and she's all shivery, anyway." The tight fit of his jeans made his arousal obvious.

Cleo took advantage of the moment he'd created to snap frame after frame, but she'd lost the instinct that had always guided her trigger finger. Although he was totally into the mood, she wasn't. She felt no connection with his fantasy because...he wasn't Tom. When the truth hit her, she almost dropped the camera.

She surged right into denial, blaming exhaustion, Jake's tone of voice, the setting, for her lack of involvement in this shoot. But in her heart, as she clicked the shutter furiously, she knew that what she'd feared the most had indeed happened. She'd broken her rule, interrupted the flow of the creative river she'd been gliding down with such success. She'd lost the magic touch for getting the shots that had made her famous. And she was never getting it back.

14

A SIXTH SENSE made Tom take a stroll on the front porch just when Cleo drove away from the ranch to shoot her thirteenth cowboy. His gut tightened, knowing the way she normally conducted those sessions. He knew that her photo shoot this morning wouldn't end up like last night's, yet he still didn't want her pointing that camera at some cowboy on the make. He didn't want her using that sultry tone of voice that made men gaze at her with lust.

But it was her job. She'd go on doing it, whether he wanted her to or not. He might as well concentrate on something productive, like trying to negotiate more time on the balloon payment. With a sigh he walked into the house and headed for his office.

By noon he'd talked to enough self-important bank officials to last him a lifetime. He went into the dining room, hoping Cleo might have decided to eat with everyone else for a change, but she wasn't there. He spoke to several of the guests, managing to laugh and talk like a normal human being even though he felt as if somebody had hollowed him out and left only the shell.

Juanita passed by with a heaping bowl of potato salad and stopped to glance over her shoulder at him. "She's taking pictures of Rosa and Peter at two in the barn, in case you'd like to know."

"Thanks." He figured Juanita could see past the front

he was putting on for the guests to the agony inside his heart. The threat of losing the ranch was bad enough. The threat of losing Cleo, too, had nearly crippled him.

"Want to sit down and have some lunch?" Juanita asked.

He shook his head.

"Make her stay, Tom."

He forced a smile. "Don't think I can."

Juanita frowned. "Try harder." Then she continued serving the guests.

He would try harder, if he only knew what might work. But he'd given her his best last night, and it hadn't been enough. Stopping to speak to a few more guests on his way out, he left the dining room. By this time tomorrow, she'd be gone. He couldn't accept it, but he didn't know how to keep it from happening.

Going out to the corral, he threw a saddle on Red and headed out, letting the big horse run as long as the terrain allowed. He rode hard, but the peace he usually found on the back of a horse wouldn't come. Finally he turned Red's nose for home, and as the ranch came into view, he saw her drive the convertible in and park it beside her cabin. He pulled his horse to a halt and leaned on the saddle horn to watch as she climbed out and went inside.

The connection between them tugged at his insides with the strength of a steer on the end of a rope. As he nudged Red into motion again, he wondered if he'd still feel that tug when she was two thousand miles away. From the power of it, he imagined he would. But she didn't want him in New York, either. She'd also made that clear.

He took his time getting back to the corral and unsaddling his horse. He didn't want to arrive at the barn before she'd had a chance to get completely involved taking pictures of the kids. But he had to see her, had to talk with her at least once more, and this might be his only chance.

The sound of childish laughter echoed inside the barn as he drew near, and he smiled. For one brief moment he allowed himself the fantasy that Cleo was in the barn taking pictures of their children, but he couldn't dwell on the fantasy too long, not when it had such a slim chance of coming true.

Juanita glanced at him when he appeared in the open barn door, but Cleo was oblivious.

"That was a *wonderful* somersault, Peter," she said. "Do another one."

"Wanna see my cartwheel?" asked Rosa, jumping up and down in the mounds of hay Cleo had spread out for them.

"You bet." Cleo dropped to one knee, clicking away as Peter tumbled in the hay. He came up grinning, pieces of hay stuck in his dark curls. "Look this way, Peter. That's good. Do you have a teddy bear?"

Peter nodded. "Freddy the Teddy."

"How big is Freddy?"

Peter raised his hands over his head as Cleo kept the camera shutter busy.

"Here goes!" shouted Rosa.

Cleo swung her attention to Rosa's earnest attempts at a cartwheel. "That's so good," she said. "I'll bet you're going to be in the Olympics someday."

"I am," said Rosa, and flung herself over again.

Tom couldn't resist coming closer. He crouched next to Juanita, who was sitting on a bale of hay, her face glowing with pride.

She leaned over and murmured in his ear. "Look how she is with them."

Oh, he was looking, all right. In between shots she'd call them over and pick hay out of their hair, running her fingers through their soft locks. Her touch lingered as she brushed a speck from Rosa's shirt, or refastened a button on Peter's overalls. He couldn't see her face, but he could hear the smile in her voice every time she spoke to them. She was entranced with these two children, and they'd fallen head over heels in love with her.

Judging from the unbearable pain in his heart, so had he.

He sat back on his heels and watched with bittersweet delight as the session continued. She was a natural with those kids, but he wasn't surprised. She might be, though.

"That's it," she said finally. "Film's all gone."

"Now you do one," Rosa said. "You promised."

"So I did." She set her camera down, walked over to the bed of hay they'd constructed and executed a decent cartwheel. "Ta-da!" She threw her arms up and back in a classic gymnast pose.

"Yeah!" Rosa clapped wildly and Peter grinned.

Cleo laughed and turned toward the bale of hay where Juanita was sitting. "Well, lady, I—" She caught sight of Tom for the first time. Her smile faded. "Hi. Didn't know you were there."

He stood. "I hope you don't mind."

"No, of course not." She ran her fingers through her hair and glanced away. "After all, it's your ranch."

Juanita gave him a sharp nudge in the ribs and angled her head in Cleo's direction. Then she hurried over to take each of her children by the hand. "Time for that homemade strawberry ice cream I promised you," she said.

"Yummy!" Rosa said. "Come on, Cleo. Ice cream!"

"Sounds great." Cleo tucked her camera in her bag and swung it to her shoulder.

"Uh, Cleo, could I talk to you a minute?" Tom asked, stepping closer to her.

She glanced toward the doorway as Juanita hustled the kids outside. "Okay." Her gaze returned to his. "But I don't think—"

His arms went around her and his mouth came down on hers before he even realized what he was doing.

She struggled at first, but not for long. He slid the camera strap from her shoulder and lowered the case gently to the ground as he tapped into her heat. Soon the resistance went out of her and she molded herself against him. Then, with an endearing little whimper, she opened her mouth for his tongue.

He longed to keep kissing her right through tomorrow, but that wasn't exactly a realistic plan. With great reluctance he lifted his mouth a fraction from hers. "Nice cartwheel."

"I thought you wanted to talk," she murmured.

"I thought I did, too." He ran his tongue over her lower lip. "God, you taste good."

"Tom, this is only going to make it harder."

As her comment sank in, he began to laugh. "It already has." He pressed her against his groin. "As I'm sure you can tell."

She shook her head and smiled. "Cowboys. Gotta love 'em."

"I'm glad you think so. And I have a much better treat in mind than strawberry ice cream."

"No." She pushed gently on his chest.

He let her go. "You're not leaving until tomorrow."

"Actually, I'm leaving in an hour. I've decided to spend my last night in Bozeman."

Pain sliced him to ribbons. "Don't."

She gazed at him, her blue eyes cloudy with unhappiness. "I can't risk another night here. I'm losing myself on this ranch."

"Or finding yourself."

"You don't understand." She combed her hair back with trembling fingers. "I'm Cleo Griffin, the woman who takes sizzling photos of men. That's the niche I've carved out for myself, and there aren't that many niches available, believe me."

"I've never asked you to stop doing that." He didn't like it, but he knew better than to ask her to give it up.

"I know you haven't." Her smile was sad. "That would have been easy. I could have laughed in your face and refused to abandon my career."

"Don't end what we have, Cleo." The tightness in his chest threatened to turn into full-fledged panic. She couldn't be leaving in an hour. Less than an hour now. "We can work something out, something that's good for both of us. Let's try at least."

She shook her head. "I came here on a manhunting expedition. I wanted the calendar subjects, of course, but I also wanted a man who would...give me what I need. And the joke is, I found him."

"I have a feeling I won't find this very funny."

"It is funny, if you just keep your perspective. I went out on a shoot this morning."

"I know."

"I've lost the ability to shoot sexy pictures, Tom."

He was ashamed of the selfish joy he found in that fact. "What happened?"

"It was pretty horrible, actually. Here was this gorgeous hunk of a cowboy, Jake Collins."

"I know Jake." And he was damn glad he hadn't realized who her thirteenth cowboy was. Jake was eligible, and he had a hell of a reputation for pleasing women.

"I tried to get into the mood, to create that chemistry that makes my calendar shots special." She gazed at him. "All I could think about was you."

Damn, he loved hearing that, but he shouldn't love it. She was telling him she might have just committed career suicide. That was the term Deidre had used to explain why she couldn't have their baby. Well, it seemed he'd contributed to career suicide once again. "Maybe... maybe you'll get the feeling back." He forced himself to say it because he knew that's what she wanted.

"That's why I'm leaving today. The sooner I get away from here, the sooner I can try to find my old self."

He had no answers for her. Even if he thought she'd be happy as a ranch wife, he was on the brink of losing the Whispering Winds. "What we had was good, Cleo. I refuse to believe it'll ruin either of us."

"Let's hope not." The white hat he'd loaned her the morning of the cattle drive was hanging from a hook on the barn wall. She retrieved it and held it out to him. "I was going to drop this by your office, but you've saved me the trouble."

He left his hands at his sides. "I don't want the hat back. I couldn't let another woman wear it, not considering the way I feel about you. If you don't want it, drop it in a trash can on your way to the airport."

She lowered her hand to her side. "You'll receive a check for...for our...photo session."

"I don't want a check."

"But—"

"Don't you dare send me money, as if what we shared was a business deal. If you do, I'll tear up the check and send you the pieces."

She swallowed. "I always knew you were stubborn, cowboy."

"I always knew you were, too, lady." He had to give her credit. She was gutting out this final scene like a trouper, even though he knew she must be dying inside, just as he was.

"Well, then, I guess this is it. Goodbye, Tom. Good luck."

"Same to you." Watching her walk away was like facing a major operation without anesthetic. He knew he was in for some of the worst pain of his life, and there wasn't a damn thing he could do to ease it.

A HOME-PREGNANCY test kit might be wrong, Cleo thought. She might have flubbed the test she administered to herself early that morning, and she really should see a doctor before going into a panic. Funny thing, though, she wasn't in a panic. Maybe that would set in later, when she faced the consequences of her behavior. Right now, sitting in her workroom and looking at the contact sheet containing pictures of her potentially viable baby's father, she was feeling the first moment of joy since she'd walked away from Tom on that warm June afternoon.

It had been a rough six weeks. Some days she had wondered if life was worth the effort. But she'd had to keep going, trying to sort everything out. Maybe she'd just been waiting for this day, even though she wasn't sure what to do with her new information.

Bernie knocked on the frame of the open workroom door. "Can we talk?"

Cleo tossed the contact sheet down and swiveled her chair around. "Sure. What about?"

Bernie threw up her hands. "*About what*, the woman

says. Cleo, it's been six weeks since you came back from Montana. I gave you time to recover from the trip. I gave you time to roam the city thinking up new calendar ideas, although I haven't heard any results from that search. Besides that, we not only don't have a cover shot chosen for the Montana calendar, we don't have a final decision on whether we're doing twelve months or thirteen. Calvin's calling here every day wanting a meeting, and we..." She paused and stared at the poster-size nude hanging on the workroom wall. Then she sauntered forward, hands on hips, and peered at it. "Sweet heaven."

Cleo smiled. "That's not one of the photos I was considering."

Bernie continued to stare at the poster. "You've done some good work, toots, but I gotta tell you, this is beyond good. I didn't know you took any nudes while you were down there."

"This was sort of..." She paused to clear her throat. "Serendipity."

"Photographic genius, is what it is. Gallery stuff. You got any more?"

"That's the best one, but there are a couple of others I like, too." Cleo picked up the contact sheet with the shots of Tom on it. She hadn't been able to look at them until last week, but once she had, she couldn't seem to look at anything else. She could spend hours, *had* spent hours, staring at those shots.

She handed Bernie the contact sheet she'd been holding back for weeks, unwilling to let anyone see the pictures of Tom until she'd decided what to do about them.

Bernie glanced quickly over the sheet and back to Cleo. "And who's this?" she asked softly.

"Tom McBride."

Bernie reached for Cleo's arm and hauled her out of

her chair. "Come into my office and pour yourself some coffee, girl, while I put the phone lines on hold. Aunt Bernie needs to find out what's been happening with her Cleo."

Sprawled in a chair across the desk from Bernie, Cleo sipped coffee that wasn't half as good as Juanita's and told Bernie the whole story, right up through the photo shoot with the kids. She'd shown Bernie the pictures of Rosa and Peter before shipping them to Juanita, but she hadn't made a big deal of them at the time.

She drained the last of the coffee, thinking that she'd have to start cutting back on it now. "I guess the bottom line is that Tom's was the last calendar session I... enjoyed." She put the empty mug on Bernie's desk. "The next day I forced myself to take those shots of Jake, but I loved every minute of shooting the kids. Can you beat that?"

Bernie looked as if she'd gone into shock.

Cleo waved her hand in front of Bernie's face. "Still in there, Bern?"

"My life is passing before my eyes."

"I know what you mean." Cleo slouched farther down in the chair. "I've been hoping for weeks that the urge to shoot hunks would come back. I even got another idea for a calendar."

"Yeah?" Bernie's expression took on more life.

"Fitness instructors, personal trainers."

"Hey, that's a dynamite concept, Cleo! Yeah. Sweat, and skimpy shorts, and bulging biceps. Let's see. We could call it *Muscle Men*, or *Barbell Brawn*, or—"

"We're not calling it anything. I have zero interest in shooting it. I visited some gyms, tried to work up the old enthusiasm, feel the old zing of sexual interest. I struck out, Bernie."

Bernie sat forward and rubbed her hands over her face. "I feel like the jockey on a Derby contender that just came up lame."

"That's why I've put off telling you. I've been hoping the problem was temporary, but I'm afraid it's not."

"I knew something had happened in Montana. You haven't been the same since you got home." Bernie sighed and sat back in her chair. "So one night of fantastic sex with Rancher McBride, and every other man is chopped liver to you, is that what you're telling me?"

"Well, there is one other little detail."

"I can't think of anything more catastrophic than this. Hit me."

"I'm pregnant."

Bernie rolled her eyes. "That would be it."

TOM SELDOM DRANK, but the evening seemed to call for a bottle of Jack Daniel's. Feet propped on his desk, he tossed back a shot of whiskey. Yeah, that was just what he'd needed.

"Tom?"

He glanced toward the door to find an amazing sight—Juanita with a tray of sandwiches. She must really be worried about him to break her own rules like this. "I figured the kitchen was closed hours ago," he said, grinning.

"You're not eating worth a damn, so I'm bringing you some food." She stalked into the room, glared at the bottle on the corner of his desk and smacked the tray down next to his booted feet. "And you'd better eat it."

He took his feet from the desk and surveyed the plate of sandwiches. It would have to be roast beef and cheese, he thought grimly. "That's pretty nice of you, Juanita."

She took a photo album from under her arm. "I finally

got the pictures Cleo sent me all fixed up nice, ready to mail to my parents. Before I do that, I thought you might like to see."

"Sure." That was about the last thing in the world he needed to look at tonight, but he knew how much it would mean to Juanita.

She opened the album and placed it in front of him. "She said she'd never taken pictures of kids before. But she's a real artist, that lady. I meant to save this for a Christmas present, but I can't stand it. I have to send them now."

Tom's heart swelled with love and pride as he studied each shot and remembered the laughter that had filled the barn that afternoon. Cleo had captured that sense of fun with her camera. Using her professional skill and her inborn talent, she'd recorded the pure joy of being a kid with nothing better to do than turn somersaults in the hay.

"Aren't they wonderful?" Juanita asked.

"Yes." Tom's voice was husky.

"You...haven't heard from her?"

"No." He'd been counting the weeks. She'd be sure one way or the other by now, and she'd tell him if there was something he should know about. Her silence meant his instincts had been wrong. So that was that.

"I can't believe she won't be back," Juanita said. "She was crazy about this place. You could see it in her eyes, in her face."

"Maybe it's just as well she doesn't come back." Tom gestured toward a chair beside his desk. "You'd better sit down. We have something to discuss."

"If it's about those chili peppers, I know they were too hot. Next time I'll—"

"It's not the chili peppers, Juanita. I wish it could be

that. I was planning to tell you about this tomorrow, but since you're here, this is as good a time as any."

Her plump hands closed into fists. "It's the ranch, isn't it?"

"You need to start looking for another job, Juanita. The bank's set up the auction to take place the day after tomorrow."

15

AFTER THE INITIAL SHOCK wore off, Bernie sent Cleo back to her workroom with instructions to pick the shots for the Montana calendar, at least. Cleo spent the day wrestling with the question of whether to use a photo of Tom, and by the end of the day she still hadn't decided. She ducked out of the office while Bernie was on the phone, figuring she'd sleep on the problem.

The next morning she was still undecided, and she fully expected Bernie to be irritated with her. Instead, her assistant suggested they take the day off to go shopping on Fifth Avenue, just as Cleo had talked about during her phone call from Montana.

"I'm not buying clothes *now*," Cleo protested.

"Then we'll buy things for the baby." Bernie shut down her computer. "Let's go. Shopping helps me think."

"I'm not keeping the baby."

"What, you're sending it back?" Bernie grabbed her purse and ushered Cleo out of the office. "I don't think it works that way, toots. No refunds, no exchanges."

"I'm sending it to Tom."

"By courier or regular mail? I suppose you can ship anything these days. They probably have a little cardboard bassinet, reinforced, of course, that you can—"

"Oh, for pity's sake! You're making it sound ridiculous."

Bernie punched the elevator button. "That's because it is ridiculous. You're a creative, loving person who's just started to make this little human being. I've seen how possessive you are about your photographs, Cleo. What makes you think you'll be able to ship this kid off to Montana?"

Cleo knew Bernie had a point. It was the same point that had been nagging her ever since she'd taken the pregnancy test. She stepped into the elevator. "I can't raise a kid. I have a career to think about."

"You just said a mouthful there."

They rode in silence to the street and Bernie whistled for a taxi. "F.A.O. Schwartz," she instructed the driver as she climbed in.

Cleo followed her into the cab. "Bernie, that's a toy store!"

"Well, the little tyke has to have something to play with, you know."

Cleo flopped against the seat. "I'm not keeping this baby."

"Sure you're not."

Two hours later they sat at a corner deli, bulging sacks taking up most of the booth. Cleo thought it was an awful lot of toys for a baby she wasn't keeping, but she'd had a terrific time. Her pastrami sandwich tasted delicious, and Bernie seemed to be in a good mood despite the disaster they faced.

Cleo swallowed a bite and glanced at her assistant. "I'll make the decisions for the Montana calendar this afternoon, Bernie. I promise."

"You can't decide whether to use Tom or not, right? Considering your rule and all?"

"That's right."

"But he said you could?"

"Yes." She remembered the bleak look in his eyes as he'd offered her the roll of film. "He doesn't want me to, but the ranch is in financial trouble and the calendar would increase business." It would also turn a personal moment into a public one, and alert single women all over the country as to his whereabouts.

"Then I advise you to use it, Cleo. The two of you are going to need all the money you can get if my latest brainstorm doesn't pan out."

Cleo didn't know which part of that statement to grab on to first. "It isn't the two of us. It's him and me, two separate people."

"Wrong. For one thing you're parents of the same child, so you'll never be separate people again. But more important than the physical mating is the psychological mating. You've found your man, Cleo, the one you've been looking for during all those photo sessions. You didn't realize it, and God knows I didn't, either, but this little run was doomed to end. It was just a matter of when."

Cleo bristled. "The hunk calendars were a creative brainstorm. It had nothing to do with seeking a mate, or whatever Freudian spin you're putting on it."

"Then why, after going to bed with this guy and *accidentally* getting pregnant, did you take the best damn kid pictures I've ever seen?"

Cleo stared at her, the sandwich forgotten. "You mean the ones of Rosa and Peter? Those were fun to do, but they weren't anything special."

Bernie took a long drink of her iced tea and patted her mouth with a napkin. "Fortunately our publisher doesn't agree. On the strength of those pictures, the company's willing to consider a calendar of kid shots next time out."

Cleo's mouth dropped open.

"You can fire me for this if you want, but when you sneaked out of there yesterday afternoon, I went into the workroom, found the contact sheet for those pictures, and took it over to our friends at Images, Inc. I told them you were headed in a new direction, and it was gonna be huge. They could either come along or we'd look elsewhere."

"Oh...my...God." Cleo put a hand over her racing heart. "I'm not a kid photographer. I don't know the first thing about—"

"Then learn, dammit." Bernie leaned across the table, her dark eyes flashing. "And it'll be easy, because that's what's in your heart now. I watched you in that toy store, which was my main motivation for going there, to confirm what I already suspected. You couldn't keep your eyes off all those cute little kids, and I'll bet your trigger finger was itching. I saw you reach for a nonexistent camera bag twice."

Cleo blushed. "Come on. That little blonde with the strawberry lollipop stain all over her mouth would make anybody long for a camera."

"She made me long for a Handi Wipe. Nope, it's your delicate condition doing this, sweets. You could've just adopted a puppy and we'd be into dog calendars, which would have made life much, much simpler. But you got pregnant. And you're in love with the father, which is very convenient, I might add. Doesn't always work that way."

"Bernie, if you're suggesting that Tom and I get married and raise this baby together, it won't work. He's not the commuter-marriage type and, although it kills me to admit this, neither am I."

Bernie grinned. "It's very satisfying to be right. So move to Montana."

"Move to...? Are you out of your mind?"

"Toots, everything you think comes out in your photographs. I also looked through the contact sheets of the Montana landscape. What's up with that psycho horse, by the way? Reminded me of Norman Bates."

Cleo smiled as she imagined Bernie scratching her head over the shots of Dynamite, sleepy-eyed one minute, wild and rearing the next. "Dynamite's a lovable little mare, a real sweetheart."

"Sure she is. Until the screeching-violin music starts. Anyway, it was obvious looking at those pictures that you adore the place. Make yourself happy and live there."

Tears pressed against the back of Cleo's eyes. Bernie was the best friend a girl ever had. "I couldn't. I couldn't leave you in the lurch like that."

"What lurch? Assuming you haven't decided to fire me for acting without orders, I'll keep the New York office open. With phone, fax, e-mail and overnight delivery, who cares where you are? You can drop in for a visit now and then, and someday I might even bring George out there." She winked. "Give him a ride on Dynamite the psycho horse."

"I...I don't know what to say." But excitement bubbled in her, even though she couldn't really do this, shouldn't even consider such a wild and crazy idea.

Bernie nodded, her own eyes suspiciously moist.

"You'll go. I booked you on the first flight leaving for Bozeman tomorrow morning."

CLEO HAD DECIDED not to call first. She'd had no communication with Tom in six weeks, and she couldn't imagine saying what was in her heart over the telephone. They'd had such a short time together, and fires that hot could burn out just as quickly. Once she looked into his eyes she'd know, but not until then.

As she drove the rental car over the winding road down through Gallatin Canyon, she couldn't decide if the queasiness in her stomach was motion sickness, morning sickness or butterflies at the prospect of seeing Tom. The drive seemed endless, and she would have given her best telephoto lens to have Tom's solid presence in the driver's seat so that she could be a passenger, as she had been on her first trip down this road, when she'd spotted the pair of eagles.

A shiver ran over her spine, remembering those eagles. She'd never believed in signs or fate, or any of that, but still, all Bernie's talk about finally finding a mate resonated in the deepest part of her soul. When she turned in at the gate leading to the Whispering Winds, she had the feeling of coming home.

Apparently lots of other folks had decided this was the place to be today, too. She stared through the windshield at the vehicles, mostly pickup trucks, crammed into the yard. People were milling around as if they were at a picnic, or at a... Her already jumpy insides twisted tighter.

She'd been so eager for the first sight of the ranch that she'd missed the small notice tacked to the right-hand side of the wooden gateway. She couldn't read everything on it, but the words at the top was enough to ram a fist of fear into her stomach. Auction—2:00 p.m.

She stared at her watch in a panic. It was nearly four! But wait, that was New York time. The rental-car clock read five minutes before two. My God. If Bernie hadn't made the reservations—but she had. Cleo leaped from the car and opened the gate. After she'd driven through, she forced herself to take the time to close the gate again.

Tom wouldn't think much of her as a ranch-wife prospect if she couldn't even remember to close his gate.

On the drive down she sent up a cloud of dust, but she didn't care. Nobody was getting this ranch away from the McBrides if she had anything to say about it. Mentally she took stock of her assets and wondered if she had enough to bail out a ranch. Maybe not, but she could buy some time, time for the Montana calendar to come out.

With a screech of brakes she stopped just behind a pickup with California plates. As she got out of the car and slapped her hat on, she noticed another California license plate, and one from Idaho. Damn, they'd come from all over the place to scoop up this piece of prime real estate. Little did they know they'd be dealing with a New York chick.

She ran up the ranch-house steps, shoved past several people standing on the porch and flung open the front door. "Tom!"

He was standing by the stone fireplace with two men who wore western-cut sport coats, despite the heat of the August day. They looked warm but official. Cleo felt light-headed at the thought that these people were here to take the ranch away from Tom.

At her entrance, his head jerked up and he stared across the room at her. "Cleo?"

She tried to read his expression to find out if he was glad to see her, but the light was wrong. "Stop the auction." She stood by the door and tried to catch her breath.

He said something to the men and came over to her, his quick strides eating up the distance. "Why didn't you tell me you were coming?"

She looked into his eyes and all she saw was deep concern. Well, she had startled him, and she did feel a little faint. He probably thought something was wrong. "I didn't know I was coming until yesterday," she said. "And I didn't want to have a phone conversation about—"

"Let's go into the office." He cupped her elbow and started in that direction.

His touch was all she needed in the world, she thought. But he needed this ranch. "Tell them to hold off on the auction, Tom."

"They won't start until I say it's okay. We have a couple of minutes. Let me get you a glass of water. You're pale."

"We don't have time for water. I'm fine."

He took her into the office and practically pushed her into a chair. "I'm getting the water. Stay there."

"Tom!"

"Dammit, stay there."

So much for tender reunions, she thought. And he was trying to order her around, as usual. She walked into the living room and over to the men in the suit coats. They both touched the brims of their expensive-looking Stetsons and gave her a murmured greeting.

"You two look like the ones in charge of this shindig," Cleo said.

"We're handling the auction, if that's what you mean, ma'am," said the taller of the two.

"There won't be an auction. Just so you know."

"Excuse me, ma'am," said the shorter one. "But there will be an auction, as soon as Tom takes care of his business with you."

"His business with me is that I'm giving him whatever money it takes to stop this auction."

"Over my dead body," Tom said from behind her.

She turned and knocked her arm against the glass of water he was holding, spilling it down his shirt. "Sorry."

He took her arm, less gently this time. "Excuse us, gentlemen. I'll only be a minute."

"Sorry about spilling water on your shirt," she said as he propelled her into his office.

"I can see you're still the same bullheaded woman you were when you left." He kicked the door closed behind him and shoved the half-full water glass at her.

"And you're still the same bullheaded man. Maybe I should throw the rest of this on you. It might cool you off."

He tossed his hat on the desk and stood glaring at her. "Did Juanita call you?"

"No."

Bracing his feet apart, he rested his hands on his hips. "Don't lie to me, Cleo. I wouldn't put it past her to call and tell you about the auction, just so you'd come out here and try to save me."

For a long moment she stood there just taking in the sight of him. He was every bit as magnificent as she'd thought when she'd stepped out of the jetway weeks ago and found him waiting for her. And behind his blustering attitude burned the flame she'd hoped to see in his gray eyes. Nothing had changed. They were going to have a wonderful future.

She took a sip of water. "Of course I'm going to save you."

"Like hell."

"You were man enough to make a woman out of me, Tom. Now let's see if you're man enough to swallow that huge pride of yours so we can get on with our life together."

He stared at her.

"I'm asking you to marry me."

"Why?"

"I think you can figure it out." She watched as the realization of why she was there swept over him.

Fierce joy flared in his eyes as he closed the gap between them and took the glass from her hand, setting it on the desk beside them. Then he swept the hat from her head and kissed her with a desperate urgency that left her gasping. He leaned his forehead against hers. "You don't have to marry me."

She chuckled. "I think that's my line."

He lifted his head and looked into her eyes. "I know you wanted me to raise the baby here, but I'll make a good life somewhere...else." He swallowed hard. "It'll be okay. You won't have to disturb your career or get tangled in some legal bind you don't want, just because we went a little crazy that night."

She sighed and rested her hands on his shoulders. "I've never asked a man to marry me before. I wore the hat you gave me, thinking that would soften you up."

His smile looked sad, but at least it was a smile. "You still look great in the hat. I'm glad you kept it. But Cleo, you don't want me."

"The hell I don't. The thing is, once your calendar comes out, I won't be the only one. So I figure I'll have to hang out at the Whispering Winds and fight off all the eligible females looking for Rancher McBride. Otherwise you'll never get anything done around here."

He cupped her face in both hands. "Look, I know the ranch came to mean something to you while you were out here, but everything has to end someday. I won't have you sacrificing yourself for some sentimental idea that the Whispering Winds has to stay the way it is."

"First of all, I'm not sacrificing anything. My career as a photographer of hunks died a natural death."

He caressed her cheeks with his thumbs. "You can't

know that yet. Maybe after you have the baby, and get back into the swing of things, you'll—"

"I don't want to get back into the swing of things. My whole focus has changed from sexy men to cute little kids, and fortunately, Bernie has already lined up a calendar deal to launch my new direction."

"Even more reason for you to stay the hell away from this sinking ship. God knows I understand your attachment to this ranch. All week I've had people in my office, some with tears in their eyes, trying to find a way to stop the auction. It can't be done. I've accepted it, and so should you. Conserve your resources for your new venture, Cleo."

"But you are my biggest resource."

"No. I'm—"

"Tom!" She looked deep into his eyes. "I'm not offering my hand in marriage because I love the Whispering Winds." She paused. "I'm offering it because I love you."

Finally, he was speechless. He looked, she thought, as if she'd whacked him over the head with a fence post.

She reached up and touched his parted lips. "Your line," she murmured, "is *I love you, too. Marry me.*"

"Cleo...." His voice was hoarse with distress. "I'm penniless. We have a baby on the way. How can I—"

"By choosing love instead of pride. By being a big enough man to match the glorious country that is so much a part of you. By admitting that you need me and allowing me to give to you, after all you've given to me. Let me be your wife, Tom, in every meaning of that word."

Slowly, the uncertainty cleared as his gray eyes began to glow with hope.

"Remember the eagles we saw the day we met?" she asked softly.

He nodded.

"I studied up on them. They mate for life."

"That's right." His voice was husky.

"That's what's happened between us, Tom. That night in June we mated for life, like those eagles. It just took me a while to figure it out."

His smile was gentle as he combed his hair back from her face. "Not me. I knew right away."

"But you didn't tell me because—"

"Because I love you. I love you so much I was determined to live without you, if that's what you needed."

Hearing him say it was so sweet she battled tears. "It's not what I need. What I need is to live here with you, and raise our children, and take my pictures, and have you kiss me and tell me you love me on a very regular basis."

"I'd say it's already been way too long since I've done that."

"Me, too."

"I love you, Cleo."

As he kissed her, she could have sworn that she heard, through the open window, the triumphant cry of an eagle.

BACHELOR FATHER

BACHELOR FATHER

Prologue

I'M GOING TO DIE. The rapids pulled her under again. Through the churning bubbles Katherine saw a tree root. She grabbed at it, but fists of water punched her away. Fighting to the surface, she gulped in more water than air. Then the current took over again and slammed her against a submerged rock. She ignored the pain and tried to get a grip on the mossy, slippery surface.

No luck. The water closed over her head. Air. She needed air. But she was so tired. So very...no, damn it! Flailing her arms, she broke the surface again and choked as she tried to breathe.

"Here!"

Rescue! The possibility ran through her like an electric charge. Nearly blinded by the water pouring from her hair into her eyes, she struggled to turn in the direction of the voice. There...just ahead...a branch being held over the tumbling water!

"Grab it!" yelled the man.

She had one chance at this, she thought. One chance at life. As the river swept her toward the branch, she offered up a quick prayer and reached for the branch with both scraped hands. Contact!

But the river wouldn't let go. It tugged and pulled, trying to work her loose from her salvation.

"Wrap your arms around it! I'll bring you in!"

Following his orders took faith. She had to loosen her handhold to wrap her arms around the branch, and she was sure she'd be swept downstream in the process of getting a better grip.

But she wasn't. Inch by painful inch he worked her toward shore, until at last he could touch her hand. Once his fingers circled her wrist, she knew he'd saved her. Dizzy with gratitude, Katherine glanced up at the man who had just become the most important person in her life.

HE COULD HAVE MISSED HER, Zeke thought with a shiver. Headed back to camp with the string of trout he planned to cook for dinner, he could just as easily have cut through the trees instead of following the river. But an uneasy feeling he'd learned not to ignore had made him skirt the banks and check the rapids.

She'd scared the hell out of him. Adrenaline pumped through his system after he hauled her out of the water and she flopped facedown on a bed of wild grass.

He crouched beside her, his heart racing. "Was anyone with you?"

She gasped a few times. "No."

He swore. Although he didn't have to worry about looking for a drowning victim downstream, he wanted to shake this idiotic woman for traipsing around in the wilderness by herself. She'd almost paid the ultimate price.

But he'd saved her, and now he had to deal with the consequences of that. He'd deliberately left his cell phone at the ranger station, figuring he was off duty. Dusk was nearly upon them.

He leaned close to her. "Do you have a camp nearby?"

"No." Her breathing was steadier, but she didn't move from where she'd landed. "Lost my pack...in the water."

Zeke recognized a New York accent. Lord deliver him from greenhorns who thought Yellowstone was a slightly more rugged version of Disneyland. He sighed. "Then I guess you'll be spending the night with me."

1

Nine months later

WHAT A CIRCUS. From the porch of the main house, Zeke surveyed the crowded grounds of the Lost Springs Ranch for Boys. In all the years he'd spent as a kid on this ranch, he'd never seen the place so packed with people. But that was the idea—to get folks involved in this bachelor auction Rex Trowbridge, an alumnus who was now on the board of directors, had cooked up to raise money for the ranch.

Zeke longed to stay where he was, comforted by the familiar feel of the porch rail under his hand. But he had maybe five minutes before he had to walk out to the arena and climb up on the auction block where a gang of ranch alumni were gathering. The aroma of barbecued ribs filled the air, and fiddle music rose above the buzz from the crowd. Even CNN had shown up to film the action, so it looked like Rex would get the corporate sponsors the ranch needed to survive.

And Zeke wanted the ranch to survive. Lost Springs was his safe place, the haven his mind returned to whenever he felt rootless and alone. His thumb on the porch rail brushed over a small, crude carving of a lone pine. When he was ten he'd used his pocketknife to cut his mark into the wood, fully expecting to get in trouble for it. But he'd wanted to put his stamp on the place so that years later he could come back and find proof that Zeke Lonetree had been here.

He hadn't been punished for carving the tree into the rail. Every time he'd returned to the ranch he'd checked that nobody had sanded it down—to reassure himself that some things in life stayed the same. The thought of Lost Springs closing was more horrible than the thought of taking part in this bachelor auction, so he'd agreed to be here. But Rex had no idea how much it was costing Zeke. Walking up on that platform would be like slicing off a chunk of his soul and offering it to the buzzards.

A piercing whistle sounded above the hubbub, followed by shouted comments directed at Zeke from the auction block.

"Yo, Lonetree!" called Shane Daniels, one of the alumni who'd become a champion bull rider and a close friend. "We ain't got all day, son."

"Yeah, get your Native American butt out here!" yelled Chance Cartwright, who'd made good as a horse breeder and trainer. "All these women saw *Last of the Mohicans* and they want you bad."

Zeke groaned and wished he could treat this auction the way Shane and Chance did, as a big joke to be enjoyed. But both of them were used to being in crowds and rubbing elbows with the rich and famous. In fact, most of the guys on the block had high-profile, public positions, while Zeke's park ranger job in Yellowstone allowed him to spend most of his time the way he preferred—alone in the wilderness.

"Move it, Lonetree." Amos Pike, a toy manufacturer, motioned Zeke over to the platform.

Zeke took a deep breath and reminded himself why he was doing this. A phone rang inside the ranch house, but unfortunately it wasn't Zeke's job to answer it. He couldn't put off the inevitable any longer. Shane had given him a new Stetson for luck. With a sigh he tugged it low over his eyes and started down the porch steps.

"Zeke?"

He turned.

Rex, the guy responsible for his current misery, pushed open the screen door. He had a cordless phone in one hand with his thumb over the mouthpiece. "Come on in for a second," Rex said.

Zeke was delighted for any delay, but still he gestured halfheartedly toward the arena. "The guys want to get started."

"I know. We will in a minute. But it looks like you're being pulled from the lineup."

Hope lightened the heaviness in Zeke's chest as he followed Rex into the cool interior of the ranch house. "Pulled?"

"Yeah. Let me finish my discussion with this lady, and then you can talk to her."

Zeke listened to Rex's end of the conversation and figured out that someone was making a large donation in order to take Zeke off the block. He didn't understand what was going on or why, but he wasn't about to complain. He might still be obligated to a woman for a date of some kind, but at least he'd be spared the agony of walking the runway. He'd take it.

"Okay," Rex said to the person on the other end of the line. "That sounds great. I'll let you work out those details with him. And thanks again for your generosity, Ms. Rutledge. You'll be helping many young boys get a better start in life. Here's Zeke." Rex handed over the phone. "Way to go, stud," he murmured.

Zeke frowned in confusion as he took the phone and

covered the mouthpiece. "I have no idea what this is about, Rex."

"Well, when you do, I hope you'll fill me in. My curiosity's killing me. Listen, even if you're out of the auction, how about hanging around, anyway? Some of the kids were hoping you'd give them an update on the wolves in the park."

"Sure." Still feeling bewildered, Zeke held the phone to his ear. "This is Zeke Lonetree."

"Ah, Mr. Lonetree. I'm Naomi Rutledge, editor in chief of *Cachet*."

Cachet. He'd heard that name somewhere, but he couldn't quite place it.

"The fashion magazine." She tossed her explanation into the silence as if she couldn't believe his ignorance.

"Oh." *Oh.* Katherine's magazine. A wave of dread washed over him. He hoped she wasn't tied into this bachelor-auction business in some way. He never wanted to see her again.

"Listen, I'll get right to the point. I believe you are acquainted with my senior fashion editor, Katherine Seymour."

Zeke closed his eyes. Surely it wasn't heartache he was feeling. He'd wiped that episode out of his memory months ago.

"Mr. Lonetree?" she prompted. "Does the name Katherine Seymour mean anything to you?"

He opened his eyes and cleared his throat. "We've met."

"Yes. So I understand. Well, she has some...personal business to discuss with you, so I would like—"

"Put her on. I'm sure we can handle it over the phone." Panic rose in Zeke's chest as he tried to fend off what he feared was coming.

"I'm afraid that's not possible. She's...unavailable."

"Is she okay?" The nature of Zeke's fear changed. He didn't want to get within two thousand miles of Katherine, but he didn't want anything bad to happen to her, either.

"She's fine. But she needs to see you, so I've arranged for her to fly out to Jackson Hole the last weekend in August. I presume that would be convenient to your place of employment."

"You can fly her anywhere you want, but I have no intention of—"

"The man I just spoke with assured me that you'd honor the terms of the bachelor auction and meet her there."

"You bought me for her?" Having a woman win him at an auction was bad enough. Having a woman procure him for someone else was ten times worse.

"I did nothing of the sort! *Cachet* is donating a generous sum to the Lost Springs Ranch for Boys, and in exchange I want you to meet Katherine in August and talk with her. It's a business arrangement. I'll even cover her expenses. Agreed?"

"Why are you doing this?"

"I'm not at liberty to discuss the reason. You need to take it up with Katherine when you see her. I'll mail you the particulars."

"Look, Ms. Rutledge, this is a complete waste of time for everyone. Katherine and I have nothing to—"

"I assure you, my donation to the ranch is *very* generous. I'm certain you wouldn't want to jeopardize that."

Zeke felt the trap closing around him, and he had no one to blame but himself. He'd acted totally out of character by making love to Katherine the night he'd saved her from the river. Then he'd made the further mistake of thinking the encounter had meant something to her. Months of her silence had convinced him otherwise. Now he was being summoned like some menial servant without being given any explanation. He longed to hang up on this bossy woman with the New York accent that reminded him of Katherine's.

But she'd practically said she'd withdraw her donation if he didn't go along with this ridiculous arrangement. He'd agreed to this damn auction to help the ranch, and now was his big chance.

"Do we have a deal, Mr. Lonetree?" she asked.

"We have a deal, Ms. Rutledge."

KATHERINE TOUCHED A FINGER to Amanda's cheek and guided the rosebud mouth to her nipple. As the baby nursed, Katherine stared at her in wonder. She couldn't believe that Amanda was nestled in her arms. So many times during the pregnancy she'd thought she would lose her. But Amanda had clung stubbornly to her chance at life, and Katherine had never known such joy as she felt now, holding her child.

"What a lovely picture you two make." Naomi smiled gently as she walked into the hospital room dressed in her usual color scheme of black and white, her silver hair perfectly coiffed, her makeup flawless.

Katherine returned her smile. "Can you believe she's really here?"

"Not quite." Naomi walked over to the bed and leaned down to stroke Amanda's tiny head. "I didn't dare count on this, not with the problems you had carrying her." She finger-combed the baby's abundant jet-black hair. "I don't think this is going to turn blond."

"Probably not." Just her luck her baby's hair would

forever remind her of that lusty night in the forest with Zeke Lonetree.

"She's beautiful, Katherine. I'm so sorry your parents didn't live to see her."

"Me, too." Her throat tightened, but as she watched Naomi tenderly smoothing Amanda's hair, she gave thanks that at least she had Naomi. "I guess this makes you a god-grandmother."

Naomi looked up, her eyes moist. "So it does." She cleared her throat and returned her attention to Amanda. "Although god-grandmother is a mouthful for a little kid. Maybe…she could just call me grandma."

Katherine's heart squeezed. "Of course she could."

Naomi gave the baby's hair one last stroke before turning to find a chair, which she pulled over to the bed. "And now that we've made it to this point, you and I have a few things to discuss."

"I plan on getting right back to work. If you have no objection, I'll bring Amanda to the office and set up a bassinet for her. I'm sure I—"

"I'm sure you can, too." Naomi laid her manicured hand on Katherine's arm. "But that's not what I want to discuss. I'm thinking of making some staff changes."

Katherine's breathing quickened. She was being demoted. Naomi might have seen her through this problem pregnancy with loving care, but she was the founder of *Cachet*, and she hadn't built the magazine into the industry giant it was by being soft. She'd decided to give Katherine's job to someone else because she didn't believe a new mother could handle the demands of being a senior editor.

Worst of all, Katherine dared not question the decision. When her parents died, Naomi had been her salvation, giving her a job at *Cachet* right out of college and promoting her regularly until she finally gained senior editor status. Katherine knew she hadn't worked up to capacity during the final months of her pregnancy, but Naomi hadn't ever complained. Under the circumstances, Katherine didn't feel she could beg for more consideration.

Feeling like a doomed prisoner, she gathered the courage to look directly into Naomi's eyes and take the bullet like a woman. "What sort of changes?"

"I want to train you to take over for me."

Katherine sighed with relief. She would work like a demon to justify Naomi's continued faith in her. "So you're going on vacation?"

"No, I want you to take over permanently."

Katherine's gasp dislodged Amanda's mouth. The baby's reedy cry of protest brought her attention back to the task and gave Katherine a moment to recover herself as she resettled Amanda at her breast. But her heart was still pounding when she finally glanced back at Naomi. "I...don't know what to say. I never in the world expected..." She stopped, at a total loss. Editor in chief. She couldn't comprehend it.

Naomi chuckled. "I can't go on forever, you know."

Katherine felt as if someone had just hit her over the head with the NYC phone book. "I guess I thought you would."

"And die in harness? Not this lady. Or worse yet, I could start losing my edge and have a staff who's afraid to tell me. No, I want to slip out of the top spot gracefully and leave someone I trust in charge."

"But what about Sylvia? Or Denise, or—"

"Darling." Naomi squeezed her arm. "You've been my choice ever since you were born."

"I have?" Katherine took a moment to digest that startling information. "No wonder you were so excited when I decided to work on the high school newspaper."

"It was all the encouragement I needed. Of course, I would have backed off if you'd chosen one of those other careers you talked about. I remember once you wanted to be an actress, and then there was your doctor-nurse period. And what was it you wanted to be when you were ten? A wilderness guide?"

Katherine smiled. "Yeah. Then I thought about all the bears I'd meet."

"Well, you made the right choice, both for you and for me. You've turned out to be a damned good writer and a highly competent businesswoman."

"Who got herself knocked up!" No matter how happy Katherine was about having Amanda, she was still embarrassed that she'd stumbled into motherhood by accident.

"Stress counteracted your birth-control pills," Naomi said briskly. "You couldn't have anticipated that." She gazed at mother and baby. "And don't tell me you're sorry, because I know you're not."

"No." Katherine dropped a kiss on the top of Amanda's head. "I'm not."

"So, are you up for some new responsibilities?"

The shock of Naomi's offer had lessened and now Katherine began to fully realize the scope of it—the confidence and the love that it implied. Her eyes filled. "You know I am."

Naomi blinked and looked away. "Good. Very good." She cleared her throat and glanced back at Katherine. "We only have one pesky detail to take care of."

A catch. Katherine wondered if she'd been premature in her gratitude. "What's that?"

"Amanda's father."

Katherine swallowed. It wasn't a comfortable subject. Many times during the past few months she'd wished she could claim immaculate conception. After promising Zeke that birth control wasn't a problem, she dreaded telling him she'd been wrong. She'd rationalized postponing the call because she'd seen no reason to involve him if she ultimately lost the baby.

"You have to tell him," Naomi said.

"I know."

"He might just relinquish all rights to her."

"Maybe." Funny how little she knew about the man who had given her life twice, first by saving her from drowning and second by fathering Amanda. He was possibly the most gentle man she'd ever known, yet beneath that gentleness burned a fierce passion. Her heart still raced whenever she allowed herself to remember their moment of joining, when she'd felt somehow *claimed*.

The next morning, though, he'd been much more cautious and withdrawn. Plagued by her own insecurities, she'd suggested that maybe she ought to get back. Instead of trying to change her mind as some men might, he'd sealed himself off completely, which had convinced her there was no hope for a relationship.

"Do you feel anything for him?" Naomi asked.

Katherine looked up to find the older woman watching her closely. It was an important question. If she still had an emotional connection to Zeke, one that could potentially lead to a relationship, then she had no business letting Naomi train her as a replacement. She might not know a lot of things about Zeke, but she was absolutely sure of one thing—he would never live in New York. During their night together he'd made clear his love of the wilderness and his aversion to cities and crowds.

"I feel gratitude." Katherine glanced at the clock on the

bedside table and decided it was time to switch Amanda to her other breast. She still felt a little clumsy handling the baby, but once she settled her in again, the tug of her small mouth felt perfect and right. "After all," she continued, "Zeke saved my life, and he inadvertently gave me Amanda."

"I'm not talking about gratitude."

Katherine tried to be objective about her emotions regarding Zeke, but it wasn't easy. That night was like a blazing comet in her life, but her reaction to him had probably been born of many factors. She'd recently been dumped by Ken, she'd just been saved from drowning, and she'd never been stranded in the wilds with a man, especially a man as virile as Zeke. Maybe the fact that he was part Sioux had tickled her romantic fantasy. And maybe it was that look he gave her across the campfire, a look that promised so much pleasure...

"Katherine?"

She blinked and glanced at Naomi. Heat rushed to her cheeks. "Okay, he's very attractive, and I have some hot memories that are tripping me up a little. But he's apparently a real loner who wants nothing but wilderness surrounding him, while all I want is to work at *Cachet*."

"But what about your vacation last year? You didn't choose the Hyatt on Maui, don't forget. You opted for your personal little Outward Bound in Yellowstone. Maybe that yearning to be a wilderness guide isn't completely gone. Maybe you have a hankering for the great outdoors yourself."

Katherine smiled, more sure of herself now. "What I have a hankering for is a crisp set of galleys, a hot cup of espresso, and a bagel slathered with cream cheese."

Naomi beamed in approval. "Good girl. Although

you'll have to go easy on the caffeine as long as you're breastfeeding."

"Decaf espresso, then." She noticed that Amanda had drifted off to sleep, her tiny hands curled into fists. "New York is what I know and love, and I've found my dream job. What could be better?"

"I can't imagine. So it's time to tidy up the situation with this man and get on with business. If he wants to surrender his parental rights, we're home free. If he wants partial custody, which I doubt, I'm sure you can work that out with him."

She made it sound so easy, Katherine thought. Something told her it wouldn't be quite that simple, but she tried to look confident as she nodded in agreement. "Right."

"Great. I've set it up so you can do exactly that."

Katherine stared at her. "Set what up?"

"He was part of a bachelor auction out in Wyoming, a benefit for a boys' ranch. I donated a chunk of money to the ranch in exchange for you spending a weekend with him in Jackson Hole at the end of August. You can tell him about Amanda then. She'll be two months old and should travel just fine."

"Naomi!" Katherine jerked, causing Amanda to startle awake.

"Or were you planning to tell him over the phone?"

"I—" Katherine paused to catch her breath and gently rock Amanda back to sleep. She should have expected something like this from Naomi. The woman had invented the term *take charge*. "I hadn't thought how I'd tell him, but..." She gazed at Naomi, still having trouble comprehending what her godmother had done. "You bought him for the weekend?"

Naomi waved a dismissive hand. "That's overdramatizing the whole thing. It's a business arrangement. I gave money to the ranch in exchange for helping my chief assistant tidy up her personal life."

"I can't imagine Zeke putting himself up for auction, let alone agreeing to spend the weekend with me simply because you paid the going price."

"I won't pretend that he was eager to comply. He tried to talk me out of it, said that the two of you had nothing to discuss. But when he realized that my sizable donation to the ranch depended on his cooperation, he gave in."

Katherine's chest grew heavy with despair. She'd been right about Zeke. He might have surrendered himself to a night of lovemaking, but he didn't want complications in his solitary life. Unfortunately, she was about to bring him a very large one.

"I still can't believe he was willing to take part in a bachelor auction in the first place," she said. "I've never met a more private man."

"He's an alumnus of the place. All the bachelors were. Quite an interesting story, really. They must have blanketed the media with invitations. Ours came quite a while ago."

"And you didn't tell me?" So Zeke had been raised on a boys' ranch. She hadn't known that. It made his lone-wolf image even more vivid.

Naomi regarded her with the same calm assurance that had kept her staff in awe of her for two decades. "You've been on an emotional roller coaster for months. Any mention of Zeke seemed to be stressful for you, and I was so afraid you'd miscarry that I decided not to bring this up. But it's worked out for the best. Going to Wyoming with Amanda is the right thing to do. You can clear the decks and then come home and settle into your new position."

"But Zeke doesn't want to see me. You said so yourself."

"He needs to see Amanda. You owe him that much, Katherine."

She gazed down at her sleeping child. Zeke's child. Naomi was right, but the thought of meeting Zeke again under these circumstances scared her to death.

"Your courage is one of the qualities that made me decide to turn over the magazine to you in the first place," Naomi said. "I'm not giving you anything you can't handle. You can do this."

Katherine lifted her head and looked into Naomi's eyes. "Yes, I can."

2

AUGUST TURNED OUT TO BE a wet month in the Tetons, and more rain looked likely as Zeke climbed into his battered king-cab pickup and headed for Jackson Lake Lodge on Friday afternoon. He spent the drive time singing "Ninety-nine Bottles of Beer on the Wall," because it reminded him of cookouts at Lost Springs and why he was putting himself through this. *Cachet's* donation would go a long way toward remodelling bunkhouses that no longer met the fire code, and Rex had already lined up a contractor for the renovation.

Naomi Rutledge had made it clear, however, that her check wouldn't be issued until after this weekend.

Zeke had never pretended to understand the thinking process of people who lived back East, but the whole deal was weird, even for New Yorkers. Painful though it had been, Zeke had combed through every moment of the night he'd spent with Katherine, searching for a clue as to what this could be about.

From the beginning, he'd tried to control his growing sexual awareness of her, which had been tough as their conversation grew more personal. He found out she'd broken up with her boyfriend, and to get her head on straight she'd decided to spend some time alone in the wilderness. She'd admitted that notion had been naive and overly dramatic.

Plucky, honest women appealed him, and this one

seemed to be available. Eventually his desire felt natural and right, something to be seriously considered even though they'd just met. But while he was debating the issue, she'd made the first move. It had only been a light touch on his arm, yet he'd felt his world shift. Then he'd turned to look into her hazel eyes. That moment when he knew that she wanted him as ferociously as he wanted her would be with him forever. A moment like that could make a man feel like a god.

This moment, however, when he was about to confront her after nearly a year of silence, when he'd been summoned to this meeting by her boss and kept in the dark about the reason, made him feel like a toadstool.

He sang another chorus of the drinking song as he pulled his beat-up truck in among the out-of-state cars and tour buses parked at Jackson Lake Lodge. But he didn't have the nerve to keep singing as he walked into the lounge where they were supposed to meet, so the jitters he'd postponed with the song struck with a vengeance. He'd always loved this high-ceilinged room with tall windows facing Jackson Lake and the jagged Tetons beyond. He hoped this meeting wouldn't ruin the place for him.

Heart pounding, he scanned the room. He didn't see her. Damn it, after all this, maybe she'd stood him up. Of course, that would be a good thing. He didn't want to see her, anyway. Except that he'd gotten himself all worked up about the prospect, and at least if he saw her, he'd find out the answer to the mystery.

"Zeke?"

He wouldn't have bet that he'd recognize Katherine's voice, but he didn't have to turn around to know she'd spoken his name. A flood of desire took him completely by surprise as his body replayed the sensation of being deep inside her. He turned to face her slowly, giving him time to regain his cool. He knew she wouldn't be wearing rumpled khakis this time, and he prepared himself for her city look.

But as he gazed at her, his brain stalled. When he finally admitted what he was seeing, his knees almost gave way.

She looked more polished than she had a year ago, but he barely noticed as his attention fastened on the canvas carrier snuggled intimately against her chest. She supported the weight of the carrier with one arm. With her free hand she cradled the head of a baby. A baby with very black hair.

While his mind shouted denials, his gut reacted with a primitive tug of certainty. *His.* He relived the dizzy ecstasy of being inside Katherine, of her warmth and a connection unlike any he'd known. When he'd finally poured himself into her, he'd experienced a sense of purpose he'd never felt with any woman. Maybe he'd known then, no matter what she'd said about birth-control pills. Maybe he'd known all along that this could be the only logical explanation for their meeting today.

"Her...her name is Amanda." Katherine sounded out of breath. "Zeke, I didn't mean for this to happen. Apparently the stress of nearly drowning short-circuited my system."

A girl. He noticed the baby's terry outfit was pink. He began to shake. A baby girl. Somehow knowing that she was a girl terrified him even more. She was asleep, her dark lashes creating a fringe above each cheek. She pursed her tiny mouth, then relaxed it again. Petrified though he was of this little bundle, he couldn't seem to look away.

"I didn't want to tell you over the phone. I realize this

comes as something of a surprise." She paused. "Zeke, I wish you would say something."

With great effort he lifted his gaze and looked at Katherine. A frown creased her high forehead. How he'd enjoyed touching the smooth planes of her face as they'd lain side by side in his small tent, his battery lantern on low so he could see her while they made love. Her golden eyes had reminded him of a mountain streambed, the kind that he could stare into for hours. He might have even told her that. He knew he'd said things to her that he'd never said to anyone before, risked more than he'd meant to risk.

Her eyes brought him no joy today. All he could see was a woman who'd taken the best he had to give, then acted as if she could hardly wait to get away from him the next morning. Admittedly he wasn't good at expressing his feelings, but that morning he'd been trying to think how he could tell her what the night had meant to him. Before he had it figured out, she'd announced she'd better leave. He'd been half expecting her rejection. In his experience, caring too much almost guaranteed being discarded like an empty fast-food sack.

And now obligation was all that had brought her here to let him know they had a baby. He wanted to call Amanda an accident, but he knew she wasn't. At the time she was conceived, he thought he'd found his mate. That belief alone might have cancelled Katherine's birth-control pills. He'd seen people will their own death, so maybe you could will life into existence, too. Maybe he'd unconsciously done that.

He cleared his throat. "I think we should find a more private spot to talk about this."

"You're right, we probably should. But just let me say this. I'm not here to ask for anything—not child support or even for you to give Amanda your name. I take full responsibility for this baby. I understand how you want to live your life, and a child doesn't fit in very well. Now that you've seen her, if you'd like to relinquish all rights and never see either of us again, that's fine."

He stared at her, hurt tearing at his insides. She knew nothing about the way he wanted to live his life, but she'd use his loner status to justify closing him away from the baby because that suited her best. Anger and self-protection followed close on the heels of his pain as he threw up the walls that had sheltered his bruised heart all his life. He kept his voice low. "Is that what you came for? To have me sign off on this kid?"

"No!"

The baby's eyes opened and she started to whimper.

Katherine rocked her gently. "I mean, yes, if that's what you want, but if—"

"You could have hired a lawyer to put that in a letter and saved us both a lot of time." He took satisfaction from the distress in her eyes.

"I thought you deserved to see her."

"How considerate." He lowered his voice even more, conscious of others in the lounge starting to listen in. "You haven't seen fit to contact me in all these months, not even when you knew you were pregnant. Now you drop out of the sky, present this baby and suggest I give up my rights. That's a great idea, but I don't need three days in a plush lodge to work that out with you. Mail me the papers." He brushed past her and walked out of the lounge, refusing to allow the baby's wail to penetrate the thickness of the wall around him.

KATHERINE STOOD in the middle of the lounge in a state of shock, automatically comforting Amanda while she tried to assimilate what had taken place. Unless she'd misunderstood, Zeke had just agreed to the very thing that Naomi wanted, and for all intents and purposes, the visit had already accomplished its goal. She should feel jubilant, ready to celebrate before catching a flight back to New York.

Instead she wanted to cry. This was wrong, all wrong. Back in New York, she'd thought such a plan would be best for everyone, but after seeing Zeke again, she knew she didn't want him to sign some papers and disappear from Amanda's life.

When she'd walked into the lounge and caught sight of him there, his broad back to her, she'd felt an unexpected rush of delight. And awe. She'd forgotten just how big a man he was. His silky black hair seemed a little longer—it touched his collar in back now. But his stance was disturbingly familiar, and the faded jeans and blue flannel shirt could have been the same ones he'd worn that night. She suspected he had lots of similar clothes.

And he certainly fit the surrounding country with his massive frame and bronzed good looks. The rugged Tetons outside the window provided the perfect backdrop for a man in flannel and denim.

In spite of the anxiety she'd felt at presenting Amanda to him, she'd looked forward to the moment he would turn around, the moment she would once again be able to admire his warrior's face with those intense dark eyes. Until now she hadn't acknowledged to herself how much she'd missed him.

And now he was gone.

But maybe she could still catch him.

Grabbing up the diaper bag she'd set down, she clutched Amanda tight and hurried out of the lodge. She made it into the parking lot just as Zeke started to climb into an old gray truck. Calling his name, she started toward him as a light rain began falling.

He turned, but there was no charity in his glance. The forbidding look in his dark eyes almost made her give up and go back inside, but Amanda's warm weight against her body was all the motivation she needed.

"Please don't leave."

His expression was totally closed. "It's raining. Take her back inside."

"Come inside with me. We'll get some coffee. We'll talk." She was begging, but she didn't care. "I don't want you to leave like this. Surely you'll want to see her once in a while, and we need to—"

"Why?"

"Because she's your daughter!"

His laugh was harsh. "You say that as if it makes a difference. I happen to know being somebody's biological kid doesn't mean a thing."

So he'd been abandoned by his parents, she thought. He hadn't admitted that when they'd talked about neither of them having any family left. She took a deep breath. "You're right, it doesn't mean a thing to some people. I had you pegged differently."

His eyes hardened even more. "Up until ten minutes ago I didn't even know this baby existed. I wish you'd done us both a favor and kept it that way, but since you haven't, I'm going to leave here and pretend I never laid eyes on her."

"Zeke, please don't."

"It's the best thing all around. Now take her back in. It's raining harder." He climbed into his truck, started the engine and backed out of the parking space.

Katherine bowed her head over Amanda to shelter her from the rain and to hide the tears that threatened to fall.

Naomi would be thrilled, she told herself, sniffing. A clean break. No strings. Lots of little girls grew up without fathers.

Amanda gurgled and waved her hand, bumping her fist against Katherine's damp cheek.

"Forgive me, sweetheart," Katherine murmured, not sure who she wanted to forgive her—Amanda or Zeke.

ZEKE STARTED OUT OF the parking lot, determined to get the hell away from the lodge as quickly as possible. But he made the mistake of looking in the rearview mirror.

Katherine stood there getting wet, her head bowed over the baby. They looked so hopelessly vulnerable, so in need of protection. Katherine was brave, but she had a reckless streak, too. That's what had nearly gotten her killed on her solo trek through Yellowstone. He remembered the stab of fear he'd felt when Naomi had called and he'd been afraid something had happened to Katherine.

Well, something had, and he'd been partly to blame for it. Would she do something foolish now just because he'd refused to talk about this baby business? He'd thought he was giving her exactly what she wanted by refusing to have anything to do with the kid, but his response seemed to have devastated her. Would he get some terrible message from Naomi Rutledge concerning Katherine and the baby's welfare?

With a muttered oath he slammed on his brakes. Slowly he backed the truck to where she was standing, pulled on the emergency brake and put the gearshift in neutral.

As he got down and rounded the truck, she was watching him cautiously, her eyes wide. She held Amanda with a protective grip. He'd been told that his size, combined with the features passed on by his Sioux ancestors, gave him a menacing air, so he deliberately relaxed his expression and unclenched his hands.

She had a large canvas diaper bag hanging from the crook of her arm. Vaguely he recognized Winnie the Pooh characters, although he'd been an adult before he knew anything about those stories. He gazed at her standing with her tiny baby, her storybook diaper bag, and an almost childlike uncertainty in her big eyes.

Damn it, he felt like rescuing her all over again. The woman kept getting herself in trouble, and he kept wanting to keep her safe. It was a bad combination. But he couldn't leave her standing here looking as if her world had suddenly stopped spinning.

"Let's take a drive," he said. "I don't feel like discussing this over a damn cup of coffee. I need to be doing something."

She peered at his old truck. "Do the seat belts work in your back seat?"

"Yeah." Then he realized that these days you didn't just decide to go for a ride with a baby. There were all sorts of rules and regulations. "Forget it. Just write me a letter when you get back to New York."

"No, I want to go for a drive with you. I brought her infant seat, just in case we did want to take her out somewhere with us. It's up in the room. Wait here."

She set the diaper bag down and hurried away before he could protest that this was all too complicated. He stood in the light rain waiting for her, the diaper bag by his feet. He'd always suspected babies were a lot of trouble, for a million reasons.

He was surprised by how quickly she returned with some contraption that she asked him to belt into the back seat so the kid was facing backward. All the baby would see was upholstery. It didn't look like much fun for the baby, but he remembered park visitors with similar child seats. He had to move some camping stuff to make room. Part of the reason he'd bought the king cab was to have a place out of the weather to keep his sleeping bag and small tent. The very tent, in fact, that Katherine had shared with him. The rain started coming down harder just as he finished.

"Let's get both of you in, then you can put her back there." He picked up the diaper bag.

"Okay."

He opened the passenger door, but it soon became obvious she'd have trouble getting in while Amanda was still strapped to her. He didn't want to touch her, but it was the expedient choice now that the rain was really sluicing down from the sky. Setting down the diaper bag, he put his hands around her waist and lifted her and the baby onto the front seat. His hands spanned her waist perfectly, just as they had when he'd lifted her on top of him and eased her down over... No, he couldn't think about that.

"Thank you." She didn't look at him.

He noticed the pulse at her throat throbbed and a pink flush tinged her cheeks. He wondered if his touch had anything to do with that. She might not want to maintain any permanent connection with him, but apparently he affected her. He'd bet she found that very inconvenient. Well, so did he.

"Watch your arms," he said. "I have to slam this to get it shut." He heaved the door closed, and by the time he climbed in, the baby was crying. He hoped to hell that wasn't going to go on very long. "What's wrong with her?" he asked.

"Just the loud noise of the door closing, I think." Katherine jiggled the baby and crooned to her. Then she lifted her out of the pouch and nuzzled her cheeks. "There, there, Mandy. You're safe. Don't be scared."

Zeke sat immobilized by her tenderness. For some stupid reason it made his throat ache to watch her cuddle that baby. You'd think he'd never seen a mother and baby before. To be honest, he hadn't been this close to many. Growing up on the ranch had meant being around lots of boys and young men. The couple who'd run the place had a daughter, little Lindsay Duncan, who now owned the place, but she was already a toddler by the time Zeke arrived.

Amanda's crying tapered off to small gasps and one hiccup. Then she quietly stared up at her mother with an unblinking gaze.

"That's my girl!" Katherine talked in a special singsong way and smiled at the baby. "Can you give Mommy a happy smile?" She tickled the side of Amanda's cheek. "Come on now, big smile. That's it. *Big* smile."

To Zeke's utter fascination, Amanda did smile, which seemed to make her cheeks look chubbier and gave her a double chin. It was the cutest thing he'd ever seen, and he knew cute when he saw it. Nothing matched a couple of tumbling bear cubs, or nothing had until now.

"Some experts say that a two-month-old isn't really smiling," Katherine said. "That it's just a reflex, or gas."

Zeke could tell from the more adult tone in her voice that Katherine was speaking to him, not Amanda. "Looks like a smile to me," he said.

"Of course it's a smile." Katherine lapsed back into her melodious baby talk. "We know a smile when we see one, don't we, Mandy? Yes, we do! Now, let's get you back in your seat." She lifted the baby from the pouch and handed her to Zeke. "Take her for a minute so I can turn around and get ready to lay her in there."

"Take her?" He pulled back as if she'd tried to give him a live grenade.

"Just for a minute."

"I don't know how to hold a baby!"

"Pipe down. You'll scare her again. Just support her head with your hand and the rest of her in the crook of your arm." She settled the baby into his arms and adjusted his hold. "Like that."

His body stiffened and his heart began to pound as he realized he had total responsibility for keeping this baby alive for the next couple of minutes. "I'm going to drop her. I just know it. Or squeeze her wrong and break something."

"I doubt that." Katherine knelt on the seat and begin fiddling with the carrier in the back.

For the first time Zeke noticed what she was wearing— a long flowered skirt and a sleeveless blouse the color of young grass. The light material of the skirt stretched tight across her bottom as she adjusted the straps on the infant seat. Zeke tried not to pay attention.

He also became aware of two very pleasant scents replacing the smell of musty canvas that usually filled his cab. One was sweet and fresh, probably baby powder, but the other had a sexy tang to it. When he'd spent the night with Katherine she'd had no toiletries at all, let alone perfume. He'd even let her borrow his toothbrush. He'd loved the natural fragrance of her body, but this other was seductive in its own way. He liked it. He liked it way too much, in fact.

Amanda made a noise and jerked her small body.

He held her tighter. "Don't do that," he instructed the baby.

She stared up at him.

He found himself staring back. Her eyes were a soft blue, yet Katherine's were hazel and his were brown. "Why are her eyes blue?" he asked.

Katherine answered as she continued to fuss with the seat. "Because she's so young. The doctor said as she gets older they'll probably turn hazel, like mine."

He continued to study the baby. Her skin wasn't as pale as Katherine's, yet not as bronzed as his. His skin-color genes and Katherine's must have combined into this shade, which was kind of nice. The thought of his genes combining with anyone's blew him away. Then he noticed the small dimple in her chin, a dimple just like...his mother's.

"Okay, hand her to me."

Zeke was so afraid of dropping the baby in transit that the process of giving her to Katherine involved a lot of physical contact. And memories—the tickle of the downy hair on her forearm, the coolness of her fingers against his skin, the rhythm of her breathing.

While she strapped the baby securely in the seat, he faced forward and took several deep breaths himself, just to get over the dizziness of being so close to Katherine.

Finally she was back and buckled herself in.

He started the engine and turned to her. "We might be gone a couple of hours. Do you have what you need?"

"Yes. I have extra diapers and I'm breast-feeding. We'll be fine."

He wished she hadn't given out that bit of information. He didn't need to be presented with a picture of her un-fastening her blouse and offering her breast to Amanda's little pink mouth. He'd be wise to get them both back to the lodge before that became necessary.

A car horn beeped and Zeke jumped. In his preoccupation with Katherine and Amanda, he'd totally forgotten his truck was sitting in a crowded parking lot blocking traffic. "Guess we'd better get rolling." Then he turned the key and ground the starter motor because he hadn't remembered the engine was already running.

Get a grip, Lonetree. Anyone who knew him would get a kick out of seeing him rattled, he thought. Among the other rangers, he was famous for never losing his cool. He'd faced bears, rattlers, even escaped convicts with calm detachment. But he'd never faced a situation like this one, and he had a feeling it was going to take every ounce of courage he could dredge up.

3

KATHERINE WATCHED the windshield wipers slap back and forth while she thought about what she'd done, running after Zeke like that. She'd have a tough time explaining herself to Naomi. She could just hear her godmother—*He was ready to give up all parental rights and you talked him out of it? Where was your brain, girl?*

Her brain had very little to do with it. She'd been operating on instinct, and right now her instincts told her this was right, for the three of them to be heading down the road together in the rain. Zeke had left the main highway to follow a narrow two-lane road with little traffic on it. Safe in the truck cab with Zeke, she felt cozy, almost peaceful. She hadn't felt that way for a long time, maybe not since the night she'd spent with him in his tent.

She glanced at Zeke and realized she'd never seen him at the wheel of a vehicle. He looked good there—competent and sexy. The day after her tumble into the river, they'd hiked to a ranger station, and another park service employee had offered to take her back to the Old Faithful Inn so Zeke could return to his campsite and get on with the solitary retreat she'd ruined.

And here she was again, invading his privacy. But for Amanda's sake, she'd brave it out and hope he'd be willing to accept some part in his daughter's life.

As if he felt her attention on him, he turned his head. "Should you check her? She seems too quiet."

"I'm sure she's asleep. She loves riding." His comment made her smile. For the first month or so of caring for Amanda she'd had the same fears. She used to wake up twenty times a night and make sure the baby was still breathing. "Sometimes when she's fussy I bundle her up in her car seat, go outside and hail a cab, just so I can settle her down. It's worth the cost of a twenty-minute ride around town."

"You don't own a car?"

"Nope. Cabs are handier when you're in Manhattan. I don't live that far from the office. A car would be more of a nuisance than an advantage."

He frowned. "But don't you ever have the urge to get away from the city?"

"Yeah. That's why I came to Yellowstone last summer."

"Couldn't you have found someplace closer?"

"Well, sure. My parents and I used to camp in the Adirondacks when I was a kid, but that seemed too...tame. Besides, I'd been hearing about Yellowstone all my life."

"So you decided to tackle it alone."

"I like a challenge."

His jaw tightened. "I'd say you have one now, with your job and the baby."

And your stubbornness, she wanted to add, but didn't.

"And speaking of your job, what's Naomi Rutledge's stake in all this?" he asked.

Katherine decided that revealing Naomi as her godmother would only confuse the issue, so she stuck to the job situation. "She's offered to let me take over the magazine when she retires. Understandably she'd like my personal life to be under control before she does that."

He stared out at the rain-swept landscape. "That

should be a no-brainer. I'll bow out of your life and Amanda's, like I said back at the lodge. Case closed."

"I think that's a mistake." She took note that his jaw now seemed carved in granite. He didn't appear to be the kind of man who would change his mind easily once it was made up. He'd given her Naomi's preferred response twice in a row, and she was no more ready to accept his decision than she had been the first time. But she wasn't sure she could explain why.

"I don't get it, Katherine."

A thrill ran through her. It was the first time he'd used her name since they'd met at the lodge, and the sound of it made a definite impact on her, reminding her of the way he'd said her name while they'd made love. "I'm not sure I get it, either," she said, picking at a loose thread in the stitching of the armrest. But she was beginning to suspect her behavior wasn't all motivated by Amanda's welfare. She'd been intrigued with Zeke a year ago. She still was. She'd told him the truth about liking challenges, and he certainly presented a huge one.

"Why didn't you contact me when you found out you were pregnant?"

At last—an easy question, one she'd been meaning to answer for him right away, but the sensual vibrations between them kept sidetracking her. "I had a very difficult time during the pregnancy," she said, glancing up. "The doctor said I was very likely to miscarry."

"All the more reason to—"

"I didn't see it that way. You were concerned about birth control that night, so I didn't think you'd welcome the idea that I was pregnant. There was no point in getting you involved unless there really would be a baby. I wasn't sure of that until the minute she was born."

His voice was tight. "That was two months ago. Did

you forget to pay your phone bill? Or maybe you ran out of stamps. That can happen."

"I couldn't picture having a conversation about this over the phone. And a letter seemed even worse." She turned in her seat to look at him squarely. "Look, we got caught by a weird set of circumstances. I've tried to do what I thought was best. Maybe I've made some mistakes, but I—"

A loud bang interrupted her sentence and the truck lurched. Automatically she swiveled toward the back seat as Amanda started to cry and Zeke started to swear.

He eased the truck to the side of the road. "Sit tight. We have a blowout." He opened his door and cool rain blew in.

"Do you have a spare?"

"I think that was the spare that just blew." He climbed down and slammed the door.

Her heartbeat quickened. No spare. Before having Amanda, she wouldn't have been all that concerned, even if they'd had to walk back to civilization in the rain. But now she couldn't afford to be stranded.

Unbuckling her seat belt, she turned around and unfastened Amanda from her car seat to bring her up to the front. The baby wailed pitifully, her face scrunched up and her arms waving in the air. Katherine glanced at her watch and decided that the loud noise wasn't the only thing that had upset Amanda. She was due for some chow.

RAIN SOAKED ZEKE'S flannel shirt as he gazed at the hole in the sidewall of the left front tire and swore some more. He hardly ever drove the truck because he used park service vehicles when he was on duty. This afternoon when he'd started for the lodge, he'd remembered he hadn't fixed the flat after a nail had punctured it a couple of months ago, but it was too late to worry about it then.

He calculated the distance back to the lodge versus the distance to his little cabin. The cabin was closer. If he drove slowly, he might make it without damaging the rim too badly. Then he could call somebody from there.

Of course, that meant dragging Katherine and the baby to his cabin. He hadn't intended to do that, even though he'd been driving in that direction. He just happened to like this road, which was one of the reasons he'd decided to buy a couple of acres out here and put up a small log house. He had no neighbors within several miles, but he did have a phone, running water and electricity. Most of the time.

With one last disgusted look at the tire, he climbed back in the truck. "I think—"

"Close the door gently if you can, so you don't startle her."

He glanced at Katherine and caught his breath. Her green blouse was unfastened, although she'd modestly pulled it around her so that her breast barely showed. Somehow that made the whole picture more erotic to Zeke. Rain drummed on the roof of the cab, but he could still hear the soft sucking noises Amanda made while she nursed.

He pulled the door closed as best he could, knowing he'd have to open it and slam it again before they started driving. Then he stared straight ahead and tried to concentrate on following the path of an individual raindrop as it slid down the windshield.

He seemed to be having trouble getting enough air, and he cracked his window open a little.

A woman nursing her child was no big deal, he told himself. He lived among wild animals who raised their young that way, and this was the very same activity. Except it wasn't even close. A year ago he'd desperately wanted this woman, and she'd desperately wanted him. Now the result of their mating that night lay in her arms, the tiny mouth fastened to her breast. God help him, he wanted this woman still.

"Is the tire done for?" she asked quietly.

"Pretty much." He cleared the hoarseness from his throat and hoped she hadn't attached any significance to his husky tone of voice. He didn't want her to know how she affected him.

"Maybe somebody will come along."

"That's not too likely." He took a deep breath and let it out. He wanted to touch her, to cradle her breasts in both hands as he once had, to taste her. "Not many people use this road, and this isn't a good day for sightseeing."

"Zeke, please don't...don't leave me here and go for help."

He glanced at her in astonishment. "It never occurred to me."

Relief shone in her eyes. "Maybe I'm being silly. If I didn't have Amanda I wouldn't mind, but—"

"I wouldn't leave you." His pulse raced as he gazed into her eyes and saw the fulfillment she drew from nursing her child. No woman had ever looked so beautiful to him, so desirable as Katherine did now. Motherhood had given her a glow that he found almost irresistible. But he would have to resist.

"What are we going to do?" she asked.

For a moment he wondered if she was asking about the flat tire or if she wanted a solution to their much bigger problem. He didn't have one for it. But she probably was talking about the tire. "We'll drive on it," he said. "I have a cabin out here. It's not far. From there we can call a tow truck."

"You live out here?" She sounded quite interested.

"Yeah, when I'm not on duty at the park. It beats renting an apartment somewhere."

She nodded. "I can't picture you in an apartment. I imagine you clearing the land and building something out of logs, like Daniel Boone or Davy Crockett."

That made him smile. "Which is exactly what I did."

She gazed at him, her expression wistful. "That's the first time you've smiled since we met at the lodge."

"Yeah, well, this experience hasn't been a laugh a minute."

"I hate that it's so painful for you. She's a beautiful little girl, and I wish you could share some of the joy I feel."

"You're really happy about this?" All along he'd thought she was being a good sport for the baby's sake.

"How could I help being happy? Maybe I was a bit shocked when the doctor told me I was pregnant, but in about five minutes the shock wore off and I started feeling excited. A new life was growing inside me. That's a miraculous thing, Zeke."

He wondered if he'd have reacted that positively if she'd called to tell him right away. Maybe not, but he'd never know. Well-meaning though she might have been, she'd cheated him out of that sense of anticipation. "But what about your career? Isn't this messing things up for you?"

"It could, if I had a different boss, but Naomi gave me all the time off I needed to make sure this baby had a chance to survive. Now that she's here, I'm able to take her to the office with me, and when she's a toddler she can stay in *Cachet's* in-house nursery while I work." She paused. "My only regret is whatever trouble I'm causing you."

"You haven't caused me any yet." She'd caused him a fair share of heartache, but she'd protected him from any inconvenience so far. He wasn't sure he thanked her for that.

"We wouldn't be stuck out on this road if it weren't for me."

"We wouldn't, but I would be. This tire would have blown on the way back home whether you were riding with me or not. And I probably would have decided to drive on it instead of hiking through the rain to the cabin."

"That makes me feel a little bit better." She glanced down at Amanda. "I think she's about finished. If you'll give me a moment, I'll burp her and put her back in her carrier so we can get going."

"Sure." He understood the message. He was supposed to stop looking at her and focus on something outside the cab so she could get herself together again. With some regret he did that, staring across a meadow to the misty forest beyond. Normally he could see the Tetons from here, but the clouds had moved in and completely covered them.

For once the landscape he'd grown to love didn't interest him. He tried to ignore the rustle of clothing as Katherine buttoned her blouse, but it was pretty tough to ignore the happy little sounds she made as she talked softly to Amanda in the process.

He wondered if his mother had ever talked to him that way, with a singsong lilt to her voice. All he remembered were the frowns and the switches made of willow, and even those memories were hazy now. He'd only been three when she'd driven him to the entrance of Lost

Springs and ordered him out of the car, but he still remembered everything about that moment—the clothes he'd had on, the smell of the dirt under his feet, the hawk circling overhead in a huge, cloudless sky.

"I'll burp her, change her diaper, and we're done," Katherine said.

Zeke took that as his cue that it was safe to look at her again. Sure enough, she was properly dressed now, with Amanda propped over her shoulder as she patted the baby's back. He'd probably never have the chance to watch her nurse Amanda again. Maybe that was best.

Amanda made a sound like a bullfrog. The magnitude of it startled Zeke. "Does that hurt her?"

"Nope." Katherine smiled. "It would hurt her if I let that gas stay in her tummy. Then she'd really scream. Listen, would you mind getting me the diaper bag from the back? This will just take a second."

He leaned over the back seat and hauled the multicolored bag up front. He placed it between them where she could reach it. "Want me to look away again?"

Katherine laughed as she placed Amanda on a pad on her lap and popped the snaps on the baby's pink jumpsuit. "Not on Amanda's account. She's a free spirit who doesn't mind in the least who sees her naked."

"Unlike her mother." After he'd led her back to his camp last summer, she'd made him hang a blanket between two trees so she could hide behind it when she took off her soaked clothes.

Her cheeks turned pink and she concentrated on untaping Amanda's disposable diaper. "I barely knew you then."

"You barely know me now."

She didn't look at him. "That's true, I guess."

"So why not make a clean break before this gets any

more complicated? It's what you decided to do last summer, isn't it?"

Her movements stilled. "I thought that's what we both decided."

"Yeah, I guess we did." Wild horses wouldn't drag the truth from him.

She glanced up, her hazel eyes troubled. "But now there's Amanda."

"Look, I'll be glad to send you a check every month if that's—"

"No. I don't want money. I thought I made that clear."

"Then what do you want?" He watched the confusion in her eyes and believed that she didn't really know. "We can't make this turn out like a storybook," he said. "You can't wave a magic wand and turn me into the daddy who goes off to the office with a briefcase every day and then comes home to play patty-cake with his daughter."

"I know that." She popped open a plastic container and ripped out a moist towelette with an angry motion.

"So given that I'm staying here and you're going back to New York with Amanda, what kind of a real father could I be?"

"I don't have all the answers, Zeke."

"But you don't want me to sign away my parental rights to this baby."

She glanced up. "No, I don't. But you still have that option. If you decide that's the best thing for you, then by all means do it."

"I do think it's for the best," he said quietly.

"All right." She swallowed and leaned down to finish diapering Amanda. "Then I guess I'd better stop trying to change your mind." She snapped the baby's jumpsuit together again. "Hold her for a minute while I get organized to put her back in her seat."

He took the baby from her, and Amanda's tiny body felt a little less foreign to him this time. She stared up at him with the same concentration as before. Then she began waving her arms and kicking with her legs.

"Hold still now," he said, trying to keep his voice gentle. He didn't want her to start crying because he was too gruff with her.

She stopped wiggling and went back to her staring routine.

"That's better." He smiled in spite of himself. She was so serious-looking for such a little thing.

Then, to his total amazement, she smiled back.

Something stirred within him and his throat grew tight. He looked away from that endearing little smile and swallowed hard. "You about ready for her?" he asked.

"Yes." Katherine leaned over and lifted Amanda from his arms.

KATHERINE REMAINED SILENT as the truck rolled jerkily along the pavement, but the ride became more jolting when Zeke turned off on a dirt road. She kept glancing into the back seat, but Amanda slept through it all. As long as she was in motion, she was content.

But someday her needs would be much more than that, and Katherine wondered if she'd be enough parent for the little girl. So long as Zeke was a faint possibility on the horizon, she hadn't really contemplated the job of raising Amanda alone, even if Naomi had thought that was the logical decision. Now that Zeke had completely rejected fatherhood, Katherine realized that she'd unconsciously counted on him to have some influence in Amanda's life, no matter what she'd told Naomi.

Besides that, his rejection felt like a personal insult,

both to her and her baby. She couldn't imagine how someone could look at Amanda and choose never to see her again. From the tender way Zeke had made love that night a year ago, Katherine had thought he had a soft heart. Apparently she'd been wrong.

The truck approached a wooden bridge that spanned a rushing creek and Zeke put on the brakes. "Damn, but that water's high."

"Are you worried about the bridge holding?"

"Not going across this time, but if the rain keeps up… Well, we'll just tell them to bring the biggest, baddest tow truck they have to get across the creek, that's all." He stepped on the gas and the truck limped across the bridge, the tires making a hollow sound on the boards.

Katherine turned to look back at the creek when they were on the other side. Brown water boiled only about a foot beneath the boards. The sight made her a little sick to her stomach as she remembered the helpless feeling of being tossed around in the rapids. Without Zeke she surely would have died that day. "Has the bridge ever washed out?"

"No, but I only built it two years ago, when I bought the property. I've never seen the creek running that high." He glanced at her. "Hey, don't worry. Forget I said anything. We'll be fine."

"I'm sure we will." Katherine faced forward again as they entered a grove of aspens, their white trunks shiny with rain.

"There it is, through the trees on the right."

She peered out her window and spotted the clearing between the glistening tree trunks. Behind the clearing rose a hillside covered with pine, and nestled against the hillside was the sweetest little log cabin she'd ever seen. It looked like something out of one of her history books in school, right down to the stone chimney and the small front porch. She almost expected to see a pioneer woman come out of the front door and wipe her hands on her apron as she waited for her visitors to arrive.

"It's charming," she said.

"Thank you." He sounded pleased with her response. He pulled the truck up beside the cabin, shut off the motor and glanced at her. "We can at least have a cup of coffee while we wait for the tow truck."

"Only if you have decaf. Everything I put in my stomach affects my breast milk, so I have to be careful."

His gaze warmed for a brief moment before he broke eye contact and cleared his throat. "Sorry. No decaf. Come on. Let's go in and make that call."

She strapped Amanda back into the baby sling and grabbed the diaper bag while he unlocked the cabin and came back out with a yellow slicker to hold over the two of them. When he helped her down from the truck, she was glad there was a baby between them. Once his hand closed over hers, she had the craziest urge to move right into his arms. As it was, they were plastered together under the slicker as they dodged puddles on the way to the front porch.

"It's really coming down," he said, shaking out the slicker. "Go on in. After I call, I'll see if I can't find something you can drink."

She stepped into the cabin and was greeted with the aroma of fresh-cut wood. The place looked as she had imagined—a single room with rustic furniture including a bed, a rocking chair, a table and two chairs. One corner contained a stove, sink and refrigerator. Another was partitioned off and was undoubtedly the bathroom. The room was neat but had no particular decorating touches, which didn't surprise her, either. Even without curtains, a tablecloth or a vase of flowers on a windowsill, the effect was still cozy and welcoming.

Zeke came in and closed the door behind him.

"It's very nice, Zeke."

"Simple." He walked over to the large window looking out on to the porch. The stationary center pane was flanked by two screened windows, which he'd left open, but now he closed them against the chill.

"Simplicity has elegance, too." Katherine said.

His grin was wry. "I wasn't going for elegance." He crossed to the wall phone hanging behind the rocker. "Have a seat," he said, gesturing to the kitchen chairs. "I'll call the towing company and then see what I have in the cupboard."

"I don't really need anything," Katherine said. It wasn't quite true. Her stomach was grumbling because she'd been too nervous to eat lunch. But she didn't want to bother him when she'd be back at the lodge in a couple of hours at the most. She'd eat then.

"Well, I'm going to have something." He picked up the receiver and started to punch out a number. He paused and clicked the hang-up button a couple of times. Then he clicked it again. Finally he replaced the receiver and turned to her. "Maybe you'd better reconsider having something to eat."

Anxiety added to the turmoil in her stomach. "What's wrong?" But she knew exactly what was wrong.

"This storm must be worse than I thought. It's knocked out the phone. Looks like we'll be here awhile."

4

"HOW LONG DO YOU THINK the phone line will be out?"
Katherine quickly calculated whether the baby's needs
could be met for the next few hours. She always packed
more than enough diapers, and she'd brought an extra
terry sleeper. Food was no problem.

Zeke sighed and walked over to peer out the window.
"No telling where the lines are down. Out here the telephone can be out quite a while before anyone notices or
reports it. It serves mostly vacation cabins, which aren't
used all the time." He turned toward her with a worried
frown. "I should have headed back to the lodge and said
to hell with the wheel rim. I'm sorry, Katherine."

"Don't worry about it." To her surprise, she wasn't
sorry at all. If he'd been able to call a tow truck they'd
have parted within a couple of hours. Now they had
more time. She wasn't sure if that would change his mind
about keeping some connection with Amanda, but it
might.

"I could hike out to the road and try to catch a ride
back to the lodge."

"That seems completely unnecessary." If he left, that
would destroy any hope that he'd bond with Amanda.

"You'd be fine. You'd be safe here and there's plenty of
food."

"I'd still rather you didn't leave us alone."

"You won't get washed away, if that's what you're thinking. We're much higher than the creek."

She was unwilling to admit why she wanted him to stay, but she could offer him a reason he might accept, one that was also true. "I wasn't thinking of water, but speaking of that, did I ever tell you how I fell in the river in the first place?"

"I don't think we got around to that."

Because we had other things on our mind. She became aware that this one-room cabin put them in close proximity to a bed. Not that she would allow herself to get involved with him in that way again. They'd created enough problems for each other as it was. It was a beautiful bed made of peeled and sanded logs, a big bed, a soft-looking bed, a—

"How did you fall in the river?" he prompted.

She blushed and turned her attention away from the bed. She hoped she didn't have a telltale lustful expression on her face. "I was crossing the river on a log. A pretty fat log, too, so I shouldn't have had any trouble making it. Then I heard a snuffling noise behind me, looked over my shoulder and saw a bear at the edge of the river."

"What kind of bear?"

"A *big* bear."

He smiled. "I meant the breed."

"I didn't stop to ask him his pedigree. I just started scrambling across that log like a squirrel with its tail on fire, only I'm not as surefooted as a squirrel, and I fell in. As I headed downstream, I thought maybe it wasn't such a bad escape method, but then I couldn't stop myself and I kept going under, so I figured I'd probably drown. But at least that was better than being eaten by a bear."

He chuckled. "Far better."

"In my opinion." She liked making him laugh. She'd forgotten that she had that power. He'd told her that not many people got him to relax enough to laugh.

"For the record, I doubt you had much to worry about from that bear," he said. "He was probably after trout, not magazine editors."

"Oh, yeah? Maybe it was a grizz." She took her hands away from Amanda's sling and lifted them menacingly, curling her fingers into claws.

"A *grizz*?" He grinned. "Are you trying to speak the lingo, New York lady?"

He'd teased her with that label last summer. As the night had progressed, he'd switched to calling her *his* New York lady. His use of the term now sent a shiver of reaction up her spine, but she tried to keep her tone light. "I'm trying to tell you that I'd rather not stay in this cabin alone with Amanda when it's possible a bear could come along and bash down your cabin door."

"That's not going to happen."

"Do you or do you not have bears around here?"

"All right, there is a black bear that hangs around this area." He stroked his chin and his dark eyes sparkled. "And maybe she's been up on the porch a couple of times, but—"

"On the *porch*?" Katherine hugged Amanda tighter. "That does it. You're staying here with us until such time as we get escorted out of here by a burly guy driving a monster tow truck. Do I make myself clear, ranger man?" If he could toss out the nickname he'd given her that night, she could toss out his.

The laughter in his eyes faded, to be replaced with something more potent. "I don't know how long we'll be here."

"I don't care. I—"

"I do."

She met his gaze. "You really want us out of your life, don't you?" she said softly.

"Yes."

ZEKE TURNED AWAY from the pain flickering in Katherine's eyes. Sometimes the truth hurt, as he well knew. There was nothing more to say, so he'd better get some food on the table. Fortunately he'd done a little shopping the day before and had most of the basics.

He walked over to the kitchen cupboard and took down a can of tuna. "How about a tuna sandwich?"

"That's fine." Her voice held none of the playfulness from a moment ago, when she'd been describing her bear experience.

For a brief time during that conversation about the bear, he'd forgotten their situation and had found himself enjoying the Katherine he'd known a year ago, the one who had caused him to lower his defenses. He'd be wise not to lower them again.

"Can I help in any way?" she asked.

"I'll take care of it." He'd really done himself in this time, Zeke thought. Although he wasn't planning to tell Katherine yet, there had been times when the phone had been out for several days. He wasn't about to stay here with her for days, though. If necessary, he'd drive the truck the way it was. He'd rather have mega-repair bills than spend that amount of time here with Katherine and the baby. He didn't want to get in any deeper than he already was.

He put on some coffee and started working on the sandwiches while Katherine talked to Amanda in that cozy way she had. When she crooned to the baby in such an intimate tone he felt closed out, which might be how she wanted him to feel after the way he'd come across about the parental rights thing. But he knew himself, and being a part-time father would tear him apart. It was a situation guaranteed to produce misunderstandings and potential rejection. He had a very low tolerance for rejection, but he wasn't going to expose himself enough to explain that to her.

Rain pelted the window over the sink as he worked on lunch. He listened to it come down and thought about the creek bridge. Most likely the beaver dam upstream had given way, and if he wanted to get back across that bridge in the truck, he'd have to make his move soon. Obviously Katherine wasn't going to let him go without her. He wasn't crazy about the idea of leaving her, either, although he thought she'd be safe enough, especially if he showed her how to fire his gun to scare off Sadie if she showed up.

But he doubted she'd agree to that procedure, and there was no way he could force her to stay behind. He decided to wait an hour. If the phone wasn't working by then, he'd suggest they drive the truck on the flat tire, get back on the main road and look for the nearest phone.

"Zeke?"

"Yeah?" He kept working on the sandwiches instead of turning around. The busier he kept himself, the better.

"I understand that you want to give up all your rights to Amanda and have no more contact with us, but I was wondering if...if you'd mind her knowing something about you."

A warning flashed in his brain. "Such as?"

"Well, that you love the outdoors, and you're part Sioux. Things like that."

The concept of Amanda being curious about her father hadn't even occurred to him. He'd been so focused on getting mother and baby out of his life that he'd forgotten Amanda wouldn't always be a baby. And kids wanted to know about their parents. He still wondered about his father and had done some fruitless research trying to find out who he was and what had happened to him.

"I could disguise the information so she wouldn't be able to track you down," Katherine said, "if that's what you're worried about."

He picked up the two sandwich plates and walked over to the table where she sat holding the baby. "Yeah, that's what I'm worried about." He also wondered how a grown-up Amanda would take the news that he hadn't wanted to have anything to do with her. Damn, but this was getting dicey.

"I think it would be better to give her some information rather than make you a big question mark," Katherine said.

"Maybe." He set down the sandwiches. "I made coffee, but I guess you can't have that. I suppose beer's out, too. I have orange juice and—"

"Actually, a beer would be fine. I have one once in a while when I'm afraid stress might have decreased my flow of milk."

His glance went immediately to her full breasts underneath the gauzy material of her green blouse. Fortunately he had the presence of mind to quickly look up again. He couldn't be caught staring at her. "I'll get you a beer." He walked over to the refrigerator and tried to ignore his memory's instant replay of Katherine poised above him, her breasts quivering with each upward thrust he made.

By the time he returned to the table with a foaming glass of beer in one hand and his mug of coffee in the other, he'd calmed himself.

"Thank you." She gave him a brief smile.

He realized that her smiles were in short supply this trip, too. He'd been proud of himself when he'd made her smile the first time after fishing her out of the river. She'd been so damned scared that she hadn't been able to stop shaking. He'd asked her country-bumpkin questions about life in the big city until at long last he'd coaxed her into smiling a little. That was the first moment he'd realized that he wanted more than a smile from her.

He'd never in a million years have guessed that such a moment could lead him to this. Silently he gazed at Katherine as she sat across the table from him. She'd taken Amanda out of the sling, and now she tucked the baby in the crook of her arm as she sipped her beer. A bit of foam clung to her upper lip and she licked it away with her tongue. An arrow of desire shot straight to Zeke's groin. He'd have to get her out of here soon.

He took a bracing drink of his coffee and realized how much he'd hate to give up coffee if he were in her shoes. A mother's self-sacrificing behavior held a certain fascination for him, probably because he hadn't experienced any from his own mother. At least none he knew of. At Lost Springs they'd tried to convince him that his mother had been self-sacrificing when she'd left him at the ranch. It hadn't felt that way then, and it still didn't.

"So what would you like me to tell Amanda about you?" Katherine asked.

He picked up his sandwich. "Persistent, aren't we?"

"I figure I won't get another shot at this."

He paused, his sandwich halfway to his mouth. "Tell her I was a selfish son-of-a-gun who wasn't cut out to be a father." He bit into the sandwich.

"I'd like to tell her that you saved my life."

He glanced up.

"Without you I wouldn't be here now," she said quietly. "And neither would she. And I don't want to deliberately lie to her. You're not selfish."

He chewed and swallowed. "Sure I am. If I weren't, I'd want some sort of joint custody."

She gazed at him. "I don't believe that you're denying yourself that out of selfishness. I think..." Her voice trailed off as her expression softened.

He didn't want to ask what she was thinking when she looked like that. He'd seen that expression before, and he was no match for it. "You'd better eat that sandwich," he said a little too gruffly. "Keep up your strength."

Almost like an obedient child she picked up the sandwich, but having only the use of one hand, she fumbled with it. Some of the filling spilled out as she tried to maneuver it to her mouth.

She obviously needed some help so she could eat properly, but Zeke didn't want to volunteer to hold Amanda. Funny things happened to his insides whenever he ended up touching that baby. "Would you like me to get her seat out of the truck?" he asked.

Katherine glanced outside where the rain cascaded off the front porch roof in a continuous waterfall. "No sense in going back out in that until it lets up. But I could put her on your bed, if you wouldn't mind."

"She won't roll off?"

"She can't roll yet." Katherine pushed back her chair and stood, holding Amanda in both arms.

"Today might be her day to start."

"Not likely. I'll put her blanket and changing pad on your bedspread to protect it."

"I'm not worried about that. I just think it's dangerous to leave her there with no rails on the bed or anything." Zeke surveyed his little cabin for a better solution. "Hang on a minute. I think I have just the thing." He walked over to the fireplace and took the kindling out of an oval copper kettle he'd bought at a garage sale. He turned the kettle upside down and tapped it to get any scraps out, then crossed to the bed and took the spread off. Folding it, he tucked it into the kettle, letting the excess spill out and pad the sides.

Feeling proud of himself, he set it down next to the table. "How's that?"

"That's..." She looked at him and her eyes started to fill. She quickly averted her face.

He was crushed. "Okay. Stupid idea. Of course you don't want to put her in an old kindling kettle. I don't know what I was thinking." He stooped down to pull the bedspread back out.

"No, stop!" She sniffed and wiped at her cheeks with her free hand. "It's a perfect idea. I love it."

He stared at her, completely at sea. "Then why are you crying?"

"Because..." She swallowed. "Because, when you put that bassinet together, it was almost as if...well, you were acting like a f-father. And I didn't realize how m-much I wanted you to...oh, forget it." She choked back a sob and crouched down to lay Amanda in the makeshift bed.

Zeke stood there, hands clenched at his sides as he fought the urge to take her in his arms and tell her he'd do whatever she needed him to. He wanted to promise that he'd do his best to shield her and the baby from whatever disasters came their way, that he'd be the anchor she so desperately seemed to want.

But he'd be making empty promises. He couldn't follow her to New York and live in her world in order to keep those promises, and he doubted she wanted him to. He wasn't the sort of warm, easygoing man that women liked to have around on a regular basis, and Katherine had proved that by leaving last summer. So he said nothing and returned to take his seat at the table.

She fussed with Amanda for quite a while, and he figured she was getting herself under control. She'd had a hard time the past few months, he was sure. She'd said the pregnancy hadn't been easy, and from what he'd heard childbirth was no picnic, either, especially when you had to face it alone. He probably didn't want to know what she'd been through bringing Amanda into the world. He'd only have the urge to make it up to her.

"There." She sat down at the table again, clear-eyed. "Shouldn't you try the phone again?"

"Yep." He got up and went over to pick up the receiver. "It's still out."

"Oh, well." She'd adopted a breezy air. "I'm sure it'll be connected soon, and then we can get out of your hair." She started on her sandwich.

"I'm sure you'll be glad to get back to New York. You must be good at your job if Naomi Rutledge wants you to take over the whole magazine." Talking about her work felt safe—it reminded him of the distance between their very different worlds.

She swallowed a bite of tuna. "She blew me away with that news. Sure, we get along well, and she's been super through this pregnancy, but I never in the world imagined she wanted me to be her replacement."

"Sounds like a lot of responsibility." He'd hate being tied down like that.

"It is." She took another sip of her beer. "And I'm sort of scared, but the time I spent in Yellowstone last year has given me more confidence in myself." She glanced at him. "Up until I fell into the river, at any rate. That was pretty inept. But before that I'd been alone for almost two days and I really had time to think and evaluate my strengths and weaknesses honestly. I decided I was more capable than I gave myself credit for."

He shoved away his empty sandwich plate. "Time alone can be a good thing."

"I would expect you to think so. I don't hunger for that kind of isolation all the time, but I learned a lot during that trip."

Maybe that had been why she'd made love to him so eagerly, he thought. Feeling self-sufficient in the wilderness could give someone a real high. Add to that the adrenaline rush of nearly dying, and it was no wonder she'd wanted the earthy physical release sex could bring. It probably had nothing to do with him. Any reasonably decent guy would have served the purpose.

"I didn't know you were raised on a boys' ranch," she said.

He grew uneasy. "That's something you probably shouldn't tell Amanda. She could trace me in no time if she knew to start at Lost Springs."

She finished her sandwich and picked up her glass of beer. "You honestly don't think you'll ever want to see her? Not even when she's an adult and wouldn't require any caretaking?"

He picked up their plates and carried them over to the sink. "Look, Katherine, I don't know the first thing about being a father. I never knew my own. The Duncans, the people who ran Lost Springs when I was there, were wonderful to all of us, but it wasn't the same as having your very own father and mother who had all your baby pictures and remembered when you said your first word and got your first tooth." He rinsed the plates. "I wouldn't have the foggiest idea how to treat a daughter, but you obviously do, so the best thing is for you to handle this alone."

"I guess you can't be any plainer than that."

He dried his hands on a towel hanging by the sink and turned back to her. "I'm trying to be as honest as I can, both with myself and with you."

Her smile was tremulous. "Same here."

"Then I guess we understand each other."

"I understand." She blinked, but there were no tears this time. Then she glanced down at the kettle where Amanda lay. "And I'll figure out some way to make her understand, too."

It was a sucker punch, and he felt it down to his toes. Amanda lay cradled by the green bedspread, fast asleep. As a kid he'd raised dozens of baby animals whose mothers were killed by predators or on the highway. As a ranger he was still doing it. Yet in all that time of nursing young wildlife, he'd never seen any creature look more vulnerable and in need of care than this tiny baby. And he was turning his back on her.

5

Sitting in a cool cabin in damp clothes gave Katherine goose bumps now that she didn't have Amanda to keep her warm. At least that's what she told herself. It couldn't be nerves, or the fact that without the baby in her arms, she began wondering what it would be like to hold Zeke again.

She looked for a thermostat on the wall and found none. She guessed that the fireplace provided the cabin's only heat, and she couldn't ask Zeke to build a fire when they could be leaving at any moment.

Picking up her beer glass, she left the table and moved around the cabin. She pretended to be interested in what she found, when her true motivation was to get rid of her jittery chilled feeling. She touched the log walls. "Did you peel the bark off yourself, or did you have some help?" She was pretty sure of the answer, but it seemed like a safe topic and she didn't like the sound of silence. She became far too aware of his body when they both stopped talking.

"I did it myself."

Of course he had. The original Lone Ranger. He might as well wear a black mask over his eyes and ride a horse named Silver. But even the Lone Ranger had Tonto. "So none of your friends from Lost Springs came over to help?"

"I invited them after I was finished."

"Oh." She gazed at the fireplace with its thick plank serving as a mantel. Something was carved into the front edge. She looked closer and saw that it was a tiny pine tree, all by itself. So Zeke had a brand, of sorts. The more she studied it, the more the carving irritated her. What right did he have to declare himself an island, especially when fate had given him a child?

And why was she being so noble about the whole thing and quietly accepting his decision to reject fatherhood completely? Naomi might think that was the best course of action, but Katherine would be the one trying to explain to Amanda that her father wanted nothing to do with her because he was a lone wolf with no ties and intended to keep it that way.

She turned toward the kitchen area, where he was straightening things up after their lunch. "I've changed my mind about something."

"Oh?" He hung the towel up and walked over to the table, but instead of sitting down, he placed both hands on the chair back, as if he needed to grip something while he heard what she had to say.

And he probably did, she thought. She had a tight hold on the beer glass herself. "I told you at the lodge that I didn't come here to get any money from you, and that's what I'd decided because I pretty much blamed myself for this pregnancy." She squared her shoulders. "But I'm not to blame. I took precautions. They just didn't work. So it's silly of me to shoulder all the financial responsibility. And besides that, if you send something every month, that will at least let Amanda know you care about her in some fashion."

He frowned. "I'll send it, but I wouldn't do it so she'd know I was thinking of her. In fact, I'd rather she didn't know where the money came from."

"Sorry." Katherine warmed to the fight. "You're overruled. And I'll tell you why. You just said yourself that not having your mother and father around when you were growing up left you unable to relate to a child. I don't want Amanda to have that problem. I want her to know that she has a father, and although he's emotionally unable to connect with her, he at least gives of himself in the form of a check every month."

He looked like a cornered animal as his dark eyes blazed. "And I suppose you'd encourage her to write to me, and eventually you'd suggest that she come here for a visit."

"Absolutely not! Do you think I'd take a chance with her fragile young ego? I wouldn't want her to get here and be brutally rejected."

"I wouldn't—"

"Wouldn't you? Every single time I've tried to bring the two of you together, you've acted as if she has some contagious disease."

"But she's a baby!" he bellowed. "I've never been around babies! I don't know anything about them. I might accidentally hurt her. Or worse!"

Amanda began to cry.

Katherine glared at him and crossed the room to pick up the baby. "You certainly know how to scare her to death."

"I didn't mean to be so loud, okay?" He stalked over to the telephone. "This just proves my point. The less she knows about me, the better. I'll only create problems for her." He picked up the receiver and put it to his ear. "Damn it to hell." He started to slam the receiver into its cradle but caught himself and replaced it carefully.

Katherine swayed gently and kissed Amanda's cheek until her crying gradually subsided. "There, there,

Mandy. It's all right." She glanced over at Zeke, who reminded her of a large caged animal as he paced back and forth in front of the window. Water still poured from the eaves. "We could be stuck here quite a while, couldn't we?" Her belligerent mood hadn't eased any.

"No." His pacing ceased. "If you'll get her ready to travel, we'll head out."

"Head out? What, you have a couple of mules stashed in a barn out back?" She figured mules would suit his stubborn personality better than horses.

"No." He stared out at the rain. "We'll just drive on the rim."

"And ruin it."

"I don't give a damn if we do."

Katherine didn't much give a damn about his precious tire rim, either. But she didn't want to get stuck out there. "Is that a safe idea?"

He rounded on her. "Yes." His voice was carefully controlled, his gaze intense. "I may be *emotionally unable to connect* with that kid, as you said, but I would give my life to keep her from harm."

She caught her breath at the power in that statement. She had no doubt that he meant it, either. He might be a difficult man to get close to, but without hesitating, he'd put his life on the line for those smaller and weaker than he. She'd always suspected that if she'd missed the branch he'd held out for her that day, he would have dove into the water after her. Either he would have saved her or they both would have drowned, but he wouldn't have stood there watching her die.

And she still owed him for that. The anger drained out of her. "Zeke, I probably came on too strong about the money thing."

"I've always said I'd be willing to pay. I just don't want you building that into something more."

"Okay. I won't make it into something more."

"How soon can you be ready to leave?"

"I should probably feed her first, just in case it takes longer than we think it might."

"Fine. Let me know when you're ready to go." He opened the front door, letting in the scent of damp earth, and went outside on the porch as if he couldn't bear to be closed in the same little space with her for a minute longer.

ZEKE LONGED FOR A HORIZON to look at, but the forest was shrouded in gray and he couldn't see much beyond the clearing. He took a deep breath, drawing in the dank, loamy air. The chill felt good on his face. He didn't like the picture Katherine was painting of him, as if he were some weird recluse who couldn't relate to anyone.

It wasn't like that. He had friends. He interacted just fine with tourists at the park. But he had grave misgivings about ever being somebody's husband, and he sure as hell wasn't equipped to be somebody's father, especially if that person happened to be a tiny little girl.

He'd never been tiny. At three he'd looked six. He could still hear his mother telling him that he was too big, that he ate too much, that he was too loud. Apparently he'd been missing whatever a kid needed to make him lovable, or she wouldn't have dumped him off at the ranch. At least there in the midst of a gang of boys, his size had been a plus. He could watch over the smaller kids.

Women still made him feel awkward, though, like a bull in a china shop—except for the night he'd spent with Katherine. On his own turf, with the immensity of the woods surrounding them, he'd felt in tune with a woman for the first time in his life, and he'd allowed himself to hope that maybe he wouldn't live his life alone. Of course he'd been wrong.

And now this—having a daughter thrust at him with no mental preparation, and then being expected to say and do the right thing on selected holidays and summer vacations, all by himself with no woman to guide him... He couldn't deal with that.

Then there was the other problem. He was still attracted to Katherine. He could feel that attraction growing like a seedling reaching for the sun. She probably thought he'd escaped to the front porch because he was angry with her. In fact he was angry with himself for shouting and waking the baby, but he'd left the room because he wasn't sure what he'd do if he stayed while she unbuttoned her blouse again to feed Amanda.

He'd bought a couple of Adirondack chairs for the porch this summer, and he sat down in one while he waited for Katherine to finish getting the baby ready. For the first time he wondered why he'd bought two chairs. He'd ordered them from a catalog, and the order for two had been automatic in his mind. It just looked right to him, and yet he'd never brought a woman to the cabin until now, and when the guys from Lost Springs came out for the annual fishing trip, two chairs wouldn't be enough.

He shook his head and muttered a swearword under his breath. Katherine really had him going, making him question every damn thing about his life, including how many chairs he'd bought for the front porch. The sooner he got her and the baby back to the lodge, the better. Maybe he'd leave his truck there and rent a Jeep so he could head for some remote place and camp for a couple of days. Yeah, that's what he'd do. Some time alone would clear away the cobwebs.

The front door opened and Katherine came out carrying Amanda in the sling with the diaper bag over one arm. "We're ready."

He stood immediately. "Let me get the slicker." He managed to move past her without touching her and went inside to discover the cabin still held the scent of her perfume. He'd definitely have to go camping and let the place air out. Otherwise this reminder of her would probably keep him awake and fully aroused all night.

After grabbing the slicker, he went back out. "Give me the diaper bag and you can have the slicker," he said.

"What about you?"

A cold shower was exactly what he needed, he thought. "I'll just move fast." He handed her the raincoat and took the diaper bag. "Let's go."

She held the slicker over her head and started down the porch steps. He followed close behind. On the bottom step her foot slipped out from under her on the wet wood and she started to go down.

His brain froze with fear, but his body reacted, grabbing at her arm and hauling her back against him, baby and all. She lost her grip on the slicker and it fell to the mud below. The weight threw him slightly off balance and he staggered but managed to stay upright as rain pelted down on them.

Panting, she turned to him, her eyes wide. "I almost—"

He couldn't seem to let go of her. Her mouth was very close, pale and pink and wet with rain. Their bodies fit so that Amanda was pretty well shielded from the downpour, but they were still getting drenched. He barely felt it. "But you didn't fall."

"No. You saved me. Us."

He watched awareness replace panic in her eyes. Her glance drifted to his mouth, then rose again to his eyes. That subtle signal was all he needed. He lowered his head.

She made a soft sound as his lips found hers. He didn't know if she meant it as a welcome or a protest, but he didn't care. Just once. Then he would get her into that truck and back where she belonged, far away from him.

He remembered the shape of her mouth. And he remembered the sweetness, remembered the slight resistance followed by a yielding that made his blood pound in his veins. For one wild moment he considered taking her back inside. Then he forced himself to leave the temptation of her mouth. He lifted his head and looked into her eyes. They were glazed with desire, probably just like his. If he asked her to stay, she might do it. And then what?

"I thought you hated me," she whispered.

"I wish I could."

"Zeke..."

"We'd better go."

She nodded.

After releasing her, he leaned down and picked up the muddy slicker. She started toward the truck, her head down, her arm protecting Amanda as best she could. He tossed the slicker on the porch and followed her.

KATHERINE FOUGHT A NEW wave of desire when Zeke lifted her and Amanda into the truck. She loved the strength that allowed him to lift her to the seat in one smooth motion. That strength had saved her life once, and just now his strong grip had kept her from falling and quite possibly hurting Amanda when she went down.

And yet she'd felt the power in those big hands become the gentle caress of a lover. She'd never been touched with such tenderness as she had the night she'd spent in his tent. She doubted she'd ever be touched that way again, and she yearned for it so much that she was trembling. His mouth on hers had awakened her body instantly. She felt pliable, moistened...ready.

He'd had to slam the door again but Amanda seemed used to the noise and didn't start to cry. Katherine was thankful she had a baby to care for right now, a task to distract her from Zeke. Removing Amanda's wet terry outfit and replacing it with a dry one from the diaper bag kept her occupied as Zeke hurried around the truck and climbed in beside her.

"I have to slam this door, too," he said.

"Go ahead. She seems to be adapting." Katherine kept her attention focused on Amanda, who had picked this moment to become squirmy and vocal. While Katherine peeled the damp material away from her chubby body, she waved her hands and legs and made little crowing noises. When Zeke slammed the door, she jerked in response but didn't cry.

Zeke started the engine.

"Don't leave yet." Katherine spoke above the drumming of the rain on the metal roof of the cab. "I don't have her in the carrier."

"I know. I'm just getting the engine warmed up so I can turn on the heater. I don't want her to catch cold."

Katherine's hands stilled as she finally understood. He wasn't rejecting Amanda because he cared too little. He was rejecting her because he cared too much. He considered himself such an unfit father that Amanda was better

off with nobody than taking a chance with him. The realization made her ache with regret for him and for
Amanda. With this sort of beginning they'd probably
never find each other.

Zeke turned the heater fan on low and tested the flow
of air with his hand. "That's better. Are you about finished?"

"Yes." She quickly finished tucking the baby into her
dry sleeper and snapped it up. "Can you take her—"

"Yeah, just a minute. Let me dry off as best I can first."

She waited while he rolled back his sleeves and took a
clean bandanna from his hip pocket to wipe his damp
hands and arms. Such big hands, such muscled arms. She
remembered that the decision to make love had come before they'd entered the tent together, so that when he'd
crawled in through the flap, he'd already stripped down
to nothing. His massive body and bronzed skin had fascinated her, and she'd spent a long time just kissing
him...all over.

"Okay, I can hold her now."

Katherine gave Zeke the baby without making eye
contact with him. Then she turned around in the seat.
The nubby upholstery was soggy from her rain-drenched
clothes. "I'm getting your seat all wet," she said.

"It'll dry."

Amanda continued with her little experimental noises,
crowing and gurgling in Zeke's arms, while Katherine
positioned the straps on the carrier. Then Katherine
heard a deep, male sound that sounded a little like
"boo." Amanda gurgled some more, and Katherine
heard a soft chuckle followed by another "boo." She was
afraid to move. Zeke was playing with Amanda.

"She has a little dimple in her chin," Zeke said.

"Yes." Katherine cleared the huskiness from her

throat. "Yes, she does. I'm not sure where she got it. Nobody in my family—"

"My mother had one."

She glanced over at him, but he was engrossed in Amanda and didn't notice her gaze. Her heart squeezed as she thought of what it must have been like for him—a small boy abandoned by his parents. She'd like him to tell her about it, but coaxing him to talk about that part of his life would take more time and trust than he was willing to give her.

"I'll take her now," she said.

He handed her the baby with great care, but she could tell he was already feeling more comfortable holding that tiny body. Katherine settled Amanda in the carrier and strapped her in tight. "Hang on, Mandy," she said. "We have a bumpy ride ahead."

"She'll probably just go to sleep," Zeke said.

"Probably." Katherine noticed the casual way he said it, as if he were already becoming somewhat of an expert on Amanda's habits. As she buckled her seat belt she wondered if he was aware that he was beginning, just a little, to behave like a parent.

"Ready?" He glanced over at her, his expression carefully neutral. But with a sharp intake of breath, his expression changed. He stared at her breasts and swore softly.

She looked down to discover that the rain had made the material of her blouse nearly transparent, and the cold had tightened her nipples under the lacy nursing bra. With the seat belt secured between her breasts, she was on display. She quickly crossed her arms over her chest. "Sorry."

Zeke swallowed and turned his attention to backing the truck around, but between his heavy breathing and hers, the windows were fogging up. Silently he switched on the defroster.

6

THE TRUCK HANDLED LIKE the tank Zeke had driven in the Persian Gulf War. That seemed appropriate, although he'd been in physical danger then, and he was in emotional danger now. Of the two, he'd been better prepared to deal with the war than this situation with Katherine. It was a damned good thing he'd decided to drive her back to civilization instead of waiting for the phone to be reconnected. Much more contact and he could predict what would happen.

Muscling the lame truck along the muddy road took all his concentration. He tried not to think about what he was doing to it in the process. Katherine sat silently beside him as they jolted along. He worked to make the ride as smooth as possible for Amanda's sake, but the baby didn't let out a peep, so she must have dropped right off to sleep.

The skies were producing a world-class rain, but it was a quiet storm with no thunder and lightning. He was grateful for that. Lightning was a ranger's nightmare, even in a wet forest.

This particular forest was mighty wet. The wipers cleared a fan of windshield glass only to have the rain obscure it again. Zeke leaned forward, watching for the first sight of the creek and the bridge. Once they made it over the bridge, he'd breathe a lot easier. If they made it past the creek, he could guarantee that he'd be free of her, and then he could start reconstructing his world.

Except it looked as if he wouldn't get over the bridge. Zeke stepped on the brake and leaned heavily against the steering wheel.

"Oh, no." Katherine put her hand over her mouth.

Quietly he surveyed the swollen creek. The bridge had been ripped in half.

Katherine turned to him, her eyes wide.

He deliberately masked his despair, afraid she might misunderstand and think he was worried about their survival. He wasn't. The cabin would shelter them for as long as necessary. But the cabin wouldn't protect them from each other. "Guess we turn around," he said.

"And wait for the phone to be fixed?"

"Well, the phone is only part of our answer now. Even a tow truck couldn't get across that creek the way it is. The only way anybody could get in here today would be with a helicopter."

"So we have to wait for the creek to go down?"

"Yep. At least enough that a four-wheel drive can get through." He put the truck in reverse and searched for the best place to back it around, but the shoulders of the road looked very unstable.

"How long could that take?"

"Hard to say. Depends on how much more rain we get." He eased the truck back slowly, cranking the wheel as far as he could. The flat tire didn't help.

"Well." Katherine took a deep breath. "I was prepared for a few hours away from the lodge with Amanda, not a couple of days."

He figured Amanda would be the least of their problems. Her food supply was always available, and she didn't do anything but eat and sleep. Oh, God. Maybe she had some condition that required medicine every so often. He'd never even thought to ask. "What are you missing?"

"If we end up being here overnight, Amanda's going to run out of disposable diapers."

Maybe it was only his relief that the baby wasn't sick, but that struck Zeke as funny. He started to laugh.

Katherine got a haughty look on her face. "I'm glad you're amused. As a man who's never changed a baby's diaper, you can't be expected to understand the problem, I suppose."

"Disposable diapers," he said, still chuckling. "If that's the biggest problem we have in the next couple of days, we'll be doing great."

"Easy for you to say. You've never—"

"I'll make you a promise. If Amanda runs out of disposable diapers, I'll figure out a solution. Now, look over on your side of the truck and tell me what's happening with the right rear wheel. I'd like to back the truck up another foot or so if the area looks solid enough."

She turned in her seat. "I can't see real well, but I think it's okay. Start going slowly, and I'll tell you if it looks like it's starting to sink."

"Okay." He took his foot off the brake and gently pressed down on the gas. "How's—"

Her sharp cry of alarm made him jump. In his agitation he hit the gas instead of the brake, and the whine of a spinning tire told him they'd just slid hub-deep into the mud. He slumped back against the seat. Terrific.

"Zeke."

At the controlled terror in her voice he turned in surprise. This was inconvenient, but not the end of the world. Then he saw the bear peering in the window. "Sit still," he said.

Her face was chalky as she stared straight ahead, not looking at him or the bear. "I want to get Amanda up here with us."

"Don't. Chances are she'll go away if we don't do anything to interest her."

"H-how do you know it's a girl f-from just her face?"

"Because I know that face. Sadie has a den around here someplace, although I haven't found it yet. But I've seen her with her cubs."

"So she's the one who's...been on your porch?"

"Yep."

"Does Sadie look hungry to you?"

"Just curious. Take it easy, Katherine. I won't let anything happen to Amanda."

"I've heard that bears can rip open cars as if they were tin cans."

"They have to be motivated. We don't have anything in here she wants."

"Except a baby!"

"She'd rather have candy. If you had a handful of chocolate, I might be worried. Now, turn your head slowly and look at me."

When she did, he gave her a reassuring smile. "You're safe, Katherine. So's Amanda. I promise." He didn't tell her why he could be so sure. If they had a real problem with Sadie, which he doubted, then he'd offer himself as a distraction while Katherine took Amanda to safety. It was a drastic solution and he didn't expect to have to use it, but it was a guarantee that mother and baby would survive.

He eased his hand across the space between the seats and took hold of hers. Her fingers were icy. He held her hand, moving his thumb up and down her cold fingers.

"Trust me," he said. "This is my territory, and I don't allow my guests to be eaten by the bears."

"But we're sitting ducks, stuck in the mud like this, and even if we weren't, we couldn't outrun her with this flat tire."

"She'll go away eventually, and when she does, I'll dig us out of the muck."

She clutched his hand. "I don't want you to go out there, even if she leaves. She could come back."

"We can't sit in this truck forever." He liked having her hold tightly to his hand. He liked it so much he almost hated to tell her that Sadie was lumbering off into the mist and he had to go dig them out as promised. "Sadie's gone," he said. "And I'm going to see about the back tire."

She clutched his hand tighter. "Wait." After she turned slowly to look out the window, she sank back against the seat with a huge sigh, but she didn't let go of his hand. "I love the wilderness, but I have to admit I'm petrified of bears. When I was a little kid, a man in our neighborhood took a trip out west. He was killed by a bear. I overheard the grown-ups talking about it, and the details were seared into my seven-year-old brain."

He stroked the back of her hand with his thumb. He remembered how much he'd loved the texture of her skin and how much fun he'd had exploring every inch of it. "So why did you decide to hike through Yellowstone last summer? You must have known there would be bears in the park."

"That was part of it, testing my courage. Then when no bears showed up the first day, I relaxed and decided there weren't any around the area where I was. Of course I was wrong. And when that bear arrived, I was just as scared as I had been at seven. I hadn't conquered anything."

"That wasn't a fair test. When a wild creature shows up all of a sudden, most people are startled, if not downright frightened. Don't be so hard on yourself."

She turned her head to gaze at him. "It's just that I needed to succeed right then. I needed a chance to feel worthy. Instead I fell into the river, and caused...all sorts of problems."

Indeed she had. But for a few wonderful hours, she'd found that sense of worthiness in his arms. He was sure of that much, just as he was sure the feeling hadn't been enough to keep her there. And now she would go on seeking fulfillment in other parts of her life, with her child and her promotion at work. And he would try to forget her.

It wouldn't be easy. Right now her eyes looked the way they had when he'd decided to make love to her— the look that reminded him of a mountain streambed. He could sit here and stare into her eyes for hours.

"I didn't mean to hurt you," she murmured.

"I know." He squeezed her hand and released it. "I'm going to dig us out of here." Opening his door, he checked the footing before he climbed down.

"I'll help."

He looked around and she already had her door open. Considering how frightened she'd been a moment ago, he was stunned by her courage. But he didn't want her out there in case Sadie did come back. He couldn't predict exactly how the bear would react, no matter how matter-of-fact he'd been with Katherine. "Uh, actually I need you to sit in the driver's seat ready to gun the motor when I get us freed up."

"But—"

"There's only one shovel." He patted the wet seat where he'd just been. "Come on over here and get set. When I tell you, step down hard on the gas and keep the front wheels turned to the left. It won't be easy."

"I can do it." She closed the passenger door, startling Amanda awake. The baby began to whimper. Turning around toward the back seat, she started to comfort the baby with some soothing words and gentle pats.

"On second thought, never mind about driving us out," Zeke said. "You have your hands full. I'll—"

"Go dig," she said. "I'll handle things in here. If necessary, Amanda can cry for a little while. It won't kill her."

"You'd let her cry?"

"If I know nothing is majorly wrong with her, sure. Now, go dig. We're wasting time."

Spoken like a New York businesswoman, Zeke thought. He started to ask her if she had an appointment to get to. Instead he closed the door and slopped through the mud to the back end of the truck where he kept some tools in a metal box. Sure, they had to get back to the cabin eventually, but if it took them all afternoon, it didn't matter anymore. They might as well resign themselves to being marooned. But then, he was used to dealing with nature's whims and she wasn't. She was probably chafing under the restraint and thinking ahead to the problems this situation might cause at her office if it lasted through Monday.

The tire had sunk deep and the digging was hard work, but Zeke welcomed the labor. Big-muscle movement calmed him as it had always done. Once he'd hollowed out a trench in front of the tire, he collected rocks to line it. Finally he decided the job was about as good as he could manage. Walking behind the truck to get another vantage point, he called out to Katherine, figuring it would take her a while to stop fussing with the baby and get organized to drive the truck out.

The engine roared immediately, and before Zeke could jump out of the way, a geyser of mud coated him from head to toe. He swiped a hand over his face and spit the dirt from his mouth. That would teach him to underestimate her efficiency. At least the tire was free.

He replaced the tools in the back of the truck and used his bandanna to clean off some of the grime as he returned to the driver's side of the cab.

She was still in the driver's seat, and when she caught sight of him she jumped and her mouth formed a round O of surprise. She quickly rolled down the window. "What happened?"

"Well, I didn't get out of the way fast enough." He noticed Amanda wasn't crying anymore. Katherine was a whiz of a mother, all right.

"Oh, my." Her eyes began to twinkle and she pressed her lips together. "You look like you belong in a minstrel show."

"I'll bet I do. Care to scoot over now so I can drive us out of here and back to the cabin?"

"I'm here now. Why don't I just drive?"

"It's hard to handle with that flat."

"I can do it."

He recognized her need to be in control of something, even if it was only his balky old truck. No creature liked the feeling of being trapped, with no power. He shrugged. "Okay." He walked around and got into the passenger seat. "Go for it."

"I may not have a car in New York, but I know how to drive."

"I believe you." He gestured down the road.

With one last glance at him, she pressed her foot slowly on the gas. The truck moved forward, back on to the road, but the steering wheel jerked out of her grip. She grabbed it again, her jaw set. "I've got it."

"I see that you do." He made himself relax against the seat and gaze out the passenger window, although he flinched every time the truck lurched, knowing the strength it took to hold it steady on the road. Once he glanced over and saw a trickle of sweat roll down her temple, but he knew she wouldn't ask him to take over.

As she fought the truck and guided them down the road toward the cabin, he wondered what the labor room scene had been like. He'd heard that first babies could be the hardest to deliver. The idea of her delicate body wrenched with the pain of childbirth made him woozy, but he was sure she'd handled it like a trouper.

"Did you have any drugs?" He hadn't meant to ask the question out loud.

"Excuse me?" She gave him a quick, worried look.

"When you had Amanda. Did you take anything for the pain?"

"No. It's better for the baby if you don't, and I still think it was for the best, but partway into it I was ready for them to give me something. Turns out it was too late." The steering wheel jerked in her hands and she tightened her hold. "There's a window of opportunity when you can give the mother a painkiller, but I'd passed that window and had to tough it out. I'm glad now that I did, but at the time it was a little rough."

He hated thinking of her going through that. "Was anyone with you? Besides the hospital staff, I mean."

"Naomi."

"You should have called me, Katherine."

"I—" She fought the wheel as the truck forged over another rut in the world. "The truth is, I didn't know you well enough."

He smiled grimly. He'd imagined that he'd opened up his soul to her that night, that he'd allowed her to know him as nobody else ever had. Maybe he hadn't told her all the details of his life, but he'd loved her without holding anything back. He'd never lost himself so completely in a woman, but then, he hadn't told her so. And he certainly couldn't tell her now.

THE TRUCK WAS A BEAST, and wrestling with it gave Katherine great satisfaction. Her shoulders ached, but she was working out a lot of her frustrations, both physical and mental.

"Big rut up ahead," Zeke warned.

"Right." Katherine steered left, hoping to avoid it altogether, but the front tire caught the edge of the rut. Fearing they'd get stuck again, she gunned the engine. The jolt made her teeth snap together, and a searing pain shot up her right wrist. Tears pricked her eyes but she held on and kept going, determined that she wouldn't wimp out on this task.

"What's wrong?" Zeke asked.

She gritted her teeth as her wrist started to throb. "I'm...fine."

"Don't give me that. Stop the truck."

"No. I'll get us there."

He reached over and turned the key. The truck lurched to a stop. "Okay, what's wrong?"

She leaned her forehead against the steering wheel and fought tears. "Damn it, damn it, damn it! Can't I do one little thing right for a change?"

His arm came around her shoulders in comfort, but his tone was stern. "Tell me what happened, Katherine."

"I think... I might have sprained my wrist when we went over that big rut."

Zeke swore softly. "Which one?"

"My right one, of course! The one I need the most to take care of Amanda! I am the biggest screwup that ever existed!"

His arm tightened around her. "Hey, stop that. If you were the biggest screwup that ever existed, Naomi Rutledge wouldn't be asking you to take over her magazine, would she?"

"She might." Katherine swallowed a sob. "She's my godmother. She probably just feels sorry for me."

"Oh, yeah, I'm sure. The woman I dealt with isn't about to hand over her magazine to a screwup, not even her goddaughter. Now, let's trade places, and I'll get us home. Then we'll see about your wrist."

Katherine lifted her head and gazed at him through watery eyes. "And if I'm incapacitated, who's going to take care of Amanda?"

"I am."

7

ZEKE DROVE THE TRUCK as carefully as he could, knowing every jolt brought Katherine fresh pain. His stomach churned as he thought about her hurting, but he forced himself to stay calm. He had no problem with his own injuries, but when another creature was hurting, human or animal, he was in agony. That trait had eliminated a career in medicine, although in preparation for becoming a ranger, he'd taken some basic emergency training. He also knew from firsthand experience that once he iced her wrist and wrapped it in an elastic bandage, she'd feel better.

Amanda stayed asleep for the rest of the trip, but the rain was coming down as hard as ever by the time they reached the cabin. He opened the driver's side door. "Stay there. I'll help you inside."

"No, you get Amanda inside." She fumbled with the door handle with her left hand. "I can manage."

"Katherine..."

She turned to him, a fierce glow in her eyes. "Get Amanda. It's only my wrist. I can walk just fine."

He'd seen that same glow in the eyes of wild animals protecting their young, and he knew better than to argue. "Okay. But wait and let me help you down." He was out of the truck in seconds and splashing through puddles in his haste to get to her door. Once he opened it he held out his hand. "Let me take a look."

"I'm sure it's nothing." Gingerly she laid her hand in his.

"It's something." He lightly traced his finger over the delicate bone structure of her wrist. The swelling had already started. "Put your other hand on my shoulder," he instructed. "I'll try to lift you down without bumping your wrist. The door's unlocked. Go in and take a bag of peas from the freezer, wrap them in a towel and put that on your wrist until I get there."

"Zeke, I'm sorry. All I seem to do is cause you problems."

"It's my fault as much as yours. I knew the truck would be hard to drive. Now turn toward me so I can get you down from there." When she complied he fit his hands around her waist. He avoided looking into her eyes as he slowly lifted her down, taking care not to jostle her wrist. God, she felt so good, so warm within his grip. Every time he touched her was like coming home. But once her feet were on the ground, he released her immediately. "I'll meet you in there," he said.

"Do you think you can work the strap on the carrier?"

He glanced at her. "Go on. I'll figure out the strap." Once he was convinced she was on her way into the cabin, he turned back to the truck cab. "Somehow."

He climbed into the passenger seat, got to his knees and leaned over into the back seat the way he'd watched Katherine do it. Amanda was awake, waving her arms and chortling as if she found her view of the upholstery fascinating. Zeke studied the situation and figured out how she was belted in.

"Okay, kiddo, let's spring you from that contraption." He managed to unfasten the strap, but Amanda started kicking in excitement and got her legs tangled in it.

"Great. Snafu right off the bat." Zeke worked to free her. "Hold still, now."

She seemed to kick and squirm even more vigorously.

Despite the chill in the air, Zeke began to sweat. He had to get her out of there so he could go inside and take care of Katherine's wrist. And the longer he took, the more worried Katherine would be. Finally his patience snapped. "Hold *still*, Amanda!"

She went rigid, at which point he was able to extricate her from the tangled strap, but as he hauled her into the front seat, she began to cry.

"Oh, hell." He cupped her against his chest and patted her back. "Now, stop. I can't take you in to your mommy while you're crying. She's got enough to worry about."

Amanda cried harder.

Zeke sighed and tried to think how Katherine had handled these situations. Of course if the baby was hungry, she was out of luck, but he didn't think that was the problem. He'd scared her by talking too rough. Maybe he could fix that mistake by trying some of the nonsense talk Katherine used.

He cleared his throat. "Oh, sweet little baby girl," he crooned. "Let's have a smile. Give Daddy a smile. Enough of the waterworks now. We have enough water coming down outside without you adding to it. Easy does it, sweetheart. I'm here, baby girl."

Amazingly, Amanda stopped crying.

"Thank God," Zeke muttered. "Lord knows how long I could have kept that up." Hunching over to shield Amanda from the rain, he climbed from the truck, grabbed the diaper bag and slogged through the mud to the porch.

Katherine was waiting at the top of the steps, shivering

in her wet clothes, a bulky ice pack clutched around her wrist. "I'm afraid I have some bad news."

His heart beat faster. "Do you think your wrist is broken?" He quickly climbed the steps and ducked under the porch roof. "Because if it is, I'm hiking out to the road."

"No, I'm sure it's just a sprain. This is still critical, though. Your electricity seems to be out."

"Oh, is that all?"

"All?" She stared at him. "Lights, refrigeration, hot water?"

He shrugged. "We'll build a fire, light the lanterns and keep the refrigerator door shut as much as possible. No big deal. It'll be like camping."

"Oh."

He gazed down at her and suddenly was reminded of what had happened the last time they'd been in a camping situation together. His breathing quickened. "Or not." The huskiness in his voice probably betrayed his thoughts. "Let's go in and get your wrist taken care of."

KATHERINE DIDN'T WANT to admit how much her wrist hurt, but she took the over-the-counter pain medication Zeke offered without any argument. He'd settled Amanda in her makeshift bassinet, and she seemed to be content to lie there and suck on her fingers.

Zeke washed up at the kitchen sink and then brought a first-aid kit to the table, where Katherine sat resting her arm with the ice pack over it. Zeke pulled his chair close. "Okay, let's take another look." He eased the ice pack away. "Let's make sure it's not broken."

Katherine flinched. "I seem to recall that involves pain."

"Some, but I have to know. If you broke anything I'm

not going to wait around for a tow truck. Breaks can get nasty if they're not taken care of quickly." He cradled her hand in his. "Tell me how this feels." He rotated her hand gently to one side.

She sucked in a breath. "Like you're shoving hot needles into my wrist."

"Good."

"*Good?*"

"Yeah. If your wrist was broken you'd be screaming at me to stop, not telling me how it feels." He laid her hand carefully back on the table and took a rolled elastic bandage out of the first-aid kit. "This won't feel wonderful, either. Try to distract yourself from what I'm doing."

"Yeah, okay." She looked away as he cradled her hand once again and positioned the bandage against her palm. "I notice you don't have a television," she said, wincing as he wound the bandage securely.

"Or a radio," he added. "Which is lucky, because they wouldn't be working now, anyway."

"So how do you spend your time?" They were huddled so close that she became aware of the pattern of his breathing and the subtle scent of his body. Both were saturated with erotic memories.

"I hike."

She glanced out the window. "I guess you won't be doing that today."

"Guess not."

Damn, but it hurt to have him wrap that thing around her wrist. "So how do you spend your evenings?"

"You should know. You spent one with me."

Her head snapped around and she stared at him, but he didn't look up from his task. She wondered if he'd meant that to be as provocative as it sounded. Heat surged through her, and her voice was tight as she struggled to form a response. "I'd imagine that was unusual."

"Thanks a lot."

She'd say this for him, he'd taken her mind off her pain. "No, I mean..." What did she mean? "I didn't mean to imply you don't spend your evenings with women. I'm sure you—"

"Have a girl at every campsite? That's me."

Now that he'd broached the subject, damned if she didn't want to know about the other women in his life and specifically if he'd been involved with anyone since...since last summer. But she didn't know how to ask. "Okay, so you're a wilderness Romeo," she said, trying to sound flip about it. "But what do you do when you're alone?"

"I read. And sometimes I just sit, stare into the fire, and think." He secured the bandage and glanced up at her.

The look in his eyes made her quiver, and she wondered if he was remembering that night by the campfire, how the conversation had grown quieter and quieter, the words further apart.

"I should probably rig up a sling for you," he said. "But first you need to get out of those wet clothes."

Uh-oh. That was exactly how she'd gotten into trouble the last time she'd been with Zeke. "I don't have a change of clothes."

"I'll get you something." He left his chair and walked over to a chest of drawers positioned against the wall at the end of the bed.

Katherine wasn't sure this was a good idea, taking off her clothes and putting on Zeke's. Too much intimacy was implied. Still, she was cold and wet, and when he laid a green flannel shirt, black drawstring sweats and heavy wool socks on the table, they looked invitingly warm and cozy.

Then she realized he was in the same wet condition, and his clothes were spattered with mud, besides. "You should change, too," she said.

"I will, once you and Amanda are all set. You can change in there." He tilted his head toward the bathroom. "Be careful of that arm, though. I'll be happier when it's supported by a sling."

She glanced up at him. "I don't know about the sling, Zeke. It'll be in the way when I nurse Amanda."

"We'll work around it when you're nursing her."

Deep inside, a coil of sexual tension tightened. Apparently he planned to be right there helping her when Amanda nursed. Her injury was knocking down the barriers between them at an alarming rate.

She stood and picked up the pile of clothes lefthanded. "I should probably wash off my feet and ankles before I put on the socks. Will you be okay out here alone with Amanda while I do that?"

"Guess so."

"I'll hurry."

"Don't hurry so much you hurt yourself."

She grimaced. "Right." She headed for the bathroom. Once she closed the door she automatically flicked on the wall switch before remembering the electricity was out. But even in the gloom of a rainy afternoon she noticed the huge claw-foot tub that dominated the room. Decked out with a utilitarian showerhead and curtain, it still looked sinfully luxurious.

As she peeled off her damp clothes and washed up as best she could in the icy tap water, she imagined what a hot bubble bath would be like in that tub. Heaven. She wondered if Zeke ever took a hot bath. Certainly he did.

Otherwise he wouldn't have installed such a thing in his cabin. It was an intriguing picture.

She was about halfway finished when Amanda began to cry. Gritting her teeth, she began working faster.

Then Amanda's crying stopped. She didn't usually stop crying by herself, so either Zeke had picked her up, or something was wrong. Immediately her imagination came up with a dozen possibilities that put Amanda in peril of her life. Zeke wasn't experienced enough to know if she was choking, or had the blanket over her nose, or...

Katherine jerked on Zeke's shirt and sweats, tied them quickly and hurried out the door to find him quietly holding Amanda in his arms.

He glanced up, a tender look in his eyes. Then he looked at Katherine's bare feet. By the time his gaze met hers again, all tenderness had vanished. "Didn't think I could handle it, did you?"

"I..." She paused and grimaced. "No. And I apologize. If you could please hold her a little longer, I'll go put on the socks." She turned back toward the bathroom, berating herself for stepping on Zeke's feelings at the very moment he was beginning to gain confidence around the baby. If she wanted him to form a relationship with Amanda, she'd have to back off and trust him.

ZEKE PACED BACK AND FORTH in front of the window, which worked off some of his frustration and seemed to keep Amanda from crying. But he didn't kid himself that he had any talent in that direction. When Katherine sprained her wrist he'd foolishly announced he'd take care of the baby. Oh, sure. And pigs could fly. Maybe he'd done okay with the smaller boys at the ranch, but he'd never been in charge of anybody this young, or this gender.

Katherine came back out of the bathroom with socks on her feet. "Zeke, I'm really sorry I reacted like that. You obviously had the situation under control."

As if to prove that wasn't true, Amanda began to fuss.

"I don't think so," Zeke said.

"She's probably hungry and needs to be changed." She hesitated. "If you're willing, I could show you how to change her."

He didn't think he had much choice. "Okay." He hoped it wouldn't be any more complicated than changing the oil in his truck. But as he glanced down at the squirming, fussy bundle in his arms, he decided it was probably more like deactivating a bomb.

He held her while Katherine used her good hand to arrange the necessary tools on the table. It all looked completely foreign to him.

"Okay, you can bring her over," Katherine said.

He walked up to the table, where she'd put a padded mat down. She moved aside and gestured toward it.

He started to put Amanda on the mat and paused with her suspended over the table. "Does it matter which end goes north and which end goes south?"

"Yes. Depending on whether you're right-handed or left-handed, her feet should be pointing in that direction."

"I'm left-handed." He turned Amanda carefully around and placed her on the mat with her head pointing right and her feet pointing left.

"You are?" Katherine glanced at him. "I didn't know that."

There was a lot she didn't know about him, he thought. "Left-handed people are supposed to be very creative," she said. "That might be one reason you wanted to build the cabin all by yourself."

"As opposed to the fact that I'm antisocial?"

"I didn't say you were antisocial."

"You came damn close." He noticed Amanda watching him carefully. "Can she pick up swearwords, do you think?"

"You mean store them up for when she can talk?" Katherine smiled. "I don't know."

"I think I'll clean up my language, just in case. Okay, what's next?"

"Keep your right hand on her at all times. She can't roll yet, but I still like to make sure there's no way she can fall. Then just unsnap the legs of her sleeper."

"Right." His fingers seemed too big for the tiny snaps and he fumbled with the task. "Damn, these are tricky," he muttered, then remembered his new resolution. "I mean, *doggone*, these are tricky." He glanced at Amanda, who was staring at him as if he'd landed from another planet. "She's probably wondering if this is going to take all day."

"Actually, I'll bet she's fascinated by seeing a new face during this procedure. She's probably sick of looking at the same lady all the time."

He doubted it, but he appreciated Katherine's attempt to be encouraging. Finally he had Amanda's chubby little legs free. Next came the really dicey part. "Now what?"

"The diaper's held on her with those adhesive tabs. Pull them free and it will come off."

He followed her instructions, while Amanda gurgled at him. At least the baby wasn't screaming in agony, so he must not be doing so bad. Katherine stood very close to him, her shoulder touching his. When she moved he caught a whiff of her perfume. And he still wanted her as much as ever.

"Fold up the wet diaper and give it to me," Katherine said. "I'll throw it away while you start cleaning her up." She started to move away from the table.

"Hold it! I'm not doing this part without supervision."

"Just take the towelette from the container and wipe carefully in all the folds." She walked over to his trash container.

"There's a hell of a lot of folds here. I mean, a *heck* of a lot of folds. What if I'm too rough? What if she decides now's a good time to go again?"

"That's why you have a pad there." She returned to his side, a smile on her face. "At least she can't squirt you in the eye like a little boy might."

"They do that?" In spite of himself, he was fascinated by the habits of these uncivilized little creatures. In some ways they were like the wild animals he related to so well.

"Boys react just like a miniature fire hose, lots of times as soon as you take the diaper off. You have to be on alert the whole time."

"How do you know about this?"

"*Cachet* is very supportive of employees with children. They bring their babies to work, so I've been present at a couple of staff meetings where babies had to be changed before we could go on with the meeting."

"Oh." Although he was happy about the magazine's policy for Amanda's sake, he didn't enjoy being reminded about Katherine's perfect job.

"So, are you going to continue?" She gestured toward Amanda, who was kicking her legs and blowing bubbles.

"Right." He remembered that Katherine had really yanked to get one of the moist towelettes out of the container, so he took an end and pulled hard. About ten came out, all linked together. He had enough length to make a scarf. "Sh—sugar!"

When Katherine started to laugh, he glared at her.

"I'm sorry," she said, sobering immediately. "I guess you don't know your own strength."

"Can you stuff them back in?"

"It's not worth the effort. Just tear off one and throw the rest away."

"Okay. Whoops. We've got leakage."

"Well, now you have a purpose for those extra towelettes."

Once he had the puddle cleaned up, he started cleaning Amanda. He was sure he was doing it all wrong and she'd start crying any minute, but she didn't. In fact, the more he worked on her, the better he felt about doing it.

Katherine cleared her throat. "That's probably good enough." She gave him a clean diaper. "I only have four of these left."

"Then what?"

"Good question. Do you have safety pins around?"

"I don't know." He'd decided he should be able to put the diaper on without asking Katherine how it went, so he studied it for a minute, then studied Amanda.

"Maybe we can use dish towels."

"Maybe." He thought he had it figured out, so he lifted up one of Amanda's legs and shoved the diaper underneath that side. Then he lifted her other leg and pulled it into place. Except now the adhesive tabs wouldn't work unless he put her facedown. So he had the damn thing backward.

Lifting her legs one at a time again, he pulled the diaper out and turned it around. There. In no time he had her taped together and the snaps done up. He turned to Katherine. "How was that?"

Her eyes were warm and sparkly. "That was great. Thank you."

"And she didn't even cry."

"Why should she?"

"Well, because I'm big, and my voice is deeper and I figured I'd scare her."

"But you're gentle and slow with her. She senses you mean well."

"Yeah." He slid one hand under her head and the other one under her bottom as he lifted her off the table. "Animals are like that, too. Even wild ones can sense if you're trying to help them." He settled Amanda into the crook of his arm. He must have smiled at her, because suddenly she grinned back at him and waved her fists in the air.

"Hey, Mandy," he said softly.

She gurgled and waved her fists some more.

His heart swelled as he gazed down at her. She was beautiful. Whether he and Katherine had been wise or foolish when they'd made love didn't matter anymore. They'd produced Amanda, and that was reason enough to bless that night they'd spent together.

He glanced up at Katherine and caught her watching him with a tenderness that took his breath away.

"I knew you'd fall in love with her if you gave yourself a chance," she murmured.

8

ZEKE WAS AFRAID KATHERINE was right, and he was falling in love with Amanda. Not a wise move. She wasn't
his to keep. But then neither were the wild baby animals
he cared for and released when they were old enough to
be on their own. He survived losing them, so he ought to
be able to survive this.

"I should probably feed her," Katherine said, holding
out her arms.

Zeke glanced at her bandaged wrist. "Let me rig up a
sling for you first." He settled Amanda in her bassinet
and she immediately began to cry.

"I'll feed her first," Katherine said.

Zeke hated hearing Amanda cry, but he put a restraining hand on Katherine's shoulder. "You need that sling.
I'll fix it in no time."

She stilled under his hand.

He could feel the current running between them and
took his hand away before his touch became a caress.
"This won't take long." He took a pillowcase from the
dresser and used his pocketknife to rip the sides open.

Katherine gasped. "You're ruining your pillowcase!"

"Doesn't matter." He walked over to her. "Bend your
arm at the elbow."

She did as he asked. "I still don't think you should
have cut open that perfectly good pillowcase."

"You need a sling for your arm more than I need that

pillowcase, and with Amanda needing to be fed, we don't have time to come up with an alternative." Concentrating on keeping the process impersonal, he slid the material under her arm and stepped behind her so he could tie the ends around her neck. But he kept getting her hair caught in the knot. "Could you lift up your hair?"

"Sure." She slid her left hand behind her neck and lifted the hair off her nape.

He hadn't expected the gesture to affect him like a fist to the gut. Yet here he was, struggling to breathe as he gazed at that exposed, tender spot at her nape.

"Zeke?" She half turned toward him. "Is anything wrong?" Then she looked into his eyes. "Oh." Her eyes grew smoky with desire, and her lips parted.

"Turn around," Zeke said roughly. "Let me tie this. Amanda needs you."

Quietly she turned her back on him.

He fastened the tie with shaking fingers and hoped he had the tension right on her arm. His throat was tight with longing. "Go sit in the rocker," he said. "I'll bring her to you."

Her whisper of agreement sent chills of need up his spine.

Resolutely he walked to the bassinet and picked up the crying baby. A few hours ago her crying would have made him anxious, but he was beginning to understand it was her method of communicating. He didn't have to worry that something was terribly wrong every time she fussed a little.

He jiggled her and made faces, which sort of worked. Her crying was reduced to stray croaks of protest. But when he glanced over to see if Katherine was ready for the baby, all his cajoling stopped. Mesmerized, he stared at Katherine, her head bowed, the blond sheen of her hair catching the light from the lantern as she concentrated on the now-difficult job of unbuttoning her shirt. The process was slow, making it all the more erotic. Zeke's body throbbed in response as he watched her finish the task.

She looked up and started to speak. The words seemed to lodge in her throat as she gazed at him. Finally she spoke, her voice strained. "I can't figure out how to manage. Maybe I should take off the sling."

"We'll prop her on a pillow." He had no idea how he knew what to do, but somehow he did. Holding Amanda in the crook of one arm, he took a pillow from the bed and brought it over to her. "Hold your arm away from your body a minute." He knelt beside the rocker and tucked the pillow on her lap, providing a nest for Amanda. Gently he laid her on the pillow, and Amanda immediately starting nuzzling at the flannel material still draped modestly over Katherine's breast.

Katherine steadied her with her left hand, but she obviously had no way to move the flannel aside.

So Zeke did it for her. "Let me," he murmured. He trembled as he cradled the weight of her milk-filled breast. Then he carefully brought it toward Amanda's seeking mouth. When the baby took the nipple greedily, he kept his hand there as long as he dared, absorbing Katherine's warmth and the rapid beat of her heart. Amanda sucked steadily, and Zeke thought it was the sweetest sound he'd ever heard.

He glanced up at Katherine, but her lashes were lowered, as if she couldn't allow him to see the emotions swirling there. He understood. When his own needs became too great, he gently slipped his hand from under her breast, stood and went over to the door.

He had to remain there a minute until his breathing

was under control and he could speak. "Call if you need me," he said finally. Then he went outside.

I NEED YOU. Katherine ached so much she wasn't sure if she could bear it. If Amanda hadn't been in her arms, she would have dragged Zeke over to the bed and demanded that he make love to her with all the vigor she knew he was capable of.

Yet making love to Zeke would be a huge mistake, putting her future in jeopardy. She could feel the danger, even without Naomi there to remind her. Naomi had sent her here to tidy up loose ends, not become more entangled.

The job Naomi expected from her required absolute focus. The two of them had made allowances for Amanda—her early childhood care could be handled right at the magazine. By the time she was in school, Katherine would have adjusted to her new duties and feel free to take part in whatever girlhood activities presented themselves with Amanda. Naomi had even hinted that she might be willing to take over as room mother or Brownie leader if the need arose. Naomi had everything mapped out, taking the demands of motherhood fully into account.

But she had not taken a love affair into consideration. For the first time Katherine wondered if Naomi had lovers. She'd divorced her husband years ago, and she was an extremely attractive woman. Now that Katherine gave herself time to think about it, she suspected Naomi did have love affairs, but obviously she chose appropriate men who would never interfere with her work.

Zeke was highly inappropriate. The passion would be too great, the distance too far, the needs too compelling. Loving Zeke could easily destroy her career. She might even be able to live with that, but she couldn't live with the prospect of sacrificing Naomi's hopes and dreams.

Still, she wanted Zeke to connect with Amanda, and that's exactly what he was doing. Unfortunately, with each step closer to Amanda, he came a step closer to stealing Katherine's heart. She desperately wanted Zeke to keep in touch with their daughter as she was growing up. But that would require her own participation. Somehow she'd have to make that participation friendly yet businesslike. Yeah, right. The task already seemed impossible. If she made love to him again, she might as well not even try.

When the time came to switch Amanda to her other breast, she gritted her teeth and managed by herself. Her wrist hurt whenever she used it, but she couldn't handle a two-month-old baby without using both hands. Naomi wasn't going to be happy about this sprained wrist, either. It would make her less effective at work.

Well, she couldn't do anything about her bum wrist now. What was done was done. But she could do something about Zeke.

He came back into the cabin just as she finished feeding Amanda. He brought in an armload of wood and the cool scent of wet pines. "The rain's stopped," he announced.

Katherine had been so absorbed in her thoughts that she hadn't noticed. "Do you think it's over?"

"Hard to say." He deposited the wood on the hearth and crouched with his back to her as he built a fire. "But even if it is, it'll take a day or so before that creek goes down enough to get a vehicle through."

She couldn't help admiring the flex of those strong shoulders as he worked. "But if the phone line is repaired, we might be able to have someone come out by tomorrow night?"

"It's possible." He stood. "Guess I'll go shower off some of this dirt and then we can think about what to have for supper."

"Okay." One night, Katherine thought to herself as Zeke walked into the bathroom. Surely she could make it through one night without giving in to temptation.

AFTER REMOVING KATHERINE'S underwear from the circular shower rod, Zeke stayed under the cold spray longer than he probably needed to rinse the mud off his body and out of his hair. He swore softly the whole time, using words he hadn't dredged up in years. He cursed unpredictable birth-control pills, the weather, his worthless bridge, flat tires and the fickle finger of fate.

But he couldn't bring himself to curse Katherine. She was as much a victim of this as he was. And she was still eager to escape. No matter that she caught fire instantly the minute he touched her—she longed to be far away from the fire itself. He sighed, knowing he wasn't the kind of guy to take advantage of a woman's weakness.

Turning off the shower, he stepped from the big tub and dried off briskly. He didn't realize until he was finished that he hadn't brought any clean clothes into the bathroom with him. Unfortunately for both of them, he'd have to go back into the main room of the cabin wearing only a towel.

He opened the door and glanced out.

Amanda dozed in Katherine's arms as she rocked back and forth, eyes closed. Maybe he could make it to the dresser and back to the bathroom without her being aware of him. But the continued rain had made the drawers stick. By the time he jerked and fought them open and tucked his pile of clothes under one arm, he glanced over his shoulder and found her watching him.

She cleared her throat. "Under the circumstances, it might be better if you didn't parade around here in a towel."

The unfairness of her implication that he was doing this on purpose irked him. "I live alone. I don't automatically think of protecting my privacy."

"I'd appreciate it if you'd start thinking about it."

"Would you?" He advanced on her. "Katherine, this is my house, and we're in the middle of the woods. Normally I don't even bother with the towel. So you see, I am making concessions."

Her cheeks grew pink.

He gestured toward the bathroom. "And maybe you'd better start thinking about the wisdom of flaunting your underwear in my face."

Her cheeks flamed, but her chin jutted defiantly. "You're the one who suggested I shouldn't sit around in wet clothes. What else was I supposed to do with them?"

He had to admit she had a point. He sighed. "Look, this is a small place. We can't get away from each other unless I pitch my tent out in the yard."

"There's a thought." A flash of humor softened her belligerent expression. "I don't mean that. And you're right, this is your house. It's just that..." Her gaze traveled over his bare chest, and when she looked back into his eyes, the hunger had returned to hers. Her voice was husky. "Please go put on your clothes."

He clamped down on his desire, turned and walked into the bathroom.

KATHERINE HADN'T MEANT to fight with Zeke, but no sooner had she vowed she could make it through one night than he'd appeared in front of her practically naked. She didn't think he'd done it on purpose, but that didn't change the surge of desire she'd had to fend off, was still fending off.

After Zeke returned, fully dressed, he moved around the cabin, taking care of the tasks that needed to be done. He made no conversation, but he made a lot of racket. It sounded like impatient noise to Katherine, and she didn't blame him.

As the watery light of afternoon faded, he lit two kerosene lanterns. Then he stoked up the fire and put on some bigger logs before getting a cast-iron kettle out of the cupboard, which Katherine assumed they'd use to heat dinner over the fire. He seemed pretty well equipped for the loss of electricity, she thought. It must happen often out here.

As she sat and rocked Amanda, lulling her to sleep, she thought of how different her life was from Zeke's. Electricity was essential in her world. It operated the elevators in her twenty-story apartment house, her answering machine, her personal computer, her microwave. Without those conveniences she wouldn't be able to exist comfortably. Without electricity, she wouldn't have any way to heat bathwater for her or Amanda.

And the forest was such a quiet place, at least when Zeke wasn't banging something or other, which he seemed to be doing pretty constantly this evening. Still, even his noise wasn't the same as the noise in her tenth-floor apartment, where traffic on the street below sent up a constant hum that she blocked out, just as she'd learned to block out the sound of doors closing and telephones ringing in other apartments. She lived in a beehive of people, while Zeke lived in almost total isolation.

She'd been so wrong to expect him to respond like a

jaded urban guy when she'd shown up with Amanda. To think that he'd sit and drink coffee while they talked over their options was insane, she now realized. In her world that might have happened. Many men she knew hid their primitive urges under a veneer of civilized behavior. Zeke wasn't quite civilized.

And that was why making love to him had been such a transforming experience. But it would be selfish of her to do that again. Still, she had a hard time resisting Zeke's wildness. When they'd made love last summer, she'd fantasized they were creatures of the forest themselves.

"Is stew okay?" Zeke asked, turning from the cupboard to glance over at her.

"Fine. I like stew." She would have eaten anything he gave her, considering how rotten she felt about putting him in this untenable position.

Yet she had to remember that despite the pain she and Zeke had caused each other, the end result had been Amanda. She gazed down at her child, never tiring of watching her. Despite the clatter Zeke was making in the kitchen, Amanda lay quietly, eyes closed as she sucked gently on her fist. Gradually her body relaxed into sleep and her hand fell away from her rosebud mouth.

She was so perfect, Katherine thought, a lump of emotion lodging in her throat. So helpless, too. Amanda depended on her to make everything turn out right, and she was determined the baby's instinctive faith wouldn't be misplaced. Amanda deserved the best life Katherine could give her, and that's what she'd get.

Gradually Katherine became aware that the cabin was completely silent except for the crackling of the fire. She glanced up, expecting Zeke to have gone out for more wood. Instead he was standing by the fireplace gazing at her and Amanda. The minute Katherine saw him there, he turned and crouched down next to the kettle hanging over the flames and began to stir the contents.

"Is there something I can do?" she asked, pretending she hadn't seen that wrenching expression of longing on his face. "Set the table or something? Amanda's asleep."

He didn't turn. "Napkins and silverware are in the top drawer next to the refrigerator." His voice had a definite huskiness to it.

Oh, God, she should never have come here, Katherine thought. She should have overruled Naomi and sent Zeke a letter, just like he'd said. Then this man who had grown up an orphan wouldn't have any picture in his mind of the little family he'd created and yet couldn't be part of.

Except he could be a part of Amanda's life, if he'd allow himself to. When she was too little to send to Wyoming, Katherine could bring her. Sure, the contact with Zeke would be tough, knowing they had no future, but if she could survive this weekend, she could survive anything. And it would be better for Amanda, and better for Zeke, who was not going to forget this little baby, not judging from the look on his face a moment ago.

She eased out of the rocker and leaned down to lay Amanda in the makeshift bassinet. The arrangement made Katherine smile. Amanda fit inside the brass kettle perfectly. Another month and she'd be too big for it, but it was exactly the right size now. Katherine had left her camera in her room at the lodge or she would have considered taking a picture of Amanda to save for when she was older. Assuming Zeke would be a viable part of her life, that was.

She walked over to the kitchen area, but when she tried to open the drawer Zeke had indicated, she realized why he'd been making so much noise. All the drawers were swollen from the rain. The silverware clattered as she put some muscle into it and pulled hard enough to get the drawer open.

"I found a box of hot cocoa mix, if you'd like that to drink," Zeke said from his position by the fire. "I've already heated water for instant coffee."

"Cocoa's fine." Katherine set the table with Zeke's utilitarian white napkins and his stainless steel. There was something appealing about his uncomplicated life-style. She was beginning to appreciate that a minimum of possessions meant more time to do other things. Unfortunately one of the things she longed to do wasn't wise.

"If you'll bring me a couple of bowls, I'll dish this out."

"Sure." She opened cupboard doors until she found the bowls and took two out. Walking over toward the fire, she took a deep sniff of warm stew and thought what a cozy setup this was, having all the conveniences in one room. If they were a couple, this night in the cabin could be a lot of fun, she thought wistfully.

ZEKE SAT ACROSS THE TABLE from Katherine and tried not to think about sex. It reminded him of an exercise a professor had given during one of his college classes. Everyone was supposed to try not to think of a pink elephant. Nobody could think of anything else *but* a pink elephant.

Katherine used her spoon to point to her bowl of stew. "This is very good."

"Homemade's better, but this is okay in a pinch." The soft light from the kerosene lantern cast the same glow that it had when they'd shared a campsite. He'd cooked her trout that night, and she'd raved about that, too, he remembered.

She took another spoonful of stew. She'd nearly polished off the bowl. "I'm not fussy. As bad a cook as I am, I can't afford to be."

He'd guessed she wasn't much of a cook when she hadn't leaped to take over his kitchen and whip up something amazing. Women who could cook, even if they'd sprained a wrist, usually liked to show off a little. "I was spoiled," he said. "Lost Springs had a great cook while I was there. I'm sure people expect boys in an orphanage to live on bread and water, but I swear Millie must have been Julia Child's clone. We ate like kings."

"What was life like there?"

"A boy's paradise. Dogs to wrestle with, horses to ride, cows to chase. We all had chores, of course, and the bigger kids were expected to take care of the smaller ones, but it was like never-ending camp, sleeping in bunkhouses with your buddies, going on roundup together, sleeping under the stars sometimes." *And sometimes you woke up crying because you dreamed about your mother driving away and leaving you with strangers.*

"And now the ranch is in financial trouble?"

"It was. The bachelor auction made a big difference."

"That's good." She picked up her cocoa and took a sip. "More stew?"

"No, thanks. I'm full and happy."

He deliberately avoided meeting her gaze. Now would come the tough part of the evening. They'd sat together like this a year ago, and after they'd satisfied their hunger for food, they'd begun to feel the pangs of that other, more erotic hunger.

Tonight would be worse, because he knew what awaited him in Katherine's arms. He wondered if sex with her would be that wonderful again, or if leftover adrenaline from her scare had made her more passionate that night. Well, unless she made a move toward him, he wouldn't find out. Damned if he'd take the blame for losing control and landing them in bed together again.

"I can't imagine you on an auction block," she said.

"I hated the idea. But I couldn't say no when everybody else was doing it. If they fell short of their goal I'd always wonder if it was my fault." He took a swallow of his coffee. "As it turned out, I didn't have to go up there."

"No." She hesitated, her shoulders tight. "Maybe now you wish you had."

He thought about that. At first he'd wished Katherine hadn't told him about the baby and had just stayed in New York, but now the idea of never seeing that little face, never touching that tiny body seemed unthinkable.

He glanced over at the kettle where Amanda lay sleeping. "No, I'm glad you brought her out here."

She sagged with relief. "Thank you for saying that. All day I've been wondering if I made a terrible mistake. I thought maybe it would have been better if you'd never seen her. Then you wouldn't have any mental pictures, and that might be easier."

"It would be easier. But not better."

She toyed with her spoon. "Zeke, couldn't we work out something where you could have contact with her? At least once in a while?"

Instinctively he threw up his barrier again. "I don't think so, Katherine. I don't know anything about taking care of kids."

"But you just said at Lost Springs the big kids were expected to take care of the small ones. You must have been a big kid at some point."

"Yeah, but they were boys."

She smiled.

He wished she wouldn't smile. Every time she did, his heart beat a little faster and his mouth went dry. When they'd made love in the tent, she'd been full of smiles. He was conditioned to expect pleasure to follow when Katherine smiled.

"Boys and girls aren't all that different," she said.

"Maybe not in New York, but out here we consider them a lot different. We even have separate bathrooms and wear different kinds of underwear, both of which are designed for those...differences."

Her skin grew rosy. "I didn't mean it like that. I meant that you can treat a little girl basically the same way you treat a little boy."

"Is that so? I'm not so sure. On Saturday nights at Lost Springs, some of us would climb in the old ranch van and go to the Isis movie theater in town. And the big guys would take care of the little guys, which meant if one of the younger ones had to go to the bathroom in the middle of the show, one of the older ones would take him and bring him back. Just how would that work with a little girl?"

"To be honest, I hadn't thought of that. But it seems like a minor problem."

"Maybe to you. Women have been hauling little boys into the women's room for generations. No man in his right mind would take a little girl into the men's room, at least not in this day and age."

"You could figure out other things to do, outdoor things like hiking and camping. I think you and Amanda—"

"Don't do this, Katherine." He was beginning to panic. He knew a ranger who was a noncustodial father, and the guy's life was a nightmare. He had to face a little stranger every summer, and about the time he got reacquainted with his son, the kid took off for his mother's house to spend the next nine months changing into yet another stranger. And that guy had more social skills than Zeke, and his kid was a boy, which helped a lot, too. Zeke pictured himself trying to keep up with dolls and dresses and makeup. He couldn't imagine being able to cope.

"But—"

"I'm glad I had a chance to see her, but this is where it needs to end. Take her back to New York and raise her there. I'll send you money, but don't ask me to twist myself into something I'm not just to suit your image of what should be."

She sighed and stood, gathering her dishes. "I'm not asking you to change anything about yourself, Zeke. Amanda would love you just the way you are."

"After growing up in New York City?" He picked up his bowl and empty coffee mug, along with the kerosene lantern, and followed her over to the sink. "You think she'd be happy spending time in this little cabin with no TV, no computer games, no friends to play with? Even you are mystified as to how I spend my time." He set the lantern on the counter. "You couldn't hack living here for days on end, so what makes you think Amanda will be excited about it? You'd be forcing something on her she didn't even want, Katherine."

She set her dishes in the sink and turned to him. "Everybody needs a father!"

"Yeah, well, everybody doesn't get a father." He dumped his dishes in with hers in an angry clatter. "Stop trying to make everything turn out perfectly for Amanda. The only way I can imagine her learning to like it here is for you to move in and raise her right in this little cabin. Are you ready for that?"

He was surprised that she didn't immediately reject his outrageous proposal. He'd meant it as a ridiculous suggestion, but she looked at him as if she might actually be thinking about it. There was a light in her eyes that hadn't been there a moment ago.

"Don't kid yourself." He started rinsing the dishes in cold water. "Don't think you could sacrifice yourself like that and be even slightly happy."

"Is it really me you're worried about?" she asked quietly, leaning on the counter. "Or would you be the one making the biggest sacrifice by allowing a woman and child into your world?"

The concept of having her and Amanda live with him was so stunningly beautiful that he couldn't speak. And because it would never happen, he put it out of his mind immediately. He scrubbed vigorously at the bits of stew in the bowls.

"It's okay, Zeke. You don't have to be afraid that I'll suddenly camp on your doorstep and ruin your peace and quiet."

He kept his attention on the dishes, cleaning them as they'd never been cleaned before. "By the way, you can take the bed tonight. I'll take the floor."

"Oh, no. I'll take the floor. I'm the uninvited guest."

He rinsed the bowls and started scouring out the sink. "Don't argue with the ranger, ma'am. I sleep on the ground a lot, so a blanket on the floor of a cabin is a step up for me. Besides, if I put you on the floor you'll toss and turn all night trying to get comfortable and keep me awake."

"I will not toss and turn."

"Yeah, you will." He looked up with a faint smile. "You did last time."

Her face filled with color. "I'm sorry. Why didn't you say something?"

"Are you kidding? I wasn't complaining, just stating a

fact." His body stirred as he gazed at her. "Restlessness has its advantages, sometimes."

She swallowed. "I'll take the bed, then."

"Good."

9

JUST AS ZEKE WAS RUNNING out of tasks to distract him
from his need for Katherine, Amanda came to the rescue
by waking up. Thankful for the interruption, he hurried
over to scoop her up from her bassinet. "Is she hungry already?" he asked, turning to Katherine.

"I doubt it. But I'll bet she wants her bath. I give her
one every night about this time."

Washing the baby would take up some time, he
thought. "Then let's heat water in the kettle and give her
one."

"I guess we could use the kitchen sink," Katherine
said. "Let me hold her while you get it ready."

Zeke carefully transferred a fretting Amanda to Katherine. While he filled the kettle and hung it over the fire,
Katherine walked around the cabin and talked to
Amanda in the sweet little singsong voice he'd tried to
imitate out in the truck. Katherine was a whole lot better
at it than he was. The sound of her voice seemed to
soothe Amanda, but it had the opposite effect on him. Of
course, anything Katherine did seemed to have a stimulating effect where he was concerned.

Too bad he couldn't take a bath so he could sleep better. He had a feeling he was in for a long, frustrating
night. As he filled the sink with water from the kettle,
steam warmed his face and neck. "This seems pretty hot.
Should I add cold?"

"Probably. It should be lukewarm. After you add some cold, you can test it by sticking your elbow in."

"My elbow, huh?" He rolled up his sleeves, figuring he'd have to do it anyway when bath time came, added some cold water and dunked his elbow in. It was amazing how it registered the temperature of the water better than his hand. Still too hot. He added cold water a little at a time until he had it the way he imagined it should be.

"How about soap?" he asked.

"I have some liquid soap in the diaper bag. And you'd better have a couple of towels ready, too. And transfer the changing pad to the counter."

"Got a rubber ducky?"

Katherine laughed. "She's not quite at that stage."

Zeke flashed back to a time at the ranch he'd forgotten about, when he'd been put in charge of giving the smallest boys their baths. He'd loved the job and had gone so far as to whittle the kids toy boats they could play with. With a start he wondered if that long-forgotten experience had been the reason he'd bought the big tub for his bathroom.

Someday Amanda would be big enough to sail toy boats in her bathwater. And he had just the tub for that kind of fun, as it turned out. But he wouldn't be making boats for her or letting her play in the big claw-foot tub.

"I think we're set."

"This time I'd better abandon the sling so I can use both hands. You don't want to deal with a slippery baby one-handed."

"Keep the sling on." Without preamble Zeke lifted Amanda into his arms. "Let me do this. You can coach from the sidelines."

THIS WAS WHAT SHE wanted, after all, Katherine thought, although it felt strange having someone else give

Amanda her bath. Zeke was definitely a fast learner, though. In short order he had Amanda's sleeper off and was working on her diaper.

He glanced over at Katherine. "So far, so good."

Amanda cooed and waved her arms.

"She knows what's coming," Katherine said. "She likes baths."

"Yeah, but she's never had one given by fumble fingers."

"Don't be silly. You're not clumsy." Quite the opposite, if she remembered correctly. *Adept* came to mind.

"I do a little better with bigger girls."

Katherine wondered if she'd just have to get used to being constantly needy until she finally left Zeke for good. She leaned against the counter. "We can't seem to avoid that subject, can we?"

"Pretty tough to avoid it when we're stuck together like this. And it's not as if we've never made love, so that barrier's been crossed."

"And we have the evidence to prove it." She saw that he was about to get the diaper off by lifting Amanda's legs one at a time again. When he'd changed her diaper before, she wouldn't have dared correct him and risk shaking his confidence, but now she felt he was less likely to give up the project if she made a gentle suggestion. "Try holding both ankles and lifting. That way you can slip the diaper out in one motion."

Zeke followed her direction. "I'll be damned—uh, doggoned. Big improvement." He gazed down at Amanda. "Smart mommy you have there, Mandy."

Too bad she enjoyed his compliments so much. She took the folded diaper he handed her. "If I'd been a little smarter, we wouldn't be here."

"You mean because you wouldn't have tried hiking Yellowstone by yourself?"

"Right." She walked over to the trash, deposited the diaper and came back to the sink. "Or I would have understood the intricacies of my birth-control pills and known we didn't dare make love that night."

Zeke put a restraining hand on the baby as he glanced at Katherine. "Oh, I think we would have made love."

"And knowingly run the risk of pregnancy? I don't think so."

"There are lots of ways to make love." His dark eyes were warm. "And we're both pretty smart, as a matter of fact. I'm sure we would have figured out something."

Her mouth grew moist and her body tightened. "Okay. Maybe you're right. But if we're both so smart, why can't we figure out a solution to this mess we're in now?"

"Oh, I think you have. You just have to be strong enough to carry it through." He regarded her quietly for a moment. "And now you'd better tell me how to do this so I don't drown our baby."

Her heart wrenched. He'd never used the term *our* before. "Well, you, uh—" A wave of emotion caught her by surprise and she had to clear her throat. "You hold her head and neck with your left hand, and—no, wait. I keep forgetting you're backwards."

"Watch your language. This little girl might be left-handed, too."

"Oops. Sorry. Let's say you're opposite from the way I am."

"That's better. So I should hold her head and neck in my right hand."

"Yes, and her bottom in your left." She hoped Amanda would be left-handed, as well as have Zeke's bravery and compassion, although she wasn't sure how much of that could be inherited and how much needed to be taught.

"Got her." He sounded nervous. "But she's getting squirmy."

"This is where your big hands help. Lower her into the water slowly and let her get used to it. Then slide your left hand out and use the washcloth on whatever you can reach. Don't worry about every nook and cranny."

"And there sure are a lot of those." Zeke eased her into the water.

"Oh, and I warn you she likes to splash. She'll be slippery when she's wet, so keep a firm grip on her."

"Okay, wiggly girl. Time to get clean." Zeke picked up the washcloth and Amanda started kicking. "Hey!" Amanda kicked harder, splashing water on Zeke's shirt. "Splashing is one thing. This kid's a motorboat."

"I probably should have told you to take off your shirt." Except Katherine didn't really want a shirtless Zeke walking around the cabin. She reached over and took hold of Amanda's flailing legs with her left hand. "Easy, baby."

Amanda stopped kicking and slapped both hands into the water, spraying Zeke's shirt again as she crowed loudly.

Katherine gave Zeke a look of apology. "She loves this, as you can tell. I usually put on my terry bathrobe when I give her a bath, so it doesn't matter."

"It doesn't matter, anyway." Zeke started washing Amanda as he grinned down at her. "Having a good time, aren't we?"

She grinned back and plopped her hands into the water again.

Zeke chuckled as he continued his gentle movements

with the washcloth. "Gonna be a swimmer when you grow up, Mandy? Win a few medals?"

"Maybe she will." Katherine stood close to Zeke and basked in this moment of togetherness. "Swimming was my sport in high school."

"I didn't go out for a team until I was in college, but it helped put me through."

"You were in swimming, too?" He certainly had the physique for it, she thought. Massive chest and long, lithe legs.

"Yeah, I was. Small world, isn't it? So, do we do her hair and face?"

"I'll rinse another washcloth out in the bathroom sink for her face, so we don't get soap in her eyes. Be right back."

"Okay." Zeke sounded unconcerned, totally unlike the last time she'd left him alone with Amanda.

In the bathroom she found a clean washcloth, dampened it and wrung it out. The cloth would be cold, but better that than a soapy one. She'd started back into the main room of the cabin when instinct made her pause.

Without her there, Zeke had entered into a private world with Amanda. Katherine knew the feeling well— the coziness of a charmed circle that included only parent and baby. Zeke leaned over the sink, his shirt soaked as he cradled Amanda in his brawny arms and smiled down at her. He dwarfed the tiny baby, which only made the picture more poignant.

"Want a ride now?" he asked.

Amanda gurgled.

"Okay. A ride it is." He swirled Amanda gently in the water. "Whee," he said softly. "See, Mandy? Fun, huh? Now we'll go the other way. Whee. Don't worry. Daddy's got you."

Daddy. Katherine's chest tightened. Damn. In another second she'd start crying. She turned and went back into the bathroom and held the cold cloth against her eyes. Her dearest wish was coming true, and Zeke was building a relationship with his daughter. Katherine vowed then and there not to let her physical attraction to Zeke jeopardize that bond.

"Hey, Katherine! What's taking you so long? This kid's starting to wrinkle!"

Caught halfway between laughter and tears, Katherine turned on the faucet to disguise the tremble in her voice. "Be right there! Couldn't find the washcloth!" Taking a deep breath, she rinsed out the cloth again and left the bathroom.

ZEKE HELPED KATHERINE tuck a sweet-smelling Amanda into the copper kettle bassinet. He'd placed it next to the bed so that Katherine would have the baby handy during the night. While they stood together gazing down at her in her fluffy nest, she fought sleep and stared back at them.

Zeke thought how normal it would be to put his arm around Katherine at a time like this, but he didn't do it. He could talk to her, though. That was still allowed. "I never thought about it before, but baby animals are all sort of the same."

"How do you mean?"

"You have to think of how they see things. They're so small, and you're so big, that you have to be real careful that you don't scare them, or they'll never trust you."

Katherine glanced over at him. "That's true, at least for Amanda. I don't know much about animal babies."

"They're a lot the same. I thought taking care of

Amanda would be more complicated, but she seems to be getting used to me."

"She's definitely used to you. Look, she's trying to stay awake, but her little eyes keep closing."

He enjoyed the low melody of Katherine's voice as she talked about the baby. He could stand here for a long time listening to Katherine and watching Amanda sleep. "She's been having too much fun. She doesn't want it to end."

"You could be right. Sometimes she fusses before she drops off at night, but maybe she likes the quiet of the woods."

"Maybe." He had an inspiration. "Since she's going off to sleep so easily, would you like to sit out on the porch for a little while? We can open one of the porch windows a bit so we'll hear her." He motioned to a couple of hooks by the door. "And I have an extra jacket you can wear if you think you'll get cold." During her moment of hesitation, he realized she might be wondering what he had planned for her on that porch. "We'll just talk, Katherine. I promise. Or sit and enjoy the crickets. It's peaceful out there."

The slight frown cleared from her brow. "Okay. That would be nice."

"Great." He crossed to the sink and grabbed a used dish towel. "Take your pick of those jackets. I'll wipe down the chairs." He felt like whistling as he went out on the porch and whisked the moisture off the Adirondacks.

She came out wearing his black nylon jacket. "Which chair?"

"Either one. Maybe you'd like the one closer to the door, in case Amanda wakes up."

"Good idea." She sat down, wincing when she

knocked her sprained wrist against the broad arm of the chair. Then she leaned back with a sigh. "Great chairs."

"Thanks." He sat down beside her, and the feeling of sharing was all he'd hoped it would be. The damp, pungent scent of a rain-drenched forest settled around them and a cricket chirped nearby. "I figured a porch needed chairs."

"Definitely. And these are perfect. They make me think of the beach. When my parents were alive we spent a couple of weeks on Long Island Sound one summer. The beach cottages had chairs like this."

"I've never been to a beach like that. Never seen the ocean, for that matter."

"Never?" She turned her head to gaze at him. "Oh, Zeke, you would love it. The waves, and the ebb and flow of the tides, and walking barefoot along a deserted beach looking for seashells. It's your type of thing."

It might be, he thought, if he could share it with her. He pictured a dark-haired little girl squatting beside the surf, a pail and shovel in her hand. Amanda would love the ocean.

"Then again, maybe you wouldn't like it." Katherine faced forward again and her voice was more subdued. "I shouldn't make those assumptions after knowing you such a short time."

"You know me better than you think you do."

"I do?"

"Maybe even better than I know myself." He took a deep breath. Once he said this, there would be no turning back. "I'm willing to consider having Amanda come and visit me once in a while, Katherine."

She turned her head quickly toward him. "Really?"

"The idea still scares the devil out of me. Maybe I've learned how to change a diaper and give her a bath, but that doesn't mean I'll know what to do when she's two, or four, or fourteen. But I'm willing to try."

"Oh, Zeke." Her voice was husky. "That means so much to me. And it will mean the world to Amanda."

"I hope you're right." His declaration was almost worth it just to see the warmth and eagerness in her expression. "I still think there could come a time when she'd rather spend her vacation with her friends back in New York instead of out in the boonies with me."

"I doubt it." Katherine swept an arm around the clearing. "Look at all you have here. Only an idiot wouldn't feel lucky to be allowed to spend time with you here."

He thought of pointing out that she was itching to hightail it out of this paradise he'd brought her to, but he didn't.

She leaned back and gazed out through the trees where the clouds were giving way to a star-speckled night sky. "Listen to the wind in the pines. And the crickets, and the drip, drip, drip of rainwater from the eaves. The combination is hypnotic."

"I guess it is." He wasn't sure he'd have said that. The night was relaxing him, but he was far from hypnotized. The more he relaxed, the more he wanted to take her to bed.

"And the air smells so...so fertile."

"Mmm." He supposed she was only speaking poetically. After all, she was a magazine editor, and she had to come up with descriptions of fashion stuff all the time. She probably hadn't meant to use a word that made him think about sex. More specifically, sex with her. She had been fertile a year ago. No doubt she was again.

"Amanda will love coming here," Katherine said.

"But she'll be the only kid. That could be lonely."

"Maybe sometimes she will be. I was, too. But that can't be helped, can it?"

God, he must be insane. What he really wanted, now that he'd committed to this fatherhood thing, was to give Amanda a baby brother or sister. And this time he could be in touch with Katherine throughout the pregnancy, and he'd be there to watch the baby being born. After all, what difference would it make whether they set up this whole scheme for one kid or two? And to make love to her again, knowing that he was trying to get her pregnant—he grew hard just thinking about it.

Of course it was an impossible dream. He cleared his throat. "No, I guess it can't be helped."

She was silent for some time after that.

He sat and tried to become as hypnotized as she apparently was by the rhythm of the wind, the chirp of the crickets and the steady drip of the water. Instead the wind reminded him of Katherine's sigh of satisfaction, and the crickets sounded like the squeak of bedsprings. The dripping water beat in the same steady tempo that gave Katherine so much pleasure when he was deep—

"Do you think...you'll get married some day?"

No, not now. "Hard to say. If I did, the woman would have to like this isolated life-style. So far every woman I've been serious about has finally admitted she'd go crazy living the way I live, and we've broken off the relationship, so I may be out of luck. Why?"

"Your comment about Amanda being an only child. I started thinking about it and realized that you might get married and have other children, so she'd have half brothers and sisters."

"Would you like that?" He wanted her to say that she'd hate it, that she never wanted another woman to lie with him the way she had.

"Well, I—suppose then Amanda wouldn't be by herself when she visited you."

He turned his head to look at her. "That isn't what I asked. Would *you* like me to get married and have other children?"

"I don't see what that has to do with anything. What difference does it make whether I would like it? If it would be good for you, and good for Amanda, then I—"

"Damn it, Katherine, stop being so civilized and reasonable. All right, I'll go first. You could do the same thing—find a New York stockbroker and have a slew of kids with the guy."

"Oh, I don't think—"

"Why not? You said the magazine office is set up for kids."

"Well, maybe, but men aren't beating down my door with marriage proposals. I'm not what you'd call a sexy woman."

He laughed.

"I'm not! Most men think I'm too tall, or too smart, or too skinny."

"Skinny? I don't think so!"

"It's true. I've been a skinny girl all my life, and I haven't even had much in the way of breasts until Amanda was born."

He gazed at her, remembering the pleasure she'd given him in the confines of his little tent last summer. Maybe her breasts were fuller now, but they'd fit his hands perfectly then, too. "You have beautiful breasts," he said. "I thought so before, and I still do." Even in the dim light from the stars he could see that her eyes darkened in response.

"So don't tell me you won't have any guys hanging around hoping you'll consider marrying them," he continued. He figured it was even more likely now, after the baby. Pregnancy and childbirth had added to Katherine's womanliness in potent, yet undefinable, ways.

"Okay, maybe somebody might show up," she said. "And I suppose if I met someone and we decided to marry, I'd have to consider whether it would be good for Amanda to have a brother or sister. But we're talking a long time from now, Zeke."

He leaned toward her. "You know how long I'd like it to be? Amanda's welfare aside?"

"No. I'm not sure I understand your point."

His blood was heating up, and he couldn't seem to help it. "I'd like it to be never, Katherine. I don't want another man to touch you the way I have, to make you pregnant, to stand beside you gazing down at the little child you've created together."

She stared at him, her eyes wide, her lips parted.

He pushed on. "The only way I'd want Amanda to have a brother or sister would be if I made you pregnant again. That's selfish and unreasonable and exactly the way I feel."

Her breath came quick and shallow as she gazed at him. "I don't know how you do it," she murmured.

"Do what?"

"Make me want you more than I've ever wanted anyone. You don't even have to touch me. All you have to do is say something like that, and I'm on fire."

A shudder passed through him. He could take her inside now, and she would go. "But you don't want to be aroused, do you?"

She shook her head.

"Then I—"

A long, melancholy howl rose on the night air. He paused to listen.

Katherine's breath caught. "A wolf," she said, almost reverently.

"Yes." The howl came again. Then others in the pack joined in, creating a primitive chorus that gave him chills of pleasure every time. A pack had migrated down from Yellowstone, and although some people in the area weren't happy about it, Zeke was thrilled.

She rose from her chair and walked over to the porch steps, as if lured by the sound. "Naomi gave me the bachelor auction brochure to read. You helped bring wolves back to this area, didn't you?"

"Yes."

"That's something to be proud of."

"They don't scare you?"

She shook her head. "Bears are the only animals that really frighten me, and I'm sure that's from that horrible story I heard when I was a kid." She grasped the smooth post beside her and leaned against it as the wolves sent up another series of plaintive cries. Then she took a deep breath. "Magnificent."

Something shifted in the region of Zeke's heart. He hadn't meant to bring her to his sanctuary, yet it seemed at this moment as if she'd been destined to come. He knew she wouldn't stay, couldn't stay, but it seemed right that she was here now, sharing the magic of crickets and raindrops and a wolf serenade.

"Zeke, look!" She pointed to the night sky.

He pushed out of his chair and moved over beside her as a falling star streaked downward and disappeared into the trees, followed by another, and another.

She lifted her face in wonder. "It's a meteor shower, isn't it?"

Zeke gazed at her, more mesmerized by the expression

on her face than the sparks of light blazing trails toward the horizon. "You've never seen one?"

"No, but I always wished I could. Oh, Zeke. This is beautiful. It seems as if it stopped raining just so we could see this."

"Yep, it does." He ached from wanting to hold her, but he kept his hands at his sides and allowed her to enjoy the show. From now on, meteor showers would be linked in his memory to the rapture on her face as she stared up into the night sky. Last summer she'd appeared like a meteor in his life, a flash of almost painful beauty that quickly disappeared. He'd worked for months to try to forget her. Now she was back, burning brighter than before.

And he would never, ever forget.

10

THE MAJORITY OF THE NIGHT threatened to ensnare Katherine, but she resisted surrendering completely. Standing here with Zeke as stars fell from the sky and wolves called to their mates wove a dangerous spell. The soft hoot of an owl echoed deep in the forest, and she recognized her susceptibility to that sound. It triggered a memory of nights spent in the Adirondacks with her parents, summer nights when she'd felt connected to the natural world and had dreamed of becoming a wilderness guide.

But she hadn't chosen that career path, and now her beloved Naomi was counting on her. She must not allow herself to fall in love tonight—not with the wilderness and not with the man. Although he stood quietly beside her, there was nothing calm about him. Heat and the pulse of unfulfilled needs bridged the space between their bodies. If she lingered, he would close that space.

A gust of wind swept across the porch as clouds began to edge out the cascading lights. Katherine smelled the pungent odor of rain on the breeze. It was her cue to break the spell.

"This has been fantastic." She forced weariness into her voice, although she was taut with the same emotions that ruled Zeke. She avoided looking at him. One glance into his dark eyes could be her undoing. "But I think I'll turn in. It's been a long day."

He cleared his throat. "Yeah."

A haunting note in his response tore at her resolve. But for the sake of everyone—Zeke, Naomi, Amanda and herself—she had to be strong. "Mind if I get ready first?"

"That's fine."

She sneaked a peek at him. He was gazing out into the clearing, his jaw rigid. "I'll be fast," she said.

"Take your time."

He had amazing control, she thought as she left him standing on the porch. Most men would have pressed the issue on a romantic night like this one.

Once inside, she walked over to gaze down at her sleeping baby. Amanda looked snug as could be in her copper kettle. The fire had burned down to flickering embers, and Zeke had turned both kerosene lanterns low. With the cozy glow from the fire warming the room and sturdy log walls surrounding her, Katherine longed to snuggle into the shelter of Zeke's arms for the rest of the night. But if she gave in to that urge, she might not find the courage to leave.

She took off Zeke's nylon jacket that carried his woodsy scent, and hung it on the hook by the door. Then she crossed the room and turned back the covers on the bed. Zeke had probably made the bed frame, peeling the logs for the head and footboard the same way he had peeled and finished the logs for the cabin walls. It was a sturdy bed, just right for...sleeping.

Because she had no night wear, she decided to take off the socks and sweats and sleep in her panties and Zeke's flannel shirt. She also removed the sling from around her arm. But once she crawled under the covers, she discovered that Zeke's scent clung to the sheets, too. She should have been prepared for that, but she wasn't. There was no escape from the sensuous pull of this man whom she longed for and couldn't have.

The scent of him aroused her, but it held some comfort, too. As she drifted off to sleep she thought how strange it was that Zeke could make her feel so safe, yet so completely unsettle her at the same time.

THE FIRE WAS OUT and the air chilly in the cabin when Katherine awoke. At first she thought Amanda had caused her to come suddenly wide-awake, but when she leaned over the side of the bed to peer at the baby, she was still fast asleep.

Then she heard a moan. Sitting straight up in bed, heart pounding, she searched the dim cabin for the source of the sound. Zeke lay on the large rag rug near the fireplace, with a blanket over him. She could see no one—or nothing—else.

Then the moan came again, and she realized it was Zeke.

"No, no," he cried out softly, twisting his body under the blanket. "No, don't make me."

The desperate plea in his voice broke her heart. She couldn't imagine Zeke ever begging that way, and when awake he never would. But in the grip of a nightmare, all his pride was stripped away. As he moaned again, she wondered if she should wake him. She could end the nightmare, but then he'd know she'd seen him at his most vulnerable. For a man like Zeke, that could be worse than any nightmare.

"Please, oh, please." His voice was choked. "Oh, please. No. No-o-o-o."

Katherine couldn't stand it. Let him hate her for knowing too much, but she couldn't bear to let him suffer like this. Slipping out of bed, she picked her way around

Amanda's bassinet and over to the fireplace where Zeke lay on his side with his back to her.

He cried out softly and muttered something that sounded like, "I'll be good. Don't, please."

Kneeling on the rug beside him, Katherine breathed in the charred scent of fireplace ashes as she put her hand on his shoulder. Such a powerful shoulder. Such a frightened man. She shook him gently. "Zeke, wake up. You're dreaming."

He jerked instantly awake and rolled to his back, nearly knocking her over. "What? What is it?"

She steadied herself by putting her right hand on his chest and noticed her sprained wrist didn't hurt quite as much now. She also noticed that she was touching bare skin, and wondered whether he'd left on any of his clothes. "You were having a nightmare."

"Oh." He put his hand over hers and exhaled slowly. "Yeah."

"I...are you okay?"

"Yeah." He gave her hand a slight squeeze. "Thanks."

His pitiful cries still echoed in her head. She couldn't make herself get up and leave him to fall asleep alone and maybe return to the same nightmare. Acting on instinct, she eased down next to him on the rug and pillowed her head on her arm. His warmth radiated out to her, taking some of the chill from the air.

For a while they lay there quietly. She could tell he was sorting his way through the nightmare as his heartbeat thudded steadily against the light pressure of her hand on his chest. If he went back to sleep, she'd slip away and return to bed. But right now, she believed he needed someone with him.

"I guess she was doing what she thought was best for

both of us," he said at last as he began to gently stroke her hand.

Katherine waited, hardly daring to breathe for fear he'd stop talking if she became too intrusive. She had the feeling he might never have revealed his nightmare to anyone before.

"I thought it was because I'd been bad, and she was punishing me. But I guess she just couldn't take care of me anymore."

Katherine was sure he must be talking about his mother, but she didn't want to ask and ruin the moment.

"That gate looked huge, like it led to a giant's house, a giant who would eat little boys. She told me to get out of the car. When I wouldn't, she yelled at me and dragged me out."

Tears gathered in Katherine's eyes, but she remained silent.

"She told me to go through that gate and down the road, that someone would take care of me there." His voice dropped to a rough whisper. "I thought they'd put me in a cage, fatten me up and have me for dinner. But I went. I had nowhere else to go."

Katherine pictured a small, scared boy walking valiantly down a dusty road to his doom. She choked back a sob.

Zeke kept hold of her hand as he rolled to face her. He touched her damp cheek. "I...I'm sorry. I shouldn't have—"

"Yes." She cleared her throat. She couldn't see his face very well in the shadows, but maybe that was best. The darkness might make him feel less exposed. "Yes, you should have."

"Katherine...I just...please let me hold you for a minute. I'm not going to..."

Silently she eased closer, wrapping her arms around him as he wrapped his around her. It was an embrace of comfort, not passion.

Zeke laid his cheek against the top of her head. "I wish I could stop the dreams."

"Maybe you can. Maybe telling me about it will help."

His voice was low, subdued. "The thing is, it came out okay. She was right. There was somebody there to take care of me, somebody who did a better job than she'd been doing. And it happened a long time ago. I should be able to forget about it."

"You'll probably never forget about it, Zeke. Being left by your mother when you're small is the scariest thing to a kid."

He took a long, shuddering breath. "It was pretty scary."

"When my parents died on the New Jersey Turnpike, I was eighteen, a nearly grown woman who should have been able to cope. But I was furious at them for months, thinking they never should have taken that trip, that it was somehow their fault that they'd died and abandoned me." She paused, realizing that it wasn't so easy for her to admit to weaknesses, either. "I have nightmares, too, sometimes."

Zeke rubbed her back lightly. "Eighteen is still pretty young."

His touch set off sensuous ripples within her, but she managed to keep her feelings pleasantly cozy, not over-heated with desire. Now wasn't the time for that. "But I wasn't as young as you were. Do you know if your mother...if she's—"

His hand stilled. "Lost Springs was notified that she died a year after she dropped me off there. But sometimes I dream that she's come back, and I tell her about my job as a park ranger."

"I know." Katherine felt the tug of an old grief. "Sometimes I dream that my parents are alive, that it was all a mistake about the wreck. And they're so proud of me for becoming an editor at *Cachet*."

"Maybe they know."

"Maybe." Her throat tightened. "The hardest part has been this past year, when I was carrying their grandchild. And now she's here, and so beautiful. I want them to see her."

"I'll bet you do." His voice was rich with understanding.

"But having her helps, in a way. Because it proves to me that life goes on. My parents live on in Amanda."

He lay quietly for a moment. "I hadn't thought of it like that."

"You said your mother had a dimple in her chin like Amanda's."

There was another long silence. "She told me it was because I kept putting my finger there," he said finally. "She said if I ever stopped, she'd lose her dimple, so every chance I got I pressed on her chin."

Katherine smiled in the darkness. "That's cute."

"I'd forgotten about that until this minute."

"You see?" She snuggled against him, which felt good. Very good. She felt her resolve slipping. But Zeke would maintain control. He always did. "Nice memories might help balance the bad ones," she said.

"They might."

"I want you to have all sorts of nice memories with Amanda."

He didn't respond.

"You haven't changed your mind about having her visit, have you?"

The silence lengthened. "She might not want to be around me that much," he said finally. "I'm not a real lovable type."

Wrong. "Who says?"

"Well, think about it. If I'd been easier to live with, my mother would have tried harder to keep me."

"Oh, Zeke." Her heart ached at his implication that he didn't deserve to be loved. Instinctively she moved closer. "Your mother didn't leave because you had problems. She left because she did. Take it from me. You're very lovable. Amanda will adore coming to visit you."

"Mmm."

"You don't believe me. But I guarantee that time spent with you in this special place will be the highlight of her year."

"If you say so." His answer sounded neutral, as if he didn't much care one way or the other.

"Okay, now what's wrong? Did I say something to upset you?"

"No."

"I must have. Look, if I've said something insensitive, I'm sorry. I didn't mean to. I'm only trying—"

"It's not what you said." He carefully took her arm from around his waist.

"Then what's going on?"

"This." He took her hand and placed it against the cotton of his briefs, which bulged with his very hard erection. Then he laced his fingers through hers and drew her hand back up between them. His voice was strained. "I wanted to stay here snuggled together the rest of the night. I thought if I concentrated on something boring like laundry, I could keep control. But I think you'd better go back to bed, Katherine.''

She ignited instantly, suddenly aware that she wore very little and he wore even less.

"I mean it." He paused, his breathing unsteady. "Unless...you've changed your mind."

She realized that was as close as he'd ever come to asking her to help him banish his demons, at least for tonight. A woman would have to be made of stone to reject the plea in his voice, and she was definitely made of flesh and blood. Warm, eager flesh and heated blood.

Slowly she lifted her face to his. "Help me change it," she murmured. "Kiss me, Zeke."

With a groan he covered her mouth with his.

SHE OFFERED OBLIVION, and he took it. When he kissed her, nothing else mattered, and he needed mindless pleasure, needed it so much he was shaking. Maybe she wouldn't love him forever, but she'd love him tonight. For a few hours she'd fill the hollow place in his heart, ease the familiar, constant pain he felt there.

She tunneled her fingers through his hair and her open mouth cradled his, inviting him deep. He grew lightheaded and crazy with desire as he sank into the remembered richness of her kiss. Cupping her head, he guided her to her back on the braided rug. The scent of smoldering embers became an aphrodisiac, stirring his pleasure centers with year-old memories of a dying campfire and a passion-drenched Katherine in his arms. The cabin floor was no softer than the canvas-covered ground where he'd taken her that first time. There was something elemental about making love on an unyielding surface that suited the way Zeke felt about Katherine.

She'd wanted him desperately then, yet her needs

seemed even more urgent now. And each little cry, each whimper soothed his battered heart. Maybe her desire for him last summer had been more than gratitude, more than a reaction to her close call in the rapids.

He unfastened the buttons of her shirt with trembling fingers and reached beneath the flannel to cup her warm breast. Her nipple was moist.

Need slammed into him with a force that made him gasp against her mouth. Lifting his head, he gazed into her shadowed eyes as he lightly squeezed her breast.

"Please," she whispered, easing herself free of the flannel shirt.

Heart hammering, he leaned down and drew her nipple into his mouth. With just the slightest pressure, warm milk pooled on his tongue. The sensation drove him wild, yet he hesitated, unsure if he could have what he sought.

In answer, she held his head and arched into his caress.

The blood rushed in his ears as he took the bounty she offered. So sweet, yet so maddeningly erotic. His groin tightened painfully as he licked and sucked, drawing equally from her warm, plump breasts.

Her breathing quickened, and her throaty moan told him she was responding as feverishly as he. He slipped his hand beneath the soft silk of her panties. She was bathed in passion, hot and ready. He nearly ripped the garment from her so that he could sink into that tropical paradise, but a scrap of sanity remained. Not yet.

Instead he caressed her there, paying homage to the throbbing nub that held the power of her release. When she quivered against him, he knew she was balanced on the edge, needing only a nudge.

He gave her that nudge. She gasped his name as the tremors took her, and he treasured the sound of it on her lips. He hadn't been a nameless wilderness fantasy to her, or an inconvenient problem when she gave birth to Amanda. She wanted him. *Him*.

Joy surged through him as he kissed her cheeks, her eyes, her mouth. He ran his hand over her quivering body. "I want to see you."

"Oh, Zeke." Her eyes fluttered open. "Childbirth... changes a woman."

He cupped her breast. "I know." His voice was thick with need. "I like it. Let me light the lantern."

"But—"

He silenced her with a kiss. "Please." Without waiting for permission he untangled himself from her and stood. It wasn't easy to leave her side when he was heavy with unsatisfied desire, but this might be the last time he made love to her, and he wouldn't be denied any part of the experience.

Moving as quietly as possible so he wouldn't wake Amanda, he lit the lantern and took a foil-wrapped package from the bottom drawer of his dresser. No matter how much he might want to give Amanda a brother or sister, he couldn't ask Katherine to go through that.

He set the lantern on the hearth, and the glow illuminated the most beautiful woman he'd ever seen. All that covered her was the small triangle of her panties, and soon that would be gone. He slipped off his briefs and knelt down beside her. "Katherine, you're so—"

"Please don't look too close," she pleaded, spreading her fingers over her stomach. "I have stretch marks. And my tummy's not flat like it was last summer."

"Lucky you." He drew her hands away and leaned down to kiss the faint white lines. "A warrior should show off her battle scars, not hide them."

"You're being nice."

"No." His voice roughened, and he realized seeing the stretch marks had created a different sort of frustration. He stroked his hand over her stomach, trying to imagine that she'd once carried Amanda there. "I missed everything about this pregnancy. I missed watching your body change, missed feeling the baby move, missed the moment when you opened your thighs and gave birth to our child." He looked into her eyes. "Don't hide the stretch marks, Katherine. I need to see them."

Moisture sparkled in her eyes. "I'm sorry," she whispered. "I'm so sorry, Zeke."

"It's over now." Yet as he eased away the panties covering her blond curls, he throbbed with the urge to start again, to plant another seed in her womb and watch the baby grow. Instead he picked up the packet from the hearth and ripped it open.

She watched his motions. "Zeke...what you said on the porch...about having another..."

He shook his head. "I was talking crazy." He finished sheathing himself and moved over her. "Just let me love you, Katherine. It will be enough."

11

KATHERINE DIDN'T THINK one night of loving Zeke would be nearly enough, considering it would have to last her a lifetime. How she ached for him.

He gazed into her eyes. "It's only been two months. I don't want to hurt you."

She wanted him so much she could barely breathe, let alone talk. "I don't...think you will. But if you don't come to me soon, I might die."

"Me, too." He clenched his jaw. "But I'm going slow, just in case."

As he slid partway inside, the pleasure of having his solid length fill her again was so intense she shuddered with joy.

Immediately he stopped, his breathing ragged. "Are you—"

"In heaven? Almost." She cupped his face in both hands. "Give me all of you, Zeke."

With a groan he sank deep.

"Yes," she whispered as unexpected tears filled her eyes.

"I'm hurting you." He started to withdraw.

She wrapped her uninjured arm around his back and her legs around his hips, holding him tight inside her. Her voice was choked. "Don't you dare."

"But you're crying."

"Because it feels so good. I don't remember it feeling this good, Zeke."

He looked into her eyes for a long moment. Slowly he shook his head. "I don't, either."

"What's happened?"

He didn't answer, just gazed at her with those knowing eyes. "Loosen up," he murmured.

She relaxed her hold on him and he began to move. Oh, how he began to move. He spoke her body's language fluently—stroking, shifting, pausing, speeding up, slowing down. He seemed to take his cues from her, yet she spoke not a word.

And all the while he watched her face, her eyes, until gradually he'd tuned himself so perfectly to her that she lost any sense of separateness. His breath became her breath, his sweat her sweat, his body her body. And always he coaxed them upward, building the momentum, tightening the tension.

She'd never shared herself with another as she was sharing herself now. When the moment came, raining wonder all around them, her cry of completion mingled with his, and tears spilled down her cheeks at the unearthly beauty of what they had created together. And she knew what he was trying, without words, to tell her. Joy and sorrow mingled in her heart as she realized that something had happened, and they might never have the courage to face it. They'd fallen in love.

DAZED BY THE POWER of the moment, Zeke wondered if he'd ever find the strength to leave the magical shelter of Katherine's arms.

Then Amanda started to cry.

Beneath him, Katherine stirred. "I—"

"I know. She's hungry." He kissed the soft skin behind

Katherine's ear before reluctantly easing away from her. "Go get back in bed. I'll change her and bring her to you. Then I'll build up the fire."

She sat up and reached for her panties.

"Don't," he murmured.

She glanced up at him and laid the panties aside.

"And leave the shirt off, too. I love to look at you."

Her eyes darkened and he wanted to make love to her again, this very minute, but Amanda needed attention. As Katherine stood, her breasts moving gently with the motion of her body, he wished he were a better artist so he could draw her. But paper and charcoal wouldn't capture her heat, or her delicious scent.

After a quick trip to the bathroom he picked up a squalling Amanda and cradled her against his chest. "Take it easy, Mandy. Your late-night snack is coming right up." He was impressed with how efficiently he managed to change her diaper, even when she continued to wiggle and cry. In no time he carried her to the shadowy bed, where Katherine had propped herself against the headboard with a pillow. God, he wanted to climb right in there with her. "Which side?"

"Let's start with the left this time."

"Good. Then I can help you when you nurse her on the other side." He laid the fussy baby carefully in the crook of her left arm.

"Thank you, Zeke."

"No problem."

Amanda nuzzled hungrily and Katherine helped her find the nipple.

Zeke stood there mesmerized by the sight of Amanda nursing. Now he knew the taste that little baby was experiencing. His mouth moistened. "I hope that I didn't...um, take more than I should have."

She smiled up at him. "No. I have plenty for her. But if you don't build up the fire pretty soon, I'll need some covers."

"Oh!" He'd been so entranced and so filled with heat watching her nurse the baby that he'd forgotten all about the fire. "Sorry." He hurried over to the hearth and soon had the blaze going again. Then he glanced at the blanket that had been tossed aside while they'd made love. Figuring he wouldn't need it now, he folded it and laid it on a chair. He might not sleep much, but he planned to spend the rest of the night in his own bed, starting now.

He brought the lantern over and set it on the bedside table before climbing into bed next to Katherine and Amanda.

She glanced over at him. "This feels a little like being at home with her."

He propped his head on his hand to get a better view of her. "You nurse her naked while a man watches you?"

She laughed. "Not hardly. I meant that I bring her to bed and nurse her there at night. But there's no man."

"Good." He was pretty sure there hadn't been anyone else in her life, but he liked hearing it all the same.

"And I wear a nightgown."

"Why?"

She glanced at him over the top of Amanda's head. "Because that's the kind of woman I am, I guess."

"I don't think so."

As she held his gaze, her eyes smoldered with passion. "You bring out a different side of me, that's for sure."

He needed to touch her, needed to feel her warmth, but while she was nursing Amanda, he'd use restraint. He slid his hand gently over her silken thigh. "Is it a different side, or the real Katherine?"

"I don't know." She sounded slightly out of breath.

Then she looked down at his hand lying quietly on her thigh. "Zeke..."

"Don't worry. I won't do anything. But I need a connection." And this made a powerful one for him—his sunbrowned hand resting against the creamy skin of her inner thigh.

"Oh."

"Does my hand there bother you too much?"

"It bothers me, but in a nice way."

He smiled at her. "Good." He hoped she felt the way he did, aroused but under control. He lay with his palm absorbing her warmth as he listened to the crackling fire and Amanda's little slurps and swallows. The baby patted her tiny hand against her mother's full breast. Remembering the pleasure to be found there made Zeke's mouth water and his groin throb. Control became a little tougher to come by.

When Katherine spoke again, her tone had become shy. "Nursing her has been a sensual thing for me. I've never admitted that to anyone."

"I'm the perfect person to tell."

"Yes." She stroked Amanda's cheek with her finger. "Wearing nightgowns and being proper is right for my apartment in New York, but I have to admit that being here like this...lying in bed with you while I feed her...seems even more right."

His chest tightened. "Dangerous talk."

"Don't be scared, Zeke. I'm not going to do anything stupid and wreck your life."

He chose his words carefully. He couldn't tell her that he wanted her to stay with him forever. He couldn't put that kind of burden on her. "I wasn't thinking about my life."

"Okay, I'm not going to do anything stupid and wreck all Naomi's plans for me at the magazine."

He lightly massaged her thigh, careful to keep his touch easy, both for her benefit and his. "We'll figure things out."

"I hope so. But I can't help thinking that the best thing for Amanda would be for her to have both of us, all the time."

The tightness in his chest moved up to his throat. He had to clear it before he could speak. "But that's not possible."

"No," she said softly.

Zeke knew there was nothing more to say. Tonight was all he'd have. Silently he watched Amanda nurse, and when Katherine started to switch her to the other breast, he helped arrange it along with a pillow to support the baby so Katherine's arm wouldn't have to take all the weight.

He longed to caress the moistened nipple Amanda had just left, but he didn't dare. He was maintaining a precarious-enough hold on his control as it was. Lying here next to Katherine was torture, but a sweet kind of torture, and he wouldn't give up these moments for anything in the world.

He couldn't decide which was worse, his physical or mental frustration. But his physical frustration would be satisfied once Amanda went back to sleep. His mental frustration seemed doomed to continue for a long time, considering that Katherine couldn't run a New York magazine from the wilderness, and he couldn't be happy in a world of glass and steel.

SOMETIME DURING THE night, Katherine heard a crack of lightning nearby and waited for the rush of rain that would surely follow. When it didn't come, she snuggled against Zeke. Maybe the creek would go down enough for them to be rescued tomorrow. Not wanting to think about that, she reached for him and lost herself in the wonder of his touch yet again.

She awoke to a gray, misty light coming through the uncurtained window over the bed, and no sound of rain on the roof. Amanda and Zeke still slept. Moving quietly so as not to wake them, Katherine slid out of bed and put on her sweats, socks and shirt. Early morning had become her private time since Amanda's birth. The baby generally slept through the dawn hours, giving Katherine precious moments to herself, and she'd become greedy for them.

She turned to look at Zeke lying peacefully in bed. She could also use this time before Amanda woke up to make love to him one more time. But they hadn't slept much during the night, and if he had to get her and the baby back to civilization today, he needed his rest. She swallowed the lump in her throat. The moment of parting was inevitable, and when it came, she couldn't be a wimp.

The chirp of birds outside the window beckoned to her. Tiptoeing to the door, she lifted the nylon jacket noiselessly from its hook before unlocking the door with slow, careful movements. She looked forward to a half hour on the porch all by herself to watch the sun come up and listen to the birds sing. Maybe it would help her come to grips with the decision she had to make.

Clean, cool air sifted into the room as she eased open the door, hoping the hinges didn't squeak. They didn't. She slipped outside, stepping onto the dew-covered porch floor. Her socks would get wet, but she didn't care. She started to close the door behind her as she gazed out into the clearing.

She stopped in mid motion and her hand tightened on the knob. The Adirondack chairs she and Zeke had sat in the night before were lying out in the yard. The arm was broken off one of them. She tried to make sense of what she was seeing.

Had there been a terrible wind in the night that had picked up the chairs and hurled them off the porch? Surely she wouldn't have slept through hurricane-force winds.

She glanced around. The birds still sang and the air smelled pure and sweet as sunlight slowly moved into the clearing, but the tranquillity she'd expected to find was gone. She stood on one leg and pulled off a sock, then repeated the process with the other leg. The boards were cold against her feet, but at least she wouldn't get the socks all muddy while she went out to retrieve the chairs.

Stuffing the socks in her jacket pocket, she started down the steps toward the first chair. Not wanting to cut her foot on a sharp rock, she watched the ground carefully. Then she gasped.

Imprinted perfectly in the mud at her feet was a giant paw print. Torn between horror and fascination, she studied the impression of a heavy pad and huge claws that had punctured awesome holes in the ground. Sadie.

ZEKE WOKE UP WITH a vague feeling that something was wrong. He sat up and looked over at the empty space where Katherine had slept. Getting to his feet, he reached for his jeans as he surveyed the cabin in one quick glance. Katherine wasn't there, although Amanda was still asleep in her bassinet.

Damn, he'd wanted to be the first one out the door this morning, but it had been an eventful night and he'd overslept. He'd heard Sadie on the porch playing around with his chairs about four o'clock, but he'd decided not to risk alarming Katherine by trying to scare Sadie away.

Fastening his jeans, he walked over to the door and opened it in time to catch Katherine staring out toward the edges of the clearing, her whole posture reminding him of a deer scenting a predator. He was pretty certain Sadie was long gone, but sure enough, the chairs were tossed in the yard as he'd expected.

"Good morning," he said softly so as not to frighten Katherine.

She jumped anyway, whirling toward the door. "Do you see what she did?"

"Yep."

"Zeke, I have to get Amanda out of here. That bear could rip the door off its hinges if she decided to. Or break through the porch window."

"She could, but I doubt she'd decide to."

"Why not? What's the difference between that and what she did to your chairs?"

Leaving the door open so they could hear Amanda, he crossed the porch. "I've been wondering if she'd decide to come and play with those chairs." He walked down the steps and stood barefoot in the cool grass next to Katherine. "Now I know I have to bring them in at night."

Katherine gestured toward the upended chairs. "You call this *playing?*"

"Sure. If you're a bear."

She stared at him. "Then maybe if you're a bear it would be even more fun to break into the cabin and maul the people inside."

"Too much work. Especially considering that it's the end of summer and she's had plenty to eat this year. If it had been a lean summer and she'd learned that cabins have food in them, then she might try that. But last night she was just being curious. I haven't had the chairs out there very long, so maybe this was the first time she's noticed them."

"You sound as if she's almost a pet!"

"No, not a pet. That's a dangerous fantasy some tourists have. I don't." He sighed. "Look, if it makes you feel any better, I have a gun in the cabin. I heard Sadie last night, and if she'd tried to get through the door or any of the windows, I would have used the gun."

Katherine's eyes widened. "A *gun?*"

"Yes. When you live out in the middle of nowhere like this, it's a good idea to have some form of protection. I keep it loaded and it's in the bottom drawer of the chest. In fact, if you want to learn how to use—"

"No!" She held up both hands and backed away from him. "I do not want to learn to use the gun. I don't even want to see the gun."

"Good Lord. It's just a tool, like any other tool."

"You can jolly well keep it to yourself, Zeke. What I want is to get my baby out of this place, where you need a gun to protect yourself from a prowling bear."

His patience was slipping fast. "Damn it, Katherine, I've never had to use that gun to protect myself from a bear in all the years I've lived and worked in this area. I never expect to have to use it, but you seemed so spooked I thought you'd want to know it's available."

"Well, I'm not comforted, okay?"

"Amanda's safer in that cabin than she is riding around in a cab in New York City, for God's sake!"

Katherine folded her arms. "Not with that bear around."

Suddenly he was tired of trying to convince her. "I'll

go see if the phone's working yet," he said. "If it is, then I'll hike to the creek and check that out."

"And what if the phone's not working and the creek's still full?"

He gazed at her in exasperation. "Maybe I'll figure out how to rebuild the bridge, and if that's not possible, I might decide to swim across with you and Amanda on my back."

"Now you're being ridiculous."

"This roller coaster ride we're on is getting to me, Katherine. Ridiculous or not, I'll find a way to get you back to the lodge. Something tells me it would be well worth the effort."

12

ZEKE FELT PERSONALLY affronted that Katherine didn't trust him to keep Sadie under control and Amanda safe. How could she think he'd let anything happen to that little baby? He stomped into the house and picked up the phone. If that was the way she felt, it was a good thing she wanted to spend her life in New York City.

The phone was still dead, so if he wanted to get Katherine and Amanda out of here, he'd have to figure out how to do it by himself. He pulled on his socks and boots and was reaching for his shirt when a soft cooing sound came from Amanda's makeshift bassinet.

He went over to investigate and found her wide-eyed and staring up at him. She waved her hands and crowed, clearly wanting to be picked up. He started to call for Katherine and paused. No, he could do this, at least up to a certain point.

"Mornin', sunshine." He crouched down and scooped the baby out of her nest. "Ready for another day?" As he cradled her in his arms, he smiled down at her, unable to resist that chubby face crowned by a shock of dark hair that proclaimed the Sioux blood flowing in her veins. She smiled back, and a warm glow surrounded his heart...until he realized his goal for the day was to get mother and baby back to the lodge. If he achieved his goal, he'd be giving up that smile.

He laid Amanda on the pad Katherine had left on the

table the last time she'd changed the baby. "Getting a little soggy in the britches, aren't you, kiddo?"

Amanda kicked her legs and started blowing bubbles at him.

This time he felt like a real pro as he unsnapped the pink sleeper and removed the wet diaper. The sleeper was also damp, so he decided to take everything off and start from scratch. Unfortunately when he looked in the diaper bag he found yesterday's sleeper, which Katherine had dried by the fire, but no diapers. As Katherine had predicted, they'd run out.

Again he started to call for Katherine but changed his mind. He'd started this project and he'd by damn finish it. "We have us a materials shortage, Mandy," he said. "But don't worry. When you've lived on a ranch full of boys like I have, you're used to running short now and again. We learned how to make do, which is how you and I will handle this temporary crisis. Right?"

Amanda crowed softly, almost as if she were having a conversation with him.

He pretended she understood everything he was saying as he cleaned her carefully with a towelette. "You know, my job as ranger makes a lot more sense now that I've met you. We always talk about saving the parks for future generations, but that was a hazy concept to me before. Now it's not."

Amanda smiled her toothless smile.

"Now I'm protecting the parks just for you." He leaned down and touched the tip of her nose with one finger. "Just for you, Amanda—" He started to add her middle name for emphasis and discovered he didn't even know what it was or if she even had one. Yeah, she probably had one. Katherine was too particular about details to leave that out, and she'd probably used Seymour for the baby's last name. Zeke hadn't admitted it to himself before, but that was another thing he resented—having no voice in choosing the baby's given name, let alone whose last name she'd carry. Fortunately he liked the name Amanda.

"Come on, sunshine." He could at least tag his own nickname on the baby, he decided, picking her up and settling her in the crook of his arm. "Let's go requisition you a diaper."

Her soft baby skin felt good against his bare chest as he walked over to a cupboard above the sink. He tucked her in a little closer, enjoying the sensation. With his free hand he opened the cupboard. "Let's see. We have a red and white stripe, a blue check and a yellow plaid." He glanced down at Amanda. "Which would you rather have? The yellow plaid? Good choice." He grabbed the dish towel out of the cupboard.

"Now we need something to hold this arrangement together. Let's go see what's in the junk drawer."

Amanda lay quietly in his arms, apparently enjoying the journey around the cabin as much as he was. He pulled out a drawer at the end of the counter and rummaged through it. "No safety pins, sunshine. Paper clips, but I don't think that's going to work. We have athletic tape in the first aid kit, but that won't hold a squirmy girl like you." He fished around in the back of the drawer. "But *this* will."

The baby gurgled happily.

Zeke grinned at her. "I knew you were the kind of gal who would appreciate the multitude of uses for duct tape. Now let's get you fixed up."

Back at the table he wasn't sure exactly how to fold the kitchen towel and he tried several versions before settling on one that seemed to cover the problem. Because he had to make sure he kept one hand on Amanda at all times, he ended up using his teeth to tear the duct tape. He was very careful to tape only the towel and not Amanda's delicate skin.

He gazed solemnly down at the baby. "Sunshine, I'm sorry to report to you that duct tape tastes like sh—uh, sheep dip. I guess. I've never tasted sheep dip, but I'm sure it's about as awful as this."

She stared at him with such worried concentration that he chuckled. "But I won't make you taste it. I promise."

Finally he had her snapped back into her dry sleeper. With a sense of great accomplishment, he picked her up and carried her outside, where Katherine was sitting on the porch in the unbroken chair.

Katherine glanced up, her eyes grave.

"I changed her," he said simply.

"Why, thank you, Zeke."

As he handed the freshly diapered baby down to her, he decided he'd never been as proud of an accomplishment in his life.

KATHERINE HAD HEARD AMANDA making her little morning noises and had started into the cabin when she noticed Zeke was already there, bending over the kettle. She'd backed quietly out of the door, retrieved the unbroken Adirondack chair from the yard and sat down on the porch to see what happened next.

She'd heard him talking to Amanda and wondered if he might be changing her. But there were no more diapers, and Katherine kept expecting Zeke to call her inside to figure out an alternative. Apparently he'd come up with one by himself.

Feeling a little out of the loop, she cuddled Amanda close. "How's my girl? Did you sleep well?" Damned if

Amanda didn't look right past her and up at Zeke, as if the baby were fascinated with her new friend. Katherine acknowledged her jealousy with a touch of shame.

Zeke stood nearby, almost hovering. "Do you... need any help?"

She'd created some distance between them by fighting with him about Sadie. Maybe she'd make it easier on both of them if she maintained that distance. "Thanks, but I'm used to working around my bum arm now," she said.

"Then I guess I'll see about fixing the other chair."

"Okay."

He went into the cabin and emerged a short time later carrying a hammer and a handful of nails. As Katherine watched him walk down the steps and out to the overturned chair, she wished he'd thought to put on a shirt and spare her the sight of all that glorious muscle. But the sun that caressed his bronzed back so lovingly had started to warm the clearing and he probably didn't need a shirt.

Unbuttoning her own shirt, Katherine used the broad arm of the chair to take some of Amanda's weight off her injured arm. The baby sucked eagerly. Maybe it was only Katherine's imagination, but Amanda seemed more content and less prone to fussing ever since Zeke had started helping to care for her.

The hollow sound of a hammer blow drifted from the far side of the clearing. Katherine looked up and discovered Zeke had taken the repair project a distance away, probably so the hammering wouldn't disturb Amanda. Yet he was still close enough that she could see the flex of his back muscles and the bulge of his biceps as he drove another nail into the arm of the chair.

A pair of jays chattered in an aspen tree and a squirrel

darted out on a pine branch near the porch. There was no end of other visual diversions for Katherine, but she couldn't seem to avoid the pull of Zeke's lithe movements. He embodied all the reasons a woman took up the art of man-watching.

She shouldn't watch him, though, she told herself. Torturing herself by admiring his body glistening in the sun was stupid, considering that she was determined to leave here today. Maybe she'd overreacted about the bear. In her heart she knew Zeke wouldn't let anything happen to Amanda. But Sadie could serve as a convenient wedge to pry Katherine and Zeke apart. Without something to fight about, they might find their inevitable separation impossible to tolerate.

Even with something to fight about, leaving would be the hardest thing she'd ever done, Katherine thought as she gazed across the clearing. God, the man sure knew how to drive a nail. She couldn't tear her attention away from Zeke until he finished the job and hooked the claw hammer in the belt loop of his jeans. Just as he picked up the chair and turned toward her, she lowered her head and concentrated on Amanda again. She hoped he hadn't caught her staring.

He brought the chair up on the porch and set it beside Katherine's. "Now that chair has some character." His manner seemed to dare her to refute that and make more disparaging remarks about the bear.

She decided to avoid the subject. "Did you check the phone?"

"Yeah." He unhooked the hammer from his belt loop and laid it on the arm of the chair before he sat down. "Still out."

Katherine tried to be discreet as she shifted Amanda to her other breast, but she had the impression Zeke noticed every little movement she made. If he was as fascinated by her as she was by him, then he would notice. "Do you really think you can fix the bridge?"

"Depends on how far down the creek is." Turning away from his quiet, but thorough, study of her as she nursed Amanda, he leaned back in the chair and focused his attention on the woods beyond the clearing. "I'll take a little hike down there after we have some breakfast and check things out."

"And leave us here?" She hadn't meant that to sound quite so panic-stricken. Except for the bear, she'd do fine here by herself. But Sadie had her a little spooked. "What I mean is, I'd like to go along. It's a beautiful day. Maybe I could help you."

"You don't have the shoes for it, Katherine."

"I could manage."

He propped his elbow on the chair and rested his chin on his hand as he gazed at her, his dark eyes growing warmer by the minute.

Conscious of that glow, she tugged her shirt to cover more of her exposed breast. "I really can manage. The shoes will be fine."

He shook his head. "If you're worried about Sadie, the chance that she'll come by in the hour or so I'm gone is practically nonexistent."

"You're probably right." She was feeling sillier by the minute. She was letting this darned bear turn her into a coward. "Never mind."

He continued to study her. "On the other hand, if that bear came by and scared you, I'd never forgive myself. Maybe your shoes will work."

She sent him a grateful look. "Thanks, Zeke."

He watched Amanda nurse for a while.

Katherine felt the heat of his gaze but didn't think she

could very well ask him to turn away. After all, Amanda was his daughter, too, and after today he wouldn't be seeing her for some time. It was just that she'd never been so conscious of the little slurping and swallowing sounds Amanda made, or of how often the baby patted her hand against Katherine's breast, drawing Zeke's attention there.

"What's her middle name?" Zeke asked quietly.

"I didn't tell you?"

"No."

"I'm sorry. It's Lorraine. My mother's name."

"Amanda Lorraine. That's nice." He paused. "I suppose her last name is Seymour?"

Katherine caught a slight challenging note in the question. "Well, yes. I had to decide, for the birth certificate, and I wasn't sure if you wanted anything to do with—"

"I understand."

The way he cut off her explanation didn't sound particularly understanding. She remembered the little pine tree carving on his mantle that indicated a certain pride in his family name of Lonetree despite, or maybe even because of, his difficult childhood. She wondered if he was beginning to feel possessive toward Amanda. "Maybe you'd like to discuss hyphenating her last name," she said.

"Maybe." His glance strayed from her for the first time in several minutes as his attention shifted to a point over her right shoulder. "Stay still."

Her pulse jumped. Oh, God. The bear. "What?" she croaked.

"Two deer, a doe and a buck. They're only about thirty yards away. You'll need to turn to see them."

She let out a long sigh. "I thought it was Sadie."

"She only comes in the late afternoon and evening. I've

never seen her around here in the morning, and most animals are creatures of habit. Now just turn slowly to your right and you'll be able to see them on the edge of the aspen grove."

Katherine loved deer, with their liquid brown eyes and graceful carriage. Amanda had begun to drift off to sleep but she continued to nurse sporadically, so Katherine kept her tucked against her as she eased around.

Sure enough, the deer grazed only a short distance beyond Zeke's truck. The buck had a fine set of antlers. He raised his head, looked around regally, then stared straight at Katherine before lowering his head to graze again.

"They're beautiful, Zeke. They look tame enough to pet."

"Fortunately, they're not. That would be dangerous for them."

As if to prove Zeke's point, the deer lifted their heads in response to a slight breeze blowing toward them from the direction of the cabin. In seconds they'd bounded off into the woods.

"I guess they caught our scent," Katherine said, gazing after them.

"Yep. They have to use all their senses to avoid predators, to find food...to mate."

The resonance in his voice triggered a response in Katherine. She turned her head to find his gaze focused on her like a laser. Her movements had dislodged the shirt somewhat, and Amanda picked that moment to doze off, releasing Katherine's nipple. Heart pounding, she pulled the shirt over her bare breast. "Whereas we've evolved past that need," she said.

"Have we?" His dark gaze grew intense. "Maybe I've been around these animals so long I'm growing to be like them. I find your scent...irresistible." He gazed at her a moment longer, then stood, looking out at the clearing. "Irresistible," he murmured, almost to himself.

His stance reminded Katherine of the buck that had recently left the clearing with his doe. When Zeke turned, a haunted expression on his face, she expected him to bolt, too, away from her.

Instead he paused in front of her chair. Slowly he leaned down, bracing both hands on the chair's wide arms, effectively imprisoning her there. "I know you have to leave." His dark eyes searched hers.

"Yes." She expected him to push away and leave her to her frustration while he dealt with his. His kiss caught her off guard.

She gasped in surprise. With a murmur of need he deepened the kiss, urging her to relax back into the chair, to accept the sweet pressure of his lips, the gentle thrust of his tongue. The bristle of his morning beard was rough against her skin, but she didn't care.

Dazed and aching, helpless to do anything but respond, she lifted her mouth, opening to his invasion. He kissed her greedily, tasting, nipping, delving again and again as his breathing grew ragged.

Finally, with a groan, he drew back, the muscles in his arms bulging as he gripped the chair arms and stared at her with eyes black as midnight. His voice was hoarse and his chest heaved. "If I don't get you out of here today..."

She was shaking. "I know."

He shoved himself away from the chair. "After breakfast."

ZEKE DIDN'T RECOGNIZE himself anymore. His famous control had disappeared. The minute Katherine walked into the cabin he wanted to put that sleepy baby in her bassinet and take her hot-blooded mother to bed. But once he did that, he could forget about getting her out of here today. And the sooner she left, the sooner he could start to heal.

So instead of seducing her, he got a small fire going and whipped up oatmeal in the cast-iron pot. In a separate pan he heated water so he could make coffee for himself and cocoa for Katherine. In the midst of all that, Katherine announced she needed to change Amanda's diaper.

"So soon?" he asked, turning from where he was stirring the oatmeal in the pot. There was another reason to get Katherine back to the lodge today. The dish towels wouldn't hold out much longer.

"I'm afraid she's ready again." She laid the baby on the changing pad and started unsnapping her sleeper. "Besides, I'm dying to find out how you—" She paused and began to laugh.

"What's so funny?" He realized he sounded a little defensive, but he couldn't help it. He was new at this, and besides, he'd run into a supply problem. "I thought it was a pretty good job."

"It's a wonderful job." She sounded as if she were trying to control herself, but her efforts weren't very successful. She kept bursting out with new giggles. "I just never would have thought of—" she tried to disguise another fit of laughter by clearing her throat elaborately "—of duct tape."

"I couldn't find any pins, and I didn't think paper clips would hold."

"Well, this duct tape holds like crazy. She may be welded into this yellow plaid diaper for life."

Zeke was quite certain he could manage his invention

a whole lot better than Katherine was doing. "Here, you stir the oatmeal and I'll change her." He leaned the spoon against the side of the pot and crossed to the table. "And you'd better put the sling back on your arm, too."

"All right." Katherine's hazel eyes sparkled with merriment as he approached. "Maybe next time you might want to use a teensy bit less of that tape, though."

He looked into her eyes and forgot all about diapers. "How come you always look so damn kissable?" He realized he sounded downright cross, and maybe he was.

She matched his irritated tone. "It's not like I'm trying to be attractive, Zeke. I mean, look at me—no makeup and clothes six sizes too big, for heaven's sake." She moved aside but kept her hand on the baby's tummy until he put his next to hers. Then she stepped back.

He started working at the duct tape. Maybe he had been a little overzealous in his application of it. "You know, when I made love to you a year ago, you weren't trying to be attractive, either." He glanced over at her. "Maybe pure, unadulterated Katherine is what turns me on."

She rolled her eyes. "Men are forever saying things like that. Then some beauty queen strolls by and their tongues hang out."

He went back to his task, made more difficult because Amanda had decided to start kicking and waving her arms. "I can't speak for the guys you know in New York, but I go in for earthy, not flashy. When you stroll by in that flannel shirt, my tongue's dragging the ground."

She didn't answer right away. When she spoke, her voice was subdued. "You're forgetting that's not the real me. Ninety percent of the time I look nothing like this, even though it's pretty much all you've seen. After all, my job involves putting out a fashion magazine."

"Good point." Depressing point.

Her voice gentled even more. "But it's good for a girl's ego to have a man say he likes her just the way she is. Thank you for that."

"Don't mention it." He struggled with the tape. "You'd better put on your sling and then go stir the oatmeal. It's no fun when it starts sticking to the pan."

"Right."

Feeling in need of a mood elevator, he leaned down and kissed the baby on the nose. "Hey, sunshine. Looks like somebody thought you needed industrial-strength diapering this morning."

Amanda gurgled at him and patted his face.

"Don't worry. I'll get you out of this sooner or later." He wondered if he could talk Katherine into strapping duct tape over her sweats. The stuff would make a terrific chastity belt. Finally he got the diaper off and turned to Katherine, who was vigorously stirring the oatmeal. "Would you please get me another dish towel? They're on the top shelf of the left-hand cupboard."

She leaned the spoon against the lip of the kettle and went over to handle his request. She had to stand on tiptoe and strain to reach the towels, even though she was a fairly tall woman. If she lived here, Zeke thought, he'd move the cupboards down a foot. But of course she'd never live here, so they could stay where they were.

"You don't have a whole lot of these," Katherine said as she handed him the red-striped towel. "It won't matter if we can get back to the lodge today, but if we can't for some reason, then—"

He took the towel. "If I can't take you back today, we'll have bigger problems than a shortage of diapers." He glanced at her. "The longer we stay in this cabin together, the tougher it'll be when you leave."

"You don't have to tell me that. We'll make it out."

Zeke gazed at her standing there, her cheeks flushed, her eyes bright as a mountain meadow. "We'll see."

13

TWO HOURS LATER, KATHERINE stood with Zeke on the banks of the turbulent creek. If anything it looked more impassable than it had the day before. Little of Zeke's bridge remained, so repairing it had only been a pipe dream.

Katherine glanced over at Zeke. He had insisted on carrying Amanda in the baby sling, arguing that he was more surefooted in his hiking boots than she was in her city shoes. He'd been right about that. She'd slipped twice but hadn't fallen down...yet.

"What do you think?" she asked, although his frown pretty much said it all.

"Let's follow the path downstream a ways. There's one wide spot where it's always more shallow. Before I built the bridge I used to take the truck across there."

"But the creek wasn't running this high, I'll bet."

"No." Zeke glanced up. Heavy clouds had begun to gather in the west. A hawk glided on the steady wind blowing the clouds in their direction.

"You think it's going to rain again, don't you?"

He nodded. "How are your feet holding up?"

"Fine," she lied. She'd crammed her shoes on over his heavy socks, which made them too tight, and she was afraid she'd rubbed more than one blister on each foot. But she'd been determined to come with him, both for the comfort his presence brought and for the chance to assess the situation firsthand. If he decided to bring the truck through, she wanted to have some idea of whether they'd get stuck in the process.

"Then let's go." He started down the trail winding beside the creek.

If she'd had hiking boots she would have thoroughly enjoyed herself, but her hiking boots were back at the hotel and her feet hurt. Still, she drew pleasure from the Christmas scent of the pines and the merry chatter of birds, squirrels and chipmunks. A red fox with a spectacular plume of a tail ran across their path, and three deer disappeared through the trees like tawny shadows.

She wished she could relax into the peaceful scene as she'd been able to do so often as a child in the Adirondacks. Instead she couldn't help worrying about how Zeke would get them back to the lodge today. In fact, she wondered when she'd ever get back to the lodge, and New York seemed a million miles away.

Naomi had booked her to return Monday so she'd be at her desk bright and early Tuesday morning to approve the next issue's layout and make assignments for the Milan show. Besides that, a feature on a new designer was due by— In her preoccupation she tripped over a tree root and barely missed falling.

Zeke turned quickly. "You okay?"

"Fine." She managed a smile.

"Your feet hurt."

"Not much."

"You're limping."

After making such a fuss about coming and insisting that her shoes were fine for the trip, Katherine wasn't about to admit to her problem. "Yes, because I just stubbed my toe on that tree root. Go on. I'm right behind you."

"We're almost there." He turned and continued along the muddy path.

Katherine took a deep breath and followed him. That's what she got for ignoring the beauty around her and worrying about some future problem. That was a lesson she'd thought she'd learned during her solo hike last summer, but apparently she needed more teaching. Good thing Zeke was carrying Amanda, who seemed totally happy with the arrangement, too.

"Here's the place," Zeke called out.

Katherine came up beside him and surveyed the rushing creek. "It doesn't look a lot better, to be honest. And how would you get the truck here?"

"There's a wider path that cuts through the trees. We can take that back to the cabin, now that we're here." He adjusted Amanda's weight against his chest as he gazed out over the creek. "The water's gone down some since early this morning. See where that debris is hanging from that low branch?"

Katherine looked where he was pointing. "Yes."

"That's where it was a few hours ago. If it doesn't rain again, it'll go down some more by this afternoon. We could probably make it."

"If it doesn't rain."

"It might not."

Katherine wouldn't have wanted to bet on it. Yet Zeke seemed to think they had a chance of driving out of here this afternoon. And that's what she wanted, of course. The woods were beautiful, and Zeke...well, Zeke was indescribable. But she had to get back to New York.

"I guess we might as well start home," he said. "I—oh, God, look at that." He stared upstream.

"What?" Katherine strained to see what he was looking at with such a worried expression, but she couldn't figure it out.

"There. On the branch coming toward us. A mother raccoon with her babies."

Finally Katherine saw a cluster of brown fur clinging to a flimsy branch. Eventually she differentiated a nose and tail and gradually made out the babies, perhaps four of them, riding precariously on the mother's back. "Will they be okay?"

"Maybe not." Zeke started unfastening Amanda's sling. "Downstream there's a waterfall. I don't think the babies could survive that. Hold Amanda for me."

Katherine took a sleeping Amanda and put on the sling, but she didn't like the looks of this. "What are you going to do?"

"Wade in and see if I can pull the branch over next to the shore, so the mother can climb off."

"Zeke, that water's really moving." Katherine didn't want the baby raccoons to drown, either, but she was more concerned about keeping Zeke in one piece.

"I'll be fine." He started down the embankment, hanging on to the trunks of saplings as he went.

Katherine tried to tell herself that Zeke did this sort of thing for a living and he would be fine, but when he put his foot into the water and slipped, she cried out.

"Don't worry!" he called over his shoulder as he righted himself and started wading into the stream.

She worried, anyway. Rushing water had nearly killed her once, and she didn't trust it. As Zeke got in over his knees, she held her breath. He might be a big man, but the current was powerful.

Amanda stirred and started to fuss.

"Not now, baby," Katherine said, jiggling her.

"Mommy has to watch out for your daddy, who is doing something brave and foolish, I'm afraid."

Zeke staggered in the swift water, and Katherine's stomach churned. Finally he reached a point that must have satisfied him, because he stopped and looked downstream, waiting for the branch to come by.

"What if they bite you?" she called.

"They don't usually carry rabies," he called back.

Rabies. She hadn't even thought of that. She'd only been concerned that he'd be wounded, not that he'd contract a potentially fatal disease. "Maybe you should just come on back, Zeke."

"They're almost here."

Amanda started crying in earnest.

"I can't feed you now, sweetheart," Katherine said, her attention glued to the drama in the middle of the stream. "Daddy's trying to save some baby raccoons, and I'm hoping I don't have to try and save Daddy."

The branch drifted slightly out of reach as it was about to pass Zeke, and he moved toward it, nearly going down and causing Katherine's stomach to flip-flop again. But he stayed upright and grabbed the very tip of the branch. Katherine was barely breathing as the mother raccoon stared at Zeke and hissed. Katherine half expected the animal to lunge for his throat. After all, she didn't know this tall creature holding the branch was trying to save her babies.

The rush of water and Amanda's crying made it difficult for Katherine to hear, but once in a while she thought she heard the low murmur of Zeke's voice. She edged to the right for a better view, and sure enough, she could see that his lips were moving. He was talking to the raccoon.

Her heart pounded as he slowly edged back toward shore, dragging the branch with the raccoons on it toward safety. All the while he kept up his steady, soft monologue. When he was ankle-deep in the water, Katherine began to breathe easier. She spoke soothingly to Amanda and the baby settled down a little.

Finally he dragged the branch through the shallow water and anchored it against the embankment with some large rocks. The mother crouched on the branch and followed every movement he made. At last Zeke stood back. "Okay, the gangplank's down whenever you're ready."

"Good job," Katherine said, feeling proud and immensely relieved. But when he turned to climb the embankment, Katherine noticed him wince and saw that his jaw was clenched. Fresh fear shot through her.

"What's wrong?" she said.

He glanced up at her. "When I slipped out there I turned my ankle wrong. But I'll be okay."

"You sprained your ankle?" If it hadn't been such a horrible possibility, she would have laughed. First her wrist and now his ankle. A couple of gimps.

He climbed to the path beside her, his breath coming in jerky gasps and his face pale. "I think so. But I'll be okay." He turned, breathing heavily, and stood with his hands on his hips while he watched the mother raccoon. "She's going. Okay, there, take it easy. That's it."

Katherine was glad to see the raccoon scramble safely to shore and disappear into the underbrush. But she was afraid Zeke had paid a hefty price.

He sighed and turned back to her with a wan smile. "Mission accomplished."

"I'm glad, but I don't like the fact you hurt your ankle."

"I'll just walk it out on the way back." His eyes reflected pain, yet he managed a grin. "Unless you want to carry me."

"I wish I could. But I'll at least take Amanda." She expected him to argue with her.

"Okay, if you don't mind."

"Sure, no problem." She glanced away so he wouldn't see the concern she knew must be shining in her eyes. It was just a slight sprain, she told herself. Nothing to be worried about. He'd probably be able to walk it off, like he said.

But she didn't really think so, not from the way he was favoring it as he started down the path. They'd taken no more than ten steps when the first drop of rain fell on Katherine's nose.

ZEKE KNEW HE HAD A BAD sprain, had known from the minute it happened. But there was no use saying that to Katherine when there wasn't a damn thing to be done except limp home. He'd considered trying to fashion a makeshift crutch before they started the hike back, but then he'd taken a look at the clouds and decided against it. Besides, Amanda was fussing and needed to be fed soon.

He wondered if he'd still be able to drive with his sprained ankle. Well, he'd just have to. That was assuming it didn't rain any more today and raise the creek again. Then the first few raindrops fell, and he began to accept the inevitable.

How ironic. It looked as if he'd be closed in the cabin with Katherine for at least another night, but judging from the pain in his ankle, he'd be in no condition to make passionate love to her. Just when he thought this situation couldn't get any worse, it did.

As the rain came faster, he stopped and turned back to

Katherine. "If I thought this would blow over, I'd say we could wait it out under a tree. But I think we'd better keep going."

"Me, too." As she pulled the lapels of her jacket closer around Amanda, the baby started squirming and crying. "And Amanda's quieter when I keep moving."

"I'm going to feel like a jerk if either one of you comes down with a cold because of this."

"Hey, I begged you to come along, so it's my fault, not yours. And breast-fed babies are pretty resistant to colds." She licked away a raindrop that had landed on her upper lip. "I've been rained on before. How's your ankle?"

He wondered how he could possibly think about sex at a time like this, but the motion of her tongue when she'd licked away the raindrop had caused a reaction in his groin. "I'll live."

Katherine jiggled Amanda as she gazed up at him. "I'd better warn you I'm a complete dunce when it comes to first aid. I never can remember when you're supposed to heat something or when you're supposed to ice it down."

He had a momentary image of her tending to his injury, her gentle hands on his skin. Nope. Bad idea. "Don't worry. I'll be able to handle it myself. How are your feet?"

"Probably in better shape than your ankle. Let's go."

Gritting his teeth against his increasing pain, he set out again. He must have torn something in there for it to hurt so damned bad. At least the raccoon family had made it, though. He'd think about that while he was walking, to take his mind off his ankle.

He remembered the day the ranch had inherited some baby raccoons when a mother was killed out on the main road. He and four other lucky kids had been allowed to raise a baby raccoon as a pet. Saving that little family to-day had been sort of a tribute to Stinky's memory, and the warm feeling that gave him took away some of the pain.

Not enough, though. By the time the cabin came in sight he was feeling dizzy from it. He stopped to catch his breath as the world wobbled a little.

"Zeke?" Katherine peered up at him. "You don't look so good."

"I'm okay." He fished in his pocket for the house key and handed it to her. "Go ahead and get Amanda out of the rain. I'm sure she's hungry."

"No, we're going in together." She took hold of his arm. "You can lean on my shoulder if you want."

He was beginning to see little white spots in front of his eyes. "That's okay. Go on. I'll be right there."

"Nope." She gave his arm a little pull. "I'm not going without you."

"Katherine, I think I—" The world went black.

THE NEXT THING ZEKE KNEW, someone was trying to take off his pants. And they were damned determined about it, too pulling, puffing and cussing a blue streak. It wasn't helping the pain in his ankle one bit, either. He slowly sat up, propping his hands on the floor behind him, and came face-to-face with Katherine.

She stopped tugging on his pants. She'd only been us-ing one hand, which explained a lot of her awkwardness. "You're conscious! Oh, thank God!"

Nearby, Amanda fretted in her bassinet.

He tried to figure things out. The last he remembered he was outside. "How did I get into the cabin?"

"I dragged you." She looked a mess, her hair soaked, mud streaking her face and the front of her shirt.

"Dragged me? With a sprained wrist? Katherine, you should never have tried to—"

"I was supposed to leave you out there?"

"Maybe not." Even though she was wet and covered with mud, she was the sexiest-looking woman he'd ever seen. "I guess I passed out."

"You went down like a felled tree." She resumed pulling at his pants.

The movement hurt like hell, but he kept his tone light. She was only trying to help. "What are you doing?"

She glanced up. "You need to get these off."

"Why?"

She frowned impatiently at him. "I don't know much about first aid, but in every movie I've ever seen, when the hero gets hurt, the heroine undresses him and puts him to bed. Besides, you're all muddy and you shouldn't get into that bed in muddy clothes. And besides *that*, your ankle is swelling, and if I don't get these jeans off soon, you'll never get them off without cutting them. These look sort of new and I didn't think you'd appreciate having them cut up."

"I don't have to get into bed."

"Are you kidding? You just passed out. You should be in bed." She gave another yank and the jeans came free. She took them to the door, opened it and tossed them outside before coming to stand over him. "I got your floor all muddy, too, but that can wait. Take off your shirt and I'll help you into bed."

He wished he could be pain-free enough to enjoy this. Then Amanda's fussing became more demanding and he realized Katherine had postponed taking care of the baby to tend to him. "Look, I appreciate what you're trying to do, but I can manage from here. I'll bet you haven't fed Amanda yet."

"No, and I'm not going to until you're in bed and we've done...well, whatever is necessary to that nasty-looking ankle. Take off your shirt. It's all muddy from where I dragged you across the yard and up the steps. I'll get a towel to get some of the dirt out of your hair."

He finally decided the best way to restore some calm to the situation was to do as she asked. She seemed to have a program in mind, and it had to proceed in order, beginning with him climbing into bed.

He glanced over at the bassinet. "Sorry, Mandy. Guess you'll have to get in line." He unbuttoned his shirt and took it off as Katherine returned with a towel and knelt down behind him.

"You really need your hair washed." With her left hand she began rubbing the towel briskly over his hair and scalp. "But we'll have to take care of that later. This will get the worst of it."

He thought of mentioning that she was working on the wrong end of him. While she was concentrating on getting the mud out of his hair, his ankle seemed to be swelling more every second. But the sensation of having her rub his head felt good, especially when she swayed close enough that her soft breasts jiggled against his shoulders. To hell with his ankle.

"There. That's better." She stood and walked around to peer down at him. "Now, do you think you can stand, or do you want me to help you?"

He was beginning to get in the swing of this. Certain things could make a guy forget he was in pain. "I might need some help."

"Okay." She crouched down beside him. "Put your arm around my shoulders. When I count to three, I'll start lifting. Put your weight on me and on your good ankle."

"I will." He put his arm around her, and she slipped her arm around his waist. Nice. Her smooth cheek was only a breath away. He watched her clench her jaw in concentration and a wave of tenderness swept over him at her earnest attempt to render aid.

"Here we go," she said. "On three. One, two, *three*." She gripped his waist and heaved.

He could tell she wasn't terribly familiar with helping people to their feet, and his bulk threatened to topple them both until he put some of his weight on his bum ankle. With a soft grunt of pain, he rebalanced himself and leaned fully on Katherine. The feel of her warm body almost made up for the sensation of someone cutting at his ankle with a chain saw.

"I'll bet it hurts," she murmured.

"Some."

"Let's get you over to the bed."

He allowed her to guide him there, where she'd already folded back the sheets and propped up one pillow as a backrest. She turned him and eased him down to a sitting position. Before he took his arm from her shoulders, he fantasized pulling her down with him. He might really screw up his ankle with a stunt like that, but his ankle wasn't much of a consideration. Amanda was, however. Her fussing had turned into an outraged wail. She needed Katherine to feed her.

"Let me lift your legs for you so you don't strain that ankle any more than necessary," she said.

"All right." He couldn't remember ever allowing someone to baby him like this. The few times he'd become injured he'd always handled the problem himself or made do with a quick trip to the emergency room. No one had ever fussed over Zeke Lonetree. And damn, but it felt nice.

She held both feet carefully as she maneuvered him fully onto the bed. "Okay, now what?"

He leaned back with a little sigh. Maybe relaxing on a comfy bed wasn't such a bad idea. "I'm fine now. You can feed Amanda."

"I know there's something more we should do with your ankle. Or is it too late?"

He grinned at her. Propped in bed with his weight off his ankle made him feel a lot feistier. "Yeah, it's too late. I think we'll have to amputate."

"Don't even joke about a thing like that. What can I do for you?"

"Well, if we elevate it with a pillow, that will probably help with the swelling."

"Makes sense. If you'll hand me the other pillow, I'll fix it up for you."

Despite the pain when she lifted his ankle, he enjoyed her hands on him way too much. The brush of her bandaged wrist reminded him that she'd probably suffered some pain dragging him into the cabin, yet she'd done it. She obviously cared about him, which made the chemistry between them even sweeter. But he tried to seem unaffected by her touch. He didn't want her to think she was arousing him and stop these gentle ministrations.

She stood back and surveyed him. "Done. What else?"

"I don't suppose the freezer's cold enough to keep anything frozen."

"Nope. I checked that right after I dragged you in here."

He smiled at her. "I thought you didn't know anything about first aid?"

"Well, duh. That's what you did for my wrist. I was pretty sure I should use some ice for your ankle if we had any. But we don't."

"Then I guess you've done all you can for now."

She gazed at him doubtfully. "Aspirin? For the pain?"

He shook his head. "Go feed the baby."

"Okay." She glanced down at her mud-spattered shirt. "Mind if I borrow another shirt and change first?"

"Be my guest. Why not let me hold her until you get ready?"

"Oh, Zeke, she needs changing and she's hungry and squirmy. I don't think—"

"Let me give it a shot. My ankle's not in great shape, but there's nothing wrong with my arms. Maybe I can settle her down some."

"Well, if you want to try, that would be very nice." She hurried over to the bassinet, picked up Amanda and held the baby away from her muddy shirt as she brought her over. "Hey, Mandy, don't cry. Daddy's going to hold you for a while until I get cleaned up. Be a good girl."

He discovered he liked the way Katherine said that— *Daddy's going to hold you*—as if Amanda should feel honored. Actually he was the one who felt honored to be able to hold her, even fussing the way she was. He cradled her against his chest and started telling her about his pet raccoon Stinky. Sure enough, she stopped crying and acted as if she were hanging on every word.

While he told his story, he was aware of Katherine opening not one, but two dresser drawers.

"So you really do have a gun in there," she said.

He interrupted his story to answer her. "Yeah. If I were a horse you could shoot me and put me out of my misery."

She paused beside the bed, a red-and-black shirt in her hands. "Does it really hurt that bad?"

"No," he lied. "I'm kidding."

Her forehead creased in worry. "Could it be broken?"

"No. Just a sprain." Except that he knew certain types of sprains could be as painful and take almost as long to heal as a broken bone. If he hadn't started out with that kind, he'd probably created it by walking on it all the way back to the cabin. "Now go change your shirt before Mandy gets bored with my stories."

"Be right back."

After she went into the bathroom, Zeke returned his attention to Amanda. "Okay, where was I? Did I ever tell you about the time that Stinky got loose in the ranch house kitchen? No? Well, I thought the cook was going to fix raccoon stew after that little episode. But it wasn't my fault. I'll tell you a secret. It was Shane Daniels who almost got Stinky barbecued. You'd like Shane. He's..."

Zeke paused as he wondered how his buddies from the ranch would react to the news about Amanda. One thing was for sure, they'd have kicked his butt if he'd refused to have anything to do with his daughter. Parenthood was pretty sacred to those guys, for obvious reasons. It was pretty sacred to Zeke, too, which was why he'd originally thought he'd rather be no parent at all than a half-assed one. But now that he'd agreed to stay in touch with Amanda, he'd just have to figure out how to be a decent father under crummy circumstances.

Amanda began to wiggle and whimper.

"I'm sorry, sunshine." He brought his attention back to the baby in his arms. "I'll bet you want me to finish the story. It was like this. Shane decided to play a joke on the cook. And that's when all the ruckus started."

14

KATHERINE KEPT THE BATHROOM door open a crack so she could hear Zeke's tales of Stinky while she washed the mud off and changed into a clean shirt.

His raccoon stories charmed her tremendously. So that's why he'd been so determined to make sure the raccoons survived. She wondered if he'd tell Amanda those stories again when she was old enough to understand them. And if Amanda would come back to New York demanding to have a raccoon for a pet.

Katherine tried to imagine what Zeke would look like by that time, closing in on forty, maybe with touches of gray in his raven-black hair. Instinctively she knew he'd only become more attractive as he grew older—his type always did. Some woman was bound to come along who fancied herself a pioneer lady ready to live in Zeke's wilderness with him.

It would be heaven. Katherine glanced guiltily in the bathroom mirror as the traitorous thought glowed like neon in her brain. She couldn't allow herself to think such things. Naomi was offering her the top job at a prestigious magazine. Anyone who turned that down would be foolish, not to mention incredibly ungrateful. Besides, Naomi would be crushed, and Katherine could never do anything to hurt her generous and loving godmother.

She nudged off her muddy shoes and peeled off her socks. Sure enough, blisters. She left the socks off. While giving her hands one last wash after handling the socks, she wondered if a soak in the icy water would be almost the same as ice on Zeke's ankle. Once Amanda was fed she'd see about that.

She ran a comb quickly through her damp hair and looked at her bandaged wrist. In order to get it somewhat clean she'd had to saturate it with water and it was soggy and uncomfortable, but she couldn't worry about that now. She left the bathroom as Zeke was winding up a story about Stinky's adventures with a ranch dog named Shep. After taking another dish towel from the cupboard to use as a diaper, she walked over to the bed, amazed at how quietly Amanda lay in Zeke's arms.

He glanced up at her. "You look good in red."

And you look good in bed, she thought. "Thanks. I'll take her now."

"She's a good baby, isn't she?"

Using her left arm, Katherine lifted Amanda and carried her over to the table to change her. "I think so. I don't have much basis of comparison except for the babies of employees at *Cachet.*" She unsnapped the sleeper. Good thing she'd washed the spare plus the soiled dish towels and dried them by the cooking fire before they left on the hike.

"I'll bet the other babies cried more than she does."

"It seems that way." She'd used considerably less duct tape on this diaper, so it wasn't such a struggle to take off. "Other mothers have told me that it's just luck when you get an even-tempered baby. I think it might also be because I keep her on a regular schedule and make her feel as secure as possible."

"Or maybe it's because of me." He sounded downright smug about it.

"You?" Katherine placed a restraining hand on

Amanda and turned toward him. "What, you passed on some calm-and-peaceful genes?"

"In a way."

Amanda had apparently run out of patience. She started to wail like a little banshee.

"Even Amanda disagrees about that." Katherine taped up the diaper and snapped Amanda into her suit as quickly as possible, considering the soggy and unwieldy bandage on her wrist. Then she picked her up and started over toward the rocker as Amanda continued to cry.

"Would you pull the rocker over here and talk to me while you feed her?" Zeke asked above the hubbub.

Katherine paused for just a heartbeat. "Sure." As she dragged the rocker closer to the bed, she wondered if he realized how revealing his request was. Her strong, silent mountain man was beginning to enjoy having company.

Because she didn't want to buy trouble, she positioned the rocker so that she was on an angle from Zeke's direct view. She knew the sight of her nursing Amanda aroused him, so she'd keep herself out of sight as much as possible.

Sitting down in the rocker, she worked at the buttons of her shirt. The wet bandage really was more clumsy than a dry one, and Amanda's squirming and crying didn't make things any easier.

"If you'll come over here, I'll unbutton that," Zeke said.

Oh, no, you don't. If he unfastened those buttons, she'd become just as aroused as he was by the process. "Thanks, but I've got it now." With a sigh of relief she gave her breast to Amanda and silence settled over the cabin.

"You can't blame her," Zeke said. "She started getting hungry back on the trail. She's had to wait a long time."

"I don't blame her." Katherine leaned her head against the back of the chair and rocked slowly while she listened to the rain. Nursing Amanda was one of the most satisfying experiences of her life, and it frustrated her almost as much as the baby when she couldn't do it on schedule.

This recent crying jag was about as bad as it ever got. Amanda had suffered no bouts with colic or unexplained illnesses. When the two of them were free to do their thing, the baby was a joy to care for. The pregnancy had been difficult, but the doctors had assured Katherine she didn't have to worry that she'd always have difficult pregnancies. The next one would probably be a breeze, they'd said.

Except there wouldn't be a next one. If all her children could be this wonderful, Katherine was a little sorry she wouldn't have any more. Although she hadn't admitted the fact to Zeke, she didn't want to have another man's child any more than he wanted her to.

Then she remembered Zeke's comment that if Amanda had a brother or sister, he wanted to be the one to father the baby. A thrill of awareness ran through her at the thought that Zeke would entertain such an idea. Of course it was crazy and she'd never follow through with it, but making a child with Zeke had been an outstanding experience.

She glanced over at him. He was watching her, a glow in his dark eyes that almost made her believe he could read her mind. Silence could be erotic, she realized, especially when it was filled with soft sucking sounds from the baby she and Zeke had created. She'd better start making some conversation, as Zeke had originally requested.

"So why do you think Amanda's temperament is all your doing?" she asked.

"Simple. It's her Sioux blood."

"And Sioux babies are all even-tempered? Come on, Zeke."

"I don't mean Sioux babies in particular. Traditionally, Native American babies had to be quiet and well-behaved. During warfare between the tribes or against the white man, a crying baby could alert the enemy."

She had no trouble picturing Zeke as a warrior—in some ways he seemed like a throwback to those days. "Yes, but that was a long time ago, and it was probably mostly conditioning after they were born, not some innate part of their makeup."

Zeke grinned. "You're probably right. But it sounded good, didn't it?"

"Sure did. It's good copy, as we say in my job. Naomi's already suggested that Amanda would make an exotic runway model with her coloring."

Zeke frowned. "A model? Don't they have to starve themselves to stay skinny enough for the camera?"

"If she inherits my metabolism she won't have to starve herself. And I think she'll be beautiful enough to make it."

Zeke still looked doubtful. "Sure, she'll be beautiful enough, but what kind of a life is that?"

She loved his parental assumption that his daughter would be gorgeous. Even more she loved his concern for Amanda's future. "Well, there can be a lot of pressure, but a lot of money, too. And if she has any interest in acting, that's a logical step from modeling."

"You mean be a movie star?"

Katherine gazed down at Amanda. "You never know."

"So many movie stars seem to have messed-up lives."

"But not all of them." Katherine glanced at him. "If

Amanda grows up with lots of self-esteem, she could handle herself in that world. But then I want her to grow up with lots of self-esteem no matter what she decides to do with her life."

"Which is where I come in."

Katherine nodded. "I think so. When I brought her out here I was confused about that. Naomi had convinced me I could raise Amanda without you."

"You could."

"Maybe. But I don't want to." She met his gaze. "And I hope you don't want me to, either."

He took a deep breath and looked into her eyes, as if making some sort of pledge. "No, I don't. Not anymore."

AFTER KATHERINE FINISHED feeding Amanda and was tucking her in for her nap, Zeke noticed how chilly the air in the cabin was. He'd been so engrossed in watching Katherine nurse the baby, he'd been oblivious to the temperature, but now that she'd buttoned her shirt, he could concentrate on something besides the temptation of her breasts.

He surveyed the small pieces of wood left on the hearth. Not enough for a decent fire. Throwing back the covers, he gritted his teeth and swung his legs to the floor.

Katherine glanced up from where she was crouched next to Amanda's bassinet. "What do you think you're doing?"

Zeke fought dizziness as he stood, balancing himself by holding on to the headboard of the bed. "We need wood."

"Get back in bed." She checked the sleeping baby once more and stood. "I'll take care of the wood."

"I feel dumb having you do all the work." Using the

mattress to steady himself, he started toward the dresser. "I'll just put on some sweats and another shirt."

"No, you won't." She stepped into his path, blocking his way.

"Katherine—"

"You should see yourself." She crossed her arms and planted her feet more firmly. "It's freezing in here and sweat's popping out on your forehead. Now, I want you to give up this macho routine and go back to bed before you pass out again."

He had to admit he didn't feel so great whenever he put the slightest weight on his ankle.

"Get back to bed and stop being ridiculous."

"Katherine, I—"

"If you don't start moving, I'm going to kick you in your bum ankle, ranger man! My goodness, what an ego you have. Nobody can do anything but you. Now get going."

He gazed down at her. She was so adorably belligerent it was hard for him not to smile. Figuring she wouldn't appreciate that, he set his mouth into a tight line and nodded. Turning, he sat down on the mattress again.

"That's better. Do you have a bucket around here?"

"Under the sink."

She walked over to the sink, opened a bottom cupboard and took out the bucket. "As long as you've moved yourself, I want you to soak your foot and ankle in cold water while I'm busy getting the wood. And wrap a blanket around your shoulders so you don't catch cold." She tipped the bucket under the faucet and started filling it.

"Yes, ma'am." While her back was to him, he allowed himself a grin. "At least you didn't tell me to soak my head."

"That's not a bad idea." It was a good-size bucket and she had to use both hands to lug it over to the bed. "But we'll start with your foot." She set the bucket down slowly, so the water wouldn't slosh out. "Put it in there."

"My foot isn't going to fit all the way in. It's too big."

"Do the best you can to cover your ankle."

He braced himself against the shock and dipped his toes in. Damn, the water was cold. But she'd come up with a good idea. The sooner the swelling went down on his ankle, the sooner he'd be able to take care of things around here. Muttering a few curses, he immersed his foot as far as possible.

"Well, now you're shivering."

He glanced up at her. "No j-joke."

"That's partly because you don't have the blanket fixed right." She reached around him with both arms, practically embracing him as she adjusted it. "You'd think somebody with Sioux blood would know how to wrap a blanket around himself."

"Very funny." Her close proximity and her tantalizing scent were really getting to him. He'd just about decided to grab her and kiss that smart mouth of hers when she stopped fiddling with the blanket and stepped back.

"Good. You've stopped shivering."

He wanted to tell her that was because his foot and ankle were completely numb and he was getting an erection from all her fondling. He thought better of it. "You sure have been bossy recently," he said.

"If you'd stop trying to be Superman I wouldn't have to boss you around." She surveyed him. "You need a sock on that other foot."

"If you say so."

"I do." She walked over to the dresser and took out a pair of wool socks. She laid one on top of the dresser and came over to kneel in front of him.

"I can put on my own sock, Katherine."

"Oh, be quiet. This is faster." She rolled the sock over his foot and up his calf.

He loved every second of the experience. He'd never realized before how sensitive that area of his body could be.

"There." She stood and put her hands on her hips. "Now I'll get the wood. After that I'll build us a fire and make you some hot coffee and me some cocoa. Then I'll fix us something for lunch. How about that?"

"Sounds good, Superwoman."

She lifted both eyebrows. "Hey, I'm not the one who passed out in the yard and then thinks he can do all his normal chores. I'm just taking care of business."

"And your wrist needs to be rebandaged."

She hesitated, looking at it. "Nope. First I'm getting the wood."

"Then take my gloves. They're in the pocket of my heavy jacket. In fact, you might want to put the jacket on, too."

She walked over to where the jackets hung and took down his heaviest one. It dwarfed her. Then she pulled the leather gloves out of the side pocket as she headed for the door. "See you in a few minutes. With firewood."

"Okay." Zeke's heart swelled as he watched her go out the door dressed awkwardly in his clothes. What a loving, bossy, vulnerable, sexy woman. He didn't regret a single moment he'd spent with her, and he wouldn't want anyone else to be the mother of his child. Thank God he'd pulled her out of the river that afternoon. He couldn't imagine a world without Katherine in it. And as that last thought sank in, he caught his breath.

No doubt about it, he was in love with her.

LEAVING HER FIRST THREE loads of wood by the door, Katherine carried the fourth stack into the cabin and set it on the hearth. She was enjoying herself, she realized with some regret. She liked building fires and walking in the woods and sitting on the porch gazing up at the night sky.

She took off Zeke's gloves and stuffed them in the pocket of his coat before hanging it up. Then she glanced over at Zeke. "Firewood's in."

He watched her, a soft expression on his face. "Thanks."

The warmth in his eyes beckoned her, and she had the biggest urge to walk over there and into his arms. Instead she turned, knelt by the hearth and began stacking kindling and pinecones to start a fire. As the kindling began to crackle she reached for a piece of the wood she'd brought in. With great satisfaction she put the wood on the fire. They would be warm tonight because of her.

She placed the fire screen in front of the blaze and stood. "Now for some lunch. How's your ankle?"

"I think the swelling's gone down some. It's probably time to wrap it with an elastic bandage. Then we'll redo yours."

Katherine glanced down at her wrist. "Do you have more of these?"

"Several. Sprains are common in the woods."

"No kidding." Walking over to the bed, she crouched down to peer into the bucket. "I think I could wrap your ankle for you. Let me get the first-aid kit and a towel to dry you off." She started toward the bathroom.

"And after you wrap my ankle, I'll change the bandage on your wrist."

She laughed. "This is beginning to sound like an episode from *General Hospital*." When she returned, she handed him the kit while she knelt down to take his foot from the bucket and dry it. His toes were starting to wrinkle, but the swelling didn't look nearly as bad around his ankle.

"We really are quite a pair of cripples, Zeke."

"Yeah, but put us together and we're awesome."

She thought about that as she dried his foot, being careful to get between his toes. They were awesome together. Where one of them had a weakness, mental or physical, the other one seemed to fill the gap. With parents like that, a kid could have it made. But she wasn't sure Zeke would be able to do his share of filling in gaps when he lived clear out in Wyoming. She wondered if telephone calls would help. Probably not much.

"I think my foot's dry," Zeke said gently.

She realized she'd been continuing to rub his foot as she considered the problem. "Oh." She glanced up at him. "Sorry."

"It felt sort of good."

"Oh," she said again, aware of a light in his dark eyes. She glanced away, afraid to hold his gaze for long. "We'd better get your ankle horizontal again and wrap it."

"Right." Laying the first-aid kit behind him, he took the blanket from around his shoulders and tossed it across the end of the bed.

His chest muscles flexed as he did so, and Katherine suddenly became aware that he wore nothing but his briefs and the sock she'd recently put on him. The sight of his bronzed body was potent medicine. She needed to get this first-aid business taken care of, and fast.

Before she could reach down to lift his feet, he swung

them up to the bed and laid his ankle on the pillow. Then he reached into the first-aid kit, took out the rolled bandage and tossed it to her. "Wrap away."

She caught the bandage and frowned at him. "You need to take it easy lifting that ankle."

"I don't like feeling like a damned invalid."

"As if I didn't know." She unfastened the clip from the bandage and sat down on the bed near his feet. "If I remember right, I wrap your instep and then wind this up around your ankle."

"That'll work. Make sure it's tight enough." He leaned back against the headboard and crossed his arms over his chest.

And did he ever look yummy posed like that, she thought. Time to get busy and then get the heck off the bed. "I'm going to prop your foot on my knee. Let me know if anything I do hurts too much."

"Okay."

"I'll bet you won't. You're such a macho type." She worked gingerly to wrap the end of the bandage around his instep.

"I wasn't exactly the macho type last night with that nightmare."

She stopped wrapping and glanced up at him. It was the first reference he'd made to it today. "That dream took you right back to being three years old. Not many little boys of three are macho."

He gazed at her, his dark eyes gentle. "I appreciate the fact that you didn't bring up the subject again. Some people might have pestered me for more details."

"I figure it's up to you when you want to talk about it."

"Thank you."

"You're welcome." She dared not look into his eyes any longer. She leaned over her work again. His skin was still cool from soaking in the water, although she could feel warmth when she lightly touched the swollen part of his ankle.

As she unrolled the bandage around the puffy part she had to cradle the weight of his calf in her other hand. Man, did he have muscles. And a sexy kneecap. He didn't have a lot of body hair, which was probably due to his Sioux heritage. Touching the back of his leg reminded her of the delicious texture of his bronzed skin... everywhere. She'd explored it thoroughly in the lantern light the night before. She didn't have a lot of experience with men, but she knew instinctively that making love to Zeke was an exotic experience by anybody's standards.

"That might be just a *little* too tight."

A quick look told her he was clenching his jaw against the pain, and when she inspected her wrapping job, she quickly started undoing it again. "I am so sorry." In her agitated state while daydreaming about Zeke's body, she must have pulled the bandage tighter and tighter. She winced when she thought of how that must have hurt him. "That was stupid of me."

"It's okay, Katherine."

"It's not okay." She started rewrapping, not looking at him. "You wouldn't be in this fix if I hadn't come into your life in the first place. Now you have all these problems like what to do about Amanda, and on top of that you sprain your ankle, and I can't even take care of it properly for you."

"I'm not sorry you came into my life."

"Yeah, well, being not sorry is a long way from being glad, and I don't blame you. Your life was going fine until—"

"I'm glad you did, then."

That brought her head up. "You are?"

"Yes."

"That's...nice." Oh, God. Whenever he looked at her like that she began to tremble. She swallowed and went back to her work. Her fingers shook as she attached the metal clip to the end of the bandage.

"There. You're done." She eased his foot off her knee and onto the pillow. Then she stood up and tossed the covers over him, more to get his body out of sight than to keep him warm. The fire was heating the room up nicely. At least she told herself it was the fire that was causing her skin to feel so toasty. "Ready for some coffee?"

"After we do something about that bandage of yours."

"Oh." She glanced down at the damp, grungy-looking elastic and had to admit it felt icky. But she wasn't sure it was wise for her to be close to him at the moment. "Later."

"If you wait, then Amanda will wake up, and I'll bet you'd like a clean bandage before you deal with her again."

He was right about that. And there was no way she could wrap it properly by herself.

Zeke patted the mattress next to him. "Come on. Let's take care of this so you can forget about it for a while."

"Let me put another log on the fire first." She walked over to the fireplace and spent a fair amount of time tending to the blaze, hoping in the process her reaction to Zeke would lessen. It didn't.

"Hey," Zeke called. "The fire's perfect. Come on over here and get your wrist taken care of."

"Now who's the bossy one?" But she went over and sat on the bed.

He cradled her hand gently and started unwinding the bandage. "If you wouldn't try to act like Superwoman, I wouldn't have to boss you around."

"Ha, ha." She tried to be nonchalant as she sat with her hand in his, but she was having a lot of trouble. His body heat seemed to reach out to her, drawing her closer. She deliberately held herself away from him.

"How does your wrist feel?" His breathing was slow and steady as he unwrapped the elastic. Apparently he wasn't bothered by being so close to her.

"It's a little sore. Not bad." She didn't know how anyone could keep from reacting to his gentle touch. All he was doing was taking a bandage from her wrist, yet it felt like a caress.

"There. It's off. Looks pretty good. Not much swelling."

"No." She gazed at her wrist. "Sort of wrinkly and white."

"That's because you left the wet bandage on so long." He held her wrist loosely and examined it. "Looks better."

"I'm sure I'll live." But his touch was driving her insane, reminding her of how it felt to have his hands all over her body. If he placed his fingers over the pulse in her wrist, he'd know what he was doing to her.

He took a new bandage from the first-aid kit and with calm precision started wrapping it around her wrist. "Amanda's sure sleeping soundly."

"Yes, she is." She wondered if he heard the quiver in her voice. She felt almost feverish. The minute he finished wrapping her wrist, she would get up and start lunch. There were lots of reasons why making love was a bad idea, starting with his injured ankle and ending with the possibility of two broken hearts.

But he seemed to be taking forever. She remembered what he'd said about scent being a part of the mating process. He must be right, because as she sat breathing in the sheer maleness of him, she grew damp and aroused.

She decided to try talking to dispel the tension growing within her. "So, what do you want for lunch?" She'd meant the question to sound bright and cheerful. Instead, a husky note had betrayed her. The question sounded downright suggestive.

He glanced up from his wrapping job, his gaze unreadable. "What are you hungry for?"

His expression gave no indication that he'd meant anything sexual by that remark. Yet heat burned in her cheeks as she thought of the answer she wanted to give. "I guess we should make it something easy."

"Good idea," he said softly, and broke eye contact so he could return to wrapping her wrist.

She wanted him so much she was afraid she might start drooling. Time for a little joke. "If there was such a thing as a wrist-wrapping contest, you'd get the prize for technique, but you'd never win in the time trials."

He finished the last couple of turns with deliberate care and reached for the clip to hold the end in place. "Got an appointment?"

"Yeah. I'm supposed to have lunch with this ranger I know."

"Sounds important." He closed the lid on the first-aid kit, but he didn't release her hand. Then he caught her gaze with his as he brought her hand up and placed a soft kiss in her palm.

As she stared into his dark and mysterious eyes, she almost forgot to breathe. Her heartbeat thundered in her ears. "He'd hate it if I...stood him up," she whispered.

"Then don't."

15

ZEKE KNEW MAKING LOVE to Katherine again wasn't a good idea. It would probably make his ankle hurt now and his heart hurt later. But he couldn't seem to help himself.

He slipped his hand up through her hair and cupped the back of her head. When his mouth touched hers, her lips were already parted, inviting him to kiss her the way she loved to be kissed. She clutched his shoulders and he thrust deep with his tongue. Her moan of delight aroused him as nothing else could. As nothing else ever would.

And so he would make love to her now because he had no choice, and he was no longer willing to give her one, either. They might part, they might live in different worlds for the rest of their lives, but she was his mate, and they were born to be joined together in a basic, primitive way. To deny it would be like trying to stop the orbit of the earth.

He couldn't seem to get enough of her mouth, but he wanted so much more. The buttons on her shirt slipped from their holes as if nothing would stand in his way now. When the shirt was open he reached for her breast. The weight of it in his hand felt so good he couldn't help the growl of satisfaction that rose in his throat.

He hadn't realized his connection to her would intensify now that she'd borne his child, now that she nursed that child with the breasts that he loved to caress. The emotion he'd experienced after their first night together had been strong, but it paled in comparison to what he felt for her now. She'd become completely, gloriously female, which made him feel more a man than ever before in his life.

He eased his thumb across her nipple, bringing forth moisture. He was the man who had made her pregnant, he thought triumphantly, the one who had caused her breasts to fill and her body to grow ripe with their daughter. He'd created a place for himself in her life no one could ever take away. He was the only man who could have given her Amanda.

Stroking his thumb across her nipple, he drew back a fraction from the sweetness of her lips. "I need you," he murmured.

"What about...your ankle?"

"We'll work around it."

"I shouldn't let you..." She sighed gently and arched her back in pleasure as he continued to stroke her breast. The lapels of the shirt fell away, revealing the dusky rose contrast of her nipples against her milk-white skin. "This is selfish of me."

His breath caught at her beauty. "No. I want you to give me memories. I'll need them."

Her eyes fluttered open. She gazed at him, her lips parted, her breathing shallow and quick. "So will I," she whispered.

His body tightened in anticipation, yet when she pulled away from him and stood, he thought perhaps he'd lost her. But when she walked to his dresser and pulled out the bottom drawer, he knew he'd won... everything.

She placed the condoms on the bedside table and

stepped back. Then she slowly took off her shirt and let it drop to the floor.

He was dazzled. He'd never been able to see her like this, standing before him in the full light of day. The gray light coming through the window outlined her body, making her seem to glow.

She untied the string holding the waist of the sweatpants. Instead of pushing them down, she allowed them to slide sensuously to her feet while she kept her attention focused on him.

His erection began to throb as he realized she was being deliberately provocative. "Am I getting...a show?"

Her voice was shy but her actions were not. "I think you deserve one." She stepped gracefully out of the sweats.

"Thank you," he said, his huskiness revealing just how grateful he was. She was no longer hesitant about revealing her body to him, stretch marks and all. He considered that a gift.

As she stood before him wearing only natural light, he allowed himself the pleasure of a long, leisurely visual trip back up that magnificent body as he anticipated running his hands over her again. He moved over to make room for her, oblivious to any pain in his ankle.

"Be careful, Zeke."

"I don't feel a thing. Come here."

Her gaze was hot, but she moved slowly as she knelt on the bed beside him. "You need to let me be in charge," she said.

His heart beat faster. "Is that right?"

"Yes. You're injured."

"According to you, injured people need to take their clothes off."

"That's right." Her smile tantalized him. Then she

glanced down at his cotton briefs, which barely contained him. "And that's what I intend to do."

He'd never had an experience like it. As she peeled his briefs down, she showered him with light, yet intimate, kisses. Her hair swung forward and tickled his heated flesh, and he thought he might go crazy from the feathery sensations created by her hair and her lips.

When she had him so worked up he thought he might explode, she paused in order to work the briefs down over his ankles. In the process her nipples brushed against his knees, and his pulse skyrocketed again. He had to fist his hands to keep from grabbing her and pushing her down to the mattress, no matter how much his ankle screamed in protest.

"I'm so afraid I'll hurt you," she murmured.

His voice was strained. "Trust me. I wouldn't care."

"Then you're having a good time?" She tossed the briefs aside and glanced at him.

He gave her a lopsided grin. "As if you couldn't tell."

Still moving carefully, she eased back up the bed and wrapped her warm fingers around his erection. "I can tell. I just like to hear you say it."

He groaned. "I'm having the time of my life. I—" He groaned again as she took him into her mouth. Pleasure this intense should be illegal, he thought, until she took away all thought and replaced it with a white-hot surge of pure feeling. He'd never trusted a woman enough to abandon himself to her. He'd always kept some measure of control.

But this time, all the barriers came down, leaving him open and vulnerable, hers to mold.

She brought him to the very edge of the precipice. Had she decided to hurl him over it, he couldn't have stopped her. But as he balanced there, she rose to her knees and kissed his mouth.

He closed his eyes and held on tight, tasting the passion on her tongue, growing dizzy from wanting her. Mindlessly he grasped her hips, urging her toward him.

"Wait," she murmured against his lips.

When she moved out of his arms he remembered they had one more step to follow. He'd been so crazed from passion that it hadn't even crossed his mind. He held out his hand for the packet. "Here. I'll—"

"No, I will." She was breathing hard, her breasts quivering, her hands shaking as she straddled his thighs and ripped open the foil.

He tried to help her, but he was trembling as much as she was. Their breathless laughter turned into moans of frustration, but they finally managed to get the condom on. The moment it was secure he cradled her hips and guided her over him. As she settled slowly down, he gasped and clenched his jaw against the urge to pour himself into her.

She clutched his shoulders, closed her eyes and tilted her head back. "Oh, Zeke."

That gesture of surrender nearly did him in. "Don't move yet," he said, his voice raspy.

"I have to." She lifted her hips.

He fought the pressure rising within him as she began a seductive rhythm. When she whimpered and quickened the pace, he lost the fight with a moan of pure ecstasy. Her cry of release echoed his as she shuddered and sagged against him.

Feeling more complete than ever in his life, he gathered her close. *I love you.* His lips silently formed the words as he pressed his cheek against her hair.

KATHERINE HEATED TOMATO SOUP over the fire for their very late lunch. Amanda continued to sleep as she brought a tray of soup and crackers to bed. *"Bon appétit, ranger man."*

He surveyed her and the tray. "Shouldn't there be a flower or something on there?"

"You want a flower?" Setting the tray down, she walked over to the door.

"Hey, I was kidding."

"You want a flower, I'll get you a flower." She was feeling wonderfully reckless as she stepped outside wearing nothing at all. At least she wouldn't get her clothes wet!

"Katherine, forget the flower."

She flashed him a grin over her shoulder and closed the door behind her. But damn, it was cold, and raining like crazy. She glanced around and saw a drenched and rain-flattened daisy near the edge of the clearing and not too far from the porch. If she stepped just right, she'd be able to jump from one tuft of grass to another and not get her feet muddy.

She braced herself for the deluge of rain as she went down the steps. Leaving the shelter of the porch felt exactly like stepping under the shower, except, of course, that she was outside. And naked.

She stood there for a second adjusting to the idea that Katherine Seymour was standing outside a Wyoming cabin in the rain in her birthday suit. Then she began to laugh as the downpour soaked her hair and cascaded over her body. Finally she let out a whoop, threw her hands in the air and lifted her face to the rain, opening her mouth to swallow the drops as they pelted down.

But as exhilarating as the experience was, the air was pretty damn cold. She located the daisy again and hopped from one grassy spot to another until she could lean down and pluck it. "A flower for m'lord's lunch tray," she said, straightening.

That was when she saw the bull moose.

The breath seemed to leave her body as she stared at him and he stared back. He was huge, bigger than the biggest draft horse she'd ever seen in a New York City parade. He stood less than twenty feet from her under the shelter of the trees, his magnificently curved antlers dripping with rain, his coat dark and wet. Even his muzzle dripped.

Fully clothed, Katherine might have felt more secure about meeting a moose in the woods. Naked, she was a little less confident. She backed up one slow step at a time. The ooze slid between her toes as she made her gradual retreat without taking her eyes off the moose.

Glancing over her shoulder, she saw that she was almost on the porch. The moose hadn't budged. He was probably as startled to see a naked woman running around in the yard as she was to see a bull moose in the midst of her flower-gathering trip.

When the back of her heel bumped the bottom step, she turned, hurried up the steps and across the porch. Yanking open the door, she stepped inside, and closed it quickly behind her. Adrenaline poured through her system. She felt wildly primitive, but also half-frozen.

She crossed to the bed and climbed in, wet hair, muddy feet and all. "I'm f-freezing to d-death."

"Can't have that. Although I could say I told you so." Zeke gathered her close.

"B-but you won't."

"No." His tone was amused. "I won't."

"Good." After a while his warmth calmed her and her teeth stopped chattering enough for her to talk. "You'll never believe what happened. While I was in the midst of picking flowers, I looked up, and I was practically nose to nose with a big ol' moose."

He began to chuckle.

"Easy for you to laugh. You weren't standing there stark naked twenty feet away from him."

"That's Elmer. He probably wanted the daisy you picked."

"Oh. The daisy. Wonder what I did with it."

Zeke peered over the edge of the bed. Reaching down, he scooped something up and held it in front of her face.

The daisy was pretty well mangled. She glanced up at him. "Sorry."

He smiled. "It's the thought that counts."

"But I messed up the sheets and the pillowcase."

He gave her a long, slow kiss before leaning back and surveying her appreciatively. "I have other sheets. Don't let being muddy stop you from climbing into my bed."

"You know what? I liked it. I liked running around naked in the rain, and even coming face-to-face with Elmer."

He looked into her eyes. "That's a good sign."

"If this keeps up, you're going to turn me into an exhibitionist."

He grinned. "As long as the exhibit's only open when I'm around."

She realized they were both talking as if they had a future, when in fact they had none. Sobering, she gazed at him. "I guess there isn't much chance I'll turn into an exhibitionist, is there?"

Quietly Katherine disentangled herself, and the exuberance that had lightened her heart turned to despair. She reheated the soup and they sat together on the bed, their backs propped against the headboard while they ate, but they remained silent throughout the meal. Katherine knew she was negotiating her way around the tricky subject of their relationship and figured he was, too. Then they spoke at the same time.

"You first," Katherine said.

"No, you."

She set down her empty bowl on the tray between them and took a deep breath. "Have you ever heard of a movie called *Same Time Next Year?*"

"No. It must not have played the Isis, and since then I haven't seen many movies."

Katherine picked up a cracker and broke it in two. "The man and woman in it each have different lives, even different partners, but they meet once a year, make love and get reacquainted. Then they separate and agree to meet again the next year, and so on."

He put his bowl on the tray and looked at her, his face devoid of expression.

"I hate it when you look like that. Inscrutable. I suppose you're going to say that's your Sioux blood coming out in you."

"No." His voice was very quiet. "It's the orphan coming out in me."

"Oh, Zeke!" She dropped the cracker and reached for him, nearly overturning the tray. Her throat tightened as she cradled his face in both hands. "Zeke, I—" She paused. *I love you. I'll always love you.* And once she said those words, what else would she say? That she would give up everything for that love?

He turned toward her and laid his hands gently on her shoulders. The mask fell away as he looked into her eyes. "I know what you're trying to do, Katherine," he said softly. "I've thought about this, too. You're hoping we can work out some sort of compromise where we can

both have what we want, what we need, and yet still..."
He massaged her shoulders and his voice grew husky.
"Still stay connected to each other."

She nodded.

He sighed. "I wish I could be that kind of man—strong
enough to see you once a year, make love to you and let
you go away again. Strong enough to believe that in a
year, you'll be back."

"Maybe...maybe a year's too long. Maybe every six
months we could—"

"No." He shook his head. "Don't kid yourself. Six
months would become three. Three would become one,
and pretty soon we'd be flying across the country every
weekend. You can't function that way and neither can I."

She swallowed the lump in her throat. He was right.
Her body still hummed from his caresses, and she
wanted him again. "We shouldn't have made love. We
should have kept things platonic, so that we wouldn't
make this any worse."

His smile was sad. "God knows I tried. I don't know
about you, but I ran out of resistance early in the game."
He slid his hands down over the tops of her breasts and
then cupped them lovingly. "I still don't have any."

"Neither do I," she said in a choked voice. "But this...
this is it, isn't it?"

"Yeah." His gaze searched hers. "This is it."

She wiped the tears from her eyes and dredged up a
watery smile. "Then if this is all we're ever going to have,
what are we doing with a tray of dirty dishes between
us?"

"Beats the hell out of me." He released her, scooped up
the tray and plopped it down on the floor on his side of
the bed. Then he gathered her into his arms.

"I suppose we should change the sheets," she murmured. "I did get things messed up with my wet hair and muddy feet."

"Why bother?" He slipped his hand between her thighs and boldly caressed her as he nibbled on her lower lip. "Now that I know running around naked in the rain like some wood sprite gets you hot, I'll probably try to get you to do it again."

ZEKE COULDN'T REMEMBER the last time he'd spent so many daylight hours in bed, or when he'd enjoyed it as much. And he'd have at least one more night with Katherine before he had to pay the piper and give her up for good. The rain had stopped at dusk, but the phone was still out and he was sure the creek was still impassable. Funny that he'd never been marooned here before, and he might never be marooned again. Yesterday he would have called it damned bad luck. Today he called it a miracle.

He would have preferred to be marooned without a bum ankle, but he was managing to get around a little bit with his walking stick. The pain always increased when he was vertical, though. And with Katherine sharing his bed, he was perfectly happy to stay prone most of the time. In fact, with Katherine "in charge," as she called it, making love hardly seemed to bother his ankle at all.

As darkness gathered outside the windows of the cabin, he lay in bed watching Katherine change Amanda after nursing her. He was really going to miss that tender, arousing scene of Amanda at Katherine's breast. Hell, he was really going to miss everything about this weekend, but he might as well not dwell on that now. Right now he still lived in paradise.

Katherine leaned over the table as she talked to Amanda. She used the same happy singsong voice, but

Zeke no longer felt left out of the charmed circle, especially when she would turn and include him in the conversation.

"Are we going to give her another bath?" he asked.

Katherine glanced over at him. "I'd love to. I'd love to give myself a bath, now that you mention it, before we put clean sheets on the bed."

"I wouldn't mind one myself. Of course, I could always take a shower."

"Come on, Zeke. That cold shower you took couldn't have been much fun."

"Okay, it wasn't much fun."

"How about if I heat up enough water to fill the bathtub? You can go in with Amanda."

"Or we could all go in together. I think we'd fit." He knew there had been a reason he'd bought that old antique tub that had come out of some silver tycoon's mansion in Casper. It was so huge that his buddies had expected him to start entering bathtub races.

"I don't want to take a chance on reinjuring your ankle."

"I'll be careful."

"I don't know, Zeke. It seems a little risky."

"No risk. I'll get in the tub first and you can hand the baby in. Then you can climb in." He had a compelling urge to have them all cradled together in the big tub, and he couldn't say exactly why. He just wanted it to happen.

"If you say so. Sounds like teenagers cramming into a phone booth to me."

"It won't be."

"Then I won't bother putting her sleeper on her yet."

"No. Just bring her over to me while you take care of heating the water." He was amazed at how eager he was to hold Amanda again. She'd slept most of the afternoon away, and when she'd woken up, she'd needed Katherine to feed her. Now at last he could get an armful of that precious little bundle.

Katherine walked over and deposited Amanda in his arms. With only her diaper on, she seemed more active, waving her arms and legs happily in the air.

He gathered her against his bare chest, enjoying the feel of her soft skin against him. "Hi there, sunshine," he said, smiling at her because he couldn't help himself. On schedule, she smiled back. Zeke glanced up at Katherine. "You can't tell me that's gas."

"No. It's not gas." Her voice sounded funny, and her eyes were moist.

"Are you okay?"

She sniffed and nodded her head. "Yeah," she said with a smile. "I'm okay."

16

ZEKE FELT GUILTY that Katherine had to carry the kettle of hot water back and forth to the bathroom, especially when she could only use one hand to do it, but she insisted the thought of a warm bath was worth the effort. The cabin grew dark enough to light the kerosene lanterns, and she placed one in the bathroom, making the room glow invitingly.

Finally she took the last kettle of hot water in and returned, looking eager. She held out her arms for Amanda. "The water temperature is perfect. Let me put her into her bassinet while I help you in there."

He handed the baby over before leaning down to unwrap the bandage from his ankle. "I can manage with the walking stick."

"Sure you can." She deposited Amanda in the bassinet. "But I'm here, so why not make use of me?"

He glanced up at her. "Because you've already had to lug all the water in. It's embarrassing to be such an invalid."

"Or is it embarrassing to be dependent on someone else?"

He looked away. She was too close to the truth for comfort. Depending on someone else wasn't only embarrassing, it was dangerous. In fact, in his experience the ones you needed the most were the ones who ended up leaving you. "I guess fending for myself is a habit after all this time."

"I can understand that," she said softly.

The tone of her voice prompted him to glance back at her. When he saw the compassion in her eyes, the solid door to his heart opened a crack. Maybe she did understand, at least a little bit. Being understood was something new to him. The ranch had been a bustling, happy place, a haven that had saved his life. But with so many boys, no one got lots of individual attention. He'd always felt he had to wrestle with his private problems alone. Looking into Katherine's eyes, he didn't feel quite so alone anymore.

But her understanding wasn't a luxury he'd have much longer. He reached for the walking stick leaning by the bed. "I'll use your help getting into the tub. God knows I don't want to fall climbing in. But let me make my own way into the bathroom."

"Zeke, for heaven's sake. I—"

"You'll be leaving soon." He gazed into her hazel eyes and thought how much he would miss being able to do that.

She studied him quietly for several seconds. "I get the point." She stepped back.

"Thank you." Standing was an effort, and without crutches he couldn't manage it without putting at least some weight on his bad ankle. He grimaced at the pain as he began the slow hobble into the bathroom. It was a symbolic gesture, and maybe an empty one, he thought. Katherine had already breached his defenses in a hundred places, and when she left he'd have to spend years repairing the damage. Considering that he'd be reminded of her whenever Amanda paid him a visit, he might never recover completely.

He stepped inside the bathroom, which looked a hundred times better in lantern light than in the light from the ordinary bulbs he'd installed over the sink. In fact, the whole cabin looked better this way. Maybe he'd forget about electric light and just go with kerosene from now on. Except the cozy glow might remind him too much of Katherine.

"*Now* will you let me help?" she said, coming in right behind him.

"Yeah." He unclenched his jaw and ran a hand over his sweaty forehead. This was one nasty sprain. He'd probably be riding a desk at work for a while until he healed. "This ankle is a damned nuisance," he muttered.

"But you saved the mother raccoon and her babies."

"Yeah, that's true." He surveyed the situation with the old-fashioned claw-foot tub. "This seemed like a great idea at the time, but I don't know how in hell I'm going to get in there without putting all my weight on my bad ankle at some point."

She pointed to the closed toilet seat. "You could sit there, put your good foot in and ease over into the water while you held on to the edge of the tub and me. You can get out the same way."

He sent her a dark look. "Sounds pretty undignified, if you ask me."

"Yeah, but it'll work."

He sat down and leaned his walking stick against the wall. "Here goes nothing." When he put his foot in the warm water, he sighed with pleasure.

"See? It'll be worth it. Now start sliding over, and I'll hold on under your arms." She moved in close. As she slipped her hands under his arms, her breasts swayed against his chest.

"I'm beginning to like this plan better." As he slid sideways, she moved sideways with him, and the friction of her body was very arousing. "Lots better," he added.

"Now is not the time to get frisky. Grab the side of the tub. Lift your other leg in. That's good. Oof. You're heavier than I thought. I—oops!"

He landed with a splash as Katherine lost her balance and tumbled against him. He caught her around the waist so she wouldn't fall headfirst into the tub, but she ended up with one breast pressed against his cheek. That sweet circumstance made up for the way the sudden movement had jolted his recent injury. Ignoring the pain in his ankle, he turned his head and nuzzled her. "Great plan," he murmured.

She braced herself by putting one hand on his shoulder. "If I weren't hanging on the edge of this tub in an incredibly awkward position, I might enjoy what you're doing."

"But you don't?" He drew her nipple into his mouth. Nectar of the gods.

She sighed. "Okay, maybe I enjoy it a little bit. But I hear Amanda fussing in there. This started out as her bath, remember?"

"Mmm." He loved having the baby around, mostly. But the idea of fondling Katherine in a tub of warm water had definite appeal. With one more tug on her nipple he drew back and placed a quick kiss on the puckered tip. "Okay. Go get the baby."

As she pushed herself upright, he saw with some satisfaction that her cheeks were pink and her breathing unsteady. She was as agitated by the encounter as he was. After she left the bathroom, he wondered for the first time how she'd take their separation. From what he'd heard, New York had plenty of distractions. Maybe she'd throw herself into the fast pace of the city and barely give him another thought.

But he didn't think so. And while she'd filled this cabin with reminders that would never go away, he'd left her with a baby, a baby with many of his features. She wouldn't easily put him out of her mind and her heart. Selfish though it might be, he didn't want her to.

KATHERINE TOOK OFF her elastic bandage. Then she unfastened Amanda's diaper and carried her into the bathroom. "Here we are, our own little nudist colony," she said. She handed the baby to Zeke.

"Hey there, sunshine! Swim time!" He cradled her against his damp chest.

Amanda responded with a loud crow and waved her hands at his face.

Laughing, he leaned down and brushed his nose against hers while she patted his cheeks and gurgled.

Katherine stood transfixed by his expression as he played with Amanda. The face that often looked as if it were carved in stone was now animated with love. And so very, very vulnerable.

Katherine wondered what she'd done.

He glanced up at her with a smile. "Coming in?"

"Are you sure there's room?"

"You bet." He moved to the far side of the tub. "You can put your feet up by my hips. Climb in. It feels great."

"Okay." She stepped, wincing slightly as the warm water made her blisters sting.

"What was that for?" he asked.

Two could play the macho game, she decided. "Nothing."

"Hmm."

"Really. It's nothing." Holding on to the edge of the

tub with her left hand, she eased into the narrow spot Zeke had provided, making sure she didn't bump his sprained ankle in the process. Once she was settled, she leaned back against the enameled surface and sighed with pleasure. "Where did this monster tub come from?"

Zeke swished Amanda through the water. "Some guy who made a fortune back in the days of the silver mines. They decided not to keep the tub when they turned the mansion into an office building, so I bought it." He swirled the baby around in the water until she wriggled with ecstasy.

"Good move." Katherine relaxed as she enjoyed the effects of the warm water, the feel of Zeke's leg aligned alongside hers, and the shared joy in their baby girl. "Look at her kick. She loves that."

"She's going to be a regular little tadpole, aren't you, sunshine?"

Amanda slapped her hands against the surface of the water, and Zeke laughed. After playing with her some more, he looked over at Katherine. "Ready to take the kid for a while, or will that be too much pressure on your wrist?"

"I can manage." She leaned forward and took the slippery baby, using mostly her left arm and hand to grip her. "Enough playtime, Mandy. Mommy's going to wash you now."

"Got her?"

"Yep." Katherine tucked Amanda in the crook of her right arm and reached for the washcloth she'd draped on the edge of the tub.

"Okay. Now I can take a look at your feet."

He'd obviously had that in mind ever since he saw her expression when she stepped in, she thought. So much for putting one over on him. He seemed to miss nothing.

He gently lifted her right foot out of the water. "Holy Toledo, Katherine. Why didn't you say something?"

"It's just a couple of blisters." Katherine washed Amanda's face while the little girl blinked and sputtered.

He lowered Katherine's foot into the water and picked up the other one. "This happened when we hiked down to the creek, didn't it?"

"Well, yeah."

"Damn it to hell." Then he glanced at Amanda. "Sorry, sunshine. But your mommy is an idiot."

"Nice talk."

He leaned over to examine her foot more carefully. "This must have really bothered you."

"Some."

"Yeah, right." He kissed her toes. "More than some. You should have said something the minute your feet started to hurt."

"And then what?" She methodically worked the washcloth over Amanda's pudgy little body. "You would have made me stay in the cabin, right?"

"Which is where you should have stayed, instead of walking all that way in those shoes."

"It was worth it. Believe it or not, I loved being out there, and besides, I thought Amanda and I should be with you."

He grew very still.

In the deafening silence, she glanced up to find him gazing at her, his dark eyes intense. When he spoke, his voice was husky. "Better be careful, Katherine. The next time that urge takes you, you might hurt more than your feet."

Her mouth grew dry. "Sounds like you're warning me away."

"That's exactly what I'm doing. Don't even think of

giving up everything so we can be a family. I don't want that responsibility."

Pain sliced through her. He'd been so loving and relaxed with Amanda that she'd imagined she was the one preventing them from forming a family unit. She'd been wrong. Her throat was tight, but she forced the words out, anyway. "Don't worry," she said. "I have no intention of saddling you with responsibility." The water had begun to chill. "If you'll hold her until I get out, then I'll take her and dry her off."

"I have some first-aid cream we can put on those blisters."

Katherine climbed out of the tub. She didn't want to cry, so she settled on anger. "Never mind. I've had blisters before. They'll heal." But she might never heal from the wound he'd just given her. He didn't want her. Although she doubted she could ever sabotage Naomi by choosing a life with Zeke over her career at the magazine, it was pointless to even think about it now. He didn't want the full-time responsibility of a wife and child.

ZEKE ACHED WITH the pain Katherine was feeling, but he'd had to say what he did. Better that she feel the pain now rather than ruin her life. Of course she wanted them all to be together. He wanted that, too, and he'd known that the emotion between them was growing stronger with every minute they spent in each other's company, in each other's arms.

But when he'd seen the blisters she'd endured without complaint, he had a horrible picture of her giving up the career opportunity of a lifetime and alienating her godmother just to hold them all together. And that was what he didn't want responsibility for.

If she interpreted his comment to mean that he didn't

want the responsibility of having her around all the time, that was okay. That would keep her on track better than the other, more complicated truth that he didn't want to be the reason she abandoned her dreams. He wasn't worth it.

She took Amanda and wrapped her in a towel. "Don't try to get out of the tub without my help. I'll be back as quickly as I can after I've put a diaper on her." She hurried out of the bathroom.

He damn well would get out of the tub without her help. A nursemaid wasn't his style. He took some time to survey the situation. Finally he decided he could get his good foot under him, push on the rim of the tub with both hands and lever himself out. In theory he shouldn't have to put any weight on his bad ankle.

In theory.

In fact, his anchor foot started to slip, and the only way he could keep from falling and possibly cracking his head against the edge of the tub was to put weight on his sprained ankle. He muffled his groan of pain behind tightly compressed lips and heaved himself onto the toilet seat.

"And you have the nerve to call me an idiot." She stood in the doorway wearing his blue flannel shirt. Her legs were bare, probably because she hadn't had time to pull on a clean pair of his sweats. She'd obviously been in the process of covering up when she heard him get out of the tub.

Panting, he pulled a towel from the rack and started drying himself. "I never said I wasn't one, too. Did you get Amanda settled in?"

"She was out like a light almost before I got her diaper and sleeper on."

He glanced at the shirt she was wearing. "Are we dressing for dinner?"

She shrugged. "It's your house. Do what you like."

He'd thought he could handle her hurt and anger, that it wouldn't tear him to bits. Maybe he was wrong. "Look, I know I didn't say what you wanted to hear, but—"

"Maybe it was exactly what I needed to hear. You've made life easier for me, Zeke. For a while there, I was confused about what I should do. Now I'm not."

"Giving up your chance at the magazine would be a terrible mistake on your part, no matter what your reasons."

She gazed at him across the short space separating them. She'd accused him of hiding his emotions, but she was doing a great job of it herself. "Of course you're right," she said tonelessly. "It's a huge opportunity, and Naomi's been planning this for years. I wouldn't dream of throwing her generosity in her face. And then there's the money to be considered. With the salary I'll be making eventually, I'll be able to afford all sorts of extras for Amanda. And there's the foreign travel. Once she's old enough I'll take her with me to Paris and London for the shows. I'm sure she'll love it."

"I'm sure she will." And the two of them would move further and further away from him, he thought. Once Amanda had become used to mingling with the rich and famous of the fashion world, she wouldn't want to spend time in a backwoods cabin like this. And that went double for Katherine. She'd been seduced by the sexual tension between them, the temporary appeal of the landscape and the romantic concept of turning him into a daddy. But none of that would last long enough to replace what she'd be giving up in New York.

"I saw a can of chili in the cupboard when I got out the

soup for lunch," she said. "Would you like me to heat it up for our dinner?"

"That would be fine."

"Um, about the sleeping situation." She cleared her throat. "I don't want you on the floor, considering your ankle."

"I don't want you on the floor, either." Actually, he wanted her on the floor, or the bed, or the dining table. He just wanted her, period. But it appeared that part of the weekend was over.

She ran her hand nervously up and down the door frame. "There's no reason we can't both sleep in the bed. But I don't think we should...make love anymore."

"If you say so." Black despair moved through him. He'd known the moment would come, the moment when they'd never make love again, but he hadn't expected to have to face it until she'd left the cabin.

"I do," she said softly. "You see, I think a relationship should be about more than just sex."

If he hadn't been hurting so bad inside, he might have laughed at that. "So do I," he said.

Little did she know that when their relationship had been about sex, he'd managed to control himself. When he finally admitted to himself how much he loved her, his control had disappeared.

"I'll go put the chili on to heat."

"Okay."

He finished drying off, which took a while. Finally he wrapped the towel around his waist before hobbling out of the bathroom. Sure enough, by the time he got into the main room, Katherine had put on another pair of his sweats. She stood by the fire stirring the chili in the kettle.

If he remembered right he had one pair of sweats left, which meant they could both be decently covered for the evening, damn it. He made his way painfully over to the dresser and took out a T-shirt and the last pair of sweats. That would have to do. Considering how tough it would be getting the pants on, he didn't want to bother with underwear.

God, he was going to miss the sight of her sweet body. Sure, he became aroused watching her walk naked around the cabin, and that was part of what he enjoyed. But he'd also loved the chance to memorize intimate details that the rest of the world wouldn't ever know about her, like the tiny mole on her right breast, and the faint birthmark on her fanny. He was just getting familiar with the line of her backbone, the curve of her thigh and the spun-gold color of the curls covering her sex.

As he stood by the dresser balanced on one leg, he figured out that in order to get dressed without offending her newfound modesty, he'd have to hobble back to the bathroom. The hell with that. If his nakedness bothered her, she'd just have to look the other way.

With his clothes tucked under his arm, he arrived back at the bed and noticed she'd changed the sheets. So they'd both be squeaky-clean, sleeping on nice clean sheets, and they weren't supposed to touch each other. Maybe he'd have to take the floor, after all. He'd be damned if he'd beg, and lying next to her all night, he might be reduced to that.

He pulled off the towel before sitting on the bed. Getting the sweatpants on was a trick, but he managed. Then he pulled the T-shirt over his head.

"I can rewrap your ankle, if you need me to."

He glanced over to where she stood by the fireplace. He had a strong suspicion she'd watched his entire performance. "I'll manage."

"Yes, but I'm sure it would be easier if I did it."

"There wouldn't be anything easy about it, considering how close you'd have to get." He watched the awareness build in her eyes. "So unless you know a way to wrap my ankle without touching me, or unless you've changed your mind about making love, you'd better keep your hands to yourself."

17

THIS WAS ALL FOR THE BEST, Katherine told herself as they ate their dinner. Zeke was in bed, a tray balanced on his knees, and she sat at the table, deliberately putting distance between them. If she thought Zeke wanted her to stay, she would have had a difficult decision to make. Now that she knew he didn't want her to, life became very easy. Or so she tried to tell herself as she forced the chili past the lump in her throat. She would have preferred not to eat, but that wouldn't be good for Amanda.

Okay, so life wasn't easy now, with Zeke less than ten feet away and the memory of their lovemaking freshly imprinted on her mind and her body. But once she was back in New York, the pain would grow less until one day she'd barely feel it. Her job and Amanda would fill her days with satisfaction and creativity. Then she remembered that Naomi had suggested she use her time in Wyoming to generate some concepts for future issues, concepts that she'd be proud to implement.

Now, there was a forward-thinking project, one that should point her in the right direction. She glanced over at Zeke. "Do you have some paper and a pen I can use?"

"Far right drawer in the kitchen. Help yourself. Oh, while you're up, would you please bring me that paper-back mystery on the far end of the bookshelf?"

"Of course." She took the book down from the shelf and walked over to hand it to him.

"Thanks." He gave her the briefest of glances, but his expression was closed.

"You're welcome. If you don't mind, I think I'll open one of the porch windows a bit. It seems stuffy in here."

"Fine."

She wanted to scream. They were treating each other like polite strangers. No, more like civilized enemies. Polite strangers would make more of an effort to be pleasant. But she was better off this way, she reminded herself again.

In the kitchen she found the unlined sheets and a collection of ballpoint pens. She chose a black one and took several sheets of paper back to the table. Then she opened the window a couple of inches to let in some fresh air.

She took a deep breath and felt her brain revive. Yes, this was more like it, she thought, sitting down at the table. No wonder she'd been in a total funk about Zeke. She hadn't given herself anything challenging to think about, focusing instead on what she was giving up—the comfort of having Zeke help with Amanda and, of course, incredible sex.

And it had been incredible. She stared off into space for a minute before bringing herself back on task with an impatient shake of her head.

Taking her cue from Zeke, she'd insisted on wrapping her wrist herself this time, and although the job wasn't as neat as his, it would do. Writing gave her some pain, but it was better than sitting there doing nothing, so she kept it up in spite of the throbbing in her wrist.

Fifteen minutes later she had a page full of ideas, all of them crossed out. She stared into the fire in frustration. Everything she came up with seemed so trivial, a waste of the staff's time and talent. Besides that, she kept glanc-

ing over at Zeke. He seemed engrossed in his book, but
she wondered if he was as serene as he appeared. She
fought the urge to go crawl into that bed and...nope. Bad
idea.

Finally she tossed the pen down and cradled her chin
in both hands as she stared at her abortive attempt to get
some work done. Maybe this wasn't the time or place to
brainstorm. Zeke's presence would make concentration
difficult for any woman with a pulse. She'd do up the
dinner dishes and then follow Zeke's example and lose
herself in a book.

She picked up her dishes and walked over to the bed to
get his.

"Thanks," he said again in that monotone that drove
her crazy. Then he returned his attention to his book.

It bothered her that he could ignore her so easily. She
should have walked away with his dishes, but she didn't.
"Is there anything else you need?"

His head snapped up and his eyes looked as if someone had tripped a switch, bringing them to full wattage.
He tossed the book aside. "Yes, as a matter of fact, there
is."

Heart pounding, she backed away. "I'm...sorry. I
didn't mean..."

His voice rumbled low. "Then don't ask, Katherine.
Not unless that's exactly what you mean."

"Right," she said breathlessly. Clutching the dishes,
she walked over to the kitchen. She set the dishes in the
sink and leaned against it while she hyperventilated.
Good Lord. And she'd thought she was holding herself
on a tight leash. Her body warmed and throbbed as she
imagined what loving him now would be like. It would
be very good.

But she'd announced to him not two hours ago that she

thought a relationship should be about more than sex. She really believed that, and going to him now would allow him to think that sex was enough for her. And it wasn't. Of course not. But when she thought about the look in Zeke's eyes just now, she had the urge to forget her principles.

She managed to wash the dishes without breaking them, although her hands trembled. When she was finished, she went through the motions of taking a book from the shelf and sitting in the rocker with it open in her lap. In the distance a wolf howled, and then another, their cries drifting in through the partially open window. The sound affected her as much as it had the night before, stirring the lusty side of her nature so recently awakened by Zeke. It promised to be a very long night.

ZEKE CONSIDERED HIMSELF a master of self-control. He prided himself on being able to hide his emotions from even those closest to him if he chose to do so. Self-preservation had taught him that lesson early, and he'd polished his skills over the years. But he'd never been tested like this.

His whole body felt drawn into a knot as he tried to keep himself from asking Katherine to reconsider. He'd been reduced to examining her every movement, her every word for some sign that she was weakening in her resolve not to make love again. Surely he was too proud to beg. He'd never lowered himself to do that for any man, woman or child since the day he'd pleaded with his mother not to make him get out of the car.

But when Katherine had asked if he needed anything else, he'd come very close to pleading with her. Very, very close. He of all people should know that it wouldn't work and he'd humiliate himself for nothing. Yet as they sat together in the silent cabin, he grew desperate to hold her in his arms one more time.

When Amanda woke up for her next feeding, Katherine nursed her so discreetly that it nearly broke his heart. How he'd loved the moments spent in the big bed with a shamelessly unclothed Katherine holding the baby to her breast. He gripped his book and resolutely turned the pages he wasn't reading while she finished and changed the baby's diaper.

From the corner of his eye he saw her approach the bed, Amanda in her arms. He glanced up into her golden eyes, and his heart beat faster.

She swallowed. "Would you...I wondered if you'd like...to hold her for a while before she goes back to sleep."

He laid down the book immediately. "Yes, yes I would. Thank you." As she placed Amanda in his arms and he adjusted to the now-familiar sensation of holding a tiny human being close to his heart, his throat tightened. The next time he saw her she wouldn't be a baby anymore. Her face blurred slightly as he gazed down at her. "Hey, sunshine."

She stared up at him in the wise way she had. During her nap she'd slept on her hair so a tuft of it stuck up from her head, making her look even cuter. Gently he pressed his thumb against the tiny dimple in her chin. "There. Now it'll stay that way for a while longer." His heart ached as he smiled at her.

She flashed him her toothless smile and polished it off with a hiccup.

"Uh-oh. Katherine?" He glanced up and discovered she hadn't moved from the spot where she'd stood to hand him the baby. "She has hiccups."

"Try putting her on your shoulder and burping her."

"I've never done that." He looked down at Amanda as she hiccupped again. "What if I do it wrong?"

"You won't. Just hold her against your shoulder. That's right. And pat her back lightly."

He tapped Amanda's back a few times, but she continued to hiccup, her small body jerking each time one hit.

"Well, pat her a little harder than that," Katherine said. "She won't break."

He increased the pressure some. "It's not working."

"A little harder. You're being too gentle."

"She's a little kid!"

"I know, but pat harder."

So he gave her a couple of harder taps and hit pay dirt. She barfed all over his shirt. And the hiccups were gone.

"Oh, dear," Katherine said. "I'm sorry. I should have given you a towel. Give her back to me. I'll get you a clean shirt and—"

"In a minute." Zeke wanted to bask in his success. He lifted Amanda away from his shoulder and tucked her into the crook of his arm. "Got rid of those hiccups, didn't you, sunshine?" He used the hem of his shirt to wipe her tiny mouth. "That's the important thing. Who cares about a little barf on the shirt? Not me. Got a smile for Daddy?"

Amanda grinned at him.

"That's it. A big smile and no more hiccups. Good combo."

"Zeke, don't you want to change your shirt?"

"Not yet." He glanced over at her. "In fact, not for a while. Amanda and I have some playing to do."

She gave him a long, thoughtful look. "Okay. I'll be over in the rocker reading my book. Call when you think she's ready to go back to sleep."

"I'll do that."

TRY AS SHE MIGHT, Katherine couldn't hear much of what went on between Zeke and Amanda. He kept his voice low while he talked to her. Every once in a while he'd laugh softly, and the sound was so intimate that Katherine got goose bumps. His whole routine with Amanda gave her goose bumps, in fact. She didn't think many men would react with such nonchalance after a baby spit up on them, let alone continue wearing the shirt while they played with the baby. Zeke was quite a daddy.

Too bad he had no interest in being a husband. Because if he did, she'd—no, there wasn't any point in thinking about that. He'd made himself clear. They would take different paths from this point on. But at least Katherine would know that when Amanda came to Wyoming to visit Zeke, she would be in the hands of a real superdad. She told herself to take comfort in that.

But weak woman that she was, the only comfort she could imagine finding at the moment was in Zeke's strong arms.

"I think she's getting sleepy," he said at last.

Katherine put down her book and went over to the bed. "Would you like me to get that shirt now?"

"No, you take care of Amanda. I'll get it. I want to go into the bathroom and wash up a bit, anyway. I think there's a little of it in my hair."

"I would be glad to—"

"Help?" A dangerous light shone in his eyes. "Do you really mean that?"

"Uh, no." She reached for Amanda and held her close to stop the sudden trembling that overcame her. "I'll tend to the baby."

"I thought so."

Katherine walked slowly away from the bed and knelt down next to Amanda's bassinet. Gently she nestled the baby inside. Amanda's eyes fluttered once and closed. She was asleep, but Katherine needed some time to collect herself. She also didn't want to leave the bassinet while Zeke was up and around, so she stayed beside it and pretended to be coaxing the baby to sleep.

When the water started running in the bathroom she relaxed a little. "You know, your daddy is a very sexy man," she murmured to the sleeping baby.

Amanda's eyelids flickered and her tiny mouth pursed.

"I wish I knew what he was talking to you about," Katherine said. "I can just picture what will happen when you're older and come out for a visit. I'll quiz you unmercifully when you get home." At least Amanda could bring her news of the man she loved.

Katherine sighed and glanced through the window that looked out on the porch. The sky must be clearing. Moonlight washed the porch and sparkled on the raindrops clinging to the pine branches overhanging the roof. Just her luck, it was probably very romantic out there tonight.

Then a shadow blocked the silvery light.

Katherine's chest grew tight as she stared out the window. The shadow moved, turned toward her. Dark eyes glittered in the light spilling through the glass.

Instinctively Katherine wrapped both arms around the bassinet. "Zeke." Her voice was faint and raspy.

Water ran in the bathroom. He couldn't hear her.

She started to call again and stopped. What was she doing? Zeke could barely hobble, yet if she alerted him, he'd come charging out here as best he could. Then he might think he had to be a superhero and go out to confront the bear, never mind the danger of facing a wild animal when he had a bad ankle.

Maybe, if she stayed perfectly still, the bear would go away. Zeke seemed to think she wouldn't try to break in. If only he could be right. Heart pounding, she watched the bear's nose twitch. Damn, she'd had to open that window a couple of inches, hadn't she? Now Sadie could get a good whiff of whatever was inside the cabin, like food, and a little baby. Katherine's arms tightened around the bassinet.

Then, to her horror, Sadie rose on her haunches. With one swipe of her paw, she ripped through the screen.

Pure instinct took over as Katherine carried the bassinet quickly over to the dresser and yanked open the bottom drawer. In less than a second the gun was in her hand.

Years ago a boyfriend had taken her to a pistol range. She'd hated it, but at least she'd shot a handgun once in her life. Fortunately Zeke's gun was similar to the one she'd used on the range. Breathing heavily, she watched Sadie drop back to all fours and stick her nose through the open window. Katherine forced herself to check and see if the gun was loaded. It was.

She stood, the gun in her right hand. Sprained wrist or not, she had to use that hand or risk a wild shot. Eons seemed to have passed since she first saw the bear, yet it had to be less than a minute. Zeke was still in the bathroom with the water running. Her heart beat at a frantic pace, but her hand on the gun was steady.

As she walked toward the door, Sadie pulled her snout free and looked at Katherine.

"I don't want to hurt you," Katherine murmured. "But I want to scare you so much you go away. And stay away." She cocked the gun.

Mouth dry, she cautiously opened the door a few inches, enough to get her right arm through. The rank scent of the bear assailed her. Both outside and in, silence fell, as if the world were holding its breath. Terror licked at the edges of her self-confidence. Refusing to give in to it, she concentrated hard on her love for Amanda and Zeke, pointed the gun away from the bear and pulled the trigger.

The blast rocked her back from the open door. The bear roared and Zeke yelled at the same time. Pure reflex caused her to lurch forward and slam the door shut just as Amanda started to scream.

"What the hell are you doing?" Despite his injury, Zeke was standing in front of her in no time, the color leached from his face.

She leaned against the door, shaking violently. "S-Sadie" was all she could say.

He took the gun from her nerveless fingers and stared at her. "You shot her?"

Katherine shook her head. Her lips felt frozen as she tried to form words. "Is she...gone?"

Zeke hobbled quickly to the window. "I don't see her." He shut the window and laid the gun on the table before limping over to Katherine. The starkness of fear had given way to a blaze of anger in his eyes. "Damn it, Katherine, why didn't you call me?"

Still trembling, she gazed at him. She longed to say she didn't call him because she loved him and wanted to protect him because he was injured. "I thought I could handle it." Her voice quivered.

"You had no idea what that bear might do! How dare you put yourself in danger like that? My God, Katherine, anything could have happened! You have no idea. No idea." He sputtered to a stop and stood there shaking his head.

Katherine watched the muscles work in his jaw and the

anger simmer in his eyes, and slowly the reason for his tirade sank in. He was furious with her because she'd risked her safety, which could only mean... Maybe their relationship was about more than sex, after all. After considering that for a moment, she had another thought. Her heart beat faster as she realized what she wanted to do.

"I don't know what the hell you were thinking," he muttered. "You just took the biggest damn chance in the universe."

She pushed away from the door. "I'll get your walking stick."

"I don't give a damn about my walking stick. Amanda needs attention."

"I'll take care of her in a minute." She retrieved his stick from the bathroom and walked over to hand it to him. Gazing into his eyes, she no longer tried to disguise her emotions. Maybe he needed to know that her feelings for him were pretty damned intense, too. "Please go over and lie down."

He met her gaze for several long seconds before he took the stick. "Okay." He winced as he started back across to the bed.

Scooping Amanda up from the bassinet, Katherine sat in the rocker and cuddled the baby until her eyes began to close. By the time Zeke had climbed back into bed, Amanda was asleep. Katherine tucked her back in the bassinet. Then she turned down the wick on the lantern she'd used to light her reading and walked over to the bed.

Zeke glanced at her. "You know, maybe I'd better take the floor tonight, after all."

"I'd like you to stay." Katherine started unbuttoning her shirt.

"Katherine..."

"I know we'll go our separate ways after we leave here." She took off the shirt and untied the drawstring on the waistband of the sweats. "And that's why I want you to make love to me tonight."

His voice was strained. "Look, you're probably not thinking straight. Adrenaline can mess with your mind, and the incident with the bear has probably caused you to—"

"I'm thinking perfectly straight." She stepped out of the pants and got into bed.

"Katherine...." He held her gaze. "God knows I'm not strong enough to talk you out of this."

She reached up and touched his cheek. "I don't want you to."

He took a shaky breath. "Then we need the box of condoms."

"No." She moved into his arms. "If this is the only time we'll have together, I want it to count. I want another baby, Zeke."

18

ZEKE LAY VERY STILL, his heartbeat drumming heavily in his ears as he held Katherine's gaze. "You're sure?"

"You were an only child. I was an only child. We both know what a brother or sister would have meant to us."

"Everything."

"Yes."

Once again he had the feeling of looking into the depths of a clear mountain stream, and he knew that she was at peace with this decision she'd made. She wanted this for herself and for Amanda. And best of all, she had confidence in him as a father.

And he couldn't deny her, not when the urge to mate rose so hot and strong. But there would be conditions this time. "If it happens—"

She nodded. "I have a feeling it will."

He thought so, too. The certainty of it made him tremble. "You'll call me the minute you know."

Her eyes were luminous with anticipation. "Yes."

"These will probably be the only two children I'll ever have." He knew beyond a shadow of a doubt that he'd never have a child with another woman, but if he started speaking in absolutes, she might not believe him.

"Me, too, Zeke."

He closed his eyes as relief and joy flooded through him. "God, how I needed to hear you say that."

She reached up to stroke his cheek. "I didn't know I

was choosing you for the father of my first child," she said softly. "But you're the only choice for the father of my second."

"I want to be there this time." The more time he spent with Amanda, the more he resented missing so much in the beginning. "I want to watch you give birth."

"You will."

"And if there are...problems, I want to be there for those, too."

She combed her fingers through his hair. "The doctor said I shouldn't have problems next time."

He captured her hand and placed a kiss on each of her fingers. "Doctors can be wrong, and I don't want you to be alone if...something goes wrong." He wanted this so much he could barely breathe, but they wouldn't go through with it unless he had her word that he wouldn't be shut out. Not again. His voice was strained as he held her hand very tight. "Give me your promise, Katherine."

"I promise, Zeke." She swallowed. "I promise to let you be part of this pregnancy. I promise that you will be by my side when I give birth to our son or daughter. I promise to honor your rights as the father of our ch—"

His kiss transformed her final word into a moan of pleasure as he drew her close. Deliberately he guided her down and started to move over her, but she struggled in his arms. He lifted his head. "What's wrong?"

Her reply was breathless. "Let me be on top. Your ankle—"

"My ankle can take it. And this time, my love, I need to be in charge."

Her sigh of surrender was all the encouragement he needed. He covered her body with his.

He wanted to memorize her, absorb her into his pores, drown in the scent and taste of her. And then, when they'd flowed so completely together that they would never be separated, no matter how far apart they traveled, he would spill his seed into her, bonding her to him forever.

He'd never kissed like this, touched like this, wanted like this. He lifted his head and gazed into her eyes to find the same intense purpose shining there.

"I'm going to love making you pregnant," he said.

She gave him the smile of a seductress, then she went still. "Do you hear the wolves?"

"No. Just my heart pounding like a freight train."

"Listen."

He paused and tried to quiet his ragged breathing. Yes, there they were, louder this time, singing their haunting tribute to the moon. "I hear them."

"I love that sound. It makes me think of you." An untamed emotion burned in her eyes. "Love me while the wolves howl, Zeke."

And he'd thought he couldn't be more aroused. Heat surged in his groin as he began an intimate exploration of her body in tune to the rhythm of the wolves' song. The wild sound wove its way into his subconscious, driving him to a primitive sensuality as he reveled in her taste, her scent, and her wordless whimpers. He longed to carry her outside in the moonlight, lay her on a bed of pine boughs and take possession of her with the swift instinctive stroke of a forest creature. He wanted to howl his triumph to the world.

Yet a part of his civilized mind still functioned, leaping ahead to a time when he wouldn't have this woman stretched beneath him, writhing with pleasure, and he longed to make this moment last forever.

But instinct seemed to rule Katherine. She tugged at his sweats, pushing them down over his hips. Then she reached for him and guided him to her, spreading her thighs, arching against him. "Zeke, now," she pleaded with choked urgency.

He felt the call of her body, the insistent pull of her womb, and he followed that call, rising above her to look down into her flushed face.

"Give me another baby," she whispered.

His erection throbbed in response, but he slipped just barely inside her and paused. "Our baby," he murmured, looking into her eyes.

"Our baby."

As the wolves' howls built to a crescendo, he held her gaze and pushed deep.

ZEKE INSISTED THAT THEY make love all night to guarantee success, and Katherine didn't argue with him. But finally even their passion for each other couldn't keep them awake. Entwined in each other's arms, they slept.

Dawn had not yet found the clearing when Katherine woke to an unusual sound, one she'd never heard in the cabin. It took her several long seconds to realize the phone was ringing, but the meaning of the ringing phone came to her more quickly. Their isolation had ended.

Zeke started to climb out of bed, but she laid a restraining hand on him. "I'll get it. I can move faster." She hurried to the phone as Amanda woke up and started to cry. Katherine picked up the receiver. "Hello?"

"Katherine?" Naomi sounded worried. "Are you okay?"

"I'm fine." Katherine stretched the cord until she could reach Amanda's bassinet.

"Is that Amanda I hear?"

"Yep." Katherine cradled the phone against her shoulder and picked up the baby.

"Is *she* okay?"

"She's fine, too, Naomi. Just a little hungry at the moment."

"I am so relieved. When I hadn't heard a word from you, I called the lodge this morning and they said they hadn't seen you since Friday. The maid reported you didn't seem to be staying there, although your clothes were still in the room. I was frantic. So I made some inquiries through Lost Springs Ranch and got this number and some idea of where this cabin might be. Apparently it's quite remote."

Katherine jiggled Amanda against her shoulder. "Yes, and the phone was knocked out. It must have just been reconnected."

"I thought you two were going to stay at the lodge."

"Well, it...didn't work out that way, Naomi."

"Good heavens. He didn't kidnap you and drag you to his lair, did he?"

"No. There was a flat tire, and a bridge that was out, and—I'll explain when I get back." She swayed with Amanda, but the baby wouldn't quiet down.

"You poor woman. You sound exhausted, and Amanda doesn't sound happy, either. What an ordeal. I understand from the people at Lost Springs that this cabin of his is quite primitive. I had no intention of putting you and Amanda through something like this."

"It really hasn't been so bad." She glanced up as Zeke left the bed.

He'd put on his sweatpants, as if the telephone call from Naomi had restored his modesty. He limped over to the rocker, sat down and held out his arms.

Stretching the phone cord, she crossed to him and leaned down so he could take Amanda. "In fact, it's been fine."

Zeke rocked the baby and murmured to her.

"Well, you're very brave to say that, but I've sent a helicopter. They should be there shortly, but I decided to call and see if I could get in touch with you to let you know they were on the way."

"You've sent a *helicopter*?" Katherine glanced at Zeke in horror. Naomi meant to snatch her away from him in less than an hour.

"Of course. They'll fly you to the airport. The lodge can ship your things back here. Believe me, it's the least I can do after subjecting you to the weekend from hell."

Katherine gazed at Zeke holding Amanda. The baby had stopped fussing and was waving her arms at Zeke. The weekend from heaven was more like it. "Can you cancel the helicopter?"

"Well, probably not, but if you're worried about the expense, don't think another thing about it. The main thing is to get you and Amanda back safely to New York. I don't mind paying a little extra to accomplish that. I hope that at least you were able to tie up your loose ends with this man."

For the first time Katherine faced the fact that she would not be in Wyoming at all if Naomi hadn't paid a lot of money to arrange for this weekend. First Naomi had bought Zeke at the bachelor auction, and then she'd paid Katherine's airfare and reserved rooms at the lodge. For that outlay Naomi expected Katherine to tidy up her life so she'd be free to run *Cachet*. Instead, Katherine's situation with Zeke was anything but tidy, considering she'd spent the whole night trying to get pregnant again.

"You *have* worked things out with him, haven't you?" Naomi asked. "I expect there's nothing much to do in that little cabin except talk."

Despite her turbulent emotions, Katherine almost

laughed. Fortunately she controlled the urge. She gazed at Zeke, and looking at him took away all the laughter and replaced it with deep sorrow. They would see each other again, but they would never share another experience like this one. They would never allow themselves the luxury of a passionate embrace or the temptation of being completely alone, because their love could go nowhere. Zeke didn't want a full-time wife and child, and Katherine couldn't turn her back on Naomi.

"We've worked things out," she said.

Zeke glanced up at her. She caught her breath at the grief in his eyes. Then his expression closed down.

"Thank God for that," Naomi said. "Well, I'd love to see you immediately when you get back, but if you'd like a day or so to rest up, feel free. Maybe we can do dinner tomorrow night. I know a lovely little place where they'll be happy to have Amanda and you won't be expected to dash into the women's room to nurse her."

Katherine forced herself to speak around the lump in her throat. "That...that sounds great."

"Good. Then we'll do it. I can hardly wait to see you. I know it hasn't been that long, but I already miss you both terribly. You're the daughter I never had, and now that Amanda's here... Well, let's just say I've come to need that cute little baby face of hers to make me happy."

Katherine swallowed. Naomi couldn't have put it any plainer than that. "We'll see you soon, then. Bye, Naomi."

"Goodbye, dear. You're a brave little soldier."

ZEKE ROCKED QUIETLY as Katherine hung up the phone and leaned her forehead against the wall. "How long do we have?" he asked finally.

She turned, her eyes brimming with tears. "Not long. She's already dispatched a helicopter."

Zeke nodded and kept rocking. He couldn't let her see that he was being slowly torn apart by their inevitable separation. "Funny how quickly a woman with money can arrange things, isn't it?"

"I could send the helicopter away."

He gazed at her, wishing she'd do exactly that, knowing it wouldn't happen. "No, you can't," he said softly. "This woman is your ticket to achieving your dreams. She thinks she's saving you from a fate worse than death. You said yourself that you couldn't throw her generosity back in her face."

Katherine wrapped her arms around her stomach. "I don't think I can, but I don't know if I can stand to leave, Zeke."

It took more strength than he thought he had, but he shoved aside his feelings of loss and concentrated on her. She had a brilliant future in front of her. He couldn't let her jeopardize it. "If I thought you couldn't stand it, I wouldn't have made love to you. Maybe it was a big mistake."

"Don't you say that!" She was crying hard now. "Making love to you last night was the best thing in my whole life! No matter what happens now, I'll never regret that!"

He wanted to cry with her, but he couldn't. She needed him to be strong. "That's good, because we can't take it back. And I'd be willing to bet my last dollar you're pregnant."

"I hope to God I am." She kept sobbing.

"You're going to need to be tough to break that news to Naomi when the time comes. She won't like it. One kid was a mistake. Two looks like a habit."

She started to laugh through her sobs, but there was a

touch of hysteria in her laughter. "Some habit. We'll never make love a—"

"Don't. Don't go down that road, Katherine." His heart twisted in anguish, but he forced his voice into a steady, soothing rhythm. "We can't think about that now. We've both made our choices. We both know those choices are the best for everyone concerned." He stood, deliberately putting pressure on his ankle. The pain helped. "Go get dressed while I change Amanda. Then maybe you'll have time to feed her before the helicopter arrives."

She stared at him, her eyes red. "Ask me to stay. Ask me to stay and I will, Zeke."

Oh, God. He struggled with the raging desire to ask her, to beg her to stay with him. Finally he won the battle. "No."

She went limp and turned away.

Stay, he screamed silently. But he kept his jaw clenched and said nothing.

She walked over to the cold, sooty fireplace, picked up the blouse and underwear she'd left draped over a chair to dry and started putting on her clothes.

WHEN KATHERINE FINALLY walked up to her apartment door late that evening, laden down with a sleeping Amanda in the canvas sling, the diaper bag and the car seat, she felt as if she'd been gone a million years instead of only three days. A huge bouquet of colorful flowers sat beside the door. Careful not to disturb Amanda, she set down the diaper bag and the car seat, walked over and plucked out the card. Her heart pounded with the hope that Zeke had—but no, the flowers were from Naomi, with congratulations for going above and beyond the call of duty.

Katherine thought she'd squeezed out every possible tear in her body, but more threatened to fall as she gazed at the flowers and wished they were from Zeke instead of Naomi. She needed some token, some sign that he was thinking of her, that he was as torn apart by this parting as she had been.

The helicopter had arrived quickly, and once it had landed, there had been no time for tender goodbyes. The last thing she'd seen as the chopper lifted off over the trees was Zeke standing on the steps of his porch, arms crossed, as he watched her leave. The sight of him there all alone had nearly killed her.

Besides, she'd rather not have flowers from Naomi. Naomi shouldn't be congratulating her. Someday Katherine planned to repay Naomi the cost of everything, including the bachelor auction. It would take years, no doubt, but Katherine needed to clear her conscience. She hadn't really operated in good faith with her godmother, and guilt lay heavy on her heart.

With a sigh she fit her key in the lock, picked up the flowers and walked inside. She returned for the car seat and the diaper bag, shut the door and secured all three locks. Zeke hadn't needed three locks, she thought. He blended with his environment instead of erecting barriers against it. While she'd been with him she'd felt that sense of unity soothe her soul. The constant sadness of losing her parents had eased, and the world had seemed more balanced.

She tucked Amanda into her crib. The baby had her own pink-and-white bedroom, one that Katherine had been proud of until now. But she couldn't help thinking how lost the little girl looked in such a big bed with so much furniture around. She'd seemed cozier in the copper kettle bassinet Zeke had created for her.

And when Katherine left the room, the separation of walls between her and her baby felt wrong. Her apartment seemed to have far too many rooms, in fact, and the noise from the street bothered her for the first time in the years she'd lived there.

Maybe she'd buy some nature music, she thought. Something with wolves howling in the background. She clutched her stomach as a wave of anguish passed through her. Zeke.

ZEKE HOBBLED OVER to the pile of wood by the fireplace and picked up another log, a log that Katherine had brought in.

After tossing it on the fire, he sat down in the rocker and picked up his beer. He still had the empty bottle from when she'd had a beer during their first lunch together. And their second lunch... He sighed and leaned his head against the back of the rocker. He'd had a total of three nights with Katherine, counting last summer. Three nights of memories to last him a lifetime.

He was probably an ungrateful son of a bitch to want more than that. He wasn't the right man for her, and he should count himself lucky that she'd been willing to love him for a little while. And she'd given him a gift. For a solitary, gruff man like him to have a sweet little daughter like Amanda was nothing short of a miracle.

Time to let Katherine go. Time to face the fact that he was who he was, and no woman would want to shut herself away in the woods with a guy like him, least of all a sophisticated lady like Katherine. She'd hooked the brass ring when she'd been born the goddaughter of Naomi Rutledge, and no way would he ever drag her down.

He wondered if she was home by now. It frustrated him that he couldn't imagine her there because he'd never seen her apartment. He didn't know where Amanda would sleep, where Katherine would sleep. He didn't know what pictures she had on the walls or what her furniture looked like. That seemed important, somehow.

Maybe one day he'd see her apartment...or maybe not. They might decide it was safer if they met in neutral territory. He'd have to be very careful not to do anything that would cause her to leave her New York job just because of their strong need for each other, which meant never, ever being alone with her again.

Naomi would not be happy when and if Katherine announced she was pregnant again. Zeke wished he could be there to give Katherine support when she made that revelation. But he'd probably only add to her stress. For the thousandth time since she'd left that morning, he worried about whether he'd done the right thing by making love to her with no protection. And whether at this very moment, their child was growing within her.

As WOLVES HOWLED in Katherine's apartment, Amanda smiled and gurgled in delight.

"Like that, don't you, Mandy?" Katherine said as she finished changing the baby's diaper. The nature CD was Amanda's favorite, and Katherine had gotten into the habit of playing it every night when she and Amanda came home from *Cachet*. It soothed them both.

And it brought Zeke closer.

Katherine carried Amanda to the rocker in her living room and nursed her while the sounds of rushing water and the cry of a hawk brought back memories of the wilderness and the man she'd left behind. She'd traveled to Wyoming twice, and each time she'd learned more about herself, gained more confidence in her ability to handle any situation.

The rugged Wyoming countryside, she realized, made her strong in ways that the city could not. To be a whole person she needed that connection with nature that had been fostered when she was a child, and although she'd probably never become a wilderness guide as she'd once fantasized, she wasn't happy living in a high-rise in Manhattan, either.

She still wasn't sure how to reconcile this latest self-knowledge with her obligation to Naomi, but she would reconcile it somehow. So much depended on whether she was pregnant again. She prayed that she was. Far from dreading the prospect of telling Naomi that news, she welcomed it as a way to start revealing her true self to her godmother.

Katherine smiled. She was definitely a braver woman these days. She had Wyoming and Zeke to thank for that, but she also owed a debt of gratitude to Sadie. Without the bear's late-night visit, Katherine might never have discovered the courage to face her worst nightmare.

She longed to confide all this to Zeke, but he hadn't contacted her, and she didn't think she should call him until she knew definitely about the pregnancy. She missed him painfully and constantly, but she worried that excessive contact with her might make their separation worse. She'd disrupted his life enough as it was, and now he needed to return to the comfort of his normal routine. She'd no doubt be doing him a favor if she exercised some restraint.

As HE DID MOST nights, Zeke walked out to the front porch and settled into a chair. He wasn't limping much these days, but he almost hated to have his ankle heal because the injury kept him connected to those two incredible days with Katherine. He hadn't been able to make himself wash the clothes that she'd borrowed even though her scent was very faint now. Somehow they'd become "Katherine's clothes," and he didn't want them disturbed.

He'd never been on a sea voyage, but he felt like the survivor of a shipwreck. Night after night he sat on his porch, searching for the peace that he'd always been able to find there, but it was gone. Everything reminded him of her—the empty Adirondack chair, the soulful howl of the wolves, the grazing deer, the hoot of an owl.

Then there was the ache that wouldn't leave, the hollow place inside that called out for his daughter. Two damned days he'd had, and she was imprinted like a brand. Once he'd accepted her presence in his life, he'd learned to hate the two months of growing he'd missed before he knew she was alive. Now that he'd come to know her smiles, her babbling and even her cries, he resented every hour that went by because it was another hour that Mandy was growing. And he wasn't there to see it.

He'd promised himself that he wouldn't interfere in Katherine's life, but he hadn't had a clue what he'd been promising. He hadn't known that she and Mandy had become as essential to him as breathing. He hadn't known that as the days stretched out before him with no prospect of seeing Katherine or Mandy, a part of him would slowly die.

KATHERINE WHIRLED AMANDA up in her arms and danced around the living room. "I'm pregnant! I'm pregnant," she sang. "You're going to have a baby sister, or a baby brother, you lucky little kid!"

Amanda grinned back at her. Now that she'd passed three months, nobody doubted that her smiles were really smiles, and she even had a start on honest-to-goodness laughter.

"Time to call Daddy!" Katherine planned to honor her promise. Zeke would be the first to know that the home pregnancy test was positive. Well, not counting Amanda, who wouldn't tell on her. She glanced at the clock. It would be very early in the morning in Wyoming.

As she allowed herself to think about Zeke, her jubilation faded a little. She'd had no communication from him, none at all. She hoped his reasons for not getting in touch were the same as hers. She'd tried many times to send a letter herself, but in the end she hadn't been able to figure out what to say. The emotions between them had been so intense that a letter seemed incredibly inadequate.

Even the phone call she was about to make seemed like the wrong way to tell him the news. She wanted to be able to see his face, see the light come into his eyes.

God, how she missed him. He was on her mind before she went to sleep at night and immediately after she awoke in the morning. He filled her dreams, and even her daydreams. She'd had some close calls at work when she'd been distracted by thoughts of Zeke and had nearly missed an important part of a meeting.

She kept hoping that the excitement of the job would kick in again and the time she'd spent with Zeke would fade somewhat in her memory. Instead, the job didn't seem able to hold her interest as it once had, and she found herself constantly reliving her days in Wyoming and wanting to be there.

She wondered if Sadie had come back and if the Adirondack chairs were still in one piece. She wondered if

Zeke had rebuilt the bridge, and if Elmer the moose had come calling. Sometimes she tried to pretend the sirens on the streets were wolves howling, but the sound wasn't really the same. So she'd bought some more nature music and played it over and over, even if sometimes it made her cry.

She sat on the couch and gazed into Amanda's eyes. The older the baby was, the more certain it became that her eyes would be hazel, like Katherine's. Maybe this new baby would have Zeke's dark eyes. Katherine wondered if the dimple in Amanda's chin inherited from Zeke's mother would show up again in her baby brother or sister.

"I can't tell your daddy something this important over the phone, Mandy," she said at last. "And I promised he'd be the first to know, so I guess we'll keep this between us until I figure out what I'm going to do about that."

She tried to picture asking Naomi if she could take another trip to Wyoming without telling her why. It wouldn't wash. Naomi was already very curious about exactly what had taken place that weekend, because Katherine hadn't given out very many details. Naomi probably suspected that a flame still burned in Katherine's heart for Zeke, and an unexplained trip to Wyoming would confirm her suspicions.

Worse than that, it wasn't a good time to be jetting around the country. Naomi was turning over more of the magazine's responsibilities every day, and Katherine didn't have a lot of free time aside from the hours she spent taking care of Amanda. She even worked weekends, although that was supposed to be temporary until the change-over was complete.

Now that the rest of the staff understood Naomi's plan,

Katherine had to be careful that she appeared responsible enough to take command. Running off to Wyoming when so many projects needed her attention wasn't going to inspire confidence in her co-workers. Announcing the pregnancy would be shock enough to everyone's system, especially considering how the last pregnancy took her out of the action.

Katherine looked down at the baby in her lap. Amanda had mirrored her mother's changed mood, and her chubby face wore a solemn expression, as if she carried the weight of the world on her baby shoulders.

"We'll figure this out, Mandy," Katherine said. "Don't worry. We managed with that bear. We will definitely figure this out. Just give me some time."

19

ZEKE TRUSTED KATHERINE. He believed she would keep her promise. Yet she'd been gone six weeks and she should have called him by now to let him know if she was pregnant. Home pregnancy tests were all the rage these days, and he figured she'd use one the minute she missed her period. They hadn't established that she'd call him if she *wasn't* pregnant, but somehow he thought that she should, as a courtesy.

Hell, he just wanted to hear from her. The loneliness was excruciating. He'd been a loner all his life, but he'd never felt as if he existed in a vacuum before. He was so desperate to relieve his agony that he'd considered selling the cabin and building another somewhere else, somewhere that wouldn't remind him of Katherine every time he turned around.

But he couldn't do that until he heard from her, one way or the other, about the baby. Sure, she could contact him at work, but he thought she might try the cabin first. He couldn't always be there because of work, but whenever possible he hung around the place, hoping that she'd call. Of course, that meant he was faced with memories of her and the baby constantly.

When the waiting and wondering and remembering threatened to drive him crazy, he decided there was only one thing to do.

WALKING ALONG FIFTH AVENUE took Zeke's breath away. He kept looking up at the buildings towering above him, which meant he was constantly bumping into people hurrying down the sidewalk. So many people, all of them in a rush. He'd nearly been run over twice by taxis.

"Hey, cowboy, watch where you're going," muttered a guy Zeke knocked with his elbow.

"Sorry." Zeke tipped his hat. He'd decided against the flannel shirts he usually wore when he was out of uniform. For this trip to the big city he'd put on a western shirt and his best jeans. At the last minute he'd added the Stetson that Shane Daniels had bought him for the bachelor auction. He could use a dose of luck. There was a nip in the air on this October morning, but he'd left his jacket in the hotel room because he thought it was too scruffy to wear to the *Cachet* office.

He'd called, and without identifying himself had asked a receptionist to direct him to the place. Now he finally stood in front of the building, heart pounding. Somewhere in that tall gray mass of stone Katherine was working. She'd have Amanda with her. Zeke was so eager to see his baby he could almost taste it, but *eager* didn't begin to describe how he felt about meeting Katherine again. His breath hitched and his palms grew sweaty.

Well, he'd come this far. Pulling the brim of his hat low over his eyes, he pushed through the revolving doors and walked into the building. The heels of his boots clicked on the marble floor as he crossed to the bank of elevators. He consulted the directory. *Cachet* took up three floors—the top three.

An elevator opened in front of him and several people got off. Others waiting with him got on and turned to stare at Zeke as he stood there and debated whether to go through with this, after all. The elevator doors closed.

He was out of his element here, a stranger in this land of skyscrapers and crowds of people. This was Katherine's territory. She probably wasn't pregnant, and so she'd decided they shouldn't communicate again until Amanda was old enough to visit him by herself. She wouldn't welcome his intrusion into her busy workday.

But the fact that she was so close drove him crazy. A ride up the elevator and he'd be able to see her again, talk with her, even if only for a few minutes. And he was damned sure going to see Amanda. To leave without quenching his soul's thirst for a glimpse of his child would probably kill him. If Katherine became upset with him for showing up like this, he could take it. After all, she'd been upset with him before. He'd endure her anger for a chance to see his daughter.

He punched the elevator button.

Moments later he stood in the reception area. He looked around with a sense of doom. Everything from the glass-and-brass receptionist's desk to the white upholstered chairs lining the wall spoke of money and sophistication. He'd known his world and Katherine's were very different, but he hadn't realized just how different.

But by God, he'd get what he came for. By the time he left this slick world of hers he'd see how Mandy had grown and he'd know whether he'd made Katherine pregnant that night or not. If he had, she might even be regretting it by now. Ice surrounded his heart at the thought that she might have changed her mind about the baby, might have…no. She wouldn't do that. He believed in her more than that. He had to.

"May I help you?" The receptionist, a well-manicured

brunette wearing a telephone headset, looked friendly enough.

"I'd like to see Katherine Seymour."

"Do you have an appointment?"

"No, but...I think she'll see me."

The receptionist gave him a long look. "And your name?"

"Zeke Lonetree."

"If you'd like to have a seat, I'll buzz her office, Mr. Lonetree."

"Thanks. I'll stand." He couldn't sit still if someone paid him to do it, he thought.

The receptionist punched a number into her phone. "Ms. Seymour? Oh, yes, Ms. Rutledge. I didn't expect to find you there. I see. Well, I have someone here who wants to see Ms. Seymour. His name is Zeke Lonetree." The receptionist fiddled with a gold pen while she listened. "All right. I'll do that. Thank you, Ms. Rutledge."

The receptionist cut the connection and glanced up at Zeke. "Ms. Seymour is in a meeting, but Ms. Rutledge will see you. She's in Ms. Seymour's office watching Amanda." She smiled, and her professional mask slipped a little. "That's Ms. Seymour's baby."

"I know." Zeke just bet Naomi would see him. She'd probably tell him to get the hell out of town. But Naomi didn't have that kind of power over him, despite her money and her connections. He'd stay until he saw Katherine, but in the meantime, he could get a look at his sweet baby girl.

The receptionist now gazed at him with frank curiosity, as if she had begun to put two and two together. "Do you know how to get up to Ms. Seymour's office?"

"No, I don't."

"Just go down that hall and take the elevator all the

way to the top. Her office is the door on the left. Her name is on it."

"Thank you." Zeke walked down a hall carpeted in a black-and-white pattern he thought was called herringbone. The walls were lined with framed *Cachet* covers. The place was a maze, he thought as he rode the elevator to the building's top floor. And standing guard to make sure he didn't penetrate it and find Katherine was Naomi Rutledge. Well, he'd open every door in the place, if necessary.

Once he stepped off the elevator he saw Katherine's office door immediately. It was partially open. A similar door with Naomi's nameplate on it was right across the hall. Cozy.

He tapped on Katherine's door.

"Come in, Zeke."

He opened the door and stepped into one of the most elegant offices he'd ever seen, but then, he didn't spend much time in elegant offices. A wall of windows looked out on Fifth Avenue, and when he stepped through the door, his boot heels sank into thick cream-colored carpeting. Naomi sat behind a delicately carved cherry desk, but he didn't waste much time looking at her. His glance went immediately to a small crib in the corner of the office where Amanda lay fast asleep. Next to the crib were a rocking chair and a changing table.

He crossed the room to gaze down at Amanda. He couldn't believe how much bigger she seemed and how much more hair she had. His throat tightened as he watched her sleep, his beautiful daughter, growing so fast. And he'd missed all those days. He wondered if she still loved to play when she took her bath, if she'd learned how to roll over, and when she'd get her first tooth.

"Hello, Zeke."

He'd forgotten anyone else was in the room. With an effort he returned his attention to Naomi. "Hello, Naomi." She was about as he'd expected, polished and attractive in her black suit. Although she might be in her sixties, she carried her age well. Not a silver hair was out of place and her skin was in excellent condition.

"I wondered if you'd show up," she said.

"And why is that?"

She motioned to a chair in front of the desk. "You can sit down, you know."

"Thanks, but I'm just here to see Katherine for a minute." He didn't want to leave his position by the crib, just in case Mandy woke up.

Naomi's eyebrows lifted. "You came all the way from Wyoming to see her for a minute?"

"I—there's something we need to discuss." Amanda stirred and he turned back to the crib. If only she would wake up, then he could hold her.

"Try not to wake her up," Naomi said. "Katherine managed to feed her and get her to sleep before the meeting, which is a small miracle that doesn't always happen."

"I won't wake her." He was bothered by Naomi's attitude, as if he couldn't be trusted around Amanda. He was the father of this kid, and if he accidentally woke her up, he knew what to do about it.

"Katherine tells me you want visitation rights," Naomi said.

"Yes." He gazed down at the sleeping child. She was so perfect. Still. The tiny dimple in her chin made her even more perfect. He thought of it as the Lonetree stamp. She made a little sucking noise in her sleep, and the sound took him back to those magic moments in the cabin when he'd watched Katherine nurse her.

"Of course, she wouldn't be able to come out and stay with you for quite a while yet," Naomi said.

"Not until she's weaned," Zeke said. He wasn't sure how long that was, but he hoped not too long.

"Oh, I'd think you'd want to wait much longer than that. I'd say when she's four or five, then she might be ready."

Zeke turned to face Naomi as a slow-burning rage seared his gut. "I have no intention of waiting four or five years to spend time with my daughter."

Naomi regarded him quietly for several long seconds. "I see. It seems you became quite attached to her while the three of you were trapped in that little cabin."

Zeke glanced around Katherine's office. "You know, traps come in all shapes and sizes."

"And what is that supposed to mean?"

"Nothing. I—" Whatever he'd been about to say disappeared from his mind as Katherine walked in the door.

"Zeke!" Her face lit up with surprise and delight, but she quickly doused the light of those emotions and glanced nervously over at Naomi. "I wasn't expecting you," she said with more composure.

He held on to her first reaction and ignored her second. She looked great, charcoal business suit and all. "I know this is a surprise. I thought about telling you I was coming, but then I just...came."

"It's good to see you." Her eyes held a special glow as she gazed at him.

He lifted his eyebrows, silently asking the question. When she smiled back, he knew. Pleasure washed over him in a wave and he started grinning like a kid with a ticket to a major league baseball game. Hot damn. Another baby.

"Zeke said he had something to discuss with you, so I should probably leave you two alone." Naomi stood and rounded the desk.

Zeke glanced at her. Once again he'd forgotten she even existed. Good thing he hadn't followed his impulse to swing Katherine up in his arms and twirl her around the room. Of course he wasn't supposed to be doing stuff like that anyway. They were officially off limits to each other now. He'd said he wanted it that way, as a matter of fact.

"Oh!" Katherine seemed similarly surprised to find Naomi still in the room. "Well, maybe that would be best."

Naomi held out her hand to Zeke. "I'm glad I finally had a chance to meet you."

He took her hand. He'd never held one with so many rings on it. "Thank you again for your contribution to the ranch. I stopped by there not long ago and construction's started on the new bunkhouses for the boys. You made that possible."

"Actually I think you made that possible. I hope you enjoy your stay in New York."

"I'm leaving this afternoon."

"Really? What a shame. It's a great city." She withdrew her hand and turned to Katherine. "May I see you when you're finished here? There's a detail that's been nagging at me concerning the layout we approved yesterday."

"Certainly. Thank you for watching Amanda."

"As always, it was my pleasure. She's the light of my life." She left with the graceful air of a queen taking leave of her subjects.

Zeke waited until she'd walked across the hall and into her own office before he turned back to Katherine. "When did you find out?"

"A week ago."

His gut tightened.

"Don't look like that. I had my hand on the phone to call you, and then it seemed so impersonal."

"Damn it, Katherine, I've been practically living by the phone!"

Katherine glanced across the hall, where Naomi's door remained open. She nudged hers shut. "I'm sorry." Her eyes pleaded for understanding. "But I wanted to tell you in person. I tried to figure out a way to get out there, but I couldn't see how I could leave again, so I mailed you a plane ticket yesterday. Believe it or not, I talked your boss into telling me when you'd have a few days off."

"I switched those days so I could come now. I couldn't stand it another minute."

She clasped her hands in front of her. "I'm really sorry. I'll be glad to reimburse you for—"

"Not on your life." He cleared his throat. "You look terrific."

Self-consciously she tucked a strand of hair behind her ear. "Thanks." She blushed. "You, too. I've never seen you so..."

"Clean?"

She laughed, but her laughter had a nervous edge to it. "Don't you think Amanda's grown a lot?"

He couldn't seem to stop looking at the color of her eyes, the texture of her hair, the shape of her lips. "I can't believe how she's grown. She's going to be a big girl."

Katherine nodded. "Tall. Like you."

"And you. Both of them will probably be tall." Excitement churned within him and he couldn't help looking down at her stomach. "And you're absolutely sure?"

"Yes. I had it confirmed by a doctor yesterday. So you're really leaving this afternoon?"

"I only came to find out. Now I know, so I can get out of your hair."

"Oh." She looked disappointed. Turning away from him, she walked over to her desk. She drummed her fingers on it a few times before wheeling back to face him. "I'm going to resign."

"You *what?*"

"I've been thinking about it all week, which is why I finally decided to mail you a ticket. I wanted to warn you that I was doing this, so it wouldn't come as a shock."

Panic rose in his chest. "Katherine, no. Don't do this. I shouldn't have made love to you again. It was selfish of me, and—"

"Look, you don't have to change any of your plans. Well, you might have to make a little more time in your life for your two children, because they'll be living in Jackson with me, instead of here in New York, so naturally I hope that you'll spend more time with them."

"What are you saying? You can't throw all this away. My God, you have a window overlooking Fifth Avenue! Do you know what that means?"

"Yes." She lifted her chin. "Not much anymore. I have a lot to work out with Naomi, and it won't be easy. I'll hate letting her down, but I need to make...other plans. I'm not asking you to marry me, or take care of me. But I will be near enough that our two children can know you, know you really well. I will find something creative and challenging to do there, something that will involve the outdoors. It's—"

"No!" He'd ruined everything for her. Ruined everything with his selfish, greedy desire to give her another child.

Amanda started to fuss, but Katherine stayed where she was, her expression filled with pain. She put a hand to her chest. "Are you saying you...don't want me to be that close to you?"

Standing in this expensive office and knowing what she'd be giving up, he decided to lie. But he had to look away to do it. "That's what I'm saying." He knew he had to get out of there, and damned fast. "Goodbye, Katherine. Keep me posted on...everything." He flung open the door and practically ran down the hall.

The elevator opened just as he arrived, and he stepped inside. He had to put as much distance between him and Katherine as he could before he got down on his knees and begged her to spend the rest of her life with him. But what he had could never compare with all of this. Never in a million years.

KATHERINE STOOD WITHOUT moving. If she moved she might break. Soon she'd go over and pick up the baby, soothe her and get her back to sleep. Soon.

"What the hell was that about?" Naomi burst into the office. "Where was he going in such a hurry?"

Katherine blinked. Her voice was strangely calm. "Away from me, I believe. I scared him to death." She gazed at Naomi. "I didn't mean this to be so abrupt, and I hate that I'm messing up everything you've planned for, but...I need to resign. I had planned to move to Wyoming, but..."

"Because you love him."

Katherine felt as if she were enveloped in some sort of thick fog. "Yes, but I didn't tell him that. Listen, Naomi,

I'm so sorry about this. You've been the most supportive, most loving, most wonderful—"

"Never mind that. Why haven't you told him you love him? It's true. And he loves you."

Katherine gazed at Naomi in confusion. "That's just it. He doesn't."

"The hell he doesn't! He's giving up everything so that you can keep the job of your dreams!" She shook her head. "Young people are so dense these days."

Katherine stared at her. "You really think he loves me?"

"I would bet my fortune on it. In fact, I think I will. I've had a pretty good idea this would happen, and I've started looking into selling the magazine."

Katherine's mouth dropped open.

"Oh, for heaven's sake, don't look so shocked. I've known from the minute you came back that you were gaga over this ranger of yours. So go get him. Chase him down before he gets out of town."

"But, Naomi, you're going to sell *Cachet?*"

"Lock, stock and barrel. Well, maybe I'll keep some stock. Then I'll travel, come to Wyoming to visit my god-grandchild and have a life. That's something you have a chance to build, by the way. Create your own dream, Katherine. Don't chain yourself to mine. Now go, go get him!"

Still Katherine hesitated. "But what about Amanda? She's fussing and probably needs to be fed."

"I'll deal with her until you come back. And don't come back without that gorgeous hunk of man. He's worth twenty jobs like this one."

"Oh, Naomi, I don't know if he really wants me."

"Have I ever steered you wrong?"

"No."

"Then let me advise you one last time. Chase that man down. Use the express elevator at the back of the building."

"Okay." Katherine began to grin. She ran down the hall and through a double door that led to the express elevator. Rumor had it that the original owner of the building had had the elevator installed so that he could slip away with his mistress if his wife was spotted coming in the front of the building. The elevator plummeted her to the ground floor quickly enough to make her stomach jump, if it hadn't already been doing cartwheels at the prospect of blatantly throwing herself at Zeke.

Once on the ground floor she dashed out another set of double doors, through the lobby and into the street. Thank God he was tall and wearing a Stetson. She spotted him a block away.

Dodging pedestrians, she ran as fast as her tight skirt and designer shoes would allow. "Zeke!" she shouted.

He turned. The minute he caught sight of her he started making his way back toward her. "What is it?" he called as he drew near. "Is Amanda okay?"

"Amanda's fine." She leaned over and put her hands on her knees while she caught her breath.

"Then why are you here?"

She straightened. Maybe she'd been too coy. Maybe, in spite of her newfound courage, she'd been too cowardly when it came to Zeke. Well, she'd do her damnedest now. "Because I love you."

He stared at her.

"Naomi seems to believe the feeling's mutual, and that the only reason you've been pushing me away is because you're thinking of me, and this job I would be giving up." She looked into his dark eyes and her courage began to falter. "I'm here because I'm taking the chance she's right."

With a groan he gathered her close and pressed her head against his shoulder. "She's right, and damn it, Katherine, you have to stay here. You'll have everything here, while with me you'll have—"

"Everything," she murmured, lifting her head to look into his eyes. "All I want is you and our children. I want to live in the wilderness with you. I love it there, Zeke. I always have, but I lost track of that when my parents died, and then Naomi kept urging me to be a journalist and work for her. Please don't push me away because you think you know what's best for me."

"All I have is a one-room cabin!"

She smiled. "I dream about that cabin every night. I dream about it in the daytime, too."

"Just the cabin?"

"No, I dream about the man in the cabin. And I wonder if he loves me as much as I love him."

Fierce emotion blazed in his eyes. "More. I love you more than I ever thought I would love another person. Oh, God, Katherine, could you really be happy out in the woods with a guy like me?"

Her heart swelled with joy. "Not just a guy *like* you, but with the one and only Zeke Lonetree? I think it could be arranged. Of course I want the whole package—the ring, the ceremony, the honeymoon."

He tightened his grip. "And where would you like to go for this honeymoon? I could probably swing Hawaii, or maybe San Francisco, but then some people like—"

"I was thinking about a little cabin in the woods."

"But you've been there."

"Yeah, and I wasted far too much time, and wore far too many clothes."

"Ah, New York lady." He cupped her chin in his hand. "I'm going to kiss you right in the middle of your precious Fifth Avenue."

"Kiss me right in the middle of my mouth, ranger man. You'll like the taste better."

People eddied around them, jostling them in their haste to get on their way, but Zeke held her tight. And as his mouth found hers, she imagined she smelled wood smoke, pine trees and rain-soaked earth. She could even swear she heard, somewhere in the distance, the proud song of the wolves.

_____ Epilogue _____

"JUST A LITTLE MORE." Zeke crooned. "That's it. Breathe...breathe. Now *push*. That's it."

In the muted light of the hospital birthing room, Katherine ignored the murmurs of her doctor, Eva, and the attending nurses. Her world had narrowed to the pain and Zeke. She focused intently on his calm, patient voice and his dark warrior's eyes made even more dramatic by the pale green surgical mask he wore. With each contraction she clutched his hand with the same urgent grip as when he'd pulled her from the rapids. He was her key to survival.

He touched a cool cloth to her forehead. "Almost there. Big push, sweetheart."

She could do this. She'd faced a bear, damn it. She could do this.

"One more push." Above the mask, his eyes seemed to glow. "Give us our baby, Katherine."

Our baby. Fighting exhaustion and pain, she closed her eyes and bore down with a loud groan.

For the first time, his voice quivered. "The baby's coming. That's it. That's it! God, how I love you, Katherine!"

She opened her eyes as a lusty wail filled the room.

"It's a girl," Eva announced as she laid the warm, wet baby on Katherine's chest. At the contact, the baby's cries slowly subsided.

"A girl." With a soft smile Katherine cradled the child they'd created. Then she gazed up at Zeke. "I'm glad."

Zeke leaned over them, his voice choked. "Yeah, me, too. I'm starting to get the hang of little girls."

"Yes, you are." She couldn't imagine ever loving him more than she did at this very moment. Yet she knew she would. Every day the bond between them grew stronger.

He swallowed and cleared his throat. Then he laid a gloved hand on the baby. "Welcome to the world, Naomi..." He paused and glanced at Katherine. "We never decided on a middle name, did we?"

"I did." Katherine had been saving her idea until this moment, hoping and praying the baby would be a girl. "I want to name her Naomi Suzanne."

He sucked in a breath and stepped back, clearly taken by surprise. "After my mother?"

Katherine nodded.

Zeke lowered his head and turned away as a tremor passed through his massive body.

At his reaction, Katherine's chest tightened with anxiety. Maybe she'd made a mistake. "Unless you don't want to," she said softly.

His head came up. His dark lashes were spiked with the tears he'd fought unsuccessfully to control. When he finally spoke, his voice was rough and unsteady. "I want to," he said. He crouched down so that he could gaze into the baby's face. Slowly he settled his big hand over the tiny body. "Welcome to the world, Naomi Suzanne."

PURE TEMPTATION

1

Summer Project: Lose Virginity.

TESS BLAKELY rocked gently on her porch swing, a yellow legal pad balanced on her knee, a glass of iced tea on the wicker table beside her. She gazed at what she'd written and sighed. The beginning of a quest was the hardest part.

It was pitiful that a twenty-six-year-old, reasonably attractive woman found herself saddled with the handicap of virginity, but there it was, on paper. And her status had to change before she left for New York at the end of the summer, or she'd risk her credibility with the high school girls she'd been hired to counsel. Besides, she wanted to experience sex. She *longed* to experience sex.

She took a sip of iced tea and continued.

Goal One: Find knowledgeable candidate willing to deflower me.
Goal Two: Swear candidate to absolute secrecy.
Goal Three: Get it on.

Tess sighed again. Writing out her goals and objectives had been her cherished method for getting what she wanted, beginning at the age of eight when she'd yearned for her very own pony. But although she wanted to lose her innocence much more than she'd wanted that pony, her current project seemed about as likely of success as a personal rocket trip to the moon.

The little town of Copperville, Arizona, wasn't exactly crawling with "knowledgeable candidates," but even the few that she'd consider had been scared off long ago by her four very large, very overprotective older brothers. And not a one of those beefy brothers had moved away or relaxed his vigilance. They all expected their little sis to save herself for her wedding night. They were stuck in the Dark Ages, as far as she was concerned, but she loved them too much to openly defy them.

That was the reason for goal number two—for absolute secrecy. Now *there* was a definite sticking point. Even if she found a man her brothers hadn't intimidated, how could she ever expect him to keep a secret in Copperville? This was a town where you could wake up with a sore throat in the morning and have three kinds of chicken soup at your doorstep by noon.

Which meant she might never arrive at the third step— Getting It On. And she was ready for number three. Extremely ready. She'd driven all the way to Phoenix to buy research books, knowing that she couldn't be caught thumbing through *One Hundred Ways to Drive Him Wild* in the Copperville Book Barn, if the local bookstore even carried such a thing, which she sincerely doubted.

So much for her list. The goals were unreachable. She tossed the legal pad on top of the stack of books lying next to her on the swing. A list might have worked for the pony, but it was probably dumb to think it could cure a resistant case of chastity.

And to be honest, a list might have helped get her that pony all those years ago, but her best friend, Jeremiah "Mac" MacDougal, had been the real key. Her family lived in town and had no room for a horse, but Mac had talked his folks into keeping Chewbacca on their ranch. Tess's older brothers had always thought they had first claim to Mac, being boys, but Tess knew better. Ever since Mac, who'd been only five at the time, had saved her from a rattlesnake, she'd known he was the best friend she'd ever have.

Mac. Mac could help her find the right guy! She mentally slapped her forehead and wondered why she hadn't thought of him before. Unlike her brothers, Mac understood why she needed to take the job in New York and prove herself an independent, capable woman. Her brothers might have laughed at her when she asked for a light saber for Christmas, but Mac had saved his allowance and bought her one.

Surely Mac would also understand that she couldn't go to New York a virgin. Coming from a small town was enough of a handicap. If the girls she'd be counseling figured out that she was sexually inexperienced, she'd be a real joke. Mac would see that right away. And he'd help her find the right man to solve her problem.

THE SUN HAD BARELY crested the mountains as Mac saddled two horses. He'd left his bed this morning with a sense of anticipation. He hadn't had an early-morning ride with Tess in months. When she'd called to suggest it, he'd been happy at the prospect, although lately he'd been feeling a little jealous of her.

As kids they'd spent hours talking about the places they'd go when they were older. This September she was actually going to do it, while he was stuck on the ranch. His folks expected him to stay around and gradually take over what they'd worked so hard to build. As the only child, he couldn't foist off that obligation on anybody else.

Tess had it easier, although she was forever complaining about how hard it was for a woman to "go on a quest," as she put it. But she was doing it, and he wasn't. Her mom and dad hated having her leave town, especially for some faraway place like New York City, but they still had four sons, their wives and seven grandchildren. With such a slew of Blakelys around, Tess didn't have to feel guilty about grabbing her chance at independence. Mac envied her that freedom.

"Top 'o the mornin' to ye, MacDougal."

He buckled the cinch on Peppermint Patty and turned to smile at Tess. She used to greet him that way for months after she'd starred in Copperville High's version of *Brigadoon*, and hearing it again brought back memories.

They'd rehearsed her lines in the tree house in her folks' backyard. At one point he'd almost kissed her, but only because the script called for it, of course. Then they'd both decided the kiss wasn't necessary for her to learn the part. He'd been relieved, of course, because kissing Tess would seem weird. But at the time he'd kind of wanted to try it, anyway.

"Aye, and it's a fine mornin', lass," he said. She looked great, as always, but there was something different about her this morning. He studied her, trying to figure it out. "Did you cut your hair?"

"Not since the last time you saw me." She used her fingers to comb it away from her face. "Why, does it look bad?"

"No. It looks fine." In twenty-three years of watching Tess create new looks with her thick brown hair, he'd lived through braids, kinky perms, supershort cuts, even red streaks. Once he'd given her a haircut himself after she got bubble gum stuck in it. Neither set of parents had been impressed with his barbering skills. He liked the way she wore it now, chin-length and simple, allowing her natural wave to show.

"Is there a spot on my shirt or something?" She glanced down at the old Copperville Miners T-shirt she wore.

"Nope." He nudged his hat to the back of his head with his thumb. "But I swear something's different about you." He stepped closer and took her chin in his hand. "Are you wearing some of that fancy department-store makeup?"

"To go riding? Now that would be stupid, wouldn't it?"

He gazed at her smooth skin and noticed that her freckles were in full view and her mouth was its normal pink color. Her eyelashes were soft and fluttery, not spiky the way they had been in high school when she'd caked on the mascara. Nope, no makeup.

But as he looked into her gray eyes, he figured out what was bothering him. They were best friends and didn't keep things from each other, or at least they hadn't until now. This morning, for whatever reason, Tess had a secret. It changed her whole expression, making her seem mysterious, almost sexy. Not that he ever thought of Tess as sexy. No way.

Despite himself, he was intrigued. Even a little excited. He didn't associate Tess with mystery, and it was a novel concept. He decided to wait and let the secret simmer in those big gray eyes of hers. It was fun to watch.

He tweaked her nose and stepped back. "I guess I'm seeing things. You're the same old Tess. Ready to mount up?" To his amazement, she blushed. Tess never blushed around him. They knew each other too well.

"Um, sure," she mumbled, heading straight for Peppermint Patty without looking at him, her cheeks still very pink. "We're burning daylight."

While he stood there trying to figure out what he'd said to make her blush, she climbed quickly into the saddle and started out. As he mounted he continued to watch her, and he could swear she shivered. With the temperature hovering around eighty-five on this June morning, he didn't think she was cold. This might be the most interesting morning ride he'd ever had with Tess.

MAYBE ASKING FOR Mac's help wouldn't be so simple, after all, Tess thought as she headed for the trail leading to the river. Here she was blushing over some offhand remark he'd made about *mounting up*. Or maybe she'd spent too much time reading *those* books, and every conversation had sexual overtones now. She certainly couldn't go to New York keyed up like this. It would be good to get this whole business over with.

Ducking an occasional overhanging mesquite branch, she rode at a trot ahead of him on the dusty trail. He knew something was up. She never could keep anything from him, so she might as well lay out her plan as soon as they got to their favorite spot by the river. As kids they'd used the sandy bank for fierce battles between their *Star Wars* action figures, and when they were older, they'd come out here to drink colas and talk about whatever was going on in their lives. Tess had never shared the hideaway with anyone else, and neither had Mac, as far as she knew.

The riverbank was where they'd gone after Chewbacca died. They'd talked about heaven, and had decided horses had to be there or they weren't interested in going. They'd headed out here after Mac broke his arm and couldn't try out for Little League, and the day Tess had won a teddy bear at the school carnival. Before either of them knew anything about sex, they'd spent time by the river talking about whether men and women made babies the same way horses and dogs and goats did.

Later on, Mac had put a stop to their discussions on that topic. Now Tess wanted to reopen the discussion, but she wasn't sure if she had the courage.

"So what's your summer project this year?" Mac called up to her. "I know you always have one."

A perfect opening, but she didn't want to blurt it out while they were riding. "I'm still thinking about it." She drew confidence from the familiar rhythm of the little mare, the friendly squeak of saddle leather and the comfort of breathing in the dry, sweet air of early morning.

"Really? Hell, you usually have something planned by April. I'll never forget that summer you got hooked on Australia—you playing that god-awful didgeridoo while you made me cook shrimp on the barbie."

"How did I know it would spook the horses?"

Mac laughed. "The sound of that thing would spook a corpse. Do you ever play it anymore, or are you taking pity on your neighbors?"

"Watch yourself, or I'll be forced to remind you of the time you mooned my brothers."

"That was totally not my fault. You could have told me the bridge club was coming out to admire your mom's roses."

Tess started to giggle. "So help me, I tried."

"Sure you did."

"The boys stopped me! I felt terrible that it happened."

"Uh-huh. That's why you busted a gut laughing and why you bring it up on a regular basis."

"Only in self-defense." She barely had to guide Peppermint Patty down the trail after all the times the horse had taken her to the river. The horses flushed a covey of quail as they trotted past.

She could smell the river ahead of them, and obviously so could Peppermint Patty. The mare picked up the pace. As always, Tess looked forward to her first glimpse of the miniature beach surrounded almost entirely by tall reeds. The perfect hideout.

As the mare reached the embankment and started down toward the sand, her hooves skidded a little on the loose dirt, but she maintained her balance, having years of experience on this particular slope. In front of them the river gurgled along, about fifty feet wide at this point. Other than a few ducks diving for breakfast and a mockingbird trilling away on a cottonwood branch across the river, the area was deserted.

There was no danger that anyone would overhear their discussion, and she trusted Mac to listen seriously without laughing as she laid out her problem and asked for his help. She couldn't have a better person in whom to place her confidence. Yet no matter how many times she told herself those things, her stomach clenched with nervousness.

MAC LET his gelding, Charlie Brown, pick his way down the embankment as Tess dismounted and led Peppermint Patty over to the river for a drink. This morning was exactly like so many other mornings he and Tess had ridden down here, and yet he couldn't shake off the feeling that this morning was like no other they'd ever spent together.

He watered his horse, then took him over to the sycamore growing beside the river. He looped the reins around the same branch Tess had used to tie Peppermint

Patty and went to sit beside Tess on a shady part of the riverbank.

He picked up a pebble and chucked it into the water. "Did you hear from that teacher at your new school?"

"Yep." Tess plucked a stem of dry grass and began shredding it between her fingers. "I got an e-mail from her and she'll be glad to let me stay with her until I can find an apartment."

Mac glanced at Tess. He'd wondered when she'd suggested the ride if she had something specific on her mind. Maybe this move had her spooked. She'd been renting a little house ever since she got the counselor's job at Copperville High, but living on her own in a small Arizona mining town with her parents three miles away was a lot different than living alone in New York City, two thousand miles from everyone she knew.

"Would this teacher rent you a room in her apartment?" he asked.

Tess shook her head. "She doesn't have the space. I'll be on the couch until I can find an apartment of my own. Besides, I want my own place. After growing up in a houseful of brothers, I've discovered I love the privacy of living alone."

"You just think you're living alone. Your family drops in on you all the time."

"I know." She sighed. "I love them, but I'm looking forward to being less convenient for a change."

Mac could understand that. It was one of the reasons he'd decided to get a private pilot's license. He looked for excuses to fly the Cessna because it was one of the few times he could be alone. "You might get lonesome," he said.

"I probably will." Tess began shredding another blade

of wild grass. "But after living in a fishbowl for twenty-six years, lonesome doesn't sound so bad."

"Yeah." Mac tossed another pebble in the water. "I hear you." He breathed in the familiar mixture of scents—the dankness of the river, the sweetness of the grass, the light, flowery cologne Tess had worn for years, and the wash-line smell of sun on denim. Dammit all, he was going to miss her. He'd avoided facing that unpleasant fact ever since he found out that she'd gotten the job, but now it hit him all of a sudden, and he didn't like it.

Tess had been part of his world for as long as he could remember. So had the rest of her family, giving him the brothers and sister he'd always longed for. But Tess had always been the one he'd felt closest to. Maybe it was all those Halloweens together when she'd insisted he be Raggedy Andy to her Raggedy Ann, Han Solo to her Princess Leia, Superman to her Lois Lane. Or maybe it was the Easter-egg hunts, or the Monopoly games that lasted for days, or tag football—Tess had been there for everything. Every Christmas she dragged him out to go caroling even though he couldn't carry a tune in a bucket.

He'd die before admitting to her how much he'd miss her. In the first place, they'd never been mushy and sentimental with each other, and in the second place, he didn't want to be a spoilsport right when she had this exciting chapter opening in her life. He was happy for her. He was jealous as hell and he'd have a hard time adjusting to her being gone, but that didn't mean he wasn't glad she had this chance.

"I'm glad you got the job," he said.

"Me, too. But I asked you to come here with me because I have this one problem, and I think you can help me."

"Sure. Anything."

"It's a different world there in New York, and I don't feel exactly...ready for it."

Her voice sounded funny as if she was having trouble getting the words out.

"You're ready." He broke off a blade of grass and chewed on the end of it. "You've been working up to this all your life. I've always known you'd go out there and do something special." He turned to her. "It's your ultimate quest, Tess. You might have butterflies, but you'll be great."

"Thanks." She smiled, but she looked preoccupied and very nervous.

He hoped she wasn't about to break their code and get sentimental. Sure, they wouldn't be able to see each other much, but they'd survive it.

She cleared her throat and turned to stare straight ahead at the river, concentrating on the water as if she'd never seen it flow before. God, he hoped she wouldn't start crying. She wasn't a crier, for which he'd always been grateful. He'd only see her cry a couple of times—when Chewbacca died and when that sleaze Bobby Hitchcock dumped her right before the senior prom. Good thing he hadn't had a date that night and had been able to fill in.

They'd had a terrific time, and he'd even considered asking her out again, for real. She'd looked so beautiful in her daffodil-yellow dress that it had made his throat tight, and to his surprise he'd been a little turned on by her when they'd danced. He'd almost kissed her on the dance floor, until he'd come to his senses and realized how that would be received by the Blakely brothers. Then, too, he might gross himself out, kissing a girl who was practically his sister.

She continued to gaze at the river. "Mac, I—"

"Hey, me, too," he said, desperate to stave off whatever sappy thing she might be about to say. If she got started down that road, no telling what sort of blubbering he'd do himself. He chewed more vigorously on the blade of grass.

"Oh, I don't think so," she said in a strained voice. "The thing is, Mac...I'm still a virgin."

In his surprise he spit the blade of grass clear into the river. Then he was taken with a fit of coughing that brought tears to his eyes.

She pounded him on the back, but the feel of her hand on him only made him cough harder. Ever since he'd discovered the wonders of sex, he'd made sure that he and Tess didn't talk about the subject. Life was a lot safer that way, and he wished to hell she hadn't decided to confess her situation to him this morning.

As he sat there wondering if he'd choke to death, she stood up and walked toward the river. Taking off her hat, she scooped water into it and brought it back to him. She held it in front of his nose. "Drink this."

He drank and then he took off his hat and poured the rest of the cool water over his head. As he shook the moisture from his eyes and drew in a deep breath, he felt marginally better.

She remained crouched in front of him, and he finally found the courage to look at her. "So what?" he said hoarsely.

"I'm *twenty-six years old.*"

"So?" His response lacked imagination, but she'd short-circuited his brain. If he'd ever thought about this, which he'd been careful not to, he'd have figured out that she was probably still a virgin. The Blakely boys had fenced her in from the day she'd entered puberty.

"I can't go to the big city like this. I can't counsel girls who've been sexually active since they were twelve if I've never, ever—"

"I get the picture." Much too graphically for his tastes. His mind had leaped ahead to a horrible possibility—that she would ask *him* to take care of her problem. And the horrible part was that he felt an urge stirring in him to grant her request. He pushed away the traitorous thought. "I think you could certainly go to New York without...experience. Chastity's catching on these days. You could be a role model."

"Oh, Mac! I don't want to be a role model for chastity! I didn't choose to be a virgin because of some deeply held belief. You know as well as I do that my brothers are the whole reason I'm in this fix."

Her brothers. God, they would skin him alive if he so much as laid a finger on her. "Well, your brothers aren't going to New York!" He knew the minute he said it that he'd stepped from the frying pan into the fire.

"No, they're not. And that's another point. I'll be clueless about sex and unchaperoned in a city full of sophisticated men. Is that what you want for me, to be swept off my feet by some fast-talking city slicker who'll play me for a fool because I don't know the score?"

This was a trap made in hell. And damned if he wasn't tempted. "Of course not, but—"

"I need a nice man, Mac. Somebody who can take care of this problem for me before I leave."

Oh, God. She was going to ask him. His heart hammered as he wondered if he'd have the strength to refuse her. "Listen, Tess. You don't know what you're saying."

"I know exactly what I'm saying. And you're the only person I trust to help me find that man."

2

"ARE YOU CRAZY?" Mac leaped to his feet so fast he knocked Tess over. The only thing worse than imagining *him* involved in this dirty deed was imagining *some other guy* involved. "Sorry." He reached down and gave her a hand up. Once she was steady on her feet, he released her hand quickly.

She dusted off the seat of her jeans. "Mac, please. I can't stay a virgin forever."

"Why not?" So he was being unreasonable. He couldn't help it. And dammit, now he'd caught himself watching her dust off her fanny and thinking that it was a very nice fanny. *Dammit.*

She sighed and lowered her head. "I was so counting on your help."

"Aw, jeez." Not only was he having inappropriate thoughts about her, he also felt as if he'd abandoned her. But he couldn't imagine how in hell he could diffuse either situation. "Tess, you know I'd do anything in the world for you, but I can't see how this would work."

Her head came up, and hope gleamed in her gray eyes.

He backed a step away from her. "Don't look at me like that."

"Here's how it will work. We'll brainstorm the possibilities and come up with a shortlist. Then you can find out if any of the guys are seeing anyone, because I don't want to break up any—"

"Whoa." Panic gripped him. "I never said I'd do this."

"You said you'd do anything for me."

"Anything but find you a lover!" Just saying it gave him the shivers. He'd worked so hard to keep from thinking of Tess in a sexual way, and now the barriers were coming down. For the first time he acknowledged the sweet stretch of her T-shirt across her breasts and the inviting curve of her hips. "I think that's a little more than a reasonable person should expect, don't you?"

"This is perfectly reasonable! Why should I search around on my own and end up with some clumsy nerdling who makes my first experience a nightmare, when I can rely on your advice and have a really nice time instead?"

There had to be a good answer to that one. He just needed a moment to think of it. And he couldn't think while he was picturing Tess having a "really nice time."

"See?" She gave him the superior little smile that she reserved for the times she'd won either an argument or a game of Monopoly. "You have to admit it makes sense."

"I don't have to admit anything. And why me? Why not one of your girlfriends? I thought women exchanged notes on guys all the time."

"They do, but you're a better source of info." She stuck her hands in her hip pockets. "You've dated more people around here than anyone I know. You'd know what women say about a guy, and you've had a chance to get to know the guys themselves and what they're really like. You'd know if they brag in the locker room, for example. Besides all that, there's not a single person, man or woman, I trust to keep my secret as much as I trust you."

He gulped. When she put it that way, he didn't know how he could refuse. And he wished she wouldn't stand like that, with her hands in her hip pockets and her chest thrust forward. He didn't like it. Okay, he liked it too much.

"Mac." She reached out and put her hand on his arm.

He tried not to flinch. Tess had put her hand on his arm a million times. She'd grabbed him for various reasons, usually to inflict injury, and he'd grabbed her back. He'd held her hand when she was a little kid and they'd gone trick-or-treating, and they'd clutched each other and screamed when they rode the Twister at the state fair. Touching had never been a big deal. Until now.

"Listen, Mac," she said. "You pulled out my first tooth, remember?"

"Different case."

"And you taught me to drive." She grinned. "You also gave me my first drink of whisky."

"You begged me for it, and then you threw up."

"And you held my head. You see, at all those important moments in my life, you were there to guide me."

"This is *way* different."

"Not if you stop being a prude."

"I'm not a—"

"What about Donny?"

"Donny Beauford?" He snorted. "You can't be serious."

"Why? What's wrong with Donny?"

Mac couldn't say exactly, except that when he thought of Donny in an intimate embrace with Tess, his skin began to crawl. He passed a hand over his face and gazed up through the leaves of the sycamore. Finally he glanced at her. "He wouldn't...take care of you."

"Oh." Her cheeks grew pink, but she faced him bravely. "You mean sexually?"

"In any way."

"Oh. Now, see, that's exactly what I need to know. How about Stu?"

"Oh, God, he's worse."

"Buck?"

"Nope."

"I know who. Jerry."

"Definitely not! Jerry's a dweeb. He'd probably—" Mac thought of some raunchy revelations he'd been privy to and decided to censor them. "Never mind. Not Jerry."

"Okay, then you make a suggestion."

He gazed at her as the silence filled with the sound of the river and the shuffling hooves of Peppermint Patty and Charlie Brown. The horses were becoming restless in the growing heat. Moisture trickled down his back, but he didn't think it was only the weather making him sweat. "I can't think of anybody." The truth was, he didn't want to think of anybody.

"Maybe you just need some time. I caught you by surprise."

"You certainly did that."

"Tell you what. Let's postpone the discussion. Maybe we could meet for dinner tonight."

"It's poker night."

"You're right. I can't, either. I'm playing pinochle at Joan's. Okay, then tomorrow night."

He decided a delay was the best he could hope for. He couldn't imagine what would occur to him to get him out of this mess in thirty-six hours, but maybe he'd stumble onto a miracle. "I'll meet you at the Nugget Café." He smiled. "It's meat-loaf night." Meat-loaf night at the Nugget was one of their shared treats.

"So it is. About six?"

"Yeah. Sounds good." He glanced up at the sun. "It's late. We'd better get back. I've got tons to do today."

"Yeah, me, too."

"Like what?"

"Research. I bought some books in Phoenix."

Mac had a feeling he shouldn't ask the question, but he did, anyway. "What sort of books?"

"On sexual techniques. When the time comes, I want to make sure I know as much as possible."

He felt as if somebody had kicked him in the stomach. "*This* is your summer project?"

"As a matter of fact, it is."

Mac groaned. It was even worse than he'd thought. When Tess settled on a summer project, a truckload of dynamite wouldn't dislodge her from her chosen path. If he knew Tess, and he thought he did, she would not be a virgin by the end of the summer. He could help her or not, but she would persevere until she'd checked off everything on her list.

TESS REALIZED how lucky she was that she liked each of the women her brothers had chosen to marry, and they liked her. When the guys got together for poker every Wednesday night, the wives hired baby-sitters and met at one of the other brothers' houses for pinochle. Tess was always invited. She'd miss the friendly, raucous evenings when she went to New York, but some sacrifices had to be made if she planned to live up to her own expectations.

Tonight the women were meeting at Rhino and Joan's. Rhino, originally named Ryan but indelibly stamped with a macho nickname in high school, was Tess's oldest brother and the acknowledged leader of the five siblings.

He'd been the first to get married, buy a house and have kids.

From the moment Tess's niece Sarah had arrived in the world, Tess had decided being an aunt was the coolest thing in the world, although she was a little tired of being a maiden aunt. She arrived at Joan's early so she could see Sarah, who was now eight, and six-year-old Joe before Joan tucked them into bed.

After giving each of the kids the game she'd bought for them in Phoenix and joining in as Joan sang them silly good-night songs, she followed her dark-haired sister-in-law downstairs to the kitchen to help her get out chips and drinks for the party.

"Thanks for bringing them the game," Joan said as she took glasses out of the cupboard. "They're really going to miss you when you go to New York."

"I'm going to miss them." Tess emptied tortilla chips into a bowl and opened the refrigerator to search for the homemade salsa Joan always kept on hand.

"Oh, I don't know. You'll be living such an exciting life, I don't know if you'll miss anything from back here."

"Sure I will. I love this place, and my family and friends."

"Me, too." Joan turned to look at her. "But I'd give anything to be in your shoes."

"Really?" Tess gazed at her sister-in-law. With Joan's Hispanic, family-oriented background and her obvious dedication to her home and children, she seemed to have found her dream. "I thought you were the original Earth Mother."

"Don't get me wrong. I'm very happy. But the challenge has gone. When we first got married, everything was new. Sex was new, and then having kids was new, and then buying this house and fixing it up was new. But now it's all just a comfortable routine. And I want—" she paused to laugh "—more worlds to conquer, I guess."

"I so understand. That's the whole reason I'm going to New York. It's my Mount Everest." She hesitated, then decided to risk a suggestion. "Have you thought of going back to school?"

"I've already got the catalogs. I'm thinking—now don't laugh—of becoming a marriage counselor."

"No kidding! Joan, that would be wonderful. Obviously you know what goes into making a good marriage."

Joan gave her a rueful glance. "I wouldn't call me an expert. But I understand what happens when a couple gets to this point and sort of loses interest in each other."

Tess's jaw dropped. "You mean..."

"I mean things are getting really dull in the bedroom. I've been thinking of driving to Phoenix and getting some how-to books. I wouldn't dare buy anything like that in Copperville or the whole town would think I'd become a nymphomaniac."

"Amen to that. You know, I—" Tess stopped herself before she offered Joan a couple of her research books. She loved and trusted Joan, but she wasn't quite ready to tell her sister-in-law about her summer project. "I think that's a good idea," she said.

"I figured you would. Listen, I'm not saying anything against your brother. He's a great guy. It's just that we could probably both use some pointers."

"Sure. Most people can."

"I mean, you know how it is. You get used to a certain way of doing things, and then it all becomes mechanical."

"Absolutely." Tess felt like an impostor, having this discussion with Joan, who assumed Tess had some experience. If she needed any further proof she was doing the right thing, here it was.

Joan came over and gave her a hug. "Thanks for listening and encouraging me. Even though you're younger than I am, I always think of you as being more sophisticated, for some reason. Maybe it's your college degree."

Tess returned the hug. "Book learning isn't everything."

"No." Joan stepped back and smiled at her. "The ideal thing would be to have both."

"I couldn't agree more." And if Mac would help her, she would have both, at last.

THE POKER GAME was held at Tiny Tim's, the youngest and the largest of the Blakely clan. Tim was a newlywed, proud to show off the new digs he shared with Suzie in an apartment complex near the edge of town.

Mac had spent the entire day worrying the subject of Tess's virginity, and the hell of it was, he could see her point. Her small-town background might make her seem unsophisticated to native New Yorkers. And if the kids she was counseling found out she had no sexual experience, either, that might become a credibility issue. Then there was the other problem—the very good possibility that some city dude, some fast-talking greenhorn, would take her virginity. Mac *really* didn't like thinking about that.

"Hey, Big Mac, are you in or not?" called Rhino from across the poker table.

Mac's head came up with a snap. Then he realized the question had to do with the cards in his hand, not whether he would help Tess find a lover for the summer. She'd sure ruined him for poker night. One of the things he loved about these weekly games was the simplicity of them. But nothing was simple tonight. No question was innocent. Even the name of the game, five card stud, had overtones he'd never noticed before.

He tossed his hand facedown on the table. "I'm out."

"Let's see what you got, Rhino," said Dozer, whose given name was Doug. Nobody called any of the brothers by their real names anymore. Doug and Hamilton, the two middle boys, had become Dozer and Hammer when they'd formed the heart of the offensive line for the Copperville High Miners.

The brothers were Mac's closest buddies, not counting Tess. Their mother and his were best friends, so the kids had naturally grown up spending a lot of time together. In high school the Blakely boys had literally covered his ass when he quarterbacked the Miners. But he saw them with new eyes tonight as he evaluated how each of them might react if they learned about the conversation he'd had with Tess this morning, and the fact that he hadn't turned her down flat.

"Read 'em and weep, Dozer," Rhino said, laying out two queens and three sevens. At the tender age of thirty he was starting to lose his hair, and so he wore baseball caps a lot, even inside. Tonight's was a black one from the Nugget Café.

Rhino didn't miss much, which made him a damn good poker player. He'd likely be the first one to figure out if Mac had lined up some guy to initiate Tess, and he'd probably organize the retaliation against Mac and the poor unfortunate guy Mac had brought into the picture.

"Aw, hell," muttered Dozer, a redhead with a temper to match. He acted first, thought about it later. He'd been known to deck a guy who so much as looked at Tess wrong. "You must be living right."

"Nah," said Tiny Tim, pushing back his chair. "He's ornery as ever. Just lucky. Who needs a beer?" Tim didn't have a mean bone in his huge body, and couldn't even go hunting because of his tender heart. He'd do anything for anybody and never took offense—except when it came to somebody bothering his sister. Then all his tenderness evaporated. Mac had seen it happen.

"Hit me," said Rhino with a tug on his cap. "And don't be bringing out any of that light crap, either."

"Yeah, he wants something to put hair on his head," said Dozer.

"Funny," said Rhino. "Real funny."

"Don't blame me for the light beer," said Tim as he headed for the kitchen. "Suzie bought it. Said I needed to watch my waistline."

"Yeah, Deena's been giving me that old song and dance, too," said Hammer, the third and smallest of the brothers, although at six-three he was no midget. He was Mac's age and they'd been in many of the same classes in school. Logically he should have been Mac's best friend in the family, but Hammer wasn't a thinker, and Mac had always found more to talk about with Tess. Mac had often suspected Hammer was a little jealous of Mac's special relationship with his sister. This new development could really set him off.

Hammer glanced at Mac. "You don't know how good you've got it, with no woman to nag you to death about your diet."

"That's the truth," added Dozer. "It's getting so bad that if I haul out a bag of chips for *Monday Night Football*, Cindy tries to grab them away."

"And you let her?" Rhino asked. "You wouldn't catch that happening in my house. I lay down the law with Joan."

Mac led the chorus of hooting laughter. "Are you kidding?" he said. "Joan's got you wrapped around her little finger!"

Rhino grinned sheepishly.

"In fact," Mac continued, "I've never seen guys crazier about marriage than you four. You could hardly wait to march down that aisle. Don't give me this bull about nagging wives. You love every minute of it." And he envied them, he realized. They'd all found happiness.

Rhino took the beer Tim handed him and popped the tab. "So when are you gonna round out this ugly bunch and make it five for five?" He watched Mac over the rim of the can as he took a drink.

Mac gave his standard answer. "When I find the right woman."

"Hell, you've had a passel of right women." Dozer brushed back a lock of red hair from his forehead. "Jenny was great. I dated Jenny, and there was nothing wrong with her."

"So why did you end up with Cindy?" Mac asked.

"Cindy knows how to handle my temper. But you don't have much of a temper, Mac. Jenny would've been fine for you."

"Yeah, she would," said Hammer. "Cute figure."

"Obviously I should have taken a poll before I broke up with her." Mac picked up his beer.

"And Babs," Rhino said. "I liked Babs, too."

Mac swallowed his beer. "Me, too. Just not enough to last forever."

"Aw, you're too picky, Mac," said Tiny Tim. "That's your problem. Nobody's gonna be perfect." He grinned. "Although Suzie's close." He ducked a shower of peanut shells.

"The newlywed nerd might have a point, though,"

Rhino said. "Maybe you are too damn picky. What kind of standards are you using, if you eliminated two nice girls like Jenny and Babs?"

Mac shelled a peanut and tossed it in his mouth. Then he glanced around the table. "You know, I'm truly touched that you all are so worried about my marriage prospects. Maybe we should hold hands and pray about it. Maybe, if we concentrate real hard, I'll see the light, and grab the next available female I run across."

Rhino's bushy eyebrows lifted and he glanced at Tiny Tim. "Seems to me this apartment complex has a pool."

"Sure does." Tim pushed back his chair, as did the other Blakely brothers.

Mac saw the look in their eyes and pushed back his chair, too. "Now don't get hasty, guys. I was just making a joke."

"So are we," said Hammer. "Right, Dozer?"

"Yeah." Dozer grinned, revealing the tooth he'd chipped in the state championship football game eleven years earlier. "I *love* jokes."

As he was carried unceremoniously out to the pool and thrown in, Mac thought he probably deserved a dunking, but not for the reason the guys were doing it.

3

TESS HADN'T SPENT much of her life in dresses, but tonight's dinner with Mac seemed to require one. She didn't want to wear anything too fussy, not when the late-afternoon temperature had topped out at a hundred and five. She ended up choosing a sundress with daisies on it because she knew Mac liked daisies.

As she stood in front of the mirror wondering if she needed jewelry, she remembered the single teardrop pearl on a gold chain that Mac had given her as a high school graduation present. She'd been touched that he'd bought something so delicate and feminine, considering the rough-and-tumble nature of their friendship. Because she saved the necklace for special occasions, she seldom took it out of the black velvet box it had come in. Tonight seemed like the perfect time to wear it.

Once she was ready, apprehension hit her again. If Mac had willingly fallen in with her plan, she would have been calmer at this point. Her project was nerve-racking enough even if Mac agreed to help. If he continued to drag his heels, she'd need to gather her self-confidence to stay on track.

Her rented bungalow wasn't far from the center of town, so she decided to walk the two blocks to the Nugget and work off some of her anxiety. She slipped on her sunglasses, hooked the strap of her purse over her shoulder and started out. A block into the walk, she knew she'd made a mistake. She'd arrive at the restaurant more cooked than the meat loaf.

Mac pulled into a parking spot in front of the Nugget as she passed the drugstore two doors down from the café. As she walked, she watched him climb out of his white pickup. Although the truck was dusty from a day spent on ranch work, Mac wasn't. He'd obviously changed into a clean shirt and jeans, and he was wearing a dove-gray Stetson she'd never seen on him before.

He looked damn good, with his cowboy-slim legs encased in crisp denim and his broad shoulders emphasized by the cut of his gray plaid western shirt. Every so often in the years they'd known each other, she'd paused to notice that her best friend was a hunk, but she hadn't done that lately. She was noticing it now.

Maybe all her reading was affecting her. She suddenly wondered what sort of lover *Mac* would be. Then she quickly put the thought out of her mind. Mac was like a fifth brother to her. She shouldn't be having such thoughts about him. He'd be horrified if he knew.

As if sensing her eyes on him, he glanced in her direction before going into the Nugget. He paused. "Did your car break down?"

"I decided to walk."

He scratched the back of his head as he stared at her. "But it's June."

"So I discovered. I have to admit I'm a little warm." Up close she could smell his aftershave and noticed there was no stubble on his square jaw. For some reason the fact that he'd showered and shaved for this dinner made her stomach fluttery.

He looked her up and down from behind his sunglasses and then shook his head. "I thought I taught you better than this. Now after that hot walk you'll hit that cold air-conditioning. It's not good for your system."

"Oh, for heaven's sake. You sound like my mother. Could you at least mention that my dress looks nice? I wore it because you like daisies."

"Your dress looks nice. And you're going to catch your death of cold in that restaurant."

It wasn't the reaction she'd expected. As her irritation grew, she realized she'd secretly hoped he'd be dazed and delighted by her appearance, the way guys in movies reacted when a tomboy type like her showed up in a dress. "Let me worry about that."

"Fine. Just don't come crying to me when you catch a summer cold."

"I promise it won't be your responsibility."

"I'm glad to know at least something's not my responsibility." He held the door open for her and the brass bells hanging from the handle jangled.

She stayed where she was. "Look, if that's going to be your attitude, maybe we should just forget the whole thing."

"And then what?"

"In or out, you two!" called Janice, a waitress who'd been working at the Nugget ever since Tess could remember. "We don't aim to air-condition the entire town of Copperville!"

Mac let the door swoosh closed again and turned back to Tess, his expression impassive. "What'll it be?"

She didn't really want to call the whole thing off. She needed Mac to help her, and besides, he'd shown up for dinner all shaved and showered. It would be a shame to waste that effort. "Let's have some meat loaf," she said.

MAC HELD THE DOOR for Tess a second time and tried not to drool as she walked past him trailing her cologne like a billowing scarf. When he'd seen her coming down the street in that flirty, daisy-covered dress he'd almost swallowed his tongue. Then she'd gotten close enough that he could see the moisture gathering in her cleavage, right where the pearl nestled.

He fought the crazy urge to lean down and lick the drop of moisture away before it disappeared into the valley between her breasts. He must be out of his mind. Fantasies like that didn't apply to Tess, the girl who could ride her bike no-hands down Suicide Hill, a girl who could throw a baseball so hard that it stung when it hit his glove. *But the girl is a woman now.* He couldn't ignore the truth any longer. He'd had glimpses of the fact over the years, like the first time he'd seen her in a bikini and she actually filled the thing out. And the prom had been another revelation, but he'd come to his senses before he'd done something stupid like kissing her. Sure they'd kissed when they were little kids, just to see what all the fuss was about, but it hadn't meant anything.

Funny, though, he still had a vivid memory of the spring day down by the river when they'd decided to try kissing. If he concentrated, he could still feel her soft little-girl's mouth that had tasted like pink bubble gum. When he'd pulled back to get her reaction, she'd looked sort of dreamy and sweet. Then she'd grinned at him and blown a big bubble that popped all over her face, destroying the moment.

He followed her through the restaurant to the back booth, the one they always took at the Nugget. Along the way he managed to return greetings from the others in the café, people he'd known all his life. But his attention was claimed by the sway of Tess's hips under the flared skirt covered with daisies. The dress zipped in the back, and he figured she had nothing but panties on under it. The combination added up to what he and his buddies used to call a good makeout dress.

Damn. He had to stop thinking like this. Late this afternoon he'd finally decided maybe he should try to fix her up with someone. He'd come up with a couple of possibilities and had told himself he'd rather have Mitch or Randy be the lucky guy than some sleaze in New York.

Now he didn't want Mitch or Randy anywhere near her.

But if he didn't help her, no telling what harebrained thing she'd do. He'd seen her get a bee in her bonnet enough times to know she wouldn't give up her summer project easily. The year she'd decided to learn how to use in-line skates, she'd sprained her ankle and bloodied both knees, but she hadn't given up. And she had learned.

He slid into the booth across from her and tried to pretend this was like all the other times they'd shared a meal or a milk shake at the Nugget.

"Hungry?" she asked.

"You bet," he lied. He wondered if he'd be able to force anything down. He'd never look at her the same way again, he realized in despair. No matter what happened, the friendship had been changed forever. He'd made the mental leap and begun to think of her as a desirable woman—more desirable than he ever would have imagined. He could hardly believe that all these years he'd managed to screen out her sexuality.

"Have you been thinking about...what we discussed?"

"Some." He blew out a breath. "A lot."

"Any ideas?"

Yeah, and all of them X-rated.

Janice sauntered over to their table, notepad in hand. "Hey, you two."

Tess smiled at her. "Hey, Janice. How's that grand-kid?"

Janice reached in the pocket of her skirt. "Take a look." She tossed a snapshot of a baby down on the table.

"Oh, Janice, she's gorgeous."

"Isn't she?"

"Cute kid," Mac said, although he was more interested in the look on Tess's face than the picture of Janice's grandchild. As Tess gazed at the photo, her expression grew soft and yearning. Only a fool would misinterpret that expression, and Mac wondered if Tess knew how much she wanted a baby of her own. Hell, that was an-other thing he'd never connected with Tess, but she'd make a great mother. Which meant she had to find some-body who'd be a great father. The whole idea depressed him.

Janice scooped the picture up and slipped it back in her pocket. "So, are you guys having meat loaf or something else?"

"Meat loaf for me," Tess said.

"Same here." Mac hoped he'd feel more like eating when their order arrived.

"The usual on the salad dressing?"

"Yep," they both said at once.

"Iced tea?"

"Yep," they said again.

Mac thought about Tess going to New York, where the waiters wouldn't automatically know she liked honey-mustard salad dressing, coffee in the winter and iced tea in the summer. He thought about her eating alone at a restaurant, or worse, eating with some guy. Some guy who would be having the same thoughts Mac was having right now.

"I'll be back with your tea and salads in a jiff." Janice headed back toward the kitchen.

Mac stared at Tess, not sure what to say for the first time in all the years he'd known her. They'd always been able to talk to each other. They'd been able to hang out without talking, too. She was the sort of girl you could take fishing, because she'd sit, her line in the water, and let the peacefulness of the day wash over her. But there was nothing peaceful in the silence between them tonight.

"It was pretty hot today," he said. Then he rolled his eyes. They'd been reduced to talking about the weather. "Forget I said that."

She smiled. "Okay." She leaned forward, which made the pearl shift and dip beneath the neckline of her dress. "Remember the time we put pennies on the train tracks?"

He gazed at the spot where the pearl had disappeared. Then he glanced up again, aware that he shouldn't be looking there. They were in a public place. Anyone could walk in and catch him at it. One of the Blakely boys, for example. "Yeah, I remember."

"I never told anybody."

"Me, neither."

"That was twenty years ago, Mac. You and I have kept that silly secret for twenty years, because we both have the same sense of honor. That's why I'm asking you for help. I know you won't tell."

"I swear, you two look like you're hatching a plot," Janice said as she set down two iced teas, then plopped a salad plate in front of each of them and a basket of rolls in the center of the table. "Aren't you a little old to be painting water towers and such?"

"My folks' anniversary is coming up," Tess said. "Thirty-five years."

"Aha! And you're going to give them a surprise party."

Tess looked secretive. "Could be."

"My lips are zipped," Janice said. "But be sure and invite me."

"I will."

After she left, Mac leaned closer to Tess. The scent of her cologne worked on him, giving him ideas he shouldn't be having, but he didn't want anyone to overhear him. "You see how complicated this can get? Now you're going to have to give your parents a party to cover your tracks!"

She shrugged, and the straps of her dress moved. "No problem. It's a good idea, anyway."

His fingers tingled as he imagined slipping those straps down. Slipping the sundress down. With a soft oath he leaned back against the booth. "I'll bet you're freezing in here, right?" He wasn't freezing, that was for sure.

"Not really." She reached up with both hands and combed her damp hair back from her face with her fingers. The motion lifted her breasts under the cotton of the dress, and there was no doubt that she was braless.

Mac told himself he wasn't getting turned on. Definitely not. "Let me get that old flannel shirt I keep in the truck."

"I don't need your old flannel shirt. I'm fine."

But he needed her to cover up. "I could get it anyway, just in case." He started to leave the booth.

"Mac, I don't want the blasted shirt, okay? I want to

get this project going. So sit down and tell me what you've got."

He stared at her, his mind in turmoil. He should tell her about Mitch and Randy. He really should.

"Meat loaf's here!" Janice announced. "Goodness, you haven't touched your salads. Must be some party you two are cooking up."

"You don't know the half of it," Tess said. She moved her salad plate to one side. "Just set it down there, and I'll eat everything together."

"Me, too," Mac said, following suit.

"Better clean your plates," Janice said. "Or no dessert for you. And Sally made fresh peach pie today."

Mac patted his stomach, which was in no mood for a meal, let alone dessert. "Sounds great. You know I love peach."

Once Janice had disappeared, Tess leaned forward again. "That reminds me," she said in an undertone. "I've been learning the most amazing things from my reading. For example, the use of flavored oils. Did you know they make peach?"

"No." His jeans started growing tight. Mind over matter wasn't working.

"Have you read any books on the subject?"

"No." He stabbed his salad, determined to get through some of this food if it killed him.

"There are some wonderful ideas in there. You might want to take a look."

He lost control of his fork and it clattered to the plate. "I don't think so."

"Oh, for heaven's sake. Men and their egos. I'll bet even you could learn something."

He picked up his fork and returned to his meal with a

vengeance. "Thanks, but I think I'll just blunder along on my own."

"Okay, but this is a perfect opportunity to check the books out without anybody knowing you're doing it. When I leave, I'll be taking those books with me and you'll be SOL."

"I won't be likely to forget you're leaving."

The light of amusement faded in her eyes. "Oh, Mac. I'm sorry. I didn't mean to say it like that. I know you'd love to do the same."

He clamped down on his emotions. There was no point in wanting what you couldn't have. "I wouldn't say that. And somebody has to take over the ranch. I noticed this past winter that my dad's already slowing down."

"Have you ever given them the slightest hint that you don't want to take over?"

"I do want to take over. They've struggled so hard to build that place and keep it going. It would kill them to have to sell it to strangers when they can't work it anymore." He looked into her eyes. "If you were an only child, would you be heading for New York?"

She seemed about to say yes, when she hesitated. Then she sighed. "Probably not. It really helps that my brothers look like they're going to stay in Copperville forever." She sent Mac a look of deep sympathy. "You can come and visit me anytime you want. I'll show you New York in style."

"Thanks. Maybe I'll take you up on that."

"We could have a great time. The top of the Empire State Building, the Statue of Liberty, Central Park, Times Square. Promise me that you'll come to visit me, Mac. It would be so wonderful to have that to look forward to."

"Okay, I promise." His heart wrenched at the thought of how much they probably would enjoy themselves.

And then he'd have to come home again and leave her there. Well, he'd just have to get over it. His life was here, and hers would be there, and that's the way it was meant to be.

"I feel so much better, knowing that you'll come to visit me." Her eyes glowed. "I guess I always pictured seeing some of those things with you. Maybe I'll wait until you get there before I do some of that tourist stuff, so we can both experience it at the same time. I've heard Ellis Island is very moving. And the Metropolitan Museum of Art will be beautiful, and we could save our money and eat at one of those pricey restaurants, at least once, and—"

"I'm not taking you to a pricey restaurant unless you can do better on the food than you're doing here."

She glanced at her plate and picked up her fork. "I guess I'm distracted. I can't seem to think of anything except this move, and getting ready for it." She pushed her food around and glanced up at him. "Mac, I know you think I'm crazy for wanting this one thing before I go."

"Not crazy." He laid down his fork and gave up all pretense of eating. God, she was beautiful. Not cute, not attractive, not passable. Beautiful. He'd never admitted that to himself before, but he'd probably always known it on some unconscious level. He'd been entranced watching her talk about their future adventures in New York.

"Then you understand?"

"Yes."

She sagged against the table, and her sigh was heavy with relief. "Thank goodness. I wondered if I'd ever convince you."

"I'm convinced."

"Then you'll help me? You'll find someone and introduce us?"

Maybe he'd known all along what he had to do. Maybe he'd just needed time for the inescapable truth to settle upon him. But now he could see no other way. It was dangerous, extremely dangerous. A great deal was at stake. Still, it was the only answer, and he was man enough to accept that, along with the consequences.

He took a deep breath. "I don't have to look for someone. I already know who will do it."

"You do?" Her eyes grew bright, her cheeks pink. "Who?"

"Me."

4

TESS GASPED and put her hand over her mouth. She felt as if someone had dumped a bucket of warm water over her. Oh, God. Mac. Could she do it? Her imagination quivered and danced around the idea, unable to focus on the possibility. Her heart beat so loudly she thought he might be able to hear it. Mac. Oh, dear. How delicious. How impossible. How frightening. How lovely.

"Unless you don't want me to."

She was having trouble breathing, let alone talking. "I—I—"

"It's okay if you don't. I might not be...what you want."

"I...have to think."

"Sure."

Although she was caught up in her own turmoil, she sensed his vulnerability. "I'm honored," she choked out.

"*Honored?*"

"That you'd even consider...that you'd even be willing..."

"Better me than anybody else I can think of."

"Is it..." She paused and squeezed her eyes shut. "Such a sacrifice, then?" At his astonished laughter, she opened her eyes.

"Are you kidding?" He stared at her in wonder. "If word got out that you were in the market, the line outside your door would stretch all the way to the Nugget."

"You think?" He'd never, ever given her such an extravagant compliment about her sex appeal. His compliments on that score had been nonexistent, come to think of it.

"You could have your pick," he said. "You don't have to settle for me. I just thought—"

"That I'd feel more comfortable with you. Thank you, Mac. And I probably would. Once I get over the shock."

"Take your time."

"You won't change your mind?"

He shook his head.

"But what about my brothers?"

He let out his breath in a great gust. "I won't pretend that won't be tough. But I've kept our secrets from them before." He gazed at her. "I guess I can do it again."

She'd never been so impressed with another human being in her life. "I don't deserve such a good friend."

He gave her a crooked smile. "Don't go giving me too much credit. This wouldn't be the worst assignment I'd ever drawn in my life."

"So you think you could have...fun?"

"I think I could manage that."

Tess leaned back in the booth and fanned herself with her hand. "Wow. This blows me away." She glanced at him with his fresh shower, shave and clothes. "Did you decide this before you showed up tonight?"

"No. I honestly didn't know what I was going to say to you when I got here. Then, while we were talking, I finally decided this was the only solution I could live with."

She hesitated, feeling unbelievably shy. "The reason I asked is that I wondered, considering that you're all cleaned up, if you thought that we'd just...take care of it."

He coughed and cleared his throat. "Is that what you want?"

She couldn't seem to control her racing pulse, and every breath was a struggle. "I don't know. I realize this is my project, but I'm not feeling very much in charge right now."

He gazed at her. "I have a suggestion."

She swallowed. He was the sexiest man she'd ever seen in her life. How had she missed that in all these years? "Okay."

He leaned forward and beckoned her to do the same. He lowered his voice and his eyes grew smoky blue. "Maybe we need to work up to this. We could take a drive, park somewhere, do some old-fashioned making out and see how it goes. And to take the pressure off, we'd agree not to go all the way this first time."

He was so close that his breath caressed her face. His hands—hands that had positioned her grip on a baseball bat, picked her up when she fell off her bike and pinched her when she'd dropped the frog down his back—had taken on a whole new significance. And they lay less than an inch from hers on the Formica tabletop. As she looked into his eyes, her heart beat so fast she thought she might have a heart attack. This was a Mac she'd never met before. "I g-guess we could do that, but..."

"But? And how were you envisioning the process?"

Her cheeks grew hot. "Honestly?"

"Honestly."

She kept her voice to a low murmur, which increased the sense of intimacy in the booth. "If you'd set me up with someone, I envisioned a one-night stand, to get it over with."

He winced. "That's a terrible idea."

"It is?"

He held her gaze with those electric eyes. "I thought you wanted to have a nice time."

"I do." She drew a shaky breath. "But couldn't I have a nice one-night stand?"

"Not you. Some women, maybe. Not you. You need to ease into it."

"That's why I've been reading all those books. And I'm a quick study."

His eyes twinkled and his mouth twitched as if he wanted to smile, but he didn't.

"What?"

"It's just so you, to thoroughly study a subject before you get into it."

He had her totally off balance, and she wasn't used to feeling that way with Mac. She tried to equalize the situation. "I could probably teach you a few things, Mr. Know-It-All!" she whispered a little louder than she'd meant to. Then she glanced around quickly to see if anyone was listening. Nobody seemed to be paying them any attention, which wasn't surprising. Seeing the two of them huddled over the table in the back booth of the Nugget was commonplace.

Mac leaned back against the worn seat, amusement in his eyes. "No doubt you could." As they continued to gaze at each other in silence, his expression became more guarded. He picked up his spoon and balanced it on his forefinger. "The question is, do you want to? Last time I checked, the ball was still in your court."

"I don't know, Mac. This is very...personal."

"That's a fact." He concentrated on the perfectly balanced spoon.

"You know me so well."

"About as well as anybody."

"Things would never be the same between us."

He laid the spoon down. "They're already different."
He glanced at her. "Am I right?"

Oh, yes. The blue eyes she'd always taken for granted
now had hidden secrets, and she was already wondering
how those eyes would look filled with passion. Passion
for her. The thought made her body tighten and throb in
ways that had nothing to do with friendship. "You're
right," she said.

"Let's get out of here."

Anticipation leaped in her, making her shiver. "What
about your dinner?"

"I wasn't hungry to begin with. But if you want, we
could have Janice box it up."

"Let's not bother. It won't last in this heat."

"Probably not." Mac reached in his back pocket for his
wallet. "We don't need a bill. As long as we've been eating this Thursday-night special, we should know what it
costs."

"Right." Tess opened her purse.

"Put your money away, Tess."

She glanced at him. "But we always split the bill. I
don't want you to think that just because—"

"New game, new rules. You're my date tonight, and
dinner's on me."

The gesture thrilled her more than she was willing to
admit. "Aren't you taking this a little too literally?"

"Nope." He slid out of the booth. "I would expect any
man in my position to have the courtesy to buy you a
meal."

Her feminist conscience pricked her. "What, as some
sort of barter arrangement?"

He took his hat from the hook at the end of the booth
and settled it on his head. "No, as an expression of gratitude."

Her breath caught in her throat at his gallantry. No wonder he'd had women falling at his feet. She'd never quite understood it, but then, he'd never turned the full force of his charm on her.

Janice ambled over toward them. "Leaving so soon?" She glanced at their plates in surprise. "Was something wrong with the meat loaf?"

"No," Tess said. "We—"

"Goodness, you're flushed." Janice put her hand against Tess's cheek. "You're feeling feverish, child. I'll bet you're coming down with the flu."

"I think she might be, too," Mac said. "That's why we decided to leave."

"My Steve came down with the flu last week. You wouldn't think a bug could survive in this heat, but it seems to be going around. Best thing to do is stay in bed."

Tess felt her face heat, and she didn't dare meet Mac's gaze. "Right."

"Look at you!" Janice exclaimed. "You're burning up! Better get on home."

"What's wrong with Tess?" called Sam Donovan from his stool at the counter.

"Flu!" Janice called back.

"Flu?" asked Mabel Bellweather, popping up from the booth where she'd been sitting with her sister Florence. She hurried to Tess's side. "Should I call your mother, honey? She'd want to know if you've come down with the flu."

"I'll call her, Mrs. Bellweather," Mac said.

Mabel patted his arm. "You're a good boy, Jeremiah MacDougal. Anybody'd think you were kin to Tess, the way you've watched out for her over the years. I know she'll be in good hands."

Tess looked at the floor, at the walls covered with Frederic Remington prints, at the golden light of sunset outside the café windows. Anywhere but at Mac.

"Just get along now," Janice said, guiding them toward the door.

Although she wanted to run out the door, Tess made herself walk like a sick person as she preceded Mac through the restaurant. They exited to a chorus of get-well wishes.

Mac helped her into the truck. "Well, at least we're being inconspicuous about this."

"We can't go through with it," Tess wailed. "Soon everybody in town will know that you took me home from the Nugget, and—"

"And what?" He started the truck and switched on the air-conditioning. "You're letting a guilty conscience run away with you. They aren't the least bit suspicious of us being together." He backed out of the parking space and headed down the street toward her house.

"You're sure?"

"I'm sure. You saw the way Mrs. Bellweather patted me and told me I was a good boy."

Tess glanced over at him. "And is that what you intend to be?"

He pulled up at the town's only stoplight and gave her a look that threatened to fry her circuits. "Depends on your definition."

STAY COOL, Mac told himself. He was supposed to be the experienced stud, the one who knew the score. If he gripped the wheel tightly enough, Tess wouldn't know that his hands were shaking. And if she noticed he was sweating, then he'd blame it on the hundred-degree temperature.

The reaction they'd gotten at the Nugget had convinced him of one thing—nobody would suspect that he and Tess had progressed to more than friends for the same reason he'd taken so long to come around to the idea. It was totally out of character for both of them. Even the Blakely brothers wouldn't guess, if he and Tess could keep from tipping them off.

But oh, God, what had he done? His whole world was turning upside down. If Tess agreed, then they would become lovers this summer, assuming he didn't turn out to be like his old dog George, who'd been taught to stay out of the living room when he was a puppy and now couldn't be dragged in there. Mac wasn't sure how deep his hands-off conditioning ran, but he might find out soon.

He'd already discovered he was more possessive about Tess than he'd ever dreamed. If he made love to her this summer, that possessiveness could get out of control. And he couldn't allow that, because she was going to New York, and she'd meet other guys there. And that would lead to...he didn't even want to think about where that would lead. He was setting himself up to go crazy, that's what he was doing.

But he couldn't see any other way around the problem.

"Are you really going to take me to my house?" she asked.

He glanced at her. She still hadn't committed to anything. "Do you want me to?"

"Not really." She was staring straight ahead, holding on to her little straw purse for dear life. Sunglasses hid her eyes, but her cheeks gave her away. They were the deep pink of the sunset lining the horizon. Her chest rose and fell quickly, making the pearl quiver in the valley where it lay against her golden skin.

The air in the cab grew sweet and thick with desire, until Mac felt as if he could lick it like a cone of soft-serve ice cream. "So you want to take that drive?" His voice was slightly hoarse.

"Yes, but I've figured out what we should do. Let's go to my house and sit in the driveway for a little while, in case anybody notices. Then I'll get down on the floor of the cab, and we can drive away to...wherever you had in mind."

Instantly he became aroused. Apparently the old dog would be able to learn new tricks. "All right."

She still didn't look at him. "You know, we might not be able to do anything. We might start laughing or something."

"Laughing's okay. Laughing usually means you're having a good time."

"I mean because we feel ridiculous."

That hadn't occurred to him. "Do you think you will? Feel ridiculous?"

"I don't know. Maybe I should pretend you're someone else."

"Don't do that." The idea incensed him more than it probably should have. "That would be insulting."

"Okay."

He pulled into her driveway and glanced at her. The pretending statement had him going. "Who would you pretend I was?"

"Nobody, because you don't want me to."

"Yeah, but if I didn't care, who would you superimpose over my face? Brad Pitt?"

She turned to him and took off her sunglasses. "I don't know. I hadn't really thought about it. Forget I said anything."

"Tom Cruise?"

"Mac, I won't be doing it, so let's drop the subject."

He couldn't drop it. He had to know who she thought was sexy. "Antonio Banderas? Mel Gibson?"

"All of them!" she said, clearly exasperated. "In a rotating sequence! With Leonardo DiCaprio thrown in for good measure! There, are you happy now?"

He stared at her. Good Lord, he was jealous that she'd imagine a movie star making love to her instead of him. He was in big trouble. "Sorry," he said. "Feel free to imagine anybody you want."

She looked at him as if he'd gone around the bend, which was pretty much true. "Okay."

"Just don't tell me about it."

"If you say so. But if you've never tried it, you might want to reconsider. Some men get very turned on by hearing their partner's fantasies about other men."

"Somehow I don't think I'd fall into that category."

"If you say so," she repeated. She seemed to be relaxing, if her superior little smile was any evidence. It was the kind of smile that told him she didn't think he had the foggiest notion what he was talking about.

Maybe he'd have to take a look at those books of hers, after all. She definitely had him at a disadvantage. Sure, he'd glanced through his share of sexy magazines when he was a teenager, but he'd been concentrating on the pictures, not the text. He'd thought he'd be the teacher and she, the student, the way it had been all their lives. The idea that she might know more about sex than he did wasn't entirely comfortable.

She unsnapped her seat belt. "I guess I'd better get down on the floor of the cab now," she said.

"Wait a minute. It's all dirty down there. You'll mess up your dress." He opened his door and reached around behind the seat where he always kept a soft blanket. He handed it to her. "Put that down first."

"I remember this! We used to make a tent with it in your backyard!"

"Yeah, that's the one."

She arranged it on the floor at her feet. "It's like meeting an old friend, seeing this blanket again, still so soft and blue. The binding's getting a little worn, though. What do you use it for, now?"

"Uh...different things." Suddenly he didn't want to tell her that he'd made love to several girls on that blanket. He kept it washed and tucked behind his seat to have handy if the weather was nice and the woman in his truck was willing. And now, dumb as it seemed, he felt as if he'd betrayed Tess by using the blanket that way.

She gazed at him. "It's all right, Mac. I know you've had a lot of women."

He shifted in his seat. "I wouldn't say I'd had a *lot*."

"Then my brothers must be lying. According to them, you've been to bed with more women than—"

"Does it matter?" He didn't like the direction the conversation was taking.

"I guess not. In a way it's a good thing. You've had lots of experience, so I assume you'll know what to do."

"And what I don't know, you'll be able to teach me."

She looked at him, eyes narrowed. "You don't like that idea much, do you, Mac?"

Damn, but she could read him like a book. She was the only woman who'd ever been able to do that. "Hey, I'm always open to new things."

"I know you. You like to be the one who has all the answers."

"That's not true. I can take suggestions as well as the next man."

"The experts all warn that sex is a sensitive topic, especially for guys. Maybe it would be best if I didn't mention any of the things I've learned. I wouldn't want to give you a complex."

That did it. "A complex! Hell, woman, make all the damn suggestions you want! My ego can take it!"

"See? You're already upset."

"I am not upset!"

She always seemed to know when to stop arguing and just gaze at him quietly, reflecting his behavior back to him.

Finally he gave her a sheepish smile. "Okay, so I'm a little intimidated."

"Wouldn't you like to learn more, if you could?"

"Sure. Only a fool wouldn't."

"Good." She looked extremely pleased with herself. "Then I can contribute something, after all."

That made him grin. "You think your biggest contribution will be from a book?"

That seemed to shake her poise and she blushed bright red. "Well, um, I guess not."

"I guess not, either."

She met his gaze for a fraction longer before she glanced away, obviously rattled. She took a deep breath. "I'm scared to death, Mac."

"Even with me?"

She nodded. "Especially with you. I know you have high standards. What if I disappoint you?"

He reached out and took her hand. It was different from any other time he'd held her hand, and they both knew it. He waited until she turned her head and looked into his eyes. "I wouldn't have offered to do this if I didn't want to, Tess. There's no chance that I'll be disappointed."

The uncertainty eased in her gray eyes. "Thank you."

He squeezed her hand and released it. "We're giving

each other the jitters, sitting here thinking about it. We'll be better off once we get started."

"You're probably right. So here goes." She turned on the seat and started hunching down so she could fit on the floor. "Take a look and make sure nobody's around to see me doing this."

He scanned the tidy little neighborhood. "I don't see anybody. Most people are probably inside having dinner right now."

She tucked herself down onto the blue blanket. "Punch it, cowboy."

And so it began. He took a deep breath and put the truck in Reverse. He'd done some wild things in his life, but this had to be the granddaddy of all risks he'd ever taken. He hoped that this time he hadn't finally bitten off more than he could chew.

5

KNEELING ON THE BLANKET on the floor of the truck, Tess felt more wild and crazy than she had in years. She had developed a taste for reckless adventure after tagging along after her brothers and Mac when she was a kid. Lately she'd been missing that adrenaline rush.

She rested her arms on the seat and pillowed her head on her arms. She had two choices—either she could look at the passenger-side door on her left or Mac's thigh on her right. With her feeling of adventure still running strong, she looked to her right.

His muscled thigh flexed as he stepped down on the gas, making the denim of his jeans move in subtle and tantalizing ways. Just beyond was the ridge of his fly. Her pulse quickened as she contemplated the ramifications of her decision. Of course, if they discovered they had no talent for making out with each other, they could call a halt to the whole program.

Mac clicked on the radio and a soft country tune filled the cab. She'd ridden in Mac's truck with the radio on hundreds of times. They'd sung along with the music, even rolled down the windows and turned up the volume when they were feeling really rowdy and wanted to stir up the neighborhood. She realized now that she'd always felt more alive when she was with Mac.

She certainly felt alive right now. Every nerve ending was checking in and registering the soft blanket under her knees, the tweed fabric of the seat beneath her arms, the waft of the air-conditioning over her bare back. The scent of Mac's aftershave used to be a comforting presence, letting her know her friend was nearby. Now it signaled something else entirely. The man who would soon take her in his arms was sitting very close to her.

"We're going to be on a dirt road in a minute," he said. "I'll try not to jolt you too much. Once we've gone a ways, you can probably sit up again."

"Where are we going?"

"A little road I found a couple of years ago. It goes out to the edge of a plateau where you have a nice view of Anvil Peak. Hold on. Here's comes the turnoff." He touched his booted foot to the brake, causing the denim to ripple again.

Watching Mac drive from this vantage point was quite an erotic experience, Tess decided.

He turned the wheel with one hand and reached over with the other to grip her shoulder as the truck bumped down off the pavement and onto the dirt. His hand was warm and sure as he held her steady. There was nothing seductive in his touch, and yet her heartbeat began to thunder in her ears and her whole body reacted to that point of contact. When he took his hand away, she wanted to have it back. Maybe his embrace wouldn't feel as awkward to her as she'd feared.

"Okay, I think you can sit up now. Nobody ever comes out here."

"Except you. You seem pretty familiar with the place." She crawled up to the seat and straightened her dress.

"I've been here a few times."

"Making out?"

"Now don't start asking me questions like that, Tess. You're going to spoil the mood for sure."

"Making out," she concluded.

He sighed and switched on the headlights.

"Well, I'm not dumb, you know. I understand the reason guys search for lonely roads." She looked around. Sure enough, there were no signs of civilization, just a road stretching to a point in the distance where the scrub-covered ground dropped away. Across the green swath of the river valley, Anvil Peak was silhouetted against a brick-red sky. To the right of that, the smokestack of the Arivaca Copper Mine sent a gentle plume into the air. "This is very pretty."

"I think so."

"So who did you bring out here?"

"Tess!"

"You pestered me about movie stars."

"And I shouldn't have. When two people are together, they should be concentrating on each other."

"Unless they want to explore the fantasy angle."

"Could we forget the fantasy angle? For all you know, being out here with you is my fantasy!"

She caught her breath and stared at him. "Is it?"

"No. Or at least I don't think so. I don't know what made me say that. Forget it."

But of course she couldn't forget it. And she remembered a dream she'd had about five years ago, one she'd put out of her mind as being silly. "Have you ever dreamed about me?"

"Of course I've dreamed about you. We see each other all the time. I dream about all the people in my life. Everybody does that."

"No, I mean, have you ever dreamed of me in a sexual way?"

He hesitated. "Yes. Once."

"So have I. About you."

He kept his attention on the dirt road. "That's probably normal."

"I didn't say it wasn't. What did you dream?"

"I...I can't remember."

"I don't believe you. Are you going to tell me what it was?"

"Nope."

"Do you want to know what I dreamed?" When he didn't answer, she smiled. "I'll take that as a yes. We'd gone out for ice cream at Creamy Cone one summer night, and mine was melting all over the place, and you'd forgotten to get napkins, like you always do."

"Not *always*."

"Most of the time. Anyway, I was a mess, and I didn't want to go home like that, so you decided the only solution was to lick the ice cream off me. We'd magically gotten down to the river by that time, and we were sitting on the sand in our special place. You started cleaning me up, like a cat would, and then...you started kissing me instead of licking, and...then you took my clothes off..." She wondered how much detail to include, but she felt dishonest leaving anything out.

"You kissed my breasts," she continued quickly, "and I said I was surprised you wanted to do that. You said you'd always wanted to, and you kissed them some more, and then you kissed me...all over." She decided to leave some details to his imagination. "Then right at the moment you were finally going to...well, you know...I woke up."

Her heart was pounding by the time she finished, and she had total recall of what she'd felt like in that dream, all warm and melting like the ice cream. She was definitely in the mood for a kiss. For more than a kiss.

Mac stopped the truck and switched off the lights and

the engine. "That's...quite a dream." His voice sounded strained.

"Now you tell me yours."

"Maybe later."

"Was it anything like mine?"

"No."

She sat in the truck as the silence grew more and more intense between them. The air-conditioning was off, but the outside heat hadn't penetrated the cab yet. The warmth she felt was all coming from inside her, and she was ready to do something about it, but she didn't know whether she should make a move or let Mac be the first one. From the corner of her eye, she could see him sitting there, staring into space. He seemed hypnotized. At last she decided to say something. "What next?"

"Give me a minute. Then we'll take the blanket in the back."

She peered at him. "Are you feeling sick or something?"

"No, I'm feeling aroused."

"You *are?*" She glanced down at his jeans but it had become too dark to see much. "Cool. Was it my dream that turned you on?"

"Sure was. But then you probably knew that would happen, after all your reading about fantasies."

"No, I didn't." She felt thrilled with herself. "I wondered if you'd laugh."

He groaned. "I guess you don't know me as well as you think you do, then."

"Then you...really want me right now?"

He looked over at her. "Yeah. I really do. What a surprise, huh?"

"Oh, Mac." She put a hand against her racing heart. "That makes me feel so good."

He gave her a slow smile. "I guess this isn't going to be as difficult as we thought."

She smiled back. "I guess not. Want me to put the blanket in the back and wait for you?"

He took a deep breath. "I'm okay now."

"Are you ever going to tell me your dream?"

He took off his hat and laid it on the dash. "Not right now. It's a little more graphic than yours."

"And you said you didn't remember!"

"I've tried my damnedest to forget all about it. I thought I had, until you started talking about dreams." He opened his door. "Stay there. I'll come around and help you out. I don't want you stepping on a snake in those sandals."

"I've lived here all my life, Mac." She picked up the blanket from the floor. "I certainly know enough to check for snakes before I get out of a vehicle after dark in the middle of nowhere." She opened her door.

"Hey." He turned back to her. "Could you pretend that you're a timid female for a few minutes and give a guy a chance to be a big brave he-man? It's good for the ego."

"Oh." She grinned and pulled her door shut again. "All right, but I think it's stupid."

He shook his head. "Maybe this will be exactly as difficult as we thought."

Tess sat obediently while Mac rounded the truck and opened her door, although waiting for him to take care of things wasn't her style. But if that made him feel more romantic, then she was all for it.

He held out his hand. "I'll take the blanket first and then come back for you."

"I can take the blanket."

"Tess."

"Oh, okay, here's the blanket, Mr. He-man, but this is dumb. We could make it in one trip."

"Yeah, if we're going for efficiency. I was after a different effect." He walked around to the back of the truck, pulled down the tailgate and climbed in.

She listened to him arranging the blanket. A couple of years ago, he'd installed an all-weather cushioned pad in the bed of his truck. At the time she'd wondered if it had anything to do with his love life, but she'd decided not to ask. Now she was pretty sure she knew the answer.

He hopped down from the truck and came back to where she was waiting.

"Can I put my dainty foot on the ground yet?" she asked.

"Not yet." He gazed up at her. "Have you ever been lifted down from a pickup?"

"Not since I was six years old. Once I could manage by myself, it seemed silly when I was perfectly capable of—*whoa!*" She gasped as he took her by the waist and lifted her out of the truck. Instinctively she put her arms on his shoulders, which was a good move because her feet still dangled in midair.

Balancing her against his chest and looking into her eyes, he let her slide down in a slow, sensuous movement. Warmth rushed through her as the friction of his body against hers gave her a complete and thoroughly arousing caress. At last her feet rested on the ground, and she let out her breath.

He held her close and gazed down at her. "Did that seem silly?"

Completely absorbed in the experience of being tucked so intimately against him, she shook her head.

"Think you're ready for a kiss?"

Oh. She gulped. "I...don't know."

"Let's try it." Holding her close with one arm, he reached up with his free hand and gently combed her hair back from her face.

She'd seen this tender side of him, usually when he was working around animals, or the times when she'd hurt herself and he'd been the one to doctor her up. But now she wasn't hurt, and his sensitive touch was meant to excite, not soothe her. He was succeeding admirably. She was trembling so much she wondered if she'd be able to stay upright.

"You're nervous."

"Yes."

"Me, too." He continued to comb her hair back, lightly massaging her scalp with his fingers.

"I can't tell." His touch felt awesome.

"Macho guys learn to hide their nerves. I'm hoping you like this."

"So am I."

He chuckled. "Do you remember the bubble-gum kiss?"

"Yes," she murmured. The more he stroked her hair, the less capable she felt of standing on her own.

"Did you like it?"

She took a shaky breath. "So much it scared me. So I started goofing around."

He began tracing the contours of her face with the tip of his finger, ending with her mouth, which he outlined slowly and with great care. "I still remember how your mouth felt that day."

She held as still as she could, considering the fine quiver that seemed to have taken over her body. She focused on his touch, wanting to record every subtle variation in pressure.

He brushed her lower lip with his thumb. "Your mouth is still as soft as it was then."

She gazed up at him, trying to make out his expression in the shadowy twilight.

He cradled her cheek. "The last time I touched you like this, I was putting an ice pack over your eye, where you got hit by a baseball."

She could barely see his smile in the darkness. "You didn't touch me like this," she murmured.

"Sure I did." He slid his hand along her jaw and leaned closer.

"No. You were rougher." Her heart thudded with anticipation. "You were mad at me."

"I was mad at myself." He tilted her head back ever so slightly. "I was the one who hit that ball."

"And I'm the one who bobbled it."

"Mmm. Your mouth looks sexy when you say *bobbled*."

"You can't even see my mouth."

"Yes, I can. There's a little bit of light left over. That's why I tilted your head back, to catch that light. I wanted to see your mouth, to know I'm going to kiss it soon. Say the word again."

Desire curled and stretched within her. "You're crazy."

"Yeah." He drifted closer. "Say it for me, Tess."

"Bobbled."

"Again."

She felt his warm breath on her mouth. "Bobble—"

His lips touched hers, and in that instant, she knew that the world as she'd known it had ceased to exist. For she was really, truly kissing Mac, and now nothing would ever be the same.

TESS HAD BEEN forbidden fruit for so long that when Mac placed his mouth on hers, he half-expected a lightning bolt to strike him dead. Instead, her velvet lips welcomed him so completely that he drew back, his heart racing. Damn, this was going to be good. Too good. A man could lose himself to a kiss like that. If he'd ever secretly wondered if she was a virgin because she wasn't sensual, he'd been dead wrong. She was on fire.

"Mac?" she whispered. "Is something—"

With a groan he returned to her full mouth, committing himself to the kiss, to what would follow the kiss. To hell with what it might cost him. But he had a sinking feeling it would cost him more than he could ever guess.

For her mouth was a perfect fit for his. He didn't have to think about kissing Tess—it happened as effortlessly as breathing. She opened to him as if they'd been doing this for years, and although his body pounded with excitement, her invitation to pleasure seemed natural, almost expected. And he accepted without hesitation—tasting her richness, probing her heat, shifting the angle so he could deepen his quest.

Joy surged within him as she responded, pressing closer, moaning softly as he made love to her mouth. He thought of all the wasted years when she'd been there, only a touch away. But she was here now, so alive and warm in his arms, so ready.

Very ready. As she molded herself to him, he could feel her nipples, tight and aroused, pressing against his chest. His erection strained against his jeans. If he didn't slow down, he'd violate the terms of tonight's agreement and make love to her out here in the desert. That couldn't happen, first of all because he believed what he'd said about not rushing the process, and second because he had no birth control with him.

With great regret he drew back, breathing hard. The

sun had gone down, and the stars didn't allow him to see her expression very well. He wished he could, but maybe it was for the best. Tonight promised to be intense enough without being able to see desire written all over her face.

"I...liked that," she said. Her breathing was about as ragged as his.

"Yeah." He rubbed her back and took a deep breath as a chorus of crickets started up in the nearby sagebrush. "Me, too."

She wound her arms around his neck and leaned back to look up at him, although she probably couldn't see his expression, either. "You're aroused again. I can tell by your voice."

"Any guy would be aroused if you kissed him like that."

"Was I too...uninhibited?" She sounded genuinely worried.

"God, no. You were great."

"I wondered, because I don't usually get so..." She paused. "Excited."

Man, he loved hearing that. "Really?"

"Especially the first time I kiss someone. You're, um, very good at this kissing business. I guess it's all your practice that gives you such good technique."

"That wasn't technique." He loved running his fingers through her hair. "That was...I don't know. You inspired me, I guess."

"Oh." There was a world of self-satisfaction in that tiny syllable.

He began itching to kiss her again. And he had all the rest of the territory labeled as "making out" to enjoy. Even knowing he wouldn't have the ultimate experience tonight didn't dampen his enthusiasm for the next step. "Ready to climb in the back of the truck?"

"I've been thinking. Are you sure you should?"

He laughed. "I think we dispensed with that a while back. No, I probably shouldn't, but I will anyway, because it's still the best solution."

"No, I mean, with the way you react when we kiss. I'll bet you're not used to just making out with a woman and not finishing the job. You're liable to get awfully frustrated."

He grinned down at her. "So are you. That's the idea—to build up to the main event, so we're really ready for it."

"I can understand that strategy for me, because of my lack of experience, but I'm afraid I'll be torturing you. I know from my reading that some men are able to draw out foreplay for a very long time, but I'm sure they extend that time gradually, so their bodies are used to delayed gratification. You wouldn't be in that category."

He sorted through that little speech until he thought he understood. "Are you saying you're willing to sacrifice yourself for my benefit?"

"I...yes, I am. We don't have to stop with just making out if you find that you're too...uncomfortable."

Oh, God. Heaven was within reach and he'd been caught unprepared. He took a deep breath. "Well, as willing as you are to make the supreme sacrifice for me tonight, it won't be possible. I don't have birth control with me."

She met his declaration with stunned silence. "You don't?"

"Of course not. What, you think I carry a supply around with me at all times, just in case I get lucky?"

"Not even in your wallet?"

"Not since high school. These days I have a much better idea of what will and won't happen with a woman, and I plan accordingly."

She seemed to be digesting that. "What about in the glove compartment of your truck?" she finally asked.

"Are you kidding? My mom's been known to borrow my truck, and she's also been known to get a speeding ticket now and then. I can imagine how much she'd love finding condoms in the glove compartment when she's digging for the registration papers."

She gazed up at him. "You know, I'm glad to find out you don't keep some around at all times."

"You had me pegged as some sort of sex machine, didn't you?"

"Not exactly a machine, but everybody thinks you installed that spongy mat in the back of your truck so you could have fun with your girlfriends."

He let out a sigh of exasperation. "I put that mat in the back of the truck when Mom started refinishing antiques, so she could haul them around without damaging the finish on the furniture."

"Not for making love?"

"No."

"And so you've never—"

"I didn't say that. And this discussion's over." He swung her up in his arms before she traveled down that road any further. Of course he'd made love in the back of the truck, but he didn't want to talk about it now.

"What are you doing?"

"I'm taking charge and carrying you to the back of the truck. It's the manly thing to do." She didn't resist, so he concluded she had faith in his self-control. He was putting a huge amount of faith in it, himself.

"Then I guess you don't want to talk about your love life anymore," she said.

"You've got that right." Specifically he didn't want to talk about or think about any other women he'd been involved with, in the back of his truck or anywhere else. They'd been wrong for him, but he hadn't realized how wrong until a few moments ago...when he'd kissed Tess.

6

TESS SAT CROSS-LEGGED on the blanket and waited for Mac to crawl into the bed of the truck and join her. The night was still very warm, but she felt shivery with delight. Maybe it was partly the blanket, reminding her of the tent she'd shared with Mac as kids. They'd hauled comic books and snacks into their hideaway, and there had been nothing sexual about the cozy intimacy of being stretched out beside him in that tent.

Or maybe there had been, and she had been too innocent to realize it. At any rate, she had a delicious sensation now that reminded her of that intimacy, only magnified a hundred times. They were alone, closed off from the world, and ready, in a sense, to play.

"The sky's so clear," Mac said as he crawled up beside her. "Let's lie on our backs and look at the stars, like we used to."

"And not do anything?" She was hungrier for him than she cared to admit.

He gave her a swift kiss on the mouth. "I'll tell you my dream."

"Oh, all *right*." She pulled the skirt of her dress down underneath her as she settled back on the blanket and looked upward. "Big Dipper, Little Dipper, North Star," she said automatically as she searched them out.

Mac lay down beside her, his arm touching hers, his

thigh against hers. "Orion's Belt, and the Seven Sisters," he added.

"And?"

"And nothing. That's all I ever learned."

"Still? I thought you took an astronomy class."

"I learned things for the test and then forgot it. I only remember what we figured out from that kid's book you had on the constellations."

"Slacker."

"Yeah."

Tess felt as if they could still be seven and nine, lying on their backs in the cool grass of the park on a summer's night. Tess's brothers would be racing around playing tag, and the grown-ups would be sitting in lawn chairs complaining about being stuffed. Meanwhile, Mac and Tess would be off by themselves looking at the stars, probably because they'd been the ones most captivated by *Star Wars* and galaxies far, far away.

She could almost imagine they'd gone back in time... until Mac reached for her hand, lacing his fingers through hers. Memories of childhood faded. They definitely weren't kids anymore, and the emotions coursing through her at the barest touch of his hand weren't the least bit childish.

But the basis of those feelings had been there all along, she thought. What was happening between them now had been simmering within her for years, waiting for a touch, a word, a gesture, to make passion flare to life. He rubbed his thumb along hers, and although it might have been an unconscious movement, she didn't think so. He had to realize that what they'd taken for childhood play had been more sensual than they'd ever admitted to each other, or themselves.

"Tell me your dream," she said.

He was silent for a moment. Then, with a little sigh that sounded like surrender, he began. "You'd been invited to a Halloween party, and you asked to borrow Peppermint Patty because you wanted to go as Lady Godiva."

"*What?* I would never do such a thing." She thought of riding bareback with no clothes on. It didn't sound comfortable, but it was sort of erotic. "Did I have long hair?"

"Down to your hips. You wanted to practice riding with no clothes on to see how it felt before you tried it at the party, so you talked me into riding along the river trail with you. You rode bareback, and you had this loose dress on with nothing on underneath. Halfway along the trail you took off the dress and tossed it into the bushes."

Tess shivered. It *was* a sexy image. "But my hair covered me up, right?"

"Not that well. And you know how the trail winds, so even though I was behind you, I got some side views. You were..." He cleared his throat. "You were beautiful. And riding like that, rocking back and forth on the horse, was turning you on."

"How could you tell?"

"Your skin was flushed, and you were breathing faster, and...your nipples were hard." Mac clutched her hand a little more tightly and cleared his throat again.

"Oh." Which described exactly the way she was feeling right now. When Mac didn't continue with the dream, she prompted him. "Did you wake up then?"

"No."

"What happened?"

"You had an orgasm."

"Oh!"

"Which turned *me* on, and I pulled you off the horse and made love to you right on the ground."

Tess wasn't sure who was holding on tighter, her or

Mac, but they had each other in a death grip. "Was it...nice?"

His voice was hoarse. "It was a dream. You can't put dreams up against the real thing."

Disappointment shot through her. "Then it wasn't nice."

"No, it wasn't nice. It was wild and primitive, no holds barred. I bit your neck and you dug your fingernails into my back. It was...fantastic."

"Wow." She wondered what he'd think if he knew how her body was throbbing this very minute. Being thrown to the ground and ravished sounded perfect. She loosened her grip when she realized she might already be digging her nails into his hand.

He released her hand and turned on his side to face her. "I don't want you to be scared by that description, Tess. I would never be that rough in real life."

She turned on her side, too, pillowing her head on her arm. But her casual posture belied her racing heart. "Too bad."

He sucked in his breath. "You'd *want* that?"

"Would I want you to be so overcome with desire that you'd pull me from my horse and make love to me on the ground? Of course I would. But as you said, it was a dream. In real life—"

"In real life I want you even more than that."

She gasped. "You *do?*"

He lifted a hand to her cheek, and as he caressed her, his hand trembled. "In real life, I want to rip that dress away and take you now, right now. But I won't. It wouldn't be fair to you."

"It would so be fair!"

His laugh sounded strained. "No, it wouldn't."

She'd never heard that edgy tone in his voice, and it

was more exciting than the tenderest of murmurs. She almost wished he would be that reckless, but of course he wouldn't, which was why she was lying here with him now. She trusted him. "But taking it slow doesn't seem fair to *you*," she said.

He slid his hand to the nape of her neck, massaging gently. "Fair doesn't even come into it. I never imagined I'd be lying here with you like this. It's like getting a present I didn't have sense enough to know I wanted." He fingered the clasp of her necklace. "What made you decide to wear this tonight?"

"It seemed right."

"It was," he murmured. His lips found hers and his kiss soon brought her to a fever pitch.

She didn't realize he'd begun unzipping her dress until the material loosened over her breasts and he drew back slightly, gently ending the kiss. She opened her eyes. His face was in shadow, but she could see the rapid rise and fall of his chest as he eased the zipper the rest of the way down.

"Stop me whenever you want," he said in a husky voice.

"I don't want to stop you." Her heart pounded as the thin strap of her dress dropped from her shoulder.

"Just know that you can." He took the strap carefully between his fingers and pulled it down, bringing the bodice of the dress with it, gradually exposing her breast. His breath caught. "Oh, Tess." He eased her to her back and expertly drew the dress down to her waist. Then he groaned and shook his head.

"What are you thinking?"

"That you're even more beautiful than in my dream. And that you've been right there, all along...."

Her mouth moistened with desire. "All covered up."

"Yeah. Damn. All these years."

"Aren't you going to...touch me?"

"I'm still caught up in looking." But at last he traced the aureole of one nipple, causing it to tighten even more. Then he cupped her so tenderly, so carefully, that she felt like precious china. She loved being cherished, but she wanted more. Perhaps she needed to show him. Arching her back, she pressed forward, filling his cupped palm.

"Ah, Tess." Taking a shaky breath, he dipped his head and brought her tight, aching nipple into his mouth.

Yes. She cupped the back of his head and lifted into his caress. Oh, yes. His was the touch she'd been waiting for—the swirl of his tongue, the nip of his teeth, the sweet pressure as he sucked, nursing the flames that licked at the tender spot between her thighs. Shamelessly she offered her other breast, and he lavished the same loving attention there while continuing to give a sweet massage to the damp nipple he'd just left.

As she twisted on the soft blanket, her skirt rode up. Or maybe he pushed it up, in that subtle way he had of making her clothes disappear. He slipped his hand between her thighs, pressing against the damp silk of her panties. The heel of his hand found the spot that ached, and pushed down. She trembled.

He kissed his way back to her mouth, then lifted a fraction away from her lips. "Do you want me to stop?"

"No," she said, panting. "But I don't...I've never..."

He paused, breathing heavily, too. "No man has ever had his hand there?"

"They didn't dare."

He leaned his forehead against hers. "But you must have done this...yourself."

"No, I—read about it."

"Not the same."

"I know but—promise not to laugh—I didn't want to be alone when it happened."

"Oh, sweetheart." He didn't laugh. Instead, he tenderly kissed her forehead, her nose, her cheeks, and finally her lips. "You're not alone now," he whispered between kisses.

And sometime in the midst of those bewitching kisses, he eased his hand beneath the waistband of her panties. When she felt his fingers slip through her damp curls, she gasped.

His hand stilled and he lifted his mouth away from hers. "Is that a no?"

She began to quiver and fought the urge to press her thighs together. His hand resting there felt wonderful, but frightening, too. "Just a...reaction."

"Should I stop?"

"No. But Mac, this is so personal."

"Yes, ma'am." There was a definite smile in his voice. "About as personal as you can get." He eased his hand down and began a slow massage.

Breathing became more difficult as her body responded to that easy stroke. "At least...it's almost completely dark."

"That can help. The first time."

She felt as if he was transforming her into a liquid, flowing state. "What if I make a fool of myself?"

"I hope you do."

"I hope I don't. You'll never let me forget it." She gasped again as one of his very talented fingers sought out the sensitive nub that sent shivers zinging through her.

"No, I probably won't," he murmured as he kept up the maddening, electrifying rhythm.

She felt like a watch being wound too tight, but she

wanted him to keep on winding. "Oh, Mac." She clutched his shoulder as the tension grew.

"Won't be long now." He leaned down and feathered a kiss against her lips. "Let go, Tess."

"I don't know how."

"Your body knows. Get out of your head and live right..." He pressed down a little harder. "Right *there*."

She moaned as the pressure became unbearable and her body arched and quivered beneath him.

He leaned over and whispered in her ear as he deepened the caress. "Remember my dream? You rode naked to the river, becoming so aroused that you climaxed, and then I pulled you down, spread your legs and—"

She cried out as the convulsions swept through her, wave upon wave of glorious release. And all through it, she held on to Mac, the man who had offered to lead her into this land of magic, and then had made a miracle happen. And he held on to her equally as tight, covering her face with kisses and laughing softly in triumph.

MAC HELD Tess and listened with pride to her sighs of satisfaction as she nestled in his arms. He was tense with unfulfilled need, but he could stand the pressure. "So you liked it."

"I adored it." Her voice was lazy and sweet, an after-the-loving voice that didn't sound like the Tess he knew, but like a Tess he'd like to know. "Mac, you used fantasy on me, after all."

"Had to get you past that wall."

"See?" Her voice was whisper-soft. "Fantasy can work."

"You made a believer of me."

She sighed again. "I'm so glad you were the one, Mac."

"Me, too." Even when Tess had announced she was

still a virgin, Mac had never dreamed that she'd never experienced what he'd just given her. Knowing that he'd introduced her to her first orgasm made him feel like a king. Of all the accomplishments in his life, this might be the one he was the most proud of.

On the downside, he was in real agony. Tess had been right that he was used to finishing something that started this way, and his body was demanding that he take care of things. Even without birth control, there were ways to gain mutual satisfaction. But she couldn't be expected to do that for him, considering her lack of experience. He wouldn't even ask.

Then he felt her fingers working at his belt buckle.

"Tess? What are you doing?"

"If you'd move back a little I could do it better." She fumbled her way through the fastenings of his button-fly jeans. It was obvious she'd never undressed a man in her life.

Suddenly he felt protective of her innocence. "Look, you're new at this, so please don't think that I expect you to—"

"Want me to stop?" She paused. "It's just that, in the dark, I feel...braver. And I want to, Mac. I really want to."

She'd nearly released him from the confines of the denim, which left only the cotton of his boxers between him and paradise. Consideration warred with urgent need. "Uh..."

"I'll confess I'm a complete novice when it comes to giving a man pleasure, but I've read extensively." Her words might be scholarly, but her tone was sexy as hell.

The combination of sex and innocence was dynamite. His erection stiffened even more, thinking of her untutored hands on him, practicing.

She rubbed him through the cotton. "Well?"

With a sigh, he kissed her deeply. "Considering it's dark and all, I'd love it," he murmured against her lips.

"Then lift your hips so I can push your clothes away. I'm too much of a beginner to deal with impediments."

His skin flushed with anticipation. He'd never in his life been approached this way, and he found it damn exciting. "Okay." He lifted up and she shoved his boxers and jeans down in one efficient movement.

"Goodness gracious." She sounded intimidated.

Well, at least he wasn't a disappointment to her. He took some satisfaction in that. "Change your mind?"

"No. I'm just...impressed. Lie back and let me get used to the idea."

He did, and realized he was quivering—like a first-timer. When she finally circled his shaft with one warm hand, he squeezed his eyes shut and gritted his teeth. He would not explode this very minute. He would not. Talk about making a fool of yourself. But even the thought of Tess holding on to him like that was enough to make him climax. The reality was so stimulating that he wondered how long he'd survive her attentions.

"Your skin here is so soft."

"Mmm."

"Let me just moisten it."

Before he realized what she was up to, she'd leaned down and started using her tongue. "Tess!"

She lifted her head. "Am I shocking you?"

"Yes! You're not ready for that stage yet."

"I'm not?" She moved her hand up and down his shaft. "Or you're not? Are you okay? Your face is all scrunched up."

"I'm trying to control myself. And when you do unexpected...things, I find it difficult."

"Oh. So you don't want this to be over too quick?"

"Right." He groaned as she settled into a rhythm that was uncannily good for someone who had never engaged in this activity. She must have some good books.

"Do you suffer from premature—"

"No!"

"Because there are techniques for that."

"Tess, I'm fine...usually." He clenched his jaw and fought the urge to erupt as she explored the tip of his penis with fluttering fingers. And he knew in a flash of certainty he was reacting this way because these were Tess's fingers touching him so intimately. "Maybe it's because I've wanted you for so long, without knowing."

"That's a nice thought." She leaned down and flicked her tongue back and forth against the spot she'd been caressing with her fingers.

He worked so hard to hold back his climax that he thought he might pass out. "Where...did you learn that?"

"A book." She blew on the damp spot. "Do you like it?"

He gripped the blanket in both fists and stared blindly up at the night sky. He'd never had an experience to equal this one. "Yeah. I like it."

"Too bad we don't have some ice."

"*Ice?*" He definitely had to get a look at those books. "What—what for?"

"It's supposed to feel fantastic during an orgasm if you put some right here." She pressed against a spot below his family jewels.

He didn't know about ice, but the pressure she was exerting was having a fantastic effect. He moaned softly.

"Having trouble holding back?"

"Yeah, you could say that."

"Then let's try this." She held him snugly at the base of his shaft with one hand, pushing down slightly, and took the tip in her mouth.

The effect was unbelievable. Intense pleasure poured through him from the action of her mouth, but her firm grip on his shaft kept his climax at bay. He moaned. He groaned. He thrashed his head from side to side.

Then she released her grip, took him completely into her mouth, and his control shattered. He tried to pull away from her, sure this wasn't what she meant to do, but she wouldn't let him. His world came apart as he surrendered to the most cataclysmic orgasm of his life. As his spinning universe slowly came back into focus, he drew her up and gathered her close to kiss her passion-flavored lips.

He felt as if he'd been poleaxed. This evening had started out to be an educational session with him as teacher and her as pupil. Somehow, in the past few minutes, she'd completely reversed their roles. And in the process she'd made him her slave.

"We can try the ice another time," she whispered.

"Sure." He held her close, unable to find the energy to do more than breathe.

7

TESS HAD NEVER SEEN Mac so still, not even the time he rode all day without a hat and ended up with sunstroke. He was usually brimming with energy, yet he lay slumped against her like an unconscious person, his eyes closed. On the other hand, the experience of loving Mac had stirred her up again. She'd finally experienced activities she'd only read about, and she felt as if a whole new world had just opened up for her. She was ready for... more. She wasn't sure exactly what form that "more" would take, but she was ready for it.

She peered into his relaxed face. "Mac, I didn't hurt you, did I?"

His mouth curved in a faint smile. "Nope."

She stroked his hair back from his forehead. "You're awfully quiet."

His lips barely moved enough to form the words. "Your books should tell you why."

"It was that good?"

"Yeah, Tess, it was."

"Cool." She smiled to herself in the darkness. "I was wondering if I'd done everything right."

"Extremely right."

"Good." She adjusted her position. "Is it okay if I kiss you again?"

His eyes drifted open. "Where?"

"On your mouth. Where did you think?"

"I wasn't sure. For a virgin, you have some amazing ideas."

She brushed her lips against his. "I'll take that as a compliment."

"It was."

She settled her mouth over his, coaxing his tongue into slow love-play with hers. At first his response was lazy, almost nonchalant, but gradually the tempo of his breathing picked up. As the temperature of his kiss changed from warm to sizzling, he cupped her breast, kneading it with sure fingers. Her body throbbed with new knowledge, and she whimpered and moved closer to his heat.

He drew his mouth back a fraction. "Oh, Tess. I'm getting hard again."

She reached downward. "Let me—"

"No." He captured her hand. "We have to stop. I thought I was so drained that I could just play around for a while more without getting too worked up. I was wrong. I don't trust myself if we get started again."

Her body tightened in anticipation. "You'd ravish me?"

"There's a good chance." He reached for the strap of her dress. "Let's put this back on."

"Mac..." She could hardly believe that she was about to make such a bold suggestion, but she wanted this night to continue forever. "I'm sure you have birth control stashed somewhere at home. You could take me back to my house, go get it, and then come back to my place."

He paused in the act of pulling the bodice of her dress back up over her breasts.

"You see, I want you, too," she murmured.

He trembled and bunched the material in his fist.

"There's still a lot of time before the sun comes up."

He drew a long, shaky breath and continued his task, reaching for the zipper of her dress. "It's probably stupid, but I want to stick with what I promised you. You'll only have the experience of giving up your virginity once in your life. I think...we should make it special."

"We could make it special tonight."

"Not special enough. Give me a chance to woo you a little. Let me bring you flowers, maybe a bottle of good wine."

Despite her frustration, she liked the picture he was painting. "Should I buy lingerie or something?"

"Lingerie would be very nice." He arranged the pearl in the cleft between her breasts. "But wear this. I love watching the way it nestles right there."

"I'll bet when you gave it to me you never imagined a scene like this."

"Not consciously." He ran a finger over the gold chain. "But maybe subconsciously. When I saw the necklace in the jewelry store, I knew immediately I wanted to get it for you for graduation." He looked into her eyes. "Maybe I wanted something that would touch you where I wasn't allowed to."

She smiled. "We seem to have overcome those restrictions without too much trouble. I'd say our makeout session was a success."

"Yeah, but now we have to go back and face the real world with all its guilt trips. And we still have the big hurdle to jump." He gazed at her. "Maybe when it comes to that final moment, I won't be able to do it."

Her smile widened. "Oh, I think you will, judging from tonight."

He grinned back. "You could be right."

"So, when?"

"Tomorrow night? Oh, wait. Damn. I promised to fly

my mom up to an antique show in Flagstaff tomorrow. Dad's going along, and he and I have appointments to look at some horses while we're up there."

She wrestled with her impatience. "How long will you be gone?"

"Three days. Until Sunday. Damn. I don't think there's any way I can get out of it, either. It's been set up for months."

"Three days sounds like an eternity."

"Tell me about it."

She traced the line of his jaw. "We could go back to my original plan and have you come back to my place tonight."

He gazed at her for a long moment and finally shook his head. "No. I really want this time to be one you'll remember."

"I don't think there's much doubt about that, no matter when it happens. And to tell the truth, I'm...afraid you'll change your mind in three days."

"After tonight? Are you kidding?"

"You had a good time tonight?"

He cupped her face in both hands. "I had the best time I've ever had in my life. And I promise you I won't change my mind."

Her heart swelled with an emotion she couldn't name, but it was strong, and it brought happy tears to her eyes. "Thank you, Mac. You're a true friend."

"I do my best."

"What time of day will you be home on Sunday?"

"Probably around noon."

"So you could come over that night."

"I could do that."

Her heart thudded in her chest. "Then I'll expect you about eight."

LEAVING TESS at her door that night was the toughest thing Mac had done in a long time. He hadn't told her, but he wouldn't have had to drive clear back to the ranch for birth control. He'd made it a practice to know where he could buy condoms on short notice, and there was a convenience store still open only five minutes from her house.

He was probably a fool for not taking her up on her suggestion and making love to her all night long. The thought of doing that made him ache. Now he had to wait three days for the chance. No matter that he'd been waiting all his life.

Wait a minute. *Waiting all his life?* Where had that come from? It couldn't be true. Surely Tess didn't have anything to do with his fruitless search for a wife. He just hadn't found the right woman yet. Oh, God. Maybe he had.

On impulse he swung into the Ore Cart Bar's parking lot and climbed out of the truck.

Suddenly a cold beer and a game of darts sounded like an excellent idea. He was still a young carefree bachelor. Bachelors were free to stop in for a beer whenever they wanted to, and he cherished that freedom.

Maybe tonight he sort of wished he could go back over to Tess's house instead of stopping for a beer, but that was only natural, considering how new the situation was. But the novelty would wear off with Tess, the way it had with all the rest.

That's what you think, taunted a voice that sounded a lot like Tess when she was bound to prove herself right and him wrong. Over the years she'd infuriated him, made him laugh until he could barely stand, and worried him sick. But she'd never bored him. Mac walked into the bar, hoping a beer would silence that know-it-all voice that told him he'd started something that he had no idea how to finish.

The bar was fairly well deserted on this weeknight, but it had one patron that made Mac consider ducking back out the door. Unfortunately Dozer Blakely saw him before he got the chance.

"Hey, Big Mac!" he called from his bar stool. "Come on over and let me buy you a cold one."

Mac walked toward the row of stools and glanced around. "Where's Cindy?"

"At home." Dozer shoved a wayward lock of red hair off his forehead with a beefy hand. "Waitin' for me to cool off. Hey, Dutch, set the man up with his favorite brand, okay?"

"Will do," the bald bartender said. "How're you doing, Mac?"

"Can't complain." Mac sat down next to Dozer, but he would have liked to put more space between them. He could still smell Tess's perfume on his clothes, and he was afraid Dozer might recognize it. "Listen, should you be fighting with Cindy, her being P.G. and all?"

Dozer smiled. "When we fight, I'm the only one who gets upset. Cindy's cool as a cucumber." His blue eyes twinkled. "Hot date tonight?"

This would be tricky, Mac decided. "Why do you ask?"

"Oh, you look a little mussed up. I figured you might have been out parking."

"Could be."

Dozer smiled and took a sip of beer. "So, did you take that dunking last night to heart and decide to make up with Jenny?"

"Uh, no." Mac grabbed the beer Dutch scooted in front of him and took a big swallow.

"Babs?"

"Nope."

"Somebody new?"

"You could say that."

"But you're not talking, are you, Big Mac?"

Mac grabbed the opening. "No, Dozer, I'm not. I don't want you guys riding herd on me with this one, pestering me as to when we're going to tie the knot." He glanced at the hefty redhead and decided to go on the offensive. "And speaking of the knot, you're a sorry poster boy for the institution of marriage, sitting down here at the Ore Cart nursing a beer while your wife sits at home."

"I'm only doing what she told me." Dozer shook his head. "She's something else. I fly off the handle, just itching for a fight, and she won't fight. She tells me to go grab a beer and come back when I have something nice to say. In the meantime, she works on her cross-stitch, calm as you please."

"How do you know?"

"Because I usually sneak back and peek in the window to see if she's pacing the floor or banging things around, at least. You know, upset because I left the house. The hell of it is, she's not. So I come down here, drink my beer, and go home. She takes me back like nothing happened, and that's the end of that."

"What was the fight about? Or I should say, the fight she refused to have with you."

"Damned if I can remember." Dozer grinned sheepishly. "Knowing me, it was probably over something dumb. I tell you, I picked the right one when I hooked up with Cindy. Any other woman would have divorced me by now, with my short fuse. But Cindy knows it's just a passing thing, and she sends me off until I get over it. I love that woman something fierce."

"I'm glad for you." Mac picked up his glass again. "Here's to you and Cindy, and your diamond anniversary."

Dozer raised his glass in Mac's direction. "I'll drink to that." He took a long swallow, draining the glass before he set it down.

"Another beer, Dozer?" Dutch called.

"Nope. One's all I need, thanks." He turned to Mac. "Of course, if she ever threw me out for good, I'd drink the place dry."

"Sure."

"I've been meaning to tell you something, Mac."

"What's that?"

Dozer fished for his wallet and pulled out some money. "All kidding aside about Babs and Jenny, I can see why you didn't end up with them. They're both nice and all, and Jenny's built real sweet." He jiggled his cupped hands out in front of his chest. "Real sweet."

Mac didn't want to think about women's breasts, either. "And your point is?"

"You're a smart guy. You need somebody with brains. Babs and Jenny could never have kept up with you. You'd have been bored in a month or two."

"So I figured."

"Well, good. So, is this new girl smart?"

"Yeah, she's smart."

Dozer nodded. "Did you score yet?"

Mac winced. The type of evening he had planned for Tess didn't even begin to fit the definition of "scoring." He tried to imagine Dozer's response if he knew they were talking about his sister.

"Guess not," Dozer said, undisturbed by Mac's reaction. "Otherwise you would've grinned when I asked that." He laid his money on the counter and slapped Mac on the back. "Well, good luck with her, buddy. You deserve to find yourself a real nice lady. Maybe this is the one."

"Maybe." *Not.* As Dozer headed home to Cindy, Mac sipped his beer, determined to think of something else besides Tess lying alone in her bed. He even carried on a conversation with Dutch about the Arizona Cardinals' chances this year. When the beer glass was empty he added another bill to what Dozer had left and walked out into the warm night thinking how great it was to be a free man. He drove home with the windows down, a song on the radio...and Tess on his mind.

THE EVAPORATIVE COOLER had reduced the heat in Tess's little bungalow by the time she walked inside that night, but the place was still plenty warm. She closed the front door and with a sense of deep regret, listened to Mac's truck drive away. If only he still carried condoms in his wallet, then he could have stayed.

To make matters worse, he hadn't even kissed her goodbye. She understood why—nosy neighbors might have seen them and passed the word. She could spend all the time she wanted in Mac's company without arousing any suspicions, but one public minute in his arms would start every tongue in town wagging.

This particular business they had between them had to be kept private. She could still hardly believe he'd offered to take care of her problem himself. He was running a big risk that could potentially ruin his relationship with her brothers. And because she appreciated that so much, she intended to protect him as best she could. So she kept their goodbyes on the porch deliberately nonchalant.

But once she was inside the door and he was truly

gone, she ran her hands over her breasts and closed her eyes, lost in remembering. Then she lifted her arms over her head and turned slowly in a circle, executing a subtle dance of celebration. By touching her and arousing her the way he had, Mac had given her a completely new sense of her body.

In the carefree days before puberty, she'd run and played with Mac and her brothers with no thought to the fact that she was a girl and they were boys. Then the changes had begun, and for the most part, she'd thought of them as a nuisance. As she developed, her body seemed to get in her way more than it helped her enjoy life. But now...now she understood what all those changes had been for. For *this*. Laughing in delight, she flung her arms out and whirled until she grew dizzy.

Feeling slightly drunk with the wonder of it all, she wandered into her bedroom, shedding her clothes as she went. She kicked off her sandals and padded barefoot into the bathroom, where she turned on the shower, adjusting the temperature until it mimicked the warmth of a lover's caress. She craved bodily sensation in a way she could never have admitted to anyone, least of all Mac.

She stepped under the spray, letting it beat down on her. Then she flung back her head and lifted her breasts to the coursing water. Her nipples tightened and she touched them gently, reawakening the memory of Mac's loving.

Then she slid both hands down her water-slicked body to the juncture of her thighs, where she throbbed for him still. Her erotic books had been very clear—she didn't need Mac or any man to give her the kind of release she'd found tonight. She could take charge of her own pleasure.

And maybe someday she'd follow that advice, she

thought, skimming her hands back up over her rib cage to cup her breasts once again. But tonight she wanted to savor the remembered sensation of his hands caressing her, coaxing her to enjoy the wonders of her body. Perhaps she was being silly, but it seemed to her that to work the miracle herself at this moment would dilute that precious memory.

She turned off the shower and toweled dry, paying careful attention to the task. Her body was no longer exclusively her domain, and the thought made her shiver with delight. She smoothed lotion over every inch of skin she could reach, taking her time, anointing herself as if she expected Mac to return.

He probably would not. He was, as she knew from years of experience, a man of his word. Once he'd decided that her initiation should proceed a certain way, he would follow through on that decision, ignoring his own needs, and even her arguments to the contrary. She wouldn't see him again until three days from now, at eight o'clock on the dot.

And perhaps he was right about this, she thought as she rubbed the scented lotion over her body. Perhaps there should be some ceremony and ritual to what they were about to do. She had three days to prepare. Three days to find tempting lingerie and turn her room into a lover's bower. Setting down the lotion, she returned to her bedroom and surveyed the situation. Most of it would have to change.

Grabbing a yellow legal pad and a pen from her desk drawer, she sprawled naked on her bed and began making a list.

8

THE NEXT AFTERNOON as Tess pulled packages from the car after her shopping trip to Phoenix, her neighbor, Hazel Nedbetter, came hurrying over with a florist's vase full of daisies. Tess quickly shoved the Naughty But Nice lingerie box under the front seat.

"I took these into my house so they wouldn't wilt on your front porch," Hazel said.

"Why, thank you, Hazel." Tess took the vase and stared at the cheerful bouquet of white and gold daisies, exactly like the ones on her dress. They could only have come from one person.

"It isn't even from the Copperville Flower Shoppe. The van was from some big florist in Phoenix. Can you imagine? The delivery fee must have been huge!"

"Probably was." At least Mac had taken some precautions, Tess thought. If he'd ordered from the local flower shop, the news would have spread by now. She was thrilled that he'd sent a bouquet, but she didn't know how in hell she'd explain it to Hazel. And Hazel would need an explanation. The more mysterious Tess was, the more Hazel would speculate and the wilder the gossip would become.

The sun beat down on them, and Tess needed to buy some time to think of what she'd say. "It must be three hundred degrees out here. Let's go into the shade," she said, starting toward her front porch. Doggone Mac, anyway. He'd put her in a precarious spot, but his reckless gesture made her smile. She could just hear him—*I wanted to send you flowers. I figured you're a smart girl. You'll think of something to tell the neighbors.*

Setting the vase on the porch rail, she turned to Hazel and used the first explanation she could think of. "I'll bet they're from my new principal in New York."

"Really? How fancy! I don't think Mr. Grimes ever sends flowers to the people he hires at Copperville High. They must do things differently back East." Hazel eyed the small white envelope secured in the arrangement with a plastic holder. Clearly she wanted Tess to take the envelope out and open it to prove that the flowers were indeed from Tess's new principal, as she'd speculated.

The envelope wasn't sealed shut, so Hazel could have looked at the card, but Tess didn't think she had. Still, it was possible, so Tess decided to go for broke.

She could pull this off, although Mac had given her quite a challenge. He knew good and well that the neighbors would notice flowers arriving at her doorstep and he was probably sitting in Flagstaff chuckling as he imagined her predicament. Even if she'd been home, the delivery van would have attracted attention. Most of her neighbors in this older section of Copperville were retired and had plenty of time to observe the activities surrounding them.

Determined to convince Hazel, Tess boldly plucked the envelope from the plastic holder. "Let's just see if I'm right." She opened the envelope, figuring whatever Mac had said, she'd tell Hazel it was indeed from her principal.

As it turned out, Mac had come to her aid. The cryptic card read *Wishing you the best as you explore new worlds—M.* Tess knew exactly what new worlds he was talking about, and they all involved the bed she was about to re-decorate. But Hazel wouldn't realize that.

"Yep, it's from my principal, all right," Tess said. She repeated the greeting for Hazel and on impulse decided she could even nail her story down a little tighter. "My principal's name is Emma Kirkwood, but most people call her Em, or they use the initial *M* for short. See?" She turned the card around for Hazel's inspection. Tess had no idea if anyone called Emma Kirkwood *Em*, let alone abbreviated the nickname to an initial, but the chances of Emma appearing in Copperville were remote.

Hazel adjusted her bifocals and peered at the card. "Sure enough." She glanced at Tess. "That's real nice, sending you a bouquet like that. Although I would have thought maybe roses or carnations would be more likely than daisies."

"M likes daisies."

Hazel nodded. "Been shopping?"

With the change of topic, Tess knew she was home free. The daisies were explained. "Yes. Picked up some things for the trip." And it would be some trip, considering the supplies she'd found today. She thought Mac would be pleased. Maybe more than pleased. She wanted him to salivate, actually.

"When does Lionel plan on putting up a For Rent sign in front of your house?" Hazel asked.

"Not until next month, I think. Don't worry, Hazel. Lionel is very particular who he rents this place to. You'll get good neighbors."

"I suppose, but I'll miss you, anyway."

"I'll miss you, too, Hazel." Tess lifted the hair off the back of her neck. Even the shade of her porch was darned warm, but if she invited Hazel in she might be there for another hour. She was a dear lady, and another time Tess might not have minded visiting with her, but at the moment she was eager to get her purchases inside before someone else showed up and noticed the lingerie box or the satin sheets.

"Your poor mother's going to cry her eyes out when you go."

"I know. I'll probably cry, too. But I have to spread my wings, Hazel. My brothers all got to be football heroes. This is a chance for me to shine."

"Oh, yes, your brothers. They might act like they don't care about such things, but they're going to hate having you so far away. And then there's Mac MacDougal. That boy's going to miss you something terrible. I noticed you two were out last night. I was surprised at that, because Mabel Bellweather told me you were feeling sick when you were at the Nugget for dinner."

Tess began to wonder if she and Mac had any chance of keeping their secret, after all. Copperville was a hotbed of gossip. "I was feeling sick, but after I left the restaurant I started feeling better, so we took a long drive. He, um, wanted to discuss the breeding program he and his father are starting. They're going to look at a few studs during that big horse show in Flagstaff this weekend. You did know they're in Flagstaff?"

Hazel nodded. "I heard. Nora's at one of her antique shows up there."

"Right." Tess decided she needed to prepare Hazel for Mac's next move. "I made Mac promise to come over when he gets home and tell me all about the trip," she said. "So you'll likely see his truck here after they get home."

"Now, see there?" Hazel wagged her finger at Tess. "You two have always been close like that, sharing your news. Who's he going to tell about his goings-on when you're in New York City?"

Tess hadn't wanted to face that, herself. "I guess we'll have to use the phone. Well, Hazel, I'd better let you get to your dinner preparations."

"Guess so." Hazel seemed reluctant to take the hint. "How was Phoenix?"

"Hot," Tess said.

"I'll bet. These nights have been so warm I can barely sleep."

Which means Mac and I had better close the blinds good and tight, Tess thought. "I know what you mean," she said. "Well, see you later, Hazel. And thanks again for preserving my bouquet."

"You're welcome. Enjoy it." Hazel headed back over the path worn in the grass between the two houses.

Tess picked up the flowers and went inside. The phone rang the minute she set the vase on her coffee table. She walked over to the little telephone table next to the sofa and picked up the cordless receiver. "Hello?"

"Where have you been?" Mac asked. "I tried about six times today and kept getting your machine."

The sound of his voice made her nipples tighten. He'd never had that effect on her before, but times had changed. "I was in Phoenix."

"Oh, really? Buying more books?"

"Not this time. This trip was for other things." Her first impulse, because it was the way they'd always interacted, was to tell him everything she'd bought. But the dynamics had changed and secrets were very appealing now.

"Anything to do with...Sunday night?"

"As a matter of fact."

"What did you buy?"

She smiled. "Oh, something very, very brief."

"Really." The timbre of his voice changed. "Care to describe it?"

"I'd rather surprise you. Use your imagination."

"That's been my problem today. I can't seem to use anything but my imagination. I've been so spaced out my dad keeps asking if I overdosed on allergy medicine, even though he knows I don't have allergies."

"So you've been thinking about me." Her body reacted, moistening and throbbing as if he were right there beside her.

"That would be an understatement. I keep thinking about that daisy dress of yours, and…everything that happened last night."

"Me, too." She stroked the petals of her floral arrangement. "But the daisies were *very* hard to explain to Hazel Nedbetter, Mac."

His laugh was low and sexy. "I'll bet you came up with a story, though, didn't you?"

"I told her they were from my new principal, whose name is Emma, but she often goes by just the initial *M*."

He laughed again. "Damn, but you're clever. I wish I'd been there to hear you spin that yarn."

"Me, too."

His voice lowered, became soft and seductive. "I wish I could be there right now."

Tess sighed. "Me, too."

"What are you wearing?"

"A sleeveless blouse and shorts." Scenarios from her reading flashed through her mind, and she had the urge to experiment with her newfound power. "But it's very hot, Mac." She picked up the vase of flowers. "I think I'll just walk back into the bedroom and take my blouse off."

"*Now?*"

"Well, sure, unless you want me to hang up."

His tone was strained. "No, I don't want you to hang up. I might not get another chance to call you today. But Tess—"

"Just unfastening the buttons will help."

In her bedroom she set the vase down and started unbuttoning her blouse. "Ah. I can feel a little breeze from the air conditioner right here, blowing on my bare skin. By the way, did you find any good studs?"

"Uh, yes. No. Maybe. Have you got your blouse off yet?"

"I'm getting there. These buttons aren't the easiest in the world. I tell you, it's so warm here, Mac. This little trickle of sweat just rolled down between my breasts. I'll bet I'd taste really salty right now."

"You're..." He cleared his throat. "You're doing this on purpose."

"What? Taking off my blouse? You bet. Ah, there. That feels so much better." The joke might be on her. By teasing him, she was becoming incredibly aroused herself.

"What...color is your bra?"

"Ivory." Her breathing quickened. "Satin mostly, but the cups are a pretty lace. I like it because it hooks in the front, which makes it easier to take off."

His voice was low and dangerous. "Take it off now."

"You know, I think I will." She unfastened it with trembling fingers and released her aching breasts. "It's...off. Oh, Mac, I wish you were here."

"Believe me, so do I."

"The daisies are so beautiful." She snapped one from its stem. "So soft." Slowly she drew the petals over her rigid nipples. "I'm stroking my breasts with one of your daisies, Mac."

He groaned.

"Little bits of yellow pollen are scattered over my breasts and nipples."

"God, Tess. How am I supposed to stand this?"

"You'll be here soon."

"Not soon enough."

She continued to administer the sweet torture of touching her breasts with the daisy. She pretended it was Mac's gentle fingers stroking her. "And if it helps, I'm aching right now, too."

"I hope so." His breathing rasped in her ear. "You deserve to be absolutely miserable."

"Are you?"

"Denim doesn't give real well, if that's what you mean."

"Too bad I'm not there to help you."

"Yeah, isn't it."

"I'm going to hang up now, Mac."

"I guess you'd better." His voice was tight with strain. "I'm at a public phone at the fairgrounds, and I'll have to stand here with the receiver to my ear and my back to the folks for a long time."

"Goodbye, Mac. Think of me."

"As if I have a choice. Goodbye, you devil woman."

She broke the connection between them and pressed the daisy against her breast. Sunday night seemed an eternity away.

MAC LISTENED to the soft click that ended the call, but he didn't put the receiver down. He hadn't been kidding about the bulge in his pants, and there was no way in hell he could turn around yet. He hadn't planned on the call turning into an erotic experience, not considering the thousands of times he'd talked to Tess on the phone.

Mostly he'd been curious about how she'd handled the delivery of the daisies and if she was pleased with them.

I guess so, MacDougal, if she's rubbing them over that sweet body of hers. But he had to get that image out of his head or he'd never be able to leave this phone. Tess was amazing. When he'd suggested himself as her summer lover, he'd had no idea what a Pandora's box he was opening.

As he stood with the silent phone to his ear, he forced himself to think about something else. The exorbitant price that Stan Henderson wanted for his stallion, for example. And the fact that his father was seriously considering paying it. Finally he was able to hang up the receiver and turn around.

His father was standing not ten feet away, watching him.

"Hey, Dad." He walked over with what he hoped was a nonchalant smile. "I figured you'd be haggling with Henderson over that stud for the rest of the afternoon."

"I decided to take a break and let him think about my last offer." Andy MacDougal was a tall, lean cowboy who didn't look his age any more than Nora MacDougal looked hers. Most people assumed Mac's parents were younger, but they'd suffered through several miscarriages before he'd come along when Nora was almost past childbearing age.

"I'm guessing you've got girl trouble," Andy said. "Am I right?"

Mac grinned. A partial truth was probably his best approach. "You could say that."

"I also have a feeling she might be a serious girlfriend this time around."

Mac didn't like hearing that. "Nah. I'm not ready to settle down."

"Oh, I think you are. I've seen the way you look at the

Blakely boys and their families. I also realize you're choosy, and that's fine. But I've never known you to be this distracted. So if the woman you've been trying to call all day long is ready for a home and family, then I suggest you go for it."

"She's not."

"Oh." Andy gazed at his son for a long moment. "Want to grab a hot dog and a beer and talk about it?"

"A hot dog and a beer sounds great, Dad, but there's really nothing to talk about."

Andy nodded. "If you say so. But the offer stands, anytime."

"I know that, Dad, and I appreciate it." Mac swung an arm over his father's shoulders. "Let's go eat. I'm starved."

THE OVERNIGHT MAIL TRUCK arrived in Tess's driveway the next morning. As she signed for the package, she noticed the Flagstaff postmark. Well, at least he hadn't sent another bouquet of flowers. She'd be hard-pressed to explain a second floral delivery from her new principal.

Once she'd bid the deliverywoman goodbye, she closed the front door and ripped open the package. Inside were a pair of unbelievably soft, furry gloves. She put them on and discovered they were too big for her, but inside one glove she encountered a folded slip of paper. She pulled it out.

Dear Tess,
I saw these in a clearance sale. I could have brought them with me Sunday night, but I decided I'd rather send them so you can spend the next thirty-six hours imagining how you will feel when I put them on and

run my hands over every inch of your naked body.
In the meantime, enjoy the daisies.

                                                              M.

With a cry of frustration she clutched the gloves to her
chest. What an evil man. What a wonderful, delicious tease
of a man. She smiled to herself. Just like when they were
kids, they always had to get each other back. He'd sent the
daisies and she'd tortured him over the phone. Now this.
The score was definitely in his favor at this moment.

She put on one of the gloves and ran it experimentally
over her bare arm. *Oh, Lord.*

"Knock, knock, can I come in?"

Tess leaped to her feet as her mother came through the
unlocked front door, a habit she'd developed that Tess
had seen no reason to change—until now. Heart pounding as if she'd been caught raiding the cookie jar when
she was five, she shoved Mac's note in the pocket of her
shorts and pasted on a welcoming smile. "Hey, Mom!
How's it going?"

"I hadn't heard from you in a few days, so I thought I'd
drop by and find out what you're up to. Darling, you
look guilty as hell. What's going on?"

"Nothing, Mom."

Debbie Blakely raised her eyebrows, obviously not
convinced. She was a small woman, and Tess had taken
after her in height and hair color, although her mother's
warm brown now came from a commercial product instead of nature. She was what Tess always thought people meant when they described someone as "pleasingly
plump." Tess wouldn't have wanted her mother to lose
an ounce, but she sure wished she'd be a little less perceptive.

Debbie glanced at the coffee table littered with the

remnants of the overnight package and then at the gloves, one on Tess's hand and the other clutched against her chest. "What's that, a joke? Gloves in the middle of a heat wave?"

Tess thought fast. "That's what it is, all right. Mac sent them. It's his way of saying, 'Nanny, nanny, boo, boo, I'm in Flagstaff where it's cool and you're not.'"

Debbie Blakely laughed. "That would be Mac. And if I know you, you're planning your revenge even as we speak. Now I may have an idea what you're looking guilty about. Don't smuggle ants into his bed this time, Tess. It took Nora weeks to get them out of the ranch house."

"Right. No ants. Maybe I'll solder his boots to the horse trough, instead."

"Well, I promise not to tell. Want to do lunch?"

"Uh, sure." She'd planned to spend the day transforming her bedroom, but she could probably take time out for lunch.

"Good. I was thinking today that I won't be able to pop over here and invite you to lunch much longer, so I'd better take advantage of your being here while I can."

Tess walked over and gave her mother a hug. "I'll come home whenever I can. And I want you and Dad to visit me in New York whenever you can get away."

"Oh, we will, but...it won't be the same. My, those gloves are soft."

Tess had forgotten she was still wearing one. "Um, yes. I might actually use them in New York."

Debbie examined the glove. "Kind of big, aren't they?"

"Well, yeah, but it's the thought that counts."

"And no doubt Mac's thought was to torture you while he's enjoying the cool mountain air. He probably didn't care if they fit or not. Men."

"Scoundrels, all of them," Tess agreed.

"But we couldn't live without them, could we?"

"Guess not." Or so Tess was discovering. This was turning into the longest three days of her life.

"If you'll excuse me, I'll freshen up in your bathroom before we go," her mother said.

"Sure. Help yourself." Tess sent thanks heavenward that she'd decided to watch a movie last night instead of starting her renovations then. Satin sheets would have been a little difficult to explain to her mother, not to mention the angled mirror she planned to install.

"Oh, so these are the flowers you got from your principal," Debbie called out as she passed through Tess's bedroom into the bathroom. "Why don't you have them out on the coffee table?"

"I was enjoying them before I went to bed last night," Tess called back. Oh, my. Word traveled as fast as always around this place. She and Mac would have to have their wits about them. But they'd had a lot of practice being co-conspirators. Maybe she could think of this secret project as an extension of the pranks they'd pulled together over the years.

She looked down at the gloves. Then again, maybe not.

9

WITH SOME EFFORT Mac managed to smuggle a small
cooler on board the Cessna Sunday morning without his
parents noticing. Inside rested the bouquet of daisies
he'd bought on the sly in Flagstaff and he'd used motel
ice to keep them fresh in the cooler. Ice had never been an
erotic substance to him until Tess had mentioned placing
it against certain parts of his anatomy. Now he couldn't
even look at an ice bucket without getting turned on.

And now, at long last, he was flying his parents back to
Copperville. His rendezvous with Tess was only a few
hours away, yet it was too many hours for his comfort.
He hadn't dared call her again, considering the condition
she'd put him in the one time he'd tried it. But she'd been
on his mind constantly. He wondered what she'd
thought of the gloves, and if she'd run them over her
skin.

Picturing her doing that, his mouth went dry. Maybe
she'd always been a sensuous person, but her reading
had stoked up the fire in her. He wasn't going home to a
timid virgin, that was for sure. But she was still a virgin,
and no matter how she plotted to drive him insane, he
had to remember to go slow and be gentle. That might
not be as easy as he'd thought at first.

When he and his folks arrived home, Mac and his father unloaded the suitcases from the car while his mother
went inside to check for messages on the answering ma-

chine. Mac walked into the kitchen in time to hear Tess's voice coming from the speaker.

This message is for Mac, she said, sounding like the Tess he'd known for twenty-three years, not the new Tess he'd just discovered. *Mac, don't bother to eat dinner before you come over tonight. I'll feed you. Something simple, finger food probably. Oh, and don't worry about ice. I have plenty. I might be out back or something when you get there, so just come look for me. See you tonight.*

Mac nearly dropped the suitcases he was carrying.

His mother turned to him with a smile. "You're seeing Tess tonight?"

"Yeah." Mac tried his best to look nonchalant, which wasn't easy while he was thinking about Tess feeding him some exotic food while dressed in whatever sexy outfit she'd bought. And then there was her subtle reference to ice, and the fact that she wanted him to walk in the unlocked door and come look for her. He'd bet a million dollars where he'd find her, and it wouldn't be "out back."

She'd cleverly created the whole message to sound normal, when it was filled with suggestive ideas that only he would understand. That was so like her. She'd done it to get him back for the gloves, no doubt. He cleared his throat. "I promised to drop by and let her know how the trip went," he added, realizing he was standing there staring into space. Not good.

Nora gazed at him, a speculative light in her blue eyes. "You're upset that she's leaving town, aren't you?"

"Not really. I'm happy for her. It's what she's always wanted."

"I know, and of course we're all happy for her, but you're agitated about it. I could tell by the expression on your face just now. Your color was high. I think you're upset because she's going off and leaving you."

"I absolutely am not." Mac set down the suitcases, walked over and took his mother by the shoulders. "That imagination of yours is working overtime." Then he gave her a quick kiss on the cheek and noticed the tiredness around her eyes. Three days of being constantly on the go had taken its toll on both her and his father. He couldn't ignore the fact that they were both nearly seventy. "I think I'll ride out and check the stock tank Dad's worried about," he said.

"Wasn't he going to do that after we got unpacked?"

"Yeah, but why don't you two take the afternoon off? You both got a lot accomplished on this trip. Relax for the rest of the day."

His mother nodded. "I'll see if I can get him to do that. I think he's more worn out than he admits." She glanced at Mac with gratitude. "Thanks. I don't know what we'd do without you."

"Hey, no problem." Mac smiled at her and headed out the door. On the way, he passed his father coming in. "Try and get Mom to take it easy for the rest of the afternoon, will you? She's bushed."

"I need to check the stock tank."

"I'll do it. No point in both of us heading out there in this heat."

His father laid a hand on his shoulder. "Thanks. If I don't watch your mother, she'll run until she's exhausted."

"My thoughts exactly." Mac crossed the back porch and started toward the corrals with a sense of relief. The solo activity was just what he needed to get him through the next few hours.

HE'D NEVER BEEN so nervous and excited in his life as he drove toward Tess's house a little before eight. The sun was down and the streetlights on, but heat from the day still rose up from the pavement and he had the truck's air conditioner going full blast. Considering his heated condition, he might have to run the air conditioner in the dead of winter if he had a negligee-clad Tess waiting at the end of the line. Which wouldn't happen, because she'd be gone by winter.

The cooler beside him with a bottle of wine inside had been easy to pass by his parents. He'd taken wine over to Tess's house before. But he'd sneaked the daisy chain he'd made into the cooler when no one was around. His mother did seem to be watching him a little more closely, so he'd have to be careful about similar preparations in the future.

The future. A terrible thought came to him. Maybe tonight was all there would be. After all, once he'd taken care of Tess's virginity problem, she wouldn't need to continue this risky business, even though she'd be in Copperville for the rest of the summer. For some reason, he hadn't figured that out. He'd been "hired" for a specific job, and after tonight the job would be over.

Hell, he couldn't think about that or he'd be too depressed to enjoy himself. And he definitely planned to enjoy himself. If her brothers ever found out about any of this, his goose was not only cooked, it was fried, so he might as well make the reward worth the risk. Tonight would be one for the record books.

He parked in her driveway and discovered he was shaking like a newborn colt. The lights in the living room were muted, but he doubted that's where she was. Heart pounding, he got out of the truck with the cooler and walked up the steps to her front porch.

Sure enough, the front door was unlocked. He walked in, his chest tight from the effort to breathe normally, and stepped on a daisy. A trail of them led from the front door down the hall. He turned and locked the door.

Quietly setting the cooler and his hat on the coffee table, he opened the cooler and took out the daisy chain and the wine. First he glanced at the unopened bottle and then at the trail of daisies leading, no doubt, to her bed. If he didn't open the bottle now, it might never be opened.

Sidestepping the daisies, he walked into the kitchen, found the corkscrew and opened the wine. His hands weren't completely steady, but he managed to take two goblets from the cupboard without dropping them. With the daisy chain looped around one arm, the wine in one hand and the glasses in the other, he took a deep breath and started down the hall, following the daisies.

He'd prepared himself for the tempting sight of Tess lounging on her bed with very little on. After all, they'd gone swimming together hundreds of times, so he knew what she looked like in a bathing suit. This wouldn't be all that different, probably.

Wrong.

The scene she'd created left him breathless. His blood hammered through his veins as he gazed at every man's fantasy—a virgin trapped in a bordello.

Red velvet swags and red bulbs in the lamps gave the room a glow of sinful pleasure. His furry gloves lay waiting on a bedside table. On the other, a tray of food that could have been plucked right out of an orgy offered plump red tomatoes, velvet-ripe peaches, chilled asparagus, and clusters of moist grapes.

Whether it was the fruit or some exotic fragrance Tess had added, the room already seemed to smell of sex, and a stereo played soft, yet subtly persuasive music with an underlying beat that mimicked the rhythm of lovemaking. Gilt-framed mirrors propped at various angles all reflected the centerpiece of the room, a bed covered in virginal white satin and mounded with satin pillows of all shapes and sizes.

Reclining on that nest of pillows was a woman Mac barely recognized. Although the scraps of white satin covering her breasts seemed inconsequential, they managed to emphasize her cleavage, where the pearl necklace lay cradled by her soft body. His gaze traveled to the white lace garter belt and panties, which defined her femaleness in ways he'd never imagined. The garters were fastened to white silk stockings with a sheen like pearls and lace tops circling her thighs. Last of all he absorbed the fact that Tess, the woman who believed in no-nonsense running shoes and well-worn boots, was wearing a pair of white sandals with four-inch heels.

Tess gave him a slow smile. "What do you think?"

"I don't—" He swallowed. "I don't believe this is about thinking."

"True." Her gaze traveled to his crotch. "I have the reaction I wanted. Would you like...to get out of those clothes? They seem a bit...tight."

"Um, yeah." He looked down and realized he was still holding the wine bottle, glasses and daisy chain, but his brain was so fuzzy he couldn't decide what to do with them. It was a wonder he hadn't poured the wine on the carpet.

She held out both hands. "I'll hold the bottle. And the daisies. I can pour us some wine if you want while you're taking off your clothes."

He gazed at her holding out her arms to him in that welcoming fashion and had the urge to toss the wine and glasses over his shoulder and join her immediately on that tempting bed. He groaned softly and shook his head to clear it. He'd need every ounce of control at his command in order to make this the slow seduction he'd planned.

"Is anything the matter?" she asked.

"Only that you've blown me away, and I'm struggling to get my bearings."

"I really did that?"

"Yeah, you really did that." He handed her the bottle and glasses. After she set them next to the tray of food, he gave her the daisy chain. "I'm usually a little more suave when I walk into a lady's bedroom with wine and flowers. I usually present them instead of waiting for her to ask."

"Oh." She grinned, and he caught a calming glimpse of the other Tess, the one who loved climbing trees and eating cotton candy. "Thank you for the wine and flowers," she said demurely. Then she put the daisies around her neck. They draped her breasts like a lei, drawing attention to the provocative swell above the tiny garment she wore. "How's that?"

"More exciting than I could have predicted."

She looked into his eyes, her own filled with an intensity to match his. "It is exciting, isn't it? Us, and...all of this. Who would have thought?"

"Not me."

She glanced at the wine. "The books say alcohol dulls sensual pleasure."

"I thought you'd need to relax." He chuckled. "Maybe I need it more than you do. You don't look nervous at all."

"I have a million butterflies inside."

"You do?"

"Of course. I've never acted this way with a man in my life."

He was humbled as he thought what a gift she was giving him. "That makes tonight very special. For me, too."

"I'm glad. You know, maybe a little wine wouldn't hurt."

"I'm so keyed up I can guarantee it won't affect me."

"And I don't want to be inhibited."

He laughed. "This is inhibited?"

"Sort of. The books say that a woman can drive a man crazy if he comes into the bedroom and finds her... touching herself."

He gulped. "Really." From the painful bulge in his jeans, the books must be right. "And some wine might encourage you along those lines?"

"Maybe."

"Then drink up."

Her cheeks grew pink. "Just a little, then." She reached over to the nightstand and poured them each half a glass. Then she picked hers up and leaned back against the pillows. "Now undress for me, Mac. And make it slow."

His jaw slackened. "What do you mean, *slow?*"

"Tease me a little. Build the suspense." She swirled her wine in her goblet and took a sip, watching him over the rim of her glass.

His body quivered in anticipation while his mind balked. "What suspense? You've seen every part of me. And I can say that with conviction after the other night. What difference does it make how I take off my clothes now?"

"Believe me, it makes a difference. And keep your eyes on me the whole time you're doing it."

Suspicion made him frown. "How do you know it makes a difference?"

"A friend of mine in college had a male stripper for her twenty-first birthday party. He was very good."

"I'm not a male stripper!"

"Your body is even nicer than his." She rubbed the wineglass slowly back and forth across her lower lip. Then she circled the rim with her tongue and licked an imaginary drop off the side of the glass. She turned to him with a smile. "I'll make it worth your while, cowboy."

He wanted to laugh and make light of her blatant attempt to remind him of what she'd accomplished the other night. But the laughter stuck in his throat as he gazed helplessly at her mouth and remembered. With that gesture of her pink tongue moving over the wineglass, she probably could have persuaded him to drink arsenic.

He settled for drinking the wine she'd poured. Walking over to the nightstand, he picked up his glass and drained it. He set down the empty glass, took off his watch and laid it next to the glass. Then he emptied the condoms out of his pocket and put those on the table, too.

She glanced at them and back at him. "I have some, you know."

"How did you know what size?"

"I had a good idea."

He remembered her hands on him, her mouth taking him in, and agreed silently that yes, she probably did know.

"So, will you strip for me, Mac?"

He gazed at her. "Swear to me you'll never tell anyone," he said as a last attempt at self-preservation.

"I swear on the tomb of old King Tut, take a willow switch to my butt."

That crazy rhyme they'd made up as kids took on

erotic meaning when spoken by a sexy wench reclining in her red velvet and white satin room of seduction. "Is that a suggestion?"

"Not exactly. I haven't done much research into spanking fantasies." She picked up a remote control and pushed a button. The volume of the music increased a fraction, the beat becoming more insistent. "Now do it, MacDougal. Make me squirm."

TESS TRIED TO LOOK composed as she lay against the pillows and waited for Mac to undress, but inside she was churning with anticipation. He had no idea what a beautiful body he had, and in the past she hadn't allowed herself to admire it much, either. But that was then. This was now.

He'd worn a long-sleeved western shirt even though it was summer. Like most cowboys, he kept mostly long-sleeved shirts in his closet, because they'd protect his arms from whipping branches on a wild cross-country ride. If he got too hot, he'd roll the sleeves back, but Mac had come to her tonight in dress mode, the sleeves snapped at his wrists.

Slowly he unsnapped them, his habitual movements executed with tantalizing care. Her heartbeat quickened. He was really going to do this for her.

She sipped her wine as he started on the top fastener of his shirt. Keeping his gaze on her, he made his way gradually down the row. Each soft pop of a snap was like the flare of a match lighting a new fuse. She hungered for each snap to release, each section of newly exposed skin.

He languidly pulled the shirt from his jeans so it hung open. She waited for him to take it off. Memories flashed by, more potent than she'd realized, of Mac stripping off his T-shirt and using it to mop his face when he'd helped her parents paint their house one summer, of Mac lying bare-chested beside the river one hot afternoon, his fishing pole anchored in the sand, his hat over his eyes.

She'd enjoyed the view then—she wanted it now. Instead, as if to gently torture her, he walked over to a chair and sat down. He drew off one boot with great deliberation, and then the other, all the while keeping his attention on her. His socks followed.

He's undressing because he's going to make love to me. The thought washed over her like a caress, moistening her with need.

He stood and walked toward her. "I've decided two can play this game."

"You have?" Her voice was breathy, not at all the way she normally sounded.

"You did a good job on the phone. If you unhook your bra for me now, I can watch."

She trembled. Darkness had protected her during their first encounter, distance and a telephone line the second. She wanted to be bold and daring this time, to experience the wonders she'd only read about. Mac was asking her to do that.

Following his lead, she drank the rest of her wine and set the empty glass on the table next to his.

"And do it slow," he murmured.

Heart pounding, she leaned back against the pillows and eased her fingers over the clasp holding the silken cups. Then she waited as he took off his shirt and she could finally admire his sculpted torso. With her eyes she traced the scar on his shoulder from a scrape with barbed wire, another on his arm from a run-in with a bull. The scars only made him seem more masculine.

He was magnificent. No wonder she'd loved wrestling

with him when they were teenagers. She wanted to do more than that now.

He stood, hands on hips, and lifted his eyebrows, clearly indicating it was her turn.

She applied pressure to the clasp and it gave way, but she held it closed as she reached up and slid one shoulder strap down. Then she slid the other strap down. Slowly, slowly she allowed the garment to part and fall away, leaving only the pearl necklace and his daisies. The chain of flowers caught on one nipple, causing it to pucker. Instinct prompted her to brush the daisy chain across her other nipple, arousing it, too.

His gaze darkened and he sucked in a breath.

She paused and flicked her glance toward his belt.

His attention never left her breasts as he eased the buckle open and pulled the belt slowly from the loops. "Now touch them," he whispered.

Her heartbeat ratcheted up another notch. Sliding both hands up her rib cage, she cradled the weight of her breasts, lifting them as if in offering. Then she drew her thumbs down over the nipples, caressing herself.

"Oh, Tess." His hands shook as he unfastened his jeans.

The effect of sliding her thumbs over her breasts while he watched was incredible. Sensation poured downward to the juncture of her thighs, pooling and throbbing there, demanding satisfaction. Now she knew what fulfillment felt like, and she wanted it again.

He shoved jeans and boxers away, no longer measuring his movements.

The sight of his aroused body brought a quiet moan from her lips. Her desire had a shape now, as instinct made her aware of a hollowness that ached for what he could provide. More than release, she wanted to be filled.

He came to the edge of the bed. "You said you'd feed me."

"Yes." Her breathing was quick and shallow. "Whatever you want."

"That's good to hear." His voice was husky as he put a knee on the satin sheets. "I see what I want." He gently moved her hand aside and replaced it with his own.

At the remembered touch, her heart thundered in her chest. "Is there...anything I can do?"

"Arch your back," he murmured.

She did, lifting her breasts.

He used his teeth to lift the daisies away. When he drew her nipple into his mouth, she gasped with the realization that she was nearly at the point of climax. He'd had to coax her before, but no longer. Apparently this time she'd need only the fantasy they created in this room to become a wild woman. She hoped Mac was ready for that.

10

FOR THREE DAYS Mac had been dreaming about Tess's body. To taste and caress her breasts, to kiss and nibble and suck to his heart's content, was heaven. As the tempo of her breathing quickened, he lightened his touch, not wanting to bring her to the brink too fast. They had hours to enjoy each other. And besides, he knew where he wanted to be when she climaxed this time.

"You're so beautiful," he murmured.

"You, too." She ran her hands over his chest, brushing his nipples until they became as taut as the rest of him. She reached lower.

"Not yet." He drew back, knowing he couldn't tolerate her hands on him there until he was more in control. He teased the daisy chain over her skin, tinged rose by the lamps, and caused her to flush even pinker. Pollen scattered over her breasts and he licked it off. Then he took the pearl in his teeth.

Still fondling her breasts, he eased up and transferred the pearl to her mouth. As it lay against her tongue, he toyed with it with his own tongue in a blatantly suggestive way. He wondered if she knew that he was telling her, if she understood what he had in mind. If not, she would find out very soon. He was hungry for her.

With one last flick of his tongue over the pearl, he lifted it from her mouth and eased downward, depositing it, moist and shining, in the valley between her breasts. "Do you know what I want now?" he whispered against her skin.

"I...think I do."

"Are you ready for that?"

Her breathing grew ragged. "If you are."

"I crave you. All of you."

Her breath caught. "But I...might go crazy."

"That was my plan." Heart racing, he began his journey, kissing his way along her downy soft skin to her navel. The scent of her cologne mixed with the perfume of crushed flowers and the heady aroma of arousal as he dipped his tongue into the small depression. She moaned and twitched beneath him.

He moved lower. The silk of her stockings and the ridiculously high heels excited him more than he wanted to admit, and he decided not to disturb any of it yet. The damp scrap of lace covering the object of his quest was easily drawn aside. Ah, she was so pretty. So drenched with need.

He touched her gently with one finger and she gasped. He kept his caress subtle as he planted lingering kisses along her inner thigh and ran his tongue over the lacy top of her stocking. Desire surged through him as he lavished the same attention on her other thigh, moving ever higher, ever closer to his goal.

At last he kissed her dark curls, and she moaned. When he finally touched his tongue to the delicate pearl nestled there waiting for him, she writhed beneath him. Suddenly impatient with the thin strip of lace denying him total access, he held it between his fingers and tore it with his teeth. Now.

Easing his shoulders under her silk-clad thighs, he sought his reward. The taste of her made him groan with delight. As her cries of pleasure filled the room, he immersed himself in sensory overload, relishing the stockings, the shoes, the rosy light, the satin sheets, the erotic music, and most of all, the passionate woman coming apart in his arms.

Her climax came quickly, too quickly for him. She lifted her hips and he took all that she offered, but as she sank back, quivering and gasping, he settled in for a more leisurely exploration. She tried to wiggle from his grasp but she was weak in the aftermath of her release. He held her easily and continued along his chosen path. Before long her slight resistance faded and she opened to him in a wanton gesture that nearly brought him to the boiling point.

And he learned her—the touch that made her whimper, the stroke that pushed her closer, the teasing flick that drove her wild. As he coaxed her toward the precipice a second time, a fierce possessiveness took over. Rational thought played no part as he boldly claimed her, drawing from her the most intimate of sounds as she gave herself up to wave upon wave of shattering convulsions.

He brought her gently back to earth with feathery touches and light kisses over her thighs and dew-sprinkled curls. At last he drew slowly up beside her and brushed the hair back from her flushed face.

She gazed up at him, her gray eyes filled with dazed wonder. Her lips parted, but no sound came out.

He smiled. She looked the way he'd felt the other night. He was gratified that he'd created that sort of expression in her eyes. He trailed a finger down the curve of her throat and over her breastbone until he encountered the pearl on its golden chain. He brought it up slowly to his lips and kissed it before settling it back between her breasts.

Her gaze grew smoky and she ran her tongue over her lips.

He was glad to see a return of desire in those gray depths, for he was far from finished. And he loved knowing that the pearl necklace had become a symbol for the intimate activity they'd just shared. If he had it his way she'd wear it forever, and each time it moved against her skin she'd relive the sensations his tongue had given her.

"How do you feel?" he asked.

Her voice was low and throaty. "Like a concubine. How do you feel?"

"Like the luckiest man on earth."

She sighed. "That was way better than they described it in the books, and the books made it sound very nice."

He brushed his finger against her lower lip. "But you're still a virgin."

Her smile was pure seduction. "Feel free to take care of that anytime, cowboy. In case you can't tell, I'm putty in your hands."

His erection throbbed. She made the next step sound almost casual, and he tried to keep the same tone in his voice. "How about now?"

"Now's fine," she said lazily. She ran a fingertip down his shaft. "Unless you'd rather have me—"

"Not this time." He heard the edge in his voice. Damn, he was strung tight as a roped calf, and he figured there was only one way he'd be able to unwind. But in the process he didn't want her to absorb his agitation and tighten up herself. The whole point behind the way he'd just loved her was to ease her into this moment. Well, part of the point. In truth he hadn't been able to help himself. She was luscious.

"Do you want me to put the music on again?" she asked.

He became aware that the music had ended. He'd been so absorbed in her that he hadn't noticed. He thought about the music, considering. "Let's not," he said, combing his fingers through her hair. "I think this is a moment when we should listen only to each other, to anything we might say, to how we breathe...and the cries we make."

Her eyes darkened. "Okay."

He reached across her and took a packet from the bedside table.

"I could put that on for you. I've practiced."

"Practiced?" Jealousy hit him, swift and unyielding. "On who?"

"Mr. Cucumber."

He started laughing. "Only you, Tess."

"You think it's funny?" She grabbed the packet from him.

"Yes, I think it's hilarious." He give her a swift kiss and made a grab for the packet, but she held it out of reach. "Give it here." He kissed her again. This was sort of fun. Then he started chuckling all over again as he thought about her sitting in her kitchen studiously rolling a condom down a cucumber, over and over, until she got it right.

"I want to show you how good I am!" she protested, ripping the packet open.

"No." He made another grab but she evaded him. "Come on, Tess. I'm too worked up. If you fumble around you could set me off."

"I won't fumble."

"You will." He tackled her in earnest, laughing and kissing her everywhere he could reach as he tried to get the condom away from her. In the process he pulled off both her shoes so she wouldn't injure anything important.

"I'm good at this. Let me do it, Mac." She used the satin sheets to her advantage, wiggling away from him.

The wrestling match was putting him in even greater danger of exploding, but between sliding around on the sheets and coming into constant contact with Tess's bare skin, he was having a great, if risky, time of it. He'd always loved wrestling with Tess. "If you don't hold still and give me that condom, I'm going to tie you to the bedposts," he warned with a grin as he paused to catch his breath.

"I don't care." She was breathing as hard as he was. "The books say that's fun. Ever done it?"

"No." He looked down at her, his pulse racing at the vivid picture of her lying spread-eagle on the white bed, silken ties holding her wrists and ankles. He could barely breathe. "I was kidding," he said hoarsely.

"I wasn't. That seems like the perfect time for you to use the furry gloves."

He gazed into her eyes and saw the fire there. "You'd let me do that?"

Her chest heaved with her rapid breathing, making her breasts quiver. "I would let you do that, Mac, because I trust you. And you would let me do the same with you. It would be exciting."

"Oh, Tess." He began to tremble as a new picture formed—Tess tying him down and then...trying out all that she'd learned in her books.

"Lie down. Let me put the condom on."

"All right." She was messing with his head, making him want to surrender his role of leader again and let her tempt him into all sorts of new and fascinating sensuality. He lay back against the pillows. "But don't...play around."

"Don't worry. I understand your problem."

"I don't have a problem! Any guy in this situation would be struggling to keep it together."

"So you've had a good time so far?"

"You don't even have to ask. I—" He nearly choked as she leaned over him and took his erection into her mouth. "Tess!"

She lifted her head and smiled at him. "Lubrication." Then she expertly rolled the condom on in less time than he'd ever managed it and lifted her hands like a cowboy in a calf-roping event. "Done."

Despite her speed, the contact made him gasp and grit his teeth.

"Wasn't that pretty good?" she asked.

"Sure was."

"Want me to be on top? I've seen pictures of how—"

"No." He grabbed her and rolled, pinning her to the mattress. Then he reached for the garters and unfastened them. "And it's time to get rid of these."

She gazed up at him, her breath shallow and her lips parted in anticipation. "If you say so, macho man."

"Sometimes a guy has to take charge." He rolled each stocking down and pulled it off. Then he worked her out of the garter belt and what was left of the panties.

Her cheeks flushed as she lay there under his gaze. "Now do you approve? Am I ready?"

He was so overcome by the picture she made wearing only the daisy chain and the pearl necklace that he could barely speak. He lifted his gaze to hers and swallowed. "You're perfect," he said in a tight voice. He swallowed again. "And I should probably let you be on top and in control, since you've never done this, but I...don't want to."

Her question was breathy, seductive. "Why not?"

"Because I think I'd feel...secondary."

"Sort of...used?"

"Exactly."

"I wouldn't want that."

"Thank you." He stroked her breast, loving the softness beneath his palm as he cradled the supple weight and brought the nipple to a firm peak. "I'll be careful."

"I know you will." She closed her eyes and arched into his caress. "Oh, Mac, I could get addicted to having you touch me like that."

He paused, unsure how to respond. "We have all summer," he said at last.

Her eyes opened slowly, and excitement glowed in their gray depths. "Do we dare risk it? Making love like this all summer?"

He would risk just about anything to spend the summer loving Tess, but he didn't want to pressure her into anything she might regret. "That's up to you. It's your project. You said all you needed was deflowering."

"That was when I thought...it would be someone else. Mmm. That's good, Mac."

He rolled her other nipple gently between his thumb and forefinger. "The more we make love, the greater the chance someone will find out."

"Mmm. Yeah." She closed her eyes again and ran her tongue over her lips. "We should think about that."

"So think about it." He leaned down and drew one pert nipple into his mouth.

She sighed and lifted upward, encouraging him to take more. "Oh, sure. While you're driving me insane."

He tried his best to do exactly that, hollowing his cheeks as he drew her more fully into his mouth, letting her experience his hunger for several long seconds before he kissed his way to her other breast. "You don't have to decide now," he murmured against her skin as he slid a hand down to the damp triangle between her legs.

"That's...good." She drew in a quick breath as he tunneled his fingers through her curls and reconnected with her flash point. "And so is that."

Caressing her now took on a different meaning, because now, at last, he would know the wonder of being inside her. His blood sang in his veins as he stroked her, preparing her for that sweet invasion. And he would be the first. God help him, he was filled with joy at that thought.

TESS SENSED the change in Mac's touch, as if the promise of completion gave new urgency to every caress. And though she'd tried to seem casual about what was about to happen, in reality she felt like a canoe being carried down the rapids toward a thundering waterfall. If anyone but Mac had been touching her, arousing her, she would have leaped from the bed, unsure if she truly wanted this change in status, after all.

But Mac was there, making her ache, making her long for the firm thrust of him, deep inside her. Perhaps there would be pain. She no longer cared if only he'd finally claim her, complete her in ways she'd never dreamed of until this moment.

He lifted his head, a question in his eyes as he slipped his finger deep inside.

It was the penetration she longed for, but not nearly enough. A sudden shyness overtook her, causing her to close her eyes before she asked for what she wanted. "More," she whispered.

He eased two fingers in, placing soft kisses on her mouth. "Tell me how that feels."

"Different." Her breath caught as he moved his fingers

gently back and forth. "Wonderful," she said, letting out a trembling sigh. "Mac, I'm going wild inside. Deflower me. Please."

His kiss was soft and lingering, but still she felt the barely leashed power of him as he moved between her thighs and propped his arms on either side of her head. Quivering with excitement, she wrapped both arms around his back and felt his muscles flex. She couldn't tell for sure because of her own trembling, but she thought he was shaking, too. His breathing was affected, at any rate, as he probed her gently with the blunt tip of his erection. She braced herself. No matter how much she might want him there, he would be substantial and might take some getting used to.

"Tess." There was a smile in his voice. "Open your eyes."

She gazed up at him, astonished by the tenderness in his blue gaze. She'd thought a man in his position would be in the grip of passion and appear much more fierce. "What?"

"You look just the way you used to before the roller coaster started. I'm going to go easy. You don't have to clench your jaw like that. And keep your eyes open. If you're looking at me, I'll be able to tell how I'm doing."

"How can you be so...calm?"

"Believe me, I'm not calm," he said quietly. "But I am paying attention."

"Oh, Mac. Thank you for being here."

"I'm here." He eased slowly forward and his eyes darkened. "Right here."

She noticed the flicker of uncontrolled desire in his eyes before she became totally absorbed by the sensation when he entered her. She registered warmth and size. He withdrew and eased in again, and she moaned in pleasure at the friction that was unlike anything he'd provided before.

"Tess?"

"That was a happy moan," she murmured, looking into his eyes. There was that flicker of primitive need again. She found it thrilling.

His breathing was labored, but he kept his movements slow. "I'm going a little deeper."

"Yes." Everything else, she began to realize, no matter how delicious, was only a lead-in to this, the ultimate connection. Nothing in her world had ever felt so right as opening her body to this man and being filled by him.

He slid forward, and met resistance. He stopped immediately and looked into her eyes. "This is it."

Her heart thudded wildly. One movement and her life would be forever changed. She would be a virgin no longer. Ah, but then she could welcome the whole length of him and know the wonder of joining intimately with another person. And not just any person, either. Mac. One movement and she could be fully with him, in every sense.

She slipped her hands down to his buttocks and gripped firmly. "Let's go for it."

As he pushed gently forward, she rose to meet him, determined to share in the moment. The sharp pain brought a cry to her lips.

"Damn." He stopped, his gaze troubled.

"It's okay." She trembled against him. "It's going away. Don't hold back. It's over now. Love me. Love me the way a man loves a woman."

With a groan he pushed deep, locking their bodies together, his hips cradled between hers. And the fierceness she'd expected to see earlier flared in the depths of his eyes as he gazed down at her.

As she met that gaze, she felt an answering intensity rise within her. She'd expected them both to be naked tonight, but she hadn't guessed he'd also strip her to the essence of her soul, and she him. She looked into his eyes and realized they were both seeing depths they'd never imagined before. And her world shifted, for she knew the connection they were making would not end with this night, or even with this summer. It would last forever.

11

PERFECT, Mac thought. He'd never been anywhere in the world that had felt so absolutely right as being here, as close as he'd ever been to Tess. It seemed as if their entire lives had been leading to this moment. Linked in spirit ever since they were children, they had finally created the ultimate link, and a sense of destiny washed over him.

Mindful of her tender condition, he moved carefully, but still he moved, needing to define and redefine that sword-to-sheath perfection they made together. "Okay?" he murmured.

"Very...okay." Her eyes shone.

He eased back and edged forward again. Yes. And again. *Oh, Tess.*

"Mac...Mac..."

The wonder in her eyes and the richness she poured into his name told him all he needed to know. She was with him. He cupped a hand beneath her bottom, steadying her as he transmitted a new, more urgent rhythm. She caught on quickly, rising to meet his thrusts. Her bottom was soft and yielding, sweet to hold, sweeter yet to knead gently with his fingers. Yet the flex of her muscles against his hand when she truly began to participate drove him wild.

Very wild. Soon. He changed the angle, brushing the tips of her breasts with his body, pressing against the sensitive nub between her thighs that would bring her with him.

Her breathing grew shallow and he knew he'd found the spot, if only he could last long enough. This first time, he wanted to give her the gift of knowing how good it could be, how much higher she could climb when he was deep within her, coaxing a response that would vibrate down to her toes.

Her eyes widened and her breathing quickened. He played to that response, urging her on. So good. He'd never dreamed making love could be like this. Her body rose to meet his thrusts, tightening around him. As the moment built in the depths of her eyes, exultant laughter bubbled from him.

"Yes," he cried.

"Oh, Mac!" She arched against him. "I'm—"

"Yes." His voice was hoarse with need. "You're a woman now." *My woman.* With one final thrust he brought heaven raining down upon them.

TESS SAT propped up against the pillows next to Mac, the tray balanced on another pillow across their laps while they sampled the snacks she'd prepared for the evening. Mac was eating with gusto, but Tess felt too happy and pleased with herself to be interested in food.

She looked at Mac for about the hundredth time, a grin on her face. "We did pretty good, huh?"

He lowered the peach he'd been about to bite into and gazed at her. A slow smile eased across his face, and he nodded. "Yep. You look damn pleased with yourself, too."

"I am." She picked up a cluster of red grapes and plucked one off its stem with her teeth. "I'm proud of us. I think we were awesome. Better than I ever expected."

After swallowing his bite of peach, he gestured around the room. "I don't know. Looking at all this, I'd say you expected a lot."

"The books say a man is a visual animal, so I was trying to make sure you'd be properly aroused."

He laughed so hard he almost choked on his peach. "Overkill," he gasped. "Major overkill."

She lifted her chin. "I don't know how you can say that, considering how well everything worked out. Maybe if I'd left the bedroom the way it was, and worn an old T-shirt and boxers, you wouldn't have been able to get an erection."

He stared at her. "Tess, I had an erection driving over here just knowing what we planned to do tonight."

"Yeah?" She smiled. "So the phone thing worked?"

"I *knew* you did that on purpose!"

"Of course. Just like you sent the gloves on purpose."

"And you put that double-meaning message on the answering machine. I stood there listening to it with my mom watching me the whole time, if you don't think that was tough!"

"Well, I didn't want you to lose interest!"

"Fat chance of that, twinkle-toes."

"Seriously, Mac. According to what I've read, women are a lot better at sustaining lustful feelings in the absence of the lover than most guys. Guys are more the out-of-sight, out-of-mind type. I didn't want you to lose interest."

"For your information, there was no chance I'd lose interest. I didn't need that phone conversation or the message on the answering machine and your cute little reference to ice in order to get excited."

"Oh! I didn't remember the ice! I was planning to give

you a special treat with that ice trick. But I was so carried away that I...forgot."

He gave her a long glance. "I'll take that as a compliment."

Her heart beat a little faster, remembering the glory of the moment when she'd felt completely united with him, as if their souls had fused. She'd lost all track of techniques and tricks in the wonder of loving Mac. "It is a compliment. I couldn't think of anything but what was happening between us." She held his gaze and heat invaded her secret places once again. "I guess we didn't need the ice."

"No. We didn't need anything but each other."

Even now, she could barely believe that he really and truly wanted her. "This is so new. Then you're really turned on by me, the girl you've known forever?"

"Uh-huh."

"Wow."

"In fact, I'm getting in the mood again."

And so was she, but she'd been hesitant to admit it. "I thought it took a while for men to recharge."

"It does. It's been a while."

"Not that long. From what the experts say, a man would probably need some stimulation before he could manage another episode."

Mac chuckled. "That reading may get you into trouble yet. Take my word for it, I could manage another episode. Maybe several. I wish I could stay here and make love to you all night, but I don't know how we'd ever explain my truck being parked outside your house all that time."

Tess glanced at the clock and sighed with regret. "You're right. The neighbors would wonder and the gossip mill would start running."

He nodded. "I could park outside somebody else's house all night with no problem, but not yours. And we sure don't want to awaken anybody's suspicions." He moved the pillow and the tray of food and swung his legs over the end of the bed.

Tess couldn't resist glancing at the part of his anatomy that had recently delivered her from her virgin status. "You *are* ready again!"

"Surprise, surprise." He reached for his clothes.

"Want a quickie?" Her blood raced at the thought.

He turned back to her, a smile on his face. "And what do you know about quickies?"

"Everything. You just forget about the foreplay and go for it." Her nipples tightened in reaction. "It makes for variety. What do you think?"

He paused, his boxers in one hand. "Sounds tempting. But I guess I need the answer to my question first."

"What question?"

He faced her. "Well, you're not a virgin anymore."

"No, I'm not."

"So your project's technically finished, right?"

Her stomach clenched with sudden anxiety. "You mean we could stop right here and never...make love again?"

"That's what I mean. I need to know if this is the end of the fun and games or not."

"What do you want to do?"

He gave her a wry grin and gestured toward his groin. "I think that's obvious."

"I'm talking about the long-term risk." But as she spoke, she wondered if she fully understood the long-term risk. She'd been concerned about their families and people in town finding out. Maybe that wasn't the biggest problem. After tonight she felt bonded to Mac in a way she'd never experienced before, and yet she'd have to break that bond at the end of the summer. The more they made love to each other, the stronger the bond would become.

"I'm willing to accept the long-term risk," Mac said quietly.

A world of meaning lived in that statement, she thought. "And we'll still be...friends?" She wondered if that was the most foolish risk of all. If they made love all summer, could they possibly continue to be just friends?

His reply was soft and deliberate. "We'll always be friends."

He looked magnificent standing there, she thought. No woman in her right mind would turn down the chance to spend the summer loving Mac, no matter what the consequences. "I wouldn't want to lose your friendship," she said.

"You won't."

"Promise?"

He smiled. "I swear on the tomb of old King Tut, take a willow switch to my butt."

She took a deep breath. "Then I guess..." She paused and blushed. "I guess I'd like to expand my summer project and get more...experience."

His smile faded, and he gazed at her with that unfamiliar fire in his eyes. "Okay. Then that's what we'll do." He started to put on his clothes.

"Wait. I thought we were going to have—"

"A quickie?" He pulled on his jeans and winced as he started buttoning his fly.

"Well, yes."

He reached for his shirt. "If tonight had been the end of the road, we would have. In fact, I might have turned it into something a little longer than that." He gazed at her as he buttoned his shirt. "But if we have all summer, then I don't want to settle for a quickie."

She wanted him so much she trembled, but she swallowed the words that would have begged him to stay. Still, she couldn't let him go without knowing when they'd make love again. Her hunger for his touch both startled her and warned her of the dangers ahead. "When are you...free again?" she asked. No matter how hard she tried, the neediness in her voice seeped through.

He crossed to the bed and sat down. Leaning toward her, his shirt half fastened, he cupped her face in one hand. "Are you going to get all prissy and try to pretend you don't want me so much you can't see straight?"

Of course he could read her like a book. She should have realized that. "I—"

"Because that's how much I want you. I'm practically blinded by how much I need you, how much I want to be inside you again. I don't want to leave tonight, but we both know I have to, and the sooner I go, the easier it'll be for both of us." His thumb brushed her lower lip. "I want to see you again tomorrow night, and the night after that, and the night after that. Hell, I want to spend all summer here in your bedroom."

"You do?"

"I can't think of anything sweeter. But we have to watch it or we'll make people suspicious. We need to wait a while before we get together again."

She moaned in frustration.

"That's better. At least you're being honest about what you want."

She gazed into his eyes, helpless in the grip of passion. "I didn't realize making love would be so...so good."

"It isn't always."

"I figured that, from the cautionary tone of the books.

The first time is supposed to be pretty awkward because the couple isn't used to each other."

He caressed her cheek. "That's where we have the advantage. We already know how the other one thinks."

"Maybe not completely. You see, I was afraid that familiarity would make me boring for you."

"Oh?" His eyebrows raised. "Why? Am I boring for you?"

"No, but I've never done this before. You have."

"But not with you."

"So having sex with me is not boring?"

He smiled. "Not by a long shot."

"Good." She smiled back. "Then how about we do it again Tuesday night?"

He shook his head. "Too soon. And Wednesday's poker night. That should be quite a test, come to think of it."

"Mac, you're torturing me."

"No more than I'm torturing myself. Listen, Thursday night's a full moon. Let's take a ride to the river."

Her pulse rate skyrocketed. "Am I supposed to wear a dress with nothing on underneath?"

He grinned. "Good memory."

"As if I could ever forget that dream of yours!"

"Well, I won't ask you to do that. You'd be uncomfortable, and your hair's too short for that particular fantasy, anyway."

"I could wear a wig."

His smile widened as he combed his fingers through her hair. "I like your hair the way it is. But you might wear as little as possible without making a big deal of it. And don't worry about being thrown to the ground. I'll bring a blanket. And a couple of towels."

"Towels?"

"Ever gone skinny-dipping?"

"Of course not. My brothers would have had a fit if they thought I was swimming nude in the river." She gazed at him. "Have you?"

"A time or two."

"With a girl?"

"Maybe."

She was insanely jealous, but she didn't want him to know. She glanced away. "It's naive of me to think you wouldn't have. Did you take them...down to our hide-away?"

He guided her chin around until she had to look at him again. "Do you honestly think I would take someone else to our spot? To go skinny-dipping and...other stuff?"

She hoped he wouldn't, but she'd never asked him not to. "It's a good spot."

"It's *our* spot. I wouldn't feel right taking someone else there. I'm insulted that you could even think such a thing."

"Oh, Mac." She couldn't help the happy smile she gave him. "I would have so hated you taking someone else there, even if you didn't go skinny-dipping or have sex with her."

"I know. That's why I'd never do that. But I want to make love to you there, on the sand. And maybe even in the water."

Her body moistened, imagining exactly that. "I don't know if I can wait until Thursday night."

"Me, neither. But we don't want to ruin everything. In the meantime..." He leaned closer and kissed her, his tongue taking firm possession of her mouth.

She grew hot and dizzy from the suggestive movement of his lips and tongue and the memory of all the pleasure

he'd given her. By the time he drew back, she was struggling for breath.

"Come to the corral about seven-thirty Thursday
night," he murmured.

"I will." She tried to pull him back for another kiss, but
he left the bed.

His voice was hoarse. "I really have to go, or we'll be
tumbling around on that bed all night and we'll both be
in trouble." He finished dressing. "I'll see you Thursday
night."

It seemed like an eternity, but she knew he was right.
People were used to them doing things together, but not
constantly. "Okay. Thursday night it is."

He started out of the room and turned back. "I suppose
you'll have to change the room, in case anybody shows
up."

"I probably should. But I could put it back again sometime if you'd like."

"Oh, I'd like. We have some unfinished business in this
room—something to do with silk ties and furry gloves."

She was going wild inside. "Mac, if you drove your
truck down to the bar, and walked back, maybe we
could—"

"No." He gripped the door frame as if to keep himself
from walking back into the room. "Leaving is best. I
don't want anybody reporting my truck was at the bar all
night, either. And there's always the chance I'd be seen
leaving your house in the early-morning hours." He
glanced at her. "If we really want this secret to keep all
summer, then we have to be careful not to blow our
cover."

She sighed. "I guess you're right."

"Aren't I always?" He gave her a cocky grin.

"No, you are not, you arrogant man!" She laughed and threw a pillow at him.

He caught it in one hand. "Your aim's off, Blakely. You must be out of practice. When was the last time you threw a baseball?"

"I don't know. Want to practice Thursday night instead?"

"Not on your life."

"Then get out of here. I have more reading to do."

The comment had the desired effect, making the flame leap again in his eyes. "You really know how to get to a guy."

"I promise to tell you all about what I've read when we get together Thursday night."

"Want to bring a flashlight and a book along? We could glance over it together."

"Sure, why not? Sort of like reading comics together in the tent after dark."

He laughed. "Not even close. Oh, and by the way, congratulations on your new status."

"Thank you. I think I'm going to like it."

"I know I am. This is by far the best summer-project idea you've ever had." With a wink, he walked down the hall.

Tess listened until she heard the front door close. Then she got up and threw on a robe before walking down the hall. Maybe he'd change his mind and come back in, needing to hold her again as much as she needed to hold him.

Unfortunately he really seemed to be leaving. After he slammed the truck door shut, the engine roared to life and the headlights flicked on. She automatically walked over and flashed the front-porch light, their goodbye signal. He flashed the headlights of his truck in return. Then he backed the truck down the driveway.

She could hardly stand to have him go. He'd taken her from innocence to knowledge, and now she craved him with an intensity bordering on obsession. Maybe she would have felt this way about any man who had introduced her to the wonders of physical love, but she doubted it.

For one thing, not any man would have known her well enough to make this such a mind-bending experience for her. Not any man would have had the tenderness and caring Mac had demonstrated every step of the way. And she couldn't imagine any other man looking so beautiful in the act of love.

As she stood in the living room listening to the fading sound of his truck's engine, she discovered the fatal flaw of her great plan. If she couldn't bear to have him leave after one night of lovemaking, what condition would she be in when the summer came to an end?

12

TESS WAS LOOKING for any distraction to get her through until Thursday night. When Hammer's wife, Deena, called Tuesday morning to suggest a day at the community pool with whichever Blakely women and kids could make it, Tess jumped at the chance.

Deena, a freckle-faced brunette who had been one of Tess's best friends in high school, was a teacher's aide. She had summers off, which was a schedule she intended to keep until five-year-old Jason and four-year-old Kimberly were older. Joan brought Sarah and Joe, and Cindy found somebody to work her shift at the auto-parts store so she could ease her pregnant self into the cool water. Only the newlywed Suzie, a bank teller, couldn't get off.

"And wouldn't you know, she's the one who looks the best in a bathing suit," Deena said as the group of women staked out a corner of the fenced pool area with lawn chairs, beach towels and a cooler containing sandwiches and juice.

"Oh, I don't know that Suzie wins the bathing-suit competition," Joan said. Like everyone else, she'd worn her suit under her T-shirt and shorts and was now stripping off her outer layer. "Tess is looking pretty buff in that red tank suit."

Tess glanced down at herself, suddenly self-conscious. "Hey, it's the same old me."

"Maybe so," Deena said. She grabbed Jason and

swiped some sunscreen lotion on him. "But you're look-ing real good, chick. Been working out or something?"

"Nope." She hoped she wasn't blushing. Surely the fact that she was no longer a virgin didn't show some-how. Inside she felt like a changed woman, but outside she must look exactly the same. Mac wasn't that much of a miracle worker.

"They're right," Cindy chimed in. "There's a certain glow about you." She laughed. "People say pregnant women get that, and I'm still waiting. Mostly I just feel fat."

"I think you're all seeing things." Tess felt desperate to get out of the spotlight. "Come on, kids! Who's ready to go for a swim with Aunt Tess?"

A chorus of *me, me, me* followed immediately.

Tess had helped teach all of them to swim, and conse-quently they were all fish, even four-year-old Kimberly. Tess gazed down at their eager faces and felt a pang of re-gret. They would grow so fast while she was gone. She must remember to cherish days like today, and not count them as time-fillers until she could see Mac again. "Last one in's a rotten egg!" she called, and leaped into the pool.

Three hours later the women gathered their tired group together, put more sunscreen on pink noses and decided the perfect ending to the day would be treats all around at the Creamy Cone. Tess pulled on her shorts and sandals, ran her fingers through her hair and de-cided not to bother with the T-shirt. In the summertime, shorts worn over a bathing suit became almost a uniform for patrons at the Creamy Cone.

Everyone piled into Joan's minivan for the four-block trip, and on the way Tess sat in the back with the kids and led them through "The Itsy Bitsy Spider" and "I'm a Little Teapot."

"Carry me, Aunt Tess," Kimberly begged when they arrived at the bustling ice-cream shop.

"Too many cannonballs into the pool for you," Tess said, hoisting the little girl out of her seat and propping her on her hip.

"I *like* cannonballs," Kimberly said, snuggling against Tess.

"Yeah, you sprayed me all the time," added her brother, Jason.

Tess laughed. "Me, too. This girl's a regular spray machine."

"Hey, look!" shouted Joe, Joan's six-year-old. "Uncle Mac's here!"

Uncle Mac. Of course the kids had always called him that, considering that he was an honorary Blakely, but today, after she'd been hearing herself referred to as Aunt Tess for hours, the title struck her differently. Aunt Tess and Uncle Mac.

The idea hit her with more force than any cannonball jump of Kimberly's. Uh-oh. She hadn't subconsciously been having *that* little fantasy, had she? If so, she could forget it right now. Mac was only helping her out. Sure, he might be having a good time in the bargain, but if he'd ever considered having a relationship with her, he would have spoken up long before this.

And he certainly could have spoken up on Sunday night, she thought as she watched him get out of his truck. Instead, he'd been more intent than she was on keeping their secret. Nope, he definitely didn't have dreams of happily-ever-after with her.

"Hey, Uncle Mac!" Joan's daughter, Sarah, called. She started to run across the parking lot.

"Sarah!" Joan yelled a warning and bolted after her as a low-slung car pulled quickly into the lot, apparently oblivious to the running girl. Sarah had a good head start on her mother.

Still holding Kimberly, Tess ran forward, too, knowing neither she nor Joan would make it in time.

At the last minute, when Tess was too horrified even to scream, Mac hurtled into the path of the car, snatched Sarah out of the way and leaped to safety.

The driver, a teenage boy, slammed on the brakes and jumped out of the car. "Oh, God! I didn't see her!" he wailed. "Is she okay?"

Mac held a quaking Sarah tight in his arms. He was breathing hard. "I think so." He leaned away from the child. "You okay, sweetheart?"

Her voice was muffled against his shirt. "I...think so."

"Sarah!" Joan reached them and wrapped her arm around the girl's shoulders. "Did you get bumped? Does anything hurt?"

"N-no." Sarah sounded close to tears.

Joan sagged with relief as Cindy and Deena came up and put comforting arms around her. Everyone started talking at once, exclaiming over the close call, while Joan took several deep breaths and the color seeped back into her face.

Finally Joan held up her hand for silence. "Put her down, please, Mac. She and I are going over to that tree and having a little talk about running in parking lots."

"I don't run," Joe announced.

"Me, neither," said Jason.

"Me, neither," piped up Kimberly from her perch in Tess's arms.

"And we're going to hold you all to that," Mac said, glancing at each of them with a stern expression.

The teenager stepped toward Joan. "I'm sorry, Mrs. Blakely. I shouldn't have driven in so fast. I just got the car today, and I was all like, wow, I want to show my friends. But if anything bad had happened to her..."

Joan took Sarah's hand and gave the teenager a weary smile. "Fortunately it didn't. It's Eddie, isn't it?"

"Yes, ma'am. Eddie Dunnett."

"Well, we're lucky, Eddie. Hopefully we've learned something without suffering a tragedy in the process. Sarah shouldn't have been running without looking, and you should probably remember how dangerous parking lots can be around here, especially this one in the summer."

"Yes, ma'am." Eddie glanced at Mac. "Thanks, Mr. MacDougal. Thanks a lot."

"I'm glad I still have some reflexes left," Mac said.

"Yeah, no quarterback at CHS could run the option play like you. My dad still talks about it."

Mac looked uncomfortable. "That was a long time ago. So, is everybody ready for some ice cream? I'll treat."

"In that case, I'll have the jumbo banana split," Deena said with a grin. "I was going to settle for a small cone, but if the gentleman's buying—"

"Okay, but I'm gonna tell Hammer you took advantage of me," Mac retorted.

Deena laughed. "You're lucky he's not here. He'd order the Earthquake."

"If he was here, I wouldn't have offered to treat. Come on, everybody. Let's see what kind of bill you can run up."

"Sarah and I will be in shortly," Joan said. "Joe, you go with the rest of them so I can talk privately with Sarah."

"Come along, Joe," said Cindy, holding out her hand.

Tess had always liked the way members of the family

accepted responsibility for all the children, not just their own. A Blakely grandchild had a host of adult role models, and from where Tess sat, they were all good ones. Then if you added Uncle Mac, a true hero, a kid would have no excuse for not turning out well.

As for Sarah, she looked completely miserable for ruining the mood of the day. For a sensitive little girl, that was punishment enough. "Come on, gang," Tess said, adjusting Kimberly on her hip. "I'm in the mood for vanilla dipped in butterscotch."

"That's my favorite," said Mac, falling in beside her. He reached over and tugged gently on Kimberly's blond curls. "How's Kimmy today?"

"Uncle Mac! You're messing up my hair!"

"It's already messed up! You've been doing cannonballs in the pool, haven't you?"

Kimberly laughed. "Yep."

Tess wondered if Mac realized that in reaching over to tease Kimberly his arm had brushed Tess's breast. But if Mac didn't realize it, Tess did. All at once she became aware of her own unkempt hair, her pink nose and her wrinkled shorts. Until a few days ago, she'd never thought about what she looked like when Mac was around. Now she wished she'd at least taken time to comb her hair.

"We all got a little messed up today," she said.

"That's okay." He reached over and tweaked Kimberly's nose, getting a squeal in response. "I like my girls messed up."

This time she was sure he was aware that he'd brushed against her. The movement might have seemed accidental to someone else, but Tess felt the deliberate nature of it. He held the door of the shop open for her, and as she walked by him, she registered the heady scent of a slightly sweaty, thoroughly masculine Mac. He wore a T-shirt and jeans today and looked sexier than any man had a right to. She fought her reaction to him, knowing that she couldn't let any of her feelings show in front of her sisters-in-law.

"So you can take a break any old time and sashay into town for ice cream?" she asked, glancing at him. Oh, but he looked good, with his hat tilted at a rakish angle and a gleam in his eye. "Must be a cushy job you have, Mac-Dougal."

"Not as cushy as yours," he said. "Frolicking in the water with this bunch all day while I'm out there busting my butt repairing fence."

Kimberly leaned over Tess's shoulder to peer behind Mac. Then she giggled. "Your butt's not busted, Uncle Mac."

That's for sure, Tess thought, remembering the muscled firmness she'd gripped when they'd...whoops. Dangerous territory. Thoughts like that would make her blush, and blushing wasn't something she normally did when Mac showed up. She stepped into line at the counter behind Cindy and Joe. Mac stood behind her, and she could feel his presence as clearly as if he'd pressed his body up against hers.

Kimberly peered over Tess's shoulder at Mac. "When I grow up, I'm gonna marry you."

"That makes me one lucky guy," Mac said.

Tess shivered, remembering those words in a far different context than playful banter with a little girl.

"Unless I marry Buddy in my Sunday school instead," Kimberly added solemnly. "He's always trying to kiss me."

Tess jiggled her and spoke with mock sternness. "Hey, you little heartbreaker. You can't propose to one guy and then announce you're marrying somebody else the next minute. You have to make up your mind."

"Okay. Then I choose Uncle Mac."

"Thanks, Kimmy. Can *I* give you a kiss?"

"Oh, sure. Just don't slobber like Buddy."

"I'll try not to." Mac leaned forward and kissed her on the cheek. "There, it's official."

They were all just kidding around, Tess told herself. There was no reason for this tightness in her chest, no reason for her to feel suddenly grief-stricken at the thought that Mac would have a real engagement one of these days. No doubt he'd even ask Tess to be in the wedding. After all, they were best friends.

Her turn came to order, and she got a butterscotch-dipped cone for herself and a chocolate-dipped one for Kimberly.

"That's all?" Mac said as she stepped aside so he could order. "No triple banana split or Earthquake for either of you?"

"I like chocolate-dipped the best. I always get that," Kimberly said with authority.

"Tess? You're going to let me get away with just a butterscotch cone?"

"Yep." She set Kimberly down and handed her the chocolate cone before taking the freshly dipped butterscotch one from the counter clerk, a young woman named Evie Jenkins. "Thanks, Evie."

As Kimberly walked over to the table where the rest of the group had gathered, Tess turned back to Mac, who looked more tempting than any ice-cream cone. She realized that her sisters-in-law were engrossed in eating their ice cream and keeping their children from becoming sticky disaster areas. They wouldn't pay any attention to her and Mac, especially considering they were used to seeing the two of them tease and joke with each other.

A devil took temporary possession of her, and she gave Mac a sultry glance. "As much as I'd like to take advantage of you, this is my all-time favorite." Then she swirled her tongue around the top of the cone.

Mac stared at her.

"Then if you nip off the top—" she bit through the butterscotch coating "—you can suck the ice cream right out." As she demonstrated her technique, she glanced up at Mac.

He continued to stare at her while gripping the counter so hard his knuckles showed white against his tan.

"Mr. MacDougal? Are you ready to order?" asked Evie.

Mac didn't take his gaze from Tess. "Uh, yeah." His voice was gravelly. "I'll have...what she's having."

"Coming up."

"I can't believe you're doing that," he murmured to Tess.

"Eating ice cream?" She smiled innocently. "That's what everyone does at the Creamy Cone."

"Not like that."

"Exactly like that. I've eaten one of these like this a million times."

"But not after we've just..."

She took a quick inventory of the area below his belt and was gratified with the slight bulge there. "I can't imagine what you're talking about."

"Oh yes you can," he said in a low voice. "Imagination is your long suit. You love to torture me, don't you?"

"What's good for the gander is good for the goose. You were playing games with me as we walked in here, while you were pretending to fool with Kimberly."

"That was only—"

"Mr. MacDougal? Here's your cone. Oh, and the other ladies said you were paying for everyone."

"That's right." It seemed to take great effort for him to turn away from Tess and focus on the task of paying the bill.

Tess moved a little closer. "I'll see you over at the table," she said softly. "And thanks for the dipped cone."

He slipped his wallet back in his pocket. "If I'd known what you were going to do with it, I never would have agreed to buy you one," he muttered without turning around.

"Fair is fair." Feeling much better than she had when she'd been mired in thoughts of his eventual marriage, Tess walked over to join the others.

MAC PLAYED abysmal poker the following night, and the Blakely brothers finally figured out that a woman must be distracting him. Although they teased him about being lovesick and pestered him for the name of his latest conquest, he managed to outmaneuver their questions. By the end of the evening no one was the wiser.

His latest conquest. He chuckled at the irony of that as he stuffed a blanket and two beach towels in his saddle-bags Thursday night in preparation for his ride with Tess. Tess had conquered *him*, more like it. He was afraid to put a name to what he was feeling in relationship to Tess, but he craved her nearly every waking minute, and that wasn't a good sign. He'd thought tonight would never get here.

No other woman had ever made him come unglued so fast. Maybe it was all the reading she'd done, or maybe she was a natural when it came to exciting a man. In any event, her instincts would do justice to some Hollywood sex kitten, and yet she had no real experience with men other than him. Oh, how he loved knowing that. He loved it way too much, considering that the status quo would change. More men lived in New York City than in all of Arizona. She had a damn good chance of finding at least one who was to her liking.

He pushed that notion out of his head, not wanting to ruin the night. And it was one hell of a beautiful night. The moon sat just below the mountains, creating a glow that threw the familiar ridge into stark silhouette. Any minute now the moon would poke its head over, looking huge and golden as it crested. Mac hoped Tess would get here before that happened, so she could see it with him.

He'd always liked sharing stuff like that with her because she was so passionate about the beauty around her. He should have known that she'd transfer that passion to anything she did, especially making love. Passion and curiosity—it was quite a combination. He wondered if she'd remember to bring any of her books.

The sound of her car pulling in beside the barn made his pulse rate go up. She rounded the barn just as a sliver of the moon eased up over the ridge.

"Come over here and see the moon," he said.

She quickened her steps. "I hoped I'd get here in time." She reached his side and leaned her forearms against the top rail of the corral as she watched the sky. "Oh, wow."

He leaned casually against the rail next to her, his arm barely brushing her arm, as if to prove to himself he could be alone with her and not grab her, as if he were in no hurry to leave and go down to the river. As if he didn't want her with every fiber of his being.

When she'd hurried toward him, he'd figured out from the lovely jiggle under her T-shirt that she wasn't wearing a bra. If he had to make a guess, he'd say she'd skipped the panties under her shorts, too. She held a book and a small flashlight in one hand. All of that made a potent combination, and he was more than ready to forget about the moon.

But he'd promised her they would always be friends, and Tess was the sort of person who remembered promises like that. She'd expect that someday they'd be able to stand here and watch the moon rise as friends, the way they'd done many times before. He might as well start practicing now.

But the air was filled with her scent, and his heart raced as he thought of holding her soft body again. He hungered for the taste of her lips, although he wouldn't dare kiss her here. Either one of his parents could come out and catch them.

"How was poker?" she asked.

"I lost every hand."

"Mac!" She turned toward him. "That's not like you. In fact, you usually come out ahead of everyone else."

"Your brothers were extremely happy about it. They wanted the name of the girl I was seeing, so they could thank her. They figured that was the only thing that would make me completely hopeless at cards."

"But it wasn't really me that was the problem, right? It was having to face my brothers after having sex with me."

"I guess so." Although he wasn't quite sure about that. He'd suffered some guilt pangs for the first half hour or so of the poker game, but after that, the guilt had seemed to wear off. From then on he'd lost because he was daydreaming about Tess, but revealing that might give away more than he wanted to right now.

"So what did you tell them?"

"Nothing. I just let them speculate."

"Do you think they'll try to find out who you're seeing?"

"Oh, they'll ask around, but I don't think anyone will think of you. As I've said before, no one would ever suspect what's going on between the two of us. We could probably kiss in the middle of the park in front of the whole town, and they'd think it was brotherly and sisterly affection going on."

"Do you feel like kissing me now?"

He stared at the moon. "Yeah, I do."

"More than kissing?"

His groin tightened. "Yep."

"I just wondered. You seem so cool and collected. Weren't you the one who told me not to get all prissy and pretend I didn't want you so much I couldn't see straight?"

He looked at her and saw a beautiful face silvered by moonlight, sparkling eyes that drew him like a moth to flame, moist lips that made him crazy to taste her again. "I want you so much I can't see straight."

"Then what are we doing standing here gaping at the moon?"

"Beats the hell out of me." He pushed away from the fence. "Let's go."

13

BEING ON A HORSE in his current condition wasn't the smartest move he'd ever made, Mac realized as they went down the trail, but riding to the river was the only option. Walking would take too long, so he had to make a compromise between speed and comfort.

The moon lit their path and gave him an arousing view of Tess moving along ahead of him, her hips swaying gently in rhythm with Peppermint Patty's brisk little walk. When the trail curved so he caught her in profile, he became more convinced that she didn't have a bra on under her shirt.

And then she took off the shirt.

He could hardly believe she was doing it and wondered if he was having another potent dream, complete with crickets chirping and an owl hooting in the distance.

A few moments later the shirt came sailing back toward him, and he was so dumbfounded he was barely able to snag it before it dropped to the ground. "Hey!"

"What?" She turned in the saddle, giving him a breathtaking view of her breast bathed in moonlight.

"What are you doing?"

Even from this distance, the mischief was obvious in her smile. "Getting you hot."

"I'm already hot!" Squirming in the saddle, to be more accurate. Panting, lusting, longing for relief from this agonizing need to be deep inside her.

"Then hotter."

"Damn, Tess." Her shirt was scented with her cologne, and something even more erotic, the fragrance of Tess, aroused and ready for love. He bunched it in one fist and held it to his nose. Oh, Lord. That scent...memories of lying between her thighs, of tasting her, whirled through his fevered brain. "Why does your shirt smell so... good?"

"A little trick I read in the book I brought along tonight."

"What trick?"

"Oh, you just find a way to convey your own...special perfume to your lover. They say it works better than any manufactured perfume from the store."

He watched her through a haze of desire. "They would be right. You're not wearing panties under your shorts, are you?"

"No."

"So you took this shirt and put it—"

"In a very special place. Then I sent it back to you. You know, the motion of this horse is...*very* nice."

Mac groaned. "Ease up on me, Tess. I'm a desperate man."

"The book says anticipation is everything."

"Bull. Anticipation is excruciating." He heard the gurgle of the river ahead. Almost there. Smelling the water, the horses picked up the pace, and he tortured himself with imagining the sweet jiggle of Tess's breasts in the moonlight. He reached down and pulled the blanket out of his saddlebag and tucked her shirt in its place. He had no intention of wasting time once they got to the river.

Tess headed Peppermint Patty down the embankment and was off her horse in no time. She left the mare ground-tied, as she and Mac always did when they came down here at night. The horses weren't going far in the dark, and they provided a good warning system for snakes.

Mac's view of Tess was blocked by her horse as he dismounted holding the blanket. But when she stepped out from behind Peppermint Patty into a pool of moonlight, Mac lost his grip on the blanket. She was naked.

"Does this come close enough to your fantasy?" she murmured.

As he gazed at her standing in the silvery light like some nymph from a fairy tale, the water rippling and flashing behind her, his throat tightened with desire. "It goes beyond it," he said huskily. "I don't think I could dream something this beautiful, so I sure hope you're real."

"I'm real." She walked toward him across the sand and he noticed the small book in her hand. "And I want to make love with you, Mac."

Make love. His throat ached with emotion as he faced the truth—making love was exactly what he'd be doing, perhaps for the first time in his life. But for Tess, this might only be a stepping stone, an initiation into pleasures she would one day enjoy with another man. He had to protect his heart. "I see you have your reference book, there," he said, trying to keep his tone light.

"You said you wanted to see it."

"Oh, I do." But technique didn't seem to matter so much now. Still, she wanted an education, and he'd been chosen to help her learn. That in itself was an amazing gift he'd been given, and to expect more would be greedy. He leaned down, picked up the blanket and shook it out, settling it on the sand. She stretched out on it while he started taking off his clothes with shaking hands.

The process took longer than he wanted because he couldn't stop looking at her lying there like some sort of nature goddess. He never would have guessed that their old meeting spot by the river could turn into such a seductive place. More than seductive. Tess made his heart ache with her beauty.

Sunday night she'd totally captivated him with her white satin and rose-colored bedroom, but there was something even wilder about this scene. Not far away a pack of coyotes howled and yipped, hunting, perhaps even mating by the light of the full moon. The sound stirred basic instincts deep within him. He'd do well to ignore them. They could only get him into more trouble.

"Coyotes," Tess said.

"Yeah." He took off the last of his clothes and reached in the pocket of his jeans.

"They sound so...primitive."

He caught the note of urgency in her voice, as if her reaction was the same as his. Heart pounding, he knelt beside her on the blanket. They were only playing at this, he told himself. He would be crazy to get serious. "So, professor, what do you want to try?"

She opened the book and leaned away so that moonlight fell across the page. "This."

The coyotes howled again as he gazed down at a black-and-white artist's drawing of a couple mating in the way that wild creatures mated. He sucked in a breath, knowing that was what had filled his mind as he'd listened to the coyotes' song, yet never imagining she would want such a thing, too. But oh, to love her like that, with the night sounds around them and the river rushing by...he ached with the wanting of it.

He glanced at her and a tremor passed through him. This primitive mating would have great significance for him, which made it dangerous, but for her it might simply be a unique experience. "You're...sure?"

Slowly she closed the book. Then she sensuously rolled to her stomach. Before he realized it, she'd risen to her hands and knees, offering her round bottom in the age-old invitation of a female to her chosen male.

His body could not refuse. Hot blood thrummed through his veins as uncivilized needs took hold of him. Grasping her hips, he moved into position behind her. A guttural, untamed sound rose from his throat and he fought the urge to drive deep and claim her in the way of the wilderness. Instead, he probed gently, not wanting to frighten her.

Desire surged in him when he found her moist and ready. Still he held back, slipping his hand around her waist and down, massaging the tight nub that heightened her response. With a little cry that was almost a plea, she tilted her hips, and he could restrain himself no more. He slid smoothly into her waiting channel.

And for the second time in his life he felt an incredible sense of connection, even stronger than the first time. And with that arose an urge he'd never known—the compulsion to pour himself into this woman and watch her grow round with child, his child. His body chafed against the barrier he'd placed between seed and womb and called for him to complete the connection and fill her with his essence.

And he could not. With a groan of pleasure mixed with deep frustration, he drew back and pushed forward with more force, lightly slapping her with his thighs. She murmured encouragement, and he increased the pace, pummeling her gently yet firmly as the sandy clearing filled with the sounds and scents of mating. They became slick with sweat in the heat of the night air as the slap of flesh against flesh grew faster and more defined. Their gasps and soft cries melded with the call of night creatures, the wind in the trees and the ripple of water over stones.

She tightened around him a moment before she was rocked with convulsions. Her undulations drew him into more frenzied movements as instinct told him now was the time, the time to plant his seed. He erupted in a forceful climax, crying out her name and holding her close to receive him. And the mating dance that had shaken him to his soul came to a powerful...and fruitless...end.

TESS LAY on the blanket, curled with her back nestled against the protective curve of Mac's body, and wondered how she'd created such a terrible problem. She'd fallen madly, passionately, desperately in love with her best friend. What had started out as fun and games, a fine adventure together before she headed off to her new life, had become more important than anything else in her world.

She didn't believe a woman should sacrifice a bright future in order to be with a man. Yet that's exactly what she wanted to do. She knew that Mac wouldn't leave Copperville as long as his parents needed him on the ranch, so any woman who wanted to be with Mac would have to stay in Copperville, too. And she wanted to be with Mac, to make love with him, to laugh and play with him and make babies with him.

Especially make babies. She wanted to be his mate, to make love again the way they had a little while ago, only without protection. She'd leaped from being a virgin only days ago to wanting it all—marriage, motherhood, years of lovemaking with this man.

It wasn't the way she'd pictured herself. From as long as she could remember, she'd been determined to escape the confines of this small town, to be sophisticated and worldly. She'd vowed to live in a big city, travel to exotic places, have many lovers.

Then, when she'd tired of all that, she'd settle down, probably right here in Copperville, and raise a family.

Now all her worldly plans seemed hollow and lonely. What good was any of it, if she couldn't have Mac there to share it with her? She'd rather stay here and be a ranch wife than lose Mac.

Not that Mac was asking. He'd never given any indication that he thought of her in those terms. He didn't act as if he wanted to settle down and marry anyone, as a matter of fact, let alone her. He'd never even been engaged.

He stroked her hip. "Whatcha thinking about, twinkle-toes?"

She decided on a partial answer. "Oh, just that it's too bad I'll be heading for New York the end of August."

He kneaded her thigh. "Because this is so much fun, you mean?"

"Yes." More than fun. She'd become involved, heart and soul, but she dared not tell him.

"It's fun, but in a way it's a good thing we have a limit on the time we can be together. We'd never be able to keep it a secret if it went beyond August."

"True." Perhaps he was happy with the secret arrangement, considering that he wanted to keep his status with her brothers intact. The only way her brothers would tolerate a sexual relationship between Mac and Tess was if they were getting married. Immediately. Mac didn't want marriage at the moment, apparently, so the secret had to be kept.

"Ready for a little skinny-dipping?"

She turned toward him. "We're really going to?"

He gave her a quick kiss. "Sure. We're all hot and sticky. It'll feel good. And besides, it's part of your education."

"Mac, I don't think we can have sex in the middle of that river."

"Why not?" His grin flashed in the moonlight. "Because it isn't in your book?"

"Because you won't have a pocket to stash your condom in."

"Tsk, tsk. You take away a girl's virginity, and suddenly she thinks sex is only about intercourse." He got to his feet and pulled her up with him. "Come on. Let's see what happens when you stand thigh-deep in rushing water without a bathing suit on." He took her hand and led her toward the riverbank.

Excitement swelled within her. That was another thing she loved about Mac. He had a heck of an imagination. Still, she wondered if he'd thought of that sort of stimulation on his own. "Have you been reading my books?"

"Nah. But I went down to the drugstore and bought one of those magazines they keep behind the counter. The article was about hot-tub jets, which we don't have, so we'll have to improvise."

And improvise he did, although there was much laughing and splashing and playful groping before he finally had her positioned the way he wanted her. He'd so awakened her sensuality that he easily convinced her to accept the river as a teasing lover. Holding her steady, adding his own caress to that of the water, he coaxed her to let the current stroke her intimately, bringing her to a crescendo of feeling. At the moment of release she couldn't tell whether the bubbling water or Mac's caress had sent her over the edge.

While she was still gasping in reaction, he swept her

into his arms and carried her back to the blanket. He made love to her while they were both still wet and slick as otters, so their bodies slid together as if they were oiled. She'd never known such triumphant freedom. She felt lithe and supple, capable of anything. They twisted and turned on the blanket, exploring different positions, alternate ways their bodies could move and shift yet still give unbelievable pleasure.

She was sure Mac was enjoying himself. His murmured words told her so, and when his tone roughened, she knew he was in the grip of fierce passion. When at last he surrendered to that passion, she held him tight and absorbed the strong tremors that shook him. She couldn't imagine living without this, without him. Perhaps, if she loved him well enough and thoroughly enough this summer, he'd realize he couldn't live without her, either.

THE SUMMER PASSED far too quickly for Tess. For every creative lovemaking scheme she dreamed up, Mac came up with one to match it. She suggested a day trip to Phoenix. They checked into the honeymoon suite of a hotel where no one would know them and spent the day in bed. He flew them up to Flagstaff where they hiked to a mountain meadow and made love in a field of daisies under a bright summer sky.

They experimented with velvet ropes, furry mittens and feather dusters. While they were in Phoenix they stopped into an X-rated boutique and dared each other to buy something. They came out of the shop with body paint and flavored massage oils.

The charged hours Tess spent with Mac seemed painted in brilliant color, while the rest of her life seemed to be cast in shades of gray. She went through the motions of a normal summer, playing cards with her sisters-in-law every Wednesday night, baby-sitting for her nieces and nephews, having lunch with her mother, planning the surprise anniversary party for her parents. But none of it seemed quite real, because she couldn't tell those she cared about that a most significant and wonderful thing had happened to her—she was completely in love with Mac MacDougal.

And she wanted to tell the world. She especially longed to confide in her mother, who would be a great source of advice. When her sisters-in-law discussed their husbands, whether in frustration or delight, Tess wanted to be a part of that conversation, to join the ranks of women openly, proudly in love.

Mac seemed just as involved with her as she was with him, although not a word of commitment ever came from his mouth. During the hot weeks of summer, they shared everything, it seemed, except a future. It was as if she were about to be shipped off to war and might never come back, so the subject of a happy-ever-after could never be broached.

Aside from that, she thought they were no different from any other couple just discovering passion and love, except that their relationship was known only to themselves. At first she'd thought secrecy was essential to her summer project. Sharing the secret with Mac had felt delicious and naughty. Now she was sick of it. But she couldn't tell. Not ever, unless Mac agreed, and she couldn't imagine him agreeing. And that made her soul ache.

BY THE FIRST WEEK in August, Mac had come to the painful conclusion that he should break up with Tess. He should have ended their affair long before this, in fact.

He was obviously good enough for her in bed, but not good enough to consider altering her career plans for, not good enough to let the world know about their love affair. He'd watched for any wavering on her decision to move to New York, and there was none.

As he headed to her house for another night of love-making, the truck splashing through puddles left by a heavy afternoon rain, he cursed himself for being weak. If he couldn't treat sex with her as a casual roll in the hay, fun while it lasted but forgotten when it was over, then he should get out now and start putting himself back together.

In fact, that's what he'd do, by God. Tonight. He wouldn't make love to her. He ignored the sick feeling of disappointment in his gut at that thought and vowed to carry through with what was right, what would ultimately save his sanity.

He'd walk into her house and tell her this activity was eating into his time, causing him to get behind on some paperwork for the ranch. That much was true. He'd taken over the books for his parents a couple of years ago, and at the moment he was making a sorry job of it.

He arrived at the town's traffic light as it turned red, and although his was the only vehicle at the intersection, he stopped anyway. As he sat waiting for the green, a horn beeped behind him.

Glancing in the rearview mirror, he spotted Rhino Blakely's truck with Rhino driving and Hammer in the passenger seat. Mac raised a hand in greeting and fought down the guilt that swept over him every time he unexpectedly met members of Tess's family. Tonight he didn't have to feel guilty, though. He was going over to Tess's house, but he wouldn't be there long. It was over.

Rhino hopped out of the truck and ran forward to knock on Mac's window.

Mac rolled it down. "What's up?"

"Joan and Deena went to a movie, and me and Hammer feel like a darts tournament at the Ore Cart tonight. What do you say?"

Mac hesitated only a split second. If he had somewhere to go, that would force him to make the break with Tess. "Sure. I have to swing by Tess's house for a few minutes, but I can be there in a half hour or so."

"Great. Light's green." Rhino ran back to his truck.

Mac rolled up the window and crossed the intersection. Fate must have stepped in to make him take this necessary step, he thought. Here he'd been thinking of what he needed to do, and along came some help in the form of Rhino and Hammer. If he ended it with Tess tonight, the brothers would never find out about the wild activities going on under their noses.

Even Tess probably needed some time to regroup before she went to New York. She might not realize it, but she'd probably have a tough time giving up what they'd shared this summer.

The rest of the way to Tess's house, Mac ran through all the reasons to end the affair. They were all good reasons, yet he felt as if someone had dropped a load of copper ore on his chest as he walked up the steps to her porch and opened the door. Walking away from another night of wonderful lovemaking and knowing he wouldn't make love to Tess ever again might be the hardest job he'd ever given himself. He'd have to be strong.

14

EXOTIC MUSIC with a pulsing beat drifted from Tess's bedroom, and automatically Mac became aroused just wondering what she had in store for him. Whatever it was, he'd resist.

Not that resisting would be easy. With each rendezvous they planned, he always wondered what she'd come up with that would surprise the hell out of him. And totally turn him on. He and Tess had tried stunts that had never crossed his mind with any other woman.

Yet now that he thought about it, sexual adventure suited Tess perfectly. She'd tempted him with bold ideas when they were kids, too. The raft they'd built and almost drowned trying to ride, the wild-horse roundup, the cave-exploration trip—Tess had thought of every one of those.

God, it wouldn't be easy walking back out of here tonight and giving up the excitement of loving Tess, the pure fun of just being with her. But that was short-term thinking. For the long term he needed to start learning to do without Tess's soft mouth, her warm, moist body, her... He stood in the doorway and felt his resolve slip away.

Tess was dancing. And not just ordinary dancing, either. She wore filmy pants that hugged her hips, a jeweled bra dripping with gold coins, a gold armband and a veil across her nose and mouth. She was a vision straight out of a sheik's harem, complete with tiny cymbals attached to her fingers. She kept time with them as she rotated her hips in the most mesmerizing rhythm he'd ever seen.

"Surprise." Her grin was faintly visible behind the veil. "I've been practicing for weeks." She continued to dance as she motioned him to a straight-backed chair in the corner of the room. She'd obviously placed it there for her audience of one. "And now I'm going to dance for you and drive you insane. Enjoy."

The light veil had the most incredible effect, emphasizing the sultry look in her eyes and making him hungry for her mouth simply because he couldn't see it very well. By covering her lips, she made them seem more exciting and forbidden, more of a prize when they were finally claimed.

Not that he would be claiming them. He had something to say, and that would eliminate the chance of kissing those temptingly disguised lips of hers.

But he couldn't make his announcement immediately. After all, she'd been practicing this dance for weeks to surprise him. He ought to at least let her show him what she could do. Courtesy demanded it.

Besides, he couldn't seem to take his eyes off the circular motion of her hips. He wondered what that would feel like if...no. He wasn't going to make love to her tonight, so it didn't matter what that would feel like. Fantastic, probably. But he was ending it. Definitely. Once she'd finished her dance.

He slouched in the chair and tried to look slightly bored as she danced slowly around him. When the beat became faster, so did the motion of her hips. He swallowed. Then she began adding a new dimension, a gentle shimmy of her breasts that made the dangling coins dance. He licked his dry lips.

She drew closer, brushing his arm with her hip as she danced. Her shimmy increased in speed, and she leaned forward, shaking her breasts so close to his face he could see the tiny drops of perspiration in her cleavage. The pearl necklace rested there, as it had all summer. And looking at it never failed to get a response from him.

"Unfasten your jeans," she whispered.

He glanced quickly into her eyes. This wasn't going at all the way he'd thought it out. "No, Tess, I—"

"Do it," she whispered more urgently, dancing around him, her hips keeping that maddening, erotic rhythm. "I want you now, Mac. And I can tell you want me."

"But—"

"Now." Still dancing, she took off the finger cymbals and reached beneath the snug band around her hips for a small package she'd obviously hidden there earlier. She swayed closer, her arms undulating with the music, and tucked a condom in his shirt pocket.

He was lost. If he didn't go along with her plan, she would be very disappointed. She had this scene all worked out and had gone to a lot of trouble to make it happen. Besides, he was so aroused he was in pain. He couldn't walk out of this room now if his life depended on it. He worked clumsily at the buttons of his fly, his heart pounding as he focused on the fascinating shimmy of her breasts and the amazing rotation of her hips.

He took the condom out of his shirt pocket. Then he nearly dropped it when she reached between her legs and somehow made the crotch of the filmy harem pants come undone without missing a beat.

"Are you impressed?" she asked softly.

"Oooh, yeah." And shaking with need. He managed to

get the condom on as she danced closer, the coins jingling from the quivering rhythm of her breasts.

"Hold perfectly still," she whispered. "I'm going to do it all."

Incredible as her body looked as it moved, he was completely captured by her eyes. Emphasized by the veil, her eyes seemed to smolder with more fire than ever before. He couldn't look away.

Still keeping time to the music with her hips, she braced both hands on his shoulders and straddled the chair. Then she slowly lowered herself in a sensuous, rotating movement that made him gasp with pleasure. Yet he wouldn't, couldn't close his eyes. As she used all the sensuous dance movements to make unbelievable love to him, he focused on the blazing heat in her eyes, searching for the depth of emotion that rocked him whenever they came together like this.

And he found it. As her rhythm increased, her eyes told him that yes, she felt what he felt, that her heart had been branded as surely as his.

"I love you," he said. For the first time in his life the words meant something special, something so real he could almost touch it.

Her eyes were pure flame. "I love you," she murmured.

Joy surged so intensely through him that at last he closed his eyes, afraid she'd see his tears of relief. She loved him. Everything would be okay. As her movements grew more uninhibited and her cry of release filled the room, he held her tight and abandoned himself to a soul-satisfying climax.

They stayed locked together for many long minutes, Tess's veiled cheek resting on Mac's shoulder. He gently stroked her back, unsure what to say next. He really wanted the first words to come from her—something along the lines of *I've decided not to go to New York. I love you and I want to stay here with you.*

They'd honeymoon in New York, he decided. They'd take lots of trips, in fact, to make up for the loss of her big adventure. They'd—

"Yo, Big Mac! Where are you, buddy?" The unmistakable sound of Rhino's voice came from the direction of the living room.

Tess scrambled from Mac's lap and ran to the bedroom door. She slammed it and plastered herself across the door frame, her eyes wide.

"Oh, God." Mac stared at her. He'd completely forgotten he'd promised to meet Rhino and Hammer at the Ore Cart, and that he'd told them where he was headed in the meantime.

"Hey, Mac!" Rhino called again, this time obviously from the hallway. "What's going on?"

Mac swung into action, jumping from the chair. "We'll... I'll be out in a minute!" he called. "Lock that," he muttered to Tess.

"Why can't you come out now?" Rhino sounded suspicious.

"Just give me a minute, okay?" When he heard the lock click Mac headed for Tess's bathroom.

"What's going on in there, Mac?" Rhino's tone had changed from suspicious to angry. "Is Tess with you?"

"Yes, I'm with him, Rhino. Go on out to the living room. We'll be there soon."

Mac finished quickly in the bathroom. "God, I'm sorry, Tess," he said as he returned, buttoning his fly on the way.

"It's not your fault." She'd taken off her jeweled bra. Topless, she pulled a plain one out of a drawer.

"Yes, it is my fault. I met them when I was driving over here. I told them I was on my way to your house but I'd meet them in a half hour for darts."

She turned in the act of fastening the front clasp of her bra. "Why would you—" She paused. "You weren't planning to stay, were you?"

"No."

Her face grew pale. "You were going to end it, weren't you?"

"Well, yes, I was, but I—"

"Never mind the long explanation." Her voice quivered and she turned away from him. "Just get out there and talk to them while I get dressed."

"Tess, dammit, I—"

"Go! I mean it, Mac!"

A knot formed in the pit of his stomach. "What do you want me to tell them?"

"You might want to start with the truth." She cleared her throat. "There's no way we can make up a story they'll buy at this stage. We got caught, Mac. There isn't any way we can pretty it up so they'll like it."

"The hell there isn't. We could tell them we're in love with each other."

She pulled a T-shirt over her head. "Thanks for the thought, but I'd rather you didn't."

Raw as he felt right now, he didn't have the courage to question her. Maybe she didn't want anyone to know she'd fallen in love with the guy who was merely doing her a service before she left for New York. And the way she was acting right now, he was pretty sure she would go. Maybe she loved him, as she'd said. But she'd leave him anyway.

Without another word, he unlocked the bedroom door and walked down the hall to face his inquisitors.

HE'D BEEN ABOUT to break up with her. Tess fought tears and struggled to get dressed. Oh, he might love her, as he'd said in the heat of passion. He'd probably told several women he loved them over the years, especially when they pleased him sexually. He still hadn't felt the urge to marry one of them. She was just another of his conquests, fun for the summer but not the one he wanted to spend a lifetime with.

There was only one thing Mac could say that would placate her brothers, and that would be to announce their engagement. And he wasn't going to do that.

Angry voices from the direction of the living room told her things weren't going well. Stuffing the harem outfit in a drawer, she ran a brush through her hair and padded barefoot down the hall.

Rhino sounded furious. "So you stand there and admit that you took advantage of our sister's innocent nature?"

Hardly, Tess thought, wondering what sort of story Mac was spinning out there.

"That's exactly what I'm saying." Mac's tone was lower and more controlled. "And if I hadn't, some city slicker in New York would have. She couldn't stay innocent forever, dammit. I convinced her she needed to be prepared before she went off to the big city."

"You *convinced* her?" Hammer bellowed. "You *seduced* her, you mean! That poor girl didn't have a chance!"

Tess hurried into the room. "I did so have a chance. I—"

"Tess." Mac turned to her. "You can't assume the responsibility for this. I took advantage of your lack of experience. Simple as that."

"You most certainly did *not*." She realized he was trying to protect her, but she couldn't let him do that. If he had any chance of saving the relationship with her brothers, the truth had to come out. She glanced at her brothers. "I don't know what he told you, but this whole summer project was my idea. I decided back in June that I wanted to lose my virginity before I left for New York."

Rhino and Hammer stared at her, their jaws slack. Rhino was the first to speak. "Summer p-project?"

Mac snorted. "Don't listen to her. You know Tess. She could always make up wild stories on the spur of the moment, and most of the time it was to save my sorry ass. She's doing it again."

"I am not! I came up with my plan and asked Mac if he could fix me up with someone. He offered to take care of it himself."

"Oh, I'll just bet he did!" Rhino advanced on Mac. "And how did she get this idea in the first place, huh? She's never been worried about stuff like that before, so who was putting ideas in her head, buddy-boy?"

Tess stepped between them. "I've been thinking about stuff like that since I was fourteen years old, Rhino! It wasn't Mac's idea, it was mine."

"He probably made you think it was your idea," Hammer said, joining his brother as they faced Mac, fists clenched. "We've always known this is one slick character when it comes to women. We just never thought he'd go behind our backs and prey on our little sister, right, Rhino?"

"That's right. Guess we have to take you outside and work you over, Mac."

"You will not!" Tess pushed a hand into each one of her brothers' substantial chests.

"I can take care of myself, Tess." Mac rolled his shoulders. "You don't have to protect me from your brothers."

"She can't stop us, anyway," Rhino said. He gently nudged Tess aside.

"Yes, I can!" Tess pushed her way between the men again. "If you touch one hair on his head, I'll tell Mom and Dad about the time you guys drove over the border, got drunk on tequila and spent the night in a Nogales jail."

"I don't care," Hammer said. "No biggie."

"And what about the time I found the marijuana in your bedroom, Hammer?" she added sweetly.

"You had pot in your room?" Mac asked. "You never told me that. God, your dad would have had a fit."

A flush spread over Hammer's face. "I only smoked a little of the damn stuff, and it made me puke!"

"So that's what I'll tell the folks," Tess said. "I'm sure they'll understand. Although they might wonder what happened to the rest of the joints, since I found about six."

Hammer's flush deepened. "I sold them at school."

Rhino turned to him, his eyes wide. "You *peddled* those things? You told me you flushed them!"

"Who flushed what?" called out Tim as he came through the front door. "And what's up with the darts tournament? Suzie said you called, so I went and picked up Dozer, but when we got to the Ore Cart they said you'd come down here."

"Yeah," Dozer said, walking in behind Tim. "Are we gonna play or not?"

Rhino crossed his arms over his chest. "It seems somebody's already been playing." He glared at Mac. "Our friend here, the one we all thought we could trust, has been playing house with our sister all summer."

"What?" Dozer looked from Tess to Mac. "Tess, is this true? Did this guy...?"

"It was a mutual decision," Tess said, "so don't go—"

"That's it." Dozer started across the room. "He's toast."

"Hold it, Dozer." Rhino grabbed his brother by the arm. "It's not that simple."

"It *is* simple," Tess said. "I'm the one to blame here, not Mac. I asked him to do this!"

"And he couldn't pronounce the word *no?*" Hammer said.

"I didn't want him to say no! I wanted to finally experience sex!"

Tim's face grew red. "Aw, Tess! What did you have to go and do that for? There's plenty of time for that after you're married!"

"Oh, really?" Tess lifted her chin and surveyed her four brothers. "And I suppose all you guys waited until after you were married?"

There was a general clearing of throats and glancing everywhere but at Tess.

"That's different," Rhino said. "We're guys."

Tess stared at them. "Hello? Can any of you say *women's rights?*" She threw up both arms and paced across the room. "I can't believe we're almost to the millennium and you're still making such outdated statements. In case you hadn't noticed, women aren't considered helpless little flowers anymore."

"Hey, we know all about that stuff," Hammer said. "We got women in the mines now. Women driving the big ore trucks. Women everywhere. But, dammit, Tess, you're our *sister.*"

"Yeah, and guys can be real sleazy!" Tim added. "We didn't want you getting hurt or anything! A lot of guys only want to fool around. They're not into the marriage thing."

"Which reminds me of a very critical point." Rhino

narrowed his eyes at Mac. "Just what are your plans, now that you've had a real fun summer fooling around with a sweet and innocent young girl?"

"I'm twenty-six, Rhino!"

"That's very young!" Rhino shouted back.

"Not *that* young," Tim said. "I'm twenty-seven."

"We're off the subject," Rhino said. He fixed Mac with an intimidating look. "What are your intentions, Mac?"

Tess panicked. She didn't want to listen to Mac fumble around and try to dodge the question. Suspecting he had no interest in her as a wife was not as bad as hearing him say it. "No plans, folks! *Nada.* Have you forgotten that I'm going to New York in a couple of weeks to start a new job? I'm in no position to make a commitment at this point. In fact, Mac and I had that understanding from the beginning, didn't we, Mac?" If she expected him to look at her with relief and gratitude, she was disappointed.

The blue eyes that had been filled with such passion not so long ago gazed at her without any expression at all. "Yes, we did."

"That probably suited lover-boy right down to the ground," Hammer muttered. He glanced at Tess. "And I still say you're covering for him and he came up with the idea first. He probably figured this deal was too sweet to pass up—a girl who was leaving town at the end of the summer. Perfect, right, Big Mac?"

Mac's nonchalant shrug broke Tess's heart. That's probably how Mac had thought of their lovemaking. A summer romance. Fun while it lasted. "Well, that was the beauty of it for me, too," she said, forcing the words past a tight throat. "I couldn't afford messy entanglements when I was about to leave."

Rhino looked at her, his gaze far too perceptive. "I don't buy it, Tess."

She squared her shoulders. "Well, I don't give a damn whether you buy it or not. It's the truth."

"Let me get this straight," Dozer said. "On the one hand we have a guy who's been romeoing his way around the county ever since he was fifteen, and on the other we have a girl who's lived like a nun until the age of twenty-six. What—"

"I didn't live like a nun by choice! You guys scared off all my prospects!"

"They were all terrible prospects!" Rhino said.

"And I'm trying to make a point, here," Dozer continued. "Tess says this is all her fault, but I wonder how that could be, considering she had zero experience and the stud-man over here has more experience than anybody in this room. I mean, who do you suppose was in control of that situation?"

"I was!" Tess said.

"Not likely." Dozer started toward Mac again. "And I'm itching to land a few punches."

"Sounds like a plan," Hammer said.

"Might as well get it over with," Rhino added.

Tess grew desperate. She couldn't have her brothers beat up the man she loved. She lowered her voice to deliver her ultimatum. It had always worked for her mother, so maybe it would work for her. "If you do this, I'm through with all of you," she said.

They turned to her with expressions of disbelief.

"I mean it. No brother of mine would gang up on an innocent man. And Mac is innocent."

"Hah!" Dozer said.

Rhino stroked his chin and gazed at her. "Does he mean that much to you, Tess?"

Trapped. There was no answer except the truth. Tears

of frustration pushed at the back of her eyes. "Yes, dammit, he does."

Rhino nodded. "Then maybe you ought to stay home and marry him instead of traipsing off to New York."

But he doesn't want that, she longed to say. Instead, she swallowed the lump of emotion in her throat and lied. "Just because you care about someone and don't want them hurt doesn't mean you're ready to give up your dream for them. My dream is to experience some other place besides Copperville, and I finally have the chance to do that." She blinked to hold back the tears.

Rhino studied her for a while longer. "Well, I guess that settles it. We can't very well beat up on Mac and make our sister cry, now, can we?"

"I wouldn't cry." She sniffed. "I just would never speak to you again."

Tim frowned and came over to put a hand on her shoulder. "You look like you might cry."

She sniffed again and glared up at him through swimming eyes. "Well, I won't."

"We've got another thing to think about," Hammer said. "Is this information going to leave this room?"

"No." Rhino fixed each of his brothers with a stern look. "Nobody tells. Not even your wives. Got that?"

Everyone nodded.

Tess gazed at them all with a heavy heart. She wanted this little scene over with. "Don't you all have a darts tournament to play?"

There was a moment of silence. Finally Rhino broke it. "Guess we do. Come on, Mac."

"Thanks," Mac said, "but I think I'll take a pass."

"Like hell you will." Hammer grabbed one of Mac's arms.

"Yeah." Dozer grabbed the other one. "You don't think we'd leave you here, do you?"

"I'll make it even plainer," Rhino said. "Unless Tess changes her mind and decides to marry you, I don't want you around this house again. You may have gotten away with it all summer, but the party's over, buddy. The Blakely brothers are back on duty. Now let's go play some darts."

Tess watched with great misgiving as they escorted Mac out of the house. "You do understand I meant what I said," she called after them as Dozer demanded Mac's keys so he could drive Mac's truck. "If you hurt him, I'll find out, and there will be hell to pay."

"We won't hurt him, Tess," Rhino promised as he climbed into his truck. "We just won't let him within ten feet of you ever again."

15

MAC WISHED the Blakely brothers *had* started swinging at him once they were out of Tess's sight. A nice little brawl would have been an improvement over what was happening at the Ore Cart. As he sat at the bar and nursed a beer, he wondered if they were trying to get him to throw the first punch. He wasn't about to do it.

He felt numb, which was another reason he'd love to get in a fight just so he could at least feel something and know he was still alive. But he wouldn't be the one to start it. Like someone in shock staring down at a gaping wound, he should be feeling tremendous pain knowing that he'd never hold Tess in his arms again. He had no doubt he would feel that pain eventually. But the reality of losing his best friend and the love of his life hadn't hit him yet.

"Hey, Benedict Arnold, you're up." Hammer pulled the darts he'd just thrown from the board and handed them to Mac, points out.

Mac took them, gazing stoically at Hammer as one of the points seemed to accidentally dig into his palm. "Thanks."

"Whoops, did I stick you with that dart? Jeez, I'm sorry, man. Oversight on my part."

"No problem."

"Check where he's putting his feet," Dozer said. "A

guy like him could edge over the line to get an advantage."

"I'm watching him," Rhino said. "All the time."

Mac clenched his jaw and threw the darts. He sensed that the brothers were testing him, trying to get him to crack. If he challenged them, either by starting a fight or leaving the bar, that would be the end of the relationship. If he stayed and took everything they had to dish out, the day of forgiveness might eventually come.

Unfortunately he was starting to win the damn darts tournament. Throwing darts felt exceedingly good right now. He'd give anything to be out on the field throwing a football right now. He could probably heave it seventy yards with no problem. He deliberately made a bad toss of the dart.

"Hey, lover-boy!" Dozer called out. "Having a little trouble with your concentration?"

"No doubt," Rhino said. "The boy has a lot of things on his mind. No wonder he hasn't been winning at poker this summer."

"I still can't believe it," Tim said. He of all the brothers seemed more hurt than angry. "I can't believe you'd sit there every Wednesday night like always."

"Sort of makes you lose your faith in your fellow man, doesn't it, Tim?" Hammer said.

Mac threw his last dart dead in the middle of the bull's-eye and turned to face the brothers. He gazed at them and pain started sneaking into his heart, like the pinpricks after an arm or leg has fallen asleep. Nothing would ever be the same. Nothing. "I'm sorry," he said softly.

They returned his gaze silently.

Finally Tim spoke. "Would you marry her if she wasn't going to New York, Mac?"

He saw nothing wrong with telling them the truth. "Yes."

Rhino made an impatient noise deep in his throat. "Then why the hell don't you get her to stay?"

"I don't think I could," Mac said.

"You could," Rhino said. "She might pretend she's one of those women who takes her fun where she finds it, but she's not. We always figured she'd fall hard for the first guy she got involved with because she's not the type to take sex lightly, no matter what she says. That's the main reason we've been protecting her all along. She could have wrecked her life with the wrong guy."

"Maybe I'm the wrong guy."

Hammer drained his glass of beer and set it down on the bar with a loud click. "Maybe. I can't say I'd relish having a lying son of a bitch for a brother-in-law."

"He didn't exactly lie," Tim said.

"No, it's more like he betrayed our trust," Rhino said. "Now, that's not good, but I'm telling you, Tess has probably lost her heart, just like we thought she would when she became involved with someone. I think you need to convince her to stay here and marry you, Mac. It's the only answer."

Mac considered the idea, and for a brief moment hope gleamed in his heart. He knew Tess loved him. If only she'd given him some indication that she didn't really want to go to New York...but she hadn't.

He took a deep breath. "You're right, I might be able to convince her to stay. But I can't do it. All her life she's talked about leaving small-town life behind and experiencing the excitement of a big city. She could easily start blaming me for taking that away from her." He should know. Despite how much he loved his parents, he couldn't completely eliminate the resentment that cropped up whenever he thought of how they'd tied him to the ranch.

"Hell. You have a point." Rhino gazed at the floor. "I hate this. I purely hate it. If you were some other guy, we could all have a great time taking you apart."

Mac laid the darts on the bar. "Have at it."

"We can't beat you up, Mac," Tim said. "Not after the way you said you were sorry, and that you'd marry Tess if you thought it would work out."

"Maybe it would work out," Dozer said. "Maybe she'd forget about this big-city thing after a while. Like the sofa Cindy wanted. She thought she'd die if she didn't get it, but we couldn't afford the darn thing. Then after she got pregnant she forgot about the sofa."

Mac's smile was sad. "I wish you were right, Dozer. But I've listened to Tess go on about this for years. You guys got so much recognition with your football that she felt overshadowed most of the time."

"Yeah, but she was in those plays," Tim said.

"I know, but Copperville folks don't get as excited about plays as they do about football games. You know she once considered trying to make it on Broadway."

Rhino groaned. "We were all having a heart attack over that plan, too."

"That Broadway idea was because of us?" Dozer asked.

"In a way. It would have made a splash. At any rate, thinking about a career on Broadway got her hooked on the idea of New York, but she finally realized she didn't want to act for a living, so she decided to get a job in New York as the next best thing. Because no one else in the family has done anything remotely like that, it'll be her badge of honor. I think she needs to go."

"I can't believe she's been jealous of us, when she was so smart, pulling down A's all the time," Hammer said.

"Pulling down A's doesn't rate a picture in the paper. Don't get me wrong. She's proud as heck of all of you, but she wants her own claim to fame. This is it."

Rhino stroked his chin. "You seem to know her pretty well."

Hammer coughed. "A little too damn well, if you want my opinion. Why didn't you just tell her you wouldn't do it, Mac?"

"I should have. God, I know I should have. But she seemed so determined to make this happen. She was considering Donny Beauford."

A strangled noise came from Rhino, and Dozer choked on his beer.

"God bless America," Hammer said. "Beauford?"

"I'd ten times rather have Mac than Beauford," Tim said. "Make that a hundred times."

A silence fell over the brothers as each of them seemed to be contemplating the horrors of Donny Beauford with their sister.

"I guess it had to be somebody, sooner or later," Tim said at last.

"We knew that," Rhino said. "But we wanted to make sure it was the right guy."

"I've been wondering about something," Mac said. "How were you planning to supervise Tess's dating life once she moved to New York?"

Rhino grinned. "We had a special picture made of all four of us and we planned to give it to her as a going-away present."

"And we had the photographer squat and point the camera up, so we all look *huge*," Tim added.

"We're going to tell her to keep it right by her bedside

to remind her of her family," Dozer said. "Any guy who sees that might think twice, especially if we pay a few surprise visits to New York now and then."

Mac shook his head. "Amazing."

"We might not have to worry so much now," Rhino said. "If we want to look on the bright side of this disaster, Mac might have done us a favor."

Hammer glared at Mac. "I can't buy that."

"Think about it," Rhino said. "You know how she is once she settles on someone or something. Like a little bulldog. If she's carrying a torch for Mac, she won't be interested in any of those city slickers."

Mac thought that was one of the best things he'd heard all night. Unfortunately it didn't change the fact that Tess would be leaving and he would be staying. His life was about to become very empty, more empty than he could imagine. So if he wanted to keep his sanity, he wouldn't even try to imagine life without Tess.

TESS KNEW that her last two weeks in Copperville would be rough, but she hadn't understood the half of it. She ached from wanting Mac, but she'd expected that. The need for him was always there, a subterranean current that sometimes bubbled to the surface and threatened to drown her. But the moments she hadn't expected were worse—moments when her first impulse was to share some little detail of her life with Mac, until she realized she could no longer do that.

There was the time she rescued Sarah's kitten from a tree, and the hysterical sight of Mrs. Nedbetter riding around on her new mower, even though she had a postage-stamp lawn. Tess would hear a good joke or read an article about a new technique for breeding horses, and pick up the phone. And then the truth would hit her. No matter what he'd promised about always being friends, their friendship was dead.

The most exquisite torture of all lay ahead of her. Her parents' anniversary party was no longer a surprise— surprises seldom worked out in Copperville. Once the secret was out, her family had decided to combine an anniversary barbecue in the park with a going-away party for Tess. Most of the population of Copperville would be there...including Mac.

By the day of the party, Tess had packed most of her belongings, including many of her clothes. Too late she realized that the only thing she hadn't packed that was festive enough for the event was her daisy-patterned dress. Mac would probably think she'd worn it on purpose. The only reason it still hung in her closet was that she hadn't gotten around to stuffing it in the bag of discards she'd collected to give to charity.

As she zipped the dress, she realized that the pearl necklace she'd continued to wear probably would be another red flag for Mac. For the past two weeks she kept meaning to take it off for good, although she couldn't make herself give it away. But each time she'd reached for the clasp so she could put the necklace back into her jewelry box, she'd decided to leave it on a little longer.

Putting the necklace away seemed so final, as if that would sever the last tie with Mac. Besides, her mother had mentioned how nice she thought it was that Tess was finally wearing the lovely gift Mac had given her. Her mother might notice the necklace was gone and comment, Tess decided. Better to leave it on. Mac would just have to deal with it.

She arrived at the park early to help her brothers and sisters-in-law with the preparations. They worked steadily for two hours in the heat, tying balloons to lampposts, firing up the barbecue grills and chasing rambunctious children. Tess welcomed the sweaty, frantic activity and pushed thoughts of Mac to the back of her mind.

But her pulse started to race right on schedule when he backed his truck up to a ramada and started unloading the kegs of beer that had been ordered for the party.

"Guess I'll go help him," Rhino said.

"Don't sample the wares until we're finished here," Joan called after her husband.

Tess kept sneaking glances at the two men as they laughed and joked with each other while unloading the kegs. Pretty soon Hammer, Dozer and Tim wandered over and joined them. Everyone acted like the best of buddies, and she began to hope that her brothers had made a temporary peace with Mac. Once she wasn't around, they might be able to put the whole incident aside.

"Hey, Dozer," Cindy called over to the group. "Time for you and Tim to start cooking. People are beginning to arrive and the anniversary couple will be here any minute."

"Coming," Dozer said.

Deena continued tying the last of the balloons on an adjacent ramada. "Hammer," she called. "I need you to check on Jason and Kimberly at the swings. Suzie's been playing with them over there, but I'll bet she could use a breather."

Hammer headed toward the swings. "Jason, let Kimberly have a turn, son!"

Tess pretended not to notice that Mac had tagged along as Tim, Dozer and Rhino approached the table. Instead, she concentrated on filling a large wading pool with ice to hold the salad bowls. She'd never followed through on her plan to use ice during lovemaking with

Mac, but ice never failed to remind her of the passionate adventures they'd shared this summer.

"Cindy, which cooler did you put the hamburgers and hot dogs in?" Dozer asked.

"The red one," Cindy said.

"*Which* red one?"

"Oh, for heaven's sake." Cindy got Dozer by one arm and Tim by the other and propelled them over to a nearby ramada. "Come on. I'll show you."

Tess dumped the last bag of ice in the wading pool. "This is ready, Joan."

"For what?" Mac asked.

Tess glanced at him and could tell by the challenging look in his eyes that he'd meant for the question to rattle her. It did. Her cheeks warmed. "We, uh—"

"It's for the salads, so you don't get poisoned by the mayonnaise," Joan said briskly.

"That's not all it's for." Rhino grabbed a piece of ice and slipped it down the back of Joan's dress.

She shrieked and scooped up a handful of ice, pelting him with it as she chased him across the park.

And just like that, Mac and Tess were alone.

He picked up an ice cube and tossed it up and down in his hand. "We never did get around to this, did we?"

Her throat felt so tight that she couldn't speak. She shook her head.

"Guess we never will." He tossed the ice on the ground and moved closer. "How are you doing?"

"Okay." She risked one look into his eyes and glanced away again. Too potent. She cleared the huskiness from her throat. "How about you?"

"Okay. I thought about calling you to see how you were holding up, but I thought that might make things worse."

"Yeah. It probably would have." She watched the ice cube melt in the grass at their feet. "Mac, did my brothers—"

"Beat me up? No. In a way I wish they had. It might have made me feel better."

Tess glanced across the park. Joan and Rhino were walking back toward them. They didn't have much time. She lowered her voice. "Dammit, I will not have you taking the blame for this. It was my idea and I should be the one feeling guilty, not you."

"Like they said, I could have turned you down."

"You knew I was going to nab somebody for the job, and you were afraid I'd end up with a dweeb."

"Yeah. And then there was that dress."

She glanced at him.

"Why did you wear it today, Tess?"

Because I was selfish enough to want you to look at me like that one more time. "I'd packed everything else."

"And what about the necklace?" he asked softly. "Didn't get around to packing that, either, did you?"

Her heart ached so fiercely she could barely breathe. "Mac, I—"

"Promise me something."

"What?"

"That you'll wear that necklace in New York."

"Loafing, are we?" Joan said with a grin as they walked up. "Boy, I can't leave my staff for a minute without discipline going to hell."

Rhino's glance shifted from Mac to Tess and he frowned. "I'll put Big Mac to work for you, sweetheart. He's probably distracting Tess so she can't get anything done."

"Oh, I don't really care," Joan said. "After all, we won't have Tess around here much longer, so I'm sure everybody wants a chance to spend a little time with her today. Technically, I shouldn't be making her work at all, since this is also supposed to be her party."

"I wouldn't feel right sitting around," Tess said. She'd caught the brief look of disapproval on her brother's face. He might have shelved his anger for the time being, but he wasn't about to let Mac spend any more time alone with her.

"None of us are going to sit around," Rhino said. "Come on, Mac. I have a bunch of lawn chairs in the van. Let's go take them out and set them up."

"Sure thing." Mac glanced at Tess.

She realized she was clutching the pearl in one hand. She released it and turned away. His request completely confused her. He knew that wearing the necklace would be a constant reminder of him, preventing her from moving on to someone else. That sort of dog-in-the-manger attitude wasn't worthy of him, and she couldn't quite believe that was his motivation. Yet she could think of no other reason he'd want her to continue wearing the necklace.

The more she thought about it, the angrier she became. Who did he think he was, branding her like that when he didn't have the slightest intention of making a commitment himself?

Her parents arrived soon afterward. Once the party was in full swing, Tess focused on making this a special day for her parents. More than once she felt the tug of tears as she realized that by next week she wouldn't be able to see them and talk to them every day as she could now. She wondered if she'd made a terrible mistake taking the job in New York, but she couldn't change her course now, and besides, she needed to get away from

Mac. If she stayed around much longer, he would surely break her heart for good.

Although the festivities took most of her attention, she couldn't forget that Mac was there, although she really tried. Despite her efforts, she always seemed to know where he was, whether he'd stripped off his shirt for the volleyball game, or had taken yet another kid for a ride on his shoulders, or was challenging one of her brothers to a game of horseshoes. His voice, his smile, his laughter drew her as if they were connected with an invisible string.

Finally she decided the pearl necklace was part of the problem. She couldn't take it to New York, let alone wear it while she was there. And Mac needed to know that.

She excused herself on the pretext that she needed to head for one of the park rest rooms. When she was away from the crowd, she took off the necklace. Unclasping it wasn't easy because her hands were shaking. Once she'd done it, she felt as if someone had wrapped her heart in barbed wire.

But this was what she had to do. She found Mac eating some of her parents' anniversary cake while he talked with a couple of ranchers who lived on the outskirts of Copperville.

"Excuse me, Mac," she said.

"Sure." He glanced at her bare neck and his gaze grew wary. "What is it?"

She reached over and dropped the necklace in his shirt pocket. "I need you to keep this for me." Choking back a sob, she turned and hurried away.

16

MAC WANTED to throw the necklace away. In the tortured days that followed, right up to the morning Tess was scheduled to leave, he tried to make himself pitch it in the garbage, in the river, over a cliff. He couldn't do it.

The day she left, he drove to a bluff overlooking the highway winding out of town and waited there until he saw her car go by. He thought he'd fling the necklace over the bluff once he knew she was really and truly gone. But long after her car and trailer had disappeared from sight, he still clutched the necklace tight in his fist.

In the weeks that followed he kept the necklace in a drawer and fell into the habit of tucking it into his jeans' pocket before starting the day. He'd meant for her to keep it on as a reminder of him and what they'd meant to each other. He'd held on to the slim hope that after some time of living in the big city she'd grow tired of it and come home. If she wore the necklace until then, he might have a chance. But she'd turned the tables on him... again.

He handled his ranch duties like a robot. The work had always seemed confining to him, but he'd been able to bear it while Tess remained in Copperville. Now the daily routine was intolerable without her. She'd been the one who had kept his life interesting, and the fact that she shared his desire to go out into the world had kept that fantasy alive for him. Now she was out there and he was left behind.

As the heat lifted in late September, he was rounding up strays down by the river one afternoon when he came to a life-changing realization. Once his parents were gone, he'd sell the ranch and travel the world. That wouldn't take the place of losing Tess, but it would have to do. And if he was planning to sell the ranch eventually anyway, his parents' dream of keeping it in the family and passing it down through the generations was doomed from the beginning.

Suddenly the whole charade seemed stupid. To pretend he wanted a ranch that he wouldn't keep after his parents died was unfair to all of them. Telling his mom and dad the truth after all these years wouldn't be easy, though. Still, he was determined to do it and end the hypocrisy.

He waited until dinner was nearly over. He'd barely been able to taste his mother's prized beef stew, but he'd forced himself to eat every bite and carry on a conversation about the antics of the stud they'd bought from Stan Henderson in Flagstaff.

From the moment he'd come into the ranch house that night he'd seen the place with new eyes. Now that he'd decided the ranch would not be his ball and chain, he could appreciate the beamed ceilings and rock fireplace, the heavy leather furniture grouped around the hearth and the carved oak table and chairs in the dining room.

It wouldn't be such a bad place to live...someday, and with the right person. But he couldn't expect his parents to keep it going without him, holding on to it for when he was ready to settle down. And before that day came, he had many things to do.

Finally he pushed his plate aside and gazed at them. "I need to talk to both of you. It's...pretty serious."

"At last," his mother said with a sigh.

Mac stared at her. "What do you mean, *at last?*"

"Your mother's been worried sick about you ever since Tess left," his father said. "I've been a mite concerned, myself. You've been moping around like you've lost your best friend, and I guess you have."

Mac felt his neck grow warm. It showed how self-absorbed he'd been lately, that he hadn't even realized how his mood had been affecting his parents. "I'm sorry if I've been a pain in the butt."

"You have," his father said.

"No, he hasn't, Andy." Nora sent her husband a reproving glance. "He's been sort of glum, that's all."

"Which translates to being a pain in the butt, in my opinion," Andy said.

"I agree," Mac said. "But I'm about to be even more of one." He took a deep breath. "I know you've both worked hard all these years to build up this ranch."

"It's been a labor of love," his mother said.

She wasn't making it any easier for him. Mac cleared his throat. "I appreciate all that you've done, and I realize the goal was to pass the ranch on to me someday, but—"

"You don't want it," his father finished, his voice husky.

Mac met his father's gaze and his resolve nearly crumbled at the deep disappointment he saw there. "I might," he said gently. "Eventually, when I get some of the wanderlust out of my system. It's a beautiful place, and tonight I really began to realize just how beautiful it is. But right now the ranch feels like an elephant sitting on my chest, choking the life out of me."

"You want to go to New York, don't you?" his mother asked quietly.

"Maybe." *Yes.* He hadn't allowed himself to get that far in his thinking, but now that his mother had put the idea into words, he knew immediately that he wanted to start with New York. He wasn't sure how Tess figured into any of this, or if she even wanted to figure in, but he would never know if he didn't go there and find out.

"What in hell would you do in New York?" his father asked. His tone of voice betrayed the depth of his hurt.

"I'm not sure." The ideas started coming to him, and he realized they'd been simmering in his subconscious for years. "I'd probably try to get on with one of the small commuter airlines there. If that didn't pan out I'd find some job at one of the major airports and work my way up until I could fly. I love airplanes, Dad. I always have."

"You have a damn airplane! You can fly it around all you want!"

"Andy." Nora laid a hand on her husband's arm. "That's not the point. He wants to go out on his own, the way Tess has. Plus, he misses her like crazy. I don't know if something more than friendship is involved, but I'm beginning to think there is." She glanced at Mac. "I didn't want to interfere, but I had a strong feeling that you and Tess went beyond the boundaries of friendship this summer. Debbie thought so, too."

"You and Tess's mom talked about it?" Mac felt the heat climb from his neck to his face.

"To be honest, a lot of people in town had their suspicions," his mother said. "We wondered if Tess might decide to stay home, after all. When she left, I felt so bad for you."

"I knew it." Andy threw his napkin on the table and pushed back his chair. "This is all about chasing after a woman. If Tess had had the good sense to stay in Copperville, then you two could get married and you wouldn't be comparing the ranch to some damn elephant."

"Don't blame it on Tess!" In his agitation, Mac rose to his feet. "I've always felt this way. Both of us have, Tess and I. We spent hours as kids talking about the places we'd see, the exciting things we'd do once we left Copperville."

"Lots of kids talk that way," his father said. "Then they grow up and realize that what they have is better than anything they could find out there!"

Mac gazed at his father and tried to put himself in Andy MacDougal's shoes. After nearly thirty years of breaking his back to create a legacy for his son, his son was rejecting that legacy. Mac hated hurting his father. "It probably is better, Dad," he said gently. "But I'll never appreciate that if I don't see something of the rest of the world."

"Of course you must," his mother said.

"Maybe we should just sell the ranch right now," Andy said. "No point in killing ourselves if it's not going to be passed on."

"Oh, Andy, for heaven's sake!" Nora looked disgusted. "Forget your hurt pride for five seconds and listen to what your son is saying. He needs time to explore. And he needs to be with the woman he loves."

Mac's heart clutched. "Now, Mom. Don't jump to—"

"I'll jump to any conclusion I want, thank you very much." She glanced at him. "And Tess feels the same about you, unless I miss my guess. I also fully believe that both of you will eventually get homesick for Copperville and come back here to raise your children."

"Children?" Mac almost choked. "Last I heard, Tess

had no intention of getting married, let alone having kids. I think you're getting ahead of yourself."

His mother smiled. "No, I think you're behind. Time to catch up. Go to New York and ask those questions. See what kind of response you get." She looked over at her husband. "All we need to do is hire someone to help out for a while, until these two come back home."

Andy scowled. "And what if they don't? Then it'll all be for nothing."

"Now that's the dumbest thing I've ever heard you say, Andy. Nothing? This ranch was your dream all along. You hoped it would be passed down, as a lot of parents do who work to build something, but you wanted it for yourself, too. You've had a wonderful time living this life, and don't you dare pretend it was nothing but selfless sacrifice for your son!"

Gradually Andy's expression changed from belligerent to sheepish. "Guess you're right, Nora. I can't imagine any other place to be. That's why I can't figure why anybody in their right mind would want to live in that rat's nest they call New York City."

"We're all different," Nora said. "As for these two, they were both born and raised here, and I say they'll be back."

"I can't make any promises," Mac said. But he couldn't help weaving a few fantasies, either. Maybe he could have it all, a few years of adventures with Tess and then a family and security right here in Copperville with the only woman he'd ever wanted. But Tess might not be interested in such a plan. After all, she had given back the necklace.

"You don't have to make any promises to us," his mother said. "But I think you need to make a few to Tess."

NEW YORK WAS EVERYTHING Tess had imagined and more. She'd used her weekends to walk Manhattan from end to end, and each excursion brought new delights. She'd become addicted to pretzels sold by sidewalk vendors, and corner deli markets, and the ride up to the top of the Empire State Building.

But she'd never expected to be so completely, utterly lonely. She'd made friends with people on the staff of her school, but *friend* didn't seem like the right word to describe someone she'd only known a couple of months. Friends were people you'd known for years, people who knew your family and all your other friends. Friends were people like...Mac.

She'd thought the ache for him would have begun to wear away by now, but if anything, it grew stronger. Today was worse than most days, because it was both Sunday, a time for families, and Halloween, a holiday she and Mac had shared for twenty-three years. They'd never considered themselves too old to dress up. A year ago they'd gone to a party together as a couple of Beanie Babies.

Tess had been invited to a party given by one of the teachers at school, and she'd accepted, but as she sat in her tiny apartment trying to come up with a costume, she couldn't get excited about it. Her simplest option was to wear the harem outfit she'd bought for the belly-dancing demonstration she'd given Mac. She thought she'd thrown it away, but she must have been in a real fog when she'd packed, because it was in the bottom of a box. Once she discovered it, she'd been so desperate for any reminders of Mac that she'd kept it.

Wearing it, however, might present a few emotional problems. Yet she didn't have any other great ideas for a costume, and this one was complete. With a sigh she started putting it on for a test run to see whether it made her cry, or worse yet made her hot and bothered. Sexual frustration had been a constant companion along with loneliness, but of the two, loneliness was the worst. She missed having Mac to talk to even more than she missed his lovemaking.

Still, she'd give anything to be held and caressed by him again, and it was definitely *his* lovemaking that she wanted. She'd turned down several dates already. The thought of even kissing someone besides Mac made her shudder.

If that attitude persisted, she might have to resign herself to staying single all her life. Damned if she wasn't beginning to believe she was a one-man woman. She'd never have believed it before the scorching events of this summer, but it seemed that Mac had taken not only her virginity, but her heart. And she wasn't getting it back.

After putting on the filmy harem pants and the jeweled bra, she stood in front of the mirror in her small bedroom and fastened the veil in place. Heat washed over her as she remembered the look in Mac's eyes as she'd danced for him. She'd never felt so sensuous as when she'd leaned over him and shimmied her breasts practically in his face.

He'd meant to end their affair that night without making love to her, but she'd tempted him beyond endurance and even made him forget he'd agreed to meet her brothers for a darts tournament. In all the turmoil that had followed, she'd forgotten that her seductive dance had succeeded beyond her wildest dreams. She had made him lose his mind. Maybe he didn't want to marry her, but for that moment, he had been completely, utterly hers.

And he'd said that he loved her. It had turned out to be an empty pledge, and now she wondered if he'd only

meant that he loved the fantastic sex they'd made together. But when he'd said it that night, he'd filled her
heart to overflowing.

She couldn't wear the harem outfit to the Halloween
party. It made her long for Mac in every conceivable
way—physically, mentally and emotionally. Maybe
she'd skip the party altogether and rent a video. She
reached for the hook on the jeweled bra just as the doorbell rang.

Probably her next-door neighbor, she thought. She'd
moved clear across the country, yet some things stayed
the same. The woman in the next apartment reminded
her so much of her neighbor, Mrs. Nedbetter, back in
Copperville, that several times she'd called her by the
wrong name.

She glanced at herself in the mirror. Oh, well, it was
Halloween. She'd explain that she was trying on cos-
tumes in preparation for a party. She really should make
herself go, she thought as she walked toward the front
door. A simple costume like a gypsy or a pirate wouldn't
be that hard to create.

The doorbell chimed again. Then a voice that made her
breath catch called out "Trick or treat."

"Mac!" She raced to the door and unlocked it, fum-
bling in her eagerness. So what if he'd only come for a
visit and would leave her worse off than she was now?
She didn't care. She flung open the door and gasped.

He was dressed as a sheik, complete with rich-looking
robes and a gold piece of braid holding a white flowing
turban on his head. When he saw her, his jaw dropped.
"Wow. This is just plain scary."

"Yeah." She held his gaze, her heart pounding. "Scary
as hell."

"Are you going to a Halloween party?"

"No. Well, maybe. I was invited and I was trying to decide if I wanted to go or not, so I put this on in case I could wear it." She gulped for air. "But I can't."

"Funny, but you seem to be wearing it. Or is that an optical illusion?"

"I—listen, come in." She stepped back from the door. "Do you have bags? How long can you stay? When did you—"

"No bags. I left them at the hotel."

Her hopes died. "H-hotel? You're not...planning to stay...with me?"

He walked through the doorway, his sheik's robes swaying, and closed the door behind him. Then he turned to her. "I didn't want to impose on you. I'm sure you have all sorts of things going on."

So he had come for a visit, with a capital *V*. He probably wanted someone to show him the sights, and she was handy, but he'd distanced himself from her by checking into a hotel. His sheik's outfit was a little joke, not a significant statement of his intentions.

"Well, of course I have things going on." She was determined to hide her pain. "But I'd be glad to adjust my schedule. If you'd told me you were coming, I might have been able to arrange a couple of days off, but on short notice, I'm not sure."

He waved a hand as if that didn't matter to him. "I don't want you to interrupt your work for me." He hesitated. "You said you were invited to a party." His voice became husky. "Do you have a date?"

For a split second she considered lying, but she'd never been good at that, especially with Mac. "No. It's just some people from work. Not a couples sort of thing."

"And you're thinking of going in *that?*"

She bristled. Deciding not to wear it because of the

memories it evoked was one thing. Having him question her choice in that tone of voice was quite another. He didn't have that right. "Why not?"

"Because it's indecent!"

"You didn't think so that night I danced for you!" She blew the veil impatiently away from her face. "You enjoyed this outfit so much your tongue was hanging out, mister!"

"And it still is! And so will every other guy's at that party!"

Her chin lifted. "What's it to you?"

He stepped forward and grabbed her. "Everything."

Her breath caught as the space surrounding them seemed to glow and pulse. She became lost in his gaze.

He squeezed his eyes shut. "Damn. I didn't mean it to come out like that."

"You didn't?" Some of the luster faded.

"No." He looked into her eyes. "I meant to go slow, find out if you had a boyfriend."

The luster returned.

"Well?" he prompted.

Wherever this conversation was leading she wanted to go along, but he'd taken his time about having this talk with her. She decided not to make it too easy and ruin the challenge for him. "Well, what?"

"Do you have a boyfriend?"

What a beautiful day. What an absolutely gorgeous day. "I think so."

"You *think* so?" He scowled down at her. "What kind of an answer is that?"

She was glad she still wore the veil. It hid her smile. "He's not being real clear about his intentions, so it's hard for me to know whether he's my boyfriend or not. But I'm pretty sure he is."

Mac's scowl darkened. "So he's one of those wishy-washy types?"

"Let's just say he's a little confused."

"And how do you feel about him?"

"I'm crazy about him."

His eyes blazed and his grip tightened on her arms. "You can't be."

"Why not? He's terrific."

"Terrific? What do you mean by that?" His eyes narrowed. "Tess, have you and this guy...made love?"

"Not recently."

"I don't give a damn if it's recent or not! Tess, how could you make love to another man? How could you—"

"In fact, I haven't made love to this guy since August," she added gently. "I was wearing this outfit at the time."

Understanding slowly softened the fierce line of his eyebrows and the glitter in his blue eyes. "Oh." He swallowed. "Did I hear you say you're crazy about this guy?"

She nodded.

"I can't imagine why." His voice was hoarse. "He's an idiot."

"No." She reached up and touched his cheek. "Just confused." She stroked the curve of his jaw with a trembling hand. She wanted him, no matter how long he could stay or what his terms might be. "Would you like to cancel that hotel reservation? No one in Copperville has to know that you stayed here during your visit, if that's what you're worried about."

"I'm not visiting."

"*What?*"

"I'm job hunting, looking into a couple of commuter airlines. I've come here to live."

She reeled from the news. "Mac! What about the ranch? What about your parents?"

"They've hired someone to take over my part of the work. Telling them that I needed to go out on my own wasn't easy, but it was the right thing to do. I should have told them sooner, but I guess I needed you to blaze a trail for me."

"I'm stunned."

His eyes grew shadowed. "Look, this puts you under no obligation. I'm not asking you to change your life just because I decided to come here. I mean, sure, I'd like to see you, and everything, but—"

"And what do you mean exactly by *and everything*?" She moved her hips boldly against his and felt his instantaneous response. "This?"

He groaned softly. "Tess, I—"

"And this?" She pushed the material of his sheik's robe aside and brushed her jeweled bra against his bare chest.

His gaze smoldered. "You drive me insane, Tess. I've missed you so much I can barely think straight."

She pressed her body against his. "If you can't think straight, then maybe you don't remember what you told me when we made love that last time."

"Oh, I remember that, all right."

She gathered her courage and continued. "I need to know if it was just something you said in the heat of passion, or if it meant more than that."

He held her tighter. "You want all my cards on the table, don't you?"

"Yes."

"Then take off that damn veil."

She reached up and unfastened it immediately, tossing it to a nearby chair.

He gazed down at her, his glance warm as it roved over her face. Then he reached beneath his robe and pulled out the pearl necklace. "I think it's time you put this back on."

Her heart thudded wildly at the implication. She trembled as he fastened the clasp around her neck and nestled the pearl between her breasts.

"Okay," he said softly. "I was going to lead up to this, but if you want everything all at once, that's what you'll get. I love you. Maybe on some level I've always known you were my mate, but so many things got in the way. I'm going to marry you someday, Tess, when you're ready. I realize that might not be for a while, but—"

"I'm ready."

"I'm willing to wait until you've experienced all..." He paused, as if finally registering what she'd said. He looked into her eyes.

She nodded.

"Oh, God." His mouth came down on hers, and he kissed her until they were both breathless. "You're sure?" He held her face in both hands, his gaze probing. "I mean, you just started this new life, and maybe you need to stay single for a couple of years, to—"

"To what? Nothing could be as exciting as living with you as your wife. I think I've known that since I was three years old. I love you, Mac, desperately, completely and forever."

His smile was tender. "Yeah, but do you swear on the tomb of old King Tut?"

"You bet. And now let me give you some vital information. The bedroom is through that door on your right. Do you think we could go in there and make mad, passionate love for about ten hours? I'm feeling very neglected."

He grinned and lifted her up in his arms. "Only ten hours?"

"For starters."

He feathered his lips over hers. "Got ice?" he murmured.

Epilogue

PLEASANTLY FULL after a meal of fried chicken and potato salad, Mac lay back on the picnic blanket, closed his eyes and sighed with contentment. No New York traffic, no jackhammers, no jet engines. Only the gurgle of the river, the call of a quail, the rustle of the breeze through the reeds.

He'd visited beaches and riverbanks in many parts of the world this past year, but he'd recognize the baked-sand and wet-moss scent of this one blindfolded. The breeze moved over him like a caress. How he loved summer nights in Arizona.

Something tickled his nose, and he swatted it away. The tickling resumed, and he opened one eye.

Leaning over him, Tess brushed a feathery tip of a wild-grass stalk over his mouth.

He gazed up and noticed that when she leaned over, her blouse gaped open quite nicely. Taking the stalk from her fingers, he slipped it down the front of her blouse and stroked it over the swell of her breasts. "They already seem fuller."

"It's probably your imagination. I'm barely three months along."

"I'll never forget the look on our folks' faces when we told them." He could see desire stirring in her eyes as he continued to tickle her breasts with the grass.

She smiled. "I think they were even happier about the baby than when we told them we were home to stay."

"I'm pretty happy about that baby, myself." He brushed the grass up the curve of her throat and tickled under her chin. "Any regrets about leaving the big city?"

"Only that we never did it on top of the Empire State Building."

"We'll visit someday and do it then."

She shook her head. "Nah. We don't have to. Making love to you for the rest of my life is all the adventure I need."

"You mean that?"

"Absolutely."

"Then take off your blouse," he murmured. The sight of Tess unfastening buttons was one of the joys of his life.

She obliged him and tossed the garment aside before gazing down at him, a question in her gray eyes.

"Keep going." His erection strained his jeans as she flipped open the front catch of her bra. In another moment her breasts spilled into view, her nipples already taut. He stroked the grass across them anyway, loving the ripple of desire that went through her, the surrender in her sigh.

His voice grew husky. "Lean down."

She moved over him and he filled both hands with the weight of her breasts, kneading gently as he began to taste her.

While he feasted, she managed to wiggle out of her shorts, open his jeans and free his erection. He groaned with pleasure as she slid down over his rigid shaft. How miraculous to make love this way, without barriers. Releasing her breasts, he guided her down for a long, satisfying kiss.

She drew back and gazed into his eyes as she initiated a slow, sensuous rhythm. "I love you, Mac."

"And I love you," he said. Above her the cottonwood

leaves dappled the twilight sky. Heaven couldn't be any better than this. "I love you more than life." His climax was building quickly, and from the way Tess was breathing, she wasn't far behind him.

"Stop," she said, panting. "I just remembered."

His fevered brain wasn't working. "Remembered what?"

"Hold on a sec." She reached toward the small picnic cooler near the edge of the blanket.

He squeezed his eyes shut, teetering on the edge. "I don't know if I can." He felt the pulsing begin. "Tess, I can't—" Something cold pressed against a critical part of his anatomy and he erupted, sensations crashing over him in waves, ripping moans of ecstasy from deep in his chest.

Finally he lay still, spent and quivering, while she sprinkled kisses over his face.

"What...was that?" he asked.

She sounded very smug. "Ice."

And the fun's not over yet. There are even more of these irresistible guys on the way...

If you still have a weakness for the strong silent type, don't miss meeting sexy Dustin Ramsey, the hero of Vicki's latest Harlequin Blaze book...

TRULY, MADLY, DEEPLY—August 2002

Ten years ago, Dustin Ramsey and Erica Mann shared their first sexual experience. And it was...a disaster. Now, Dustin's determined to find—and seduce—Erica again, to prove to her, and himself, that he can do better. Much, much better. Only little does he guess that Erica's got a similar agenda...

Here's a preview...

1

DUSTIN RAMSEY STOOD OUTSIDE a three-story brick apartment complex on McKinney Avenue, the results of Jennifer Madison's investigation tucked into his briefcase. The sweat trickling down his backbone had little to do with the August heat and a lot to do with anxiety. Because of the ninety-five-degree temperature he'd left off the tie, but a business deal required a jacket as a bare minimum, and he'd also worn his best snakeskin boots.

He might feel like a fraud on the inside, but on the outside he would look like a professional businessman he should be, given his heritage. People in Dallas paid attention to clothes. He'd left Midland at dawn, and the knot of tension in his gut had tightened with every mile.

No doubt about it, he was in deep shit. If he'd asked to be involved in the family business instead of screwing around on the amateur auto-racing circuit, he'd have known that his dad was flushing the family fortune down the toilet. It was a common story in west Texas—oil barons unable to compete with the cheap crude coming out of the Middle East.

As if that wasn't disaster enough, Clayton Ramsey had used precious money to buy two weekly newspapers, one in San Antonio and one in Houston. Apparently Dustin's father had always longed to be a newspaperman. Dustin had been oblivious to everything until eight months ago, when a stroke had left his father unable to talk.

Thrust into power, Dustin had considered auctioning the land to developers, selling both newspapers, setting his parents up in a townhome and calling it good. But the tears in his mother's eyes and the hopeless droop of his father's shoulders changed his mind. He'd used the land as collateral to rebuild Ramsey Enterprises and hang on to his father's newspapers. Somehow.

The notice for his ten-year high school reunion had come about that time, which had started him thinking about Erica. He'd goofed off in every class, barely passing, until the semester he took chemistry and ended up as Erica's lab partner. She'd challenged him to do better, and by God, he had. It was his lone A in a crowd of C's.

He must have had some dumb idea that his performance in that chemistry class would transfer to his seduction of Erica in the back of the Mustang. She'd been blond, leggy, slightly drunk and unbelievably sensuous. He'd been...a virgin. A bumbling, eager, too-quick-to-come virgin. While all his jock buddies had managed to get laid in some form or fashion by the time they were juniors, Dustin hadn't.

Naturally he'd let everyone assume otherwise, shy about revealing the romantic streak that had made him want to wait until the moment felt exactly right. That moment hadn't arrived until April of his senior year during a keg party at Jeremy's house. Jeremy threw a party every time his parents left town, and usually the guests were limited to football players and cheerleaders.

But in honor of his senior year, Jeremy had invited the whole damn school, including the brainiacs like Erica. A couple hours into the party, Dustin had come up with the brilliant idea of asking her to take a drive into the country, and they'd ended up in the back seat together.

He still winced every time he thought about his abysmal performance that night. What a total disappointment he must have been for a knowledgeable girl like Erica. What a deep disappointment he'd been to himself. To think that the homecoming king, star running back and most eligible bachelor in school was a lousy lover. He hadn't been able to face Erica after that.

Ten years later he could forgive himself a little bit. He'd been naive to think that he could be instantly good at sex the way he'd been instantly good at every sport he'd ever tried. Hand-eye coordination was all well and good, but sex involved coordinating a trickier part of his anatomy. Besides that, he'd been intimidated by Erica. He'd tried too hard.

Okay, now he was better at sex. Without bragging, he could say that he was damn good at it. Several women had told him so. He should be able to forget he hadn't given Erica Deutchmann, his first lover, an orgasm. But he couldn't forget, and he wanted a rematch. That was a big part of why he was here.

It wasn't, however, the main reason. His reputation as a party animal had attracted other party animals. Now when he had to get serious, he had no friends to rely on. But during that chemistry class, he'd learned that he could rely on Erica. She was intelligent and ambitious, just the sort of person he needed on his side during this business crisis.

He wasn't at all surprised to find her publishing a wildly successful newsletter for singles all by herself. Once Jennifer had uncovered the information about *Dateline: Dallas*, Dustin had contacted a couple of his racing buddies who lived here, and they'd said everybody over eighteen and under forty knew about the newsletter. It was savvy, sexy and just plain fun.

Erica had tapped into a gold mine, and that was exactly the kind of drive and initiative he needed as part of his campaign to reorganize Ramsey Enterprises. He already had printing capability in San Antonio and Houston. Revenue from a hot newsletter could shore up the bottom line for the weeklies his father was so attached to.

Plus, if everything worked out, Dustin would have many opportunities to erase old memories and create new ones with Erica. It was a good plan, and it had to work. Yeah, the strategy might look like a Hail Mary pass in the last minutes of the game, but it was all he had going for him.

He took a deep breath and headed for the set of glass double doors leading into the building. Before he left Dallas, he would prove to Erica that he was capable of excellence in business *and* pleasure.

Inside the building he discovered stairs and no elevator. Damn. He liked the idea of whisking up to the third floor in an elevator before he could lose his nerve. Taking off his jacket, he started up.

By the second flight he'd convinced himself that this was the most insane idea he'd ever had. Erica wouldn't be interested in sharing either business or pleasure with him. She'd sounded sort of distant on the phone. He'd been obsessing about her for years and it was possible she barely remembered him.

Still, he'd see this through. He might have screwed around most of his life, but he wasn't a quitter. That's why he'd scored so many touchdowns in high school—point him toward a goal and he was unstoppable. He'd just never seen any other goals worth the effort. Until now.

On the third floor he paused and put on his coat. Hefting his briefcase again, he started down the carpeted hallway toward number 310. His heart pounded like a sonofabitch, and not from the climb, either. He hadn't been this nervous since...since driving out into the country with Erica.

He stood in front of her door for a good thirty seconds, working up to pushing her doorbell. Finally he squared his shoulders and did the deed. Footsteps sounded on the other side of the door.

When she opened it, he managed an automatic smile. He was a Ramsey, and Ramseys always led with a big, Texas-style grin. But he was afraid his eyes popped.

At the high school reunion a month ago, he'd had a chance to see how ten years had treated his classmates, and not one of them had blossomed like this. Erica had been pretty back in high school but not especially stylish, wearing both her blond hair and her denim skirts long. Now both were short. Very short.

Her hair was cut in the jaunty style so popular now, and her jungle-print skirt and black tank were the kind of seductive clothes that women wore these days. Not many wore them with this kind of flair, though, because not many had been blessed with a long-legged, full-breasted figure that would never go out of style. She wore large wooden earrings and open-toed mules. Urban chick all the way.

He quickly checked her left hand and found bright red nails but no engagement ring. That was a relief.

"Hey, Dustin. It's been along time, huh?"

Way too long. "Sure has. You're looking terrific." It was lame, but the best he could do considering his jangled brain and dry throat.

"You, too." Her tone was cautious. "Come on in." She stepped back and gestured for him to enter.

"Thanks." He could understand her caution. She wouldn't want him to get the wrong idea, like maybe she was interested in a date. Assuming she remembered their history, he'd be the last person on earth she'd want to date, old instant-o-matic Ramsey. Although he was mesmerized by the curve of her breasts and intoxicated by the exotic fragrance she wore, he managed to walk past her and into the room with what he hoped was confident ease.

He kept his voice casual. "So why didn't you come to the reunion?" She'd cost him precious money by staying away. He'd expected to hook up with her there. When she hadn't shown up and nobody had known her whereabouts, he'd tried the phone listings in various Texas cities, never suspecting she'd shortened her last name to Mann. He'd had to hire Jennifer to dig up that information.

"Reunion? Oh, yeah, I guess it is ten years, isn't it? I didn't get the notice, probably because of my name change."

"I wondered why you decided to change it." He inhaled her perfume with relish. It was much more blatant and sexy than what she'd used in high school. Her makeup was more out there, too—pouting red lips and dramatic black lashes, even though he knew for a fact she was a natural blonde. While taking off his Jockeys in his room after that fateful night with her, he'd found a blond hair tangled in his darker ones.

"When I was in journalism at UT I decided I wanted a more dramatic byline."

He nodded. "That sounds like you." Dazed as he was by Erica, he had trouble focusing on his surroundings.

Vaguely he registered a bright, sunny living room with lots of bookshelves, rattan furniture that gave the apartment a tropical look, a counter defining a small kitchen to his left and a hallway leading to the bedroom and bath to his right. Over her sofa hung a huge picture of some kind of flower. The rosy colors inside the flower made him think of sex, but anything would make him think of sex right now.

On an old wooden desk sat her computer, still turned on. The desk was cluttered with paper and advertising flyers. "I see you've been working on the newsletter."

"Yeah, deadline coming up."

He set down his briefcase and wandered over to the desk. He'd already seen a couple of issues, and he knew the advice column was the juiciest part, with the letters usually focused on sex. He glanced at the screen.

Dear Frustrated Franny, You deserve long and delicious bouts of sex with many orgasms. Teach your guy to go the distance. Here's one technique:

"Would you like some iced tea?"

He glanced up into those gray eyes of hers and swallowed. He'd give his cherished Harley jacket to know what she was thinking, now that they were face-to-face again. He'd become more experienced, but so had she. For example, she knew techniques for prolonging an erection.

He might not have the edge, after all.

SILHOUETTE *Romance*™

Escape to a place where a kiss is still a kiss...
Feel the breathless connection...
Fall in love as though it were
the very first time...
Experience the power of love!

Come to where favorite authors—such as
Diana Palmer, Stella Bagwell,
Marie Ferrarella and many more—
deliver heart-warming romance and genuine
emotion, time after time after time....

Silhouette Romance—
stories straight from the heart!

Silhouette®
Where love comes alive™

SPECIAL EDITION™
Emotional, compelling stories that capture the intensity of living, loving and creating a family in today's world.

Silhouette® Desire
A highly passionate, emotionally powerful and always provocative read.

Silhouette®
Where love comes alive™

INTIMATE MOMENTS™
A roller-coaster read that delivers romantic thrills in a world of suspense, adventure and more.

SILHOUETTE Romance
From first love to forever, these love stories are for today's woman with traditional values.

Visit Silhouette at www.eHarlequin.com

SILGENINT